**Praise for *New York Times* bestselling author
Heather Graham**

"An incredible storyteller."
—*Los Angeles Daily News*

"Graham stands at the top of the romantic
suspense category."
—*Publishers Weekly*

"Graham is a master at world building and her
latest is a thrilling, dark, and deadly tale of
romantic suspense."
—*Booklist*, starred review, on *Haunted Destiny*

**Praise for *New York Times* bestselling author
B.J. Daniels**

"B.J. Daniels is a sharpshooter; her books hit the
target every time."
—#1 *New York Times* bestselling author
Linda Lael Miller

"B.J. Daniels spins a tight story full of suspects
and danger sure to keep you guessing."
—*RT Book Reviews* on *Hotshot P.I.*

New York Times and *USA TODAY* bestselling author **Heather Graham** has written more than a hundred novels, many of which have been featured by the Doubleday Book Club and the Literary Guild. An avid scuba diver and ballroom dancer, and a mother of five, she still enjoys her South Florida home, but loves to travel, from locations such as Cairo, Egypt, to the Florida Keys. Reading, however, is the pastime she loves best, and she is a member of many writing groups. She's a winner of the Romance Writers of America's Lifetime Achievement Award and the International Thriller Writers's Silver Bullet. She is an active member of International Thriller Writers and Mystery Writers of America, and the founder of The Slush Pile Players, an author band and theatrical group. Heather annually hosts the Writers for New Orleans conference to benefit both the city, which is near and dear to her heart, and various other causes, and she hosts a ball each year at the RT Booklovers Convention to benefit pediatric AIDS foundations.

New York Times and *USA TODAY* bestselling author **B.J. Daniels** lives in Montana with her husband, Parker, and three springer spaniels. When not writing, she quilts, boats and plays tennis. Contact her at bjdaniels.com, on Facebook or on Twitter, @bjdanielsauthor.

New York Times Bestselling Author

HEATHER GRAHAM

PICTURE ME DEAD

HHARLEQUIN® BESTSELLING AUTHOR COLLECTION

ISBN-13: 978-1-335-58002-3

Picture Me Dead

Copyright © 2018 by Harlequin Books S.A.

The publisher acknowledges the copyright holders of the individual works as follows:

Picture Me Dead
Copyright © 2003 by Heather Graham Pozzessere

Hotshot P.I.
Copyright © 1997 by Barbara Johnson Smith

Recycling programs for this product may not exist in your area.

This edition published by arrangement with Harlequin Books S.A.

For questions and comments about the quality of this book, please contact us at CustomerService@Harlequin.com.

® and TM are trademarks of Harlequin Enterprises Limited or its corporate affiliates. Trademarks indicated with ® are registered in the United States Patent and Trademark Office, the Canadian Intellectual Property Office and in other countries.

⊕ HARLEQUIN®
™ www.Harlequin.com

Printed in U.S.A.

CONTENTS

PICTURE ME DEAD

Heather Graham

Acknowledgments

First and foremost, for Robert Merrill, forensic artist, Miami-Dade Police.

For the great folks with the South Miami Police: Pam Stack, victim advocate; Lillian Gilbert, communications officer; and Detective Kathleen Sorensen.

With thanks as well to some of the wonderful people who keep life fun and challenging in the midst of all else, the very talented staff and instructors at Arthur Murray Studios, Coral Gables, Florida: Wayne Smith, Kene Bayliss, Ana Chacon-Bayliss, Mauricio Ferreira, Romney Reyes, Christina Davo, Adrian Persad (and Rhea!), Shaine Taylor, Liz Myers and Carolina Francesehi, and definitely, above all, the one who keeps us all moving and in shape, Nelida Nunez. Thanks also to a number of fellow students who have been tolerant, kind and kept a lot of nights filled with camaraderie and laughter: Adriana Alvarez, Carolina Alvarez, Dyann Alvarez, Sean Abreu, Silvia Curiati, Judith Camposano, Lauren Carroll, Larry Durham, Enrique Gonzalez, Majo Gomez, Stella Gomez, Denise Herrera, Yvette Herrera, Raymond King, Barbara Mishaan, Vanessa Monlina, Garry Norris, Kristy Pino, Susanna Robles, Samantha Rodriguez, David and Lynn Squillacote, Jim and Dee Bowers, Kim and Angie Wahlstrom, Sergio Alcantara, Brianne Grafton, Rosans Winarto, Jan Svenson, Merle Roe, Sean Lawrence, Ben Wisz, Miguel Sandoval and last, but never least, Kenda Avery, who gives new dimensions to swing and also loves to read.

Prologue

She stared into the darkness of the room by night, suddenly and acutely aware of where she was—and the man at her side. Her mind sped up as she tried to retrace the last hours...but nothing would come to her. She had thought herself so aware, so savvy, and yet she had been taken in.

She listened. In time, she was certain she heard the slow deep breathing indicating that he was asleep.

No time to consider just what she had done, how far she had taken her quest. No time to consider the ramifications of her actions. There was no time to think of anything now....

Other than escape.

Carefully, she rolled to her side. Still careful, she rose. With the greatest quiet, she dressed.

"Going somewhere?"

She turned in the moonlight. He was resting on one elbow, watching her.

She laughed softly, came back to the bed, eased a hip on to it and leaned over to kiss his forehead. "What a night," she said softly. "Wow. But now… I have the strangest craving for ice cream. And coffee. I'm in such a blur," she said. Her nightly habits shouldn't seem too strange to him; she had just made it here, into the inner sanctum.

"I'm sure there's ice cream in the freezer. And we always have coffee."

"But I don't want just any ice cream. I want some of that new stuff they're serving at Denny's," she said. "Thank God it's Denny's, or else it wouldn't be open now. And, of course, I'm feeling a little strange. About being here. With you."

She stood, slipped on her shoes, and went for her shoulder bag. It felt strangely light.

"I'm sorry," he said quietly. "You're not going anywhere."

He rose in the darkness. She didn't underestimate the extraordinary shape he was in. Being in shape was one of life's passions for him. Along with a few others.

"I just want ice cream," she said.

He walked toward her. There was no malice evident in his face, rather a form of sorrow. "You're such a liar. I have a feeling you've had what you wanted now, what you really came to achieve. And I'm so sorry, but you're not going to leave."

She felt in the large leather handbag for her sidearm.

"The gun is gone," he said softly.

He took another step toward her. The gun *was* gone.

The terror of that simple fact registered in her mind, along with a change of gears. Run. Get the hell out.

"What are you going to do to me?"

"I really don't want to hurt you, you know."

The bastard. He *didn't* want to hurt her. *Just kill her.*

He took a step toward her. She decided to use the bag as a weapon, swinging it with practiced force. She caught his head dead center, then stepped forward and brutally slammed a knee into him. She heard the ragged intake of his breath; he doubled over.

And she burst out the bedroom door.

She ran desperately through the house and out to the front room, seeking the exit. Then she stopped dead still, stunned, staring at a person she had never expected to see blocking her way. In a flash, it made sense. The fact that she had been recognized for what she was... known.

"You...cockroach," she managed to whisper.

"*Rich* cockroach now."

Bile rose in her; sick fury rose to her lips. Now she knew the extremity of the position into which she had put herself. There was nothing she could say to describe the depths of her revulsion and rage.

Nothing that would change what she had discovered.

Instinct and common sense kicked in. There was only one thing she could do now, and that was fight desperately for self-preservation.

She ran.

She streaked through the front room. Reached the door, fumbled with the locks and was out. There was no alarm.

Of course not. Alarms brought....

The police.

Hysteria threatened to overwhelm her.

Within seconds she was racing down the drive. She could hear shouting echoing through the house behind her.

She knew she would never make it into the garage, never reach her car before they were on her. She had to run, hope to reach the street.

Maybe there would be an early riser driving on the highway.

She sped down the long drive, never having known before just how quickly she could move when necessary. No, not when necessary. When desperate. She dug into her bag for her cell phone as she tried to maintain speed. Eureka! It was there.

She hit 9-1-1. Nothing. They'd left her the phone. They'd just removed the battery.

She kept running, moving like a sprinter, no thought of saving energy, driven by adrenaline and instinct, the desire to live.

She became aware of a terrible rasping sound.

And then she realized that the rasping sound was the ragged inhalation and exhalation of her own lungs. She had escaped the house, probably more than they had ever thought she could do. A small victory. Her only hope was covering enough distance, finding help, before they caught up with her.

She swallowed hard, ignoring the fire and agony that seared through her lungs and limbs. She was well aware that she had a long way to go. The pain didn't matter. Hysteria began to rise in her. She forced it down.

She made it to the road, her feet hitting the pavement, and realized just how dark it could be in the country.

She had grown up in the city; there had always been light. But out here...

She hadn't gone that far, and already she could feel her muscles burning; her lungs were on fire.

Lights flared in front of her, sudden and blinding out of the darkness. A car! A car coming down the road just when she needed help so badly. She stumbled to a halt, dizzy with the fact that a miracle had occurred. She raced to the driver's door. "Oh, thank God! Move over. Quickly—"

She felt the gun wedged against her ribs from behind. And she heard his whisper. He wasn't even winded. "Game's up."

She went dead still. She looked at the driver. Saw the slow smile and realized she knew the face. Her heart sank.

She prayed. She asked for forgiveness for all her sins. Pride and self-confidence had been strong within her.

Oh, Lord, yes. Far too much pride. And determination. She had wanted to be the one to find the truth— and she had wanted the glory.

The glory! That was a laugh now.

Amazing how someone with so much self-confidence could be so frightened.

Don't panic, don't give up, she warned herself. Think of all the right things, reason, remember all the tricks, human psychology, everything you've been taught....

How to survive this...

How to pray. Lord, she was so deeply sorry for those she had hurt.

"Let's go," he told her icily.

"Shoot me right here."

"Well, I could. But I think you're going to do what I

say. As long as you're living and breathing, there's hope, right? The faintest hope that you might turn the tide on me. So…start moving. Get in the car. Now. Front seat, slow and careful. I'm right behind you."

She did as she was told. Because he was right. She would fight to the very last second, as long as there was a breath in her body. She was shoved in next to the driver while he got into the rear seat, keeping the gun on her all the while. Her mind worked hard. What was his plan? How would he see to it that there was no evidence of the fact that she had been here, had been with him?

As they neared the house, the garage door opened. The car they were in stopped; she was dragged out. He indicated that she should walk ahead of him. "Time for another ride, I'm afraid."

She looked at him.

He smiled at her. Grimly.

"One last ride. I am sorry."

The door to her own car was open. The muzzle of the gun pressed hard into her back, she got into the car. She had no choice. Because he was right. She wouldn't give up while she still had breath. Still had hope.

An unknown figure, a silent accomplice, was awaiting them. As she was forced into the driver's seat, the accomplice slid into the back.

He joined her in the front seat and told her to drive.

Hope…

She twisted the key in the ignition, one step closer to her own demise.

She had to cling to hope.

She talked, because she was afraid and didn't want to be afraid, and at the very least didn't want them to know she was.

"You really are the worst kinds of bastards. All this had nothing to do with religion. You used so many lost souls, promising them salvation."

"Well, there you go. You have us. Such a smart girl. Too smart. You just weren't smart enough to see the forest for the trees."

She glanced into the rearview mirror, trying to discern if she knew the person sitting in the back, if, indeed, it was her betrayer. *She'd been so stupid!* She should have seen…and yet no one else had realized the truth, either, because there had been no reason to expect anything so heinous from someone so apparently decent.

Chills crept along her spine. If only she knew…

She spoke, impatiently and with authority. "You could both get out of this now, without threat of the death penalty. You should drive me straight to police headquarters. Tell the truth. You'd have a chance to plea-bargain."

"We could never let you go," the man at her side said, and his tone was oddly soft. "I'm sorry."

She realized then that he really didn't want to hurt her. That he actually felt sorrow over what he was doing. And she also realized, at that very minute, that he wasn't the one calling the shots.

"If something happens to me, it will never end. Dilessio will be after you until the day he dies."

A swift explosion of guttural fury from the rear should have silenced her. "Dilessio will never be able to prove a thing."

"You see, they'll have to find you first," said the man at her side, his tone still soft.

He was afraid himself, she realized, just as she realized that not even she had really discovered the true depths of what was going on.

Too late to puzzle it out now.

Such a smart girl. Oh, yeah.

In the darkness, as she was directed toward their destination, she began to pray silently. Begging God to welcome her, to forgive her the many sins she had committed.

There was one thing she could do, she realized. Jerk the car off the road, kill them all.

She started to, but the wheel was grabbed from her hand. The sudden pressure on her fingers was so intensely painful that she forgot her purpose. The car rolled to a halt.

"We're parked. This will do," the one in the back said.

The pain in her hand was still excruciating. She fought it, still thinking desperately, wondering what move she could make to disarm the two men who held her at their mercy.

There was none.

Oh, God…

A split second movement from the back sent her head careening with deadly force against the windshield. As all light faded, as even pain ebbed to nothingness, she heard his voice, a sound as soft as the oblivion that reached out to welcome her.

"I really never wanted to hurt you. I am so sorry. Truly…sorry."

God, forgive me.

The prayer filled her mind.

Fragmented like crystal…

And was gone.

Chapter 1

Five years later

What happened, Ashley admitted to herself later, was at least partly her own fault. But another part of it was that he startled her. And being startled was closely akin to being *scared*. She hated to admit to being afraid over silly things, though. It just didn't fit with the life she had chosen.

So…

It might well have been her fault. But it wasn't even 6:00 a.m. Nick did have a few old-timers who arrived early now and then, tapping at the door at the crack of dawn because they knew he would be up, but she hadn't been expecting to run into any of them before the sun had even begun to peek out.

It was dark. Still the middle of the night to some people.

She was on her cell phone, as well. When it had rung, she had been certain it was Karen or Jan, making sure that she was up and almost out of the house. Naturally she answered it while juggling her coffee, purse, keys and overnight bag. It wasn't Karen or Jan, though, but her friend Len Green, who had been with the metro force for some time now and watched over her progress like a mother hen. He was calling because he knew she was leaving. He joked that he'd called to tell her to have a great vacation and, out of kindness to Jan and Karen, since Ashley had opted to do the driving, make sure she was actually up and ready to swing by for them at approximately the right time. She laughed, thanking Len for calling, and indignantly informed him that she was always up on time. He mentioned briefly that he might be driving up that night after work with some friends on the Broward fire rescue team, so maybe they would run into one another. She had clicked the end-call button as she opened the door, but the phone was still in her hand.

There had been no tapping on the door. No hint of a knock at all. She was leaving, so she simply struggled with the lock and all she held, opened the door and barged right out.

And into *him*.

Into. Straight into. With impetus.

In the darkness, with the shadows of early morning broken only by the pale lights from the house, she walked right into him. She nearly screamed, as her overnight bag fell on his feet. One of the tins of cookies she had been carrying went flying. Her coffee cup, held in the same hand as her keys, was violently jostled, sending the hot liquid flying over both of them.

"Shit!"

"Shit!"

He was wearing a short-sleeved, open denim shirt, so the coffee hit his flesh. He swore—an instinctive response to being scalded. When *he* swore, *she* swore. She felt herself being steadied and stepped back quickly, still wondering if she should scream like the bloody blazes. But apparently he offered her no threat.

He looked something like a large, toned beach bum.

"What the fu—hell!" she stuttered.

"Yeah, what the hell?" he repeated, brushing at his chest, where her coffee had spattered. "I'm looking for Nick."

"At this time of the morning?"

"Excuse me, but he told me to come at 'this time of the morning.'"

The man was definitely aggravated. A friend of Nick's, huh? She took another step back, frowning as she eyed him. Could be. She'd seen him before. Not all that often. He wasn't one of the guys who sat around the bar, sharing their lives as they played armchair football during the Sunday games. Quieter. Actually, he had seemed like the brooding, silent type, the few times she had seen him. Dress him up differently and he could be Heathcliff, out walking the moors. When she had noticed him before, he had been sitting. Now she saw that he was tall, six-two or three. He had dark hair, dark eyes, strong features, and he was somewhere in his late twenties to mid-thirties. He had a rough, outdoor-type look to him, but then, most of the people around the marina had that look. Deeply tanned and well muscled—easy to see, since he was wearing cutoffs and his shirt was open, probably just thrown on as a concession to the fact that he was arriving at the private entrance to an eating establishment where shirts and shoes were required by Florida law.

"You should have knocked," she said, then was aggravated at herself, because she sounded defensive. She *lived* here, damn it.

"Well, you know, I was about to do just that—before being attacked by flying coffee."

He was suggesting, of course, that she should be apologizing. No way. She had been, frankly, scared, and that had made her angry. This was her home, and there was no reason in hell why she should have expected a man to be standing there. Not to mention that she was wearing coffee, as well. So no way was she about to apologize.

"Damn!" she said, realizing that half the cookies were a total loss, already attracting sea birds. She stared at him again. "You've broken my cookies."

"I broke your cookies?" he said. She didn't like his tone at all. Or the way his facial features tightened, more with slough-it-off contempt than with any anger. He was incredulous, as if her cookies couldn't matter in the least.

Well, they did matter. They were a present. Sharon had left the containers on the counter with a big bow on them, suggesting she have a wonderful weekend.

"My cookies are all over the ground. Good cookies. Home-baked cookies. Cookies that were a present." She tried to stop herself. She was sounding ridiculous—over cookies. "My keys are somewhere, I'm late, and now I have to change. We don't open here until eleven—for your future reference. Nick is awake, however. I'll tell him that you're here."

"You forgot something in your assessment of the damage."

"What?"

"Your coffee just burned my chest. I could sue."

"I would say your attempt to barge into *my* home caused me to ruin my own shirt."

"And your cookies, of course."

"And my cookies. So go ahead. Sue. You just do that."

She turned back into the house, intentionally closing the door in his face. "Nick!" she called to her uncle. "Someone to see you." Beneath her breath, she added, "Major-league, overgrown *ass* here to see you."

She didn't wait to see if Nick responded. In a hurry, she raced through the private quarters that abutted the restaurant to her bedroom, changed quickly and started back out again. Apparently Nick had heard her, because the man was standing in the kitchen now. Nick did seem to know the guy, because they were discussing something over coffee. As she breezed through, they both stopped talking. The dark-haired man watched her, coolly appraising, judging her, she was certain, but as to what his judgment might be, she had no idea, nor did she care. Nick had certainly never required that she—or any of his employees—be nice to people simply because they were customers.

"Ashley…" Nick began.

"Where's Sharon? Is she up yet? I need to thank her for the cookies," she said, staring back at the newcomer. She got a better look at him now. Tough guy, strong body, good-looking face, easy, powerful, controlled manner. Probably thought he was God's gift to the women of the world.

She purposely looked away from him and at her uncle.

"Sharon didn't stay last night. She was getting ready for some campaign work this morning," Nick said. "Ashley, if you'll take a second—"

"Can't. I'll hit all the traffic if I wait. Love you."

Rude, perhaps, but she was in no mood for an introduction and pleasantries.

"Drive carefully," Nick admonished.

"Absolutely. You know me." She kissed his cheek. "'Bye. Love you."

Outside, she retrieved everything that she had dropped, except, of course, the cookies that had spilled and fed a half dozen gulls.

She could hear Nick apologizing to the man on her behalf. "I don't know what's with her this morning. Ash is usually the most courteous young woman you'd ever want to meet."

Sorry, Nick, she thought. She hoped the guy wasn't a really good friend of his.

She was about fifteen minutes late picking up Karen, which made her about twenty-five minutes late picking up Jan. Yet once they were all in the car, it didn't seem to matter so much, and the tension and anger she had been feeling ebbed quickly. They were still a good fifteen to twenty minutes ahead of the real start of rush hour. Both Karen and Jan were in terrific moods, delighted that they were heading off on their few days' vacation together. There had been one container of cookies left, and Jan had happily dived right into them.

"Hey, pass the cookies up here," Karen said to Jan.

"Excuse me, you got shotgun, I got the cookies," Jan responded, grinning, then passed the tin of homemade chocolate chip cookies up to Karen in the front seat. Karen offered them first to Ashley, who was driving.

Ashley shook her head. "No, thanks." Her eyes were on the road. So far they were clipping nicely along I-95. It didn't seem to matter that they had started out later than intended. Not that much later, she told herself.

"That's how Ashley stays thin," Jan noted. "She has the 'just say no' thing down pat."

"It's because she's going to be a cop," Karen said.

Ashley laughed. "It's because she gorged on them before leaving the house," she told the two of them. That was true. Before the one container had gone to the birds, she'd eaten a number of them.

"Think they might be dietetic cookies?" Karen asked hopefully.

"No way. Nothing that tastes this good is dietetic," Jan said with a sigh. "We'll make it up, though. We'll check into the hotel, go to the pool, swim like the dickens and walk it all off at the parks."

"We'll just eat more junk at the parks," Jan said woefully. "Boy, Ashley, you just had to bring these cookies, huh?"

"If I hadn't brought the cookies, we just would have stopped and ordered something really greasy at one of the rest stops," Ashley assured her. "There should have been more cookies, actually. Enough to last the trip."

"What happened?"

"I dropped them. Actually, I banged into some guy looking for Nick and they went flying. His fault, not mine."

"We're going to have to stop anyway—coffee to go with the cookies," Karen reminded her. "In fact, I'm stopping here and now. Not one more bite until we get the coffee to go with the cookies."

"Milk would be good," Jan said.

"Milk goes with Oreos," Karen said. "Coffee goes with chocolate chips."

"I actually had coffee, but then...oh, well," Ashley murmured.

"You dropped *it*, too?"

"Yeah, I dropped it." She grinned at Jan via the mirror. "Actually, I spilled it all over him. And myself. I had to change. That's why I was so late."

"Was it a good friend of Nick's?" Jan asked. "Was he ticked?"

"Hey, was he cute, or one of the old salts?" Karen asked.

"I don't think he's a good friend, but I've seen him around before. I guess he was ticked. But it was his fault."

"That you spilled coffee on him?" Jan said.

"Well, he was just there—practically in the doorway. Who expects to open their door to a hulking stranger before six in the morning?"

"Well, actually, you should," Karen pointed out. "All those aging old tars living in the houseboats at the marina know Nick is up early, and they'd rather have your coffee than make their own."

"So, Ash, you started the morning off by burning an old geezer?" Jan said. "That isn't like you. Most of the people who frequent that place think you're the most wonderful little darling in the entire world and that Nick is lucky to have you."

"I hope you didn't cause an old guy's pacemaker to stop," Karen told her.

"I don't think this guy has a pacemaker."

"He wasn't an old geezer?" Jan said, perking up.

"He was a young asshole," Ashley told her.

"Hey, you never answered me, if he was cute or not," Karen said.

Ashley hesitated, frowning slightly. She didn't pay a ton of attention to everyone who came into Nick's—she didn't help out now anywhere near as much as she had done in years past. But she was usually observant. She noticed faces, because she loved to draw. And she usually remembered features very clearly. It seemed strange to her now that she had seen the man before and really not taken that much notice of him.

"I would never describe him as 'cute,'" she assured Karen.

"Too bad. I was thinking there might be someone hot and new at Nick's to observe," Jan said sadly.

Ashley was silent for a minute.

"Hey, she didn't say that he wasn't hot," Karen observed.

"I don't think he's the type I'd want to take an interest in," Ashley said.

"Because he was rude?" Jan asked. "It didn't sound to me as if you were in the mood to be Miss Manners yourself."

Ashley shook her head. "I wasn't rude. All right, yes, I *was* rude. Maybe I should even have apologized. But I was just in a hurry, and he startled me—even scared me there for a few seconds. He's just...dark."

"Dark? Hispanic, Latin, Afro-American?" Karen said, confused.

"No, dark, as in...intense."

"Ah, intense," Karen said.

"Well, I mean, he's dark, too. Dark-haired, dark-eyed. Tanned. Apparently likes boats, or water, or the sun."

"Um. Sounds sexy. The *dark* type."

"Did he have a bod?" Karen demanded.

"Yeah, I guess."

"Maybe I'll start hanging around Nick's more," Karen said.

"Oh, right, like you need to go looking for men," Jan said.

"Yeah, I do. Who do I meet at a grade school? You've got it made, because you stand up in front of hordes of people in great outfits and sing. You're the one who doesn't need to go looking for men."

"Looking is easy. They're all over. Finding good ones is tough," Jan said.

"Well, forget Nick's, then. Don't all the psychologists say never to look for a date in a bar? You're supposed to meet them by bowling or something," Ashley said.

"I hate bowling," Karen commented.

"Then bowling probably wouldn't be a great way for you to meet a guy," Jan observed. "There you have it, how not to date in a nutshell. Put the three of us together, and we can really solve the major problems in the world," she said ruefully.

"Hey, I solve the problems of six- to ten-year-olds on a daily basis," Karen reminded her. "I'm responsible for molding the minds and morals of the future voters of a country in need of the best next generation in history. Ashley spends her days learning how to shoot and deal with the scum of the earth. This weekend, I think we should leave the serious stuff behind and worry about the next best serious stuff—our tans and the size of our butts."

"We won't set our goals too high," Jan said. "If we can just find a few strangers who have bathed and are halfway articulate and don't mind a few minutes on a dance floor, we'll call it social triumph. I need a cookie."

"Works for me," Karen agreed. "But...butt size, huh? I think I have to have one more cookie, too, before the coffee, since it's going to be at least twenty minutes before we reach the rest stop."

Ashley noted, with a quick glance at her friend, that Karen delicately bit off a tiny piece of cookie and chewed slowly, savoring every nuance. That, she decided, was how Karen stayed the nearest thing to perfect. She ate everything, but had the art of nibbling down pat. One cookie could last Karen an hour. She was petite, a perfect size two, with huge sky-blue eyes and a sweep of natural, near-platinum hair, testimony to a distant Norse heritage, along with her family name, Ericson. Jan, on the other hand, was dark-haired, dark-eyed, five-nine and as fiery as her Latin surname, Hevia, suggested she might be. Ashley referred to them often by the fairy-tale names they had gained as children: Rose White and Rose Red. She was a green-eyed redhead herself, the coloration courtesy of her mother's family, the McMartins, since her last name was Montague. Her father's family had been mainly French, with a little Cherokee or Seminole thrown in, which meant that she had only a small spattering of freckles on her nose and the ability to acquire a fairly decent tan without burning like a beet first. She was the medium between Jan and Karen at five feet six. The two had playfully labeled her the thorn in the roses. The three had been friends since grade school, and had shared dreams, victories and heartaches ever since. This weekend was something they had been looking forward to for a long time, since their adult lives had taken them in very different directions. Karen was teaching and going to school for her master's degree. Jan was a singer, and though she doubted she was ever going to achieve mega-star status, she didn't care. She loved singing and songwriting, and her career was beginning to take off nicely, if modestly. She and her accompanist were being booked as an opening act for shows across the country. Ashley was in her third month at the metro police academy, and she had thrown herself wholeheartedly into every class, every subtlety of the law, rights and self-defense that could be learned.

"Think Sharon and your uncle Nick are going to get married?" Jan asked, leaning forward.

Sharon Dupre, the baker of the divine cookies, had been seeing Nick for almost a year now. They were definitely a hot item.

"Maybe. Who knows," Ashley replied, watching the clock and the road. "Nick is such a dyed-in-the-wool bachelor. He loves his fishing and his restaurant, and I guess, as long as Sharon tolerates his habits, it could happen."

"Well, Nick is going to have to tolerate Sharon's weird real estate hours," Karen said.

"True," Ashley agreed. "He seems to deal with it all okay. Nick is a live-and-let-live guy." She knew that well, having grown up with her uncle. She was often sad to realize that she barely remembered her parents. They had been killed in an automobile accident when she had been three. She adored Nick; he had filled the roles of both parents with love and tenderness, and there was nothing she wanted more for him than the laid-back happiness with which he had always lived. Whether that included marriage to Sharon or not was a decision he was going to have to make himself.

"Hey, there's a great pair of pants in this ad," Jan said, sitting forward to show the magazine she was reading to Karen. "Think they'd look good on someone with fat thighs?"

"They *are* great pants," Karen said.

Jan tapped her on the arm with the magazine in mock anger. "You're supposed to tell me that I don't have fat thighs," she informed her friend.

"Sorry. You don't have fat thighs. And I think they'd be great on me, too—a little person with a bubble butt."

"Great pants all around," Jan said.

"You're supposed to tell me I don't have a bubble butt."

"I'm jealous, considering I'm all thighs and no butt," Jan said, then switched subjects abruptly. "You should have joined the Coral Gables force, or even South Miami, rather than metro, Ashley. What were you thinking? Coral Gables has some really cute guys. And they're nice."

"Yeah, the metro guys can be assholes," Karen agreed.

Ashley arched a brow, meeting Karen's gaze. "You just think they're assholes because you got a mega-ticket from one," she said. "I wanted to be on the metro force." Miami-Dade County, also known as the Greater Miami area, was made up of more than two dozen small cities, villages and municipalities. Some had their own large forces, with departments dealing with everything from jaywalking to murder, while others depended on the metropolitan force, which covered the entire county, for their homicide and forensic divisions. She had always wanted to work where she could cover the full scope of the area where she had lived all her life. "There are good officers—*and* even cute ones on all the forces."

"And you were whizzing down the highway when you got that ticket," Jan said. "Oh, look, Ashley is bristling. When she's in her patrol car after graduation and needs to give out tickets, you'll have to watch out. All she'll need to do is park near your house and wait for you to leave the driveway at ninety."

"I do not speed that badly," Karen protested. "And look—Ashley is speeding now!"

"She's going two miles over the limit," Jan said. "And watch it, or we'll wind up crawling the whole way to Orlando."

Even as Jan spoke, Ashley began to press on the brake.

"See," Jan said.

"No, no, there's something going on up there," Ashley said, frowning.

The cars ahead of her were suddenly squealing and braking. Behind her, two cars, in attempting to stop, nearly plowed into the median.

They were almost at the turnpike. The highway was five lanes each way here, with turnpike access just ahead, and the ramp for the east-west expressway also branching off. The early morning traffic, which had been so smooth, was suddenly a mess.

"What the hell is going on?" Ashley murmured. Creeping in line behind the cars directly ahead of her, she saw that two cars had apparently been involved in an accident. She was off duty and still just in the academy, but if there had been an accident and there were no other officers at the scene, by the book, she was obliged to stop until someone on duty could arrive.

But just as the thought occurred to her, Karen, who had toyed with the idea of going into law instead of education, read her mind.

"No, we don't need to stop. There's already a cop car at the scene—just ahead. He must have just gotten there."

Whatever had caused the accident, they had missed it by no more than a few minutes. The lanes weren't blocked off yet, which meant the officer really had just arrived. The drivers of the vehicles were both out of their cars. One was sitting on the median, a man with his face in his hands. The other, who had apparently struck the first, was standing by his car, just staring at the road.

The accident had occurred in the far left lane. Ashley was driving in the lane directly next to it. As she moved along, she looked to her left, noting gratefully that neither driver appeared to have been hurt.

But someone had.

As she crept along in her lane, she suddenly gasped.

There was a man on the highway. Sprawled in the lane, naked except for a pair of white briefs. He was facedown, head twisted to the side, apparently dead.

She'd gone through everything necessary to become a cop. Taken the tests and seen all the videos featuring the types of horrors a policeman was likely to be up against at some point in his career or hers. But the sight of the man sprawled on the highway, naked except for his underwear, was still shocking and terrible.

"Oh, my God," Karen breathed at her side.

"What?" Jan demanded.

Ashley's hands were glued around the steering wheel as she fixed the entire scene in her mind. The immediate area first. The position of the two cars involved. The cop and the cop car that had just arrived. The body. Sprawled. Naked except for the white briefs. The head, twisted. The blood that seemed surreal against flesh and asphalt.

The cars, still veering off toward the median. And, across the median, cars slowing, braking, the screech of brakes. Far across the opposing lanes, someone standing, staring at all the traffic as if waiting for a light to change.

She moved past the body. It was still imprinted in her mind. As crystal clear and vivid as a photograph. The rest merging, blurring. The cars in the opposing lanes a kaleidoscope of color. The figure standing, watching the scene…

Just someone. Faceless. Dressed in…black, she thought. Man? Woman? She didn't know. Part of what had happened? A friend of the man who had been struck?

"What? What the hell is it?" Jan demanded from the back seat.

"A body. A body on the highway," Karen said, her voice faltering.

"A body?" Jan swung around.

They were past it now.

"Maybe I should turn around," Ashley said.

"The hell you should! The cop trying to deal with the situation and the traffic would be pissed as hell to have something else to deal with," Karen said. And she was right. There was already an officer on the scene. Traffic was knotting into serious snarls as it was. By the time she could safely reach an exit, turn around and get back to the scene, an ambulance would have arrived, and more on-duty officers, probably even those specializing in traffic accidents and fatalities, would be on hand.

"You've got to forget it, just forget it," Karen said sternly. "Please, Ashley. How many vacations do we get together? And get serious, there are accidents every damn day down here. Fatal ones, too. It's sad but true. You are not on duty. You're not even a full-fledged cop. And if you start taking every single event you witness to heart, you're going to be a lousy cop, because you'll be too emotionally involved with each incident when you're required to be alert to everything."

Karen was making a great deal of sense.

"I didn't even see the body," Jan said.

"You're lucky," Karen countered, swallowing.

Ashley was glad that, despite her words, Karen had been equally affected by the sight.

"There are accidents every single day," Karen repeated. "People die, and they're going to continue to die," she told Ashley sternly.

Ashley glanced at her quickly. "They don't die naked except for their underwear, on the highway, every day," she countered.

"Did he come from one of the cars?" Jan asked.

"Maybe, but how?" Karen said.

"Perhaps he was in one of the passenger seats and was thrown out when the accident occurred," Jan said.

"He was riding around in his underwear?" Ashley said.

"Hey, this is South Florida. Spend a little more time at the clubs on South Beach," Jan said. "He might have been riding around stark naked, who the hell knows?"

"I don't think he was in one of the cars," Ashley

said, remembering the relative positions of the cars, and the body.

"So he was walking across the highway in his underwear?" Jan said.

"Maybe there will be something on the news," Karen said, switching the radio channel from the popular rock frequency they'd had on to the twenty-four-hour news station. The commentator was giving a rundown of events in Washington, but then switched over to local traffic.

"There's been an accident on I-95, northbound, a pedestrian struck by oncoming traffic," a pleasant female voice said over the airwaves. "Both left-hand lanes are now closed, so use caution and slow down while approaching the turnpike interchange. For all you folks traveling from north Dade and Broward on your way to work in the downtown Miami area, be on the alert for slowing traffic on the southbound side. The turnpike is still running smoothly to that point, but to the south, we've got an accident on the off ramp from the Palmetto to Miller Drive."

The traffic report ended, and then a different newscaster came on to give a report about boating conditions.

By then they had reached the entrance to the turnpike. Ashley threw her coins into the bucket at the toll booth and moved into traffic, aware that Karen was staring at her.

"We're going to put it out of our minds and have a good time," Karen insisted firmly.

Ashley nodded. She tried to keep silent, then said, "It's just too bizarre. What was a man doing running across the highway in his underwear?"

"He must have been doped up," Jan said from the back.

"That must be it," Karen agreed. "Why the hell else would you try to cross at least ten lanes of traffic—dressed to the teeth *or* half-naked?"

"Ashley, when you go back to the academy Monday morning, I'm sure you'll be able to find someone who knows something about it," Jan said.

"Yeah, you're right."

"And until then, there's nothing you can do," Karen said.

"Yes, there is," Ashley said.

"What's that?"

"Stop at the first rest station, buy a big cappuccino, a horrible, greasy breakfast sandwich and stop shaking," Ashley said.

"All right, I'm up for that," Jan said. "I'll stick with regular coffee and these cookies, though."

They reached the service plaza less than thirty miles later, still subdued, but trying to rekindle the light mood that had been with them as they'd started out. While Ashley and Jan stood in line for coffee and food, Karen gathered brochures for Orlando and its multitude of tourist attractions. When they were finally seated, Jan pounced on the brochure for Arabian Knights. "I've never been there. I loved Medieval Times, though, and this place has horses, too."

"And *men*," Karen said. "But I thought we were going to go dancing? You know, to Pleasure Island or someplace like that."

"One night dancing, one night watching gorgeous men on horseback," Jan said.

Ashley was barely listening. She had taken out a pencil and was sketching on her napkin.

A hand fell over hers, stopping the movement of

her pencil mid-slide. She looked up and met Karen's. "That's chilling—too close to what we just saw," Karen said.

Jan drew the napkin from her and shuddered. "What are we going to do, Ashley? You've got to let it drop." She gazed down at the sketch again. "Thank God I was busy looking at pants that would look good on people with fat thighs," she said, trying to draw a smile. "I'm haunted just by the picture."

"You should have stayed in art school," Karen said. "A drawing on a napkin...and it's just like the real thing. Please, Ashley..."

Ashley crumpled up the napkin. "Sorry," she murmured guiltily. Her friends were right. There was nothing she could do about what had happened.

And she was destined to see much worse during her career as a cop.

"You haven't really given up on art, have you?" Jan asked her. "I mean, you're good. Really good. I've never seen anyone who can sketch people so well."

"I'll never give it up," Ashley said. "I love to draw. It's just that..."

"She likes the concept of a paycheck," Karen told Jan with a sigh.

"You could have gotten a paycheck as an artist. I know it," Jan said.

"Art school just cost too much," Ashley said.

"You didn't take that scholarship because you were too afraid Nick would want to help you and he couldn't afford it," Karen mused sagely.

"Nick would never stop me from pursuing any dream," Ashley said a little defensively. And it was true. She knew Nick had been disappointed when she turned down the scholarship that had been offered to her by a prestigious Manhattan art college. But even with the scholarship, the money necessary to live and study in New York—even in a dorm—would have been too much. She could have gotten a part-time job, but it wouldn't have been enough. Nick would have tried to help, but with tourism suffering, he would probably have just about sent himself into bankruptcy.

"Look, I love art, but I always wanted to be a cop. My dad was a cop, remember?"

"None of us really *remembers*," Karen said. "It was so long ago."

"I remember that I loved my folks and admired my dad," Ashley said. "And police work is fascinating."

"Yeah, real fascinating. You're going to be in a patrol car, trying to chase down speeders, like Karen," Jan said.

"Cute, Jan, really cute," Karen said.

"Sorry."

"Honest to God, I'm doing exactly what I want to be doing," Ashley said.

"So, horses or dancing tonight?" Karen said.

"Let's just flip a coin—we'll fit them both in," she promised. She crumpled up the wrapper from her sandwich along with the napkin on which she'd been drawing. "Ready to hit the road?"

"Want me to drive?" Karen asked.

"Good God, no!" Jan piped in. "She'll be arresting you—or giving you a warning speech, at the very least—from the passenger seat. Hey, can you write a ticket if you're sitting next to someone who's driving your own car?"

"Jan," Karen said firmly. "I'm going to throttle you

in a minute. Your precious little throat will be wounded, and you'll sound like a dying 'gator rather than a song-bird."

"Hey, you heard that—she's threatening me!" Jan said.

"Oh, will you two please stop?" Ashley begged, a smile twitching her lips.

"Seriously, want one of us to drive?" Karen said.

Ashley shook her head. "No, I'm fine."

As far as driving went, she *was* fine.

But...

It felt as if the body on the highway would be etched into her mind forever.

Chapter 2

Nick was behind the bar, washing glasses, when Sharon Dupre returned. She hurried in, hoping he wasn't going to ask about where she'd been. She had said that she would arrive to help with the lunch crowd, but she hadn't managed to get back in time.

He didn't question her. She should have known he wouldn't, she thought as he looked up at her with his customary grin. Nick wasn't the jealous type. If she wasn't enjoying his company and wanted out, she was welcome to leave at any time. If she was happy with him, well, then, she should be there, and he would be delighted.

"Hey, how was your day?" he asked.

"Great."

"Sell anything?"

"Showed two expensive places, but I don't have any bites—yet."

"It takes time."

"Has Ashley called? Did the girls reach their hotel yet?"

Nick shook his head. "She won't call me today unless there's a problem. I'll probably hear from her tomorrow. Hey, she loved the cookies. She'll tell you herself, when she gets back."

"Good, I'm glad."

She set her purse down behind the bar and gave him a kiss, wishing she didn't feel so nervous. It wasn't like her. She was never uneasy. Never. She was always in control.

She started to leave, but he pulled her back, giving her a stronger, much more suggestive kiss. When he released her, she flushed. "Sandy Reilly just came in, and he's staring at us!"

"Sandy's as old as the hills, and we're stirring memories of adventure and excitement and raw sexual thrills for him," Nick replied.

"Chill, you two," Sandy called out. "And break it up. Let's have some service around this place. The old-as-the-hills guy has perfect hearing, and he needs a beer."

Sharon and Nick broke apart, both of them laughing. Nick called out, "Beer's on the house, Sandy."

"Thank the good Lord for some things in life," Sandy said, shaking his white head. "I could really use a cold one."

"You sound desperate, Sandy."

"I am. Now I know why I stick to boats. Just went to pay some bills, and it felt as if I were on the road forever. The traffic sucks."

"Worse than usual?" Nick said.

"Hell yes, seems like every psycho in the world is out there today, and I ain't driving again. Line 'em up for me, Nick. Line 'em up."

Beneath the water, Jake Dilessio could hear the sound of the scraper against the boat. Strange sound, more like rubbing than scratching. He finished with the last of the stubborn barnacles just as his air was giving out. He rose the few feet to the surface, grabbed the *Gwendolyn*'s back ladder, inhaled a deep breath and drew his mask from his face in a single fluid motion. Dripping, he climbed the ladder and stepped onto his houseboat.

He sensed the whirl of motion before his attacker came after him. Tension, years of training and a rush of adrenaline kicked in.

As a fist shot out, he ducked, then bolted straight up, sending out his own left jab. Luck was with him, and he caught his mystery opponent straight in the jaw.

To his amazement, the man—wearing a tailored white dress shirt, tie, seamed navy pants and leather loafers—stayed down, something like a sob escaping him as he heaved in a breath and balanced on one hand and his knees, rubbing his jaw.

"Ah, hell," Jake muttered softly. "Brian?"

"You were sleeping with her," the man said.

Jake reached down, helping his attacker to his feet. The man was almost his height, slim, well built and usually attractive, a blue-eyed, blond surfer type, the kind of guy to whom women tended to flock. Right now, however, his blue eyes were red-rimmed and puffed up from crying, and his jaw was swelling, disrupting the usual classic line of his features.

"Brian, what the hell are you doing here?" he asked quietly. The adrenaline had ebbed from his body as if he'd been deflated. "Come inside, I'll get some ice for your jaw."

Brian Lassiter started to pull away, then followed Jake into the living room of his houseboat. Efficiently designed, the *Gwendolyn* offered a broad main room/ kitchen/dining room area all in one, while a set of stairs led down to an aft cabin and another few steps led up to the main cabin at the fore.

He drew Brian in, setting him on a bar stool, and opened the freezer to get ice. He wrapped a number of cubes in a bar towel and walked over to his visitor, shoving the bundle at him. "Here, put this on your jaw. I'll make coffee."

"I don't need coffee."

"You sure as hell do."

"As if you've never had a few too many to drink."

"I've had a few too many to drink a few too many times. *And* I've done some stupid ass stuff. But coming at me like that...hell, you could have gotten yourself killed."

"I just wanted to deck you once," Brian said. His voice dropped to a whisper-like sob. "Just once. You were sleeping with her."

Jake had started brewing coffee. He flicked the switch on the machine hard and turned around. "Brian, I wasn't sleeping with her. And she never told you I was."

"You're lying. There's no reason for you to tell me the truth now, because Nancy is dead."

"That's right," Jake said, his voice lethally quiet. "Nancy is dead."

"And if you *had* been sleeping with her, you'd never tell me, 'cause now there's no way I could know for sure."

Jake held his temper. "I think we both remember the inquest. It was a nasty, dirty affair. But it proved one thing, Brian. She wasn't with me that night." She'd had what the medical examiner had deemed consensual sex with someone that night. He'd volunteered to be tested, proving that it hadn't been with him.

"She sure as hell wasn't with me," Brian responded bitterly. "But even if she wasn't with you that night, she loved you."

"We were friends, Brian."

"Friends. Yeah." He was silent for a moment. "*You* still think *I* was responsible."

"I never said that."

"You never said that? Like hell. Every time you looked at me during the inquest, you fucking accused me with your eyes."

Brian really had been drinking heavily. Jake shook his head. He understood the feeling. Now and then, he still felt like heading out on a major bender himself.

"Brian, you're wrong. You couldn't be more wrong."

"Accident. They said it was an accident. But you… you never believed that."

"Brian, I think you were responsible for being a real idiot now and then, but not for your wife's death, all right?"

"I didn't make her do shit, man. I never made her do drugs, and when we were together, we never got plastered."

"Brian, you're on a crying jag of a drunk right now. You're not thinking straight. No one ever suggested that you made anyone do anything. You were an ass, and hell yes, she was mad at you a lot. But she loved you, got it? Jesus, Brian, it was all a long time ago now. What the hell brought this on?"

"You don't know? Man, how could you have forgotten?"

Jake stared at Brian. He knew. He knew every damn year. "Her birthday," he said softly.

"Yeah. She'd have been thirty, Jake. Thirty. Shit. She was twenty-five."

Jake leaned against the counter, feeling as if hot wire were coiling in his stomach. "Twenty-five, and there's not a damned thing either of us can do about it now. She's been dead for nearly five years, Brian. And if I've heard right, you've been living for the past two of those years with a flight attendant."

"Yeah, I've been living with a flight attendant," Brian agreed. He shook his head. "Nice girl. I should marry her. But every time I get too close…." His words trailed off, and a pained expression having nothing to do with his swollen jaw crossed his features. "Well, hell, I start to wonder if Nancy will live with me forever, if I won't keep on waking up nights and thinking she's staring at me, thinking that if… Well, hell."

The coffee was ready. Jake turned away from Brian and poured him a cup. Brian had hit a nail right on the head—for the two of them, though Brian couldn't know that.

Jake felt the same. As if something of Nancy continued to haunt him, as well, after all these years.

He brought Brian the coffee. "Brian, nothing is going

to bring Nancy back. And get a grip. Do you know how much time has passed? No one thinks you killed her."

"No. Not that I killed her. That I made her kill herself."

"She didn't kill herself. *I* know it, and *you* know it."

Brian lowered his head and inhaled deeply. "You know, Jake, there are people out there who think you're one heck of a big shit and not the great distinguished powerhouse you always look like in the press."

"There's not a damned thing I can do about what people think, Brian," Jake said evenly.

"Yeah, that's right. You can't arrest them for thinking you're a shit, can you?"

"Brian, drink your coffee, and please tell me you didn't drive down here."

"Why, you gonna arrest me for that?" Brian said belligerently, staring at him.

"No, I'm just going to pray there aren't any broken bodies along the way."

Brian lowered his head. "No, I didn't drive. I had a few drinks at a bar downtown and got a ride to Nick's from a friend. Sat out on the porch and had another few beers there. I didn't drive."

"Good. Finish that and I'll take you home."

Brian stared at him, shaking his head. "I know that Nancy came to you all the time. So sometimes I wonder… hell, with everything she must have said…why don't you just go ahead and tear me to pieces?"

"It would be illegal for me to kill you. And I'm a cop. That would make it really bad."

Brian tried to form a smile; it came out more like a grimace.

"Yeah, but you could beat the shit out of me. Self-defense. I've given you cause a time or two. Why don't you do it? Would it make you feel guilty?"

"No," Jake said flatly.

"Then…?"

"Because she loved you. And I loved her." The other man looked up, startled, and Jake hastened to add, "I didn't say that I'd slept with her, Brian, just that I loved her. And she always believed there was something decent in you. Damned if I can see it, but it must be there. So…finish that coffee and I'll get you home."

Brian stared at him, bowed his head again and nodded. He drank the coffee and quietly asked for another cup. After that, he went into the head and cleaned himself up a bit.

Brian had left his jacket at Nick's; they stopped for it.

Nick was behind the bar, working with Sharon, the woman he'd been dating for nearly a year, and with whom, Nick had informed Jake, he'd fallen in love. At his age. Love. She tolerated his almost twenty-four-hour work schedule. In fact, it was fine with her, since she was into real estate. She put in long days herself, sometimes—sometimes followed by days and days with little or nothing to do. She liked politics, though, and was planning on learning a lot more. She wanted to run for local office.

They hadn't seemed like a pair to hit it off so well. But then, who the hell was he to tell?

Nick arched a brow when Jake walked in with Brian. "Everything all right?"

"Just fine."

"Couldn't be better," Brian said.

"You didn't come for another drink?" Sharon asked Brian warily.

"I'm going to drive Brian home. He left his jacket here. We just came to pick it up."

"Oh," Nick said, looking from one of them to the other.

"I can drive him, if you like, Jake," Sharon offered quietly.

"No, thanks, I'll get him back home."

Brian threw an arm around his shoulders. "Yeah, we're fine. Jake and me, we're like brothers." He grinned. "I'd get him home if he'd had a few too many. You know—share and share alike."

"Let's go, Brian."

Luckily, Brian remembered directions, since he was in a new apartment. The flight attendant's name was Norma. She seemed like a decent woman, coming to the door with concern in her eyes when Brian couldn't quite work the key. Brian managed to introduce Jake without making snide comments. She was nothing like Nancy. Norma was short, fair and incredibly soft spoken. Jake realized that he'd met her once on a trip upstate; she laughed and told him she remembered him, as well.

"Well, hell, why not?" Brian muttered. Those words brought a frown of confusion to the young woman's brow, and Jake was tempted to deck him again.

"I'll get him into bed for you and get his shoes off," Jake said instead.

"The first door upstairs," Norma said. "I think I'll get him a few aspirin and some water. That might help him tomorrow morning. Did he fall?"

Jake pretended he didn't hear. Brian was leaning on him heavily. He tripped up the first step. Jake shifted his arm, lifting Brian's feet in the air, and moved quickly. Brian grinned at him when they hit the landing.

"Did I fall?" he said, laughing, but the sound was pathetic, bitter, and directed against himself. "Hell, yeah, I fell. Into your fist, right?"

"Brian, give yourself a fucking break," Jake muttered.

Jake dropped Brian on the king-sized bed and did as he'd said, getting his shoes off. He was about to walk out when Brian said, "So...you know Norma."

"I saw her on a flight, Brian."

"I bet she'd rather sleep with you, too."

"Quit being such a royal pain," Jake told him. "You're one lucky bastard. You had a great wife, and now...seems this girl loves you. Don't mess this one up. You've got another chance. Don't be an idiot."

He started out.

"So what's it been like for you, Jake?" Brian called to him.

He turned back. Brian was smiling ruefully. "The D.A.'s assistant. She was a real beauty. That lasted, what, three months? I hear there was a Hooters' waitress—girl who was pure body. Ten dates, maybe? You're still pining after Nan, too, aren't you?"

"Brian, sleep it off. Five years is a long time."

He went down the stairs as Norma was coming up them. "Thanks for bringing him home."

"Sure."

"Something like this went down last year, too. His wife's birthday...that's really all he ever says. I knew, soon after we met, of course, that she had died in a tragic accident. He must have really loved her. Anyway, thanks. A man who's dealt with something like that needs help now and then. Hey, would you like coffee or something before heading out?"

"Thank you, no."

"Well, thanks again. This was really good of you."

"No problem."

"Hey, I do remember you from a flight, you know. You're a cop, right?"

"Yeah, that's right."

"So you knew his wife."

"Yes, I did. I was her partner."

Jake didn't say anything more, just continued down the stairs and let himself out. When he returned to his houseboat, he discovered that Nick and Sharon had left him a covered dish of shrimp and pasta.

Good. He was hungry. The long weekend had allowed him a day off, but moving the boat had given him plenty to do. He ate, realizing he was starved.

He fell into bed, exhausted, but knew damned well it would be a while before he slept. Nancy's birthday. She would have been thirty. Hell.

It was usually good to sleep on a houseboat. The light rocking of the waves. Ocean air. Both usually eased his tensions.

Not tonight.

He tossed around for a while, thinking that maybe he shouldn't have opted to spend the night alone. And he thought about Brian's words.

The D.A.'s assistant.

The waitress.

Yeah, there had been women in his life. But still, he would go so far…and back away. Hell, yes. He'd been in love with Nancy. Then. And now…

Now she was a ghost in his life. A phantom. A memory, a scent. Sometimes, he would swear he could still hear her laughter.

He compared every woman he met to her. And he'd never found anyone even remotely like her.

Around two, he fell asleep. He awoke later in a sweat, having slid into the nightmare again. He'd been in the water. The clear ocean water. It had been a beautiful day. Light shone through. Then clouds covered it. The water grew murky. It was canal water, and he was in it, trying to backpedal, knowing what he was going to see. And he'd heard her voice....

He got out of bed, made his way to the kitchen, took a beer from the refrigerator, then went out to stand on deck. He needed to feel the ocean breeze in the night. He all but inhaled the beer, and he knew he was no more over any of this than Brian was.

She would be lost, so feminine, so beautiful, quasi-tragic, talking to him about her personal life....

Then so tough. She was capable in any situation, and she was as good as any guy on the force.

She was his partner. She couldn't keep things from him. If she knew anything, suspected anything...

She hadn't. At least, she had insisted that she hadn't. But maybe she had been in a position to find out.

What the hell had she been doing? He'd never known. And he should have. He'd been her partner, for Christ's sake! She'd died in a car, remnants of alcohol and narcotics in her bloodstream. Accidental death, that had been the ruling. She'd lost control of her car. There had been no evidence of foul play. Even so, during the inquest, all the dirt had come out. Her troubled marriage. Her close friendship—more than friendship?—with Jake.

She was gone.

The victim of a terrible accident. He hadn't believed it. Not then. Not now.

And he'd never met anyone like her.

Something suddenly stirred in his mind.

A brief flash, an odd and fleeting sensation. Then he knew…. Earlier, he'd felt a strange sense of déjà vu. A sense of…

Memory.

Earlier that day. Maybe it had been because on some subconscious level he'd known it was Nancy's birthday. But he had come across someone who reminded him of Nancy. Strange, too, because Nan had been tall, five-ten, dark, willowy. He hadn't seen anyone like that.

It hadn't been that the girl *looked* like Nancy, he realized. It had been something in her manner, her self-confidence, her assurance. She'd had Nancy's ability to stand her ground, undaunted, speak her mind…not back down, fight it out and still, somehow, leave a trace of magnetism behind.

Nick's niece. The redhead he'd bumped into that morning. Not small, but at best she was about five-six. He'd seen her before…but not often. Years ago she'd been around the place more, but she'd looked different back then, not much more than a kid. Gangly as a palm tree, a pile of flyaway hair, enormous green eyes, always running somewhere. Time had gone by; he hadn't hung around Nick's all that much lately. Not in almost five years, though he had applied for the new slip at the marina, the one he'd just moved into, almost a year ago now.

She'd changed. She wasn't gangly anymore. She was curved in all the right places, and her flyaway hair was more like a sexual beacon now. Attractive, yes. But what he remembered was her voice. Her indignation. Cool, aloof, even in anger, those eyes able to sizzle into someone with total condemnation.

She was in the academy, Nick had told him.

So the kid was going to be on the force. Great.

With something about her that was so much like Nancy...

Shit. It felt as if he'd suddenly been wrapped in ice.

He hoped to hell she wasn't too much like Nancy. A woman with too many ethics, too much determination— and not enough sense to be afraid.

He didn't even know her. Her life was none of his damned business. And maybe she wasn't that much like Nancy; maybe he had just made the association because it was Nancy's birthday.

He felt a strong sense of sympathy for Brian.

He drained the last of the beer. He wanted another.

No, not a beer. A single-malt Scotch.

Hell, he wasn't going anywhere tonight.

He went back into the kitchen, poured a shot, made it a double.

Somehow, he was damned well going to sleep that night.

Ashley, Karen and Jan had reached the hotel with no further trouble. They'd checked in and spent a few hours sipping piña coladas at the pool. After talking it over, they opted for the show that night and dancing the following evening.

The horses were magnificent, and the entire show was a lot of fun. Ashley found a message waiting on her phone when the show was over. Len had indeed decided to drive up with his firefighting friends. They would be at a late-night swing club.

"Fire guys?" Karen inquired.

"They're not all incredibly buff and good-looking," Jan warned.

"We could take a chance," Karen said.

And so they did.

Len was there with two friends, as if he'd made an effort to round out the party. Len was tall and built like a rock himself. He had told Ashley that he had gotten into physical fitness when he'd applied for the force, then kept it up. He was sandy-haired, and green-eyed, with a few freckles, thirty-one years old, and a genuinely nice guy. She knew he wanted their relationship to go beyond friendship, but she didn't. As nice as he was, she simply wasn't attracted to him. She knew that she couldn't say that, since nothing would be quite so devastating to a man with an ego, so she kept their relationship platonic by insisting that nothing was more important to her than getting onto the force and keeping up with a few art classes in between.

He seemed to have accepted that they were limited to friendship. Sometimes he even made her laugh, telling her about his disastrous dates, his quest for the right woman.

Both the men with him, Kyle Avery and Mario Menendez, perfectly fit the public's idea of what a rugged young firefighter should look like.

"Ashley, you do know how to pick 'em," Karen told her. "He's to die for."

"Which one?"

Karen was silent for a minute. "Actually, all of them.

Especially your friend Len. I don't understand why you don't scoop him right up."

"Because it isn't there."

"What isn't there? He sure looks like he's got everything to me."

"Go for him, then," Ashley said.

Karen shook her head. "Too awkward. He's got the hots for you."

"He's a friend, Karen. If you make him happy, you'll make me happy."

"C'mon, you two. This is a dance club," Jan interrupted. "Let's dance, then we'll sort out the psychology of it all, hmm?"

After a few hours of swing, changing partners frequently and dancing with others, as well, Karen claimed exhaustion. She, Jan and Ashley made for the ladies' room while the men ordered drinks.

"Ashley, I'm flirting away with your buddy, making myself very happy and keeping you in the clear, but you're not showing the least sign of interest in anyone," Karen stated.

Ashley sighed. "I'm in the middle of the academy and trying to help Nick out now and then. I don't want to be involved. And it's getting late. I may opt out of the rest of the evening and head back."

"It's not that late. And you don't have to get involved with anyone. Just have fun, Ashley. I'm a teacher. I spend my life with little kids. I do the ABCs and two plus two, and wash little hands and help blow little noses all day. It's been almost a year since I had what you'd actually call a real boyfriend—and I don't miss *that* creep! But I do miss…company. Okay, and sex. Don't you ever just want to have sex?"

"Karen, sex is a great thing. But maybe you want to get to know him a little."

"I don't know," Jan teased, checking her lipstick. "Sometimes guys are a lot better before you get to know them."

"He lives in Miami. She should get to know him," Ashley said.

"Mother Superior has spoken," Karen acknowledged. "But let's not call it quits already, huh? I gave him my phone number. And if he calls me once we're home... great. Or he may start pining for you all over again."

"Karen, we're friends. That's all."

"I hope that's true. I hope he does call. He has a respectable job. He's nice as hell. He drinks, but not a lot, and he dances swing. Don't you dare insist we leave right now. And be nice."

"Be nice? He's my friend. I'm always nice."

Karen sighed, her chest heaving with impatience. "I mean, be nice to all of them. Please... Jan may not admit it, but she's saving all her quality flirting for Kyle, so just be decent to Mario so we can try to keep their threesome together. With us."

"I told you, I'll be nice."

"Ashley, you're crazy. Have you ever really looked at your *friend's* buns?"

"No, Karen, I haven't actually stared at his butt, but if you say so, I'm sure his buns are great."

Karen shook her head again. "She's crazy," she told Jan.

"No, I understand her perfectly," Jan said. "It's either there or not. I can't really explain what 'it' is, chemistry or whatever, but if it isn't there, it isn't there. So quit feeling guilty and checking with Ashley to make sure she's really not romantically interested. She isn't. And we're wasting time here, discussing this all in a bathroom."

"Right, let's get back there," Karen said. "And you, Ashley, start talking to Mario. Talk shop if you have to."

"I'm in the police academy, not fire rescue."

"It's almost the same," Karen insisted.

Ashley discovered that she was actually able to have a nice conversation with Mario, who was somewhat shy and reserved. He was married and was just out with his single friends for the weekend because his wife was in Connecticut for two weeks visiting her folks. He was relieved to tell her about being a newlywed, since his friends had been afraid he was going to ruin a fun night for them.

Ashley told him about the accident they had witnessed, and he told her stories about calls they'd taken on I-95, some tragic, some simply bizarre. When the others rejoined them at the table after dancing, she found herself repeating the story, knowing Len might be interested, since it had occurred in their neck of the woods.

"Ashley, you're going to see things like that more and more often," Len said. "Bad things happen on the highways."

"Hey," Karen said. "We all decided we were not going to focus on that awful scene." She stared at Ashley, who hadn't even realized she had a pen out, or that she was sketching the highway scene on a cocktail napkin.

"Ashley is an artist," Karen announced. She kept her eyes glued sternly on Ashley and flipped the napkin over.

"An excellent artist," Jan said. "Draw a face, Ashley. Draw Kyle."

Ashley obediently began a sketch of the firefighter. The others rose and stood behind her, staring over her shoulder as she drew.

"Wow!" Kyle said, looking at her with new respect. "That's great. Sign it. I want to keep it."

"Will you do one for me, too, please?" Mario asked.

"How about Karen and Jan?" Len asked when she was finished, handing her a stack of napkins.

"I've drawn them dozens of times."

"But maybe Kyle and I would like to keep them," Len said.

Karen covertly jabbed her. "Of course," Ashley said.

She finished the pictures and passed them out. Kyle shook his head. "So... Len says you're going to be a cop, right? I mean, there's nothing wrong with being a cop but...these are great."

"And she has a photographic memory. Draw someone from today—show them," Jan insisted.

Karen placed a hand over Ashley's. "*Not* the highway," she said.

Ashley shrugged. "All right."

"You go ahead, I'll get the check," Len said.

"Hey, Len, that's not necessary."

"You've fed me plenty of times, Ash, at Nick's place."

"That means my uncle fed you," she protested.

"Don't argue with an officer of the law," he teased and walked to the bar. Ashley watched him go, shook her head and set her pen to the paper. She hesitated, then started another face. She was startled herself when she saw what she was doing. Strong, craggy features, dark hair, dark eyes, square jawline, high, broad cheekbones, and the mouth…drawn into something of a tight line, but a good mouth…

"Wow. Cool. Who is it?" Karen asked, picking up the napkin.

"The guy I spilled the coffee on this morning."

"Good-looking son of a gun," Karen murmured.

"See, photographic memory," Jan said, pleased.

"Not really. But I like to draw faces. I always have," Ashley said to the two firefighters. Kyle whistled softly. She stared down at her own drawing, oddly stirred by it. *Good-looking son of a gun.* Yeah, he had been. Walking aggression and testosterone, but…hmm. There was something about him. A beckoning power or strength or sensuality. Maybe all of them. She hated the saying, but *animal attraction* might just be the right phrase to describe him.

He did have something that…

Something that, for her, Len just didn't.

Don't you ever just want to have sex?

She looked back at her drawing. His type probably had lots of sex. He wasn't the kind of man with whom she would ever want to become involved. Not that she wanted to be involved.

With luck, she wouldn't even run into him again. Literally or otherwise. Even though he did seem to know Nick, and she had actually seen him around the place before. Lots of customers came and went, some of them frequently, some of them not so frequently.

"You're good. You shouldn't waste this kind of talent," Kyle said, interrupting her introspection.

She exhaled, glad to return to the present. "Thanks," she said, then crumpled up the napkin.

"You destroyed it!" Mario protested.

"She didn't like him very much," Jan said, grinning.

Len returned from paying the check. They talked as they exited the dance hall, Len expressing his regret that they were heading back the next afternoon, since Mario and Kyle went back on duty the next day.

They parted outside to head for their respective hotels, but not before Kyle and Jan exchanged numbers. As they walked back, Karen suddenly linked arms with Ashley and let out a soft whistle. "Wasn't it a great evening?"

"Yes, I had a good time, and I really hope you and Len do keep seeing each other."

"Yes, a guy like Len shouldn't go to waste," Jan said. "And, Ashley, your guy was mature…a little scary. But…appealing."

Ashley stared at her, frowning as she arched a brow. "Definitely a nice guy. And married," she informed her.

Karen laughed, throwing an arm around her shoulder. "I don't think Jan means the firefighter. She means the guy in the sketch."

"He isn't my guy!" Ashley insisted, startled.

"Oh, yeah? You should have taken a good look at that picture you drew. You saw something in that guy," Karen told her.

"I don't even know him. And with any luck, I won't."

"There's nothing like a mystery man," Jan teased.

"Oh, yeah, right, nothing like one."

As soon as they reached the suite, they headed for bed. But Ashley couldn't sleep. When both Karen and Jan were deeply out, she was still wide awake. So she closed the door over to the bedroom, went out to the living area to make a cup of tea, and picked up her sketch pad from the coffee table.

* * *

When the three men reached the room they'd rented for the night, Len suddenly drew back as Kyle fumbled with the plastic card that had replaced the use of keys at most hotels.

"Hey, you know what? I'm suddenly dying for a burger."

"You want us to come with you?" Mario asked. "I guess I could eat a burger."

"Hell, no, you don't really want a burger, and I don't need help to take a ride to Denny's," Len said cheerfully.

"You sure?" Mario asked. He yawned. "Hell, I'm beat."

"Get to sleep. I won't be long, and I'll try not to make a racket when I get back."

"Last man in gets the cot," Kyle reminded him.

"Yeah, well, one of us had to get it, right?"

He grinned, turned and headed back for the car.

He didn't drive to Denny's. He turned his car toward the girls' hotel and parked.

Karen had given him their room number, and mentioned that they'd wound up on the first floor, so the sliding glass doors at the back opened up to a little courtyard and garden area.

He headed for the courtyard and figured out which room it would be.

The lights were on. One person was moving inside. He knew it was Ashley.

The drapes were thin, the light behind them bright. He could see her every movement. She walked around, paused by the window, drew the curtain back and looked out.

He flattened himself against a gardenia tree.

She was holding a cup of something, just gazing out. She was wearing a long T-shirt that clung to her. In the artificial light, her hair blazed. The wavy ends seemed to curl protectively around her breasts. The knit shirt hugged the length of her. She never could have imagined just how provocative she looked.

His fingers wound into his palms, and tension streaked through the length of him. *You don't know just how well I know you, Ashley*, he thought. *I knew you'd be the one who was awake, I knew I could come here and see you. And one day, Ashley, you'll find out just what you've made me feel all this time.*

One day.

The sliders were open, only the screen in place, letting in the breeze.

That one day...

Could be tonight.

No. Not tonight. Tonight, he would just watch.

But soon. Soon she would know. He'd make her know.

The night was beautiful. Just beautiful. But not even the stars in the sky or the soft glow of moonlight on the exquisite little garden could draw her attention.

She stepped back into the room and went over to the desk. She'd already taken her sketch pad out.

She started to draw. First, the body...the body on the highway.

A man, young, muscle structure taut beneath...the spatters of blood. His hair covering his face, a soft ash blond.

Around him...the officer who had arrived on the

scene. The police car. The two drivers. Their cars. The traffic slowing, veering…nearly hitting the median.

The median. The opposing traffic…

The figure across the expanse of lanes.

She sketched, shading in until, even in black and white and shades of gray, the scene was eerily real. And everything detailed except…the figure. The vague figure across the many lanes. For the life of her, she couldn't remember any details…

It was all as she had remembered it, how the camera in her mind's eye had frozen the image.

Everything so specific—except for the dark figure who seemed to be watching…looking…

For what?

Assurance that the man—the poor, pathetic man, near-naked and bloodied—was, indeed, dead?

A chill suddenly swept over her.

A breeze…

More than a breeze. Something that made her slightly…uneasy.

She turned quickly, then felt foolish. Even so, she walked over to the doors, then closed and locked them. She looked at the thin drapes, frowning, thinking that the sun would come rushing in the next morning.

The next morning. It *was* morning, and that sun would be coming soon.

Pulling the light draperies back, she saw the set of lightproof draperies, pulled them, then checked the lock once again and went to lie down on the couch.

She closed her eyes, but the image of the body on the highway still haunted her.

Swearing, she pounded her pillow. Counting sheep had always seemed like such a ridiculous thing to do….

And yet she was desperate.
She counted horses instead.

Strange dream. There was fog and sunlight. She was walking toward him in the dream. Sometimes they were on a beach, and sometimes she was moving toward him in the cabin of the Gwendolyn. *Hair spilling down her back, flesh...yeah, naked flesh, all of it being touched by the sun and by the shadow.*

Nancy...

He'd dreamed often that she'd been there, with him, trying to tell him something. Except that it hadn't been like this. Before, they'd just been talking. Discussing the case. The frustrations, the dead ends. But she'd known something. Reckless, restless, unhappy in her married life, she was determined to throw her heart into her work.

They were good partners.

Not good enough. There had been something more, something she had suspected, something she had thought of doing to break the wall they were up against.

Then he dreamed of her face as it had looked, on the autopsy table, after they had found her. And that would always strike such a chord of horror in his heart and mind that he awakened.

Not tonight, though. Tonight that image didn't appear.

He couldn't see her clearly. Her hair wasn't dark; it was red in the light.

It wasn't Nancy. Just someone like her. Who moved something like her...

It was Nick's girl. Walking with a slow, confident, easy rhythm. She reached him. The dream progressed.

Memory faded, the now took hold. She was different, very much alive, real, vibrant. She was...reaching him. Touching him. She was...

He awoke abruptly, in a cold sweat. The alarm was ringing.

Fuck.

No. Not the alarm, the phone. Hell, what time was it? The middle of the night. And still, bleary, wretched, he was glad of the sound. It had drawn him from the depths of the most bizarre wet dream...about Nick's kid. He needed to stay the hell away from her. Far away.

Shouldn't be hard, not after the way they had just reacquainted themselves.

The phone...

Still ringing, like a hammer pounding inside his head.

He picked up the phone. Listened. And his knuckles went white against the receiver.

Chapter 3

"There's not a lot left of the face," Martin Moore said, nodding to the uniformed officer who allowed him and Jake through the crime tape to the off-road location where the body had been discovered.

"I think the recent rains washed her down here. She was probably buried in a shallow grave farther in from the road."

It was the crack of dawn, Saturday morning.

He wished he hadn't switched to Scotch the night before.

And he wished he had one then. Marty's call had been way beyond bizarre.

So much for the long weekend off. But since the case had never been officially closed, he had been called in. Marty had been in vice, the narcotics squad, five years ago, when the first murders had occurred, but he had worked with Jake for a long time now and knew the past history of what were still referred to as the Bordon murders—as well as anyone. He also lived in the area, so he'd reached the scene first.

Police floodlights helped illuminate the area, which was still dark. Inky dark. Much of this part of the county had been developed out of land that was really part of the Everglades. The dirt was rich here and the foliage thick. Lights were few and far between. Before dawn, the darkness could be a strange ebony, as if the Glades had reclaimed what was really part of a no man's land.

Jake paused a few feet from the corpse, taking his first look at the body that had been discovered that morning by a jogger. A foolish jogger, he thought, running at a time when the night still held sway in an area where the obsidian shadows and undergrowth could hide many a sin.

The jogger, he noted, was still on the scene. She was a middle-aged woman with a pretty, too-skinny face, a sweatband around her forehead, and the typical shorts, T-shirt and sneakers found among those who chose the quiet paths out in the farm district for their morning rituals. She was badly shaken by her discovery. He could hear her sobbing softly, speaking to the officers, who had supplied her with a blanket and hot coffee.

"My God, I was just running and then…there she was. I saw her…and it was so dark, I didn't even realize at first. And so I doubled back. And I was so frightened I could barely punch the numbers into my cell phone. Thank God for cell phones! I know now that I'll never go out jogging when it isn't full light again. I don't care if I have to learn to run around my own living room, I'll never, never come out like that again. It's so terrifying.

But then, of course…she was just left on the road, right? She might not have been killed there, right?"

Jake could hear one of the uniformed officers telling her that they had no facts right then, but that she didn't need to worry, one of the officers would get her back home.

Lady, you shouldn't go out jogging along this path alone before the sun is up in any way, shape or form, Jake thought. They were in what most people in the county considered to be the country. Far south in Miami-Dade, an area where the old encroached on the new, where waterways connected to the deep river of grass that was Everglades. There was good land out here. Some people kept large tracts with beautiful homes, and some had acreage where they grew strawberries, tomatoes and other produce.

Good earth for growing intermingled with sawgrass, deep dark muck and tangled trees.

Much of the land, such as this immediate area, was county owned. It was often heavily wooded, and where there weren't actually trees, the foliage was thick and dense.

A good place to dispose of human remains, a place where nature could inflict tremendous damage on a corpse and render many of the clues it might have given up hard to discern, even destroy them. Over the years, a number of criminals had tried to dispose of bodies and evidence on land much like this. And, God knew, many of them had succeeded.

The jogger was just the poor civilian who had happened upon the physical remnants of a brutal crime. There would be little, if anything, she could tell him.

Still, he would speak with her himself for a moment. Later.

For now...

The victim.

"Where's the M.E.?" he asked.

"Right over there, talking with Pentillo, who was first officer on the scene. The M.E. is Tristan Gannet. Mandy's taking the last of the pictures he requested right now."

"Good. I'm glad we've got Gannet and Nightingale."

Mandy Nightingale, one of their best photographers, was snapping photos as they carefully approached the position of the body.

"Hi, Jake," she said, acknowledging his arrival with a quick nod before she snapped another photo.

"Mandy, good to see you here."

They had worked together many times. She was thin as a wraith, with steel gray, close-cropped hair, and a strong, Native-American facial structure that defied age entirely. She was quick and efficient, careful to snap a crime scene in its entirety, to make sure that she not only got excellent photographs of the body but of the surrounding elements, as well.

"Thanks, Jake. I'll be out of your way in just a second."

"Take your time, Mandy," he told her. "There's no hurry for this one now."

"I think I've gotten just about everything I can and everything that Dr. Gannet specified," she assured them, squatting low to focus on a last photograph. "I'll be over with Pentillo, hanging around 'til the M.E. moves the body and I can take the rest of the shots," she told them.

"Thanks, Mandy."

She nodded. "I think Dr. Gannet knows you're here. I'll send him right over."

Jake hunkered down on the balls of his feet to study the body in the position in which it had been found.

He didn't need the medical examiner to tell him that the woman had been dead for some time. She had been exposed to the elements and to the small animals that called the area home. There were places where she was down to no more than bone, and places where flesh clung precariously to the body. It appeared that she had been left without clothing of any kind. A quick look, using his pen to shift fallen foliage for a better view, showed that unfortunately the hands had decomposed almost fully, as had much of the face.

Another murder in the county. It happened. Put millions of people together, and murder happened.

But he knew exactly why Martin had been so tense when he had called him, urging him to reach the scene as quickly as possible.

The face, though maintaining few of the qualities that marked men and women as human, had apparently not taken the same abuse as the hands.

And it was apparent that what had once been the ears had been slashed.

A chill crept through him, along with a bitterness he could actually taste.

Déjà vu.

Peter Bordon, also known as Papa Pierre, had been locked up for a long time now. Five years. But even a seconds-long, cursory inspection of this body was eerily reminiscent of the victims that had been discovered during Bordon's reign as leader of the bizarre cult called People for Principle.

"Yes, he's still in prison," Martin said, reading his partner's mind.

"You're sure?"

"Yeah. I called and checked the moment I saw the body, right after I called you," Martin said. "He's in prison—whether it really matters or not, that's where he is."

"Sorry," Jake murmured. He couldn't quite help having a tense attitude on this one. Peter Bordon had garnered a group around him as if he had been a true modern-day prophet. He had preached about community, working for the benefit of all mankind and giving up the luxuries of a sinful life. For most of his followers, that had meant donating everything they had ever worked for to Bordon's own bank account.

Three of his alleged followers had wound up dead. Discovered in fields and canals.

With their ears slashed.

No weapons had ever been found. No real leads had ever been discovered. Bordon had been the only suspect, but there had been nothing whatsoever to prove he might be guilty. The police had managed to obtain a search warrant for his holdings, but nothing had been found except for some illegal financial activity, which in the end had been enough to earn him jail time.

Late one night, an itinerant man had come bursting into one of the small precinct stations, confessing to the murders.

While homicide was being notified of his arrival and confession, the young man had hanged himself with his belt in his cell.

And that should have been it.

But Jake and most of his task force hadn't believed

that one crazed man had been responsible for a series of killings that had been so meticulously carried out. The case had never been officially closed, but with the death of the man who had confessed, the imprisonment of Bordon based on what they were able to bring into court, and the fact that no more bodies had been discovered, they had been forced to move on to new investigations.

Jake had never been satisfied, though. For him, it had never ended.

They hadn't gotten Bordon on murder.

Bordon had been involved. He was sure of it. But there was no proof. Jake had never thought that Bordon had physically carried out the crimes; they had been done at his command.

Now he was in prison, but there was no reason in hell why he couldn't be calling the shots from his cell.

Bordon had a power far greater than strength or any material weapon. He had the ability to manipulate men and women. To get into their minds.

He didn't need to dirty his own hands with the blood of others.

Planning a murder, however, could bring the same penalties as the act of carrying out the deed. But complicity had to be proven.

Five years ago, the task force had plowed through Bordon's records, desperate to get him on something. They had never gotten him for ordering the killings, but just as, decades ago, the law had managed to put away the infamous Al Capone, they had at last gotten him on tax evasion and fraud.

Unsatisfactory, but at least he'd been locked away.

The murders had stopped. Most people seemed to assume that had been because the man who had confessed to the killings had committed suicide in a jail cell.

But now it seemed that the killings *hadn't* stopped.

There had just been a hiatus, because here was another body, jarringly reminiscent of those they had found in the past.

"Jesus, Jake, don't look like that," Martin said softly. "Maybe you shouldn't even be on this case."

Jake stared at him, dark eyes hard as coal.

"All right, all right. Sorry."

"Gentlemen, may I get back in there? I'll give you my initial findings."

Jake turned. Dr. Tristan Gannet made his way back over to them. Jake was glad that it was Gannet on the case. He had been with the M.E.'s office almost twenty years and had had experience with the previous murders.

"Glad to see you, Gannet," Jake said. He quickly scanned the scene again himself before joining Gannet down by the body. No apparent materials or fabrics. No sign of footprints, but if they were right and the body had washed down here with the rain, there wouldn't be. No obvious sign of cause of death, most likely because the body was so decomposed. Victim was most probably a young woman, a few strands of long dark hair remaining. The first patrolman to arrive on the scene had done a damned good job of taping the scene off and keeping it untainted. This was no instance of a dozen officers arriving and contaminating the area. There was just so little to be found when a body had been given time to decompose. Of course, there was always the hope that the specialized crime scene investigators could find a clue that wasn't visible to the naked eye.

Jake had a feeling this one would be hard work for the crime scene investigators. When a murderer was careful and knew that minuscule clues could give his or her identity away, there was often little to go on.

There was still hope, of course. His associates might find a hair, a fiber, trace evidence. Doc Gannet might find a microscopic clue on the pathetic remains.

No chance of finding flesh beneath the fingernails, though. The fingernails were gone. For that matter, there would be no identification through fingerprints— no flesh remained on a single finger or on the thumbs.

"And no one will recognize her from her face," he murmured.

"Dental records are usually our best bet anyway, often," Gannet said. "We're lucky here, I think. I'm willing to bet the flesh was cut from the fingers, before the animals and the environment had a chance to do their work." He looked at Jake for a moment, and he knew they were both thinking along the same line.

In the previous murders, the ears had been slashed, and the flesh had been cut from the fingers. Why bother destroying fingerprints, then leaving the head and teeth so that an identity could be culled from dental records?

Were they back to where they had started?

Or was there a copycat killer out there?

"Could be a copycat," Gannet said, as if Jake had actually voiced his thoughts.

"Yeah," Jake said.

Gannet stared down at the remains, sorrow in his face. Real emotion, but under complete control. That was another thing Jake liked about Gannet. He did his work well. And though he didn't take every single case to heart so that he couldn't sleep at night, he had never, in all his years of work, lost compassion for the victims, whether of accident or violence. "We'll find out who she is," he assured Jake.

"I need your findings on this as fast as possible," Jake said.

Gannet nodded. "Naturally," he said, a slight touch of sarcasm in his voice. Unfortunately, untimely deaths occurred with a certain frequency in the county. He looked up at Jake again. "Don't worry. I intend to get right on this one." He stared at Jake a moment longer. Maybe he knew Gannet too well, Jake thought.

During the last spate of similar murders, Jake had worked the case aggressively on behalf of the victims. Even after the suicide of the "confessed" killer. And even after Bordon's incarceration.

For the victims.

And because he'd suspected that Bordon had been involved in another death, as well.

Another death... Nothing like this. But far too close to home. Nancy's death.

Not too many others on the force had agreed with him on that one. They'd thought he was creating scenarios of Bordon's guilt because he had to find a guilty party and couldn't accept a verdict of accidental death in the case of a fellow cop.

Or even suicide, as some had suggested.

Suicide. Never. It was a theory to be rejected entirely. No one who'd known her could ever even begin to accept such a possibility.

"Are you going to be all right with this?" Gannet asked softly.

"You bet. I'm a professional, Gannet. And if we do need to make comparisons to past cases, there's no one out there who knows both the facts and the theories better than I do."

"Yeah, you're right," Gannet said. Gloves on, he looked over the remains. Two assistants from the morgue had arrived to take the body when Gannet and the scene-of-crime investigators had finished their site inspection. Gannet nodded an acknowledgment to the others and quietly asked them to make sure they included the dirt and scrub around the body when they removed it from the site.

"Any idea on the actual cause of death?" Jake asked.

"Not natural," Gannet said.

"Wow. I don't have a medical degree, and I knew that."

Gannet grimaced at him. "Knife…big knife. Maybe a machete."

Jake looked at him in surprise. "There's not enough flesh—"

"A few courses in forensics and you'd see this just fine."

"I've had a few forensics courses," Jake reminded him dryly.

"Maybe. But the condition of the corpse makes it hard to see the forest for the trees. Almost literally. Shift this foliage and filth around a little and you get a good look at the bone. Yeah, yeah, I know it's covered with dirt. But see? If you look really closely…the scratch there? I have to do a full autopsy, but I'd bet we're talking a very large blade. And you'd need a blade to do that to the ears…and the features. The animals have been at her, but still…those aren't teeth marks. Definitely made by a blade. And, as we've both seen, the flesh was removed from the fingers. You've been at this a while, and you seem to know more than you let on most of the time, because you want me to make what you're already pretty damned sure you do know, official. Yeah, animals have been at her. But the flesh from her fingers was cut off, not gnawed away, or simply decomposed."

"Hell. This is more than déjà vu. We could definitely be talking the same—" Jake began.

"From what I see so far, yes, but don't go taking anything as absolute yet. Let me get her down to the morgue. And don't forget, Jake, what we both already know, as well. There can be copycats out there. There have been cases where murders have been researched and studied and duplicated almost perfectly. There are victims assumed to have been murdered by one serial killer who in reality were killed by someone else entirely."

Jake arched a brow to him.

"Hey," Gannet said with a grin. "You learn more about autopsies every year, and I learn about cop work." He was quiet again for a moment, eyes on the victim. When he spoke again, his tone was serious and flat. "Like I said, I'll get right on it. You can meet me at the morgue. Hey, I heard you're moving your houseboat."

"I moved it. Yesterday."

Gannet was watching him carefully. "Well, I'm glad to hear that. A change of scenery is always good."

"It's still the same old boat," Jake said dryly.

"Still…a new marina. You wake up to a different view."

"Yeah." He didn't say more. He had the feeling that Gannet—like others around him—believed he'd shared more than a patrol car with Nancy, so, a change of pace now was a good thing. Even if it had been almost five years since Nancy's death.

He could have said something, he supposed, could have come to his own defense, though he wasn't being attacked, he knew.

And he had no need to excuse or defend himself to anyone. The inquest had cleared him—as far as that night went, anyway. The general and even logical consensus had been that Nancy, feeling desperate over the disintegration of her marriage and the pressures of her job, had just gone wild for a night. She'd met someone, done some drinking, popped a few pills…and found her way into the canal. But there was one factor he and Brian had in common—they'd both known Nancy well. The year after her death, even with the breakup of Bordon's cult, had been a bitch for Jake. He'd been like a dog with a bone, determined to connect the two. He'd come close to crossing the line between investigation and harassment, and he'd been called on it. He'd resented his time with the police psychiatrist, though it was common practice for cops to receive such counseling after the death of a partner. He'd realized after a while that he would have to take a step back. Outwardly, he'd become a practical and methodical cop again, following the rules as closely as he could.

But he'd never changed his mind about the truth of the situation. Or his determination to see it come out one day.

"I'd like to live on the water," Gannet said. "Maybe one day."

"You should come by on a Sunday sometime. I keep a little motorboat, as well. Fishing is good for the soul."

"Yeah, I'd like that." Gannet grimaced. "Maybe my wife will let me come."

"Bring her."

"She's not big on beer."

"We'll get her a bottle of wine."

"I'll take you up on it, one way or the other, soon enough," Gannet assured him.

"Dr. Gannet, Detective Dilessio?"

Jake turned. Mandy Nightingale was back. "Are you ready to move the body and let me get the rest of the scene?"

"I'm good to go, Mandy," Gannet said.

"Jake?" she inquired.

He nodded. "If Gannet's ready, so am I."

"Good. You should know then, Jake," she said softly, "that they're holding back a slew of reporters over there."

"Want me to handle them?" Marty asked Jake.

Jake shook his head. "No, it's all right. Get some of our men started on a door-to-door. I know the doors are pretty far apart around here, but someone might have seen something. I'll take care of the press."

"Are you sure? I saw your eyes. It's all coming back, and you took the entire thing way too personally before—"

"Martin, I'm all right. We're talking about something that happened five years ago. I'm a cop, this is my job. Just keep an eye on things here, Marty. We can't let anything, not the most minute clue, slip away."

Martin nodded. Jake walked from the scene and across the road, where the uniformed officers were holding the onslaught of reporters at bay.

"A murder, right? A young woman?" Jayne Gray, from one of the local stations, called to him.

"Jayne, I'm afraid there's not too much we can say right now. We've got the body of a woman who has apparently been dead several weeks, even a few months. We've yet to determine anything else as fact, but as soon as the M.E.'s office has further information, I know they'll share it. And when that happens, you know that a police spokesperson will be telling you all that they can. There's nothing else you can learn here right now, folks."

"But, Detective Dilessio, there must be more you can give us." Bryan Jay, an obnoxious, heavy-set man from the local paper, called out. "It's a murder, right? You've found the victim of a murder, in the mud, off the side of the road."

He was tempted to give Jay a real wise-ass reply. *Hell, no. She decided to drop herself off there, lie down and die.*

"Mr. Jay, give the medical examiner time to do his work," Jake said firmly.

"Right," Jay replied dryly. "Come on, Jake, give us something."

"I've already explained that we have the body of a woman, Mr. Jay."

"Think we have a single crime here, or do we have a serial killer on the loose? Isn't this the way the first victim was found in those serial killings years ago? Are there any mutilations?"

Leave it to Jay to home in on an uncomfortable suspicion of his own, Jake thought.

"Unfortunately, this is a big city. We have a lot of murders every year."

"Still, this seems awfully similar to me. The kid who

supposedly did the killing back then is dead though, right?"

"A man who claimed to have committed the murders committed suicide, yes."

"But the case was never officially closed, right?"

"No, Mr. Jay, it was not."

"The police cracked down on the local cults back then. Papa Pierre, alias Peter Bordon, was a suspect, right? But he's been locked up for years now, right?"

Jake heard the blood rushing in his ears. He gritted his teeth, desperately fighting the temptation to step forward and bash Bryan Jay in his smug, jowly face.

"Come on, Jake!" another woman called out.

He knew her, too. Crime beat from a Broward paper. She'd moved fast to get down here, he thought.

"Peter Bordon is in prison in the center of the state. As anyone on the crime beat is surely aware, he was never tried for or convicted of murder," he said.

"That's right. Neither was the crazy guy who killed himself in jail. Harry Tennant. He was just a homeless junkie, huh? He claimed to have been the murderer, but then, lots of sickos like to claim they're responsible for sensational murders."

"Due to Mr. Tennant's death, we weren't able to investigate his story, Mr. Jay."

"Looks like he wasn't a killer, though, huh? You guys didn't follow up, and it looks like the murderer is out there and at it again," Jay said.

"Mr. Jay, I'm sorry, we're trying to deal in fact, not supposition. There's nothing else I can give you right now," Jake said firmly. He forced himself to speak a level tone. "We live in a great country, and I respect the press beyond all measure. I will not, however, stand here and spout off a bunch of theories when I haven't got any facts. Journalism deals in facts, right? As soon as we've got something to give you, we will. Thanks, and that's all for right now. We like to let you do your work, and we're damned appreciative when you let us do ours."

He turned and walked away. First thing on his list was a long talk with the jogger who had found the body—before the press got to her. Then he had to work this like a regular case. Swallow the haunting images and bitterness of the past.

The forensics experts would study soil samples and any microscopic clue that the crime scene investigators could bring in. Gannet would do the autopsy. They had good people working on the case; they would have more to go on as the reports came in. He depended on his associates. He knew that they could practically pull rabbits out of hats. Still, they weren't magicians, and they couldn't work miracles.

As to the obvious…

A woman had been murdered. Brutally.

She had been dead for at least several weeks, maybe several months.

Her ears had been slashed, as if it had been a ritualistic killing.

He knew damned well that he had to be careful; he couldn't assume that her death was a continuation of a killing spree from the past. Every possibility had to be explored.

"Copycat!" Bryan Jay shouted out as he walked away. "There could be a copycat killer out there as well, right?"

He refused to respond.

Copycat…

Yeah, copycat...

Maybe. And maybe not.

As he once again approached the murder scene, he saw that Marty, Doc Gannet and Mandy Nightingale were talking together.

Marty glanced his way, and he knew. They were talking about him. Worrying about him.

Well, there was no need.

He was fine.

This time, he damned well meant to catch the real killer.

Chapter 4

First thing Monday morning, Ashley was busy digging through the stacks of newspaper Nick had bundled neatly at the back door, ready to go out with the recycling. She was startled when she heard her uncle behind her. "Ashley, what are you doing?"

She jumped, sorry that she had woken him in her frenzy. The stacks were no longer neat. She had tried first for Saturday's paper, thinking the accident would surely have been written up in the local section. But she hadn't been able to find it.

She grimaced. "Hey, sorry I woke you. We saw an accident on our way up to Orlando. I was trying to find out what happened. Did you hear anything?"

Nick scratched the overnight growth of stubble on his chin. At fifty-two, he was a great-looking man, with lots of character sketched into the lines of his face. He didn't look particularly young—a lifetime in the sun and wind had seen to that. But his bone structure was excellent, and all time had done was weather in an appeal that hinted at an intriguing life lived to the fullest. The gray streaks coming into his sandy hair fit well with the original coloring, and he had cool blue eyes that seemed to hold an ancient wisdom.

Wisdom be damned. At that moment, he shrugged, shook his head and yawned. He was wearing a bathrobe over pajama pants and knotted the robe as he made his way to the coffee brewer, reached for the pot and found it empty. He stared at her blankly. She always made coffee.

"Sorry, I'm afraid this accident has been haunting me," she said, reaching behind him for a filter in the cabinet while he poured water into the carafe.

"No, no…it's all right. I *am* capable of making coffee, you know," he said, his tone a bit indignant. Of course, that was Nick. He was an independent man. He'd raised her. And he could damn well take care of himself. Nick was impatient with anyone who couldn't manage the basics of getting by on their own.

"You really didn't hear anything about an accident?" she asked him.

"Hey, it's Miami. There are lots of accidents. In fact, it's a strange day where there isn't a pile-up on one of the highways," he reminded her.

"Do you know where the local section from Saturday is? There ought to be a blurb or something. I mean, a man was killed. At least, I'm pretty sure he was dead."

"Um…yeah, I'll get it for you. It's in the bedroom."

"I can go."

"Sharon is in the shower, I think," he murmured.

"Oh. Well, I can wait until you have your first cup of coffee. It's just been bugging me all weekend."

"You didn't have fun?"

"Of course I had fun."

"Thinking about a dead man on the highway the whole time?" he queried. "You want some toast or something."

"No, thanks, I'm not hungry."

"You're going off to a full day at the academy. You should eat."

"I had something ghastly late last night at a rest stop," she told him. "That will do me until lunch."

"Something ghastly?"

"I think it was supposed to be a hamburger."

"Ah, so you young ladies crawled in really late. Of course, I figured it had to be late, since we keep the place open 'til twelve on Sundays and I didn't turn in until after one."

"Three," Ashley admitted.

"Great," he said, mildly sarcastic. "You've had lots of sleep, and you probably have a full day ahead."

"Every day is a full day," Ashley admitted. "But I'm young. I'm sure I can deal with lack of sleep at this point in my life."

Nick arched a brow, trying to decide if her response was in respect to the fact that he wasn't quite so young anymore and decided he wasn't going to wait any longer for coffee. He pulled the carafe out from beneath the dripping coffee and slid in a large mug in its place. He was quick—only a few drops missed the mug and hit the heating unit below.

"I'm pouring you a cup anyway, because you may be young—and implying that I'm *old*—but you sure as hell look as if you're going to need it. Did you sleep at all on that trip?"

She laughed. "I would never dream of implying that you're old. You're in your prime. And, yes, honestly, we did get some sleep. We went to a show on Friday night, then went to one of the dance clubs, got in late and slept until three the next afternoon. We didn't stay out so late the next night and still slept until twelve, which put Karen into a panic, because she didn't want to get charged for an extra night. So I'm actually in pretty good shape—even if your comment implied that I'm looking *haggard*."

He sipped his coffee, leaned on an elbow and grinned. "Most of the good cops I know look haggard. Goes with the territory."

"So you think I'm going to be a good cop?"

"You'd better be. And I'll get that paper for you. Good almost-cops don't show up at the academy late. Hop in the shower and get dressed. I'll find the local news from Saturday for you."

She nodded, drained the coffee he'd poured for her, and headed off for her room and a shower.

Nick's had been there forever. In one of those strange twists of fate, her uncle had bought the place from another Nicholas, an old-time seafarer who had bought the house and restaurant on the beach in the nineteen-twenties, when the Greater Miami area was still in its small-town infancy. Times had changed since then, and the land value had risen quite high. But Nick's remained the same. It was largely built out of Dade County pine, wood that was now rare and valuable. A dock led straight to the restaurant from the marina, where many people kept pleasure craft and some maintained houseboats.

The long bar and restaurant area were at the front, facing the marina. The more intimate family kitchen and an expansive living room for the main house could be accessed from both the restaurant kitchen and the office, which sat behind the bar. Nick's bedroom suite was above the living room, while Ashley had her own wing on the ground floor. She could get to it through the living room or through a small private entrance to the right of the restaurant. Like the rest of the place, it appealed to her. There was a rustic feel to the entire setup, but just the same, Nick was a stickler for cleanliness, codes and organization, so though it all had a comfortable, homey feel, it was also well-kept and aesthetically pleasing—at least to anyone fond of the sea and nautical decor. Above the entrance from the living room to her wing, the teeth and jaws from a great white shark had been mounted, and a nineteenth century ship's bell sat encased in a show cabinet beside it. The wall itself was lined with photographs—as well as mounted fish—and she loved them. There were many of her parents, some of her mom and Nick when they'd been growing up, some of her with her folks. One of her favorites was her with her dad in his uniform, and another was of her with both her mother and her father on the day she'd caught her first big snapper in a children's tournament.

Of course, such an old place had its downfalls. Like hot water in the shower. She remembered that Nick had said Sharon was in the shower the minute she stepped under the lukewarm water. No matter, it made her hurry. Afterward she briskly toweled herself dry. There was nothing wrong with their air-conditioning system. Nick had maintained it well, knowing that his lunch crowd didn't want to come in from a blistering morning in the hot sun and not find a spot of sweet cool solace.

Dressed and ready in fifteen minutes, she hurried back out to the kitchen. She was surprised to see that Nick, too, had already managed a quick—and probably downright chilly—shower. He was in cutoffs and a polo shirt, leaning over the kitchen counter, a grim look on his face as he scanned the newspaper in front of him. Sharon was standing beside him, gravely regarding the newspaper, as well. Her uncle's girlfriend of nearly a year was an incredibly attractive woman. Petite, no more than five foot two, and that was in shoes with at least a wedge of heel, she was also slender. She loved a rigorous workout, though, and her efforts showed in the elegance of her compact figure. She was probably a few years younger than Nick—in fact, she could almost pass for thirty—and often seemed too elegant and refined for the dockside bar where she spent so many nights. She could be a tiger in pursuit of a business deal or in regard to her newest passion: politics. But she was pleasant to Ashley at every turn, showing a real interest in her life. She wore her hair in a natural style that just brushed her shoulders. It was almost platinum, which went well with her huge blue eyes. She was an arresting woman, assertive rather than aggressive, intelligent, and a great deal of fun, as well. She was up for any adventure, which made her a good companion for Nick.

"Hey, you all found an article on the accident?" Ashley said.

Nick looked up, startled. He caught her eyes and nodded, that serious look still drawing his face.

"Morning, dear, and we're so sorry," Sharon said,

those great blue eyes of hers on Ashley then, full of compassion.

"Sorry? What is it?" she asked.

"It took some doing to find the article—there was a storm on Saturday night, and there were two fatal accidents, as well as that pedestrian being struck on the highway. But there is an article in the local section. The body you passed, Ashley," Nick said. "It's a kid you went to school with. He's not dead, though. In a coma, suffered lots of internal injuries, and the doctors are offering his family little hope."

"What? Who?" she asked, frowning as she looked from one to the other of them, then walked to the counter herself, anxious to see the story in black and white.

"Stuart Fresia," Nick said.

"Stuart?"

"I understand he was a good friend of yours," Sharon said.

Ashley was startled as she took the paper, quickly gazing over the words and finding them hard to comprehend.

Stuart.

Not just a kid she had gone to school with, an old friend. Granted, she hadn't seen him lately, not in a few years. But he'd been a smart kid, the kind to turn into a smart adult. He'd been one of those people able to tread the lines between popularity, peer pressure and academics. He'd always talked about law school. He'd known how to go out, sneak a few drinks when they'd gotten hold of some beer, and never get wasted. He'd smoked cigarettes—and a cigar on occasion—but never become entangled in drugs. She'd envied him sometimes. While it seemed that she lived vicariously through the heartache of divorce—and sometimes re-marriage and divorce and remarriage again—with the parents of a number of her friends, she'd gone home with Stuart many times to find two people who still loved one another, and their son, more than anything else in life.

And despite the natural scrapes he had gotten into while growing up, he had adored his folks. He'd recognized a certain responsibility at an early age, being an only child.

Stuart. On the highway. In his underwear. It didn't make sense.

Neither did the article. Not to Ashley.

She read it through several times. According to eye-witnesses—and the heartbroken driver who had hit him—Stuart had simply started sprinting across the highway, heedless of traffic. No one knew where he had come from, other than the far side of the highway. His car had not been nearby. He had not carried any identification. He had just been there, in that pair of white briefs, on the highway. He had sustained numerous injuries, including severe damage to the skull. After hours of surgery, he was in a coma, clinging to life with the assistance of machines. Doctors were doing everything they could, though it was unlikely he would make it. Still, the surgeon also stated that with a young man in the prime of life, and with a will and natural instinct to survive, there was always hope.

As to how the accident had happened, what had made him go racing across the highway, heroin seemed to be the answer. Blood and urine tests had come up positive for the drug.

"No," Ashley murmured.

"I'm sorry," Nick told her softly, standing behind her to place supportive hands on her shoulders.

"No, no, I mean, it's all wrong. Stuart on heroin? He wasn't a junkie."

"Ashley, it's been a while since you've seen him, right?"

She set the paper down and looked at Nick. "It's been a while, but I still can't believe it."

"People change, Ashley," Sharon said.

Ashley shook her head, frowning. "Stuart always wanted to give blood when they had all those drives at church or school when a disaster struck. They always turned him down, because he was one of those people who fainted when you came at him with a needle. This is all wrong."

Nick took her into his arms and gave her a warm hug. "Ashley, it happened. You saw the body, and you've read the article. Maybe Stuart was a good kid, a great kid. Maybe he's still basically a really good man and he just got in with the wrong people. But…hey, he is still alive. There's hope."

"You're right. At the moment, anyway, he's still alive. If he's made it since Saturday. What if he hasn't?" She stared at Nick in horror. "I'll go through the—the death notices for Sunday and today…that's today's paper over there, isn't it?"

"I checked already—there's no notice," Sharon said.

"Thanks," Ashley told her.

Nick said, "Listen, you have to get to work. I'll call the hospital, ask for his condition and leave a message on your phone, and you can check it when there's a break. All right?"

She nodded. "Great, Nick. Thanks, both of you."

She started out the kitchen door. When she opened it, she found a man standing there.

It seemed to be happening on a daily basis now.

But she knew Sandy Reilly well. He'd been hanging around Nick's for at least seven years. He looked as if he were about ninety, he was so weathered and wrinkled. She thought he was probably more like seventy, but no one ever asked him, and he never offered information regarding his age. He lived in one of the houseboats down along the pier, or, at least, he supposedly lived in his houseboat. But he spent most of his time at Nick's.

"Hi, Sandy."

"Hey there, kid, you're looking spiffy in that uniform."

"Thanks, Sandy."

"Cops, cops, cops, we got 'em all over the place."

"We do?"

Sandy laughed.

"You don't know how many cops come in here all the time?"

"I know of several, of course. Not as many as you seem to think we get. But this is a public establishment, Sandy. We don't ask people what they do for a living when they come in."

"Curtis Markham, the gray-haired guy who drinks Coors and sits in the corner with his son, a boy about twelve. Plays a lot of pool. He's a South Miami cop. Tommy Thistle—you know Tommy. Miami Beach police."

"Yep, I know Tommy. And Curtis. I put them both on my list of references."

"Then there's Jake."

"Jake?"

"You'd know him if you saw him."

"I would?"

"Yeah, sure. Well, he's not actually a regular—or he hasn't been. But he stops by some Sundays. Tall guy. Dark. In top shape. He's Miami-Dade. Homicide. A detective. Something of a bigshot, so they say. If you don't know him now, maybe you should get to know him. Come to think of it, I'm sure you'll get to know him. Now that his boat is here at Nick's, he'll be around more and more."

Sandy kept talking, but she didn't hear a word after Jake. Tall. Dark. Miami-Dade homicide.

And, of course, she knew right away. The guy she had scalded with her coffee while rushing out on Saturday.

So he was with Miami-Dade. Great. Just great.

"Isn't it great? I really do know everyone, if you think you need a more formal introduction."

"Thanks," Ashley said. "I do know the man you're talking about. I mean, I've seen him in here. Jake. That's his name?"

"Jake Dilessio. Detective Dilessio. And like I said, I'll hang around one day and introduce you. Well, of course, Nick could do that, too."

"It's okay, I don't need a formal introduction." Better to leave things as they were. She wasn't going to be a suck-up.

She might be a lot more courteous the next time she saw the guy, but she wasn't going to turn into a doormat just because now she knew who he was.

"You okay, Ashley?"

"Of course."

"You're looking a little funny. Did I say something wrong?"

Leave it to old Sandy. He probably had the lowdown on everyone who ever came into Nick's. "No, Sandy. I'm fine. Just thinking how good it is to hear the place is full of cops—and how weird that I've spent most of my formative years here and you know more about the clientele than I do."

"Well, heck, you're gone a lot, and before that, you were a kid, and Nick was always careful to kind of keep you out of the bar. Me, I'm retired, with nothing left to do but watch who comes and goes."

"Do you think that's it? I was an art major for a while. I'm supposed to be a lot more observant. But anyway, that sounds good. It's nice, knowing there are lots of people around I can ask for help now and then. But how do you feel about it? Is it good to have lots of cops around?"

"You bet. I feel nice and safe. And here's hoping you'll soon be one of them. I know you'll be one of the ten to fourteen who makes it."

"One of the ten to fourteen?" she said blankly, still coming to terms with the fact that she had scalded a detective with the same force she planned to join.

"Sure, those are the statistics, Ashley. Okay, maybe a few more, a few less, now and then. About one third of each class actually makes it onto the force, and through their first year as a cop."

"Oh, yeah. They give us those statistics, along with how many cops are killed each year, when we go to orientation. But how come you're so up on the statistics?"

"Well, I may be old as time, but the good Lord has seen fit to leave me with eyes as sharp as a hawk's and ears that pick up just about everything out there. And if I learned anything in all my time on this here earth,

I learned to listen. And I listen to the cops in Nick's place."

"I'm still feeling amazed. I grew up here, Sandy, and I don't know as much as you do about who hangs out here."

"That's because you've got your mind somewhere else most of the time when you're around. Anyway, cops don't walk around on their days off with their badges hanging around their necks or pinned to their fishing shirts. Cops are just people. They like to have a day off. And they don't always like to go around introduc ing themselves as cops. Especially around a place like Nick's. People hang out here to enjoy the water, their boats, and talk about fishing."

"But they talk to *you* and tell *you* what they do for a living," she said smiling.

"Sure, 'cause I talk to them. I'm an old geezer. Curiosity is all I've got left, and what I find out is what makes life interesting."

"Hey, Sandy," Nick said from behind her. "You'll have to fill Ashley in about the customers later. She won't be a cop if she's late to the academy too often. And by the way, we're not open yet, Sandy."

"Well, now, hell, I know that. You tell me that every morning. But you still have coffee brewing, and if you give me a cup, I'll get the place set up before those scrawny young whippersnappers you call employees even make it into work."

Ashley smiled. It was true. Old Sandy did come early several mornings a week.

But never before six-thirty. And he didn't bother a soul. He just liked to get his cup of coffee, set up and sit out on the porch, looking out at the boats and the water.

And so did some of the other folks who lived on their boats at the marina—including homicide detectives, it seemed.

"Ashley, you all right? You're looking kind of pale," Nick said.

"I'm fine. Nick," she said, staring reproachfully at her uncle. "But you didn't tell me that our early-morning visitor the other day was a cop. A homicide cop. With Miami-Dade."

"Honey, you were moving faster than a twister. You didn't give me a chance."

"Right. Of course."

"He's a good man."

"I'll bet."

"You sure you're all right?" Nick persisted, frowning.

"I'm just fine. Honest. I swear. I've got to move. 'Bye, all," Ashley said. She managed a smile for Sandy, then headed out to her car.

Once she was on her way to the highway, she found that the smile she'd had for Sandy faded. She didn't even dwell on the fact that she had scalded a superior officer on the Miami-Dade force. With luck, he would never run into her there, though homicide was situated at headquarters, where her academy classes also took place.

It was a large force, for a county with a large population.

But no logic could keep her from thinking about Stuart again and feeling both a tremendous sorrow and complete disbelief.

He wasn't a druggie. He just wasn't. He couldn't have become a junkie. He'd always had a good head on his shoulders. He'd cared about his folks; he'd wanted them to be proud of him. He wasn't a perfect kid; he'd had his moments. He could be a prankster. Once, when she'd had a crush on someone else, he'd managed to get her talking on a speaker phone about the object of her affections. She could have killed him herself at the time, but he'd apologized up and down—and the other guy had asked her out.

Too bad, actually. She'd wound up dating the jerk for two years.

It had been a wretched relationship, but that hadn't been Stuart's fault. The guy had been what she had wanted, and Stuart had managed to get them together.

She smiled, remembering how he had looked so pleased, like the cat that had eaten the canary. Once, long ago, in a different world, before they'd all realized what life meant once you grew up, they'd been friends. Good friends.

She remembered that after graduation, he'd been offered a number of scholarships. He'd been one of the most creative people she'd ever known, dragging her into doing a film for a final project that had been selected as the best in the school and shown, to the delight of their fellow students, several times in the auditorium. It had been a piece called "Discipline—Now and Then," and while sending out a definite message, it had been hysterically funny, as well.

Despite his interests in film, literature and the arts, he'd opted for a business degree. He'd chosen a Florida state school for both the financial feasibility and to be able to get back to see his parents frequently. She frowned as she drove, remembering that she'd been invited to his graduation party when he'd made it out in the requisite four years. She hadn't been able to go, because she'd taken a summer job as a mate on a sail-boat heading out to the islands. He was going to take a job working on and selling Web pages, but he was also planning on going back to school and getting into some form of either writing or film.

Funny, she couldn't remember what he'd finally decided to focus on when he went for his master's degree. She should remember something like that. All she could remember right now was his voice, always low and steady, sober and clear. And she could remember that they had promised to get together when the summer was over. They had met for lunch. And they had meant to stay close. But he had been heading up to New York to look at a few schools in the city.

And she'd been starting classes herself then. And though they had promised to keep up and call often, like so many promises, that one had become lost in day-to-day life.

Stuart...

As she drove, she saw the road before her, just as it was.

But in her mind's eye...

There was the body on the highway. And now she knew.

It was Stuart's body.

Chapter 5

It had been one hell of a long weekend.

Jake had spent half of it doing research on the lives of the followers of Peter Bordon since the break-up of his cult and the other half getting settled after the move from one marina to another. As for the research, he had some of the information he wanted in his own files, and for follow-up, he had some really good assistance. Hank Anderson, one of the best men he had ever known for divining facts from a computer, had done a lot of delving for him, though a lot of the information duplicated what he already had. It had become something of a compulsion for him to keep up on the case. He had kept quiet about his persistence, since his fellow officers might consider him obsessive and think his determination not to let matters lie bordered on police harassment.

Captain Blake, head of homicide, had called him on

Saturday afternoon, giving him a stern speech. Good detectives put in all kinds of hours. They worked way beyond their pay. But they learned how to stay sane, as well. They learned how to go home and how to have a life.

Jake agreed with his every word.

Their latest victim had been dead quite a while. Insanely rushing about could do nothing for her. Steady, dogged work to bring her killer to justice was the greatest service they could do for her.

That said, Blake reminded him, he was to remain rational, work hard—and make sure he took time off and kept his mind fresh. A cop who was overtired, overstressed and obsessive was no good to anyone.

Granted.

There was simply a lot Jake wanted to do himself.

First, the autopsy. Gannet, as promised, had gotten right on it, and Jake had been there.

Then Jake had gone in and spent hours with Hank while they went over the old cases and delved into what they could find on the new. Saturday evening, he and Marty made a few calls on past followers of Bordon's cult. Interviewing them all was going to take time, and Saturday night was a washout. The first woman they interviewed was married now, with a three-year-old, and her association with the cult was a tremendous embarrassment; her husband knew nothing about it. Nor, she swore, had she even known the victims or been part of the hierarchy of the cult at all. They both sensed she was telling the truth.

Their second call bore no greater results. The young man had only attended a few of the sermons. He had since become a born-again Christian and spent most of his days working at a local homeless shelter, a story that checked out.

Sunday afternoon had traditionally been Jake's kick-back time. It was when a lot of his friends and casual acquaintances went to a sports bar, sometimes to Nick's, drank beer, told fish stories and watched football on television. Not that Sunday. He'd been too busy with electrical and water hookups. He hadn't even crawled in to Nick's at night; he had gone to see his father, who, though his mom had been gone for nearly two years, spent too much of his time sitting alone in the darkness, telling everyone he was doing just fine.

In a way, he'd done as ordered. The problem was that no command, no sense, no logic, could keep him from thinking, puzzling and planning.

Obsessing.

He had barely reached his desk on Monday morning when he received a call from Neil Austen in the forensics unit.

"I just wanted to let you know we're doing what we can to get an I.D. on Friday's Jane Doe. Our best bet is a dental match, but so far we've got nothing. I don't think she was a local. If she was, no one reported her missing. Or else she never went to a dentist. And maybe she didn't—the poor girl died with perfect teeth. Perfect. Her wisdom teeth came in without a hitch. She didn't have a cavity. We have the information out, so hopefully someone out there will be able to get us a match. How many people reach their mid-twenties with perfect teeth?"

"Thanks for the effort and the information, Neil," Jake told him.

"I wish I could give you more. Unfortunately, these things usually take time." They both knew the sorry truth of that statement. There were many cases when just discovering the identity of a victim in such a condition could take weeks or months.

And there were times when bodies went unidentified forever. But thanks to forensics and computers, there were some occasions when identification came quickly.

"Can you give me anything else? Mid-twenties, perfect teeth…?"

"She probably stood about five foot six. Medium build. Never had a child. Gannet says it looks like a ritual murder."

"Same as…?"

"Yeah, same as." Neil gave a soft, regretful sigh. "She was probably a pretty young thing. The guys up here have given her a nickname. Cinderella. She's not actually covered in ash, but the way she was found… Funny, you see case after case, and some are still especially hard. I'll send you the reports on what we have. Oh, and Gannet says she's been dead two to four months."

"Thanks, Neil."

"Yep. I'll update you immediately on anything new we can come up with."

"Great."

Jake hung up the phone and pulled out the file on the last of the victims who had been killed five years before. A picture of a young woman with a shy smile was clipped to the right of the page.

Dana Renaldo.

She, too, had been in her mid-twenties. Twenty-seven, actually, five foot six, one hundred and twenty pounds, an eager, attractive young woman. Her parents had been deceased. She had been reported missing by a cousin almost a year before her body had been discovered. She'd come from Clearwater. The police had investigated at the time but hadn't followed up on the missing persons report because of the findings of their investigation. She had packed up her bags and cleaned out her bank accounts. Three months prior to her disappearance, she had gone through a messy divorce. There had been no children involved, so—until her body had been discovered in Miami-Dade—it had appeared to her local authorities that she had chosen to take off and start over again. It was legal for an adult to be missing if that person so chose. Prior to her disappearance, Dana had worked in real estate and insurance, and, immediately before she had left, she had been a paralegal at a law firm in Tampa. She had sent a letter of resignation and it was in her handwriting, according to the lawyer for whom she had been working.

Their Jane Doe—or Cinderella, as the forensics guys were calling her—sounded very similar in appearance.

He switched files.

Eleanore "Ellie" Thorn had been nothing like Dana Renaldo or their latest victim. She'd hailed from Omaha, and had failed to return home after a vacation in Fort Lauderdale. She hadn't taken a job, had cleared out her bank account at a local branch, and had been seen now and then around town. She had attended Bordon's prayer services. She had often stayed at the communal property. Nearly five feet ten, she had been blond and athletic. Like the others, she hadn't been found until both time and the elements had wreaked havoc on her remains.

The first of the earlier three victims had earned a degree in architecture at Tulane. She had been bright and, according to friends, determined. She'd been an orphan, raised from an early age in foster homes. She'd gotten through school with hard work and scholarships. Twenty-six at the time of her death, she'd been petite, five foot two, and a bare hundred pounds. She'd been living on Miami Beach and had loved the architecture of the area. Deeply religious, in need of spiritual solace, she had probably been an easy mark for Peter Bordon, a.k.a. Papa Pierre.

As he hung up, Marty arrived in front of him, tossing a manila folder on his desk. "Peter Bordon is still very definitely locked up in the middle of the state."

"Marty, I never suggested that he wasn't."

"But listen to this. He's been a model prisoner. He's due for release soon. Exemplary behavior. And, of course, he's in there for a nonviolent crime. Everyone who's worked with him there has found him courteous and polite. Read the report. No, maybe you shouldn't—it'll probably make you want to vomit. Well, hell, vomit or not, you've got to read it. There's a section from the prison psychologist you're really going to like. 'Mr. Bordon is a man regretful of his assumption that his method of bookkeeping did society no harm. His manner is that of a person determined to pay his debts. He is certainly no danger to society. He is deeply religious, has been a friend to many in extreme circumstances, and is a favorite among his fellow inmates.'"

Jake just stared at Marty, feeling the muscles in his neck tighten as if he were being throttled. He sighed and picked up the file.

"Jake, he sure isn't committing murder himself."

"We know that."

"He was definitely in prison when our newest Jane Doe was killed. According to what Gannet told us, she's been dead two to four months."

"I've spoken to forensics. I attended the autopsy. Jane Doe…." Jake murmured, irritated. He stared glumly at Marty. "They're calling her Cinderella. Those guys see so much that's so bad, and yet she seems to have gotten under everyone's skin."

"Like I said, Bordon was incarcerated all that time."

Jake expelled a long breath. "And like I said, Marty, when you told me before you were certain Bordon was still in prison, I believed you. The point is, that doesn't mean a damned thing. Wherever he was *physically* five years ago didn't matter at the time. And it doesn't matter now. We have another dead woman. And somehow, that asshole is involved."

"We don't know that, Jake."

"Gut feeling."

"Can't give the D.A. a gut feeling, Jake."

"Hell, Marty, I know that."

Marty sat at his own desk, which faced Jake's. "Another dead woman with slashed ears. Cinderella. They just had to give her a nickname. Man, these cases suck. And you know, it's strange, isn't it? We don't even know her real name yet, but they go and give her a nickname, and it's suddenly all personal, and that makes it all the harder."

Yeah, no matter what, it got harder with every little nuance that brought a victim's life more clearly into focus. Jake remembered standing at the table during the autopsy finding a renewed respect for Gannet. Their victim had been badly decomposed, but there had still been those little things that made her an individual. The tiny tattoo, just visible at her ankle. The mole that could still be seen on what was left of her shoulder. Even the color of her hair, a lock of it slipping from the table and looking like…a lock of hair that might fall across the pillow when a girl was just sleeping the night away. But then the whole picture came into focus. The chill of the autopsy room. The scent that always seemed to linger in the morgue, real or imagined. The body…the entire length of the naked body…so sadly decomposed. First mutilated, then gnawed by animals. A home to nature. Part of Gannet's determination on time of death had been due to the incubation period of flies and the stages of larvae. When Jake had seen the last victim from five years ago, Dana, on the autopsy table, it was as if her humanity had been stripped away. She looked like a creature made in a special effects lab for a horror film. Gannet was one good man, though. Determined that he would do his best to find out all he could. To return her soul, at the very least. To speak for her, help fight those who had so brutally stolen her young life.

Jane Doe/Cinderella. Mid-twenties. A lifetime ahead of her.

What had brought her to such a brutal death in South Florida?

Anything was possible. Maybe she'd been killed by a boyfriend who had struck the mortal blows in passion, realized his act and been smart enough to know that—despite a lot of fiction to the contrary—the police weren't complete assholes and might well follow a trail of clues to him. Maybe the guy had read about the cases involving members of Peter Bordon's cult.

Maybe.

Or maybe someone was taking up where Bordon had left off.

Or maybe…

He was back to the possibility that Bordon himself was involved.

There was no reason why he couldn't be calling the shots from prison.

"Who was she? Where did she come from? Why did she die?" Marty murmured, thinking aloud. "A young woman, just trying to live her life, making a wrong turn in the road somewhere."

Marty's words made Jake wince inwardly. This was business, his job; he wasn't a rookie. He was a seasoned homicide cop, who—if he hadn't seen it all—had certainly seen enough. The world, hell, the county, had enough homicides to keep cops moving.

And it was what he had wanted. From the time he had joined the force, he had wanted to go into homicide.

He'd always wanted to be a cop. Not because he'd grown up in a family where joining the force had been tradition, because he hadn't. His father and grandfather had both been attorneys.

He'd wanted to be a cop because the guy who had become one of his best friends in life had been a cop. The guy who had shown up when, at the age of eighteen, Jake had wrapped his graduation gift, a brand-new Firebird, around a tree in Coconut Grove.

He'd been driving under the influence.

Too many times, his dad had gotten him off on speeding tickets. Of course, his father never knew he got behind the wheel while drinking. When he drank with his buds, he usually stayed out. That night, however...

He'd decided to drive. To show off. His family had been thinking about buying a house at the end of the street. He'd wanted to show it to a girl. He could race his Firebird around a few blocks without any damage being done.

Like hell.

He was supposedly a pretty tough kid. Football, soccer, baseball, a star player on every team. Grades high enough to see that he got into the right college. He usually knew when to play and when to keep himself straight as an arrow. But not that night. That night he was exactly what the cop called him when he reached the accident. A snot-nosed rich kid, thinking he could buy his way out of everything.

Carlos Mendez had been a police officer for nearly twenty-five years the night he had come upon Jake in his folded-up Firebird. He could have taken him in for DUI. But he didn't. He told him off—and when Jake tried to tell him that he wanted to call his father, an attorney, Carlos had said that he'd get his every right, his phone call, his attorney, the whole nine yards—when the time was right. He'd told him what he thought of him—and where he was going to wind up. And that however rich he might be, he was going to spend one night in jail.

He hadn't been mean, hadn't raised his voice. But something about the way he'd spoken, so soft and so sure, had scared the hell out of Jake. He'd realized he could have killed not only himself but his date.

"You know, kid, you're in trouble. But you ought to be on your knees, thanking God. You slaughtered a palm tree. That was it—the only fatality. You could be in a morgue now. Or you could have killed that pretty young girl you were with. So be thankful, accept what you get and try to make it mean something," Carlos had told him.

Jake had listened. And at some point, he wasn't sure when, Carlos Mendez had realized he'd had a real effect on the snot-nosed rich kid. He hadn't charged him with DUI, only with the lesser charge of failure to have his vehicle under control. His leniency had come with strings—promises Jake made that night to Carlos. Of course, Carlos had no guarantees that Jake would abide by his promises. He later told Jake that he had gone on gut instinct—the most important tool a cop could have, no matter what technology offered.

Jake kept all his promises, grateful not to have had to spend a night in jail. He'd even been sober and somewhat cleaned up before he reached his parents' house, before his mother cried and his father yelled. He'd promised Carlos Mendez an afternoon at the station and fifty hours of community service. He'd put in the hours working for Habitat for Humanity and in downtown Miami at a soup kitchen for the homeless. He'd seen some of the worst the city had to offer there, men and women so strung out on drugs that life had lost all meaning, and the kids who paid the real price for their parents' addictions. Toddlers with no futures because they'd been born with AIDS. He saw, as well, those few whose lives were changed by others. The junkie thief who'd gone straight because of a decent cop and opened a home for abused children. The prostitute who had changed her ways because of a down-to-earth priest. Even the crooked accountant who had gotten out of jail to do tax forms and apply for assistance for the elderly.

And down at the station, with Carlos, he'd seen videos more horrible than anything ever concocted by the minds of filmmakers. Photos taken after traffic fatalities. Most of them accidents caused by alcohol.

In the process of it all, he met others Carlos could have arrested and sent to prison for long years of their lives but hadn't.

He'd gambled.

And his bet had paid off.

Jake had been about to leave, having earned the grades good enough to get him into almost any college in the country. He'd been accepted to his father's alma mater, Harvard.

He hadn't gone.

Once again, his mother had cried and his father had yelled. But he'd loved his parents, and they'd loved him. In the end, they'd accepted his decision to stay home, take criminology at the local college and apply to the force.

He'd never regretted it, not once. And even his father had been proud of him. No one had been more congratulatory when he had been promoted to detective. He'd known he'd wanted to work homicide because of Carlos. Not because Carlos had worked homicide, but because, while still in college, he'd been with Carlos one day when he had suddenly veered over to the side of the road. He'd spotted a body in a field.

"Shouldn't you call it in?" Jake had asked. "You're off duty."

"I'll be calling it in, as soon as I know what we've got, and as soon as I've secured the scene. And a cop is never really off duty, Jake. You know that."

Carlos was pretty damned amazing, and that was something Jake *did* know. He wouldn't ever have noticed the prone figure, inert and shielded by long grass and carelessly tossed garbage, soda cans and beer bottles.

Carlos had an eye. He assured Jake that, with a little experience, he would have that eye himself.

That afternoon, Carlos had called in the information as soon as he had determined that the victim was stone cold, beyond help.

The guy had looked like an old itinerant or a drunk. At the time, Jake had seen nothing to suggest foul play. Of course, he'd kept his distance, too, because Carlos hadn't been about to let anyone taint what might be a crime scene.

Later, when the detectives and crime scene people had arrived, Jake and Carlos watched them work. Carlos had remarked quietly then that he'd been certain right away—gut instinct—that the man had met with foul play. He was dead, silenced, no longer able to speak for himself. And yet, always, the dead, in that terrible silence, cried out for justice. Their fellow men owed them that justice. The cops and the medical examiners were all they had left. And even if the victim had been an old drunk, he deserved the same attention as any other human being.

It turned out that he had been a migrant worker and that he had been murdered. The detective on the case had it solved within a matter of weeks—mainly because Carlos had been so careful at the scene of the crime. His yellow tape had preserved footprints that had led to the arrest of a middle-aged thug who had killed the old man for the fifty dollars in his pockets.

Since that day, Jake had wanted to be in homicide. It had seemed like an important role in life—being the champion of the dead.

His decision, and his effort to reach his goal, had drawn him closer than ever to his father, who had always played the devil's advocate, telling him how a good attorney could make mincemeat out of evidence if it wasn't collected properly.

There had been more to the idea of moving into homicide. Not just to weep for the dead, or even to be their spokesman. With every year of experience, he realized that his most important role was to stop a killer before he or she could claim more victims. He and his fellow officers worked many cases that turned out to be domestic— husbands, ex-husbands, wives, lovers, killing in passion. Guns and knives were the prevalent weapons in cases like that. Then, of course, there were the little ones, kids brutalized by their parents or trusted caregivers. Those were hard to deal with. He'd never met a cop who could just blink and call it business when he or she was called to handle the death of a child.

But there were also cases that weren't crimes of passion, anger or jealousy. There were psychopaths in the world who killed because it gave them a rush. And there were also those who killed because they thought themselves superior, who appeared to be totally sane, to whom murder was a calculated risk. There were those who killed for pleasure, for sport and for personal gain.

He had handled many of those, as well. He'd done so professionally, not letting anger, pain, pity or disgust get in the way of his sworn duty.

This particular case, though, was so damned acrid he could taste it on his tongue.

So damned painful and bitter.

He inhaled deeply, gaining control.

He knew damned well that he couldn't let his emotions get out of control, nor could he visibly display them in any way—he would even have to be careful with Marty. He didn't want to be pulled from this case.

"Did you finish up the paperwork on the Trena case?" Marty asked.

"There, on top of the out box."

"I'll send it on over to the D.A. with my report. Seems Trena's lawyer told him to plea-bargain after he saw the evidence against him."

Jake looked at Marty, then paused to thank the officer who stopped by with the envelope that contained the information on the girl they were calling Cinderella. There was other business to finish up.

"Trena was smart to plea-bargain," he said, unwinding the string securing the envelope. "His gun, his fingerprints, bullets charged on his credit card in his wife's head—I think a plea bargain would be a hell of a lot better than a death sentence."

Marty smiled without humor. "Well, remember the guy who put five bullets into his buddy's stomach? His attorney got the jury to believe his gun just went off *accidentally*—five times."

"True. I'm still glad to hear Trena is going with a plea bargain. Hopefully he'll be locked up for a while."

Marty started to collect papers and folders while Jake opened the envelope he'd been given. He scanned the information. Without looking up, he told Marty, "Let's follow up on the rest of Bordon's known followers, find out what they're doing these days, check into their activities. We can work the door-to-door angle, as well, but I don't think we're going to get anywhere. We don't have a lot to work with right now. If we can just get an I.D. on the victim, it will give us more to go on." He paused, then said softly, "I think I'm going to take a ride up to the middle of the state this week."

"You want company, or you think I should stay here?"

"I think one of us should be here."

"You'd be happier if you were the one here, interviewing Bordon's old people. You like to be hands-on, Jake, and you know it. Sure you don't want me to be the one to take the drive up?"

Jake shook his head. "No, but thanks. I want to talk to Bordon myself."

Marty shuffled his feet uncomfortably. "You've talked to Bordon before."

He had. And if it hadn't been for Marty, he might have blown his entire career. He had almost gone for the man's throat. Marty and a uniformed officer had pulled him back. Marty knew how deep his feelings ran against Bordon, even if he didn't personally believe that Nancy's death had anything to do with the case. He felt the same pain. On duty with a fellow officer in the area, he had been one of the first people on the scene when Nancy's car had been found.

"I'll be all right."

"If that kid hadn't been a weight lifter, I might not have kept you from strangling the man."

"Marty, I was wrong. I was overemotional, but I swear to you, I'm in control now. I can't kill Bordon."

"What do you mean, you *can't* kill him? I'm willing to bet you can. He isn't short, and he isn't a skinny wimp, but you've got a few pounds on him—all muscle—and the adrenaline rush you had going that day was frightening. You sure as hell *can* kill him, and I'm not so sure you can control your temper."

"I can and I will."

"But—"

"I can't kill him, Marty. I really can't. I need him alive."

"You *need* him alive? We both think he's a killer, even if he never dirties his hands himself. So why is it that you *need* him alive?"

"Because we need to find out what really went on back then, and if it's recurring now. We were missing something—I mean, it seemed obvious that Bordon was calling the shots, and that there were more people involved in the deaths. Hell, maybe Harry Tennant *was* in on the murders, but I don't believe for a second that he committed them alone. Marty, we've got to find out the truth, or we're never going to be free of this case." He was silent for a minute; then he grimaced and spoke flatly, with an open honesty his partner could well understand. "I need the truth. Or *I'll* never be free of this."

After a moment, Marty nodded. "Yeah, I understand. But you're sure you'll be all right going up alone? Captain Blake will be setting up a task force again—reinvigorating it, since we never officially closed the inquiry down. There will be other officers down here getting moving on research, questioning, digging, legwork. I can come upstate with you if you want."

"I want one of *us* here. Paying attention to everything, to little details that might slip by someone else. We need to get every piece of information we've got on file and to keep digging up everything new we can find on Bordon's old followers, everything we've got on his hierarchy—the names of everyone involved in the cult, and a bio on what they've been doing since Bordon went to jail."

Jake's desk phone rang. He picked up.

It was Captain Blake, head of homicide, on the other end.

"I understand you've been busy this weekend."

"I took Sunday off."

"To read files all day?"

"I went to see my dad."

"Good. All right. I've seen the forensic reports on the girl that jogger found Friday. And yes, it's similar to the murders five years ago. And yes, we'll reinvigorate the task force. And if you can swear you'll keep a level head and unproven *speculations* to yourself, you'll head it again, Detective."

"I can keep a level head." He hesitated. "Thanks."

"No one knew what was going on back then the way you did. It's always been your case, and it only makes sense to keep it that way. Of course, this whole thing could be some kind of a—"

"Copycat killing? Yes, sir, we all know that."

"And you're not the Lone Ranger, Jake. We solve things by being a team."

"Yes, sir."

"All right, then. Meeting at ten-thirty, my office."

"Yes, Captain."

"Franklin will be in from the FBI. You have a problem with that?"

"No, sir." He did, but he wasn't about to tell that to Blake. And he was damned determined that he wasn't going to tell Franklin, either.

"Belk, Rosario, MacDonald and Rizzo will round out the group. You can always call in whatever uniformed personnel you need."

"Sounds like we've got a good team and good backup."

"Ten-thirty," Captain Blake repeated.

"Yes, sir, we'll be there."

He hung up, staring thoughtfully at the receiver.

"Well?" Marty said.

Jake shrugged. Marty was a big fan of Sir Conan Doyle.

"As your Victorian super sleuth liked to say, Marty, the game is afoot." He added, "Ten-thirty, Captain Blake's office. He's called in the other shifts for a meeting. We're reinvigorating the old task force, using the same crew. We've got Belk and Rosario, MacDonald and Rizzo. Oh, and Franklin from the FBI."

"Franklin?" Marty said with dismay.

"You got a problem with that?" Jake said.

"Problem? Me? Hell, no," Marty said, starting around from Jake's desk to take a seat at his own.

"Yep, hell no, no problem," Jake said.

"Fuck," Marty moaned.

"Yeah, I know."

"Fuck," Marty repeated. He shook his head. "Franklin," he said. He looked bleakly at Jake. "We got a problem."

"We'll get past it."

"Yeah, sure," Marty said. He punched information into his computer, ready to search the available records. He was still shaking his head.

"Fuck. *Franklin,*" he repeated.

"I hear you, Marty," Jake assured him.

"We'll get past it," Marty aped.

"We'll get past it, because nothing, *nothing*, is going to take us off this case. Nothing—and no one."

"Right. Nothing and no one," Marty agreed.

Later, after they'd both spent the early morning reviewing reports and researching the records, Jake rose to tell Marty it was time for the task force meeting.

He was still shaking his head. And when he rose, reached for his jacket, and joined Jake for the walk to the captain's office, he said again, "Fuck. Franklin."

Jake stared at him.

"Last time. That was it," Marty swore.

"You sure? 'Cause if not, get it out—now."

"Fucking *Franklin*?" he said vehemently. Then he grinned. "All right. I got it out." He shrugged. "The guy is efficient. He's just such a…prick. He even walks like he's got a broom up his ass. But he is good with a computer."

"Right. Ten-twenty-eight. Let's get in there."

"Fucking Franklin."

Chapter 6

"Basics," Sergeant Brennan announced firmly to his class. "Basics. Why do we harp so much on the basics?" It was a rhetorical question. "Because you forget those basics, and every bit of hard work done by a score of cops and technical support personnel is down the damned drain. We're law enforcement officers. We're not the law. And nothing works without the law. You people have all passed your tests to get into this class. You've made it through your background checks, and you're months along now. Hell, we've given you real bullets. In another few months, you'll graduate, and you'll be looking to make your careers as police officers. You've all come into this with different dreams, different goals. None of it will amount to crap if you ever forget the basics. First, what the hell are we here for? Jacoby, that question is for you."

Brennan pointed to Arne Jacoby, in the seat next to Ashley. Jacoby had a look that could make him appear to be the best protector in the world—or the meanest son of a bitch. He was six foot four and pushing three hundred pounds of pure muscle. He was a handsome guy, not just black, but ebony, with a shaven head and great features. Against the almost shimmering dark beauty of his skin color, he had startling green eyes.

Jacoby grinned. Although each academy class learned from a variety of experts in different fields, Brennan was their sergeant, their main instructor for their journey through training. He was a good guy; the class liked him. He could be tough, he didn't tolerate much, and he spoke often about the morality expected from a police officer. He believed passionately in everything he said. But despite his propensity for waxing on at length about tenets, ethics and morals, Jacoby had been paying close attention.

He stood.

The class, in their chairs, looked up by rote.

"To protect and serve," Jacoby told Brennan.

"There you have it. Thank you, Jacoby. That's our main function. Not to harass the law-abiding, not to seek out crimes where they don't exist. To protect and serve. However, we all know that there are criminals out there, people who set no value whatsoever on human life. You've seen the tapes. You know the statistics. You know that cops have pulled people over on traffic violations and been shot in the face because they've happened to pull over a perp guilty of another crime or just a plain old psycho. But say you know you've got someone ahead of you in a car with an APB out on them.

There's a warrant out for this person's arrest. What's the most important thing to remember?"

"Not to get yourself shot in the face?" Jacoby asked.

Brennan grinned, allowing Jacoby the pure logic of that one.

"And after that?"

"Reading the guy—or the woman—their rights."

"Hallelujah!" Brennan said. "In the past weeks, you've listened to specialists on many aspects of crime scene investigation. You'll hear from more. Anthropologists, entomologists, dactyloscopists, botanists, chemists, ballistics experts, mathematicians, profilers, serologists, psychologists and linguists. In today's law enforcement, the work of all these people is incredibly important. But all their work means nothing if police work is shoddy at the ground level. That's when your basics come in. Someone tell me about Miranda warnings. Montague, you're up."

Ashley stood as Arne Jacoby sat and began to go through the cautions delivered to every suspect—and familiar to anyone who'd ever been to the movies or watched a crime drama on TV.

"Very good, Montague. What about 'the fruit of the poisonous tree'?"

"Say an officer failed to give a suspect in a murder case a Miranda warning. In talking to the suspect, the officer found out where the murder weapon was hidden and discovered the weapon. A judge could bar the weapon from being admitted as evidence, because it was located from information gained before the suspect had been informed of his rights."

Brennan nodded, indicating that Ashley should sit again. "You all know these things. I know you all know them. You've come a long way. You've taken poly-graphs, you had to study to pass your tests to get into the academy. My point this morning isn't to teach you new things. My point is that you must never forget the basics of good police work. Maybe you'll never join the vice squad, maybe the last thing you ever want to be is a homicide detective. But what's important is this simple fact—you never know when you're going to be the first officer called to a crime scene. What you do in those first moments can make or break a case. Whatever de-tails you may learn in the future, whatever expertise you gain, remember that the most carefully gleaned information can be thrown right out of court if the ba-sics of law enforcement are forgotten or neglected. All right, ladies and gentlemen, that's it for now. Lunch break. This afternoon, we'll be listening to a serologist and blood spatter specialist. Get out of here. Go eat hot dogs or *arroz con pollo* and think about what I've said."

The class began to rise and filter out. "Hey, Mon-tague, you want the hot dog or the *arroz con pollo*?" Jacoby called to her. "Whoops, what was Brennan thinking? They don't even have *arroz con pollo* at the roach coach. What'll it be, hot dog or mystery meat sandwich?"

"Hot dog," she said to him. "Except I have to check my messages, make a few phone calls."

"Hey, you know what? I'll splurge and buy the hot dog for you. We'll be out at the tables. Want a Coke?"

"Sounds good. I'll get you next time."

"Buy me a beer one Sunday at your uncle's place."

"It's a deal."

Jacoby went off to procure their food. Ashley stood

to one side as she checked her cell phone for her messages.

True to his word, Nick had called the hospital. Stuart was still in intensive care. Only family members were allowed to visit.

He was, however, hanging in. Nick apologized at the end of the message, telling her he was sorry he hadn't been able to glean more information.

It was not much, but Stuart was still hanging in. He was alive. And while he was alive...

There was hope.

And still...

She felt no better. It was wrong, simply wrong. People changed, yes. It was a tough world, drugs were rife. But... Stuart? She whispered a quick prayer that he would continue to hang on, that he would live, that he would awaken and explain what had happened. Clear himself, his name, his reputation.

But what if he didn't wake up?

"Well?" Jake said.

Marty had just hung up. After the meeting, they had spent hours on the phone.

Marty nodded at him. "We're not going to get anywhere chasing after John Mast, Bordon's old office manager."

"No? He got out of prison six months ago. He was working at a halfway house in Delray."

Marty looked surprised. "How did you know that? Sorry, stupid me. You never let it go, did you, Jake?"

"I knew where he was, yeah. I've made it my business to at least know where people were. That's why I had you checking on him."

"Well, don't go thinking we can get anything on him."

"Why not?"

"He'd been out of prison less than two months when the plane he was on went down just north of Haiti."

So he was dead. Jake was irritated with himself. He'd been following people, but he hadn't followed John Mast closely enough.

"We really need an I.D. on the new victim."

"In the next few days, they'll start doing a facial reconstruction. There's no way we can use a picture, but a good artist's rendering may get us a few bites."

Jake picked up the telephone again, telling Marty, "I'm talking to the guys at the paper. We'll make sure we've got them ready to help in every way. We'll get the picture out there in print, *big*, and we'll get it to the news stations, as well. Someone had to have seen her down here."

As he dialed, one of the other lines rang. Marty picked it up, covered the receiver quickly and said, "I'll take the newspaper. You probably want to deal with this."

Jake frowned, hit the line button and said, "Dilessio."

"Jake?"

Inwardly, he winced. "Yeah, Brian."

"I saw the story in the paper. There's a new murder victim."

"I know that, Brian."

"Maybe Nancy did know something she shouldn't have known."

"You know I've worked that angle damned hard."

"Yeah, but now you've got another dead woman on your hands."

"I'm aware of that."

"Yeah, I know…just thought I should check in with you. And… I'm sorry about the other night."

"It's all right."

"If you ever need me to help out on this, in any way…"

"I'll call you. I really will," he added.

"I know how to do research, how to dig."

"Brian, trust me, I'm hitting some major dead ends. I'd call for help in a second."

"Thanks."

"Sure."

Brian hung up.

"You two getting to be buddy-buddy now?" Marty asked, frowning.

"No—he showed up drunk on my boat the other night, ready to beat me up."

"Ah. So he still believes…"

"Well, there is one thing we both believe. Nancy would never have killed herself. And she wasn't prone to accidents."

"Yeah, well," Marty murmured, looking down at one of the old files. "Man, this drawing really sucked. We have to get someone better than Dankins."

Jake glanced at the drawing done before they'd been able to identify their first victim. It must have been a hell of an assignment for the forensic artist, with so little of the face left, but there didn't seem to have been much effort put into the likeness.

"Dankins was let go about two months ago," he told Marty.

"I hadn't heard."

"That *is* a lousy likeness. Could be anyone."

"Yeah, it looks like my aunt Betty—and drunk on Halloween at that."

Jake stood and reached for his jacket. "You ready? We'll start today with Mary Simmons."

"Housemother for the old cult?"

"Yep, I found her. She's joined with the Hare Krishnas, and she's agreed to speak with us this afternoon."

"You found her?" Marty asked quietly. "Or you've known where she's been all along?"

"Does it make any difference?" Jake asked.

"Hell, no. I just love that music and visiting people in robes and Mohawks. Sounds like a great afternoon," Marty said. "Can't wait. Let's get to some legwork."

Finished with her messages, Ashley went to join a number of her classmates at the picnic tables. Arne had gotten her a hot dog and an array of little condiment packets. She thanked him as she sat. Besides Arne, Gwyn Mendoza, Dale Halloran and Izzy Rodriquez were also seated at the table.

As she sat, she was surprised to see Len Green striding toward them. He waved to the group as he came up to join them, smoothing back his hair. Despite the fact that he kept it fairly short, unruly dark blond strands were flying away. He had a good face, though, lean and aesthetic. He was an excellent subject for a drawing.

"Hey, Len," Izzy called.

As he joined them, Ashley wondered if he and Karen might not make a good match. Len was dedicated to his job, and so was Karen. They both believed in what they were doing. Karen had gone directly for her goal, once she had decided she wanted to teach young children. Len had told her he'd joined the academy after acquiring a business degree and spending a few years traveling for work. Business, he said, hadn't suited him, despite the fact that he'd stuck out the four years for his degree. He was working now in a patrol car with a senior partner and loved it.

"Don't look, it's a real cop," Gwyn teased. "What brings you here? Aren't you supposed to be solving crime down in south Dade?"

He made a face. "Paperwork. I wonder if the public knows how much paperwork we have to do? A guy sneezes at the wrong time during an arrest and it turns into twenty pages of paperwork. No, no, don't go quitting the academy. I'm exaggerating."

Ashley laughed with the others. Len had never been one of the regulars at Nick's, but that was where she had met him. He wasn't actually a boater or fisherman. He'd been out with a friend for a day, and when they'd come into Nick's after long hot hours on the boat, he'd noticed her studying the requirements for entry into the academy. They'd started talking, and then he'd come back a few weeks later, and that time, he'd asked her out.

By then she'd been scheduled to take the test for the academy, and she'd been able to tell him that she didn't want to date anyone until she'd completed her training. He'd asked her if they could have a meal together now and then, and maybe take in a movie. They'd done so, and she'd valued the friendship. And now it would be great if he and Karen did hit it off.

"Hey, kid, how's it going?" he asked her.

Arne Jacoby sniffed. "How's it going? She's a star student. Ever get a one-word answer out of this girl? Nope. No matter what the question, she's done the research."

"Actually, I wasn't talking about the academy," Len said. "Did she tell you about the body she passed on the highway the other week? There was an article in the paper about it. I kept it for you, Ashley, in case you hadn't been able to get a hold of a copy."

"I found the article, Len, and it's worse than what I knew."

"What are you talking about?" Arne demanded. "You're losing us. Start from the beginning. There was an accident?"

"Yes, a kind of freaky—and sad—accident, as it turns out," she added, looking at Len, then explaining to them all. "I went to Orlando with some friends for the weekend, and we passed an accident on I-95. A pedestrian had been struck. Apparently he'd been walking across the expressway. In his underwear. Turned out he was someone I know. Knew well, as a matter of fact, years ago."

"You knew the guy?" Len said.

"I think I heard some mention of that accident on a traffic report," Gwyn said, frowning. "There was an article in the paper the other morning, too."

"Strange case. The guy was in his underwear, running across the highway. Well, it is Miami…. He wasn't in a fraternity or anything, pulling off a stunt?" Len asked.

"No, not Stuart. He's out of school, working. He was the kind who graduated with honors, more of a…well, more of a nerd than a fraternity type."

"So…" Gwyn persisted. "What was he doing?"

"They're saying he was all doped up," Len explained quietly. "But that's about all I've heard about the incident. It was probably handled by the North Miami guys, or maybe North Miami Beach. Or maybe County. I'm

sure someone can find out. We can check with vehicu-
lar homicide—no, sorry, the guy wasn't killed, right?
He's in a coma. From what I read, though, he was *really* doped up."

"Was he a junkie when you knew him?" Izzy asked,
his tone soft, consoling.

"No!" Ashley said indignantly. "And that's the point.
I don't think he's a junkie now."

"When was the last time you saw him?" Arne asked
quietly.

"A few years ago," she admitted. She realized that
everyone around the table was looking at her the same
way. Sadly. As if they didn't want to state the obvious.
She hadn't seen the guy in a long time. Human beings
were fragile. There was nothing to say that he hadn't become a dope addict in the years since she had seen him.

"I'd still like to find out more about the accident,"
she said.

"Ask Brennan—maybe he knows something or can
at least point you in the right direction," Len suggested.

"Good idea," Gwyn said. She smiled at Ashley. Ashley liked Gwyn. Gwyn was tough and careful. She was
a black woman—tawny gold, actually—and she had
been born in Cuba. Raised a Catholic, she had once
told Ashley she had considered converting to Judaism,
just to make sure she had a foot in every local minor-
ity out there. With public institutions required to have
quotas, she was determined to prove she was more than
a statistical offering. She studied hard, worked hard and
meant to be the best at what she did. "If you need help,
or just moral support, let me know. I'm happy to oblige."

"Thanks."

"Any of us would help you out, Ashley," Arne said.

"Ditto," Izzy told her.

"Thanks," she repeated.

"I'll ask around, too," Len assured her. He rose. "I've got to get back to my station. And you guys need to get back to class. I know Brennan. He's a stickler for people being on time."

He gave Ashley a kiss on the cheek, waving to the others as he walked toward the parking lot.

Arne offered Ashley a hand. "Ready to head back in?"

"We've still got some time," Gwyn said.

"A few minutes," Arne said. "No more."

"You know what? I'm going to make another quick phone call. Excuse me," Ashley told them. Rising, she discarded her trash and walked halfway toward the building. She dialed Karen's cell phone number and was glad when her friend picked up the phone. Karen had recognized her cell number on caller I.D and spoke before Ashley could say a word. "Hey, you read the paper, I guess. Can you believe that it was *Stuart*? We drove by a body on the highway, and it was just a body—I don't mean that badly, it was horrible, no matter what—but we drove past right after it happened, and it was Stuart Fresia."

"I know. That's why I was calling."

"I'm glad you called. I wanted to talk to you, but I can't call you during the day because you're in class. But I can't believe it. I mean, he's got to be one of the nicest, straightest, most decent kids we ever knew. How the hell could this have happened?"

"I don't know. I wish I did. But I'm going to ask some questions."

"Well, yeah. You're a cop. Or almost a cop. You should be able to get some answers from someone."

"I'll try."

"I hope…"

"What?"

"I hope he's still alive," Karen said.

"He is—or was as of this morning. Nick called the hospital. He's still in intensive care. No one can get in to see him but family."

"No, and I guess it wouldn't do any good even if we could get in. He's in a coma."

"I've got to get back into class. I just wanted to touch base with you."

"Thanks. And promise to call me if you learn anything at all."

"Promise."

Ashley hung up and realized that the others had preceded her into the building. She glanced at her watch and noticed with dismay that although it had seemed before as if she had plenty of time to get to class, she was just going to make it.

She hurried along the halls to the right room, sliding in just as the minute hand swung. The rest of the class were already seated. She walked quickly to her own seat, noting that Captain Murray, head of personnel, had chosen that afternoon to come in and take a look at the current class. Her heart sank. She felt like a sore thumb, threading through the seats to reach her own.

She knew, of course, that he was watching her, even as he spoke with Brennan. She kept her eyes ahead, on him and Brennan, praying she showed no emotion. Certainly not guilt. She'd actually made it in time.

Neither of them singled her out. Brennan spoke to the

class for a few minutes, telling them that Shelly Garcia from forensics was going to give them a talk on blood splatter and crime scene scope, and then Captain Murray would talk about some of the directions in which they might want to go after they graduated.

Brennan sat after introducing the woman from forensics. The talk was fascinating, and Ashley was intent on what she was hearing. Then Murray stood at the front of the room and talked about various specialties within the department. She had a pad and took notes, as did the others. But she found her thoughts wandering on occasion, as well.

Without noticing, she began drawing the scene of the accident once again.

She caught herself and was careful to look up frequently as she began filling in substance and shadow in her drawing.

And once again…

The figure. Just a black figure, far across the many lanes, but watching…

Watching from the other side of the road.

Mary Simmons was sitting in the rear of the property, waiting for them. She smiled when she saw them, then rose, and welcomed them. She was thirty-five and looked ten years younger, very much at peace with herself. The garden area of the temple's property was pretty, with greenery surrounding small benches. Jake had to admit it was a serene setting.

"Thanks for seeing us, Mary."

"Sure." She glanced at Jake. "As long as you don't intend to harass the Krishnas…?"

"This place has been here as long as I can remember, Mary. We know it's legit."

She shrugged, looking at him. "I'm not sure what I can say that I haven't told you many times before." Her gaze went from Jake to Marty. Marty looked at Jake, realizing that his friend had seen Mary several times during the years that had gone by.

"Anything you can remember. Anyone we might have missed."

She nodded. "Well... Papa Pierre—sorry, Peter Bordon—always seemed to be the only one really running anything. He preached to us, had the property, brought us in, and yes, suggested that whatever we had must be given up for the benefit of all. What you all don't see, though, is that he was kind and loving, and we all believed in him. And it was a simple way of life. We worked the garden, growing all our own food, and..." She paused, smiling, "Luckily I'm a vegetarian, because we also ate fish from the canal out back, and it's likely that half the fish out there were diseased or tainted. To get back to the point, it was a simple way of life. He could befriend men, but in retrospect, he preferred women. And if there was dissent among us— seldom spoken, of course, because of our share-all philosophy—it was over who Peter would have with him each night. I kept house a lot. I was one of his first recruits. And yet, not even I really knew what went on at the house. We slept in the dorms, the cabins on the property. Unless we were chosen for the evening."

She looked at Jake. "We knew that cars came at night. I heard him talking to people in the house sometimes. But I never knew who was there. And I never suspected anything. When we learned that our friends had been murdered, we were appalled. And truly, we believed that the girls had been killed by people who hated Peter, our way of life, our beliefs. Peter even suggested to us once that we be very careful, because the police hated him, hated us, because they didn't understand the depths of our faith and how we could live so completely for one another." She shrugged. "But now... well, it seems so obvious that Peter liked money and sex. And naturally, he didn't like the police himself, because he did have us all brainwashed. But still... I honestly don't believe that Peter killed anyone. Or ordered that anyone be killed. He was greedy, he used us, but I don't believe he was a killer."

"Mary," Jake said patiently, "three women were killed. All three were associated with the cult. Peter was the head of the cult."

"Yes. But... Peter is the one with the answers, if there are any. I told you, people came and went that we never saw. Maybe they came for the money Peter received from us, I don't know."

"What about Harry Tennant?" Jake asked her.

"He had no money, so he wasn't someone you'd expect Peter to foster. He only spent a few nights on the property. Well, that I know of, anyway. In retrospect, Detective Dilessio, the more I think about it, I do believe he might have committed those horrible crimes. He was strange. I mean, really strange. He wanted to be like Peter so badly, maybe not in a religious sense, but...he wanted the power that Peter had over people." She shrugged. "He wanted women. Sex. He came on to all of us. Peter never discouraged anyone else from soliciting a relationship. It wasn't as if he felt we were his private harem or anything. And God knew, none of us seemed to know what it was that first brought us into his bed. Every person in the group was interviewed separately at one time or another. One minute you'd be talking about the good that could be done by a simple life...and the next thing you knew, you were exalting in all that was natural and beautiful in human existence. Created in God's form—we were still mortal, still animals, and natural instincts were not something to be abhorred, but celebrated. So, looking back, it's easy to see that Harry took a look at Peter, went wild with jealousy and maybe formed a psychotic hatred for the girls for wanting Peter and not him."

"Mary, I know that you've gone over this with us time and again, but please, bear with us, because another girl is dead. When the girls who were killed disappeared, didn't you worry? Didn't Peter worry?"

She shook her head. "There were no ties binding us to the place. We were free to come and go as we chose." She hesitated. "Yes, when the third girl was found, I was afraid. The police started to come by, and Peter encouraged us all to talk, so... Then Harry Tennant killed himself, and...well, you've got to understand that when you believe in teachings like Peter's, deeply believe, death is not the end but a beginning."

"Those girls were tortured. Murdered."

"Their ears were slashed," Mary said.

"Because they didn't hear, presumably. And if Peter wasn't the one they weren't hearing, Mary, then who was?"

She shook her head. Then she frowned. "I think Harry Tennant might have been more psychotic, and even smarter in his demented way, than you might want to believe, Detective."

"Why is that?" Jake asked.

She smiled sadly at them both. "I think he heard voices. He talked about Lazarus."

"Lazarus?" Marty said.

"Lazarus...who rose from the dead," Jake said. He smiled at Mary, speaking softly. "Mary, you've never mentioned this to me before."

"I never thought of it before. I believed that Harry was really crazy. And so much time has passed... I don't know what is going on now, Detective Dilessio, but I know that I spoke the truth years ago when I told the police I didn't believe Peter had ever killed anyone. I believed that Harry was responsible. He just acted crazy. One night... I woke up, and he was out by the canal, staring at the water. And he said that Lazarus had risen. That Lazarus had told him to go to the water. I admit, he gave me the creeps. So I left him there and hurried back to the dorm. Would you all like some herbal tea?"

They thanked her and declined. Jake rose and started to reach into his pocket.

"I have your card, Detective, and honestly, if I can remember anything else that might be helpful, I swear I'll call you." She stood as well, smiled, and gave him a little kiss on his cheek. "I promise. I know you're trying your best."

"Thanks."

"You didn't ask me the one question you usually do," she said.

He arched a brow.

She gazed at him with tremendous empathy. "I swear, I never saw your partner, Detective Dilessio. If she ever came out to the property, I never saw her. And I pray that you believe me. I wouldn't lie. It's against everything in my faith."

"I know that, Mary," Jake said. "Thanks. And don't forget—"

"I'll call you. No problem. I like to see you, Detective."

They left. Marty had turned down tea, but he wanted coffee. Jake agreed. There was a Starbucks down the street. Marty ordered espresso. Jake opted for a double.

"We're not getting anywhere," Marty said. "Bordon had complete control of that cult. I think those girls were hypnotized. They lived on the property owned by the People for Principle but never saw, heard or spoke any evil."

"I keep going in circles. There's got to be a straight line in there somewhere, though. And we're going to get to it," Jake said, a grim look on his face.

The class began clapping. Ashley quickly set her pencil down and did the same. To her amazement, they were breaking for the afternoon. Feeling guilty, she clapped hard. When they were dismissed and the class began to rise, she started to join them to file out, then remembered that she wanted to ask Sergeant Brennan if he could get her whatever information there was to be had on Stuart's accident. She wadded up the papers with her sketches and tossed them into the trash can as she approached the front of the room. Murray and Brennan were talking to one another again as she approached, but both men saw her coming and fell silent, awaiting her question.

"Hello. Montague, isn't it?" Captain Murray said.

"Yes, sir."

"You're more than halfway through. Are you still pleased to be in the academy?"

"Oh, yes, very pleased," she said.

"Well, good, I'm glad to hear it. Sergeant Brennan says this is one of the best classes he's ever taught."

"Thank you, on behalf of all of us," she said.

"Did you have a question about any of the material covered today?" Brennan asked her.

"Actually, I have a question about something that happened a few days ago. There was an accident on I-95. I was traveling north with some friends and went by just a few minutes after it occurred. When I got home, I found out that the man who was struck was an old friend of mine, and the papers have reported that he was apparently high on heroin. That just doesn't sound right to me. I was hoping that maybe one of you could direct me to the officer in charge of the investigation, and that he or she might be willing to talk to me."

She was glad that neither of them was inclined to inform her that apparently her old friend *had* gotten into drugs. They both continued to stare at her politely. Murray answered.

"Yes, I heard about the incident you're talking about. It was handled by Miami-Dade and FHP. I'll find out what officer was assigned to the investigation. I'm sure that whoever it is won't have a problem discussing the known facts with you. I'll make a few calls and give Sergeant Brennan the information for you."

"Thank you very much, sir," she told him.

"No problem."

She smiled, clutched her books, walked backward for a moment, then turned to exit the room. As she left, she was certain that both men kept their eyes on her.

She wondered if they were reflecting on her request—or thinking she had difficulty with punctuality? Or, worse, did they somehow know she had been drawing in class?

Great. So far she had offended a respected homicide officer, made those responsible for her think she might have a problem with timeliness, and maybe they had even realized she spent half of her class time doodling. No…they wouldn't have been so polite, she was certain, if they were about to tell her she wasn't up to par.

As she exited the building, she found herself in the middle of a crowd of people. There were three shifts, or platoons; eight to four, four to midnight, midnight to eight. The "day" shift always left when class broke.

She had come to recognize many people as they made their way to their cars. She had found "waving to" and "smiling at" friends among them. Not people she really knew; just people she saw every day. There was a certain brotherhood to be found at headquarters. Clicking her car open with the remote, she smiled at one of the women from records. The woman smiled back.

That was when Ashley saw him again. And knew now, of course, who he was. Detective Jake Dilessio. He was leaving with another man, and they were carrying on a conversation as they walked across the lot. She hurried on toward her car. But before she could open the door, the detective turned. He looked different in a suit. Taller. Older. More official. More like he could get her into trouble. She quelled the thought and remembered that everyone was entitled to their privacy—even cops. She wasn't sure how that fit with spilling coffee over someone who happened to be standing in *her* doorway, but she still didn't want to turn herself into a cowering little kiss-ass.

With luck, he wouldn't notice her. She was probably just one of a horde of ants to him. Lots of officers didn't take the students seriously until they'd actually graduated from the academy.

He was wearing sunglasses, dark glasses over dark eyes, shielded by a stray thatch of dark hair. He glanced her way but made no acknowledgment whatsoever. He obviously hadn't seen her.

But as she slid into the driver's seat, she was aware that he was still looking in her direction. He *had* seen her.

But he sure as hell hadn't waved or begun to crack anything like a casual-acquaintance smile.

He'd stared.

Wishing she could slide beneath her seat, she slid her glasses on, buckled her seat belt, switched on the ignition and eased her car from the lot.

Once on the road, she recalled that Sandy had told her that the detective had just moved his houseboat to Nick's marina.

It wasn't Nick's marina, of course. It belonged to the city. People just called it Nick's marina because Nick's restaurant had been there so long.

As she drove homeward, she realized that the detective's car was behind her own for quite some time. She recognized him in her rearview mirror. Then, somewhere on the highway, he turned off.

She entered the house through the kitchen door and could tell that it was a busy afternoon at Nick's; she could hear voices and laughter even over the sound of the jukebox. She made her way through the house to her own wing and stripped out of her uniform, jumped quickly into the shower and let the hot water pour over her for a long time. She wished she could stop think-ing about Stuart Fresia, but she couldn't. She wondered if it was guilt—she hadn't kept up with old friends the way she should have. She wondered, too, if it was just that what people claimed had happened was so jarring that she simply couldn't put it aside.

Showered, somewhat refreshed, yet dolefully aware that her long weekend and its late hours was beginning to tell on her, she went through the back entrance into the restaurant. Nick was behind the bar, helping out Betsy, the weeknight bartender. The place was jumping—odd for a Monday night.

"Hey, kid!" Nick called to her. "You bushed? Or can you give me a hand for a few minutes? Kara called in sick, so I've only got David out on the floor. There's a food pickup for table twenty-four. Can you grab it?"

"Sure."

She moved to the counter that separated the kitchen from the service area. The food pickup was just one plate, broiled snapper, with baked potatoes and broc-coli. She set the plate on a tray, added a few lemons and a paper cup of tartar sauce, and headed to the outside porch area, where tables eighteen to twenty-six could be found.

Table twenty-four was a two-seater, off around the L of the porch, often chosen by those in a romantic mood—those who knew of its existence, of course. As she walked around the corner, she saw that, as expected, tonight there was only a single occupant at the table. A man, dark-haired, head bent low, intensely interested in whatever he was reading.

As she set the plate down, she went into waitress mode by rote.

"Good evening. Here's your broiled snapper. Can I get you anything else?"

He looked up. She froze for a moment, recognizing the customer in the chair. Detective Dilessio. Since leaving police headquarters, he had changed into swim trunks and a T-shirt. The T-shirt was dry; his dark hair was wet. He'd been in the water, apparently, or maybe he'd just showered and dressed down, the same as she had. He hadn't left work altogether, though, or so it seemed. What had apparently demanded such grave attention from him was a manila file filled with papers.

He recognized her, as well, his eyes running from the top of her red head to the sandals she had slipped into.

"Anything else?" he murmured. "Hmm. The snapper is safely on the table. Dare I ask for coffee? Not to wear, to drink."

She flushed slightly. "I can do my best to safely set a cup in front of you," she assured him. He was still watching her. He didn't appear angry, only slightly amused. She hesitated. "You're Jake Dilessio, right? Detective Dilessio? Miami-Dade?"

"Yep. Why, were you going to apologize now that you know who I am?"

She felt a sizzle of temper rise, then tamped it down, determined to hold her own. "Because of who you are? Really, Detective, I'm taught on a daily basis that my function will be to protect and serve, not intimidate the public and expect special treatment. Actually, I was merely going to introduce myself. But if you were interested in apologizing for barging into me on my own doorstep, I'm certainly happy to listen."

"Ah, that's right. You're in the academy, I understand," he said.

"Yes. Are you suggesting I shouldn't be?"

"Not in the least. And if that comment meant, was I going to try to get you kicked out for scalding me, the answer is no. For one thing, if you're good, your future is far beyond any power of mine to control. I have to say, though, as you mentioned, our motto is protect and serve. Not to bully. I hope you are a bit...calmer with the law-abiding citizens of our county."

"I try. But they haven't set me loose on the streets yet, you know."

"Ah, well, then, there's time—and hope."

"I guess I should be grateful that you didn't decide to bring me in for attacking an officer of the law."

"Well, you're Nick's niece, right?"

"I wouldn't want favors from anyone because I'm Nick's niece."

"In truth, you wouldn't get any."

"Ah! So that means I was in the right."

"I don't recall saying that."

"But I was," she insisted, then wondered what the hell she was doing, standing out here arguing with him. She didn't seem to be able to leave without having the last word. And she didn't seem to be able to draw herself away, to stop studying the man, either. He was definitely interesting. No pretty-boy good looks to him, but something beyond that. Very strong bone structure. Weathered, in good shape. He had an arresting appearance, and she could well imagine that if he looked at suspects with that darkly intense stare of his, he could make them tell the truth simply because they might believe he was seeing right through them.

The way he was staring at her now.

She suddenly felt awkward.

He smiled slowly. The action changed his face. He wasn't just arresting; he was as attractive as all hell.

"Is there more?" he inquired.

"We…we could wind up on *The People's Court*. Take the matter to Judge Judy or something like that," she said lightly.

"Either that, or you could just bring me my coffee."

"Yes, I guess I could."

So much for his smile.

Ass! she thought.

Too bad she was going to have to just deliver the coffee. She would have loved to dump a full pot over his head.

Chapter 7

Jake continued reading through the list of those who had been associated with Peter Bordon. He knew the list. It was all old business. Didn't matter. He was missing something, he was certain, and when he discovered what...

Names suddenly blurred before his eyes.

Disillusioned people, most of them young, looking for something meaningful in life, thinking they had found it. All had moved on.

One of the young men was in a Catholic seminary in Tennessee.

Many had moved out of state.

He rubbed his temples, thinking back to the visits he had made to Bordon all those years ago. A young woman had answered the door. Cary Smith. They'd already checked her out. She'd moved to Seattle, married a guy who worked for a fish plant, and now had two children. At the time, he was certain, she had believed she was serving a prophet, a man who intended to make the world a better place by distributing food to those in desperate need.

Then there was John Mast, Bordon's right-hand man. He'd gone down for fraud, as well. He would have been high on the list of suspects.

But he was dead.

Jake closed the file.

Don't get obsessed, he reminded himself. He wasn't the Lone Ranger. Hell, they'd had the help of Ethan Franklin, an FBI agent, too, and though Franklin might be swaggering, arrogant and irritating beyond all measure, he knew his business.

Tomorrow they were due to meet again. Franklin was studying murder reports across the country, trying to find out if there had been similar killings anywhere else. Then, as they had today, they would hash it all out for an hour or so, go through the endless sheets of information and compare notes. All they had from the past and from the present.

And what the hell did they have from the present? A body. A body with clear evidence of a brutal death, that mocked the means of murders from the past. The body of an unknown woman who had been found in a severe state of decomposition, washed from a shallow mud grave.

And from the past…

Nancy.

He could remember her standing on the deck of the *Gwendolyn.* "I don't believe that poor kid murdered anyone. We'll keep finding them, Jake. Bodies, more and more of them. Unless that cult is stopped. I think Peter Bordon has a God complex. He thinks he has the right to take human lives. He thinks he's God's hand, or will, or something like that."

"We've gone after him hard, and we will lock him up," Jake assured her.

"We won't really get him—not until someone can get the D.A. evidence to take to trial to prove that he's the power behind the deaths." She'd glanced at her watch then. "I have to go!"

Something about her manner had bothered him that night.

"Where are you going?"

"Home. I have a husband, remember?"

But she hadn't gone home. And the next morning had been the first time Brian Lassiter had arrived on the *Gwendolyn*, ready to take him on.

But she hadn't been there. And then...

The tension. The fear. The accusations. The hunt.

It had been several weeks before she had been found, despite the fact that she'd been a cop and that every law enforcement officer in the state had been looking for her. But then, she'd gone deep into the canal. What faint tire tracks the best people in the field were able to find indicated that she had lost control of her car.

And between the time she'd disappeared and the time she'd been found, Bordon had been arrested for fraud and tax evasion, and been locked up. He'd been free, however, when Nancy had disappeared, when she had died.

Every muscle in his body seemed to knot up.

Don't get fucking obsessed, he reminded himself again.

He swore suddenly and looked at the empty glass of iced tea in front of him. Where was that coffee he'd asked for? What the hell had happened to the service at Nick's?

Nick's was busy. Ashley was stopped several times as she walked through the restaurant, heading for the coffeepot to fulfill Detective Dilessio's so graciously stated order. When she at last made it back to the service station near the right end of the bar, she ran into Curtis Markham, a South Miami police officer.

"Hey, kiddo! How are the classes going?" he asked her.

Curtis was definitely a nice guy. Around thirty, he was married, with one son. His wife worked for one of the airlines. They often came in together, and sometimes, when she worked Sundays, he took his small sailboat out with his son, Chris, then came in to Nick's to catch the end of a game or teach Chris the finer points of pool. His sandy hair was graying, but, thanks, perhaps, to his determination to keep up with his son, he was slim and wiry. Curtis only drank one day a week—Sunday. Tonight, sitting at the bar, he was drinking a diet soda while munching on fried fish tidbits.

"Classes are great, Curtis," she told him. "Thanks."

"Good. I was afraid you were going to regret joining the force," he told her.

"Why?"

He shrugged. "The academy's hard work. Then you get out and spend your days dealing with the scum of humanity. You put your life on the line every day, and you get paid pennies. I was afraid you'd maybe come to think it was a thankless job."

She smiled. "Do you feel that way?"

"Only sometimes." He grinned. "Usually what I see on the streets just makes me think I'm a lucky guy. I go home and thank the Lord that I've got a good kid and a beautiful wife."

She laughed. "You may be the only really cheerful cop I know, I have to say."

He arched a brow. "We've got grouchy cops around here?" he asked softly, looking around the place.

She whispered in return. "Outside. A Miami-Dade detective. Jake Dilessio. Temperamental. Then again, maybe it's just me. I don't think he likes me very much."

"Jake is outside?" Curtis asked.

She nodded. "In fact, I think I'd better get his coffee to him fast."

"If he's grouchy now, he may have good reason."

"Oh yeah?"

"There were some cult-related murders here about five years ago. Do you remember?"

"Vaguely—someone confessed but killed himself while in holding. There was speculation at the time that the man who confessed hadn't really done the killing, but as far as I recall, no more bodies were ever found."

"Well, a new one's been found now."

Ashley frowned. "There was a cult leader who was a suspect, but nothing could be proven against him. He went to prison for something, though, right?"

"Yeah, and he's still there. Anyway, Jake is going to be taking a lot of heat right now. That's why he's so grouchy."

"We all take heat. That doesn't mean we have to be miserable to others," she said.

Curtis suddenly gave his head a little shake, staring at her hard. Puzzled, she turned. Jake Dilessio was standing behind her.

"Came in for the coffee myself," he told her.

"Sorry."

"The service at Nick's is usually pretty good."

"How are you doing, Jake?" Curtis broke in.

"Hey, Curtis. Fine, thanks."

"Heard you took a slip here at the marina."

"Moved her in this weekend. Guess I could head back down to my own boat for coffee," he said wryly.

Ashley picked up the coffeepot, grabbed a cup from the shelf on the wall and quickly filled it.

"Sorry, it's my fault your coffee was held up," Curtis said. "I was just asking Ashley about the academy."

"I'm sure Miss Montague is just zipping right along," Jake said dryly. "She's so quick."

"Why don't I just get you a carafe of coffee and bring it out there, and then you can have a refill any time you want? And when you're done, you don't have to wait for the check—Nick wanted your meal to be on the house, a 'welcome to the marina' gesture," she said pleasantly, going for a carafe.

"Nick already gave me a welcoming meal, and I always pay my way," Dilessio told her. "*And* I like my coffee poured hot." He turned away from her. "Curtis, how are Sandra and Chris?"

"Doing great, thanks. They're up visiting her mom in Delray. Means I'm eating at Nick's for the next few days."

"Not a bad substitute, though Sandra makes a mean lasagna," Jake said. Taking his coffee cup, he started back out. Ashley noted that he hadn't let his files lie alone when he came in; the manila folder was tucked beneath his arm.

Curtis must have noticed the way Ashley watched him as he left. "Hey, the guy is really all right. You two just got off on the wrong foot."

"And it might be a good thing to have a big, bad detective living so near the place," said an amused, feminine voice.

Ashley spun around. Sharon Dupre was standing next to her, looking together and elegant, as usual. She was in a tailored navy suit, pumps and a soft blue blouse. Her eyes were twinkling as she watched Ashley.

"Mmm, it's just terrific," Ashley agreed. "Will you refill his coffee and bring him his check?"

"You bet. In fact, you ought to sit down and eat, young lady. I've heard all about the 'roach coach' where you guys have lunch."

"But you worked all day."

"I only showed one house."

"Sharon, Nick's a little busy, short some help. Do you mind helping out tonight? I was thinking that, even if Stuart Fresia is in intensive care and not allowed to have visitors, I'd like to take a run by the hospital, maybe see his family."

"Fresia…? Why do I know that name?" Curtis asked.

Ashley explained about the accident, how she had driven by right after a man had been struck, and then came home to find out that the victim was an old friend. She went on to tell him just how unbelievable it seemed that he could have gotten so heavily into drugs.

"People change. And drugs are seductive," Curtis said, and she nodded, having heard the same basic response over and over.

"Right. But not Stuart. Anyway, I'd really like to at least see for myself how he's doing."

Sharon looked concerned. "Ashley, you're still in the academy. Should you be getting involved?"

Nick had come over to the end of the bar. "She's just going out to see a friend, Sharon. That doesn't mean she's going to try to wrest the case from the investigating officer. I think it's a great idea. But first, sit down and eat, Ashley, take a breather, before you head on over to the hospital. The snapper's so fresh it's still snapping," he teased.

"Sit, Ash, tell me all about life," Curtis said, patting the bar stool at his side.

She sat. Nick poured her a soda, while Sharon went off to tell Herve, the cook, that they needed a snapper plate.

"You could tell me more about your friend," Curtis said.

Twirling her straw, Ashley shrugged. "Smart, solid, down to earth."

"Were you a twosome in high school?"

She shook her head. "We were good friends for years. If he'd just been a hot romance, I wouldn't have known him so well. Curtis, I'm not kidding—Stuart just wasn't the type to get into drugs. He wasn't even a heavy drinker. Ever."

Nick had come to stand at the end of the bar again, listening as he dried a glass then slid it back on the shelf. "Ashley, maybe it will all work out. Maybe he'll come to, and then he can tell the police what happened, what he was doing."

"I hope so. And I hope I feel a little better myself, once I see his family. I'm sure they'll be there. Oh, God.

He's an only child. His parents loved him so much. *Love* him so much. And still, I'm telling you both, no matter how people change, it doesn't make sense."

"Honey, there are lots of things in this world that don't make sense," Nick told her. "But I think you're right. Once you go to the hospital, you'll feel better, I'm sure, if you just bring some comfort to his family."

"Maybe." Sharon brought a plate of snapper to the bar. "Eat up, Ash." She rolled her eyes and winked. "I'll take more coffee to the ogre outside."

Sharon walked away. Nick frowned. "The ogre outside?"

"Dilessio," Curtis supplied.

"Jake isn't an ogre. He's a decent sort."

"And he lives here now," Ashley said, grimacing.

"He put his name on a waiting list for that slip about a year ago," Nick told her. "People love this marina. Vacancies are hard to come by. And it's good to have lots of cops around. Keeps trouble down."

"Of course. But you've got an almost-cop right on the premises. I know, don't say it. The more the merrier, right?"

"He's not a bad guy to know in the department," Nick said seriously.

"Thank God it's a big department," Ashley murmured. She ate her snapper. "Nick, if you're sure you're all right, I'm out of here. I want to get down there and then actually get some sleep tonight. We fledgling cops have to be in at seven. Curtis, take care. See you soon." Ashley slid from her bar stool.

Curtis put a hand on her arm. "Ashley, seriously, if you think something might be up with your friend's accident, you ought to talk to Jake."

"He's homicide. My friend isn't dead. Yet," she added softly.

"He knows his stuff," Curtis said. "And he's respected in the department. You are still in the academy. You try calling someone, they may just give you a line. Dilessio calls a fellow officer, he'll talk away."

Ashley hesitated for a moment. Dilessio was a jerk, and he obviously didn't like her. But, then, this wasn't about her. This was about Stuart.

"Maybe you're right," she said. "Okay, wish me luck with the ogre."

Curtis gave her a thumbs-up.

She took the coffeepot and headed outside. Jake Dilessio was still reading his files. He didn't look up as she refilled his cup, just murmured, "Thanks."

She stood there, then slid into the seat opposite him, forcing him to look up.

"I understand you're in homicide."

"Yes." He looked back at his files.

She cleared her throat. After a second, he looked up again. She plunged in.

"There was an accident on Friday morning, right after I left here. I drove by it right after it occurred. A pedestrian was struck on I-95. I saw him lying on the highway. He was wearing underwear, and that was it. This morning I read the article on what had happened. It turns out that he was an old friend of mine. The article says he was high on heroin. I knew Stuart too well to believe he did that to himself. He fainted at the sight of a needle."

She had his attention, at least. He was staring at her, eyes dark and brooding.

"I'm homicide, Ashley. Your friend was the victim

of a traffic accident—apparently, he was the cause of the accident. I remember seeing something about it. The guys investigating it are good, I'm certain. And just because this guy was afraid of needles once, that doesn't mean he didn't get into drugs later."

"I know there's something really wrong with this picture," she insisted.

"You think you know—because this man was your friend." He didn't speak cruelly, just matter-of-factly.

She shook her head. "Where did he come from? He must have come from somewhere to start walking across the highway in his underwear."

"Ashley, I've been a cop a long time, in homicide a long time. On one of my first cases, a couple got high on cocaine and heroin together. They thought they had put their infant to bed. But they set the baby in their microwave and cooked it. Finding what was left of that little corpse is one picture that will stay in my mind all my life, no matter how many cases I work. If your friend even began to get into drugs, he could have gotten hooked badly and done almost anything."

She was going to get the same reaction, no matter what. And it was incredibly irritating that everyone jumped to assumptions so quickly.

"Why is it so easy for everyone just to accept what *should* be the same sad story but may not be? I know Stuart. He didn't slip into drugs. There's something very wrong with what seems to be the obvious explanation. I've been told you're a respected detective. I thought you'd be interested in the truth."

She saw his fingers tighten on the papers he held, his only visible reaction. "You're in the academy. You know the size and scope of the county, and what goes on every day. I'm homicide. And right now, I have a full plate in front of me. I'm sorry, but even if I wanted to, there wouldn't be any difference I could make. There are already people working the investigation. If you'll excuse me, I'm working, too. On a truly brutal murder."

Dismissed again, she stood. "Yes, of course. I've been told how very important you are. Thanks for your time."

So much for assistance from the great and esteemed Jake Dilessio, she thought.

A few minutes later, she had her purse and keys and was on her way to see how Stuart was doing.

Stuart was at the county hospital, a place where the emergency room could be a zoo, where you could wait endless hours for assistance, but where the quality of care was top-notch. Ashley knew that if she were ever seriously wounded, it was where she would want to go.

A volunteer sent her up to the intensive care waiting room.

There were several people there. A young man about her own age with his face behind a newspaper, an Hispanic couple, holding hands and whispering softly to one another, a handsome, thirty-something black woman with a toddler in her arms, walking back and forth. There was another young woman who stared straight ahead at whatever was on the television, and a man who might have been about thirty, working on a notebook computer. Stuart's parents were seated together, staring into space, looking like a pair of lost children. In their mid-fifties, they were a handsome couple. Lucy Fresia had always been considered one of the most attractive mothers among their group, but now her delicate features looked pinched, and her appearance was that of a far older woman. Nathan Fresia was a tall man, nearly six-three, appearing even taller because he was slender, as well. Like Lucy, his appearance was worn and broken, and it seemed as if thirty years had gone by since she had seen him, rather than the two or three that it had really been.

"Mr. and Mrs. Fresia?" she called softly. Lucy's head jerked up, as if she was terrified that a doctor was coming in to give her bad news. She stared blankly at Ashley for a long moment, then jumped to her feet, recognizing her.

"Ashley Montague," she said, and a hesitant smile lit her features. Then she burst into tears, stretching her arms out. "Oh, Ashley!"

Ashley hurried forward, embracing the tiny woman. She felt Lucy's body shaking with the force of her tears. But then Lucy drew away, trying to wipe her eyes. "Nathan, look who's here. It's Ashley."

"Young lady, it's good to see you." Nathan bent to offer her a warm, endearing hug, as well. He didn't sob as his wife did, but his cheeks were wet.

"Stuart is…hanging in there, right?"

"Oh, yes," Lucy said. She glanced at her husband. "The doctors say he's incredible. He must have a tremendous will to survive. The nurses are in there with him now. That's why we're both out here. We never leave him alone, not for a minute. They say that we should talk to him, so of course we do. I even brought his old copy of *Green Eggs and Ham* and read it to him. He loved that book as a kid. He always said he'd read it to his own kids one day, the way we always read it to him." Her eyes filled with tears again.

"Lucy, he may still be reading that book to his kids," Ashley said softly.

"Ashley, you know that Stuart is in a coma, right?" Nathan said worriedly. "Only his mother and I are allowed in—"

"We could tell them that Ashley is family," Lucy said.

"It's okay. If he gets a little bit better, we can think of a way for me to get in to see him," Ashley said.

"But you've come all this way," Lucy said.

"Actually, it's not far for me at all, and I really came to see the two of you. My uncle called the hospital for me today, so I knew I couldn't get in to see Stuart."

Lucy wiped her cheeks, smiling slowly. "You came to see the two of us? That's so sweet, Ashley."

Ashley smiled. "Do you know how many times you had me to dinner? How many snacks you made me, and how many times you took me trick-or-treating?"

"This is still so kind of you. It's bad enough that he's lying there, not moving, so injured," Lucy said. "But what they're saying! It's impossible, it's horrible…and it can't be true. Oh, you should see the way people look at us. As if we're silly parents, completely blinded. Almost as if we're stupid. And we're not. But—"

"Lucy, please," Nathan said softly.

Lucy flushed, realizing that her voice had grown loud.

Then she looked wide-eyed at Ashley again, shaking her head. She lowered her voice to little more than a whisper. "They're saying he was into drugs. He had heroin in his bloodstream. Now he's lying there…practically dead. And he could be charged with that accident if…if he ever comes to. Ashley, we were never stupid parents. We were never blind to the drug scene. My Lord! We grew up when drugs were more prevalent than soda pop. And Stuart wasn't an angel or a perfect child, but he was our child, and we did know him. But no matter what I say to the cops, or even to the hospital personnel, they just stare at me. Their eyes get so sad, and they stutter, and I can tell they're thinking, 'That poor woman. She thinks she knew her child, but she didn't really.' Ashley, of course I didn't know everything about Stuart, and he wouldn't talk about his latest project, but he still kept in touch with me, and he was *not on drugs*."

"I believe you," Ashley said.

Lucy caught both her hands, squeezing them so hard Ashley almost winced.

"You do?"

"Of course I do. Stuart was one of my best friends for years."

"Ashley," Nathan said suddenly, "I'd heard you'd joined the police force."

"I'm in the academy," Ashley said. "I haven't been sworn in yet."

"But still…"

They were both staring at her hopefully.

"Please…don't expect too much," she said. "I asked my sergeant today if he'd ask the officer in charge if I could talk to him. I mean, I'm not sure what I can do, if I can find out anything, but I can assure people that I knew Stuart really well, too, and that I know he would never have voluntarily done drugs."

A nurse appeared in the doorway. "Mrs. Fresia, you're welcome to sit with your son again, if you wish."

"Thank you." Lucy looked at Ashley, smiling ruefully. "Excuse me, dear. I think it's so important that one of us is with him at all times. Please come back. I can't tell you what your coming here has meant to us."

"Of course I'll be back."

"We'll introduce you as a cousin, Ashley," Nathan said to her. "Perhaps your voice will mean something to him. His mother and I...we don't intend to give up."

"And," Lucy added, "the police do come here to talk to us...to check on Stuart, and see how he's doing. It's not that any of the officers has been cruel or mean.... They just can't seem to believe that we know Stuart wasn't on drugs. Forgive me, dear, I'm getting back to my son."

"Of course." Ashley kissed her cheek and gave her a big hug. Lucy left with the nurse. Ashley hesitated, then sat down next to Nathan. "Nathan, what has Stuart been up to? I'm sorry to say that I haven't talked to him in a long while."

He stared down at his folded hands for several seconds, then looked around the waiting room.

"Have you eaten?" he asked her.

"Yes, thanks, I ate at the restaurant before coming."

"Let's get coffee anyway."

Realizing that he didn't want to talk in the waiting room, Ashley agreed. They went down to the hospital cafeteria.

"I'm glad you're not hungry," he told her dolefully.

"The food isn't very good here, is it?"

"Well, the care is great, definitely some of the finest in the nation." He offered her a weak grimace. "Maybe it's not a bad thing to lose a few pounds."

"When I come tomorrow, I'll bring you dinner from Nick's," Ashley offered.

"You don't have to come tomorrow, Ashley. Lucy and I are holding up as well as can be expected."

"I'd like to come."

"How do you like your coffee?"

"Black, usually. Unless it's from what we call the 'roach coach'—the food wagon where we get lunch during the day. Then I put some of the powdered stuff in it—makes it bearable."

He smiled, and Ashley allowed him to buy them both cups of coffee. He had tossed his old one. He had stared at it until it had grown cold, he told her.

When they were seated, he ran his fingers through his hair, then looked at her. "I haven't the least idea what Stuart was up to lately," he said.

She frowned. "Stuart was always anxious to please you and his mom. Not pressured to please you—I don't mean that. He loves you so much."

"Yes, well…he was writing. Which was, of course, what he always wanted to do. Freelance. He hasn't been able to get in with a major paper the way he wanted to, but he wasn't troubled by that. He said that he was going to get the stories and get them out there, and then people would be coming to him. And he was making a living. Not getting rich, but making a living. He sold articles to a number of publications. One of them was *In Depth*." He wagged a finger at Ashley before she could say anything. "Yes, it's a rag. One of those papers that has headlines like, 'I was abducted by a two-headed alien gladiator.' But they pay well, give their reporters lots of freedom—well, obviously—and sometimes, sometimes, they come up with the kind of story that gets real attention. He'd been living at home with us but a few months ago, he said he was moving out for a while.

That he was writing and wouldn't be seeing much of us. And he meant it. We hadn't seen him since."

Ashley sat back, frowning. "Did you tell this to the police?"

"Of course."

"And they still think he just got himself involved with a bad crowd?"

"I don't know what they think. They've promised that they're looking into the situation. So…" He ran his thumb over the rim of his coffee cup, staring at the coffee, then up at her. "So if there's anything you can find out, his mother and I would greatly appreciate the help."

"I'm not even a rookie," she told him.

"You must have friends higher up in the force?" he said hopefully.

"I do. And I swear, I'll do all I can."

"Let's go!" Nathan said, suddenly sounding angry.

"What's the matter?" Ashley said, looking around. Then she noticed the man who had gotten Nathan so upset. He was the man about her own age who'd had his head buried in the newspaper in the waiting room. Dark-haired, light-eyed, he looked like a decent sort. But then again, the most decent appearing people could be the slimiest.

"That leech—another would-be reporter. Claims he knew Stuart. But he can't seem to give us anything. They talked to him at first, and he came up with a bunch of wild stories. The police asked questions, and he did nothing but infuriate a lot of important people and make it harder for them to take Stu's mom seriously. The media people have been obnoxious, trying to prove we're unfit parents or something, and that tragedy of Stuart's upbringing caused his descent into the pitfalls of drugs. I've gotten rid of them time after time, and one of the fellows on the case, Sergeant Carnegie, has been great, warning them away from us. This guy is trying to get a story out of us, and I don't intend to turn Stuart's trauma into a sensational headline."

Ashley rose along with Nathan. When they reached the hall, she told him that she was going to go home and get some sleep, but that she would be back the following night.

"Ashley, that's kind of you. Come on up for just a minute. We can get you in for a second, I'm certain."

She went back upstairs with Nathan. When they reached Stuart's room and looked through the window, Lucy was by his bed, holding his hand.

Tears welled in Ashley's eyes as she saw her friend. He was connected to several monitors. There were tubes in his nose and mouth. An IV line dripped fluids into his veins. His face was bluish and swollen. A bandage was around his head.

And yet his hand...

The hand his mother held looked so incredibly normal. Stuart had beautiful hands, with long fingers and neatly clipped nails. Strong, masculine hands.

Lucy glanced up and saw them. She rose and came to the door. "Ashley, I'll get you a smock, then you can go in for a few minutes." Her voice dropped to a whisper. "I said you're my niece, our closest relative...go in, dear. Talk to Stuart."

Ashley nodded, because it seemed to mean so much to Lucy. She didn't think Stuart would even know she was there.

At Stuart's side, just as Lucy had, she sat and held his hand. He seemed cold, cold as death, she thought, then forced herself to banish the idea. It was awkward at first, but then she began to talk to him. "Listen, you stuck-up little would-be literary giant, you hang in there. You've got everything in the world, including the world's most wonderful parents. I mean, Nick is great, but... We've talked about this before, but I like to imagine that my parents would have been like yours. And I'm going to find out what the heck you were up to, Stu, so help me. I know you're not a junkie, and I'm going to prove it, I swear."

She thought she felt a squeeze. The slightest squeeze. She stared at his monitors. She didn't know how to read them, but she was certain that nothing had changed.

Neither had he. With the help of a machine, his breath rose and fell.

And yet...

Had she felt...something? Maybe they were right, and maybe he did hear her.

She decided not to say anything. She didn't want to hurt Lucy or Nathan with anything that resembled false hope.

She stood, kissed his forehead and whispered that she'd been a lousy friend, but she did love him.

She looked toward the door. Neither Lucy nor Nathan was there. The nurse noticed her, though, and slipped in, telling her that the Fresias were back out in the hallway, talking to one of the police officers.

When Ashley got in sight of them, she nearly stopped dead in her tracks.

The officer they were speaking to was none other than Jake Dilessio.

Chapter 8

Dilessio's grave nod indicated acknowledgment. Lucy turned to her with hope written all over her face.

"Ashley, thank you so much. I see that you've used your position to get us some more assistance," she said.

Ashley instantly felt her cheeks grow pink. She had no position, and she was more surprised than they were to find this particular detective showing an interest in the case.

"I can't promise you anything," Dilessio told them. "I'll speak with the investigating officers and do whatever I can to find out why your son was out there. I'll tell you whatever I find out. But you have to be prepared for the fact that you may not like the answers."

Lucy smiled, looking very strong for a moment. "Detective Dilessio, everyone I've come across so far pities me for not seeming to understand that my son could have become an addict and gotten into very bad things in the matter of a few months. I don't deny that those things can happen, but my husband and I always enjoyed an exceptional relationship with our son. I'm going to believe in him until someone proves otherwise. *And* I'm going to believe with my whole heart that he's going to come out of that coma, and then we'll all know the truth."

"My prayers are with you both," Dilessio said. "And I certainly hope you're proven right. I admire your faith." Ashley was startled when he spoke to her next. "Were you heading home soon, Miss Montague?"

"I, uh, yes." She smiled apologetically at Lucy and Nathan. "We start at seven at the academy, I really do need to go," she told them.

"Great. Then I can hitch a ride," Dilessio said.

She must have looked at him; surprised, because he continued, "Marty dropped me off here. My partner."

"Oh. Well, of course I can give you a ride."

Nathan kissed her cheek. "Thanks so much for coming, dear."

"I'll be back."

"You're so busy, and there's so little you can do," Lucy said.

"I can be here," Ashley said. She gave Lucy a quick hug. "Well, Detective Dilessio, if you're ready…?"

"Good night," he said to the Fresias.

"Thank you, thank you again. So much," Lucy said.

Ashley started down the hall, moving quickly to keep up with Dilessio's long steps.

She turned back to see that Nathan and Lucy were watching them go. Nathan had his arm protectively around his wife's shoulders. Despite the terrible pain they were in at the moment, Ashley felt a strange little twinge of envy for them. They'd been married so many years, and they had a bond of love and commitment that would help see them through even this terrible time.

She waved and turned back, brushing against Dilessio. She quickly straightened and put some distance between them.

"Nice couple," he said.

"Very nice. And I was just thinking—" She broke off, flushing again, and angry with herself for it.

"Thinking what?"

She shrugged. It would be worse not to answer. "I don't know. Marriage doesn't get a lot of respect these days, but despite their heartache, they have one another, someone to lean on through all this."

He kept walking. For a moment she thought he wasn't going to reply, that she had revealed too much to a man she barely knew.

"I don't know. My folks were really committed to each other."

"Were?"

"My mother died a few years ago. Now Dad roams around like a lost puppy. I've seen a fair number of good relationships. Then again…" He shrugged. "I've seen a few pretty rotten ones, too. The Fresias appear to be pretty decent types, devoted to their son as well as to one another."

"They are. And if you only knew Stuart…"

"I warned them. The truth may be that Stuart got caught up in something bad."

"I can tell you that isn't so."

"Oh?" He paused, staring at her. "Then what is your scenario?"

She stood still, lifting her chin slightly, not about to let him patronize her.

"Let's start with what we know, Detective. He suddenly appeared, a pedestrian, on a highway with at least four lanes of speeding traffic in both directions. He had to come from somewhere."

"Right. A house, an apartment, somewhere near the highway. Or from a car."

"Exactly. But if he'd been living in the area, it's likely someone would have seen him walking around in his underwear, something I'm sure the investigating officer looked into. Someone would have come forward with information. This may be Miami, but men don't walk along the highway in their underwear every day. I believe he was in a car. That someone let him out or pushed him."

"Well, Miss Montague, I actually believe the same thing. Maybe there was an argument, and in his drugged state, he just got out and started walking. Maybe he was with his supplier, and in that case, the guy sure as hell wasn't going to hang around to see what happened."

"Then again, maybe someone pushed him out on the highway, assuming he'd be killed."

"A murderer who *assumes* his victim will be killed?"

She stood her ground. "I'm sure it's happened."

He turned and started walking again. She followed. "You must have an inkling something was wrong or else you wouldn't have come here."

He stopped again. "It's a strange enough story. But I wasn't blowing smoke when I said I have a full plate at the moment. I'll talk to Carnegie—he's the lead officer on this case—and find out what I can. But you need to remember this. You're not even a patrol cop yet. You're in the academy. Don't go thinking you're Detective Sipowicz, okay? You could be walking into danger you're not experienced enough to deal with."

"So," she said triumphantly, "you *do* think—"

He stopped again, impatient. "I think that if he was involved with heavy drugs, you could get yourself in a mess. Remember where we are. A lot of the worst stuff that goes down here goes down because of drugs. So if you want to help your friend, visit him when you can, keep your nose to the grindstone in your classes and leave the investigating to experienced officers."

Ashley walked ahead of him. "Yes, sir, Detective Dilessio." She reached the door to the hospital parking garage. "But since the experienced officers are really busy and don't believe in Stuart the way that I do, I've hit a bit of a wall, haven't I?"

"Carnegie is good," he said flatly. "Look, Ashley, you go with what you've got. It's not unusual that most people are going to think your friend got into drugs— his bloodstream was filled with heroin when he came in here. So don't get angry because people look at the case from that angle. Maybe what you're saying *is* true. If so, we'll find that out. We're not magicians, but we do come up with the answers even in the really tough cases, most of the time. So have a little faith, all right?"

"Of course," she said stiffly.

He opened the door. She led the way to her car, used the remote to spring the locks and got in, all too aware of him sitting next to her. It bugged her to realize she was being incredibly precise with every move she made as a driver, just because he was in the car. She jerked to a stop at the booth to pay, wincing as she did so. Shit.

The guy was going to think she wasn't even capable of driving.

He hadn't said a word by the time they reached the road. To break the awkward silence, she asked, "So... how do you like your new slip?"

"It's great. Convenient. I'm not much of a cook, so it's good to have the restaurant right there."

"I guess you've known Nick a long time."

"Seven or eight years."

"I'm surprised I didn't know you.... Well, I'd seen you a few times, I guess. You've been coming into Nick's that long?"

He shrugged. "Sunday afternoons now and then, but not too often, really."

"I know most of the cops who come in, and when I was applying to the academy, they were helpful. I'm surprised Nick didn't tell me to talk to you."

"I probably wasn't around, and if I had been, I might not have encouraged you."

"Oh?"

He didn't reply. And he'd just started to seem so human.

"You don't think women should be on the force?"

"I didn't say that."

"Then what *are* you saying?" she persisted.

He turned to her, studying her in the shadows, in the flash and glare of the streetlights. "Maybe *you're* not the type," he told her. "You're persistent—"

"I'd think that's a plus," she murmured.

"Persistence needs to come with patience. It's a team effort out there on the streets. You don't seem too willing to let your teammates carry the ball."

"Meaning?"

"Meaning you should keep your nose out of this investigation. Don't go hanging out in bad neighborhoods thinking you're going to find the key that unlocks the case. You're not ready for that kind of investigation. Trust people to do their jobs."

She stared straight ahead at the road. "Because that's how you are, right? That's why you can't even eat dinner without a file open in front of you."

"I've been at this a long time. Ten years," he told her. "You just missed the turnoff," he commented.

"Maybe I go a different way," she said defensively. But of course he was right. She *had* missed the turnoff.

Better to just admit it, and turn around. She did so. To his credit, he didn't say a word.

At last they got to Nick's. She parked in her spot and they got out of the car. "Well," she said, sounding only a little bit stiff, "I do thank you for taking the time to come down to the hospital."

He nodded. "I'll talk to Sergeant Carnegie and emphasize that your friend really wasn't the kind of kid to have gotten into that much trouble on his own. Maybe he'll have some information."

"Thanks. And, Detective...?"

"Yeah?"

"Stuart isn't a kid. He's twenty-five, and he's always been a responsible guy."

"Sure. Good night."

He waved a hand her way and started toward his slip. Ashley watched him go.

She felt tired and drained, more restless than ever about Stuart. Letting herself in through the private kitchen, she hoped the house would be empty. She didn't feel like talking right now, even with Nick.

The house *was* empty. She could hear the sounds of talking and music on her way to her own wing. Obviously Nick was still busy. He would understand if she just came in and went to bed. As would Sharon, if she were there. Which she probably was, as lately she spent most of her nights with Nick.

In her room, Ashley flicked on the television, brushed her hair, washed her face and got ready for bed while listening to the news. The anchor went from the national news to the local. That evening, there had been a big pile-up in Broward, on 595. A pop star had been arrested for drug possession on the beach. Two visiting movie moguls had been involved in a disturbance at a club.

There were still no leads on the murder victim discovered Friday in the southwest area of the county, though the police were working hard to discover her identity. The medical examiner and metro homicide departments had released the information that she had been killed in a manner reminiscent of a series of homicides that had taken place five years earlier.

Ashley set her toothbrush in its holder and left the bathroom, sitting on the foot of the bed to watch the rest of the newscast. The anchor went on to warn women to take extreme care, despite the fact that the previous killings had been associated with a defunct cult and there was no evidence of current danger.

The anchor went on to report speculation by some citizens at the time that the police and the judicial system had been lacking in the pursuit of the killer, taking the easy way out when a young itinerant had confessed to the slayings before taking his own life.

He continued speaking over a shot of Peter Bordon,

known as Papa Pierre, now in federal prison in the center of the state. The victims of the previous killings had all been associated with his sect, but Bordon had denied any involvement in the deaths. He had been convicted instead of fraud and income tax evasion.

Then he turned it over to a perky blond weather girl, who spoke about the mild and beautiful evening and days to come.

Ashley turned off the television, then found herself walking to her private outside door. She stepped outside, gazing at the boats in their slips. Glancing down the length of the dock, she noted the *Gwendolyn.*

Detective Dilessio's boat.

He was handling the new murder case. Perhaps that was why he was so testy. There had been a few occasions when he had seemed almost human, so it was possible he simply had a lot on his mind.

Well, the perky weather girl had been right. The night was beautiful, with a fresh breeze off the water, enough to make it balmy, not sticky hot, not too cool. She stood outside a while longer, then ducked back when she saw a figure emerge on the bow of the houseboat.

Dilessio.

Half in and half out of her doorway, she counted on the shadows to hide her presence. She wondered what he was doing. Maybe he had listened to the perky weather girl, too, and come out to see what the night was like. He'd stripped down to cutoffs. She could see the moonlight glinting on his chest.

She could just imagine having Karen and Jan with her. He would have been thoroughly assessed by now, legs, butt, face…maybe even feet. Of course, she couldn't see him all that clearly from here, but…

Yes, the guy was good-looking. Strong face, deep voice, good eyes and yes, great buns.

"Hey, Ash, too much work and not enough play," she murmured to herself. She forced herself to slip into her room, to close and lock the door. What the hell was she thinking?

For some reason, she didn't seem able to help herself. She kept thinking about her conversation with Karen.

Don't you ever just want to have sex?

It wasn't as if she'd just met him, but still, she certainly didn't *know* him.

Still, she found him attractive. Too attractive, especially because he could sure as hell be an overbearing jerk. Not to mention that she was in the academy and he was a detective. It was the stupidest thing she'd ever thought of in her life.

But then, it didn't really have a lot to do with thought. She had sat next to him in a car, and her palms had gone damp. Not because he was a detective. Because he'd been next to her.

She'd seen him just standing on his boat.

And...

Okay, he was physically appealing. And she'd been leading a dull life, work, study, work, study, and... he had the right parts, put together quite well, with a voice...

She groaned. It was getting late. The alarm would ring well before six, and every class was very important. There was a lot she had to prove—to herself, and to others, she suddenly realized.

She lay on her bed, oddly aware that a man who both infuriated and tempted her was just yards away.

The Twilight Zone, Nick at Nite, AMC. She needed

to watch something entertaining that would capture her mind and then let her sleep.

She started flicking through the channels. Cooking…no. Alligators in the swamp…not tonight. She went through more of the premium cable stations.

She stopped, her eyes widening.

She wasn't certain when they had started putting soft porn *that graphic* on television. She could feel the heat in her cheeks, even though she was sitting there alone.

That wouldn't help at all. She quickly switched the channel.

A rerun of *I Love Lucy* turned up. Much safer. Ashley slammed her pillow, determined that she was going to relax and go to sleep.

Eventually, she did.

Jake didn't always lock the door to the cabin of the *Gwendolyn*, but he could have sworn he had tonight. But when he'd automatically set the key in the lock, the knob had twisted before the key had been turned.

He held still for a minute, listening, but there were no sounds other than the lapping of the water against the boat and the distant, blended noises of the bar. He held very still, drew his gun, and flattened himself against the exterior of the cabin as he threw the door open.

Again…nothing.

He entered slowly and carefully. The living room, galley, dining area…all empty. He went aft and down, checking the small head, the closets, every crawl space. He traveled back through the main rooms and went into the master cabin, going through the same routine. Nothing.

Nothing…but a feeling. Someone had been there.

Puzzled, he paused at his desk. Small, compact, neat. There was just space on top for his laptop and a small printer, and the desk itself offered drawers where he stowed files on the cases he was working on. He opened the drawers; everything seemed to be in place. The computer was off, as he had left it.

Nothing appeared to be out of order....

Just slightly...different.

Feeling a sense of invasion that couldn't be pinpointed, he assured himself that the door was locked—double bolted. In his cabin, he stripped down to a pair of cut-offs and sat at his computer for a moment, drawing up the old files he had been obsessively rereading. Then he hesitated, feeling that his computer had been invaded, as well. Yet nothing was different.

He went out and stood on deck, searching along the dock and the rows of boats. No one seemed to be stirring. There were still lights on at Nick's.

Though barefoot and bare-chested, he sprang to the dock and walked the short distance to the bar. The door remained open, though the Closed sign had been set out. Entering, he found Nick behind the bar, wiping down the old polished wood. Just a few customers remained at the tables, drinking coffee. Nick had a cut-off policy where liquor was concerned; he didn't intend to be responsible for drunk drivers. An old John Denver song finished playing on the jukebox as Jake approached Nick.

"Jake, hey. What can I do for you?" Nick asked, surprised to see him. He frowned and teased, "Shirts and shoes required, you know. Florida law."

"Yeah, sorry," Jake said. "Nick, I needed to ask

you…that key I asked you to keep—did you use it to-night for any reason?"

Nick shook his head. "No, it was busy here tonight. I never left."

"This is awkward, but…are you sure you keep it in a safe place?"

"Hell, yes."

"It's not here, accessible to anyone in the bar?"

Nick glanced across the room. "Hey, y'all!" he called to the remaining customers. "Thanks for coming, but it's time for you to head out."

Jake waited while Nick showed the customers out. When the door was closed and locked, Nick said, "Come on in the house. I'll make sure the key is exactly where I left it."

Nick led the way behind the bar, through the office and into the living room. Dim night-lights cast the room in soft shadow.

"Was something wrong at the boat?" Nick asked.

"No, not really."

"Okay, well, just give me a minute," Nick said. He wasn't the type to pry, even if a few questions were warranted.

"I just had a feeling someone had been on the *Gwendolyn*," Jake offered. "I could have sworn I locked her when I left, but the door was open when I got back. There's nothing gone—I may be imagining that some-one was there. Hell, maybe I thought I locked it and didn't." His tone made it clear that he didn't believe that. "Since I could see the lights from the bar and knew you were still up, I thought I'd ask about the key."

"No problem. And hey, if you're uncomfortable about my having it…"

"I'm not. I appreciate your having it for workmen, deliveries, whatever. I'd just kind of like to make sure it's here."

"I'm sure it is. The house is off-limits to customers, you know. But you're right, it can't hurt to check. Hey, help yourself, if you want a drink, coffee, whatever. You know where the kitchen is."

"Thanks."

Nick disappeared down a hall to the right.

Ashley's sleep was troubled by dreams. Stuart was in them, talking to her, walking around in his white briefs as if it were completely normal. As if they had become the new office attire.

Stuart faded....

Dilessio was back in her dreams. He wasn't even wearing briefs. She kept trying to meet his eyes, rather than looking down, pretending that there was nothing abnormal about him walking around naked. She was with him, topside on his houseboat, telling him just how graphic cable was these days.

She awoke suddenly, feeling drenched and chilled at the same time. The dream images faded, and she sat up in her bed, trying to discern what had awakened her.

It was late. There was no muted noise from the bar. The television was showing yet another episode of *I Love Lucy*.

She stood, stretched, and wondered what could have bothered her. Walking to one of the two windows that flanked the door to the docks, she looked out. The docks themselves were empty, the boats rocking gently in their slips.

Still uneasy, Ashley walked silently in her bare feet

to the door that led to the house. She opened the door and listened. Nothing.

The bar had closed. Nick had probably gone on in to bed.

Nothing…and then…

A noise. Just a noise. Something shifting…somewhere in the house.

She went into the living room. Nick never left the place in total darkness, so dim night-lights cast eerie shadows over the room.

The mounted fish seemed to glare at her, furious at being out of the water, stuffed and hanging on a wall.

She'd lived here a long time. The fish had never seemed to be a menace before.

Again…that noise…

And it was coming from the kitchen. She walked swiftly and silently through the house to the kitchen, dropping low behind the counter, listening again. It could be Nick, of course. Or Sharon. But why would they walk so stealthily through their own house?

She moved along behind the counter, toward the end, from where she could get a full view of the room.

Too late she realized that someone, moving as silently as she, had come up behind her. A scream rose in her throat as rough arms suddenly grabbed her around her waist.

"Who the hell are you, and what the fuck are you doing?"

She tried to spin and fight, lost her balance and fell. The figure came down heavily on top of her. The oversized T-shirt in which she had been sleeping rucked up between them.

Before she could even struggle, the kitchen was suddenly flooded with light.

"What the hell…?"

It was Nick speaking. And she was staring up into the tense features of their newest neighbor and the star of her recent dream: Detective Jake Dilessio.

To her pleasure, he looked as awkward as she felt. For a moment they were caught there, almost in an embrace.

Then he quickly scrambled up, offering her a hand.

He wasn't naked, but it was close enough. Just those cutoffs. And in their brief moments on the floor together, they had made a contact she could still feel. She seemed to be burning from her flushed features to her toes. But then again, despite his tan, he had taken on a more crimson hue, as well.

"I thought someone was sneaking through the house," he said.

"Ditto," she murmured, still meeting his eyes.

"Didn't occur to either one of you just to call out, huh?" Nick said.

"Well, if someone *were* actually sneaking around the house…" Ashley began.

"You were doing exactly that," Jake told Ashley with a grin.

"I live here!" she reminded him. "What were you doing in here?"

"He was with me," Nick said.

"He was in the kitchen—you weren't," Ashley pointed out.

"He told me to help myself to something to drink," Jake informed her. "I was getting a glass of iced tea."

"Cops," Nick said with a sigh. "Everything has to be a big mystery." He shook his head, as if perplexed by a different species. "Let's put the kettle on. Hot tea might be good now. Decaf for me, since I do intend to sleep sometime tonight."

He walked around to the stove. Ashley and Jake were left standing almost on top of one another. Ashley backed off a little. She wished suddenly she slept in something a little more...dignified. Her T-shirt advertised a rock band from the last concert she'd been to and didn't even fall to mid-thigh.

"I should get a robe," she murmured.

"Listen, Nick, I'll just get back to the *Gwendolyn*," Jake said. "If you've checked on that little matter for me?"

"I did." He reached into the pocket of his jeans and produced a key. "It was right where it should have been."

Frowning, Ashley stared at Jake. Apparently he didn't feel he needed to give her an explanation.

"Are there any others out there?" Nick asked.

"No," Jake said, then hesitated. "Actually...yes. I hadn't thought about it in...a long time. I'd forgotten. But yes, you're right. There is another one out there."

He looked grim. Not the kind of guy you would want to mess with.

"Hey, Ash, grab some mugs, will you?" Nick said.

She walked around the counter and opened the cabinet. As she did so, Sharon walked into the kitchen, yawning, stretching. She was in a long, midnight-blue silk gown and robe. She had no makeup on, her hair was tousled, and she looked like a million bucks. Ashley knew her own hair was snarled around her face. And her T-shirt was...a T-shirt.

"We having a party in here?" Sharon inquired, smiling but obviously a little confused.

"Just tea," Nick told her. He kissed her on the forehead. "Sorry we woke you. Cops. Everything is a drama, you know."

"Cops? Did we have a problem?" she asked.

"No, a lack of communication," Nick said, smiling. "And now we're all awake. Like I said, sorry."

"It's okay, I don't have to be anywhere until eleven. But, Ashley," she said, concern on her features. "You have to be in class at seven."

"Oh, she's all right. She told me she's still young enough to go without sleep," Nick informed her cheerfully. "Hey, we're in good shape, Sharon. We have Miami-Dade's finest stalking one another in our kitchen."

The kettle began to whistle.

"I'll get milk and sugar," Sharon offered. "There's hot chocolate, too, if anyone would rather have that. Jake, would you like herbal tea?"

"No, thank you. I'm just going to head back."

"The water's boiled, and we're all here," Sharon said.

"Just tea then, thank you, regular tea."

"Okay, one black tea. Ashley, here you go, and the sugar and milk. She takes loads of both," Sharon told Jake, smiling.

"Two cops," Nick murmured, getting his own cup. "We're lucky you two didn't shoot each other!"

"Hey, speaking of business," Sharon said. "Jake, it was nice of you to go to the hospital tonight. That was your partner who picked you up earlier, right? Marty?"

"He comes in and talks to Sandy now and then. Sandy loves to keep up on what's going on in his city."

"Sandy is a bright old guy."

"Is there anything you can do to help Ashley's friend?" Sharon asked anxiously.

"I can ask a few questions, find out how the investigation is going," Jake told her. "But it's not my case, not even my area."

"Still, it's nice of you to help," Sharon said, then stretched and yawned and looked at Nick affectionately. "Busy night, huh? Oh, Ashley, a few friends of yours came by, too."

Ashley frowned, remembering that she should have called Karen and Jan, and brought them up to date on Stuart's situation. But would they have come by Nick's?

"From the academy," Sharon said.

"No, the one kid is already a cop," Nick corrected her. "What's his name? Len Green, I think. Officer Green. He was here with that really big, good-looking black fellow, Arne."

"Did they want anything?" Ashley asked.

"Hamburgers," Nick said.

"Nick, I meant—"

"They asked for you," Sharon said, smiling. "I guess they were just hungry, and figured they might be able to get a bite to eat and pay a social call at the same time. Anyway, I explained that you'd gone to the hospital to see a friend."

"Thanks. Well, if they needed anything, I'll see them tomorrow. Arne, at least. I don't see Len Green every day—he works down south. But if there was anything important, Arne will tell me."

"Nice guys," Sharon commented. "They spent some time talking with Sandy, too. He seemed to enjoy them."

"Good," Ashley murmured, feeling a little uncomfortable that Jake was listening to the conversation. It was such a casual conversation, surely it couldn't matter. She still felt uncomfortable.

He set down his empty cup. "Thanks for the tea, and sorry for the disruption," he said. "Good night, all. I'll let everyone get some sleep." He started out the side door, then turned back. Ashley thought he might be about to apologize for tackling her. He wasn't. "I will see what I can find out about your friend's case," he said.

"Thank you."

He exited, and Nick rose to secure the door.

"I guess I'd better go and get what sleep I can," Ashley murmured.

"Of course. Good night, dear," Sharon said.

Ashley blew Nick a kiss and started back through the house. She should have been exhausted, but she felt wired instead, and found herself wondering why Nick had brought Jake into the house at that hour of the night. Neither of them had explained.

Her television was still on, and Lucy and Ethel were at it again.

She plunged into bed, then rose and went back to the window to the right of the door. Pulling back the drapes, she looked out.

Detective Dilessio was standing on the deck of his houseboat again, hands on his hips, studying the bar.

Why?

She watched him for a few moments, once again noticing the way the moonlight fell on him. She gritted her teeth and gave herself a mental shake. He was the last man on earth to whom she should feel the slightest attraction.

But she did. It wasn't physically possible, but she could still feel where his body had been against hers in those few moments when they had been locked in a fierce embrace on the kitchen floor.

She had always been the practical one among her friends. If it isn't good for you, don't do it. Don't take a puff of a cigarette. Why start, when you know it's bad? Don't take a chance on a guy you know is bad news. If you don't start...

She wasn't starting anything. She went back to bed and stared at the television. Once again, she eventually drifted back to sleep.

Not even sleep could help her over-exhaustion. She started dreaming again, knowing she was dreaming....

She was there again, on his houseboat. They were discussing white briefs, though once again he wasn't wearing any. She kept trying to look into his eyes, to keep her gaze from dropping downward....

She wanted to talk to him about something very important, but she couldn't remember what it was, because she couldn't keep her eyes on his.

The alarm rang. She was jerked out of the dream, still painfully aware of it, the vision of him clear in her mind.

She bolted upright, miserable, feeling as if she'd never gone to sleep. Shit!

She just knew it was going to be a wretched day.

Chapter 9

The room wasn't small, but it felt confining. Stifling. There was a brown table. The walls were a sanitarium green—two different shades of sanitarium green. There was nothing in the room other than the table and two chairs.

Peter Bordon sat in one, staring across the table at Jake, who sat in the other. A guard was right outside the door. Jake didn't think he'd be crying out for backup—Bordon wasn't impressive in any physical sense. He was about five feet ten inches tall, and no more than a hundred and eighty. He was tight and compact, but not in any way heavily muscled.

Even now, so many years later, he had that strange power in his eyes. Scary, in a way. Very creepy. He had smiled with secretive amusement when he first saw

Jake, and the guard had promised he would be just outside the door.

"Guess he doesn't know *you* once beat the shit out
of *me*," Bordon said.

"I didn't beat the shit out of you," Jake countered.

Bordon inclined his head to the side, shrugging off
the comment. "Sorry, you were strangling me, I think."

"You look alive and well to me."

"I *am* well. Very well, thanks."

Only a few hints of gray teased at his light brown
hair. Those strange eyes were hazel, and it often seemed
as if Bordon could lighten and darken them at will. He
had an ability to focus on a person that was almost hypnotic. His voice was low, but full. He was soft-spoken,
but there was a strength in his tone that could cover
tremendous distance.

"Maybe I shouldn't call you Jake? Is that too personal? Me, using your first name? I should be calling
you Detective Dilessio. But then, I feel that I came to
know you so well. I know you'd be pleased if I was
dying of a slow and painful disease, choking daily on
my own vomit. There's so much anger and hatred in
your heart. But I forgive you."

"Fuck your forgiveness," Jake said, then gritted his
teeth. Bordon was baiting him, a talent of his. Jake
swore then that he wasn't going to rise to that bait again.

He reached into his jacket and drew out one of the
crime scene photos of the dead girl, sliding it in front
of Bordon. "How'd she die, Peter? And why?"

Bordon looked dispassionately at the photograph,
then met Jake's eyes again. He slowly made the sign of
the cross. "Obviously, Detective, she was murdered or

you wouldn't be here. Why, I don't know. I will pray for her soul, though."

"Peter, her throat was slit and her ears were slashed. The tips of her fingers were cut away. She died in agony. Just like those women who died five years ago."

"I never killed anyone."

"You ordered the killings."

"No, Detective, you're wrong. I would never order one human being to take the life of another."

Jake shook his head. "We might not have had proof, but everyone knows you conspired to commit murder."

"Perhaps I was angry with the women who died…or perhaps I didn't particularly like them, and though, in my deep belief, I would try not to let my feelings show, perhaps others saw my disappointment in the women, and therefore…they died."

Jake leaned forward. "Papa Pierre. That's what they called you. The foolish and the lost gathered around you, hanging on your every word, your sermons or the bliss of immortality for those who learned the true Word during their time on earth. For those who gave their all to the church—your church—and themselves—all of themselves, of course—over to you."

Bordon grinned, suddenly down to earth, the practiced hypnotic quality of his eyes and voice gone. "I fleeced a few people. I was guilty of fraud and income tax evasion. I'm serving my time. And yes, I had sex with a few women. All right. Lots of women. Lots of beautiful women. Jealous, Jake? You don't have to be, you know. You reek of testosterone. Women must practically reach out to grab you when you walk by. So don't begrudge me a little carnal amusement, Jake. We both know that there's no law against consensual sex between adults."

Jake sat back. Bordon hadn't changed a hair. He was calm and serene through every word, every lie, he spoke. He met Bordon's stare and waited a long moment. "What happened to Nancy?" he demanded, his voice as soft, as deadly, as Bordon's could ever be.

Bordon stared at him, shaking his head. "Jake, Jake, Jake. You're like a tired-out old record player. She was your partner, but she didn't come with you when you came out to harass me. I knew about her, though. She was a computer whiz, right? And at the trial, it came out that she was the one who suggested investigating me for crimes other than murder. But I don't know what happened to her. I know they found her in her car in a canal, but that's all I know. Seriously, Jake, get a grip on yourself. I'm a smart man. I can read between the lines. I know what was going on with your partner. Hell, I made a business out of knowing what people's weaknesses were. You come up here, the determined, compassionate cop, afraid that this new victim is just the first of more to come…but you don't really give a rat's ass about that girl, do you? After all this time, you still want to wrap your fingers around my neck and kill me, because maybe that will let you believe that your lover didn't kill herself because she was miserable, between her two-timing husband and you."

This time, Jake held his temper. "Nancy didn't kill herself, Bordon. She was my partner, not my lover, but that's really not the point. She was a strong woman, and she wouldn't have killed herself over me, her husband or any other man. She was murdered. And no matter what you say, I believe you ordered her murder, because she knew something. *What was it that she knew, Peter?* Whatever it was, it is the key to what is happening now. You and I both know it."

"What's happening now? Other than that you've got a new body on your hands?"

"There's something going on. More than we've seen yet. I think that you know something, something that could prevent more deaths."

"You have another dead girl. What makes you think there's some kind of conspiracy? People die down there all the time."

"But the victims aren't usually found with their fingertips gone and their throat—and ears slashed. And there's something else, Peter. I think you're conspiring with someone who's still out there. Someone who was on my boat last night."

"Breaking and entering? What was taken?"

"Nothing."

"Maybe you're losing it, Jake. Imagining this conspiracy thing. Maybe no one was there."

"No, Peter. Someone was on my boat. Looking for something."

"Well, let's see, you're the detective. Couldn't have been me—the guards will swear to that. So who could it have been? I'll just bet that late partner of yours had a key to your houseboat."

Jake gasped, and Bordon smiled in satisfaction.

"She did, I knew it. Maybe you'd better look into that husband of hers."

"I talked to Nancy's husband. He says he doesn't know a thing about the key."

"You know, you make a cuckold out of a guy, and

it's not surprising if he's out to get you for the rest of his life."

"Actually, I think he's out to get *you*. And he isn't sworn to uphold the law or anything like that. He could get a gun and shoot you dead on the spot, then claim temporary insanity because grief has haunted his life all these years."

"Maybe you ought to find out more about that young man, Jake. Maybe he's crazier than I am."

"It would help if you told me what you know about the victim we just discovered—and about Nancy. You'll never convince me that she didn't disappear because of what went down five years ago."

Bordon kept his eyes on Jake, never blinking. He shook his head sadly. "She disappeared while you were busy harassing me and my group. You want to associate the two things, but you've got no reason for doing so. I'll bet your superiors agree. Poor Jake, he wants to believe there's a reason, that it's anyone's fault but his own. You know accidents happen. Bad roads, bad weather. Sometimes people, even cops, drive too fast. People can be distraught, not themselves. There are dozens of possibilities. But you know what, Jake? I really am sorry."

"I see. You'd help me if you could."

Bordon drummed his fingers on the table, his expression never wavering. "Do you ever go to magic shows, Jake?"

"What?"

"You know, a magic show. It's all smoke and mirrors. Sleight of hand. People don't see what's really happening, because their vision is drawn a different way. You see the magician, you see the beautiful, skimpily clad assistant at his side."

"Bordon, what the hell are you talking about?"

"You know, I've spent my time here doing a lot of reading. I've counseled some of the other prisoners." For a moment his gaze flickered and a rueful smile touched his lips. "I've found God and the simple beauty of life itself."

"You've *found* God? You were a preacher, with a loyal-unto-*death* following. But now you've found God?"

Bordon waved a hand in the air. "I fleeced people out of a lot of money. I'm a charismatic man. A magician, if you will, a showman. But now...well, I just want to live, Jake. I'm getting out of here soon. It's almost a guarantee. I've been a model prisoner—but I'm sure you know that."

"You know I'd do anything in my power to throw you right back in here."

"Thankfully, you're a detective, not a judge and jury. Funny thing is, I like you, Jake. And you're good, you know. Maybe too good. I'm not frightened of you myself, but...you can be a damned scary man. Watch yourself, Jake."

"Are you threatening me, Bordon?"

"Me? No, not at all. We both know I never killed anyone. That's truer than you can begin to accept. I'm just saying you're a good detective, that's all. But no one wins every time, Jake. Maybe you should accept that."

Jake shook his head. "Not every time, but I don't intend to lose this one."

"Well, Jake, you're sitting here barking up the wrong tree with me. I've been locked up a long time now."

He shrugged. "Hell, who knows if that wiped-out kid, Harry Tennant, killed those girls five years ago or not. I saw him a few times, and I thought I had one really sad bastard on my hands. He wanted to find meaning in life so badly, and he was furious with the girls who didn't seem to be as committed to a way of life as he was. Or maybe he was impotent, and hated anyone who could lead a normal life. Maybe he was psychotic."

"I don't think he was bright enough to be as organized as the killer," Jake said. "The killer was smart— removing fingertips, delaying identification of the victims. Hiding them in the deepest muck in the city, letting nature do her work on the corpses and any hope of trace evidence. That took someone with cunning and knowledge. That points to you, I'd say."

"If you're hoping for a belated confession, that I'm going to break down and tell you, hell yes I did it, I've kept a thriving group going in my absence, and I control the hearts and minds of men and women far away— you're veering way off course. I told you, I've spent my time repenting my evil ways. I've found God."

"Oh, yeah, right, Bordon. If you found God, you'd be confessing anything you knew, trying to make sure more people weren't brutally murdered."

Bordon stared at him. "Smoke and mirrors, Jake. The world is full of smoke and mirrors."

To Jake's surprise, Bordon looked upset after making that last statement. "I don't want to talk anymore. I won't talk anymore. I don't have to talk to you."

"Wrong. You're in prison, and I have the warden's permission to be here."

"I'm not accused of anything more. I'm serving my

time. I just want to live, Jake. And I want a lawyer before I say another word to you."

"Guilty, are you?"

Bordon's cool fell back around him like a cloak. "I'm doing my time, Jake, just doing my time. I've said everything to you that I can. You're the detective. You take it from here."

Jake was disappointed. Bordon had put an end to the interview. He wasn't sure what he'd thought he could get the man to say. Maybe he hadn't expected him to say anything. He'd just been certain that if he saw Bordon, he would know. Know if the man was somehow involved again from behind bars.

Instead, he found himself no more certain than he had been before.

He pulled a card from his pocket. "If you decide you want to talk to me…"

"Yeah, yeah, I know the drill," Bordon said. He stared at the card in Jake's hand for a minute, then reached out and took it. He stared at Jake. Jake waited.

"Sure. Maybe I'll call you sometime, Detective. As I said before, I actually kind of like you. Watch it driving home. It's a long way. Over two hundred miles. How long did it take you to get here? Four, five hours? Or are Miami-Dade cops allowed to speed through other counties?"

"It took some time to get here," Jake said evenly.

After a minute, Bordon shrugged. "I've got your card," he said. "If I can think of anything that will help you, I'll call."

This particular interview was at an end, and Jake knew it. He stood and tapped at the glass for the guard to come to the door.

As he left the prison, he went over the interview in his mind. Step by step, word by word. *Smoke and mirrors. Magicians. Distracting the attention of the audience...*

What the hell had Bordon been talking about?

Other statements came back to mind.

...I just want to live, Jake.

He passed the barbed-wire fence, nearing his car, when he stopped short. *I just want to live, Jake.*

Was Bordon himself afraid of someone?

In his pocket, his cell phone went off. He pulled it out and answered, "Dilessio."

"Detective, it's Carnegie. Paddy Carnegie. Sorry it took so long to get back to you. You wanted to ask me some questions about the Fresia case?"

The Fresia case. Why the hell had he gotten involved?

No real question there. Because of Ashley Montague. Because...

She seemed to know she was right about her friend. The same way he knew that he was right about Nancy...

Because there was that something about her that reminded him of Nancy. And because...

Hell, admit it. Because he dreamed of her at night.

"Carnegie, thanks for getting back to me. I'm in the middle of the state right now, but I'm heading back south. Can we meet?"

Throughout the morning, Ashley found herself sketching during her lectures. Stuart in his hospital bed. His folks, holding close to one another. Jake Dilessio, standing on the deck of his houseboat. She sketched Arne, sitting next to her now. She remembered the words he had spoken to her as they'd both slipped into their chairs earlier.

"Hey, we ate at your uncle's place last night," he'd told her.

"I heard. You and Len, right?"

"Yeah, I met up with him at the target range. We thought we'd come by, grab a bite to eat and try to cheer you up. You seemed so down about your friend. Didn't occur to us that you'd be at the hospital, the guy being in a coma and all. But it didn't matter that we missed you—we needed dinner and the food at Nick's is good."

"Thanks," she said, feeling suddenly hungry but by then Sergeant Brennan was talking, so she figured she would hold off until lunch time and went back to drawing.

When the class ended, she set her pencil down and looked up. Shit. Brennan was staring at her.

He'd seen her sketching. He thought she hadn't been paying attention. She felt a chill creep along her spine. Just last week, two of her classmates had been dismissed. They had failed one question too many on a test.

Her test scores had been fine, she reminded herself.

At lunch, she told her friends about Stuart's condition, and that someone had told her to ask Dilessio if he could do anything. "I talked to him, and he basically said he couldn't do anything. But then he showed up at the hospital. And he's going to the cop who's handling the case."

"Did he give you any hope?" Gwyn asked.

"Not really, still…there's more here than it looks like. I just pray that Stuart… I pray that Stuart comes to soon. And can help."

"Brennan might have some information for you," Gwyn said.

"Why do you think that?" Ashley asked.

"Because he was staring at you all morning."

"You think?" Damn, he really *had* noticed her sketching.

"I know."

She returned to class feeling unnerved.

To make matters worse, Captain Murray came in after the lunch break. He wasn't speaking to the class; he was just observing.

It seemed to Ashley that he, too, was staring at her.

At one point she leaned across to Arne and whispered, "Am I crazy? Now it seems like Murray is watching me like a hawk, too."

Arne wiggled a brow. "Maybe he's got a thing for you."

"Get serious."

"You are cute, Montague."

"Arne, I'm going to deck you after class."

He just grinned. Gwyn leaned forward from the seat behind him. "I don't know, Ash. Do you have a truck-load of hidden parking tickets or something? You're right. Brennan was staring earlier, and now they're both watching you."

She tried hard to pay attention during the rest of the class. To keep her fingers off her pencil and sketch no more that day.

At last the afternoon drew to an end. Part of her wanted to stay after and ask if they'd gotten any information about the accident, but mostly she just wanted to get out.

She didn't have to decide, however. As soon as she stood, Murray spoke to her.

"Montague?"

"Yes, sir?"

"I need to speak with you. Now, please."

Carnegie was a decent sort, more than willing to meet Jake at a coffeehouse on the Miami-Dade county line at four and talk about his investigation.

Driving straight through, Jake just made it.

Carnegie was in his fifties, probably close to retirement. Despite the time they'd both spent on the force, they'd never met. From the start, though, the meeting went well. There was something of a brotherhood between them, since they were both somewhat jaded and yet were survivors.

"You know, though," he told Jake right off, "the parents have been hounding me all along, insisting I have to find out *something* because their boy just didn't do drugs."

"I've met them," Jake said.

"No parents want to find out their kid went bad. I've investigated fatalities where there's evidence, an eyewitness proving a kid was driving recklessly, and the parents still don't want to believe it 'Not my son—he aced driver's ed. Not my daughter, she would never exceed the limit.'"

"I understand that," Jake said. "But I know one of this kid's old friends, and she says he wasn't the type, either."

Carnegie had bright blue eyes, snow-white hair and a face crinkled by years in the sun. He was a big man, not given to fat, but with an appearance as solid as a wall. Yet he didn't look like a hard-ass. There was compassion in his features when he winced.

"I'd like to give them something, honest-to-God, I would. I'd be more than willing to see it their way. It's just that, hell, I haven't got a damned thing to go on. The kid was in the middle of the highway, dressed in his damn underwear. God knows what he was seeing as he walked into traffic, because he was lucky he was alive to begin with, there was so much shit in his bloodstream. The fellow who hit him is a basket case, swears he didn't see him until he was right in front of him. Two more cars cracked up because they couldn't stop fast enough, but neither of them saw a thing. The driver of the first car checks out completely. He owns a furniture gallery in North Dade, has three kids, coaches soccer and goes to church every Sunday. Ex-Navy man, saw action in the Middle East. Never even got a parking ticket. He didn't see anything until the kid crossed the median and was right in his lane. Too late for him to stop, though he tried. He didn't know if the kid walked across from the other side, or fell out of the sky or jumped out of a car. We've had every cop in the area asking questions at nearby houses and businesses. We took out an ad, asking for anyone who knows anything to call us with any information whatsoever. We've asked the parents, but they don't know what their son was up to. He'd more or less dropped off the face of the earth a few months ago, decided to take up writing. He wanted to go around incognito or something. So far, he'd sold a few things to a rag called *In Depth*. I've been to the office. The managing editor liked Fresia and was sick to hear what had happened. He thought the kid was excited about something he was writing but had said he wasn't going to tell anyone what he was doing until he had more information. Sure could have gotten into something doing research, I suppose. Believe me, it's not that we haven't worked this case, worked it hard. We're just at one of those dead ends. We've got nowhere to go."

"I understand. The thing that's true, though, is this—the kid had to come from somewhere."

"Right. He had to come from somewhere. We just don't know where. We've tried the records from the local hotels and motels. Nothing. If he were in a private residence in the area, no one is admitting it. If he came out of a car, no one saw him. We're praying for some kind of a lead. We haven't given up."

"There's still the hope the kid will come out of the coma, too," Jake said.

"Oh, yeah, now that's a hope. A desperate hope," Carnegie said. Then he was ready to change the subject. "How are you doing? I read about the body that was just discovered. Heard you never really closed the old task force down or accepted that deranged boy's confession as final proof that the murders were solved, what was it…four, five years ago?"

"Five. Almost five."

Carnegie was staring at him hard.

"Think they're related?"

"I think there's a good possibility. Of course, there's also the possibility that someone wanted to get rid of the girl, knew the particulars of the cult murders and decided that a copycat killing would be a good way to dispose of the remains. We don't know much of anything yet. We don't even have an identification on the victim."

Carnegie nodded, looked at him, appeared as if he wasn't going to speak for a moment, then said, "How about the death of your partner? Was there ever anything new on that?"

Jake shook his head, feeling a certain weariness. The old guy had apparently heard all the rumors, too. Well, who the hell hadn't? There had been an inquest.

"No," he said simply.

"Sorry, I was so sorry...we're always sorry to hear about an officer down, but...well, she sounded like a fine woman. But then, no matter how hard you try, there will always be cases where you just don't get an answer."

"There will always be some," Jake agreed flatly. "But not this one. I'm going to stick to this one until the day I keel over." He rose, stretching out a hand, thanking Carnegie. "If anything breaks, will you let me know right away?"

"Sure. And if you think you can find any answers for me, go right ahead. I'm not a new guy, I don't protect my turf, and I'm happy to get any help I can."

This was it. For some unknown reason, Ashley thought, she was out. She had done something wrong somewhere. Sergeant Brennan and Captain Murray were both staring at her very strangely.

"Sit, relax, please, Miss Montague," Murray said.

She sat. She didn't relax.

"I've studied your file," Murray told her. Apparently, he was the one who was going to do the talking. But then, he was head of personnel.

"Yes?" she said, waiting.

"You spent several years studying toward an art major."

"Yes."

"Why didn't you complete that degree?"

She frowned. "I decided to apply for the academy."

"Why?"

Her frown deepened. "Because I have an interest in law enforcement. My father was a police officer."

"But you've maintained your interest in art."

It was a statement. She felt a cool wave of unease coming over her. They *had* seen her sketching in class—probably once too often.

She shrugged, trying very hard to remain casual, yet attentive and respectful. "I love art. Of course I'll always maintain an interest. But I don't think that's a deterrent for a police officer. Most police officers have other interests in life, just like anyone involved in any other career. I have friends on the force who...who love boating, and a few who are really outstanding at karaoke. They might have had singing careers, but their real love is law enforcement."

She was puzzled to see them both smiling.

She stiffened. "If I'm out for some reason, please, just tell me."

"You're not out," Brennan assured her. "You're an exceptional student, as a matter of fact."

"You would be leaving your class," Murray said. "But you could pick up where you left off at any time in the future."

"I'm sorry. I'm completely lost."

"I have a proposition for you. We need someone in forensic art. You'd be taking a civilian position, and you'd be directly beneath Commander Allen, who is also a civilian in the employ of the department."

"It's a job many people would covet," Brennan added quietly.

"But I… I've had just the basics in forensics," she told them. "What…what does the work entail?"

"Sketching from eyewitness descriptions, mostly. Photography. Eventually, reconstruction of skeletal remains."

"I've done some photography, but—"

"It's far easier to teach someone to take photos than it is to find someone with such an incredible talent for human faces."

She stared at him blankly, trying to take in what he was saying.

Murray smiled. "Forgive me. I reached into the garbage the other day when you tossed a few of your drawings." He produced a smoothed paper, a sketch she had done of Jake Dilessio. She felt her cheeks burning. "This is an incredible likeness of Jake. There's more of the man in this than I've seen in many photographs."

"He's an interesting subject," she heard herself say.

"Yes. I believe that you're dedicated to being a cop, Ashley. And as I said, you can always finish up, go back and pick up where you left off. You won't graduate with your class, but I assure you, nothing you've done will be wasted. The job is incredibly interesting—and tough. But no more difficult than it can be out on the streets. And it's well paid." He named a yearly salary above what she could make starting out on the streets, and even above what she would be making in several years.

They were both watching her.

"I… I'm a bit overwhelmed at the moment," she said.

"We don't expect you to make a decision right now. But you are needed. If you like, you can meet with Commander Allen in the morning and then decide."

She nodded slowly. "I would like to do that," she said.

"Great." He told her where to be, eight o'clock sharp. "Commander Allen or one of his staff can give you a great deal more information about the particulars of the job than I can. I showed him your work, and he was impressed, told me he'd love to have you work with him. It's very important work. You should know that. And I wouldn't be speaking with you if I didn't think you'd be perfect for it."

"Thank you."

"Or that you have an enormous talent," Brennan said. "And it's not that easy for me to suggest you leave the academy. I enjoy having you in my class."

She thanked Brennan, as well. Though they were both still watching her, reading her reaction to their proposition, she knew she had been dismissed.

"Eight o'clock," she said.

Brennan grinned. "No matter what you decide, you get to sleep an extra hour tomorrow morning."

"There you go, a plus already," she said. She thanked them again and said goodbye. Both men watched her leave the room.

Arne and Gwyn were waiting for her in the parking lot. "My God, what happened? They couldn't have kicked you out—they couldn't have!" Gwyn said vehemently.

She shook her head. "They—they do want me to leave the academy."

"What?" Arne said indignantly.

She explained. Both stared at her dumbfounded.

"Wow," Gwyn said after a moment. Then she laughed. "Heck, if they'd caught me drawing in class, they'd have fired my ass."

"Yeah, me too," Arne agreed. "Cool. That's a major coup."

"But I wouldn't be a cop."

"They said you could always go back and finish up, right? Don't be silly, girl. Ashley, it's your dream job—art plus law enforcement. Take it. We lowly peons will all be looking at you with envy," Gwyn teased.

"I guess...."

"Hell! Gwyn's right—jump on it."

"I have tonight to think about it."

"What's to think about?" Gwyn said. She gave Ashley a quick hug. "Congratulations. That's all I can think of to say."

"I've got to get out of here. It's my mom's birthday," Arne said. "Don't forget us while you're busy dealing with the brass, okay?"

"Don't be silly, she won't forget us," Gwyn said. "Once she realizes what she's been offered and officially takes the position, we'll celebrate."

"Of course—*if I* decide to take the position," Ashley said. But it was beginning to dawn on her just how much had been offered to her. She would be a fool if she didn't accept. "I've got to get out of here, too. I've got to get home and change, and go back to the hospital."

"Your friend's still hanging in?"

She nodded. They waved goodbye and headed for their respective cars.

When Ashley reached Nick's, she was glad to see that the place was quiet. There were a few diners, both inside and out, but there were plenty of staff to take care of them. Nick, Sharon and Sandy were seated at a table together. Ashley didn't change right away but went straight over to them, anxious to tell her uncle what had happened.

She got the same reaction from all three.

"Wow," Nick said.

"Incredible," Sharon told her.

"Great news," Sandy said with a grin.

"So should I take it?" she asked anxiously, looking at Nick.

"Honey, I don't see what you've got to lose," he told her. "The captain of personnel said you could pick up where you left off at any time."

"But I could also finish with my class."

"And the position might not still be open by then," Nick countered. "Ashley, a chance to really use a God-given talent to help other people? Think about it!"

"I guess you're right. Absolutely," she said, returning Sandy's grin. She hopped up. "Nick, what's on special? I want to take a couple of plates to Stuart's folks at the hospital."

"Mahimahi Francese."

"Great. Can I get a couple of orders packed up? I want to change."

"Sure," Nick said.

"You change, and we'll get three orders packed up," Sharon said. "You've got to have some dinner yourself, especially since you get your lunch from that thing you call the 'roach coach.'"

"I can't eat with the Fresias," she said. "I want to sit with Stuart and let them eat together."

"Then there will be a plate right here before you leave," Sharon said firmly.

"Okay, okay," she said with a laugh. She kissed her uncle on the cheek, then Sharon and, because he was there, Sandy.

"Hell, I know lots of cops," Sandy said. "Now I know a forensic artist."

She grinned and started from the table, then paused. "Have you seen Detective Dilessio this evening?" she asked.

"Nope," Nick said. "Saw him early this morning, though. He had some business upstate."

"Oh," she said, trying to keep the disappointment from her voice.

"Why?" Sharon asked. "I can take a quick walk over to his boat and see if he's gotten back."

"He was going to try and get some information for me," Ashley explained. "But please don't go down there. I don't want him to think I'm pressuring him. Yet. I'll see if he's there when I get back from the hospital."

"I'll tell him you're looking for him if he comes in," Sharon assured her.

"Great, thanks."

This time, when she reached the hospital, Lucy Fresia was in the waiting room. She seemed surprised but pleased to see Ashley, welcoming her with a hug. "Honey, you really didn't have to come. Nathan and I... we just sit here."

"You're not going to 'just sit here' right now," Ashley said. "I'm going to sit with Stuart, and you and Nathan are going to go and eat Nick's nightly specialty of the house."

"Ashley, how sweet." It looked as if tears were going to well in her eyes. "Thank you."

"Don't worry about it. While you eat, I'll have a talk with Stu."

Ashley felt guilty. She wondered if things might have been different if she'd kept up with Stuart's life.

And known herself just what was going on during his days.

She and Lucy went down the hall to Stuart's room, and Ashley slipped in while Nathan slipped out. Sitting next to Stuart, she took his hand. She talked. She told him about the job offer, expressed her fear that she would be inadequate and then her excitement. Stuart didn't answer, and she didn't feel a response that night. It didn't matter. She kept talking. It was good to be able to say anything that came to mind. Good to know, too, that if he were awake and aware, she would be able to spill her heart out equally easily.

She didn't know how long she had been there when the door opened and Lucy came in to take her place. Outside, Nathan thanked her for the food, for coming and for getting Dilessio involved.

"Has he called you?" she asked Nathan.

"Not yet. Hey, I don't expect miracles."

She nodded. "Things do take time."

"Get home, young lady. I know your days are busy."

She opened her mouth, ready to tell him that the day she'd just spent had been more remarkable than busy, but she was anxious to get home just in case Dilessio had found out anything and was back at his boat. She decided to tell the Fresias about the possible change in her career plans the next day.

She bade them both good-night. As she passed the waiting room, she noted again that the same people seemed to be there—including the man Nathan had pointed out to her as being a reporter out for a hot scoop.

She hurried on by.

It wasn't late when she left the hospital, but the night seemed exceptionally dark. She wasn't thinking about it, since her thoughts were focused on the fact that she hadn't called either Karen or Jan to bring them up to speed on what was happening with Stuart. She made a mental note to give them both a call.

She would wait, though, until she'd had a chance to talk to Dilessio. Hopefully tonight.

Oddly, there was no one in sight when she entered the garage. As she walked across the cement, she became aware of the sound of footsteps that seemed almost an echo of her own. She paused, a strange, uneasy feeling creeping along her spine.

When she stopped, the sound stopped. She looked around. The garage was lit, but pillars and cars cast dark shadows in many places. Her car was at the far end. She hadn't thought anything about it when she had parked. There had been a number of people getting in and out of cars then.

She slowly spun around, searching the shadows. Nothing.

She started walking again. At first she heard nothing. Then that eerie echo of her own footsteps, so close…

She stopped and spun around again. Nothing. But goose pimples had risen on her arms. Instinct seemed to be sounding a warning in her blood, as strident as the wail of a siren.

She had her keys out and her fingers on the remote, ready to hit the panic button. She stared around again at the cars, at the shadows.

She nearly jumped at the sound of an electronic ping. Spinning, she saw a couple come out of the elevator. The sense of panic eased from her as the two spoke, intent on reaching their own vehicle. Ashley began to walk again, telling herself she had been silly.

The couple had managed to procure a spot right by the elevator. Their car roared to life and was gone. She was still a good distance from her own. She walked fast, the remote in a death grip in her hand.

She hadn't imagined it. She heard the echo of footsteps again.

She turned, and shouted out, lying, "I'm a cop, I've got a gun, and I know how to use it!"

Nothing...

She was shouting to an empty garage. Maybe she had simply imagined the sounds of someone following her.

She turned and started for her car.

This time there was no possibility that she had imagined the sound. The footsteps were at a distance, but she could hear them running. She saw the figure coming toward her, wearing scrubs and a surgical mask.

She turned and ran, hitting the panic button on her clicker. Nothing! There were too many cars in the way, blocking the signal. She kept running, aware that her pursuer was close, that the garage was empty, that the footsteps were amplified, as if her pursuer were running across a cement tomb.

The stalker ran after her, his footsteps louder.

Closer.

Chapter 10

Ashley neared her car and hit the panic button on the remote again. This time the lights flashed and the alarm went off loudly.

She could no longer hear the footsteps and didn't know how close the stalker might be. She raced for the car, wrenched the door open and jumped into the driver's seat, slamming the door shut and starting the engine. She backed instantly from her space and spun her car around, aware that her pursuer might be carrying a gun, or a crowbar ready to smash in her window. She hit the gas.

As she did so, her eyes searched the garage. She saw nothing. The person in the scrubs and mask was gone. Gone...

Or hidden in shadow.

Shaking, she drove far too fast to the exit then she

stopped at the gate to tell the attendant what had happened.

"You sure you were chased, lady?"

"Yes!" she said indignantly.

"Want me to call the cops?"

"Yes, I want you to call the cops. The person might be lying in wait up there, ready to attack someone else!"

Angry, she pulled her car to the side, got out and waited.

Two uniformed officers arrived. The first, Officer Mica, starting writing a report. When she described the person, he stopped writing.

"The person was in hospital scrubs?" he said.

"Yes. And a surgical mask."

He had quit writing.

"What's the matter?" she asked.

He shrugged. "Garages can be scary at night, Miss Montague. Footsteps echo, the lighting isn't great. Are you certain the person was chasing you?"

"Yes."

He still wasn't writing.

He sighed. "It might have been just a worn-out surgeon trying to get to his car. Or a nurse. It's easy to imagine things."

"I told you, Officer, I'm in the academy myself. I'm not easily spooked or prone to imagining boogeymen in the shadows. I was being chased. Somebody might get held up or raped because they expected to see someone in scrubs in a hospital parking lot."

She was losing her temper, which wasn't going to get her anywhere.

"All right," Officer Mica said. "We'll take a look for

someone in scrubs. We'll be stopping an entire shift change, but don't worry, we'll look into it."

He scribbled more on the page and gave her the report to sign. He had put it down as she had said it, but she knew he still thought she had imagined a worn-out doctor walking after her because his own car was parked near hers.

"Thank you," she told him, her words to him as sincere as his promise to her. She felt completely frustrated, but she had done all she could do.

Officer Mica repeated wearily that they would do a search. He gave her his card, telling her she was welcome to call and he would inform her if they'd managed to find her stalker.

"If this person really was up to no good, most likely he's gone by now," Mica's partner told her gently. "And if he was in scrubs...all he'd had to do was slip back into the hospital. But we'll call you if we find out anything at all and warn hospital security to keep a lookout."

Ashley looked at his badge. Officer Creighton. She liked him much better than Officer Mica.

"Thanks very much," she told him. "May I have your card, as well?"

He obliged. Mica held his tongue.

Not at all reassured, Ashley drove home. Now that the danger was over, she was more angry than scared. She'd gotten away. Someone else might not be so lucky. And she was really irritated by Mica's attitude. She tried to rationalize that her story might have sounded strange. And she realized even if they had believed her, looking for a stalker in hospital scrubs in a hospital was a pretty absurd task.

When she reached Nick's, she saw that someone had

parked in her spot, despite the "Reserved" sign that usually kept it vacant. She swore and parked farther down, aware that her car was past the reach of the security lights.

She might leave the academy and have to turn in her gun, but she had the damned thing now and knew how to use it—why the hell hadn't she brought it with her?

Because she'd lived here all her life and had never been in a situation when she needed a gun, she reminded herself.

Still…

When she got out of the car, she automatically looked around, mistrustful of the shadows.

She hurried along the gravel path to Nick's. She thought about using her key and slipping through the private entrance, but she headed instead to the dockside entrance in the rear.

She saw that a few diners remained on the outside porch overlooking the dock and the boats. She slowed her footsteps, still angry, then paused, looking down the length of the dock.

She saw Dilessio's boat. And there were lights on inside.

She started down the dock at a brisk pace. Then, as she neared his boat, her footsteps slowed and she stopped for a moment. She didn't want to be an annoyance, hounding him if he really was taking all possible steps.

Screw that. Stuart was in the hospital, in a coma. His parents were aging by the hour.

She started moving again, then nearly jumped when she saw that he was actually outside on the deck. He was seated in a rattan chair, his legs stretched out, bare feet on the rail in front of him. A bottle of beer in his hands, he seemed to be staring at the nothingness where the darkness of the sky met the darkness of the water. She didn't know if he saw her coming; he didn't move. She thought maybe he had dozed off—one beer too many?—he was so still. She wondered about retreating, but as she slowed down again, he called out to her.

"Good evening, Miss Montague. Do come aboard."

"I hesitate, Detective, since I see you are *so* busy, pursuing your cases around the clock."

"Actually, I *am* pursuing a case right now."

"I always thought that if I grew up to be a homicide detective, drinking beer and staring out at the water would definitely be the best method of approach."

"Come aboard," he told her.

She stepped from the dock to the deck.

"Help yourself to a beer, Coke, whatever," he told her.

"With an invitation that gracious, I might."

"Duck down a bit when you go in—the cabin door is low," he told her.

She didn't really want anything to drink, but the invitation to enter the inner sanctum of his home was too tempting. She went into the main cabin. Galley, dining room and living area blended in a surprising display of spaciousness. The place was organized, neat and clean, not cluttered, but not sterile. She entered the galley area and dug into the small refrigerator. Soda, juice, beer, water.

"Break down, Montague—have a beer," he called to her.

She reached for a bottle of Miller Lite, then went back outside to join him on the deck.

He had hardly moved. He was all but lying down between the chair and the railing.

"Nice night, isn't it?" he said.

"The weather is good."

"And the last thing you want to do is talk about it, right?"

"Were you able to talk to the investigator on Stuart's case?"

"Yes."

She leaned against the railing, staring at him, then lifted a hand.

"And?"

"He's a good guy, Paddy Carnegie. Old-timer. He knows what he's doing."

She let out a sigh of exasperation. "And what did he say?"

"He said he's doing everything he can. He likes the Fresias, and he wants them to be right. But he has no witnesses. No one has come forward and admitted so much as having seen your friend walk onto the highway. The driver who hit him saw him the minute he stepped in front of him, not before."

She must have shown her dismay, because he was suddenly impatient.

"What were you expecting? Instant gratification? That's not the way it works. Trust me, you can put years into a case, and it may still never be solved. There's a chance here, at least, that there will be answers down the line. Your friend may survive."

"Not may survive, *will* survive," she said, and was dismayed at the rather pathetic quality of her words when she had meant for them to be so strong.

To her surprise, he let out an impatient sound, something of a derisive snort. "Because what? You slept with this guy once, he's going to survive and the truth will be known. He'll be totally vindicated and all will be well. Wish it worked that way."

She stared at him coldly and stepped away from the rail. She wasn't going to dignify his assumption with a denial. "Are you drunk?"

"No, Montague, I'm telling you the way it is. And sometimes, there's nothing you can do about it."

"You really are an asshole, you know?" she spat out, and started off the boat.

"Montague!" he called.

She paused; she wasn't sure why. She didn't owe him anything.

"You've got one smart-ass tongue on you. How about, 'Thanks, Detective, for taking the time to get involved'?"

"Wow, thanks, Detective. You've been just great."

"Look, it's just that I understand Carnegie's frustration. He needs a break in the case or he's up against a stone wall. No one knows what Stuart was doing over the last several months. His parents didn't know what he was doing. They referred Carnegie to a rag called *In Depth*. He was working on a story he didn't want to share with anyone. The managing editor didn't have the least idea what he was doing."

Ashley stared at him. "Well, there it is—an answer."

"An answer? Do you know what he was doing?"

"No. But it's obvious. He tried to investigate something, the people found out—and they tried to kill him. We've got to find out what he was investigating."

Dilessio stood then in an abrupt, fluid motion, belying any thought that he might have been anywhere near inebriated.

"We've got to find out? You're not even a cop yet. And I'm homicide. Carnegie has this information, and, like I said, he's a good cop. And if you *do* find out anything, you take it straight to Carnegie." He exhaled a breath of irritated impatience. "Or tell me. Hell, just make sure you tell someone, and don't go looking into anything yourself, understand? And don't kid yourself. He might just have joined a bunch of rich club kids and gotten into dope. Whether you like it or not, believe it or not, it's not out of the realm of possibility."

She was startled to find herself almost pinned against the rail by him. He wasn't threatening in any way, just determined. He didn't yell or speak loudly. His voice was low, but the vehemence behind it was startling.

She lifted her chin, ignoring the lack of space between them.

"I can tell you right now, Stuart was on to something. Someone came after me in the garage tonight, after I went to see him."

"What?" Puzzled, he backed away slightly.

"I didn't realize there could be a connection, not until this very minute. But I was parked in the hospital garage. When I walked out to my car, someone came after me. I made it to my car and he disappeared. I had thought it was a random incident, that I just happened to be a woman walking alone in the garage when he was there. But maybe it was personal—maybe I was about to be attacked because I do know Stuart, because I spent time with him alone. And maybe whoever did this to him realizes that they didn't succeed, that Stuart is hanging in and may wake up any day."

"A person was after you…who? What did they look like? Vagrant? White? Black? Hispanic? Old? Young?"

She shook her head, sorry she had spoken. "It was someone in hospital scrubs. And a surgical mask.… I can't even say if they were male or female, though I have a feeling it was a man."

"You were chased by someone in hospital scrubs—at the hospital?"

She exhaled on a note of impatience. "Yes."

He was silent a long time. Moments in which she became aware of the very little bit of distance between them. He smelled of a recent shower and the sea breeze, along with a whiff of beer. His skin was bronzed, his chest swirled with dark hair, and his muscle structure was clearly evident. His face, that great face for a drawing, was enigmatic. She didn't know what lines she might have made with a pencil then. She wasn't breathing, she realized. She forced herself to do so. Being close was difficult, made more so by his size and something kinetic he seemed to create in the air around him. But then he shook his head, still so close.

"Look, you shouldn't go creating scenarios just because your friend is hurt and you're on edge."

"I didn't create the scenario. It happened. I filed a report."

"Then you shouldn't go to the hospital alone anymore."

"I'm going to be a cop." Actually, maybe she wasn't, not soon anyway. The forensic position did seem too good to turn down. But she wasn't about to tell Dilessio that now.

"But you were scared tonight."

"I wasn't expecting any danger at the hospital. I wasn't armed."

"And you weren't scared enough, maybe," he said, suddenly angry.

"Why does a conversation with you always turn into a fight?" she demanded.

"This isn't a fight. I'm just trying to teach you how not to be a fool."

"What's your problem with me?"

"I don't have a problem with you—except that you're an arrogant beginner with the illusion you're the only one out there who gives a shit or can make things happen."

She felt as if she were turning into a pillar of ice. She didn't blink but kept her eyes on his. "Gee, thanks. Well, thanks for the help, Detective. Excuse me. I think I'll call it a night."

"I'll walk you back to Nick's."

"You don't need to. I'll be inside in two minutes."

"I'll walk you."

"Why?"

"You thought you were being followed tonight. Cops watch out for cops, Montague."

"Great. Should I walk you back to your boat after-wards? We can just keep walking back and forth all night."

"Listen to yourself. You haven't listened to a single warning I've given you."

"What do you expect from an arrogant beginner with delusions of grandeur?"

He drew back. She thought she could hear his teeth grating, his muscles snapping with tension. "All right, Montague. I'm sorry if I'm blunt. You're a cute kid, with a lot of the right stuff. I'm older, worn, jaded and I've seen way too much stuff go down, okay? Humor me."

He started past her, taking her arm. He didn't jerk her, but he had one firm hold. She walked along—stumbled first—after him, smarting anew from his words.

Cute kid?

"There's a door to my wing right there."

"Great."

He scissored over the low wooden wall that separated the dock from the shore. She followed suit, and he walked her to her door.

"Thanks for the escort. We cute kids are always grateful to make it home safe."

"Great."

"Well?"

"Open the door and get inside."

She threw up her hands, reached into her purse... and couldn't find her keys to save her life. She fumbled blindly through the contents. He was still standing there. Impatient, she went down to her knees and dumped the contents out on the walkway. Miraculously, her keys appeared immediately.

He bent down to help her throw the wallet, pens, lipsticks, compact and other paraphernalia back in.

"I've got it, thanks," she said.

He stood, not replying. She twisted the key in her lock and went inside. "Okay, I'm in now."

"Good night."

He turned and started back for his boat. She bit her lip, watching his back. Well, that was it, he was leaving. Over and done. After giving her nothing but facts and discouragement. Had she envisioned another scenario? Him welcoming her onto his boat, discussing the case seriously with her, telling her that together, somehow, they would find the answers?

Of course not.

But she also hadn't thought he would walk her to the house as if she were indeed a child. That he would stay, make sure she had the key, that she got inside safely.

Had she hoped that he was going to follow her in, check out the room, move close to her again, talk softly in that gruff voice?

Stay?

Cute kid. Why on earth did that asshole appeal to her so much?

She'd never thought of herself as cute. She wasn't small; she didn't have a round face or dimple. She might not be a raving beauty, but she knew she was attractive, that her posture was good, that she had, at the least, some essence of sophistication.

He was such a jerk.

But when she stood there, close to him…

Don't you ever just want to have sex?

Yes, Karen! At the moment, rather desperately, I'm afraid…. With a royal jerk.

When he stood there, insulting her, she just took it all in with indignation, all the time thinking that she liked the darkness of his eyes, the structure of his face. His flesh. His *naked* flesh. He just had to live on a house-boat, where it was the most natural thing in the world to sit around on deck in nothing but cutoffs.

He turned, and she was still standing there at the door, watching him go.

"Get in and lock that door," he shouted impatiently.

She closed the door and locked it.

To Jake's amazement, he returned to the *Gwendolyn* feeling an unreasonable tension and anger. His neck was sore. It had been a long drive up and back in the one day. And all he felt was frustration, both with the Bordon case—and Fresia's.

Frustration…with Nick's niece. She had to slow down.

Frustration…because he wanted to shake her. Only because he wanted to keep her from harm.

No. Because he wanted a lot more. He wasn't sure why it had taken him so long to notice that Ashley Montague's eyes weren't just green. They switched from a cool lime to a deep emerald when she spoke, when she grew angry. She wasn't just slim, lean and agile; she had really great curves. She smelled subtly of a soft, deep, underlying perfume. Her hair wasn't carrot red or flaming; it was deeper, like her scent, seductive as a soft, hot whisper.

He opened the refrigerator, meant to take another beer.

He closed the refrigerator.

He looked around the living area of the houseboat. He was sure there had been someone on the *Gwendolyn* the other night. Nothing was gone, but he knew someone had been here.

And now Ashley had said she'd been nearly accosted in the parking garage.

There could be no relation between the two incidents. Still…

Jake put on a pot of coffee and sat in front of his computer. He pulled up the records he'd been keeping for years.

Was that it?

Had someone come onto the boat to examine his private files, knowing that he'd kept much of his research on his private computer, rather than at work? Maybe.

Tomorrow he would get someone out to change the locks. He should have had that done today.

He laced his fingers behind his head, remembering his conversation with Bordon.

Smoke and mirrors...

Mary Simmons was convinced Harry Tennant had been crazy. That he listened to voices. Lazarus. *Lazarus... awakened from the dead.*

Stuart Fresia had been writing a story.

Ashley Montague had the greenest eyes he'd ever seen, with sparks of fire. Great breasts. Really nice, tight ass.

He swore out loud, stared at his computer screen and began to type, back taut and painfully tense. He rubbed his nape. Impressions, notes, things that had been said that somehow seemed important, jarring.

Lazarus. The kid had been crazy; he'd listened to voices.

Smoke and mirrors.

Stuart Fresia had been working on a story.

Ashley Montague had great—

He erased the last. Called himself every name in the book. Turned off the computer. Then went back outside to stand on the *Gwendolyn*'s deck.

Damn, she was close. Right across the grass.

Good. Not good. She shouldn't be a cop. She didn't have the patience. She didn't have...

Not true. She would probably make a great cop. Like Nancy. But Nancy had made a mistake and now she was dead. Other cops had made mistakes. They, too, were dead.

Smoke and mirrors...

Lazarus.

What if the kid hadn't been crazy? Maybe he hadn't

been listening to voices. One of the sect members might have been called Lazarus.

He wished he had Bordon in front of him again. Wished it were legal to put the man on the rack, force him to tell what he knew.

It wasn't. But it was galling, because he was certain there was an answer right in front of him that he wasn't seeing. Smoke and mirrors. Bordon had sworn he'd had nothing to do with Nancy. Jake had never taken her with him when he'd questioned the People for Principle members. He'd taken two trips out there—alone. The first time, she'd gone to question the tourist who had stumbled on the second body. The second time, she'd been busy tracing Bordon's financial sheets.

Then…she'd been gone.

Strange. Bordon hadn't met her, but he seemed to know all about her. All about her problems with Brian. *Smoke and mirrors. Lazarus.*

Sleep on it, he told himself wearily. Maybe something would make sense by morning.

He locked up the *Gwendolyn* and went to bed. Sleep eluded him for a long time.

He dreamed again that night.

He was in a forest, a forest filled with mirrors. An old man in long white robes was walking through the trees. Lazarus. Awakened from the dead.

The mirrors dissolved into crystal. Like powder, they drifted onto the breeze. The forest faded away and he was staring at the shore next to the marina. A woman was walking toward him. Slim, lithe, sensual, moving slowly, provocatively. Soft flesh shimmering in the moonlight. Hair seemingly afire.

She was naked.

She walked slowly down the dock.

A moment later, she was on the boat. On him. Another moment later...

He woke abruptly, sweating, swearing.

The dream had been so damned vivid, he was drenched. He shook himself fully awake. Hell, no more coming straight home. He was obsessed. He had to get out. Tonight he would take himself to a club on the beach.

He sat still, listening. Had the dream awakened him? Or a sound? He slid out of bed silently. Padded through the houseboat, listening. He focused on sensual recall. A sound...not on the boat. Just somewhere...near.

Well, hell, he didn't live out here alone. Someone else had been coming home, boarding their own boat. Or someone had left Nick's. Or Nick had thrown out his trash.

He went to his bedside drawer and pulled out his gun. He walked through the living area and opened the door to the deck.

He walked out. The night was silent, other than the lapping of the water against the boats, the soft thumping when the tide brought the vessels against the bumpers.

He walked onto the dock and looked down the length of it. All seemed quiet.

He looked across the grass.

Ashley Montague was out there, just outside her door. She was wearing a long T-shirt with a cartoon character and something written on it.

It was the most erotic outfit he'd ever seen.

He stood for a moment, staring at her, knowing she was staring at him.

He leapt over the rail and strode over to her. She

looked at the gun in his hand, then at him, but she didn't move.

"Are you going to arrest me?" she asked him.

"No. What are you doing out?"

"I heard something. What are you doing out?"

"I heard something."

"Think we heard each other?" she asked.

"Maybe."

The night breeze moved by, soft, cool. They continued to stare at one another. He could hear her breathing, see the rise and fall of her breasts beneath the gently hugging cotton.

"You have your gun."

"The safety is on."

"Good." She moistened her lips, her eyes, very emerald, on his. "So...?"

He shrugged. He felt like a tower of lava himself. Mount Etna on a bad day. He was nowhere near touching her, but it felt as if little sparks were shooting from her, filling the air between them like diamond dust.

"Fuck," he muttered, shaking his head. What the hell was he doing?

Then she said, "Your place or mine?"

A whisper. Not as ballsy as she had intended, he was certain. Then she shook her head, and he thought she was going to renege, withdraw.

She didn't.

"Your place," she said, and grimaced. "This is still my uncle's house."

He didn't reply, just took her arm with his free hand, starting back across the grass.

Chapter 11

Red.

All he could see was red. The richness of it spread across his pillow, a mane of it, tangling and inviting, as tempting as original sin.

Jake was sure he was insane, of course. But it didn't matter. They were both insane.

Maybe one madness canceled out the other.

She was simply, at that moment, the most beautiful woman he had ever seen. The most desirable. She moved as no other woman had ever moved. Her eyes were green fire, her lips…he'd never seen a mouth so perfect. The air was filled with electricity wherever she stepped. No one had ever, ever, made a cotton T-shirt appear so blatantly erotic.

God, she was perfect.

What the hell was she doing? Ashley wondered.

Then she rejected the question. She had dreamed of this, dreamed of him. And God, he was perfect. Rugged face, with lines that still bordered on the classical. Handsome, but still dripping with rugged machismo. Broad shoulders and chest, hard flat stomach, lean hips, muscles rippling, golden, catching the moonlight. And the scent of him… So compelling. Sea, salt, soap…some distant aftershave, elusively tantalizing, beckoning…

Jake argued with himself that she could have stopped, could have pulled back, could have spoken. Because it would take a far better, stronger man than he to back away now.

She didn't speak.

In fact, they hadn't exchanged another word. Not as they walked to the *Gwendolyn*, not as he paused to lock his door behind them, and not even when he indicated the few steps to the master cabin. He hadn't spoken when she'd doffed the T-shirt, couldn't have, because his breathing had gone so erratic. The black lace thong she wore was in direct contrast to the silly cotton T-shirt.

A contrast that sent a rush of adrenaline erupting through him like a geyser.

He'd ripped the covers from the bed with the expertise of a magician, revealing the clean sheets beneath, and it was there that she had crawled, lying back, waiting, all but blinding him in the maze of red, a red he felt, as if he could see it pumping through his bloodstream, just as he could see it splayed across the white sheets of his bed.

At last he spoke. "Jesus," he whispered. One word. Not blasphemous. Awed.

He forgot his own cutoffs in his haste to join her. His attention went from the red of her hair, to the tiny wisp of black lace. *Straight to the point, eh, buddy?* he mocked himself, but what the hell, it wasn't as if they were in the midst of a slow seduction. He crawled atop her, met her eyes briefly...

Color, more color. Green, cat green, and as sensuous as ever those of a feline had been. Half closed, lashes low.

And her lips...moist, parted, her breath emerging in quick little pants. She touched her lips again with her tongue. Perhaps in anticipation. He ignored her mouth, no matter how appealing. He had a one-track mind.

He lowered his head against her, breathed in the sweet scent of her flesh. Tasted her from the valley between her breasts downward with the tip of his tongue. God, that strip of lace. He paused briefly at her navel. He was in love with whatever soap she used, whatever lotion, perfume. Maybe it was just the scent of her flesh. The touch of it, the feel of it. Like silk, but hot, so alive. Lower, his tongue moved finding the lace, teasing at the band, stroking over the sudden roughness. He was aware of the intake of her breath. Just a brush of his mouth at first, over silk, over lace. His fingers gripped the elastic then, moving fabric, sliding beneath. He gripped the band, drew it away.

Red.

His mind exploded as if the color shot through it. Her fingers ploughed into his hair. She was saying something then, but words made no sense. Maybe there were no words, just sounds, whispers, moaning. She moved, she moved...arching, sinuous, sensuous. Elastic snapped in his fingers. The wisp of silk and lace was gone, and he teased, tasted, laved, teased again, breathed.... He was unaware at first that her grip on his hair was achingly powerful. She had filled his senses. His blood raced through him as if pounding out a staccato beat; his entire being and concentration were filled with the taste and scent of her. He was aware of the way she moved, aware of the sounds escaping her, aware that she had reached the brink, strained like a cat, exploded into drifting crystal. Her fingers lost their death grip. He crawled atop her, looking down. Her eyes were half closed again, lashes sweeping her cheeks in midnight... red....

Then there was her mouth. He kissed her, and she burst back to life. Arms around him, fingers kneading his shoulders, and her tongue, caught with his, twisted, wet, hot, even more seductive. Yet even as she returned the moist heat of his passion, she was pushing him away, determined that her lips would discover more, as well. To his amazement, he found that the red fire was sweeping down his body. What she could do with her lips against his flesh, the tip of her tongue teasing against the dark hair on his chest, swirling against him as she followed his natural curves, and that mane of red hair tangled over his flesh with every movement.

Her fingers fell to the band of his button-fly cutoffs, dexterous, slow...torturously, deliciously slow. Her hand slipped beneath the band. Fingers curled around the pulse of his erection. He prayed suddenly for restraint. The blood beating like thunder in his system threatened to deny him. He eased himself from her, shed the cutoffs and caught her in his arms, taking her lips again before she could inflict a madness he couldn't resist and slid into her. She was soft, passionate, mercury, fire. He didn't remember ever moving with such a rampant surge of desire, feeling such sweet, exquisite torture in every second that led toward climax. Madness was stilled only by a fleeting roar of pride inside.

She tensed beneath him, arching as taut as a bowstring, letting out a cry that she quickly smothered against his neck. And he let the blood-thunder-drum seize him, climaxing himself in a rush of release that, for a moment, seemed to steal every ounce of life from his body, every breath from his lungs. Sated, drenched, heavy with the aftermath of release...

That realization brought life to his limbs, and he eased off her, drawing her against the length of his body. She was still shaking. He held her. They both began to breathe.

A moment later, he said softly, "Do you want to talk?"

"No."

Plain, simple, in a nutshell.

But she didn't make a move to leave. Nor did he draw away.

The lights were dim; the boat was rocking. She felt so sensual in his arms. Fire draped over his flesh, soft, the mane of her hair. She was still silk. Vibrant silk, so alive, so real. He drew his hand along her arm, down the length of her spine.

Damn, what a spine.

His fingers brushed over the rise of her buttocks.

Seconds later, he pulled her against him hard, the flow of blood sending his heart into overdrive. She was wet, hot, tight and arced, and she moved as if to the most erotic salsa beat. His fingers gripped her midriff, curved around her breasts, stroked, solicited...fell to her hips and held hard until the explosion burst upon them both again. Even then, he was loathe to withdraw, so he stayed inside her, calming slowly in a glove of heat.

In time he smoothed his fingers over her shoulder, smoothed the fiery hair that teased his nose. She seemed no more inclined to talk, so he remained silent himself, holding her. And it was then that he realized he hadn't felt so comfortable in eons, had never felt as much pleasure in holding a woman when the deed was done as when he was in the midst of it. The surf lapped against the bow, slight, gentle. He closed his eyes.

Lucy Fresia sat in the hospital chair at her son's side. He hadn't improved, but she had no intention of giving up on him. Stuart was in there somewhere, and he had a will of steel. She just kept telling him over and over again that she loved him.

She held his hand, leaned back. It was late. She closed her eyes. In seconds, despite the constant trauma that raged in her heart, she found herself drifting off.

She heard a click…a slight clicking sound, and it jolted her into awareness. She sat up, looking around. Nathan had come to spell her, to tell her to go home for the night. Or the sweet nurse was coming to check on him, to do whatever she could to make him more comfortable.

She glanced at the door. Through the glass, she could make out a figure in green hospital scrubs. She started to straighten, to force her smile, to greet the newcomer with all the spirit she could muster.

The figure saw her; she was certain of that, despite the fact that she was really tired and blinking away sleep.

The door didn't open. There was a pause, and the

person walked away. Puzzled, Lucy rose and walked to the door. She opened it, and looked out, but saw no one down the corridor. With a shrug, she returned to her vigil, drawing her chair closer to her son. She spoke softly. "You will make it, Stu. You will! You have to, you know." Despite the fact that she'd been there day and night, new tears welled in her eyes. "You have to, Stu. Your dad and I…your dad and I love you so much. You're everything in the world to us, Stu…please, Stu."

The rise and fall of the respirator was her only answer. She squeezed his hand. "We'll never give up. We'll be here, no matter what."

The sound of the alarm was painful.

Jake bolted up, pressing his hands against his temples.

"Shit."

"Shit," echoed from his side.

She was half sitting up as well, sheet clutched to her, hair tangled and full, spilling around her face like wildfire.

By morning's light, she was even more desirable. Stunning, sensual…and somehow vulnerable.

But morning's light was far too real, as well.

They stared at one another.

What the hell had he been thinking? Jake wondered. She was Nick's niece. Arrogant, too sure of herself, bound to get into trouble. He needed her the way he needed to walk around with a dagger sticking into his side. Hell, it had been sex. Just sex. Spontaneous but consensual. Good sex, damned good sex, but just sex.

Wrong. Not with this woman. She'd gotten under his skin before he'd ever touched her. He wondered how he'd gone so many years, passing by once in a blue moon, noticing her from a distance, maybe even getting a beer from her from time to time. He'd thought of her only as Nick's niece. As a kid. Well, she was definitely not a kid. She was a simmering blaze, and he should have felt the lick of the flames.

God, he was an idiot. She was still Nick's niece, and in the academy, besides. It wasn't against the rules for officers to date, so long as they kept their relationships for their personal time. But she was still in the damned academy. And they weren't dating. They'd had sex.

Arrogant trouble.

And she was staring at him now with something akin to pure horror.

What the hell had she been thinking? Ashley wondered. Obviously her mind hadn't been any part of it. His hair was tousled, his flesh bronze, and damned if his ass wasn't just perfect as she'd expected, but...

He was Detective Jake Dilessio.

And she didn't do things like this. Karen did, once in a while, and she'd thought about it, but...she didn't do things like jump into bed with a complete stranger.

"Shit," he said again. He seemed to be looking at her as if he had awakened next to a cobra.

"Shit," she repeated, then bounded out of the bed, searching for her underwear and sleep shirt. "What time is it?"

"Six-thirty. You'll have to hustle to make class by seven."

"I don't have to be there at seven. I have until eight." The thong was a loss. She would have to streak across the grass with a bare butt under the T-shirt.

"Why?"

"I—I've got a meeting. You'd better hustle. Oh, no, that's right. You're Detective Dilessio. You make your own hours, do your own thing. But you're right, I have to get moving."

Ashley slid into the T-shirt and hurried down the two steps, through the living area and over to the front door. She was pleased with her exit.

Except that she couldn't work the lock. He came up behind her, clad again in his cutoffs, and unlocked the door.

"Ashley?"

She didn't look at him.

"What? I do need to hurry."

But she *felt* him there, and lifted her head to meet his gaze.

"Be careful, all right? Don't go thinking you can solve the problems of the world—or even solve the mystery about your friend."

"I am careful."

He nodded. She stood there, chafing beneath his gaze, feeling her face redden. He was going to give her some speech about last night not having meant anything.

But he didn't. He smiled. And his voice was soft. "Thanks for coming. That was one of the nicest nights I've had in as long as I can remember."

Her eyes widened. "Oh, well…thank you."

"Great sex," he told her. The door opened.

She didn't know what happened then, what caused her lips to move or the words to come out. "The best I ever had," she said.

She could have kicked herself, but since the door was open, she fled, instead.

* * *

Ashley's morning was mind-boggling, but made pleasant largely because she had been handed over almost immediately to a wonderful woman named Mandy Nightingale, who was warm, friendly and incredibly professional. Mandy—who insisted on being on a first-name basis—explained to her many different areas of forensic expertise and introduced her around the department. She talked about the horrors they often encountered, clearly waiting to make sure Ashley was up for it. Ashley explained that photography was something she had dabbled in, but that she was no expert. That didn't seem to bother Mandy, who promised to take her under her wing and teach her everything she knew.

"I can teach photography," she said, "but I've seen your drawings. That kind of talent is hard to find." She went on to explain that Ashley would work as a civilian employee of the Miami-Dade Police Department, and that yes, certainly she would be able to go back and finish the academy at any time. "The thing is, and I'm not trying to twist your arm, positions like this really don't come open that often."

Ashley nodded, although her mind was pretty much made up already. "The other skill I'm a little worried about is reconstruction. I've never done anything remotely similar."

"That's something you can learn, as well."

They talked a while longer. Then, midmorning, Captain Murray returned, and Ashley told him yes, she would like to take the position.

That began several hours of paperwork. After that, Murray told her she was free to take the afternoon off. She would start training with Mandy the following day.

* * *

Marty called in, apologizing profusely; said he would catch up with Jake later in the day—he hoped. He'd either eaten something bad or picked up a virus, and he wasn't able to stay out of the can for more than fifteen minutes at a time.

Jake missed his partner during the task force meeting, though the other men were good, solid cops. Belk was forty-five, seasoned, reasonable, and had a calm about him under any circumstances that made him all but magic with witnesses. Rosario was just a few years younger; they had worked together for years. Where Belk was calm, Rosario could bluster, and between them, they could glean an incredible amount of information. Rizzo and MacDonald were younger, but still experienced, having both been in homicide for over seven years. Rizzo had a nose for research, while MacDonald could size up a crime scene like few other men. They all discussed their interviews, went through the reports on the door-to-door questioning, and once again, analyzed the medical examiner's report.

Then there was Franklin. Once again, he spoke about his experience with what he considered a far more important agency, but his experience that day seemed to signify only that he should tell them not to neglect the rest of their work, that they had close to zilch to go on, that he had combed the FBI computer and spoken to law enforcement officers across the country, and hadn't found the break they needed. Franklin was tall, dark-haired and considered himself extremely knowledgeable—and suave. He gloried in the fact that he had been asked to share his incredible knowledge on various television shows. "Until we get an I.D. on that girl, we're spinning our wheels," he said, staring at them all. "We really need an I.D. on her."

Jake refrained from speaking. He glanced at Rosario and almost grinned, because he was so certain they were thinking the same thing.

Duh, asshole!

"The FBI has no magic solution for this one," Franklin said. "What it will take is really good police work on your part."

Jake felt like a dog with his hackles up. To the best of his knowledge, the case was still under the jurisdiction of the county.

Jake stood then, but held his temper.

"Jake?" Captain Blake said, frowning. He was seated on the edge of his desk, since they'd met in his office so he could review their work on the case.

"Special Agent Franklin is correct," Jake heard himself say politely. "Gentlemen, let's get back to work."

Blake knew him—knew he didn't have one good thing to say about Franklin. But he had spoken with an almost flattering conviction.

Jake escaped. He made a call to forensics, then to Dr. Gannet. He looked at his watch and knew he had time to head south, even though he would have a long drive back to the morgue.

A moment later, he grabbed his jacket and briefcase and was out the door.

"Mr. Bordon?"

"Yes?"

Peter Bordon was sitting outside in the exercise yard, feeling the sun on his face. The guard spoke to him politely. Hell, most of the guards were polite. They had no reason not to be. He was unerringly respectful, truly a model of good behavior.

"There's a phone call for you. You have permission to take it."

"Who is it?"

"Your cousin Richard. There's an illness in your family, I'm sorry to say."

"Ah."

"You'll be out soon, right?" the young guard asked him.

"If the parole board says so."

"Well, good luck."

"Thank you, Thomas, is it?"

"Yes, Mr. Bordon."

"Thank you, Thomas."

He was led to the phone. Peter picked up the receiver. "Peter Bordon."

"So the cop has been to see you."

His fingers tensed. He allowed himself no outward expression. "Yeah."

"And?"

"He's got nothing."

"Let's hope it stays that way."

"It will."

"Yeah, we'll see that it does."

The phone went dead in his hand. His escort was waiting. "Not so bad," he told the guard. "My nephew is ill, but he's coming around."

"I'm sorry."

"He's a tough little guy."

Back out in the yard, Peter felt the sun again. It wasn't as warm. He thought back to his arrest. The cops were allowed to lie to suspects during interrogation. And Dilessio *had* lied. Because he had known something. Damn him, he'd known something.

But Peter hadn't cracked. He'd taken a lie detector test and passed with flying colors. Even so, he'd wound up in prison for fraud and tax evasion.

He smiled, lifting his chin. He didn't mind so much. He'd determined from the beginning not to plan any stupid escape attempts, just to do his time. And now he was glad.

After all, he'd found God.

He just wished he'd found a little more courage, as well. Dilessio was still out there. And he was like a damned terrier with a bone. The others didn't quite get it yet. He would never let go.

Unless he was dead.

Outside the building, Ashley called Karen to tell her about Stuart and about her own change in direction. Karen insisted that she wanted to go to the hospital that night herself, and said she would call Jan. At the very least, they could give more moral support to the Fresias. Ashley agreed. After that, Karen allowed her happiness for Ashley to burst through.

"It's perfect. You're with the police—"

"I'll be a civilian employee, until I go back and finish up at the academy."

"You'll still be with the police. But you'll be using your artistic talent, learning so much, *and* getting paid. Well paid."

"That's a definite plus. I intend to go back and finish the academy, though." She hesitated. "Homicide detectives and some of the other specialists can do even better."

"But that could well be ten years or so down the road. And if you decide at some point that you want to apply for homicide or whatever, you'll have this incredible body of experience behind you."

Ashley had to agree. She ended the call, telling Karen she would be by for her around six.

Just as she hit the end button, she felt a whoosh of air coming from behind her. Startled, she gave a little cry and spun around. Arne and Gwyn had come up behind her. Arne threw her into the air as if she weighed no more than ten pounds, then caught her on the way down. Gwyn caught her face and kissed her on both cheeks.

"Hey, promotion girl!" Arne said.

"We heard it was official, that you've put in the paperwork and you're going to become a forensic artist," Gwyn told her.

Ashley nodded. "It did seem like an offer I couldn't refuse."

"Refuse? Do you know how many people apply for a position like that?" Arne said, shaking his head. "We want to take you out to celebrate."

"That's great of you guys. I'd love it."

"Tonight?" Gwyn asked her.

"Not tonight, I just promised to go to the hospital with a couple of friends."

"Has there been any change in your friend's condition?" Arne asked.

Ashley shook her head. "No, but I feel so much better, getting to see his folks."

As she spoke, she felt arms curl around her waist. She turned, surprised to see Len Green.

"Hey, boy!" she teased. "Did you give up your patrol car?"

"No, young lady, not at all. I'm just in one of those paperwork hell places that come along now and then. And, actually, I'm glad of that for once. I just heard about your promotion."

"Well, it's not exactly a promotion—" Ashley began.

"Like hell!" He waved a hand in the air. "It's incredible. You still going to talk to a lowly patrolman now that you've soared past me?"

She laughed. "I didn't soar past anyone," she protested. "I changed course."

"However you want to look at it, it's wonderful," he told her sincerely.

"More training than ever," she heard herself say hastily.

"We're going to get the class squad together and take her out to celebrate," Arne told Len. "You want to join us?"

"Sure, of course, if I can. When?" Len asked.

"We're working on that right now," Gwyn said.

"How about Friday, Ash?" Arne said.

"Friday sounds good. Unless…well, unless, you know, something happens with Stuart."

"Hey," Gwyn said. "You can't move in there, you know. You said his parents are there around the clock. But they're his parents. You can't let yourself get obsessed with this."

"I know that. But I do feel I'm doing some good. But, yes, Friday night celebration. That sounds wonderful," Ashley said. "I think I'll bring a few friends. You remember Karen and Jan."

"He knows Karen and Jan?" Arne said.

"Len was up in Orlando when we were there," Ashley explained. She shrugged, watching Len's reaction.

She wished so badly that he would focus on Karen. "He met them then."

Arne made a teasing, disgruntled sound.

"They cute?"

"Well, hell, yes, my friends are cute," she told him.

"Then I'm glad I'll get to meet them Friday night. The more the merrier."

"Great," she said, and looked at Len.

She couldn't read anything in his expression, but he told her, "Good. I'll look forward to it—and of course to seeing the girls again. Do we know where we're going?"

"Bennigans, out on US1. It's good, it's fun, and it's affordable—since we're not all getting raises," Gwyn said.

"I'll treat you guys," Ashley told her.

"Hell, no, you won't. We're going to suck up big-time, just in case you become one of those famous people on *America's Most Wanted* or something like that," Gwyn said. "We do still get paychecks, you know."

Ashley laughed. "Sounds great."

"We have to get back to class," Arne warned. "Since we're just poor slobs who would have gotten our asses fired if we'd been caught drawing in class."

"Quit that," Ashley protested, but they were both grinning at her. They were new friends, but good ones. They sincerely wished her well.

"I have to get back, too," Len said. "I just saw you here and couldn't leave without stopping to say con-gratulations."

"Don't you have to go draw something?" Gwyn asked.

Ashley laughed. "No, I have the afternoon off."

"Well, isn't she special?" Gwyn joked, shaking her head.

"I don't think you're off anymore," Len said, staring over Ashley's head toward the entrance of the building.

She spun around. Captain Murray was walking toward her. A pleasant, cordial man who drew respect despite his easy manner and low voice, he greeted the others, who voiced their pleasure that Ashley had ended up in a perfect place.

"She is," Murray said. "Except that I told her she could have an afternoon off and now I want to renege."

She arched a brow.

"Well?"

She had to smile. "I haven't had a chance to plan an afternoon at the beach or anything. And if I had made a plan, I'd drop it like a hot coal if you asked, Captain Murray."

"Come on, then. I'll explain as we go."

She waved to the others and matched her footsteps to Murray's no-nonsense stride.

"Where are we going?" she asked.

"County morgue," he told her briefly.

The room was sterile; the occupants might be dead, but the place was cleaner than any hospital Jake had ever been in. Tile and chrome, and personnel in white uniforms.

The girl had been brought out by the time he arrived when he looked through the glass door, Gannet was the first person he saw. To his surprise, Captain Murray, head of personnel, was at the doctor's side. When he opened the door and walked in, he saw that Nightingale was there, too. His heart sank somewhat—she was one of the best crime scene photographers he'd ever worked with, but her art skills were lacking.

Then, despite himself, his jaw nearly dropped.

Ashley Montague was standing at Nightingale's side. Her eyes met his. She had known he was coming.

He looked from Gannet to Murray, expecting an explanation.

"Jake, you're here. I gather you know Ashley Montague already, that you're neighbors," Murray said.

"Yes." But what the hell was she doing here now? This case was far too important for them to be dragging in would-be cops from the academy.

"Ms. Montague is joining the civilian forensics team. Her paperwork hasn't been processed yet, but when Gannet called us, we asked her to come in with us."

He stared at Ashley. She returned his gaze steadily. "Because…?"

"She's the best sketch artist I've come across in years," Murray said.

He realized then that Ashley was holding a pad and pencil. Their Jane Doe, their poor Cinderella, was lying exposed before her.

"I'm going to clean the skull, and Mason in forensics will be doing the reconstruction, as planned, but since you're so anxious that we get something out in the paper, Ms. Montague seemed like our best recourse for the moment," Gannet told him.

Feeling as stiff as a steel pipe, Jake folded his hands behind his back and nodded. The gaze he turned on Ashley then was close to hostile, he knew.

Couldn't help it. He didn't like surprises.

"Since you recommend she give it a try, we'll see what she can do," he heard himself say. He couldn't help but be glad that Ashley Montague looked a little bit green. He knew what she'd seen and gone through to have gotten where she was in the academy. She'd undoubtedly witnessed an autopsy.

But there were few corpses that displayed the violence that had been done to this one.

Nightingale had a pad, as well. Seemingly oblivious to the tension in the room, she walked around to Jake. "Here's a first rendering, Detective."

He accepted the drawing and bit down hard on his lip.

It was good. Incredibly good. He looked from the sketch in his hand to the decayed remains of the face of the woman on the table.

Somehow Ashley had found the humanity in the girl. She had built upon patches of flesh. The left eye had suffered severe deterioration; the right eye had not. The mouth had been discolored and bruised more to one side. Ashley had evened it out. She had, he was certain, been forced to rely on instinct and imagination in some areas, but when he looked from the battered remains of the poor dead girl to the page, he had to admit—he saw her alive.

He handed the sketch back to Nightingale.

"Not bad. I assume you're doing more?" he said to Ashley.

"Yes, that's what they've asked for," she replied.

He nodded. "Fine. I'll be back in an hour."

"Jake, I can see that the sketches are delivered to headquarters—" Gannet began.

Jake shook his head. "No, thanks, that's all right. I want to compare them to the girl myself, make sure I've got the very best likeness. I'll be back."

He left the room, amazed to discover that he had to unclench his fingers to open the door.

He knew the morgue too well. Knew where to go for coffee.

He sat down, drew out a folder of notes, certain if he read and reread, he would find the thread he needed. Smoke and mirrors.

Fuck. He couldn't concentrate. He was furious.

Why?

She'd known this, known that she *wasn't* going to be a cop, not for now, anyway. She must have known she was going into forensics, and she hadn't said a damn thing.

Not that they'd really carried on a conversation....

Fuck.

She should have told him. Still, it was a good thing, a damned good thing. Now she wouldn't be on the streets.

There were lots of women cops. He wasn't a chauvinist. He had no right to want her off the streets. Hell, he hadn't even known she was an artist.

He took a sip of his coffee. It had grown cold. Impatiently, he put his notes back into the folder and started back down the corridor anxious to see the drawings.

There were several. All of them good. And all of them representing a living, breathing young woman, one who'd been attractive in life. Surely someone had loved her. Someone who shouldn't have to wake up and realize that not only was she dead, but she'd died in a particularly horrible way.

"Detective? Changes, suggestions?" Nightingale asked.

He wanted to say something. Wanted something to be wrong.

Hell, no, he didn't. He wanted the case solved. He

just didn't want Ashley Montague to be…so damned good.

No. They needed good people. He just hated surprises.

"Jake?" Mandy Nightingale persisted.

"No. They're good," he said, and added the drawings to the contents of his briefcase.

He didn't thank the artist, though he knew he should have done so. He nodded an acknowledgment to Gannet and the others, including Ashley, and turned to leave. He forced himself to turn back.

"Thank you all. I'll choose one of these for tomorrow's paper."

That was as much as he could manage. He turned and exited, further aggravated to discover he had to unclench his hands again to open the door.

Chapter 12

Ashley should have felt a deep sense of accomplishment and pride. Gannet, Nightingale and Murray had applauded her artistic efforts with a great deal of satisfaction—even smug satisfaction, on Murray's part. Well, his job was personnel. He was supposed to know people, their talents, their weaknesses and just where they could best serve the public interest. Mandy Nightingale was also wonderful, telling her not to worry, all the other skills she needed would come, but that she'd already performed a very important service—and her paperwork hadn't even gone through. Even Dr. Gannet had been extremely kind, shaking his head with a little bit of awe that she had been able to create such a plausible likeness from the pathetically damaged face of the corpse.

The corpse.

Oh, Lord.

Yes, she'd seen a lot, most of it on video, but she'd been to an autopsy. She'd never come near to passing out or vomiting. She had stood her ground; knowing that no matter how something made her feel, it would be her job to do the best for the injured and the dead.

But she hadn't seen, or even imagined, anything close to the horror of seeing a body like that of Jane Doe. She had felt bile rising in her throat. The air had gone still around her, and for long moments she had felt as if she couldn't breathe. Somehow she had swallowed the bile, then pinched herself to keep from seeing the spots growing before her eyes. She had forced herself to think as an artist, to find the features that would lead her to the true vision of the woman as she had been in life. But all the time, every minute of it, she had longed to throw the sketch pad down and run screaming from the room.

She hadn't run, though. She had done the sketches, and they were good. *She* was good, and she should have been pleased by what she had accomplished. But as she drove away from the morgue—desperate for a shower and fresh clothing before picking up Karen and Jan— she grew angry with herself for not feeling a greater sense of achievement. The hell with him.

It hurt to feel that after last night. No. That had been nothing more than a moment's insanity, almost like coming up for a gulp of air after being under water too long. He certainly felt nothing toward her. It was almost as if he still *disliked* her.

She pulled into the parking lot, grateful that her own space was available, still so deep in thought that she hardly noticed her surroundings.

"Hey, Ashley, congratulations!"

Startled, she looked up. She'd seen the single man

seated at one of the outside tables—before. Probably in his mid-thirties, he had a stocky build, dark hair and a pleasant, squarish face. She was sure he could see her mind working as she tried to remember just how she knew him. He'd been in before, of course. But she'd also seen him with Dilessio, she realized. He was Jake's partner.

"Thanks," she told him.

She walked over to the table. He grinned. "I'm Martin Moore, by way of an official introduction."

She grinned. "Nice to meet you—officially. Actually, I think I remember you from here, as well. Jack Black and water on Saturday nights, right?"

He leaned back, amused. "Good memory. I'm not here all that often. Guess I'll be around more now, with Jake having a slip here."

"Great." She tried to keep her smile in place.

"Lord, has my pain in the ass partner been around here already?" he asked.

She shook her head. "No…it's just that…"

"I heard you sketched our Jane Doe this afternoon. Good work, I hear. Everyone has high hopes that someone out there will identify her once the likeness appears in the papers."

"News travels quickly," she said.

"Oh, not that quickly." As she arched a brow, he told her, "I'm here to meet Jake. He told me. I would have been there, but I ate something yesterday that did my stomach in."

"I'm sorry. Hope your dinner went down okay."

"It did. You have a sweet—and rather attractive— mother hen in there. She recommended bread, broth and a grilled chicken breast. I'm feeling better already."

"Sharon Dupre," Ashley told him. "Nick's girlfriend. She makes wonderful cookies, too."

"It's a great place. I can see why it's always been so popular. Comfortable atmosphere, near the water and a lot of your uncle's laid-back personality."

"I've always liked it."

"That's good to hear. A lot of young people…they can't wait to move on. Have their own place, you know."

Ashley shrugged. "My parents have been dead since I was very young. I've had a wing of the place to myself since I was ten. Nick and I get along great. I was never a trouble-prone teenager, and he was never a down-your-throat guardian. I love where I live."

"You like the water, too, huh?"

"Love it."

"Old Jake couldn't be dragged away from it," Marty said. Then he laughed. "You sure he hasn't been a pain?"

"No. All right, a little bit—but just to me."

Marty grew serious for a moment, studying her. "He may be trying to help Nick with the guardian bit."

"Why me? It's not like I'm the only woman in law enforcement."

Marty shrugged with rueful knowledge, forming his words carefully. "Before me, Jake had a woman partner, did you know?"

"I had no idea."

"She was a good cop."

"And…?"

"She died."

"Oh, God! How?"

"Her car went into a canal. It was almost five years ago. Right after a series of three really nasty homicides."

Ashley nodded. "I heard about the case when Murray asked me to come down to the morgue today."

Marty nodded. "Jake never believed Nancy Lassiter went into that canal on her own. He was sure she knew something about the murders and was killed because of it. She died of a blunt trauma to the head, which was consistent with the way she would have been thrown against the windshield. She wasn't wearing her seat belt."

"I'm so sorry. That's terrible."

Marty hesitated. He winced, then said, "Maybe I shouldn't be telling you this, because we just met. But there's obviously some tension between you and Jake. You live here, and you'll probably wind up working a lot with him, so I'll dish up some past history. Nancy Lassiter was married. Her husband comes around here now and then, too. There was a lot of friction in the marriage, and Brian—Nancy's husband—was certain she was sleeping with Jake. They *were* close. Jake never gets on a soapbox about the past, but... I guess lots of people in the department thought their relationship was a little *too* close. Anyway, despite all evidence to the contrary, Jake will never accept the fact that Nancy killed herself. He feels a lot of guilt over it for not forcing her to share the information she'd found and she got herself killed because of it. Anyway, the point I'm making here is, you're Nick's niece. Maybe he's afraid you'll get into trouble, too, because you're so determined to prove yourself."

She shook her head. "He ought to be pleased, then. I've taken a step back. I'm going right into civilian employ. I won't become a cop for a long time, not until

I've worked a while, then go back into the academy and finish up."

"Did he know what you were doing today?"

"*I* didn't know what I was doing today—until I was on the way to the morgue."

"Don't worry. It will all shake out."

"Yes, I'm sure it will. And it's a huge force. I'm sure there are lots of cops out there who have to work together and aren't always so terribly fond of each other."

"Sure. And hey, I haven't seen the drawings yet, but I hear that they're beyond good. I'll get to see them soon, though. I'm meeting Jake here in—" He glanced at his watch. "—about five minutes."

"Good. I hope you're happy when you see them. I'm going to run. I have to shower and pick up some friends to go visit another friend in the hospital."

"The kid who was hit on the highway?"

"Yes. You know about it?"

"I dropped Jake off at the hospital the other night. I hear you think there's something fishy about the accident."

"I do."

"Well, be careful, then."

She smiled. She decided she liked Marty a lot. He didn't try to give the same-old, same-old speech about drugs.

"See you, then. And thanks."

She waved and hurried off, crossing the terrace, hopping the rail and hurrying across the grass to her dockside door. She glanced at her own watch, then stripped down, throwing things helter-skelter as she headed for the shower. Once the hot water was pouring down over her, she found herself just standing still, savoring the warmth that seeped into her body. It had been a long day. A triumph, some would say. Except, on a professional level, she knew she was going to have to find a way to stop seeing the image of the dead woman lying on the gurney. This was something she had chosen, something she wanted to do, and she couldn't let this haunt her.

She just felt…fractured inside. Attracted to someone with the kind of almost ridiculous passion and urgency she hadn't felt since…ever. It was akin to a high school crush, but she wasn't in school. She'd been crazy if she'd thought she could indulge her senses in one night and walk away unscathed. Insane. She'd been drawn to him ever since they'd had the run-in with the coffee.

She forced herself to turn the water off, towel dry furiously and get dressed. She decided to go through the restaurant quickly and let Nick know she was home, that she was leaving, and that she had a million things to tell him about her day, but not until later.

As she walked through the restaurant, she saw that Katie, a long-time server and more or less assistant manager was behind the bar. She waved to Ashley, looking relieved to see her. "Hey, can you help on the floor?"

"Oh, Katie," she said with dismay. She liked the woman a lot. Of Irish descent, she had dark eyes, dark hair and beautiful creamy skin. She had a gift for laughter—and for getting things done. Somewhere around forty, she had lost her husband, a firefighter, over ten years ago, and raised a family of five on her own by working for Nick. Her children, once they had become teenagers, had come in now and then to bus tables. "Katie, I'm sorry, but I really can't. I'm picking people up to go to the hospital. I have a friend—"

"I know, I know, that's where Nick and Sharon have gone," Katie said with a sigh. "There was no one here— no one at all—and I told them that if they felt like going down to see your friend's folks, they should do it. And now, it's getting busy."

Sandy was sitting at the bar. "Keep your apron on, Katie. I'll get the food out."

"Sandy, you're a customer," Katie said firmly.

"I'm not a customer—I'm a fixture," he said with a grin. "Get out of here, Ashley. And mind you, I expect payment for this."

"Of course."

"I don't mean money. I want to hear about your new career."

She looked at him, startled.

"Nick has cops for customers, remember?" he said, grinning.

She gave him a kiss on the cheek. "I'll pay you off big-time. I'll talk your ears off," she assured him. Katie gave her a wave. She left then, choosing to go through the office and the house to the parking lot, rather than risk seeing Jake Dilessio out on the terrace with his partner.

Karen was outside waiting for her when she got to her friend's house.

"I know, I'm late."

"Just by a few minutes," Karen said. "Not late at all for normal people, but since you've got such a talent for being on time…"

"I think I'm beginning to fall off on that punctuality thing," Ashley murmured.

"Hey, you have the right. What a week, huh? I called the hospital a little while ago. They won't give much information over the phone, but it seems Stu is holding his own, anyway."

"Yes, he's hanging in there."

"So tell me, did you get some rest and relaxation this afternoon?" Karen demanded.

"No. I went on my first assignment."

"You're kidding!"

"No. Let's get Jan, and then I'll tell you all about it."

They had to beep a few times; then Jan came running out to the car, apologizing, telling them that she'd been on the phone, pretending she was her own publicity agent, trying to get a promotion together for a concert. They all laughed when she treated them to her "publicity agent voice." Then Karen told her that Ashley had already had her first assignment, and Ashley explained how she'd spent her afternoon.

"Ugh!" Jan announced from the back.

"What do you mean, ugh?" Karen demanded. "Yesterday she was a nobody. Today she's a working forensic artist."

"The artist part is great," Jan said. "But will you get to sketch live people?"

"Sure. Witnesses will tell me about someone they saw at a crime scene and I'll sketch them. This was… they couldn't put a photo of the woman in the paper, not the way she looked."

They talked about Ashley's job for a few minutes more, then Jan said, "They won't actually let us in to see Stu, will they?"

"I got in the other night. The Fresias told the hospital staff I was a relative."

"Think, he can have another couple of cousins?" Karen asked.

"Maybe. Hey, you know what, though? I went to tell Nick I was headed down here, and Katie told me Nick and Sharon were already on their way."

"To the hospital?" Jan said.

"Yes."

"I'll bet Sharon is bringing a truckload of food," Karen said.

"Maybe."

"She doesn't even know the Fresias. Of course, Nick does. Remember all the school fairs he worked with Nathan Fresia? They were the only two fathers willing to go in the dunk tank. Okay, Nick was an uncle, but you know what I mean," Jan said.

"Sharon tries really hard to be like…" Karen began.

"Like what?" Ashley glanced over to the passenger seat to meet Karen's eyes.

"Like a stepmother, I guess. I mean, she goes out of her way to…to be around. Part of the family."

Ashley shrugged. "She doesn't need to impress me. I'm twenty-five, all grown up."

"But you're everything to Nick," Jan put in.

"And," Karen said, "she's running for local office."

Ashley laughed. "You think she makes us cookies and visits people in the hospital to get a political wedge in?"

"Who knows?" Karen said.

"Well, who cares?" Jan said. "They're darn good cookies."

"She wouldn't need to butter up the Fresias," Ashley said, still amused. "They're not even in the same district."

"True," Karen agreed. "Okay, maybe she has no ulterior motive at all. Time will tell."

"Hey, by the way, you two are invited out with me and a few fellow academy friends Friday night."

"Ex-academy friends," Karen reminded her. "What's the occasion?"

"We're celebrating my new job."

"Great!"

"Oh, yeah," Jan agreed dryly. "Now she gets to draw corpses. Ugh."

"Jan, remember, one man's trash is another man's treasure."

"Yeah, and it's too bad she isn't sketching trash."

"Who knows? She may get to sketch trash one day."

Ashley groaned and pulled into the parking garage, frowning. "Hey, you know what happened the other night?" she said, then went on to tell them about the person who had stalked her.

"Great. Now she tells us," Karen said.

"Ashley, they were scrubs? It was probably someone who worked at the hospital, just in a hurry to get to their car," Jan said.

"Jan, I went through that with the cops," Ashley said.

Jan shrugged, and Ashley shook her head. Her own friend was thinking like all the others. "Jan, I know when I'm being chased."

"Then Karen is right—great," she said sarcastically. "We're parking in the same garage, right?"

"I'm sure if someone was stalking people in the garage then, they've moved on by now. Especially since Ashley called the police. Hey, did you hear anything back?"

"Not yet, and I'm afraid I didn't pursue it."

She parked the car and they all got out. The three of them looked around uneasily.

"We're close to the elevator," Ashley said. "And there are three of us."

"And she's almost a cop," Karen said.

"Not anymore," Jan protested. "Ashley, did you bring your gun?"

"Actually...no. I'm supposed to turn my gun and badge in. I'm a civilian employee now."

"It's all right. It's not like we're alone," Jan said, indicating a large party heading toward the elevator. They were equipped with flowers, packages and a large balloon that announced "It's a Boy!"

Smiling, everyone crowded into the elevator together. In a few minutes they were walking down the hall to the ICU waiting room. When they walked in, they saw that Lucy was there with Nick and Sharon. All three looked up, stood and came forward to greet them. Karen and Jan gave Lucy Fresia their warmest hugs, and Lucy thanked them all for being such good friends.

"I can't believe the support we've received," Lucy said. "Nick has been great. And Sharon. A new friend, but a kind one. We get to have shrimp for dinner tonight, and home-baked cookies."

"Her cookies are the best," Ashley said, grinning at Sharon, who smiled in return.

"I pay her to say that," Sharon teased.

"Is that your dinner in the bag over there?" Ashley asked. "Where's Nathan? You two should go eat while it's hot."

"I'll just go get him, Ashley, now that you're here. I can't help but feel that Stuart knows when his friends are with him." She glanced at Karen and Jan. She shrugged. "They'll know I'm lying, but we'll just say Stu has a few more relatives. Excuse me, and I'll talk to the nurse. Nick, Sharon, will you join us in the cafeteria?"

"Lucy, I'd love to stay," Nick said. "I should get back to the bar, though."

"Yes, we should get going," Sharon agreed.

Nick gave Ashley and the girls a quick peck on the cheek. Jan nudged Ashley and whispered, "I was hoping he'd be around to walk us back to the car."

Karen nudged Jan. "It's all right. Ashley may not have her gun, but I have mace in my purse."

"What's the whispering about?" Sharon asked. "Is everything all right?"

"Yes, it's fine," Ashley lied quickly. She didn't want to say anything to either of them about what had happened the other night. "I have to admit, I'm glad you're heading back. Katie seemed to be in a bit of a bind, and I felt guilty leaving her."

"I've got to get more help," Nick murmured.

"Sandy was pitching in."

"Sandy?" Nick said.

"Hey, he probably knows what everyone in that place drinks better than we do," Sharon assured him. "All right, girls, drive carefully, okay?"

Lucy reappeared with Nathan, who greeted them all warmly, his pleasure at seeing his son's friends apparent. At his urging, Nick and Sharon agreed to join him and Lucy in the cafeteria for a few minutes, even though Nick looked a little impatient. Ashley wished that she hadn't spoken.

"Girls, only two at a time, but they've let me give them the relative story," Lucy advised them. "And we won't be gone long," she said a little anxiously.

"We'll be here when you get back," Jan said.

The older couples left, and Ashley said, "You two go on in. I got to see him yesterday."

Karen nodded, and she and Jan started down the hall. Ashley looked around, saw a magazine, picked it up and took a seat.

Until then, she had barely noticed the man in the waiting room with the paper in front of him. Once she was seated, she nearly jumped when he put his paper down and joined her.

He was the man Nathan had pointed out, the obnoxious reporter.

"What do you want?" she demanded sharply. She didn't bother to keep her voice down, since they were the only people left in the waiting room.

"Don't yell," he said. "Everyone thinks I'm out to write a sordid story. Even the Fresias don't want to believe I'm a friend of their son's."

"*I've* never met you," she told him.

"Yeah, well, and how much of Stuart have you seen lately?" he demanded.

That hit home.

"Why don't they believe you're his friend?"

He sighed. "Because I write for a tabloid even though they know that he was selling stuff to the same paper. I don't know, maybe they feel I'm responsible. I think they know I introduced Stuart to the managing editor, and that's when he disappeared from their lives. They had the police question me, and man, did they question me. I guess I'm just not the Fresias' type. They don't trust me. Unfortunately, I'm famous for headlines like *I was spirited away by aliens who kidnapped my two-headed child.*"

"Wow. What journalism."

"Hey, it pays the bills, you know?"

"If you knew Stuart and have an idea what he was doing, why didn't you tell the police?"

"I did tell them. I told them he told me he was interested in the economy, agriculture and what big business was doing to the Everglades. And that's what he was doing. Finding out about the waterways, pollution… you know, an environmental piece. But he was really excited. He thought he had something going that was much bigger. The thing is, I have no idea who he was after, and what I can't figure is how he was looking into the environment and wound up on drugs."

Ashley took a good look at him. He was about her own age, with medium brown hair, rather long. His eyes were large, very blue, and sincere. He was in a tailored shirt and jacket, and seemed both too concerned and far too intelligent to be writing about two-headed alien babies.

"I talked to the police, and they talked to the managing editor. I knew the names of a few local bigwigs Stu had been talking to before he went completely undercover. The police talked to them, but can you believe it? They all came out as pure as the driven snow. After that the police told me to shut up and butt out. I doubt I'll ever be able to tell the police anything they'd take seriously."

"So why are you talking to me? Why would I want to get involved with you, when you've done nothing but cause trouble?"

He shrugged and grinned, a nice, rueful grin. "I heard you're in the academy, and I know you don't believe that Stu was a dope addict. So I figured if anybody would really be able to fight for him, it would be you."

She studied him. He seemed sincere. He'd tried to help, and it had backfired on him.

He believed in Stuart. That mattered to her. And though she knew better than to make snap judgments, she couldn't help but feel he was more ethical than Nathan Fresia believed.

She smiled at last. "Sorry. I'm afraid I'm not in the academy anymore."

He frowned. "You washed out? I can't believe it. Not after everything Stu said about you."

"He talked about me to you?"

"Yeah, you know, just casual conversation. We went by your uncle's place one night—maybe a year ago. You weren't there. Your uncle wasn't even working. But he talked about what good friends you'd been growing up, and that he needed to give you a call so you two could get together. The bartender said you were looking into the academy." He gave her another sincere smile. "I'd like to help. I'm a good investigator."

"And you think that you can come up with something the police can't?"

"I already have," he told her.

Chapter 13

Jake was still sitting on the terrace; Marty had been gone a good twenty minutes. Catching him up on things hadn't taken long. He'd told him he'd gotten the urge to go back to the property where the cult had once had its headquarters. The farmer who owned the place now had been more than agreeable to letting him walk around. His neatly plotted fields ended where the canal began. Jake had stared at the water for a long time, reflecting that the property was a long way from where the latest victim had been found.

It was only a few miles west of where Nancy's car had gone into the canal, though. Not that there was anything strange in that. Most of the residential homesteads and farms in the southwest sector of the county had been forged out of the Everglades. Canals and waterways were a major part of the ecosystem. They crisscrossed the entire area.

The farmer's wife had come up to him as he'd been walking around.

"We bought this place for a song, you know," she told him, her eyes anxious. "You don't think that's because we'll stumble on a corpse one day, do you?"

"I certainly hope not," Jake had told her.

Even Marty had wondered what he'd thought he would find now, when People for Principle had been gone for so many years.

"I don't know. I just know that we're staring right at something and we're still not seeing it," Jake had said. Marty didn't buy it. But then, Marty hadn't been with him when he'd talked to Bordon and heard him talk about smoke and mirrors.

So he'd moved on to the task force meeting, then his trip to the morgue.

"The drawing will run in the paper tomorrow. And when it does, we'll have something. I'm certain," Jake had finished.

Marty had stared at him strangely. "The sketches were that good, huh?"

"Exceptional. If she was from around here, we'll get something back."

"So why were you such an ass to the artist?"

Jake had stiffened. "She told you that?"

"No. I just…well, hell, Jake, I'm a detective, too. I can read people."

Soon after that, Marty left. Jake had stayed, staring at his empty coffee cup.

"Hey, Jake. Can I buy you a beer?" Sandy said.

Jake gave a start. Where had the old guy come from?

"On the house," Sandy added proudly. "I'm helping out tonight."

"How come?"

"Everyone's at the hospital, seeing that kid."

"Nick and Sharon, too?"

"Yep. So Katie's running the joint, and I'm pitching in."

"They went together?" Jake asked, wondering why it mattered.

"No, no, Nick had it in his head to go before Ashley even got home. I think Sharon put the little bee in his bonnet. She'd been baking again. Thought the parents could use something warm and home-cooked. So she and Nick took off first. Ash was picking up a couple of friends, I think. What about that beer?"

"Thanks, Sandy, but no. I've got work to do. I'm not even sure why I'm still sitting here."

"The mind is working, Jake."

"Not working hard enough, I'm afraid."

Sandy looked hesitant, his white furry brows drawn into a frown. "Hey, Jake," he said quietly, "this ain't any of my business, but…take it easy on yourself. Everyone knows you…well, hell, that you still feel responsible for your old partner, and that this new case you've got going is bringing it up all over again, like a smack in the face."

"Sandy, you know too much."

"I don't have much to do except take interest in those around me. You're a good man, a real good man, but give yourself a break. Everyone makes mistakes, and everyone gets down. I saw you in here with Brian Lassiter the other night. He's the asshole who cheated on his wife, made her miserable, so…even if you were—" Sandy broke off.

"You weren't responsible, Jake. And sometime you're going to have to let it go."

"Thanks for the advice, Sandy, and the support." He rose. "I'll take you up on that beer another time."

"Sure, take me up on it when I'm going to have to pay."

"Wouldn't want to insult you by implying you couldn't afford it," Jake told him, grinning. He wandered down the dock until he reached the *Gwendolyn*. As was his custom lately, he checked the lock and the door before inserting his key. He still hadn't gotten around to changing the lock.

Inside, he logged on to the computer, called up a list of names, scrolled down. John Mast. That one jumped out at him.

But Mast was dead.

Smoke and mirrors.

Fifteen minutes later, he realized he was just staring at the screen.

Damn it, everyone out there thought he was blowing smoke. An accident. It was the logical conclusion in Nancy's death. But he just knew...

He knew. Hell, he knew.

And he was doing the same damned thing to Ashley Montague that other people were doing to him.

Being sane, logical, reasonable. But sometimes being sane, logical and reasonable meant shit.

Thoughtfully, he switched off his computer.

"Shit! Sorry," the man at Ashley's side said suddenly, rising. She noticed then what he had already heard, the sound of people coming down the hall. "I've got to go."

"No!" Ashley said. He'd started something here, and

even if he wrote for a rag of a paper, alarm bells were ringing in her head. She stood, as well. "You can't go yet. You didn't tell me—"

"I've got to get out of here before someone thinks I'm harassing you."

"Oh, no, you don't! I have to hear whatever else you have to say."

"I'll find you again, don't worry," he said, already at the doorway.

"Wait, damn it!" She followed him quickly to the door, but to her frustration, he'd already managed to disappear down the hallway. She saw the Fresias coming back. Nick and Sharon weren't with them; they'd probably headed back to the bar.

"That was quick," she said.

"We don't like to be gone long," Lucy explained.

"Karen and Jan are still in there with Stuart," Ashley told them. "I'll just walk down and see if they're ready to come out."

"Take your time, sweetheart. I'm going to go in later and sleep in that recliner they've got. Nathan is going to head home to shower and change, see to a few things and come back. I'll do the same thing in the morning."

Ashley excused herself and went down the hall and replaced Jan and Karen by Stuart's side. There was no change in Stuart's condition, but she felt a little encouraged to see that his color seemed to have improved. She took his hand, the one without the IV needle, and told him about her day. She talked to him about Dilessio, admitting the stupid surge of desire that had sent her over in the night, and her feeling of being an idiot now. But in her confidential whispers to him, she also admitted that she was fascinated, she was a fool...she couldn't help it. She told him how sometimes, you met someone who appealed to you, who attracted you…and made you care, just when you shouldn't. When she was done, she was quiet for a moment, out of things to say.

"Oh! Some friend of yours from the paper—well, he claims to be a friend of yours—started telling me something. I don't even know his name, but I can find out. I won't ask your dad, though, 'cuz he really doesn't like him. I want to talk to him again."

She glanced at her watch. She'd been with him for longer than she'd thought. But it had been a relief to pour out her heart to a friend, even though he was unconscious. She had never been able to talk easily about personal, intimate matters, not even to Jan and Karen, who were always quick to solicit others' opinions about their love lives.

"I'm going to get out of here so your mom can come in and get some sleep." She kissed him on the forehead, squeezed his hand, held it a moment, then left.

When she reached the waiting room, she was startled to see that Len Green had joined the others there.

"Hey," she said.

"Hey back. I thought I'd come show solidarity. I told the Fresias I'm just a beat cop, but if I can do anything, they're more than welcome to let me know."

"Great. That was really nice of you."

"And now we have an escort through the parking garage," Jan said happily.

"A tall, handsome escort," Karen said lightly. "Who has his gun."

"You need a gun in the parking garage?" Lucy said, troubled.

"Oh, you know, dark and shadowy out there," Ash-

ley said, frowning at Karen. She didn't want the Fresias worrying about her coming to see Stuart at night.
"We'll get out of here now, let you get your rest," she
told the Fresias. Goodbye hugs and kisses were shared
all around, and they departed.

"Ashley," Karen said, when they stepped out of the
elevator into the parking garage, "don't you think you
should tell the Fresias you thought you were being
stalked in the parking garage?"

"You didn't tell me anything about that," Len said
reproachfully.

"I never had a chance," Ashley told him. "And what
am I going to say? Everyone thinks I'm nuts, thinking
I was being stalked by someone in hospital greens in
a hospital."

"I've never thought you were nuts," Len told her.

"I don't want them to worry needlessly. They've got
enough going on," Ashley said.

As they walked, Karen suddenly came to a dead stop.
"Shush!" she said.

"What?" Jan demanded.

"Footsteps. Coming this way."

"I *am* armed," Len said. He spoke in a low tone.
Then they fell silent.

"They're coming from the elevator," Karen whispered.

"Can you see?" Jan asked.

"Too many pillars in the way," Ashley murmured.

"Stay still," Len commanded, reaching beneath his
windbreaker. He must be wearing a shoulder holster,
Ashley thought.

"They're still coming this way," Karen breathed.

Yes, they were, Ashley thought. But they were firm, not *stalking* footsteps.

A figure appeared, coming closer, silhouetted by a spill of light from the overhead fluorescent lights.

Tall, dark…broad-shouldered.

Then he stepped closer and was illuminated by the full pool of the light.

"Jake Dilessio," Ashley said, exhaling.

He saw them as they saw him, and his long strides continued in a no-nonsense fashion in their direction.

"It's that guy you were drawing," Karen said.

"He's a cop," Len said.

Ashley stared at him then. "You know him? Why didn't you tell me he was a cop when we were in Orlando?"

He frowned at her. "I don't know what you're talking about. He was in Orlando?"

"No, no, I drew a picture of him. That night, at the club."

Len was still frowning, totally puzzled.

"When I did the other sketches," she said.

"He was paying the bill, Ash," Karen said.

Then they all fell silent as he reached them.

"Detective Dilessio," Len said. "What are you doing here?"

Dilessio arched a brow at Len. "I came by to check on Stuart Fresia. How about you?"

"Ditto. I'm a friend of Ashley's," Len explained.

"I see."

"And these are two of my other friends, Karen and Jan," Ashley said quickly. "I, uh, I didn't know you and Len were acquainted."

They all stared at her.

"They're both cops, Ashley," Karen said.

"There are thousands of cops in the city. They can't all know one another," Ashley said, defending herself quickly.

"I think everyone knows Detective Dilessio. He gave a number of crime scene lectures when I was in the academy," Len said.

"You're working in the south section of town now, right?" Jake asked Len.

He certainly seemed pleasant enough tonight, Ashley thought. Not the ogre she had encountered at the morgue.

"Yes, sir, I am."

"You still like the work?"

"Absolutely."

"Did you find out anything new to tell the Fresias?" Ashley asked.

Dilessio turned his dark eyes on her. "No, I'm sorry. But I went by to tell them I'd spoken to Carnegie and would do what I could. They told me that you had just left. I was hoping to catch you."

"Oh?"

"I can see you're with friends, though. We can talk later."

"I'm dropping off Karen and Jan, and heading back to Nick's," she said.

"Great. I'll take off and talk to you later. Karen, Jan, a pleasure to meet you. Len, nice to see you."

"You, too, Detective," Len said.

Dilessio walked off.

"What was that all about?"

"I did a sketch for him today. He probably wants something redone."

"He shouldn't track you down on your off hours for something like that," Len said indignantly.

"No…no… I asked him to see if he could come up with any information on Stuart's case for me," Ashley explained quickly. "But I'm sure I can catch him when I get back to Nick's."

"Hey, if you want to get back quickly, we can just grab a cab," Karen said.

Len stepped in gallantly with the obvious. "Don't be silly. We can escort Ashley to her car, and then I'll be happy to drive you both home."

"Len, you're a sweetheart. Are you sure you don't mind?" Ashley asked. "I really am anxious to find out what he wanted."

"Sure, no problem."

They walked her to her car, and as soon as she had managed to say goodbye, she was gone.

She had a hard time sticking near the speed limit. She couldn't wait to get home.

Len Green dropped Jan off first. Then, once he was alone with Karen, he took the conversation to a more personal level.

"Ashley's doing really well in the department, even if she's going to be a civilian employee for a while. Dilessio is one of the most respected men on the force."

"And a hunk, too," Karen commented, then turned to him. "Not that everyone likes the brooding type, you know. I mean, I'm not sure he's the type to ever loosen up, just have fun. I don't even know the guy. But… well, you know…he seems very serious. And take you. You're a cop, dedicated to your work, but yet look how much fun we had the other night. I hope I remembered to thank you for such a great evening."

Len smiled at her. "You did," he said softly. She was close to him. Friendly, warm…eager? He suddenly wanted to know her better. A lot better. "So…you're coming with us to celebrate Ashley's promotion, huh?"

"Of course, since we're invited. We don't mean to horn in."

"You won't be horning in at all."

"There's my place," Karen pointed out.

He pulled into the driveway. "Cute little place. You live alone?"

"I do. It's not a mansion, but I own it. Well, the bank and I own it."

"Great."

"Want to come in and see it?"

"I'd love to. Are you sure it isn't too late?"

"No, no, not at all. I get up about six-thirty every morning, but I never go to sleep before midnight. Please, come on in. I can make coffee, tea…whatever. Or you're welcome to a beer. Whoops, sorry, you're a cop, and you're driving…."

"We could have a beer—and then the coffee," Len said.

Karen smiled slowly. "Sure."

They went in. Karen proudly showed him her place. It was small, but nice, and old, considering the area.

"There are a number of places from the late twenties around here. Back then, of course, we would have been in the boondocks, the eye of the swamp. No, what am I saying? The Everglades isn't really a swamp since the water is always moving."

He laughed. "I get what you mean."

"Well, I'll get that beer…and put the coffee on for after," Karen said.

She got the beer, turned on the stereo, and they sat on the antique sofa in her living room, talking about their jobs. After a while, she caught him staring at his empty bottle. "I'd offer you another, but…driving under the influence and all."

"Well, yeah, another glass would be good, but…"

"Hey, this is a fold-out bed. You're welcome to stay."

She was right beside him, her long legs curled beneath her. Their faces were close. He touched her chin. "I don't know that I could make myself stay on the sofa," he said softly.

He heard the soft inhalation of her breath. "I'm not sure I'd want you to stay on the sofa," she told him.

He leaned close and kissed her lightly. When they broke apart, her lips were moist, her breathing erratic.

"I'll get you that beer," she murmured.

She disappeared in the kitchen for what seemed like a long time. Then he heard her call his name, and he turned. She was in the doorway to the bedroom. No subterfuge. She was naked. Long, lean, beautiful—and naked.

He wondered why he felt such a sudden surge of fury.

Seemed like all women were sluts these days.

The tension in him increased.

He rose, feeling his fingers knot at his sides in anger.

"I've got your beer in here," she said. Soft voice, sexy, sensual.

Slut.

"Is it?" he replied, just as softly. She left the doorway. He followed. She had moved to the bed and she was stretched out invitingly. He stared at her for a long moment, feeling every muscle in his body tighten. This was Ashley's friend. *Ashley.*

"Officer?" she teased softly.

He moved toward her. And then she screamed.

But only for an instant.

Ashley parked her car in her spot, then went around the back, hoping the terrace would be empty. A few of the tables held customers, but they all seemed to be couples, out for an intimate evening. She ignored the walkway to the terrace and hurried along the path to the docks instead.

As she neared Jake's houseboat, she slowed her footsteps, hesitant. He had said he wanted to talk to her, but still, she felt awkward.

She didn't realize she was barely inching forward, her steps silent. She stared at the boat. The drapes were drawn, but she was certain the lights were on inside. An uneasy feeling crept over her, and she moved more slowly still.

When she reached the boat, her heart was hammering. She stepped carefully from the dock to the deck, then stood still for several long seconds before she walked to the door, hesitated, then raised her hand to knock. The door swung inward.

She'd been wrong. There were no lights on inside. Just as she was ready to call out his name, she heard a whoosh of noise, a warning that came too late. She tried to turn, tried to scream but she was caught from behind, unable to see a face, the breath knocked out of her and her scream turned to a soundless gasp.

She found herself flying through the air, and she landed hard, a massive weight like living rock on top of her. She opened her mouth to scream again, desperately gulping in air, trying to shake off the brilliant burst of stars that had shot through her head when she landed.

A hand clamped over her mouth.

Her scream died in her throat.

Lucy Fresia awoke suddenly, not knowing what had roused her. She looked around the darkened room and saw nothing.

She gave herself a rueful shake, half smiling. Their constant vigil was beginning to wear on her nerves.

She leaned back in her chair. Stuart lay on his bed, in the same position he had maintained since he had been brought in. The room was quiet, the muted night-light dim, and all was silent.

She bolted up suddenly.

Silent.

It shouldn't be silent! She should be hearing the sound of the respirator, that slow, even, constant whooshing that had been a part of her world for what seemed like forever now.

She flew to her son's side. His face was turning blue.

She stared at the monitors. Dead.

Stuart wasn't breathing. His heart wasn't beating.

Dead...

No!

She raced to the door, threw it open and screamed for help. Stuart's nurse came flying down the corridor. She saw the situation and shouted for someone at the nurses' station to call a code. Lucy was shoved out of the way as hospital personnel came running down the hall and into the room.

Lucy started to scream, the life seeming to drain

from her own limbs. She began to sink to the floor, still screaming in disbelief.

Sobs shook her. She couldn't even pray.

She just kept screaming, "No!" until someone came by with a hypodermic needle and stuck it into her arm.

"Ashley?"

The hand moved from her mouth.

"Jake?" she said incredulously.

The living rock moved aside. A hand came down and found hers in the darkness, pulling her to her feet. For a moment, even the darkness seemed to spin.

A light came on, flooding the *Gwendolyn*. She was staring at Jake. He was wearing swim trunks and nothing else. His hands were on his hips, and his eyes were hard. "What the hell were you doing snooping around?" he demanded.

"I wasn't snooping!" she returned indignantly. "You said you wanted to talk. What the hell were *you* doing? Do you beat up everyone who comes to visit you?"

"You were tiptoeing on board. And ever since someone broke in…"

"It was dark. I wasn't sure if you were here, if you were sleeping, if…what do you mean, someone broke in?"

"Someone broke in the other night. And they've been here again. I can tell."

"Were you robbed?"

"Don't be ridiculous."

"Don't tell me not to be ridiculous. That's a perfectly logical supposition. Why would anyone come just to invade the precious domain of the great Detective Dilessio? Just so they can say they were on his houseboat?"

He stared at her with irritation and turned, walking up the few steps to the deck. She followed him. He was pacing the narrow deck surrounding the cabin of the houseboat. He paused, staring down the length of the dock toward Nick's. Ashley stared, too.

Nothing moved.

He turned suddenly. "Are you all right?"

"Sure. I like being body slammed against the floor. And it's just great when your whole head is ringing."

She nearly ducked in fear when he stretched out a hand to touch her. She managed not to. His fingers found her skull and massaged.

"Seriously, are you all right?"

"Shaken, but fine," she said. His tone could change so quickly.

His hand dropped. He stared into the night again.

"Jake, what the hell is going on?"

"I don't know."

"Then...?"

"This is the second time someone has been on the boat."

"And nothing's gone?"

"No. Not that I can see."

"Then why would someone come aboard?"

"I don't know. They must be looking for something."

"What?"

He shook his head. "I don't know."

"Did you lock your door?"

"Yes."

"Was the lock picked?"

"No."

"Then...."

"This time, it's really my own fault. I should have had the locks changed."

She hesitated. "Who else has a key?"

After a long moment, he shrugged. "Nick keeps one."

She felt her spine stiffen, her jaw start to lock. "Nick would never, ever come aboard your boat without your permission. And if you think he's careless with your key, you'd better take the damned thing back. I'm sure the only reason he has your key is so he can help you out, let workmen in when you're not here, or—"

"I have complete and absolute faith in Nick," he interrupted.

She fell silent for a moment. "Then?"

He shrugged. "Years ago... I had another key." His lashes fell over his eyes for a minute. "My partner had one. A long time ago. Not Marty...a different partner."

"The woman who died?" Ashley said softly.

His eyes pinned hers. "Yes." He looked back to the lights that softly illuminated the area around the bar. Then he shrugged again. "I didn't even think about it then. I didn't think about it at all...until recently. I thought her husband might have it...but he denies it."

"Maybe he's not telling the truth."

"Maybe he's not."

"Why don't you get a fingerprint team out here, see if they can find anything?"

He nodded, but he didn't seem convinced.

His eyes touched hers. "I'm willing to bet whoever's been aboard the *Gwendolyn* won't have left any prints. Whoever it is was wearing gloves."

Ashley was silent for a minute. "Nothing was missing when you came in, but you're certain someone has been aboard. Wearing gloves. I really don't want to doubt you, but do you think you could be feeling a little paranoid because…well, because an old case that most people considered over and done has arisen again?"

He smiled, a little ruefully, and said, "No, I'm not paranoid, though I may be a little obsessive/compulsive. I live alone. I know where things are. And I know when they've shifted…just a little. You know, things have moved. The papers on my desk are at more of an angle. The rug at the bottom of the stairs is off a fraction of an inch. Stuff like that."

"But why?"

"I don't know. Someone must think I have something. But I don't have the least idea what."

He turned and started back inside the houseboat. She frowned, watching him. He paused and turned back. "Are you coming?"

"I, well, I just came because—"

He'd already gone back into the cabin. She slowly followed him.

"Are you staying?" he asked her.

She was startled by the bluntness of the question. She didn't know whether to be indignant that he had tackled her, concerned that he seemed so convinced his living space had been invaded, or simply angry that they could be so intimate that they should, at the very least, be friends— and that he had treated her like garbage at the morgue.

"Why did you want to talk to me?" she asked, forcing a certain sharpness into her voice.

He arched a brow. "To apologize, of course."

Her outrage melted like ice on a summer's day. She shouldn't have been so quick to forgive.

"Are you staying?" he repeated.

She found herself nodding.

Chapter 14

Jake stepped toward her, and she found herself in his arms. His lips were almost bruising, lava wet and hot, and his tongue did things to the inside of her mouth that seemed to lick into her insides. He made love with a kiss in a way that touched her where he did not, made her ache inside, wanting, longing, hoping to prolong, desperate to have everything, *him, inside her*, instantly. She struggled to put some distance between them. The hardness of his erection was instantly evident beneath the thin fabric of the bathing trunks he wore. Her fingers rimmed the elastic band, lowering it, eliciting a low groan like a growl from the back of his throat, even as his tongue thrust more deeply into her mouth. He continued to kiss her, his own hands moving beneath the fabric of her knit blouse, beneath the lace of her bra, fingers moving against her flesh, finding the nipple, rotating with an erotic pressure over and around it. She somewhat fought the sensations, intent on her own quest, until her hands closed around him. Stroked. He was smooth, pulsing like thunder.

Their kiss broke; her blouse wound up over her head, tossed somewhere within the cabin. Then his lips were at her throat. She clung to his shoulders, aware she was off the ground, then sitting on the kitchen counter as the clasp of her bra was set free with a deft movement. She struggled to kick off her shoes, aware of his hands on the button of her jeans. She was suddenly sliding against him as he dipped both his hands beneath the denim of her pants, cupping her buttocks as he slid the jeans from her body. His trunks were already on the floor. She was lifted high again, his arms locked around her, then lowered onto the pulsing heat of his erection and held there against him for several long seconds before she found herself seated on the counter again, the world spinning around, aware of nothing but the insanity of needing him there, part of her, hard and vibrant within her. Tears sprang to her eyes as she gave herself up to the urgency of wanting him. Her arms were so tightly wrapped around his shoulders that he had to strain to set her away far enough that he could press his lips to her shoulders, seize her breath, tempt her with the hotness of lips, teeth and tongue, devour her with hands and mouth, even as the erotic tempo maddened to insanity.

A bomb could have exploded outside and she wouldn't have known. The sound and pulse of her heart eclipsed reality. She was only vaguely aware of their damp flesh, the ripple and stretch of his muscle and form against her, the reality of the counter on which she sat. She was locked around him, tense, desperate, sounds escaping her, no words. She strived and arched, pressed, writhed, with ever greater insanity, touching sweetness, reaching higher until she tightened around him in a vise, spiraling into a climax so volatile, she was amazed not to feel herself fly apart. As he shuddered into climactic expulsion himself, his grip upon her was a powerful force that locked them together in a seizure of shattering ecstasy that seemed to rip through them both like violent waves of aftershock.

Her head fell against his shoulder. She couldn't be sorry she had forgiven so easily, fallen so quickly, for she didn't think that she'd ever been touched so tenderly as when he lifted her against him and held her like a cocoon of silk, maneuvering the few steps to his cabin as if he held the most precious cargo. She landed on his bed, which was still disheveled from the night before, and a second later he was lying beside her. His arms curled around her, and she smiled. After several moments, she turned back to him.

His eyes were hard and serious, and for a moment she was caught in whatever deeper emotion darkened his stare, but she found she had to ask softly, "I forgot to ask whether you were apologizing for tackling me when I came aboard or for being such a jerk when I saw you at the morgue."

A bit alarmed by her own statement, she held her breath, uncomfortably aware of everything physical around them, the feel of the bed and the sheets, the damp power of his arms around her, the planes of his face, the fall of his hair, the darkness of his eyes.

"Both," he said after a moment. He reached over, moving a damp lock of hair that had glued itself to her cheek. "Both. You took me by surprise this afternoon.

I didn't even know you owned a pencil, much less had such an incredible talent. I guess I was angry because I should have known. Come to think of it, you owe me an apology."

"*I* owe you an apology?"

"You could have told me that you were considering a move from the academy into the civilian force."

"Well…" Her voice sounded scratchy. "It's not like we've been best friends for years or anything. As if I really know you…or you know me."

She was surprised by the ruefulness of the smile that touched his lips.

"Maybe I felt I did know you a bit. I mean, think about it. How many guys in the force know you have a tiny flower tattoo at the base of your spine? Or about that little scar on the inside of your upper thigh?"

She flushed, wishing she didn't do so with such embarrassing speed.

"Actually, I wasn't certain you even liked me."

He laughed, pulling her closer. "You do have one hell of a temper on you, Ms. Montague." His laughter faded; his eyes were serious. "And the tenacity of a bull terrier."

"And you're pure walking tact and charm?"

He shrugged. "You scalded me, you know."

"I see no scars. Nothing permanent."

He was silent for a long moment. Then he said quietly, "More permanent than you know." The simple statement left her with a strange feeling of euphoria. And his lips brushing against hers were more intimate, it seemed, than anything they had previously shared.

The kiss deepened. He pulled away, leaned on an elbow, studying her.

"I didn't know that's what I was going to do. I hadn't even decided to take the position when we…when I saw you. I had a meeting this morning to find out more about it. I couldn't have said anything, because I didn't know anything." He remained silent, watching her. She was talking too much, she knew, as if she had to keep going. "I know seeing me there, doing something so important for your investigation… I'm sure it was surprising. But I didn't know a thing about it until we were on the way to the morgue. I was an art major for a long time. And…well, usually people have a relationship first and then sex, rather than sex and then…"

Her voice trailed off. She still wasn't sure they had a relationship.

"Ms. Montague?"

"Yes?"

"Shut up," he commanded before his lips touched hers again. The tenderness was still there, along with a raw edge of urgency. And with that one touch, she was electrified. She turned into his arms, pressed her lips to his flesh. And felt his tongue moving into her mouth with that intimacy that seemed to suggest the most carnal acts to follow. She was bathed in the warmth of his body, the extraordinary expertise of his lightest touch, and the greater force of the urgency replaced sensual finesse. She lost all concept of time, place or reality. Later, as she lay quietly at his side once again, she drifted to sleep, awakened, knew that he, too, was awake.

"Jake?"

"Yeah?"

"How come you came to the hospital tonight? Have you learned anything?"

"No, I'm sorry." He didn't turn toward her.

"But you believe me? That there's got to be more behind what happened to Stuart?"

He was silent for a few moments, then turned toward her. "Ashley... I don't know what to believe. I do know that Carnegie is a good cop. I can do some investigating on my own, especially where that paper he'd been freelancing for is concerned, but...you have to think long and hard about whether what you're feeling is absolutely solid, or if..."

"If what?"

He rose on one elbow as he spoke seriously. "If maybe you just feel a certain guilt or something because you slept with him and then lost touch."

She felt as if she'd been drenched with a bucket of ice water. She stiffened, coming up one elbow so she was face to face with him. She was *not* going to dignify his incorrect assumption by even responding to it. "Oh, really? The way you think there are people breaking into your boat but really it's all tied up with the fact that you were sleeping with your partner?"

She was startled by the violence of his reaction. Not that he touched her. But he withdrew with such force that it felt as if a whirlwind had gone through the bedroom. Up and on his feet, he padded out of the cabin naked, presumably in search of his swim trunks.

Ashley lay there for several seconds, feeling the sudden chill in the air. She bit her lip, sat up and decided that their insane, instantaneous, affair—was over. As to what emotion that evoked in her heart...she couldn't even fathom it. She just knew that she had to get out.

She reached for her clothing and realized that it, too, was all over the living room. Summoning what dignity she could, she walked out of the bedroom, taking the two steps down to the living area. The door to the deck was open. A soft breeze was drifting in, touched with the scent of the salt and the sea. As she searched frantically for her things, she was startled when she heard him speak.

"Don't go."

She'd just found her bra. She turned and stood at the sound of his voice and cracked her temple against the counter. He reentered the cabin, closing the door behind him. He walked straight to her, heedless of the scrap of clothing she was clutching over her chest. His palms cupped her skull, and he looked into her eyes. "Don't go. I'd like you to listen to me, if you're willing." She nodded as best she could with his fingers threaded so tensely through her hair. He wasn't hurting her; she didn't want him to think that he was.

"I'm listening," she said softly.

"I never slept with Nancy. Never. I don't know who told you I did, but it doesn't matter—a lot of people thought we were an item. But it never happened. She was married. I was in love with her, yes, but we never slept together. We came close a few times, but one or the other of us always withdrew. She, because she still believed in her vows. Me, because I loved her. And she had to either make it with Brian or decide on a divorce without me being involved. She really was one of my best friends. I knew her like I've seldom known anyone in my life. I stick like glue to my conviction that something's going on because I knew her—not because I slept with her. She didn't commit suicide. And she didn't decide to go out for a wild night of drinking and drugs because she was depressed. I don't care what the police psychologist considers a plausible scenario. That's not what happened."

He stopped speaking. His eyes had such an intense quality. They could give away nothing, or, like now, they could blaze with vehemence and conviction.

"Do you know what?" she said.

He started, frowning slightly, expecting a different reaction.

"What?"

"I never slept with Stuart. He was my friend, my best friend."

The fingers knotting in her hair eased. And he smiled slowly. "Hmm. I guess that means I'm supposed to be sorry again."

"Yeah, you should be."

"I *am* sorry. You were so passionate in his defense, but I should have realized that could have been because of friendship. We're more alike than I'd ever begun to realize," he said. She found herself released. "I'm going to lock up and set the timer on the coffee for the morning."

"Okay."

She stood still, letting the bra she had retrieved drop back to the floor.

A moment later, the houseboat was secured and the coffee had been set for the following morning. In the bedroom, Ashley found herself telling Jake about her friendship with Stuart, how she had adored his parents.

"So you two were that close but never high school sweeties?" he queried.

She laughed. "It was a big public school," she reminded him. "We all hung in the same crowd. We weren't the wild crowd, we weren't quite nerds. I had a thing for a football player, though. Stu made this announcement about it. I was totally humiliated, but the guy liked it, and we went together for several years. I guess that was my big high school romance."

"But it ended?"

"Oh, you bet. He wound up being the biggest, most insufferable jerk I'd ever met."

"Including me?"

She smiled ruefully. "Well, you did remind me of him a bit. He wanted to get married right after school. Live at Nick's with me, and let me work to put him through college. He had a football scholarship, but it didn't pay for everything. He thought art was a hobby, not a career. And he thought he should be able to go to bars, hang out with the guys—and the college girls, of course— because he was a guy. I should have been grateful just to have a guy like him and turn a blind eye to whatever he did. Luckily for me, in those insane moments when I was ready to buy into his line, Stuart was there, telling me I was an idiot if I didn't see my own value, that I'd be insane not to pursue art. So I did. But then... I don't know. I really did feel the urge to become a cop. Because of my dad, I guess. Maybe I thought I could get closer to him, somehow. And I still want to go through and finish the academy, but I know the on-the-job training I can get from this position is going to be incredible."

"It will be incredible," he told her. "I think it was just hard for an old-timer like me to see such talent from an upstart."

"Upstart?"

"You're supposed to protest that I'm not an old-timer."

"How old are you?"

"Nearly thirty-six. Thirteen years on the force."

"You always knew what you wanted to be?"

"Nope. I was supposed to grow up to be a lawyer. In some ways, I was like that asshole football player you dated."

"You *are* a chauvinist."

"Not at all, not anymore. Except...."

"Except when it comes to me?"

He hesitated even longer then. Before he spoke, he gritted his teeth and shrugged. "There's something about you that reminds me of Nancy."

"She was a cop. A homicide cop. Your partner. And you loved her."

"Right. But I know—I *know*—that she went off on her own, and that's what got her killed. She made a mistake."

"A male cop can make a mistake. *You* could make a mistake," she reminded him.

He smiled. "Yeah, I could."

"But you stay out there."

"You bet."

"So...?"

"You know what?" He turned to her, face bronze against his pillow. "Cops can be assholes. Male, female, gay, straight, you name it. Macho guys with big guns, women with chips on their shoulders...cops are human. Some guys have gone bad, really bad. But most cops really are the good guys. I met one when I was a kid. He straightened me out, and I saw that he could make a difference. That's what this job is to me. Making a difference. I see guys doing it all the time, sometimes just in small ways. I know there are times when we won't get the answers. Doesn't mean we stop trying. If you'll keep it a secret, I'll even admit I'm obsessed with the Bordon case. And I know our Jane Doe is connected somehow.

I'm sure I have the missing piece of the puzzle some-where. I just don't know what it is. Maybe that's why I understand your conviction about Stuart, why I'll ask some questions and do some investigating on my own. But when your drawing hits the papers tomorrow, I'm willing to bet we get an identification on Jane Doe, and that means I'm going to be busy as all hell, so you'll have to understand if it takes me a little time."

She drew a line down his cheek with her fingertip. "I'm grateful for whatever you can do."

He caught her finger. Teased it with his tongue. "Hey, you wouldn't be here because you think I'm a good in-vestigator and can get you answers, would you?"

She felt her lips curving into a smile. "I'm here be-cause I think you're very good at something else."

"Great. Just after my body."

"Brains or body. Pick one," she told him. "And hey—am I here because I can draw? Or because I'm conve-nient and have the right body parts?"

"Convenient, the right body parts…and hair. I'm a sucker for a redhead."

She laughed, and he drew her closer. His knuckles moved down her back; his fingertips teased the flesh of her hip. A thought crossed her mind.

Or am I here because I remind you of Nancy?

She didn't ask him.

As his lips joined his fingertips against her naked flesh, she didn't want to think at all.

The alarm hadn't gone off. Ashley was certain it was still night, but the pounding at Jake's door would have roused the dead.

"What the hell…?" he muttered, jumping up and reaching for his trunks.

"Jake!"

"It's Marty," Jake murmured briefly, before heading out of the cabin.

Ashley sat up, still crawling out of the depths of sleep, blinking. She heard Jake undo the locks, heard Marty burst in.

"We've got it," Marty said.

"What?"

"The newspaper has barely hit the streets, and we've got an identification on Cinderella."

Nathan Fresia sat in the hospital chair, his head sunk into his hands. The depths of his despair were almost overwhelming.

Lucy had been admitted to the hospital, as well. Her blood pressure had risen sky high, and she was a prime candidate for a full-scale heart attack. She was sedated, sleeping in a different wing of the hospital. He felt torn. He should be with her, but she had insisted that he be here, that he not leave their son's side.

"Mr. Fresia?"

He looked up. Dr. Ontkean, the neurologist in charge of Stuart's case, was standing quietly before him.

He must have looked really horrible, because the doctor knelt down before him. "Mr. Fresia, the important factor here is that your son is a real trouper. His will to live may actually pull him through."

Nathan nodded, realizing that, despite everything, he needed to be grateful. Stuart had been brought back to life. Not to consciousness, but he was still hanging on.

"Your wife's cardiologist has assured me that as long as she gets some real rest, she's going to be fine, too."

"Thank you." He heard the words, though it didn't sound like his voice speaking at all.

The doctor cleared his throat. "But now, I need your help. We nearly lost your son last night because a plug was pulled out of the wall. There are just too many people coming through to see him. Thank God he is the fighter he is—he hung on breathing on his own for a long time. We don't even know how long, but…it's a good sign, and also a good warning. This is an intensive care unit. He can't have a parade going through, do you understand?"

Nathan nodded. "Yes, yes, of course."

"Mr. Fresia? You need some sleep yourself."

"I can't leave my boy. I won't leave my boy."

Ontkean nodded. Maybe he had kids himself. "Sleep in the recliner, then. I'll check with you later," he said. He departed.

Nathan listened to the sound of the respirator and closed his eyes, thanking God.

And kept his vigil.

"Jake, I—" Marty broke off suddenly. "Oh, jeez, you're not alone. Man, I'm sorry."

"What?" Jake said. He followed the direction of Marty's eyes and saw Ashley's bra on the floor. He swore silently to himself.

"Don't worry about it. Cinderella. Who is she?"

"The night guys got the call right after the morning edition was published," Marty began. But before he got any further, they both heard a sudden scream coming from the direction of Nick's place.

They both started instantly for the door.

* * *

Len Green parked some distance from the lot that belonged to Nick Montague, exited his car and walked silently toward the building. He meant to take a circuitous route around the back of the establishment. The sun hadn't really hit the horizon yet, and there were plenty of trees and bushes for cover. He was sure he could make it to Ashley's door without being seen.

Then he stopped dead in his tracks as a blood-curdling scream split the morning air.

Ashley's cell phone was ringing. She could hear it, but she had no idea where she'd dropped her purse last night. All she knew was that her clothes were strewn all over the living area, and both Marty and Jake had gone racing out the front door at the sound of the scream.

She scrambled quickly, forgetting her shoes and her underwear, hopping her way into her jeans and drawing her shirt over her head even as she reached the door and pelted barefoot across the deck. She leapt to the dock, then saw that Jake, Marty, Nick and Sharon were out on the terrace.

As she raced toward the foursome, Sandy, scratching his white head, emerged from his houseboat.

"What? My God, what?" Ashley cried, reaching them.

It felt as if they were all staring at her. Except, of course, Jake, who was staring at Sharon.

"Ashley!" Sharon said.

"Was that you screaming? Why?" Ashley demanded.

"She was worried," Nick said flatly.

"Worried?"

"I saw your drawing in the paper," Sharon explained. "I recognized the woman immediately. I went to your room, but you weren't there…and then I screamed. I was so scared."

"Why were you frightened for Ashley?" Jake asked.

"We didn't even know you took the job," Nick said, staring at his niece. Ashley felt her heart sink. No, of course, he hadn't known. He'd raised her. He'd been a best friend. And she hadn't told him about one of the most important decisions of her life.

"I'm sorry."

"Is her name on the drawing?" Marty asked, bewildered. But he, too, stared at Ashley. She wondered if she should just have a sign made for her forehead: *Yes, I'm sleeping with Jake Dilessio.*

"I'd recognize Ashley's work anywhere," Nick said with dignity, and a touch of reproach.

"I would, too," Sharon added.

"Nick, it just happened yesterday," Ashley explained.

"Who is the woman?" Jake demanded, his tone impatient as he cut into the conversation.

Sharon's eyes turned to him. "Her name is—was—Cassie Sewell."

"And you recognize her because…?"

"She was a Realtor down here for a little while. She came down from the center of the state several months ago, and I met her because we were both involved in the sale of a place out by the Redlands."

"Why wasn't she reported missing?" Marty asked.

"Well, from what I heard…" She took a deep breath, then went on. "I almost had a deal, then the whole thing went up in smoke because the sellers felt they weren't being represented properly. And when I tried to get hold of her, a fellow she worked with told me she'd just come in and quit. She said she was changing her lifestyle or something. Fred Hampton, a guy in the office, said it was like she had fallen in love. That's all I know. Naturally, I wasn't that fond of her—she blew a deal for me—but when I saw her face…and Ash's drawing…"

"What's the name of the company she was working for?" Jake demanded.

"Algemon and Palacio," Sharon supplied.

Jake turned to Marty. "I'm heading straight over there. You head in and see what the night guys have."

"Right," Marty agreed.

Jake turned and started back for his boat. Nick and Sharon stared at Ashley, who braced herself to hear what her uncle had to say.

But he didn't speak. He simply turned around without a word and headed back toward the bar.

"It—it's all right, dear," Sharon said.

"No, no, it's not," Ashley said, shaking her head.

She hurried after Nick. He was behind the bar, pouring coffee. He knew she was there, but he still didn't speak.

"Nick, I'm sorry."

"You're twenty-five. You want to keep your career—and your love life—private, it's your concern."

"Nick! Please!"

She walked around the bar and put her arms around him, resting her head against his chest as she had since she was a child. "I'm so sorry. I didn't get a chance to talk to you last night because you'd already left to see Stuart. And then, when I came back…"

"Oh, yeah. When you came back."

He moved away from her.

She was quiet a minute. "I thought you liked Jake Dilessio."

"I did. That was before he was sleeping with my niece."

She held very still. "Nick, like you said, I'm twenty-five. And…well, you must have known that I… I have had…"

"Sex?" he said bluntly, turning to stare at her. "Well, yeah, I guess I knew. There was that jock when you were in high school. I'm not an idiot, you know. And yes, you're twenty-five. It's just that…well, hell! I'd like to think I mean a little more to you than a cop who just moved in down the dock."

"Oh, Nick. I know I should have talked to you. I realize you must have been doubly shocked when you saw the drawing. But everything happened so fast."

"Want to tell me about it now?"

She stared into his eyes, nodded and took a seat at the bar. "Would you pour me coffee?"

"Yeah."

He brought her a cup.

"Nick, it was amazing."

"I don't want to hear the details on your night with the cop."

"Not that—the job. I accepted, just like you said I should. And then, before I even officially started, they decided to take me down to the morgue to do the sketch. It all happened so fast, Nick."

"Like this thing with Dilessio?" Nick said softly.

She exhaled. "Yes."

"You don't even know him."

"I thought he was your friend. That you liked him."

"I like him all right. But you don't know him. He's obsessive. Tough. A workaholic. I can admire a man like that, but I don't know if he's right for you. Ashley, there were all kinds of rumors going around—"

"I know about the rumors."

"Ashley—"

He broke off. Sharon had come in. She was standing hesitantly just inside the room. "Excuse me, you two. I'm sorry. I know this is personal, it's just that…well, I need to get to the bedroom and get out of this robe and into work clothes."

"Sharon, don't be ridiculous," Ashley said. "Go right through."

Sharon gazed at Nick, empathy in her eyes, and she smiled. "Love you both," she said, and hurried past.

"Young lady," Nick began, setting his cup on the bar and leaning close. "I don't want you getting hurt. I don't want you getting mixed up with someone who's a great guy from a man's point of view, but maybe a little jaded when it comes to women, I—"

He broke off again. She turned and followed his gaze to the door. She smiled despite the gravity of their talk. Sandy was standing there in bare feet and cutoffs, carrying Ashley's purse.

"Sorry, Dilessio asked me to bring this to you, Ash," he said.

"Bring it in," Nick said sighing.

Sandy came over. "You got coffee, Nick?"

Nick and Ashley looked at one another. "Think I could have a dinner date sometime soon, away from here, with my own niece?" he asked her.

She grinned, leaned across the counter and kissed him on the cheek.

"You bet."

Her cell phone started ringing. In all the excitement

she'd forgotten that someone had tried to call her. Were they trying again now? Sandy plopped next to her at the bar as she dug for the phone.

"Ashley? Ashley Montague?"

"Yes?"

"It's me. David Wharton, the guy you met at the hospital. I need to see you. Someone tried to kill Stuart."

Chapter 15

Ashley met with David at the News Café in Coconut Grove. It was his suggestion. They were out in the open, on the sidewalk, in plain view of others and far from alone.

Before she had even returned to her room for a shower, she had gone through twenty minutes of trying to get through to Mr. Fresia at the hospital. A volunteer had given her Stuart's condition as recorded on his records. According to them nothing had changed. The nurse in the unit had refused to put her through to the room. She had finally discovered Nathan Fresia's cell phone number in an old address book, and when she dialed it, she was gratified to find it hadn't changed.

But speaking to Nathan had done little good. He had sounded exhausted, and though he had been as kind as ever, he had insisted that she not come to the hospital—

there had been so many people in and out and so much commotion the night before that a plug had been pulled out of the wall, with nearly fatal consequences.

Ashley couldn't believe what she was hearing. She had been the last of their group to visit Stuart, and she knew she hadn't pulled any plugs from the wall. She also knew that Stuart's respirator had been running just fine. When she tried to say that to Nathan, he snapped, telling her that his wife was now hospitalized, and whether she wanted to believe it or not, it had happened. Then he apologized for barking at her but insisted again that they needed to be alone, at least for a few days.

Stunned, she showered, then drove to the Grove to meet David Wharton.

He greeted her cordially and took a seat opposite her. As soon as they had coffee, he started right in. "Word is one of you girls pulled out a plug last night."

"The hell we did!" she said indignantly. "But you know something and you'd damned well better tell me right now."

"Hey, I called to talk to you, didn't I? If you don't get rid of that cop attitude fast, I'll walk away right now."

Ashley sat back, letting out a sigh and staring at him. "We didn't pull any plug. So what happened?"

"How the hell do I know?"

"You were there, apparently."

"Right. But not in his room. Do you think they'd let me in?" he asked, shaking his head. "But I can tell you this, Lucy Fresia isn't a sicko, losing her mind and longing— somewhere in the deep recesses of her subconscious— to let him go. I may not have been in the room, but I was hanging out awfully darn close, watching the hallways and what was going on. And only his parents and hospital personnel were in and out of that room."

"How can you be so certain? You didn't go down for coffee once last night?"

He exhaled, staring at her, not about to admit he might have missed something. "I'm pretty darned good at what I set out to do."

"So someone from the hospital is trying to kill him?"

"I doubt it."

"Isn't that what you just said?"

"I should have said that only people who *looked* like hospital personnel were in and out of the room."

He fell silent because their waitress was coming to take their breakfast order. Ashley had been planning to stick with coffee, but she suddenly realized she was starving. She ordered a large breakfast, while her companion opted for orange juice and toast. He seemed somewhat amused by her appetite.

"You eat like that all the time?"

"Only when I'm hungry." The waitress had moved away. She didn't really need to lean forward, but she did. "In other words, you think someone dressed like a doctor or a nurse and went into Stuart's room and pulled the plug."

"Yes, that's exactly what I mean. And don't go telling me I've seen too many movies, okay?"

"I wasn't about to say that." She believed him. Completely. Just as she believed she had been stalked through the parking lot by someone dressed like a doctor. "I believe you, which scares the hell out of me. So someone in scrubs went in and pulled the plug. But wouldn't Lucy have noticed?"

"Not if she was sound asleep in the chair by the bed."

"She'd wake up."

"There's no guarantee of that. The poor woman must be exhausted beyond the breaking point. And whoever is doing this is good, slips in looking like anyone else, and wouldn't be noticed. He or she has it down pat."

Ashley was silent for a moment. It sounded very far-fetched, but she knew that it had also seemed far-fetched when she tried to convince the police she had been stalked in the parking garage. And if the one was true, the other could certainly be true, as well.

"If what you're saying is true, Stuart is in danger even as we speak."

"I know. But it's daylight—more people around. And his father is in there right now. Besides, I thought that you could go back to the hospital."

Ashley shook her head. "Nathan Fresia thinks Karen, Jan or I pulled out the plug by accident."

"Maybe if you talked to him."

"Maybe if we got to the truth." She leaned toward him. "The other night you said you knew something, that you have something. What is it?"

He hesitated. "If I talk to you, you have to promise to find evidence to support what I have to tell you before officially bringing it before the police."

"But if you have something solid…"

"I don't know what I have. I gave them as much information as I had on what Stu was doing. There is a state congresswoman he's sure is in bed with the special interests, but when the cops checked her out, she was furious and reminded them that every citizen has a right to an opinion about the importance of business over the ecosystem or vice versa. She checked out clean." He shrugged. "From what police could find out, she hadn't done anything illegal in any way." He hesitated. "She also lost a child to drugs a few years ago, so she's a real crusader against drug abuse in the county. There were a few other ideas picked up from Stu's notes. The police checked out a major hotshot with one of the sugar companies, but they couldn't come up with anything there, either. So you see, so far I've come off as nothing but a major troublemaker. The police aren't about to listen to anything else I have to say." He stared at her, drumming his fingers on the table. "Sure, I want a story out of this, I'd be lying to say otherwise. But I'm telling you the truth. Stu really is a friend. Hell, I've done nothing but bug the cops and stake out the hospital since he was hit."

Ashley digested the information he had given her, sipping her coffee slowly. She shook her head. "I don't know what I can do."

"I've got an address. You can check it out. Hell, *we* can check it out."

"An address? An address for what? And if you had an address, why didn't you give it to the police?"

"I just found it, going through some more notes of Stu's I uncovered. And I haven't had a chance to get out there yet. Also, since last night…well, hell, I don't know what to do. Me sitting at the hospital doesn't seem to do any good, but I'm afraid of what will happen now that I'm not there."

"Where is this address?"

"The far southwest. Farm country."

Ashley stared at him. What could it hurt to take a drive? And yet he was right. She couldn't set aside the idea that Stuart might be in real danger.

"I'm not sure what to do, either," he murmured.

She was startled when he reached across the table,

gently touching her hand. "Okay, you're not a cop any-more. But…surely, you can do something, get some-one to listen."

She hesitated. In his way, Jake listened. Maybe he only listened to her because he felt obligated to do so, though, seeing as they were sleeping together.

She didn't want anyone feeling obligated to her. But she also didn't want her pride to get in the way of help-ing Stuart. Especially when there was a possibility that he was in real danger.

Dilessio wasn't going to want to speak to her today. His victim had been identified. He would be busy, like a bloodhound out on a trail.

Still…she needed his help.

She realized she had no idea how to get hold of Jake when he was away from his desk, but at least she knew people who would.

"Hang on a minute," she told David, rising.

She was getting truly paranoid, she realized with dismay. She was suddenly afraid that anyone around her might be listening in on her conversation. She walked to the corner, put through a call to the forensics depart-ment and asked to speak with Mandy Nightingale. She was put on hold for several moments, and then Mandy answered, so full of congratulations for the success of the sketch in the paper that Ashley couldn't even man-age to say hello. After that, though, she was able to give Ashley Jake's cell phone number.

Jake's phone rang several times before he answered, barking "Dilessio" as if he were impatient with the very fact that his phone had rung.

"Jake, it's Ashley."

"Ashley." For a moment it seemed as if he didn't recognize the name. Then he said quickly, "Yes, Ashley, what? I'm really busy."

"I know, I know... I'll talk quickly. I'm asking a lot, but... Stuart nearly died last night. Not because of his injuries," she said quickly, "but because his respirator was unplugged. The hospital blames it on too many people going in and out, but I know—I *know*—we didn't pull that plug out of the wall. I believe Stuart is in real danger. Is there any way, any way at all—I mean, if you use off-duty guys, I'll pay them myself—you can get a couple of guys in there to watch his room? And to make sure any hospital personnel going in really *are* hospital personnel?"

There was silence for a minute. "Ashley, I'm in the middle of a murder investigation."

"I know that, Jake. But I'm not a silly paranoid seeing spooks in the closet. I'm trying to prevent another murder. Jake, please! Remember how we talked about the fact that you can *know* things about people just because you know those particular people? Please, I don't know where else to turn. Look, I know what you're up against. I wouldn't bother you if I weren't desperate. Help me."

"I'll see what I can do."

He hung up before she could say more. She stared at the phone, biting her lip, not at all sure what direction she should take now.

But even as she turned back toward the table where David was still sitting, she received a return call.

It wasn't Jake, but Marty. He wanted the particulars, needed to hear the story again. She gave it to him as best she could, and he promised to set up three shifts of off-duty officers, and that he would talk to Carnegie and Nathan Fresia himself.

"Ashley, the off-duty guys will do it cheap for another cop—and because they might want recommendations from a couple of homicide guys sometime—but it's still going to cost."

"I know." She hesitated. "Don't worry. We'll pay it." He was silent on the other end for a minute, so she went on. "Listen, Marty, I'm sorry... I'm sorry to bother you with this."

"That's not it, Ashley. We take care of our own. I wish we could do it for nothing, there's no way we can get anyone to approve the manpower when the physicians are convinced a careless visitor pulled the plug. So private is the way to go—if you're certain the danger exists."

"I understand, Marty. And I just have a feeling about this."

She could hear him snort, though she was certain he didn't realize she heard. She thanked him and hung up. The Fresias might not be millionaires, but they were comfortable, and once she explained the situation she was sure they would be willing to help pay for security. She had a small savings account, and once her paperwork went through, she would be making a decent salary, so she could help, too. It would work out.

She walked back to the table and sank into her chair, feeling oddly exhausted already.

"I've got off-duty cops doing guard duty," she said.

David arched a brow, looking at her as if she had performed a miracle. Then he frowned. "Did you warn them about hospital personnel?"

"Yes."

He leaned back, smiling. "Then I think we ought to

take a ride south together. You want to drive, or you want me to? I'm in the mall garage across the street."

"I'm at a meter—with the time probably about to run out. We'll take my car."

Rona Palacio had been one of several people who called police headquarters the moment she'd seen the drawing of her one-time employee in the newspaper. When Jake arrived, she was eager to talk, distressed to know that such a horrible thing had happened to one of her people—and devoid of answers.

"She was barely here at all," Rona said, sitting behind her desk, nervously tapping the eraser end of a pencil. "When she came in, she was lovely, bright, vivacious, willing to work all hours, and she seemed a perfect addition to the company. You certainly don't have to be attractive to sell real estate—I mean, people want someone efficient who can get answers, who knows codes and is capable—but as pretty as she was, with so much energy…well, it didn't hurt." Rona Palacio was an attractive woman herself, Jake thought. Middle-aged, with perfectly coifed silver hair, slim and handsomely dressed in designer attire. Appearances definitely counted in her book.

"Apparently," Rona continued, "she had no family, no close family, anyway—at least that's what she said when she explained her move to this area. She said she'd been working in the middle of the state. All of her references checked out. She'd come to Miami because she'd some friends down here, and because no matter what was going on in the world, people were going to want to live in Miami. She was here maybe three weeks, and she had just started selling…and then she called in and said the world had changed, she was going in a different direction. I tried to talk to her about it, of course. But that's all she would say. I never met any of her friends, and I don't think any of the other agents did, either. I have her last known address in the files, and a list of our people so you can talk to them yourself... but I don't know what else to give you. I would love to help, what happened must have been so horrible.... If there's no family, the firm will handle the funeral. Not that she was with us long, but...it seems like the right thing to do."

"That's up to you, Ms. Palacio," he said. "What about her work area?"

"I'll show you her desk and her computer. But we've had other agents working there since she left, of course."

"Of course. But anything might be helpful."

Minutes later, he had lists of agents and an address, and had been escorted to Cassie Sewell's former work station. A friendly young assistant with wide eyes and a definite empathy for the dead woman helped him go through the computer and find the properties she had been representing. With another list in his hands, he knew that the legwork and interviews were now going to be endless. Well, they'd wanted something to go on; now they had it.

He spent much of the morning speaking with Cassie Sewell's fellow agents. The company wasn't large, and the people who had worked with her were more than willing to talk to him; unfortunately, they had little to tell him beyond what he had already learned from Rona Palacio. Cassie had been lovely, friendly and yet, in her way, a loner. She had only talked to two of them before she left, telling them what she'd told Rona: that she'd chosen a different life and was leaving the company.

No one had ever seen her with a friend. She hadn't even spoken about friends, other than saying she had some in the Miami area.

Franklin from the FBI called while he was in the middle of a session with one of the real estate agents, and he excused himself. He had to hand it to Franklin; the man had been through endless files, put agents in the middle of the state to work and already knew a great deal about their victim. The national computer had compared their crime to several others around the country, but nothing matched—other than the cases from five years earlier. He'd discovered that Cassie had worked real estate in Orange County as well, and people there had gotten to know her better than her co-workers in Miami had. She had been friendly and thoughtful, religious, and at one time had considered becoming a nun. She had been greatly liked by those with whom she worked. She had resigned, letting everyone know she was moving down to Miami because she had made some new friends from the area, and thought that she might have a better opportunity to meet the right kind of man in a church group. However, after running through the parishioner lists of several local Catholic churches, they had so far come up with nothing. He decided to visit a number of priests in person that afternoon, bringing the picture with him.

"Think she got mixed up in something that promised more than Catholicism?" Franklin asked. "Listening to her profile, it seems the obvious conclusion. And since you're going by the theory that something has been reawakened down here..."

"You don't sound convinced."

"We'll get something now that we know who this woman was," Franklin said.

"I've gotta tell you something, Franklin. I'm impressed with what you've discovered in so little time."

"You're a good cop, Jake, and I know you think I'm an asshole. I don't have your touch with people, it's true. But I had a masters in criminology before I even entered Quantico. And you can't imagine the training we go through there. Hell, we spend days learning to fold paper just right so we don't lose a microfiber while transferring evidence. I've worked hard." He was quiet a minute, then said ruefully, "I don't mean to be a dickhead."

"You're not a dickhead," Jake told him, and wondered if he'd ever thought of Franklin with *exactly* that word.

"Yeah, well, when it comes to details, I've got it covered. The instinct thing...well, that's your ballpark. So if you get any of those instincts going, let me know. I can work the evidence end of them."

"Sure. Though right now, I don't have squat," Jake told him. He was lying though. He knew he was missing something. Something in front of him. *Smoke and mirrors.*

"Anything else?" Jake asked, breaking his own train of thought.

"Yeah, just wanted to make sure you knew—Peter Bordon comes up for parole and may be out by the first of next week."

"I knew it was coming up. Thanks."

They hung up. Jake continued with his interviews. While the young assistant gathered details on the property lists, Jake called forensics and asked an old friend, Skip Conrad, for a favor.

"Hell, Jake, I can't get out there until tonight. And your place will be a mess when I'm through. You know that. You certain you want me to do it?"

"Yes. I don't care if the place comes out pitch-black. I'll owe you. And do me another favor—don't say anything to anyone else. Oh, and if I'm not there, Nick Montague, at the bar, has a key."

Skip was quiet for a minute. "You sure Nick hasn't been in your place?"

"I'm not sure of anything."

"What about Brian Lassiter?"

"No, I can't guarantee he hasn't been in there, either."

A moment later, he thanked Skip and hung up. Hell, Skip was bound to find Brian's prints. The guy had been on his boat, drunk as a skunk, touching everything in sight. Finding Brian's prints wouldn't mean a damned thing. He rubbed his temples wearily.

His phone rang again. It was Marty. "I'm at the last known residence of Cassie Sewell. The place is rented to a family, but they don't mind us looking around."

"I'm on my way."

Jake gathered the lists and left. In his car, he glanced at the addresses.

They all bordered the Glades.

And they were all too damn close to the place where, nearly five years ago, Nancy Lassiter had gone into a canal and died with whatever secrets she might have discovered.

There were long moments in which Ashley questioned her own sanity as she drove. She didn't know the man sitting next to her, and she didn't even really know where she was going—or why. David was definitely a normal enough looking man, a handsome one even, with shrewd eyes and a quick smile. He was in jeans and a knit shirt that day, again, very normal. His hair was worn a little long, but people wore their hair all different lengths these days. As she drove, she noted that for a journalist, he was in great physical shape. He must spend time in the gym to maintain the breadth of his shoulders and chest, tapering to trim hips and long legs.

"I think the turnpike is best," he said as they started out.

"Probably," she agreed. "Where exactly did you find this address? And how come it took you so long to find?"

"Stu left some magazines at my place. They all had articles about the Everglades. When I was flipping through, trying to see what he was actually after, I found a piece of paper. He'd written a few names on it, names I'd already given the police," he said ruefully. "But when I flipped it over, I saw he had written down an address, as well. Took me some time to see it. He'd written in pencil, and it had smudged."

"So are you sure we're even going to the right place?"

"Of course," he said. "I think." He turned in the seat. "Hey, do you think you ought to try talking to Nathan Fresia again? When those cops show up to play body-guard, he's going to wonder why."

"All right. I'll try to get him. Hand me my phone, would you?"

Nathan sounded somewhat better, but wary, when he came on the line. She talked quickly, explaining that since they were all worried about Stuart, and since she was certain she hadn't pulled any plugs, she'd thought that having a few off-duty officers guarding Stuart wouldn't be a bad thing. Nathan told her that the first cop had already arrived, and that he'd assumed Carnegie had set it up. After a moment he thanked Ashley and told her that she was welcome at the hospital, but to please come alone, because he wasn't sure if they would be letting anyone else in with Stuart for a few days.

She rang off and looked at David. "The first cop is already there."

"You really do know the right people."

She decided that she should call Jan and Karen. Even if she couldn't get them, she could leave messages about the latest events. She called Karen's school, only to be told that Karen had called in sick. She didn't answer at home or on her cell, and Ashley remembered that Len Green had taken her home the night before. So she left a message, then tried Len at his station and was told that he, too, had called in sick.

"What's up?" David asked her.

"A budding romance, I think," she said, and called Jan. Jan didn't answer, either, so Ashley left another message.

"I think we should take this exit," David said, as they came in sight of a turnoff.

"Have you been out here before?"

"Well, I've been in the area before."

"But you don't really know where we're going?"

"No."

He moved forward, adjusting in the seat. His knee hit the glove compartment door, and it popped open. Ashley's gun and badge were there; she hadn't had a chance to bring them back down to headquarters and turn them in, as required, since she had accepted the civilian position.

"Hey, that's cool. We're armed and dangerous," he said.

"Shut that."

"I'll bet you can use that gun, too."

"Yes, I can."

He smiled, closing the glove compartment. She felt an edge of unease at his expression and made a mental note to put the gun in her handbag and keep it on her at all times until she turned it in.

"Are you familiar with guns?" she asked him, trying to sound casual.

"A crack shot," he told her. She glanced his way and he shrugged. "ROTC." He pointed to the right.

"There…let's try following west, then turn south."

She did as he suggested. They hit a canal and had to turn back.

"Great directions," she muttered.

"Is it my fault we're practically in a primeval swamp and there are canals everywhere?"

After a number of false starts, they found a road that went through, and at last reached what they thought was the address. At least, by the numbers, it had to be somewhere within the long expanse of fields they had arrived at.

Ashley pulled over to the side of the road, which itself was scarcely more than dirt and gravel. Maybe it had been paved once. There seemed to be the remnants of asphalt beneath the tires.

As she turned off the engine, they both stared out the windows. "It's a big farm," Ashley said.

"I don't even see a house," David murmured.

"Yes…back there. And see…there's not exactly a barn, but it's an outbuilding of some kind. Maybe a silo."

"A silo? That's not a silo."

"Then what is it?"

"Not a silo. They're growing strawberries."

"What is that building, then?"

He stared at it and shrugged. What they saw appeared to be a round tower attached to some kind of storage shed or barn.

"It might be a big tower with a window so that the farmer can watch his strawberries grow," David said with a sigh. "I don't know. Wish we could get into it. Wanna look?"

"It's not legal for us to go traipsing around on someone's property, David."

He stared at her and grinned slowly. "I'm a journalist. I'm supposed to be heedless of the law. You're a—an ex-cadet or something."

"David, we have no right—"

He ignored her. "Up farther...closer to the house. That looks like a vegetable garden. That's a big house. Looks like they grow a *lot* of food."

"David, farmers grow a lot of food. That's how they make their money," she said irritably.

"They have a lot of the place planted...yet look, if you really look across the fields, the back is a big tangle of trees and underbrush."

"Amazing," Ashley said. "They can't stop the underbrush from growing on what may not be their property."

He stared at her. "The place really looks like a farm. They've made it look like a farm."

"It *is* a farm. We've solved it, and the owners should definitely be arrested," she murmured sarcastically. "David, listen to yourself. We've found a farm that we're not sure is even the right address. What do we do now that's legal and makes sense?" Ashley said, more to herself than to David.

"We get out and look around."

"We can't just walk around on private property."

"*I* can."

"Listen, we need more information, David."

"Yes, and I intend to get it."

Ashley was startled when he opened the car door and got out. She swore, starting to open her own door to follow him. But there was one thing she and David Wharton agreed on, and that was the fact that Stuart hadn't wound up half-dead on the highway of his own volition.

She opened her glove compartment, knowing that her police-issue gun should have been turned in and definitely shouldn't be in service.

She was glad to have it anyway, she thought as she pulled it from the glove compartment and put it into her leather over-the-shoulder handbag.

David was already moving along the front edge of the property. At the moment, she thought, they could easily be seen across the low growing fields.

"David, where the hell are you going?" she demanded.

"To that line of trees."

"We're sneaking up on someone, right? David, if someone is looking right now, we're pretty damn obvious."

"Then get down."

"The car is visible."

He stopped dead. "Right. Go back and get it. Pull up behind those trees there, on the property line. Hurry."

"You're insane. No wonder the police are furious at you. I should just drive away."

"But you won't. You won't leave me—and you know that Stuart was on to something."

He lengthened his stride as he headed for the cover of the trees. Ashley swore and went back for the car, moving as quickly as she could. She cursed thinking that if anyone was watching, they looked incredibly suspicious.

She quickly moved the car down the road. What was apparently the far east line of the property had a stretch of fence along it, and the fence was bordered by trees and foliage. She exited the car, looking at the long line of trees.

"David?" she said, and realized she was whispering. As far as she could tell, no one was anywhere nearby. "David?" she said again, louder, her tone almost angry.

Gritting her teeth, she started walking along the line of trees, moving quickly. The fence was barbed wire, but she saw no sign of it being electrified. In fact, it seemed to be no more than a marker. Trees and foliage grew on both sides of the barrier. As she kept walking southward, the property line made a sudden jog to the right. After that, the neat rows of field suddenly disappeared, and it seemed as if she was in an overgrown jungle. A mosquito buzzed around her cheek. Swearing, she slapped at it.

"David, you damned idiot," she snapped angrily, twisting around to head back. She was going to leave him. Her sense of responsibility didn't cover maniacs who dragged her into something, and then deserted her.

She turned back in what she thought was the right direction. A moment later, she found herself in a field. Tomatoes. There was a man bent over a plant working, wearing jeans and a denim work shirt with the sleeves cut off. A cotton kerchief was tied around his neck, and he wore a baseball cap against the sun. Before Ashley could duck back into the trees, the man straightened. He was young; as he lifted his cap to wipe his brow, she saw that his hair was sandy-colored and short-cropped. He smiled at her. "Well, hey. Where did you come from?"

"I...wow... I'm sorry. I'm lost."

His smile became one of polite skepticism. "You're lost in the back of a field of tomatoes?"

He started walking toward her. There was nothing threatening in his behavior; he kept smiling. She noted that there was a basket containing bright red tomatoes where he had been standing. There was a bulge just below his hip. She was tempted to call out in Mae West fashion, *Is that a pistol in your pocket, or are you just happy to see me?*

It was a knife. He came close enough for her to realize that he had a leather sheath attached to his belt. It looked like a big knife.

It was daylight. The sun was streaming down on a stretch of lazy farmland. The man was about her own age, smiling, apparently pleasant, and not alarmed at a trespassing visitor, merely amused.

She was still glad of the .38-caliber gun in her shoulder bag.

"So you're lost...well, welcome anyway. Do you need to use a phone? Would you like to come up to the house for a glass of water or anything?"

"I have a cell phone, thanks."

He nodded. "Can I get you something to drink? The sun can be brutal out here."

No! All she wanted to do was get the hell away. She was torn between feeling like an idiot and suffering from a tremendous sense of unease. But if anything terrible was going on around here, it was unlikely that the young man would have invited her in for a glass of water.

And what an opportunity. She could talk to the man and see inside the house.

"I'm really sorry to have bothered you," she said quickly. "I was looking for some property, and out here, well, finding a street address is nearly impossible. I'd thought that maybe, if I followed the fence... I thought the place next door might be the address I was looking for."

"I doubt that," the young man said. He extended a hand to her. "I'm Caleb. Caleb Harrison. Come on up to the house. It looks like a trek, but it's not really so far."

"Really, I don't mean to bother you."

"You're not bothering me. Living way out here, I don't see too many people, so I'm glad for the interruption. This is a back-to-basics kind of life. A lot of hard work, but time to smell the roses, too, you know?"

"Yes." She was standing dead still, reminding herself that she had a gun, and she knew how to use it. And she would be an idiot to miss a chance to see the property. She extended a hand. "I'm Monica Shipping," she said, using the first name that came into her mind. "And thanks, I'd love a glass of water."

As they walked, he pointed out his tomatoes and strawberries. "Up by the house, there are all kinds of vegetables. They grow great here. Our neighbors have citrus trees. Not a great place for them, but they seem determined." As they neared the house, she noted the numerous buildings that stretched out behind it, toward the rear of the property. "See here?" he said, stopping by the garden. "Cabbage, carrots, you name it. We're completely self-sufficient. We're all vegetarians, so that makes it easy, really."

"All?" Ashley inquired with a smile. "How many of you live here?"

"Right now? There are eight of us."

"Are you married? That's a big family."

"More like a group of friends."

"A...religious group?"

He laughed. "No. More like a commune. Just a group of people who enjoy farming, being together—and out of the mainstream bustle and trauma of life."

"Sounds interesting."

"Are you interested?"

She smiled carefully. "I don't know.... I have to admit, I've never thought about anything like this."

"Well, come in. See the place."

He brought her to a step that led up to a little porch. There was a screen door, which was closed, but the wooden door behind it was wide open. There was no air-conditioning, she noticed. The day was bright, but they weren't in the dead heat of summer, so inside, the temperature was pleasant enough.

She felt as if she had walked into a New England farmhouse. There was a knit rug before a hearth, and comfortable-looking, if slightly worn, overstuffed sofas with homey throws tossed over them. There were two rocking chairs, a basket of someone's knitting and a pile of magazines. The titles she could see included something about cabinetry and home gardening.

"Come in the kitchen," he invited.

She did so. Vegetables littered the counter. Someone was getting ready to prepare a large meal. A large vegetarian meal, she realized.

They might be self-sufficient, and they might have eschewed air-conditioning, but they did have electricity. He opened the refrigerator. "Water, and lots of juice."

She was thinking that at the moment, she could use

a double espresso, which she was sure was entirely out of the question here. "Water would be fine, thanks."

He poured her a glass of cold water, then indicated a seat at the kitchen table. She sat and looked around. The place really was charming. Copper pots and accessories hung from ceiling hooks. Mason jars filled with various preserves lined the windowsills. The chairs were covered with handmade cushions in a cheerful blue.

"Thank you," she told him.

"My pleasure." He smiled. "I get to see tomatoes in that field all day. You're the first beautiful woman who's ever appeared. It's a bit unreal."

"Thanks again," she said.

"So what do you do?"

"I'm an artist. I do sketches."

"For tourists?"

She didn't correct him.

"But you're looking for property in this area?"

She laughed. "Yes. But I'm afraid I'm not as idealistic as you seem to be. I thought I'd just like a lot of land, some space."

He nodded. "A lot of people feel that way. You must be good, though, if you can afford a plot of land this big."

"Well…you know tourists. It's all in the perception. You get one person saying they must have a sketch by a certain artist, and whether you're any good or not, your work is the hot item to bring home."

"If you ever need a bunch of tomatoes to sketch, let me know."

"I will." She set her glass down. "I really have to get back."

"I'll walk you to your car."

"No, no. I've taken way too much of your time."

"It's been a pleasure. Please, I hope you come back. Hey, on Saturday nights, Maggie—our resident folk guitarist—plays some great stuff. Please come back by and see us, if you're free."

"Thanks. Maybe I will."

He walked back out with her, but when she insisted she could find her car, he headed back to his tomatoes, while she kept walking toward the road. She knew she was being watched and fought the temptation to look back. It struck her as strange that eight people supposedly lived there, but she hadn't seen anyone else.

She kept her eyes on the road, then walked along it to the barbed wire fence to reach her car. She didn't see hide nor hair of David, and she was cursing him when she slid into the driver's seat. She revved the engine and started driving slowly down the road.

"Where the hell are you, you idiot?" she muttered. At that moment, he suddenly burst out of a group of trees about twenty yards in front of her. She drove closer and stopped, switching off the engine while she watched him work his way through the tangled landscape. Once he reached her, he hopped in swiftly.

He touched his face, giving a sigh of relief. "I was about to call for backup."

"Backup?"

"Well, I guess I should have said I was about to call the cops, but since you're still kind of an almost-cop, I said backup."

"I should have left you here, you idiot. I got caught traipsing around out there."

"Yeah, I saw you with some guy."

"I ran into him in a tomato field. I was trespassing, but he was decent about it."

"Tell me everything."

"It's a nice house, clean as a whistle. He says he lives there with seven other people. They're doing their best to live off the land. It's a commune."

"What were the others like?"

"I didn't see any of the others."

"Then where the hell were they?"

"I don't know. Maybe they have day jobs before they turn back into hippies at night. He didn't threaten me in any way, I didn't see any marijuana growing in the midst of his tomatoes. So...all that, and I didn't really get a damned thing."

"We need to find out who owns the place," David said.

"The guy told me his name was Caleb Harrison."

"Biblical."

"He said the place had nothing to do with religion. I know all kinds of guys down here named Jesus—it's a popular Hispanic name, you know—and they're not religious fanatics in the least."

"I think we should look around some more."

"I think we should get off this road and then argue about where to go from here," Ashley said firmly, turning the key in the ignition again.

David didn't get a chance to answer. There was a thump on the back of the car.

Ashley twisted in her seat. There was a tall man in coveralls and a straw hat behind them, staring at them with narrowed eyes.

He was carrying a shotgun.

Chapter 16

There was little to be done at Cassie Sewell's last known residence. A family was now renting the three-bedroom apartment, and the wife assured the police that when they had rented, the last occupant had been out completely. The walls had been repainted, and new carpeting had been put down.

A crime scene unit would still test to see if she had met her demise in the apartment itself.

Jake doubted that she had. He was certain Cassie had quit her job, cleaned out her home, gone on…and then met her fate.

When they finished at the apartment, leaving the crime scene inspectors there to do their work, Jake and Marty stood outside in the sunshine for a few minutes.

"Want me to go back and follow the paper trail?" Marty asked.

"Yes, find out to whom she wrote her last check and where she made her last credit card purchases. She had a car, a BMW, which seems to have disappeared, as well. Check the history on that."

"What are you going to do?" Marty asked him.

"Go for a drive."

"A drive?"

"I'm going to take a look at all the properties that were listed," Jake told him. Then he added, "Hey, I forgot to thank you for getting the off-duty guys at the hospital for me."

"Personally I think it's unnecessary, but if it's what they want, hey, who knows? Maybe someone *is* out to get the kid."

"Well, thanks anyway."

"Not a problem. I'll go get on the real case now."

"Call me with anything pertinent."

"Ditto," Marty told him.

That was what he meant to do. But after Marty had headed back toward headquarters, Jake decided to stop back by the *Gwendolyn*. Passing Nick's, he saw a number of customers parked in the lot and a few diners out on the terrace. He walked along the dock, waving to Sandy, who was seated on the deck of his boat, legs stretched out in the sun. The old geezer looked good, tanned and athletic. A life spent fishing and sailing could turn the skin brown and wrinkle it one hell of a lot, but apparently it kept a man fit, as well.

Sandy waved back to him, eased his hat over his white head and leaned back.

Jake climbed aboard his boat, irritated that he was apprehensive every time he did so now. Once inside, however, he was certain that everything was just as he had left it—including the mess. Coffee cup in the sink, bed torn askew…and a piece of red lace sticking out from underneath his pillow. He'd seen to it that Ashley had gotten her purse back, but sending Sandy over with her underwear would have been tasteless in the extreme. He'd thrown the wisps of silk and lace beneath his pillow, instead.

After walking over to the bed, he lifted the pillow and felt the fabric between his fingers. Her scent seemed to drift up to him. A knot formed in his stomach, and a little constriction of desire tugged at him with the sensory memories that invaded his mind and body. He tucked the lace back beneath the pillow, wondering again if they weren't both insane, then realizing that although Ashley had gone pale with everyone staring at her that morning, she hadn't backed down, hadn't made apologies or excuses. Yet he couldn't help but wonder if she would roam his way so quickly that evening.

The tightness remained. He couldn't believe it. He wanted her here. Well, hell, of course. She moved like magic. There were moments with Ashley when the entire world could collide with the sun, and he wouldn't even know he was dying. She was naturally sensual, instinctive, a knockout in bed. But that wasn't it. Or wasn't all of it, anyway. She had challenged him and, somehow, shaken him, everything about him. He didn't just want to sleep with her; he liked waking up beside her. In the past, he had felt crowded when a woman stayed too long, but he felt an emptiness when Ashley wasn't there. She could be all business, cool, efficient. She could be aloof, angry and speak her mind. But she was always sensual and compelling, whether she meant to be or not. And persistent.

He hesitated, wondering if it wasn't the growing feeling of…*need* inside him that had made him so quick to respond to her request for help. Of course, it was, damn it. She'd entered his life like a whirlwind. And like a whirlwind, she had changed it. She had changed *him*, he thought.

Thinking of Ashley, Jake gave a quick call to Carnegie, who assured him that he didn't mind at all if the family wanted their son guarded.

"Anything new on the case?" Jake asked him.

"Zilch. The only people who believe there's a mystery behind it are the parents, the friend who involved you in the whole thing, and that nutcase who did some stories for the tabloid and got the cops digging in all the wrong places. But we're still working it."

"Thanks. Listen, I'm dealing with a mountain of shit today, but I may talk with the folks at that rag myself, if you don't mind."

"Be my guest. Like I said, I've been around too many years to let pride get in the way of truth. I take anything I can get."

When Jake hung up, he was irritated with himself. The day was going fast. He didn't need to be here; he had to get moving, had to check out the properties. He shook his head, thinking that he couldn't afford to spend any more time on a case that wasn't even his.

He sat at his desk, rubbing his temples for a moment, swore, then got up and dug in his medicine chest for something to cure a headache. He sat at his desk again, turned on his computer and began to bring up his records.

He was certain that whoever had been on the boat

hadn't been out to rob him. They had been searching for information.

Therefore, he had information worth looking for.

What the hell was it?

Words, numbers, names, swam before his eyes. *Smoke and mirrors.* Corpses, descriptions of the damage done to the bodies. The most glaring common factor to be found among the murdered women, the slashing of the ears.

A religious cult.

The ears slashed—like Custer's had been at Little Bighorn, because he hadn't *heard* the words of the Sioux, hadn't listened. Obvious.

What if it wasn't so obvious?

What if the ears had been slashed because of what the victims *had* heard, rather than what they hadn't heeded? He hesitated, thought of the list of properties that Cassie Sewell had shown or represented, and made a phone call. His mind worked as he waited for someone to pick up.

Smoke and mirrors.

Back to the obvious. The dead women had been associated with the cult. Had they died because they hadn't pleased their cult leader, had they revolted against his leadership, not listened to his commandments?

What if the cult itself had been nothing but smoke?

"Sharon, you here?" Nick Montague called. The bar was quiet; Katie was handling the few customers. It still bothered him that he hadn't known Ashley had taken the new position until he had seen the drawing. He felt as if she was slipping away.

Sharon's car was out in the lot. She wasn't in the bar,

so she had to be in the house. Sharon had been acting very strange lately, now that he thought about it. She came and went frequently because of her work, but in the past, he always knew where she was. She'd made a point of saying she was showing such-and-such a place, maybe taking clients to lunch or going to a closing. But lately...she'd been very affectionate one minute, quiet and moody the next.

He was crazy to put as much time into working the place himself as he did. In the last several months the business had been doing exceptionally well. Maybe it was time he stopped focussing so much on the restaurant and focussed more on the important people in his life.

He needed some time with his niece. Quality time, as they called it. And he sure as hell needed more time with Sharon, too.

His palms felt a little sweaty. He might well be a little bit crazy. Sharon was beautiful. Bright. Fun to be with. And he was awfully casual about their relationship. But then, until his brother had died and he'd become Ashley's guardian, he'd been awfully casual about living in general. The bar had been good because it kept him close to boats, which had been his life until then. The water, fishing, sailing to the islands, soaking up the sun, just getting by. He'd never been interested in maintaining a relationship; the world had seemed too large, and far too full of bikini-clad women to ever make him want to settle down with just one. Then the unimaginable had happened when his brother had died and he'd had to pick up Ashley from the neighbor who had been baby-sitting, and try to explain to her that her folks weren't coming home. Those green eyes had filled with tears, and he had held her, forced down the magnitude of his loss, and when she had clung to him, his world had changed. For years, making Nick's place a success—had been his driving goal. Being a father-figure had become the only commitment of his life.

His love for her had paid off. He believed with his whole heart that he had raised an intelligent young woman capable of being on her own. She had her own wing of the house because, now that she was an adult, that allowed her to enjoy independence as well as his protection and guidance. And he, of course, totally re-spected the fact that she was an adult.

Yeah, right.

He was worried as hell about this thing she had going with Jake Dilessio. Sure, he liked Jake—as long as he wasn't messing with his niece. Jake had gone through women like a roll of paper towels since the episode with Nancy Lassiter years ago. Ashley didn't understand a guy like that, good at his work, almost married to his job. A guy who made no other commitments because the world was out there. Nick did know and understand. He'd been that guy.

Nick walked into the kitchen, puzzled. He pulled a bottle of water from the refrigerator, walked to his bed-room, back to the living room. "Sharon?"

"Here, coming!" Sharon called in return at last, emerging from Ashley's room.

Nick frowned, surprised to see that she had been in Ashley's wing of the house. Not that there are any great barriers set up; Ashley never locked the door to her room. Even so, he never entered without a reason, or even without knocking. He'd never seen Sharon in Ashley's room before at all.

Sharon must have noticed his confusion, because she quickly explained. "Some of Ashley's things were mingled in with ours when I did the wash. I took them in for her."

"Ah."

"I'm sorry. If you were calling, I didn't hear you."

"It's all right."

"What's up?"

"Up?" Nick was startled to realize he had forgotten. Then he quickly remembered. "Well, actually, I was thinking... Katie's got the bar, and it looks like it's going to be a slow afternoon. I thought maybe you'd like to go for a spin out on the water. Just you and me. Then again, considering you stare at water all the time because of me, you might want to dress up for dinner. We could drive down to the Keys, or up to Fort Lauderdale. Somewhere that serves food that looks good on a plate, where they have linen tablecloths and a real wine cellar."

"I think Nick's carries excellent wine."

He laughed. "I think we carry a lot of good old domestic beer. How about something a little bit more elegant?"

"That would be lovely," she told him. "One problem," she said apologetically. "I may have to show a property this evening, around eight. I didn't know that you might decide to ditch your second child—the restaurant, I mean—tonight, and I'm afraid I'm committed. If the buyer decides tonight's his only free time, I have to go."

"We'll use the time we've got," he told her with a wolfish grin.

"Oh, yes. We should use the time we've got," she answered, wrapping her arms around his neck.

* * *

The man with the shotgun walked around to the driver's window. Ashley had judged him to be an older man at first—maybe it had been his *American Gothic* attire. She felt as if she'd been swept from the semitropics to Midwest farm country. When he got closer, she could see that the man wasn't very old at all…thirties, maybe forties. He was wiry, with deeply tanned skin and blond hair beneath the straw of his hat.

"Can I help you?" The question was amazingly polite.

Before Ashley could answer, David leaned past her to reply. "I think we're a bit lost." She was startled when he slid an arm around her. "The wife and I are out house hunting. And we were given this address." He held up the paper and quoted the address wrong.

What the hell was David doing now? She held her tongue. Maybe he was right to put on a charade. The man was carrying a shotgun.

"Wrong place," the man told them. He patted the shotgun. "Sorry, didn't mean to scare you folks. We get some weird people out here at times. I have a license for her and all—the gun, I mean. There's a state prison not too far from here, you know. Still, it's a mighty fine neighborhood, but you're way off. You need to be several miles east. You'll have to follow your tracks back to the main road."

"I knew you had it all wrong," David said to Ashley. "The little woman…she's just gotten her driver's license. Can you imagine?"

"Not a problem," the man said. "You can turn around right over there."

"Thanks," Ashley said.

When they were headed back down the road, she could see that the man was still in the middle of the street, staring after them.

"You asshole," she told David.

"Why, darling, every man knows that women can't drive."

She shot him an evil stare. "Oh, yeah, right. What a waste of time. I poked around in a field, met a hippie, then a farmer with a shotgun. God knows, there's probably a pit bull around somewhere, too. We acted like a couple of idiots in front of a guy just out to give us directions. And what the hell did we find out? Stuart was after strawberry farmers."

"You're wrong. There's something going on there, and we both know it."

"No, we both don't know it."

"We need to get back onto that property. And maybe check out the adjoining fields."

"All right, Mr. Journalist, you get onto any property you want to explore and get buckshot riddled through your hide. I'm going to find out who owns that place."

David was silent.

"Well?" she demanded.

"Good idea," he said meekly, smiled, then shrugged.

Jesse Crane had once been with the Miami-Dade police, though that had been some time ago. He was still a law enforcement officer, but, after the death of his wife, he had returned to his roots.

Out along the Tamiami Trail, the Miccosukee Indians owned much of the county land and spread out over much of the no-man's land of the next county, as well. The Miccosukees had their own police force.

Sometimes there were conflicts between the sovereign rights of the Indians and the laws of the county, state and country. Jesse, however, had a way of handling disputes that seemed to bring out the best in everyone. He had a knack of knowing what he could handle himself and when he needed to bring in the more extensive facilities of the county force.

Tall, taut, lithe as melted steel, he exuded a quiet power and knowledge. He knew every dangerous creature in the Glades, could mix a potion that truly kept mosquitoes at bay, and maneuvered the hammocks and waterways of the Glades with greater dexterity than an otter. He was an arresting man with his mixture of Native American and European features, straight, ink-dark hair and hazel eyes.

For a long time, the roar of the airboat kept them from engaging in conversation. Then Jesse cut the motor, and the flat-bottomed vehicle drifted along in a sudden silence. It looked as if they were floating over the land, but they weren't. The sawgrass was so high, though, that it stretched far above the surface of the water, which ranged from two to ten feet in depth.

Jesse pointed across the terrain. "There's your 'residential' area," he said to Jake.

"You could bring the boat up to within about fifty yards of the rear of the property, right?"

Jesse shrugged. "Well, a boat like this. Or a canoe. Nothing major. But then…" He shrugged and looked at Jake. "Hell, a lot of illegal stuff gets transported around this area in small craft and airboats. If you know what you're doing, you can go for miles and if you bump into someone else, it's by sheer accident. What exactly is it that you're looking for?" he asked. "I read about the body that was discovered, but… I thought you'd be looking into religious cults, like the last time."

"I was."

Jesse was silent. The boat kept drifting.

"What do people usually do with property this far west and south?" Jake asked.

Jesse shrugged. "Well, it's not really great for livestock. Too muddy. You get a hurricane like Andrew or just a wet storm through here, and you'd be wading in muck for weeks, months maybe. Not that people don't buy the land and get a few horses, cows, chickens pigs, even. There are a lot of growers out here. The earth is actually incredibly rich in many places. My ancestors grew pumpkins, you know. Haven't seen many pumpkin patches, but…there are a lot of berry farms. You can even do some citrus. Then again, there are those people who just want to have a huge estate. You know, lots of land. They can get it far cheaper out here than anywhere nearer the city. And you can build a huge house, tennis courts, pool, the works. Some people like to be out in the sticks. There are some incredible mansions along some of the trails."

Jake was the silent one then, studying the landscape. From this vantage point, he could see a fair distance. Houses sat far back from the water's edge, though for all he knew the property lines were actually under water. The water could take a man a good distance, could easily get him out of the "swamp" and into civilization.

"Two things go on out here most frequently," Jesse said, still staring at him. "Drug running and murder. Sometimes they go hand in hand."

Jake nodded but was silent.

"Those women who were killed out here…their ears

were slashed, weren't they?" Jesse said. "And they belonged to a cult."

"Uh-huh."

"The slashed ears might have meant the girls weren't heeding the word of their master or maybe it meant they had heard too much. Their ears had betrayed them. An eye for an eye kind of a deal. Or maybe it was just something to throw the police off completely."

Startled, Jake looked at Jesse. "That's exactly what I've been thinking."

"What made you come to that conclusion?"

"I paid a visit to Peter Bordon."

"Oh? And he gave you something?"

"*'Smoke and mirrors,'*" Jake quoted. "I just know there's something I'm missing. It's like I can't see the forest for the trees."

"Well," Jesse said, shrugging, "look that way and you'll see plenty of trees. Hope you can find the forest soon, 'cuz I just heard that Peter Bordon might be released."

Ashley drove David Wharton back to the garage where his car was parked. He intended to head straight down to city hall and procure the property records.

"Small world, actually," she murmured, thinking that it had only been that morning when Jake's Jane Doe had been identified, and she had been involved with property, too.

"Small world?" David said.

She shrugged. "Nothing, really." She didn't want to talk about Jake's case, especially not to a reporter.

"Call my cell," she told him. "I'm going to the hospital."

"I thought Nathan Fresia didn't want you there?"

"He doesn't, but…well, he's got the police there now. I don't have to go to Stuart's room to find out how he's doing. And I'll pick up some flowers for Lucy."

"All right. I have to hurry. I don't know how early they're closing these days."

Ashley nodded and let him go. She drove straight to the hospital. As she parked in the garage, she felt the old unease creeping over her. But it was still daylight, and there were plenty of people walking from their cars to the elevators. She decided to take a minute to call Nick, having remembered on the way that he had said something about dinner. She called the bar, and Katie answered. She told her that Nick had gone out with Sharon for the day.

"Thrown over for another woman," Ashley said.

"Nah…he'll never throw you over. Did you actually make a date with your uncle?"

"No, we just agreed that we were going to make a date, I guess. Thanks, Katie. Hope everyone shows up—if there's a problem, call me. I'm heading back to the hospital."

The garage remained busy as she walked to the elevators. She went to the information desk and was given a room number for Lucy Fresia. She was relieved to find the gift shop open, and she bought her some flowers.

In contrast to Nathan's coolness earlier, Lucy was glad to see her. She was impatient and fretful, eager to get up and see her son, but Nathan had insisted that she wasn't to move, that she had to rest—then *he* could fall apart.

"Lucy, I know the girls and I couldn't possibly have

tripped over a cord and unplugged anything in that room," Ashley said earnestly.

Lucy smiled grimly. "My dear, Nathan still believes in accidents. I don't. It wasn't an accident that Stuart is here, no matter how those cops look at me sometimes. And I don't believe that plug was pulled by accident, either. Oh, and thank God you thought of hiring them. I didn't even think of hiring security. I suppose, if the police really believed someone had been trying to kill Stuart, they would have had someone guarding him already. And I'm sure you promised to pay those men, but Nathan and I can certainly afford it, so don't you even think about it."

"Lucy, really, that's something we can worry about later."

She squeezed Lucy's hand. "Let's pray Stuart comes to soon, and that will solve everything."

"Absolutely." Lucy ran her fingers over the hospital sheet. "They won't discharge me until the morning. Of course, the good thing is, I won't have far to go to be with Stuart again."

"Right."

"Now, Nathan may give you a problem, but if you've got the time, go on up and see him. Tell him he must leave long enough to come give me a kiss and a hug and convince me that Stuart is doing just fine."

"Certainly."

Ashley kissed Lucy goodbye, then headed down a floor and over. She reflected that she was getting to know the hospital far too well.

When she got to Stuart's floor, the waiting room was empty. She walked tentatively down the hall to his room, hoping the curtains would be open and Nathan would see her, even come out to talk to her.

But as she approached the room, she came to a dead halt. There was a chair in front of the room, with an off-duty police officer in it, just as there should have been.

She was stunned to see that the officer was Len Green.

"Len!"

"Hey, sweetheart." He stood, a slow smile on his face as he walked over to give her a kiss on the cheek.

She pulled back, looking at him. "Aren't you supposed to be on duty?"

He shook his head. "I've only been here a few minutes."

"But…how…?"

"I heard Marty put out a call, and when I heard what he wanted, I volunteered right away." He lowered his voice. "I didn't know the money situation with…well, with these people, but since I assumed that you were the one to get the whole thing started, I figured I could put in a few hours for free."

"That's great of you, Len."

"Not a problem."

"But the Fresias can afford to pay, and unless you've won the lottery lately, I'm sure you could use the money."

Before he could respond, the door opened. Nathan—thinning hair sticking straight up, clothing sadly rumpled—had apparently seen her. She braced herself, not knowing what her welcome would be.

"How's he doing?" she asked softly.

"No better, but no worse," he said, and seemed relieved by that small wonder. "Ashley, I didn't mean to be rude before, but the doctors…well, they were convinced we were letting too many people in, and that someone must have tripped over the cord without knowing it. Of course, the good news is that the machine was off and he was making it on his own. That's an encouraging sign."

"That's great, Nathan," Ashley said. "And by the way, I've just received instructions from your wife. She wants to see you. If you trust me, I'll stay with Stuart."

He took her by the shoulders. He didn't speak but kissed her on the forehead.

"I'm off, then," he said. He grinned ruefully, proving he was keeping something of a sense of humor. "Maybe I can meet some new friends along the way. I'm starting to think of this place as home."

She and Len watched him walk down the hall. "Len, bless you for coming. I'm going to go in with him."

"I'll be here."

Ashley went into Stuart's room. She glanced at her phone quickly to make sure she hadn't missed a call, then set it for vibrate so it wouldn't make a shattering noise in the quiet room.

Sitting by Stuart, she listened to the drone, wheeze and hiss of his machines. She took his hand, and, as had become her custom, she began to talk to him, telling him all about her day, and that she and David Wharton were on the trail, though she really didn't know just what trail they were on yet.

She glanced up. Len was standing outside, arms crossed over his chest, watching her, watching the room.

She felt somehow uneasy and wondered if Len had been able to hear any of her conversation. She hadn't been speaking loudly, but neither had she whispered.

Len looked grim, but when he caught her eyes on him, he smiled and waved, then brought his hand above his eyes and looked off in each direction, as if he were a lookout on a sailing ship. She smiled and gave him a thumbs-up sign.

Nathan was gone a long time. Ashley didn't mind— she was more than willing to sit vigil—she was just surprised.

When he returned at last, she realized the reason for the delay. Lucy had apparently talked him into driving home for a shower. His hair was combed, and he was wearing clean clothing. He motioned her to come out, and when she did so, he immediately apologized for taking so long.

"I should have come to tell you, but Lucy said you wouldn't mind."

"Nathan, I'd sit here all night if you needed," she assured him.

"Well, I'm here now. And you're free." He kissed her forehead. "Thank you, Ashley. And you, young man," he told Len, "Thank you, too."

"Sir, it's my pleasure," Len assured him.

Nathan went into Stuart's room, closing the door behind him.

"Think he's really going to pull through?" Len asked Ashley softly.

"I *know* he's going to pull through," she responded, perhaps too vehemently.

"Hey, it's going to be all right."

"Sorry, I didn't mean to bite."

"It's all right. By the way, congratulations. I heard your drawing brought results. We'll have a lot to celebrate tomorrow night."

"Tomorrow night?"

"We're going out to celebrate your promotion, remember?"

"Yes, I guess I'd forgotten. Oh, by the way, was everything all right when you dropped Karen off last night?"

She thought for a moment that his eyes turned guarded. "What do you mean?" he asked, and it seemed to be his turn to sound sharp.

"Karen called in sick today. I tried to reach her at school."

He shook his head. "Maybe she just wanted a day off. She definitely wasn't sick." He smiled, and she thought his smile was just a little plastic.

"I guess you're right, then—she must just have wanted a day off. Oh, well, I'm going to go ahead and get out of here," she told him. "Len, how late are you staying? Don't you have to be to work early tomorrow?"

"I won't be staying late. A woman from my station is coming in after her husband heads to work. She has Thursdays off, so she'll stay until tomorrow morning."

"Thanks again, Len. Thanks very much." She rose on her toes to kiss his cheek. He moved as she did, and his lips brushed hers.

She drew back quickly, smiling a plastic smile of her own. "Well, see you tomorrow night, then."

He nodded, and Ashley started down the hallway. She turned and saw that he was still watching her, so she waved and hurried off.

When she reached the elevators, she realized that she'd set her phone on vibrate, then stuck it in her purse without thinking, so there was no telling how many calls she'd missed. And it was long past five, David Wharton must have left city hall a long time ago.

She checked. As she had feared, she'd missed his call.

She swore to herself, punching the elevator button, then getting into the empty car, thinking nothing of it. As she followed the instructions to get her messages, she stepped out into the parking garage.

Automatically, she started walking toward her car just as she opened David Wharton's message. He sounded excited.

"Ashley! Damn it, how can you be not answering your phone? Anyway, the owner of the property is listed as Caleb Harrison. But get this. You're not going to believe who last sold that property. You are just not going to believe it!"

Chapter 17

Ashley was so stunned when she heard the name that she stood dead still.

And it was then that she heard the sound of footsteps coming from behind her.

Goose bumps instantly broke out as if something inside was warning her that it wasn't just a noise, it was a *menace*. She turned around slowly. There were a lot of cars in the garage, the shadows they cast creating great pools of darkness. But she saw nothing. No one moving. No one coming toward her.

A sharp slam sounded from ahead, and she realized that a young woman in a nurse's uniform had just gotten out of her car. Ashley still hadn't moved. The woman offered her a smile as she passed by.

Ashley gave herself a shake and started walking again. She heard an echo of footsteps. Not sharp, just an echo…as if someone was being as furtive as possible. She stopped and turned and looked around, fingering the strap of her bag. She still had the gun on her. "Who is it?" she called out, spinning around.

Again, nothing. She started walking once again. And again she heard the footsteps.…

She was almost at her car. She could hear the sound, growing closer, close.…

She stopped, pulled the gun out and spun around, both hands on her weapon, just as a car came around the corner. The woman driving widened her eyes and let out a scream. Ashley quickly lowered the weapon, damning herself.

"It's all right, police business!" she shouted, wincing. Police business? Like hell. She was a forensic artist, not a sworn officer of the law, wielding a weapon in a public garage. She had to get a grip.

She stopped and then…

Heard the footsteps. Flat and hard, coming from behind her. She turned, her hands still on the gun, but she didn't raise it.

Thank God.

She let out a sigh. "Len! What the hell are you doing here? You're supposed to be on guard duty. You scared the hell out of me."

"Me! I scared *you*? You're the one with a gun. Are you still supposed to have that weapon, Ashley? Shouldn't you have turned it in when you went civilian?"

"Yes, I have to turn it in."

"What happened? Was there another incident? Why are you so spooked?"

"Why aren't you on guard duty?"

"My replacement came early, so I came chasing after you for a ride home, since I got dropped off in a patrol car today. Now, your turn. What are you doing with that gun?"

"I thought I heard…"

"Ashley, even assuming someone *was* following you the other night, they have to be long gone by now. Why are you still so afraid?"

"Because there's still something seriously wrong where Stuart is concerned. I know it. And I'm afraid someone doesn't want me pursuing it."

"Wow," he murmured, looking at her eyes. "You really are worried."

"I'm all right. I'm just going to find out what is going on."

Len looked around the garage. "Ashley, you've got to be careful with that gun. This is a busy place."

"No, Len, it's not. Not when it's late. Then it's a big place full of shadows where you have no idea who might be skulking around behind the cars."

He sighed. "You working tomorrow?"

"Yes."

"They're going to make you give that gun back."

"Yes, I suppose they will. Len, if you need a ride, come on."

"Sure."

She clicked her car open and they walked the few feet remaining to reach it. Len settled in next to her. "You're very mysterious, you know."

"Just tired."

"Tense. Want to stop somewhere for a drink?"

"I never drink and drive."

"You can drink, and I'll drive."

She found herself cracking a smile at last as she looked at him. "That wouldn't help. This is my car. You'd be stuck at Nick's."

He looked straight ahead. "I wouldn't mind being stuck at Nick's."

Ashley caught her breath, keeping her eyes on the road. "Len…"

"Yeah, I know. You were too busy with the academy to be interested in a relationship. Well, you're out of the academy now."

"And starting a new job. The training is overwhelming."

"Overwhelming. Right. You know how many times someone gets offered a position like that out of the blue? When dozens of people would love to have it? You may find you've made some enemies, Ashley."

She frowned, feeling his bitterness. "I also spent my first day as a civilian employee in the morgue on one of the most god-awful assignments I may ever get. And for your information, I worked my ass off in the academy, and I'll be working it off again now!"

"Right. Getting buddy-buddy with the big-time detectives."

Her breath caught. His manner was strange, as if she had betrayed him in some way. "Forensic artists probably do work frequently with the detectives. It only makes sense."

"I think we both know what I mean."

"What do you want me to say, Len? I never wanted to hurt you, but I never encouraged you. Besides, I have a gorgeous friend who's crazy about you, and you're completely cavalier about her."

"Karen," he murmured.

"Yes, Karen." She took a breath. "Len, look. I guess it's good that we're having this out. I like you. You're a good guy, and I'd like to be your good friend. But…"

"I'm not man enough for you, is that it?"

"Len, what is the matter with you?"

"Sorry." He looked straight ahead. "Man, I *am* being a jerk."

"Karen is nuts about you, you know."

"Oh, yeah. Karen."

She shook her head. "Len…where am I taking you?"

"Just drive to Nick's. I'm off duty. I'm going to have a drink."

"And how are you going to get home?"

"There's this thing called a taxicab. If all else fails, I'll call one. Don't worry, I won't be coming after you to give me a ride later."

"I don't mind giving you a ride, but…"

She hesitated. But she had things to do tonight.

"I'm just really tired tonight," she told him.

"Ashley, it doesn't matter. I told you, if all else fails, I'll grab a cab."

"All right."

She drove to Nick's and parked. Len was still stiff as he got out of the car. He followed Ashley as she walked across the terrace and into the bar. Katie was behind it.

"Are Nick and Sharon back?" Ashley asked.

"No, sorry. They haven't returned yet."

Ashley nodded, hiding her disappointment. She slid around behind the bar to get Len a beer, hoping he would have a drink and lose his grudge, then head on home. She noticed that he was at the counter between Sandy and Curtis. The three of them were already talking about an accident that had occurred that day on the Palmetto Expressway.

He thanked her for the beer. She nodded, and said hello to the others. Then she asked Katie if things were all right, and when Katie assured her that everything was completely under control, she slipped on through the back to the house.

For a long moment she stood in the living room.

Sharon.

Sharon Dupre had sold the property to its current owner. She had nearly dropped clear through the asphalt. And now, when she really needed to talk to Sharon, she and Nick had apparently decided on a long romantic evening out.

She walked to the door of her uncle's bedroom, wondering if Sharon had some kind of filing system in the house—she spent almost all her time here now. But she didn't want to impose on her uncle's domain. It didn't seem right.

She didn't walk in. Instead, she crossed through the house and went into her own room. As soon as she stepped through the door, she had a strange feeling. Her pillow had been moved. A drawer in the antique nightstand was just slightly ajar.

Frowning, she leaned against the door.

Maybe she was just going off the deep end. She sat down and dialed David Wharton's number but only got his answering machine. Frustrated, she hung up without leaving a message. Then she tried calling Karen and got her answering machine, as well. As soon as she hung up, a call came through. It was Jan.

"Jan, hey, I needed to talk to you," she said, and went on to tell her friend about the plug being pulled at the hospital, about Nathan's initial reaction, and then, how they had gotten off-duty officers to guard the room.

"Well, thank God, because I know I didn't trip over anything," Jan said indignantly. "And there should have been police officers watching him all along."

"Actually, I don't think our convictions are being overlooked." She was amazed to find herself defending those who were investigating the accident.

"It's just that the police are having a very hard time. No one saw anything, just a guy in his underwear on the highway. And you can't begin to imagine the number of accidents that happen every day in this county."

"Not too many that involve a guy in his underwear wandering on the highway," Jan reminded her. "And they must realize now, since someone attacked Stuart in the hospital, that he knows something that will put someone in jail."

"Unfortunately, Stuart's doctor really believes we were careless. No one but us thinks someone pulled that plug on purpose. Anyway, Stu is being watched over now."

"Karen will go ballistic when she hears—actually, that's why I called you. I can't get hold of her. She called in sick, but I can't get her at home, either."

"I know. Strange, isn't it?"

Jan giggled. "Maybe she got her cop. Maybe they went off to have a romantic fling."

"No, I'm afraid not."

"How do you know?"

"I've seen the cop. Len is here, at the bar, right now. He went to work, and then after work he came in for a few hours to be the cop on duty at the hospital."

"Oh," Jan said, perplexed.

"Maybe we should go to her place."

"It's not like we haven't seen her in forever," Ashley reminded Jan.

"With Karen, it is. She always returns my phone calls."

"Mine, too," Ashley admitted. "Maybe we *should* take a drive over to her house."

"I'm working tonight. I just took a break to call you. Do you think…you don't think anything is really wrong, do you?"

"No, of course not. Listen, I'll just take a drive over and check on her, in case she's so sick she's not answering her phone. Although, actually, maybe we should just give her parents a call. Maybe she's with them for some reason."

"I already tried that. I played it casual. I didn't want to get her mother worried."

"I'll just drive over, then."

"You have a key to her house? Because I do, if you don't."

"I have a key. And I know the alarm code, too, so I'll be fine."

"All right, then. I should be going with you. I don't like you going alone."

"I've had police training, remember?"

"Yeah, I know. But call me the minute you find out anything. I may not get the call right away, but I'll check my messages every chance I get."

"I'm sure we're overreacting."

Jan was silent for a second. "If the cop had disappeared, too, I'd say she was off being romantic. But you said you know where the cop is."

"Yes, I do. I just left him sitting there. But I'll go ask

him if Karen said anything to him about taking off, and then I'll take a ride out to her place. I'll call you after I've gotten there and just leave a message if you're in the middle of a set."

"Great. Thanks."

They hung up. Ashley started out of the room, then hesitated. *Nothing was missing, things were just... moved.*

She was definitely getting obsessed with little things. Maybe Nick had been in for some reason. She didn't lock the door. Maybe Sharon had been in. Sharon, who had sold the property at the address that had been found scratched on a piece of paper belonging to Stuart Fresia, who was in the hospital, fighting for his life.

And now... Karen.

Reflecting on the state of her room wasn't solving anything. Feeling for the gun in her handbag, she hurried on out.

Jesse didn't seem to mind traversing the waterways, giving up his time for what might be a major miscalculation on Jake's part. They spent hours on the airboat, returning at last to Jesse's place deep in a hammock off the Trail. A private, unmarked road led to the house, so only those who'd been invited even knew there was a dwelling behind the trees.

Jesse offered him food and drink, since they'd been out a long time.

"What have you got?" Jake asked him.

Jesse laughed. "What are you expecting? Finger porridge—koonti root goop? Nope, sorry, nothing ethnic. I've got ham and cheese, salami and cheese, or corn flakes. I think there's some fruit."

Jake opted for a sandwich over corn flakes, and made it himself while Jesse dragged out maps of the tip of the state.

Spreading the maps out on the table, Jesse said, "So your meeting with Peter Bordon has gotten you thinking the cult idea is a blind?"

"I think it's an idea. Think about it. We've had men checking out every religious group we can find, giving special attention to any group new to the area. The most we've found are some questionable Santeria groups, but we're looking for people who kill other people, and so far, our Santeria groups are only guilty of chicken sacrifices. So far we haven't found anything that remotely smacks of the kind of cult Bordon was running. And we don't even have any proof that his cult was involved in those killings. Bordon was never indicted for murder."

"True. Still...most people believe he ordered the killings."

"I believed it, too."

"You don't believe it anymore?"

"I believe he was involved. But I'm starting to doubt my conviction that he was the mastermind. The latest victim was a Realtor. Her properties were all on the edge of civilization. Bordon's place was also in that area. The only connection I can think of is that all the properties are along waterways that can be reached through the Everglades. We both know that smugglers, murderers, thieves and worse have taken sanctuary in the Glades. We're talking expanses that no one has ever been able to patrol completely. So I can't help thinking the case has to do with something coming into the country."

"Drugs? They're the most prevalent. People, smuggled in to get around the INS," Jesse said. "Arms. The weapons trade is massive."

Jake nodded. "Running weapons calls for large scale transportation. Same with people. I'm betting on drugs."

"I'll have my people keep an eye out."

"My money says we're talking heroin or cocaine, where small packages mean big money."

"Like I said, we'll be watching."

"Great, thanks."

Leaving Jesse's, Jake frowned, checking his phone. It hadn't rung in hours. The damn thing didn't work out in the swamp—no cell towers around. He had to drive east for thirty minutes before he could access his own messages.

Franklin had called in, as had Marty, but nobody had anything to report. Uniformed officers were combing the area with the sketch, trying to find locals who might know something about the victim's last days.

His third message was a startling one. He didn't know the voice, nor did he recognize the name. The man spoke in a hushed and nervous tone.

"I'm calling on behalf of Peter Bordon. He wants to talk to you. Without fanfare, if you know what I mean. Bring a posse and it's off. He'll talk to you and only you."

That was it. The nervous, unknown caller had hung up.

Len was still at the bar, sandwiched between Sandy and Curtis. After a couple of quick hellos, she got to the point. "Len, has Karen called you by any chance?"

He shook his head. "Should she have called me? I just saw her last night."

"She didn't go to work today, and neither Jan nor I have been able to reach her by phone."

"I'm sorry, I haven't heard from her."

"Did she say she had something to do today? That she was going to call in sick?"

"Ashley, I'm sorry, she didn't say anything about it at all."

"It's all right, thanks. I think I'll go check on her, though."

She turned away, slipping back through the office and into the house, then out through the kitchen.

In the car, she slipped Karen's house key onto her ring before turning her own key in the ignition, so she wouldn't get there and be scrambling to discover what she'd done with it.

Leaving the marina behind, she told herself that she and Jan were being alarmists. It wasn't an emergency because someone had missed one day of work and didn't seem to be home. And yet, it was true that Karen always returned their calls.

As she passed the lights of the city, she thought for a moment that Miami was truly beautiful by night. Night hid the areas that weren't so nice. Moonlight fell on the waterways and added an aura of soft mystique.

And yet, it was under cover of darkness that so much of the city's crime took place.

First Stuart. Now Karen.

No. She refused to believe that anything had happened to her friend.

But when she drove up to the house, Karen's little Toyota was right where she kept it in the driveway. Both sides of her property line were bordered with cherry hedges. A large poinciana tree took up much of the front lawn. Karen had planted bougainvillea all around the little trellised entrance to her home. Everything looked the same as always. So why wasn't Karen answering her phone?

Ashley stared at the house for several seconds before getting out of the car. There were lights on inside, but they were dim. She got out of the car at last and headed up the walk. The outside light that usually lit up the entrance area was not on. She found herself gritting her teeth as she stared into the shadows of the trellised entryway, silently cursing Karen for not leaving the light on.

She was an almost-cop, as David Wharton had dubbed her. She still had her gun in her shoulder bag.

Before trying the key, she rang the bell, banged on the knocker and called Karen's name. There was no reply. At last, she got out her key and twisted it in the lock. Opening the door, she called out for Karen again. Still no reply.

She went in, deactivated the alarm, then locked the door. Even that act made her a little nervous. What if someone had attacked Karen? What if that someone was still in the house? She might have locked herself in with a predator.

She gave herself a serious mental shake. She and Jan were overreacting to a situation that probably didn't even exist.

"Karen!" she said.

The living room was as charming as ever. She could see both the kitchen area and the little tiled family room behind the dining room. She walked through the living room, noticing that the living room was as organized as Karen always kept it. Neat as a pin. Nothing was disheveled or out of place. On top of a bookcase there were several pictures. Karen with her mom and dad, with her sister and brother. Karen with the large family hound, Otter, taken when the beloved pet had still been alive.

Karen, herself and Jan, strapped into bungee cords at the Dade County Youth Fair, several years before.

"Karen!" she called out again, and moved into the kitchen. Nothing out of order. Dishes done, put away. She was definitely the neatest and most organized of the three of them.

Ashley ducked her head into the small hallway bath. Empty. She forced herself at last into the guest bedroom, which Karen used as a computer room. Clean and neat, every paper in its place, her incoming and outgoing boxes filled, but even the envelopes in them aligned.

Ashley's feet were dragging as she headed for Karen's bedroom door.

It was shut.

"Karen?" she called out softly. Still no reply. She put her hand on the knob. But before she could twist it, she was startled by a loud and violent pounding on the front door. She jumped. As she pulled back, the knob twisted in her hand. The door squealed on its hinges and inched ajar.

The room was dark.

The pounding came again....

Ashley ignored the noise, and turned on the light.

Sunsets on the road were often glorious. The sky turned to incredible pastel shades, with streaks of gold flashing through them as the last rays of day disappeared. When darkness came, though, it felt infinite, especially out in the Everglades.

Night had long fallen. The world had boiled down to nothing but the lights of approaching cars and those of the vehicles that followed behind Jake.

Then, ahead of him, the world became bathed in the glow of the city again as he neared the Miccosukee casino and crossed back over to an area that was increasingly more inhabited. If he kept going long enough, he would reach the strip where too many prostitutes had once plied their trade. Many of them had wound up strangled, their mangled bodies usually discovered within days. They had been killed by a man who had made mistakes, not as clever, as he'd thought he was. He had given himself away and been caught. Farther down, closing in on downtown, the street would lose its English orientation and become known as Calle Ocho. Crimes closer to downtown often had to do with passion or with deals gone sour. There were often witnesses to street violence, and clues aplenty.

There were always clues. No crime was perfect. Even so, despite the best efforts of law enforcement and modern forensics, some crimes went unsolved.

Not this one. He felt he had something. All the pieces to a jigsaw puzzle. They just had to be put together.

Tomorrow he would be taking a long drive. The call might have been a hoax, but thanks to caller identification, he knew that at least it had come from the prison.

His instinct told him that the call had indeed been made at Bordon's request. Bordon had always had the answers. Until now, he hadn't been willing to give them, to admit to anything.

Had he changed his mind? If so, why?

Fear? Of someone on the outside? Or the inside?

Then again, Bordon was a master manipulator. There were no guarantees. The man might enjoy the prospect of having the power to bring him north time and again, working him like a yo-yo.

There was no sense of going insane now. He would make a call to the prison later, and head up first thing in the morning. Waiting would be a bitch.

Once in town, Jake didn't take the left that would have brought him to police headquarters, nor did he continue on to the marina. Despite the time, and the fact that he would arrive unannounced, he had decided to pay another visit to Mary Simmons.

The Hare Krishna building was a nice one, off a street near a dog park, where the residents had always enjoyed their lush foliage, an asset of the area that was maintained vigilantly. The shrubs and trees were not as manicured as they tended to be in Coral Gables, but they had a defiant charm all their own. At night, just blocks down, the area came alive with its shops, restaurants and clubs. The Krishnas often chanted their way down those populated streets, gathering what donations they could along the way.

When he arrived, though, the building itself seemed quiet. He was welcomed at the door by a fellow whose head was entirely shaved, except for the long tail of hair that grew from his pate. He was young, with idealistic eyes and the manner of one who had decided that he was going to be at peace with the world, whether he really understood his doctrine or not. He was polite and eager to help Jake, even before Jake showed him his badge.

He went to retrieve Mary.

She didn't seem too surprised to see Jake, and welcomed him, telling him that they could talk outside. He joined her in a little garden area and got right to the point. "Mary, I understand Bordon had whichever woman he chose each night and that there wasn't any jealousy, that the women could also sleep with others, if they chose."

She nodded, then gave him something of a sad smile. "We all wanted Peter, of course. It's hard to describe to someone else how a man could…could make women want him that much when they were sharing him. There were other men. John Mast, for one." She sighed, pleating the folds of the long orange robe she was wearing. "John is dead. I know that, of course." She looked up, suddenly vehement. "And don't go thinking that John Mast had those women killed because he was jealous of Peter. John was a believer. A true believer in what we were doing, in sharing the good of God's earth…in loving one another. He was a good man. Smart. I think he knew he was eventually going to get in trouble over the finances, because I heard him argue with Peter a few times. He was always worried. But Peter didn't listen to him. And John wasn't invited around when the doors were closed. I feel very badly about John. He went to prison without saying a word, just for doing what he'd been told. And then he died."

"I'm sorry, too, Mary. But I didn't come here to talk to you because I'm convinced one of your…friends was evil. I think something else was going on. Something maybe none of you knew about."

She shrugged. "Well, that could be. But whatever was going on, Peter would have known. He told us when we had to be in, and when we had to be out, working."

"Did boats ever come through the canals?"

"Sure. Every day." She smiled. "I'm sure lots of boats are still going by. Little boats. Canoes, rowboats, small motorboats. That's why people like to live along the waterways, Detective Dilessio."

He smiled back. "Of course, Mary. Did any of those boats ever pull up at the back of the property? Did Peter Bordon have anything delivered that way?"

She shrugged. "Could be. I don't know. I was never asked to help unload anything from a boat. How much could you actually bring in by boat? Only small vessels could get through. And airboats, of course. But they're so loud.... I heard one every now and then. But they never stopped. Not that I can remember."

"How about canoes?"

She hesitated. "Maybe. Sometimes...late at night, when I was in the common room, I would hear noises. But we knew not to leave, you see. We all had a place, and we all kept to our place. That's the way it was."

"Maybe everyone didn't keep to her place, Mary. And maybe that's why those girls died."

A flicker of pain crossed her features. "Maybe," she agreed.

"You had drugs available, right? Lots of drugs?"

"Lots of aphrodisiacs," she murmured. Then she met his eyes. "Sure. Lots of drugs. We didn't shoot up or anything.... At least, I didn't. I'm clean as a whistle, Jake. So is everybody here."

"I'm not attacking the Krishnas, Mary. I'm looking for a killer."

She nodded. "Drugs were always available."

"Thanks, Mary. And if you think of anything else—"

"I'll call you. Detective, I'd really like to help you. Honestly."

"I believe you."

He started to head out. She followed him. "Detective?"

"Yes?"

She hesitated. "I know how you've always felt...what you've always believed, that Peter might have been... somehow involved. But I don't believe he ever slit a woman's throat."

"Thanks, Mary. Actually, I never believed he carried out the murders himself. But he knows who did. I'm sure of it. And one way or another, I'm going to find out."

Chapter 18

Nothing.

Karen's room was, like the rest of the house, as neat as a pin. Beneath the overhead lighting, the quilt was straight and even, the pillows leaned against the head-board, and everything appeared to be in perfect order.

The thunderous pounding on the door continued, then stopped abruptly. Ashley turned away from the bed and started back through the house. At the door, she peered through the peephole. There was no one there. She bit her lower lip. She heard a sound, someone coming around the side of the house. Then silence...followed by a noise at the living room window. She drew the gun from her bag and walked to the front door, opening it.

As she stepped out on the porch, someone came back around from the side of the house. "Stop right there!" she said.

"Ashley?"

She let out a rush of air and lowered the weapon. "Len? Len, what the hell are you doing, sneaking around the yard?"

"Me? What the hell are *you* doing? It's as if you're determined to get off a shot at me tonight." He walked toward her, shaking his head. "I pounded at the door. You didn't answer. You got me worried about Karen, then you went to her house and didn't answer when my pounding should have wakened the dead."

"I was in the other room, Len."

"Is anything out of order?" he asked.

"No," she said softly. "I don't think so. I'm going to check around one more time." She frowned. "How did you get here?"

"Don't give me that frown. I wasn't drinking and driving. I made Sandy drop me off."

"Great, you had Sandy drinking and driving."

"No, he was drinking non-alcoholic beer tonight. Honest."

"But why did you have him bring you out here?"

"I was worried about you coming out here alone."

"Len, don't you get started. Are you going to worry about every female on the force?"

"You're not on the force. You're a civilian employee. And you're forgetting that officers are supposed to have backup when they might be facing a dangerous situation."

She believed that, in his way, he really was trying to help. "All right, come in for a few minutes. I just want to take one more walk through the place."

Len followed her back in. Ashley walked through the computer room and the bedroom one more time.

She hesitated, realizing that she hadn't checked out the bathroom off the master bedroom. She did so, aware that Len was right behind her.

At first glance, the bathroom appeared to be as spotless as the rest of the house. As a last thought, she pulled back the shower curtain. The tile was as clean as everything else.

Then she saw the little specks on the bottom of the tub. She knelt down. There were just three. Three little specks of something that looked like rust.

Rust—or blood.

Ashley's heart careened into her throat. She told herself that they could be anything. They were tiny little specks. It wasn't as if the bathroom had been sprayed with blood. She didn't even know if it *was* blood. And if it was, the amount was minute. Karen might just have nicked herself while shaving.

Still...

She stood abruptly and walked into the kitchen. Rummaging in a cabinet, she found a box of plastic sandwich bags, then procured a white plastic knife from the drawer where Karen kept her picnic paraphernalia.

"What is it?" Len asked her.

"Probably nothing," she said. But she walked past him and went back into the bathroom, then knelt down, scraped the speck from the tub and bagged it, along with the plastic knife. She slid the plastic bag into her purse and stood. Len was in the doorway, staring at her. "What's wrong?"

"Nothing. I'm probably just overreacting."

"But what are you doing?"

"Just checking the tub." He was so tall, she thought.

His shoulders filled the doorway. Her imagination ran wild. What if Len were a killer? Cops did go bad.

She had a .38 Special in her bag, and they both knew she could use it. "Let's get out of here. Karen definitely isn't home."

For a moment it seemed as if he would stay in the doorway. Stop her from exiting. Then he shook his head, moving aside. "I know you know your friend much better than I do, but I think you're right about overreacting. I'm sure she's all right. Even your best friend can have secrets."

"That's possible, of course."

"Ashley, all she did was call in sick and not answer her phone."

"I'm sure you're right. And I'll try not to go off the deep end needlessly. I need some sleep," she said. She waited for him to precede her out of the house. He hesitated, then did so.

"I'll take you home," she told him.

"No need. Curtis is waiting at Nick's. He said he'd drop me off later."

"All right."

They drove in silence for a while. Then Len said, "Doesn't she have other friends, besides you and Jan?"

"Of course."

"Well then?"

"You're absolutely right. She must be out with someone else."

Ashley almost jumped when her phone rang. She dug into her purse and answered quickly. It was Jan.

"Well?"

"She wasn't home, her car is in the drive, and the house is as neat as a pin." *And there were little specks of what might have been blood in her bathtub.* She didn't say that, though. There was no reason to alarm Jan further. Not until she actually knew what she had found.

And she *would* know. Tomorrow morning, she would pour her heart out to Mandy Nightingale, who would help her. She hadn't been under Mandy's wing that long, but she knew the woman would listen to her and help her, not mock her. And in a pinch, there was always Jake.

"Are you all right?" Jan asked anxiously. "I shouldn't have let you go there alone."

"I wasn't alone. I'm not alone."

"Oh?"

"Len Green is with me."

"Oh, good. You're with a cop."

A cop who might have turned bad. *What the hell was she thinking, and why on earth should she be thinking it?*

"So what do we do now?" Jan asked.

"See if she comes home tonight. And if we don't hear from her tomorrow, we fill out a missing persons report. And get people who know what they're doing in on it."

"She hasn't even been gone twenty-four hours," Len reminded her gently, interrupting the conversation.

"We'll both keep trying her tonight," Ashley said, ignoring him. Jan agreed, and they hung up.

A few minutes later, they reached Nick's. Before Ashley turned off the engine, she said, "You're certain you have a ride."

"Yep. Curtis and Sandy both thought it was a good idea if I went to check on you. Sandy was going out, so he dropped me, and Curtis promised to wait until we were back."

"Okay, I'm going to bed then."

They both got out, and Len looked at her over the roof of the car. He saluted. "Good night, then. I'll just go find Curtis."

She nodded, then felt ridiculous and guilty. "Len?"

"Yeah?"

"Thanks for coming after me."

"Sure. Keep me posted. I—I do like her, too, you know."

He walked around to the terrace entrance. Ashley let herself in by the side door. "Sharon?" she called, as she walked in. "Nick?"

No one replied, and she didn't want to go back through the bar to see if they were there. She went into her own room. This time, nothing had changed. She shook her head, still convinced that someone had been in there earlier. She flopped down on her bed, exhausted, though it wasn't even that late. She and Jan might have been ridiculous, checking up on Karen so quickly. Still...there were those spots in the bathtub.

Jake hadn't even reached his car before his cell phone rang. He was surprised to hear Carnegie on the other end. "Jake, I just wanted to let you know I'm real glad you arranged for those off-duty guys to stand guard at the hospital."

"Has something else happened?" He felt more than a twinge of guilt. He had told Ashley that he would look into the case, but his own affairs had taken such precedence that he hadn't even thought about the Stuart Fresia investigation since he'd handed the matter over to Marty.

"Not really, but I decided to talk to that guy again,

the one who was writing for the same paper Fresia was. Guess what I found out? He doesn't exist."

"What do you mean, he doesn't exist? I thought he was screaming louder than anyone that people needed to look into the accident, that Stuart Fresia had been on to something."

"Yes, that's true. But when I went to call him today, the number he gave me was a pizza parlor. So I went to the paper, talked to personnel and got his social security number. Checked up on that, and it belonged to a guy killed in World War Two. I went back to the hospital, where he'd been hanging around like a leech. All of a sudden, he's nowhere to be seen. What it means exactly, I don't know. But I've got the department picking up the bill for round-the-clock protection. I just wanted to let you know."

"Thanks, Carnegie. Thanks a lot. I'm going to be out of town the first half of tomorrow, at least, but I'll have my cell phone. If you get anything else, let me know. And if you don't mind, I'll do some prying myself when I get back. And if you think of anything specific I can do, just yell."

"All right. I'll keep you posted."

"You're working late," Jake said, glancing at his watch.

"Not that late. And hey, I'm willing to bet you didn't knock off according to the clock."

"Think we'll die young?"

A chuckle came over the wire. "Too late for me," Carnegie said wryly. "But you—you watch your back."

"Will do."

They rang off. Jake thought about calling Marty to let him know he would be out in the morning, then decided against it. Marty probably had gone home or gone out. After all, he had a life.

A life…

Suddenly he was anxious to get home. He had a reason to see Ashley.

As he drove, he called Blake, letting the captain know his intentions and receiving a reminder that he wasn't working the case alone, and that Blake wanted every step of his investigation duly noted on his report. He admitted to Blake that the call might have been a hoax, but if so, it had been a hoax perpetrated at the prison. And if it was real, it seemed that Bordon was afraid of everyone except for his confidant. Either way, Blake agreed that he had to go.

As soon as he finished his conversation with Blake, who had been in the middle of algebra homework with his daughter, Jake called the prison and made arrangements to see Bordon privately first thing in the morning.

Bordon held the key. He knew it.

Hours of interrogation had never made the man give up his secrets. Threats of the death penalty, of years of incarceration, had never made him break his silence. Oddly, now, the prospect of being free had made him willing to talk.

Jake felt his palms grow damp as he drove. He wondered if he would be able to keep his hands off the man if Bordon admitted his complicity in the murders of the young women.

And Nancy.

Ashley had thought she was so tired that she could go to sleep without even getting ready for bed. But instead, her mind was racing. Restless, she rose. Tonight, of all nights, when she was anxious to question Sharon, she and Nick were out doing the town. She couldn't get hold of David Wharton, and Karen still wasn't home or returning any calls.

She called the hospital and asked about Stuart's condition, which was unchanged. She tried calling David Wharton again but got no answer. As she hung up, it occurred to her that Jake might have learned something.

And even if he hadn't, the night would still be better if she could see him.

She let herself out by the door that led to the docks, looking down the line of boats to Jake's *Gwendolyn*. She hesitated, then crossed the little patch of sand and grass to the docks, scissored over the ropes and headed down the dock. She hesitated when she saw that Jake's cabin door was ajar.

"Jake?"

The door opened fully. She recognized the man coming out. The case he was carrying was familiar, as well. She had met him during her whirlwind tour of forensics the other day. His name was Skip Conrad, and he was a fingerprint expert.

He saw her as she walked over to the boat. "Hey, Ashley," he said a little awkwardly. "You live here, too, huh?"

"Nick is my uncle."

"Nick is your uncle?" He was a slim man, with thinning brown hair, dimples and a boyish look, despite the shiny circle on his pate. "Go figure. I didn't know Nick's last name was Montague."

"Well, the signs do just say 'Nick's,'" she said with a smile. "You're working late. Very late. You're usually day shift, right? You dusted Jake's boat for prints?"

"Not officially," he said.

She smiled. Maybe she *was* paranoid, but so was Jake Dilessio—and he was a seasoned homicide detective. "I know he thought someone had been on the boat. He's a friend."

"Jake's a friend of mine, too," Skip said with a shrug. "No matter what he's got going, he takes time if someone else is in trouble, so…well, I figured helping him unofficially was the least I could do." He shrugged again. "Can't say as how I'm really going to help him, though. I didn't get much of anything. Looked as if everything on his desk had been pretty carefully wiped clean—which is what I think he suspected. I've got a few prints, but I bet good money that they're going to prove to be Jake's."

"Well, anyway, helping him out is good of you."

"Yeah?" He looked relieved that she apparently didn't intend to tell anyone else at headquarters what he'd been up to. "Since you live here, you can give Jake back his key for me, right?"

"Sure."

"Actually, will you lock her up for me, too?"

"No problem."

"Well…good to see you." The way he looked at her as he handed her the key, she wasn't sure he was glad to have seen her at all.

"Nice to see you, too, Mr. Conrad."

He grinned then. "Actually, I am 'Officer' Conrad. But call me Skip."

"You went all the way through the academy before getting into the forensics department?"

He shook his head, offering a rueful grin. "I hopped into this position the first opportunity I had. When I became an expert everyone seemed to need, I finished up my studies. You'll do it, too. And congratulations. I hear we've hired Rembrandt."

"I'm not that good," she assured him.

"Well, we're glad to have you anyway. Good night."

He waved and walked off the boat and down the dock. Ashley turned to lock up, then took a look inside the cabin and winced. Fingerprinting was a messy exercise. She hesitated, then decided that she should clean up.

She wondered if he would be angry that she was invading his realm.

She should just lock it up and go....

But she didn't. She went in, closed the door, headed to the kitchen, and dug around until she could find a sponge and cleanser. When she'd finished with the kitchen, she went on to the living area, the master cabin and the second bedroom. She had to admit, the place looked really good when she was done.

She was crazy, she knew. She should head back to her room and get some sleep, but she was too restless.

She walked back into the kitchen area and helped herself to a bottle of juice from the refrigerator, then leaned against the counter. A pad and pencil lay by the counter phone. She picked up the pencil and began drawing idly.

A picture of Karen.

She flicked the page. A picture of Len.

Once again she turned the page, then sketched the scene of the accident, putting in every detail she could recall. This sketch, she realized, was her best. Time had made her mind clearer. She'd wanted details—and she had them. They just didn't seem to help her.

She turned the page again and drew a head study of David Wharton.

Then she grew impatient with herself and anxious for Jake to get back. She set down the pencil and looked around the cabin. She'd done a good job.

Except for the carpet.

She hesitated, then shrugged. She'd gone this far. Surely he had a vacuum cleaner.

He did. She found it stowed in the cabin closet.

The machine roared to life. Satisfied at last, she switched off the vacuum. As she did so, she heard footsteps on the deck.

"Jake?"

There was no answer. She frowned, wondering if she'd been imagining that someone was after her all along. She stayed very still for a long time and heard nothing at all.

Shaking her head, she returned the vacuum to its place. But she felt uneasy in the confines of the houseboat, so she hurried out on deck. She locked the door, pocketed the key, then hesitated again.

Lights and noise were coming from the bar. Someone with a yen for country music had been popping their quarters into the jukebox.

The water seemed peaceful and serene. The boats rocked in their slips, water lapping against their hulls.

She found herself walking around the narrow deck that circled the cabin. After a full circuit, she looked up toward the bar again. The terrace was still lit, but there were no customers sitting in the night-lights and moonglow.

She heard a splash and turned quickly.

As she did, she felt a rush of wind, then a powerful surge against her back. It lifted and threw her.

Caught off guard, she went flying over the port side of the boat into the expanse of ebony water that rippled eerily in the shadow and glow of the moonlit evening.

As she plunged into the darkness, she heard a whoosh and felt something plunge behind her.

Chapter 19

It was at the end of dinner, just before lock-up time for the night, when everything was simply going by rote, that the siege of panic swept over Peter Bordon. His fork was halfway to his mouth, the din in the large hall was customary, and men were moving about, getting ready to return to their cells, when something suddenly changed. But only inside him. To his left, Carson and Byers were arguing about cigarettes. To his right, Sanders, the one-time CPA for a major corporation, was taking delight in a basket he had shot during his exercise session. There was nothing obvious going on to create such a sudden terror in his bloodstream.

He set his fork down, afraid that the mystery meat they called an entree would go flying across the room otherwise. His muscles were tense, his hands, his feet. He was afraid that his lungs would lock, that his heart would freeze and cease to beat. In his life, he'd never felt such an insane, unreasoning fear.

Maybe it had been coming on for a long time. He'd never been a man to know fear. He'd spent years believing in his own invincibility, his charisma, his ability to manipulate the minds of others. He didn't feel fear, he created it.

But, like everything else, it had been an illusion.

And there, with just days to go before he knew he would appease the parole board and be set free, he learned not just fear, but absolute terror. Suddenly the freedom he had craved, worked for, planned for, was a chilling prospect.

Sweat was breaking out on his brow.

Sanders, at his side, stopped speaking about basketball and the fact that, if nothing else, prison had taken away the paunch he had gained in his twenties. He was staring at Peter.

"Hey, you all right, Mr. Bordon?"

"Fine. Hit a piece of gristle in this mess," he managed to mutter. Once again, he looked around. Every one of his fellow inmates looked like a menacing killer. Sanders's smile made him look like a madman. Carson was grinning and looked like a werewolf about to devour its prey.

Peter forced himself to calm down. The police didn't know. There had been no proof. Nothing left behind. He had always known how to be careful.

But it wasn't the prospect of the police discovering the truth that had sent the terror out to paralyze his system.

After all this time.

And all these years.

* * *

Ashley kicked hard, trying to create space between herself and the threat. Her lungs were burning. She'd been caught off guard. She had to get a gulp of air.

She propelled herself beneath the boat, then broke the surface on the starboard side. A second later, she gasped out a scream, then sucked in a massive lungful of air as viselike arms wrapped around her legs and dragged her under. Squirming and fighting wildly, she went down. She couldn't see in the water.

Then, suddenly, she was released. She kicked upwards, breaking the surface in time to see a head bobbing in front of her.

"Ashley?"

"Jake?"

"Damn you, Ashley."

"Why are you yelling at me? You attacked me!"

"Why were you skulking around my boat in the dark?"

"I wasn't."

"Looked to me like you were."

She wanted to kick him, but he was too far away. Besides, her legs wouldn't have the power to hurt him against the pressure of the water. He was already swimming the few feet to grasp the ladder at the back of the boat. She followed him. When he reached a hand down to help her up, she was too affronted to accept. She ignored him and climbed on board under her own power, straightening to confront him where he waited, dripping onto the deck.

"Someone pushed me off the boat," she told him.

He shook his head. "There's no one here. Except for you, and when I came aboard, you were already in the water. I assumed you were whoever has been coming aboard the *Gwendolyn*."

She was dripping, as well. She pulled a piece of stray seaweed from her hair.

"I came by to ask if you'd found out anything. Your friend, the fingerprint man was here."

"Skip."

"Yes, Officer Conrad. Like an idiot, I got it into my head to try to clean the place up for you. Then I came topside, and I heard something. I went to see, and I was pushed overboard."

"Ashley…look for yourself. The docks are empty. There's no one here."

She folded her hands over her chest. "Right. So if I were to go by logic and appearances, *you* pushed me."

"You know I didn't."

"Right. But you think someone has been on your boat. That's why you had the fingerprint guy out. So why should it surprise you that they were skulking around and pushed me overboard? And then disappeared. Somewhere."

He turned, staring at the water. "Shit," he said softly. He left her standing there and leapt to the dock with a lithe, flying leap that would have done a martial artist proud. He ran along the dock, still staring at the water. She stood there, shivering and uneasy.

When he returned, it wasn't by the dock. She saw him dive into the water, then start swimming back in her direction.

"What are you doing?" she demanded when he was close enough to hear her.

He climbed aboard.

"If someone was here and didn't leave by the dock, then he—or she—had to swim away."

"Then you believe I was pushed?"

"I only go in the water here to scrape the hull. I can't imagine you'd jump in for a pleasure swim."

"What do you think the person is looking for?"

"I don't know," he said. "Something I have that I don't know I have. Or something they think I have that I don't."

"Did you find anything?"

He shook his head. "Nothing. If they'd come up here, there should have been wet footprints on the dock, but there aren't any. The problem is, whoever it was could have stayed in the water a long time and come up almost anywhere in either direction. Not to mention the fact that there are hundreds of boats in the vicinity. But I will find out what's going on."

"I'm sure you will. And how very kind of you to believe I might have known what I was talking about."

He turned, heading for the door to the cabin. "Do you want to stand there dripping all night?"

She was about to tell him exactly what to do with himself, but he added, "You're welcome to the first shower."

She shook her head, gritting her teeth, and walked forward. Water streamed from his pocket as he reached for his keys. His eyes touched hers as he opened the door. "Sorry. I just hated thinking I had a criminal and then found out I'd tackled you instead."

"I'll just bet it feels better to tackle a criminal."

"I didn't say anything about how it feels," he returned.

She ducked slightly as she entered the cabin. He

came in behind her, heading to the galley area to peel off his soaked jacket and kick off his ruined shoes. "The best shower is in my room."

"Actually, I think I'll just sprint back to my own room. I don't have any dry clothes here," she reminded him.

"I own a clothes dryer," he told her.

"Wow. Tempting."

He unbuttoned his shirt and let it fall, then moved toward her. "I know something that's even more tempting."

"You're being just a little bit egotistical, aren't you?"

"I wasn't referring to me."

He reached her, pulling her close and slipping her sodden shirt over her head. "My wet shirt is tempting?" she inquired skeptically.

"You bet." A spiral of heat shot through her as he lowered his lips to her throat.

"Not that wet trousers aren't tempting, too. And," she added lightly, "the seaweed on your socks and that smell of motor oil... I'm all aquiver."

"You are, you know."

She ignored that. He was tugging on the wet button of her jeans, too frustrated with his task to volunteer more. She slipped her arms around him. Her breath was coming a little too fast. "Detective, you're keeping something from me."

"Not on purpose."

"Jake."

His arms enfolded her. His fingers slipped up her back, finding the hook of her bra. "This stuff you wear..." His words were husky and garbled as he lowered his head, nuzzling the rise of her breasts above the lace of the bra. "Great underwear." He gently fingered the shoulder straps then, causing the garment to fall to the floor at their feet.

"Jake..."

He moved back an inch. "Okay, how about I seduce you with my eloquence? Carnegie has arranged for twenty-four-hour official police protection for your friend."

Her heart skipped a beat. "Really?"

"Absolutely."

"He's doing this for you?"

"If I say yes, will you be more tempted to stay?"

"I'm staying no matter what you tell me," she informed him huskily.

It was Jake who paused then, not moving away, but taking the time to talk to her. "I have to take off really early tomorrow. I want to be on the road by four. I got a message from one of Bordon's fellow inmates. I checked out the number, and it was legitimate. I think Bordon is afraid of someone, and he said he wants to talk to me. Unless he's pulling some kind of a con on me. Whatever the situation, I have to go. But I'll be back tomorrow night. Maybe late, but I'll be back. And then I'll look into the situation with your friend, Stuart Fresia. Carnegie has some information that I need to look into more deeply. I promise you, I swear to you, that we'll get it figured out."

Her limbs seemed to grow cold again. She should take whatever she could get. She needed the help, and there was no reason to refuse it. Except...except for the way she felt about him.

"You—you don't have to do that, you know," she heard herself say stiffly. "You don't have to take on work that isn't yours for my benefit. Looking into Stuart's case just because he's my friend," she added. She could have kicked herself. She needed and wanted all the help she could get. "I won't let it go," she told him. "I'll never let it go, because I know Stuart. But you're not...required to feel the same way."

"Don't you go doing anything," he told her flatly.

She felt her temper bristle. "I'm obviously not an idiot. I was one of the top trainees in my class."

"Ashley, no one is doubting your intelligence. But diving into things without knowing what you're doing is dangerous."

"Because I'm a woman."

"For anyone. Anyone without experience and training."

"Right. 'Cuz you started out with experience, of course."

"Ashley, do me a favor. Sit back and give me a lousy few days. I don't want you diving in headfirst because you really don't know what you're doing. And, yes, I *do* know. And as to Stuart's case, taking it on won't just be a favor to you. I'll look into it because it might have been an attempted homicide. And I'm hoping that by tomorrow I'll have some answers regarding the Bordon murders. And Cassie Sewell."

"And your partner?" she asked quietly.

He nodded. "And Nancy."

They were both still standing there, dripping. Almost touching. Seconds ticked by, and they remained, staring at one another.

"You really need those answers, don't you?" she asked.

"I really want those answers," he replied.

She was quiet for a moment, watching him.

He still wasn't touching her, but he was so close she could feel his warmth; the dampness of his flesh seemed to brush her own. He leaned forward, pressing her against the wall behind her, bracing them both, where they stood, and when he spoke, there was emotion in his voice, as if the moments of banter had been cast aside. "I want the answers, yes, because if anyone ever deserved for the truth to be known, it was Nancy."

She lowered her head suddenly afraid. She had rushed into this, thinking she could indulge in reckless desire and come out unscathed. She wasn't even hearing what he was saying to her; she was far too hypnotized by the aura of this man she had known for so brief a time. But that time had been intense. She knew she had been attracted to him from more than a physical standpoint, though that particular appeal was in the ascendant at this particular moment. But there was so much else about him to admire. She knew he took work seriously, that he wouldn't take the time to humor a whim of hers no matter what he felt for her sexually.

She also knew that there had been something lacking in him. An ability to give himself completely, maybe, because the past had been shadowing him no matter how he had tried to shake it. She wondered if his words were a strange form of commitment to her, but she didn't want to try to test them. She was shaken, frightened of the passion, of her own desire to be with him. Not just to sleep with him, but to *be* with him.

"Ashley?"

He lifted her chin, then slid a hand around her nape, bent and kissed her lips. Against the chill of the air-conditioned cabin, the warmth of his lips was electric.

The ills of the world seemed to slip from her shoulders. The hair-roughened texture of his chest rubbed against her naked breasts, and that light contact seemed to arouse a roiling lava bed in the pit of her stomach.

When he moved away from her, his lips remained close as he whispered, "You know, you looked good in those trainee blues of yours, you look darn good in jeans, and you even look fantastic in seaweed. But I'm willing to bet you look even better all lathered in soap."

A smile crept into her lips. "I'm assuming this boat has a *small* shower."

"Small can be good."

"And too tight to move."

"Tight can be good, too."

"And awkward."

"You never know until you investigate the situation."

"True. And, of course, you're known for your investigative technique."

"Thank you, ma'am."

"My pleasure." She slipped from beneath his arm, shed the jeans that had given him so much trouble, took a step and eased out of her thong panties. She cast a glance over her shoulder. "Head…master cabin… shower. I'm on my way."

It wasn't that small a shower. The *Gwendolyn* was a houseboat, after all, not a pleasure craft. Tight, yes, but the shower did offer room for two. Two who stood very close. Almost touching, skin to skin. Yet when she took hold of the bar of soap, she didn't have the room to slide it freely down the length of her form. Apparently he'd been anticipating such a dilemma. His darkly bronzed fingers slid over her own and took the bar of soap from her grip. He started with her throat. "We investigators don't like to miss a thing."

"Your entire case could fall apart if you did."

"I like to be thorough."

The bar of soap, wielded so deftly in his hands, moved over her breasts, the hardness of the bar excruciating against the sensitivity of her nipples. She felt them quickening, shaking with little spasms centered deeper in her body. The water in the tiny stall sluiced continually against the foam he created. Steam misted and rose quickly. His hands, slick and sure, moved slowly down the length of her, caressing her ribs and midriff, the plane of her abdomen, over her hips, then erotically flat and low, sliding between the length of her legs. Her breath caught. She felt she would have fallen had there been room to do so. The slide and swiftness of his fingers seared and teased with each seductive touch and stroke. The soap fell between them. They both went to retrieve it, crashed, laughed, left it…locked into an embrace instead, mouths glued and hungry, tongues sweeping, soap still sluicing over them both as the water rained down and the steam rose, enveloping them both.

Ashley clung to him for a moment, needing more, ran her fingers down his back, following the muscled curve of his buttocks, gripping the length of his erection. Sound growled from the depths of his throat, and he kicked open the door. Soaked and slick, she was somehow wrested into his arms and they were both laughing. A moment later they were falling on the expanse of the bed. As he rose over her then, the laughter they had shared faded. His eyes sought hers; his body pressed against hers. His hand slid down the length of her, again, and he thrust inside her with a movement that itself nearly sent her over the edge. She clung to him and felt for a moment the dampness of her skin, the coolness of the covers, the slight rocking of the boat in its slip. She closed her eyes and felt the hot vital structure of the man, the strength of his arms, the power of his hips and thighs locked around her, and then nothing but the fever inside her, the rise of honeyed fire, the yearning, reaching, stretching, desperate wanting....

Explosions seemed to rocket through her body with the force of her climax, followed by delicious little electric shocks, sweeping through her time and time again. She felt the force of his urgency, as well, each movement winding her tighter, taking her higher, a burst of heat like lava warming the insides of her, filling something deeper than a sexual need. He held her, locked in his warm embrace, and she clung to him as if her limbs had frozen around him. There was something so fierce in being with him that it was frightening, something beyond thought and logic and reality. She was terrified to realize that she felt far too deeply as if she belonged here, as if she had known him forever and was meant to be nowhere but with him for eternity.

She was startled when he spoke, though he still didn't pull away from her. "Ashley, stay out of things until I get back. I mean it."

She caught her breath, wincing. A moment later, he rolled to his side, coming up on an elbow.

She stroked his cheek. "I don't care what you say. You *are* a chauvinist. You're afraid for me because Nancy's dead."

"It has nothing to do with Nancy," he said impatiently.

"Jake, I didn't go into the academy because I didn't

have the money for a ritzy art school, but because I really wanted to be a cop."

"Like your father."

"Not just because of my father. I believe in law and order, and in the protecting and serving part of it, too. Okay, the way that things worked out, I'm not a cop. But I do work for the police force. And I'm going to face really bad things, we both know that. Jake, I have the stomach and the nerve for it."

"But do you have the common sense for it?" he asked irritably.

"I resent that," she told him.

"Resent away, but what I'm asking you is important. You get the bit between your teeth and you're determined to run with it, the hell with the consequences."

"I'm not like that at all! And what makes you think I am?"

"You're making judgments based on what you feel in your heart, not what you can see, feel and touch, as hard evidence."

"You do that all the time. It's supposedly what makes you good at your work."

"What I do is different."

"Why?"

"Why?" He ran his fingers through his hair. "Because I started with one of the best beat cops in history. Because I took all the steps to get me where I am today. You draw pictures, Ashley. You've got a real talent, so stick with that. If you go on a wild-goose chase of some kind, all you'll do is get yourself killed."

"Jake, stop it! What is your problem with me?"

"You're a kid, a kid with an incredible talent, who is still soaking wet behind the ears. And my problem is that—" He broke off abruptly, shaking his head in anger. "You're too frigging naive to even understand what I'm saying to you."

She started to roll away, ready to rise, torn between her realization of how deeply she had let her emotions tumble and her need to be her own person.

He caught her hand.

"There you go, flying off the handle."

"You're the one who's yelling."

His eyes narrowed. "I'm not yelling. I just want to talk to you. And I'm not letting go until you listen."

She felt the tension in her rise. "At this precise second, I could probably kick you in the balls hard enough to leave you screaming for the next thousand years."

The threat didn't work. In an instant he was on top of her; she couldn't have moved a knee if her life depended on it. His point, she knew.

"Well?" he said softly.

"Get the hell off me, Dilessio. I'm leaving. I've got things to do, too."

"You had no intention of leaving now."

"Maybe I didn't before, but I do now. Jake, I can't stay here if you think you can humor me, manipulate me…make me promise to stay in a little glass case because you fell in love with a policewoman once before." She held up a hand to stop him when he would have spoken. "Whether you slept with her or not, you were in love with her. You might have spent the last five years forcing her case into the background while you went ahead and worked hard on what was happening each day, but you've never really stepped back. That's understandable. But you can't envision the future based on what happened in the past."

He rose, leaving her on the bed. "I'll toss your stuff in the dryer. You can stay, shower and leave at your leisure—go do whatever things you need to do in the middle of the night. I've got to get out of here."

He didn't have to leave that quickly, she knew. He had told her that he didn't need to be on the road until four. She was restless and angry. She wanted to argue, remind him that she could be out of his hair in a matter of minutes, but he was already up and headed back for the tiny shower stall—alone.

The door closed. She wasn't going to stand outside and argue with him over the roar of the water.

That wasn't actually the temptation that gnawed at her, of course. She longed to slip back in and laugh again as the soap slid against her skin, as...

Something seized at her heart. It was wrong, all wrong. She couldn't be what he wanted or needed, couldn't say the words now that would be lies in the future.

She struggled into her wet clothing, then hesitated. She could still hear the water running. If she wrote him a note, it would be a cop-out. If she waited and spoke to him...

She hurried to the notepad by the phone and flipped past the pages that held her drawings. She started writing.

Dear Jake...

Nothing came to mind. The water wouldn't run forever.

This won't work.

Again the words she needed eluded her. There was so much she could say. *I can't keep my nose out of things that involve me?* No.

I understand how you feel. Perhaps not completely, but I know enough about the past. I'm so sorry for what happened to Nancy, but I'm sure that whatever she was doing, she felt it was important and something she had to do. But I can't be a hothouse flower. You can't spend your life trying to protect me because you care about me.

Was that too presumptuous?

Maybe she was attributing way too much meaning to what was just a hot and heavy sexual relationship to him. No. He cared about her. She knew that. And she cared too much. Dare she write the truth? *I'm falling in love with you, enough to sell my soul, my future, my belief in myself....*

No. She wasn't about to write that. She settled for *I can't see you anymore.*

There was more. So much more she could put down on paper. Too much. But right now she had even greater concerns. Karen. She had to find out what was happening with her friend. She was afraid, but she had to do things herself, make the right moves.

She had said what needed to be said to Jake.

The water stopped running. Ashley didn't sign the page; she simply dropped it and ran, fleeing the houseboat before he could stop her.

Chapter 20

It all started with a food fight, something that didn't even draw Peter Bordon's attention immediately, since it started far down at the end of the breakfast table.

Violence seldom occurred in the area of the prison where he was incarcerated. The men here were mostly white-collar criminals. They wanted to get out. They had families. Some dreamed of going straight.

They were rarely unruly, much less violent.

It started with flying eggs, but in seconds, there was a melee going. He had no intention of getting involved. He didn't care if he wore egg or not.

Then someone had him by the shirt collar and he was being dragged across the table. The next thing he knew, he was on the floor, and there were a dozen men on top of him. He could hear whistles and shouts as the guards came rushing in to break it up, but he was more concerned with the elbow slammed into his face, thudding his head against the floor. Punches were raining down all over his body. He was smothering. He yelled, furious, trying to get the men off him. He returned their punches as best he could with the weight on him.

At first he wasn't even aware of the blade sliding into him....

Then, beneath the pile-up, he *knew.*

The food fight was a performance, acted out for his benefit alone. Someone knew about the phone call. Any of them might have betrayed him. There was big money involved. Hell, it didn't even matter who had turned on him. There was always someone who could be bought, no questions asked.

The blade inside him twisted. He screamed, but his voice and his lungs were failing. He had blacked out by the time the guards at last pulled the other prisoners from him.

It had all taken just a few moments of time.

"The coffee is made—and aren't you running late?" Nick asked as Ashley made her way through the main house.

"I don't have to report in until eight now," she told him.

"Ah, well, that's good. You look like hell—well, for being young and beautiful, you look like hell, anyway."

"Thanks—kind of."

"Look, Ashley, I'm not going to presume to tell you what to do, but you might want to take things a little slower with Dilessio."

"Um, I might." Was a dead standstill going to be slow enough? She already regretted her note. For some reason, she had thought he might pound on her door and say something. Hardly likely, and it hadn't happened. He was on his way up to the center of the state, maybe finally solving the mystery that had plagued him for so long. For his sake, she hoped he found the answers. But she didn't think that was going to change him.

His concern for the woman he'd loved in the past was greater than any feelings he had for her.

"How was your night out?" she asked her uncle.

"Great. Sharon's appointment got cancelled, so we went to South Beach for stone crabs, took in a movie on Lincoln Road and walked on the beach."

"Very romantic."

"Yeah, it was," Nick admitted, shrugging like a jock caught sending a frilly Valentine. "Sharon is…beyond great. Hey, did you get your laundry?"

"My laundry?"

"Sharon said she put some of your things in your room for you."

"She did?" Ashley murmured. "Is she awake yet?"

"She doesn't have anything today until a closing at noon. She was going back to sleep when I left her."

Ashley smiled at her uncle. "I think I'll just give a knock and see if she's still awake."

She hurried away before he could stop her. He'd left his door ajar, and Sharon hadn't risen to close it. Ashley knocked.

"Nick?" Sharon's sleepy voice had a note of curiosity in it. Of course, why would Nick be knocking?

"Sharon, it's me. Ashley. May I speak with you?"

"One sec."

Sharon pulled the door fully open a moment later, tying a bathrobe around her waist as she did so. She was a beautiful woman. First thing in the morning, hair tousled, no makeup—she was still stunning with her soft tresses, petite size and classic features. No wonder Nick thought he was a lucky man.

"Ashley?" she said curiously.

Ashley didn't have time to beat around the bush. "Two things. First, what were you really doing in my room? I knew someone had been there, and Nick mentioned that you had brought in some laundry, but…no laundry."

Sharon's cheeks went bloodred. "I lied to him. I'm sorry."

"Then…?"

"I was trying to get to know you a bit better."

"We could have gone shopping or had lunch," Ashley said.

Sharon shook her head. "Ashley… I have an appointment on Saturday morning. If you'll just bear with me until then, I'll explain myself completely, and I hope you'll understand."

"You're being very mysterious."

"Not mysterious. Just a little…well, you'll understand when I tell you. What was the second thing?"

"I need to know about a property you sold."

Sharon frowned. "A property?"

"Way southwest. Almost in the Glades."

"I've sold a number of properties out there. Which one?"

Ashley gave her the address. Sharon still stared at her blankly.

"A big house, lots of land and several outbuildings," Ashley said.

"That could be a couple of places. I can't access old files from the house, but I'll look it up for you once I get to work."

"Are you going in? Nick just said you don't have anything 'til a closing at twelve."

"Ashley, if you need information, I'll make a point to go in and get it for you."

"Thanks."

"What do you need?"

"Anything and everything you can give me."

Sharon nodded. "I'll have it by tonight."

"I probably won't be home until late tonight. I'm supposed to be celebrating with friends." Of course, she wouldn't be celebrating if she didn't find one of her friends by that evening. "If you can, leave whatever you dig up on my bed."

"Sure."

They stood staring at one another for a moment. "Ashley, I shouldn't have been in your room, it wasn't my place, and I'm really sorry, but I hope you'll understand when I've had a chance to tell you…what's going on."

"I hope so, too," Ashley said. She turned and started to walk away.

"Ashley?" Sharon called after her. Ashley turned. "You know that Nick adores you. He couldn't love you more, or be prouder of you, if you were his own child."

"He's everything to me, as well," Ashley said, curious that Sharon would have stopped her with such a comment. "If you get that information, I'll be really grateful."

"I'll definitely retrieve the file."

Ashley walked back into the kitchen. Nick was looking at her curiously as she headed for the coffeepot. "Is everything all right?"

"Absolutely," Ashley said. She set her cup down on

the counter and told him a white lie. "I just wanted to thank her for the laundry."

"Good," Nick said. "Hey, your cell phone is ringing."

"What?"

"I can hear it. In the bedroom."

Once Nick had said it, she could hear the faint tones of her phone, as well. She thanked him quickly as she went running into her bedroom, digging into her bag for her phone. Jan's number. She caught it quickly.

"Jan!" she said breathlessly.

"Hey. I guess we *were* being silly about Karen, though why she hasn't called one of us back yet, I don't know."

"What are you talking about?"

"She called in to work again already—still sick."

"Then why isn't she sick at home? And why is her car in the drive?"

"I don't know. We can ask her next time we see her, I guess."

"I think I'll run by her place again after work."

"You don't need to bother. She's supposed to be celebrating your new job with us tonight. If she doesn't show up for that, it will be time to call in the troops."

"You have a point there. All right." She didn't mention the scrapings she had taken from Karen's tub. There was no reason to make her worry needlessly. And if Karen had called in to work again, then she had to be okay.

Or someone was calling the school on her behalf.

"See you tonight, then," Ashley told Jan, and rang off.

She showered quickly and dressed for work, feeling strange now that she didn't have to put on her trainee blues in the morning. When she got out to the kitchen, Sharon had apparently given up the idea of going back to sleep; she was with Nick, leaning against him where he sat on a counter stool, both of them gazing at the newspaper.

"Have a good day, kid," Nick told her.

"Thanks. You too."

Jake thought he had probably made the drive to the prison in record time, and it still seemed like the longest drive he had made in his life.

As the first miles had gone by, he'd spent the time being angry, longing to do something physical to shake Ashley and make her understand.

The second half of the drive, he'd begun to question himself. Was he fanatical? Or did he have a right to be concerned? *How do you not care when you're starting to find that every moment that really matters is with someone who is determined to put her life on the line?*

He arrived far too early and had to find the closest twenty-four-hour restaurant to the prison to sit and nurse eggs and coffee for an hour. As he ate, he jotted down notes on things he'd been thinking of. He drew diagrams of the area in which the bodies had been found. All the bodies. Bordon held the key. He'd always known it. And still, he found himself writing down information. Fact: the cult had existed. Three women associated with it had died. Fact: they had not found another group in any way similar to the People for Principle. Fact: most of the members of the cult had seemed truly oblivious of any wrongdoing, including murder. They had been humiliated and chagrined to discover that they had been fleeced. They had been eager to put the past behind them.

Fact: another woman was dead.

Fact: Nancy Lassiter, his partner, had been on the case. Had died during the investigation, though she had never been out to the property. Not that he knew about, anyway.

Fact: she had left his boat alive. And she hadn't been seen again until her car had been discovered in a canal weeks later.

In a canal, near the property.

Fact...

He'd always felt that, of the members, if anyone could tell them anything, it would have been John Mast, who had vehemently denied any knowledge of any of the deaths, but who had admitted that he didn't understand a great deal of the bookkeeping in the office he was supposed to manage. Mast had known something.

Fact: Mast was dead. He had perished in a plane crash. Or had he?

He drummed his fingers on the table for a moment, then pulled out his cell phone and dialed headquarters. Marty wouldn't be at work yet; he might well still be sleeping. But one of the task force would be available.

He was connected with Belk, who assured him that he would investigate the plane crash immediately and find out if all the bodies had been positively identified.

He turned back the page of his notepad, rereading the note Ashley had left him. She was right. They needed to back off. He did want to stop her from becoming a cop, and he knew she still meant to go back and finish up at the academy someday. He couldn't remember the exact figures, but he knew that somewhere in the United States, a law enforcement official was killed around every fifty-eight hours. Part of the job. He didn't want her to be part of that job. Even if he was himself.

Idly, he flipped the notebook to the top page. There was a briefly executed but excellent drawing of an accident.

The accident she had passed on the highway, the one that had left Stuart Fresia in a coma. He frowned, studying the drawing. There was a figure in black, staring at the road. At the accident. A figure in black...

Black, like the members of People for Principle had worn.

As he stared at the drawing, his cell phone rang. To his surprise, it was the warden from the prison. His face grew grave as he listened.

"Is he dead?" he asked, his tongue thick as he formed the words.

"Living, but barely," the warden replied. "They're rushing him into surgery. I know how important you felt this meeting was. Come straight to the hospital. The doctors don't give him much chance. He hasn't been conscious and he may never be conscious again, but I'll let you sit with him once he's out of surgery, just in case."

"Thanks."

Jake ended the call, paid for his breakfast and headed out, feeling ill, fighting alternating waves of anger, disappointment and bitterness.

For Ashley, the morning was a blur. First she'd gone to hand in her badge and gun. She hated to do it, but it was necessary. She was no longer in the academy.

Then, after signing some papers and meeting with Personnel, she had been sent in to study computer comparisons of bullet striations. She had, however, managed to meet with Mandy Nightingale. She hadn't hesitated but had explained the situation to the woman, and Mandy had listened thoughtfully. First she had said that Ashley shouldn't panic, especially since Karen had called in to work that morning. But she had agreed as well to do a discreet test and let Ashley know if the substance she'd found in the tub was blood or not.

"If Karen doesn't show up tonight, though…"

"Then I'll have to admit that I've already tested the substance for you," Mandy told her.

Ashley smiled and thanked her.

At lunchtime, Mandy came to tell her that the substance was blood, but that she still shouldn't panic. It was likely that Karen had simply cut herself shaving. There had been no spatter pattern, for one thing. "Then again, sometimes a killer cleans up so thoroughly that even with chemicals and special lighting, it's hard for us to detect any traces. Hey! Don't go pale on me. We're not going to worry yet, remember?"

"We're not going to worry," Ashley agreed. But her heart was racing and she was trembling with fear.

"You *are* worried," Mandy said sympathetically. "Ashley, you can go and fill out a missing persons report now, if you want. The department will waive the waiting period for you. But if you do that, her parents will be notified, her place of business will be investigated. And anyone and everyone who has seen her lately will be investigated."

"We'll wait until tonight."

Jan called her soon after. "Have you heard from Karen yet?"

"No."

"Neither have I. I'm going to kill her!"

Ashley kept silent, afraid that her friend might already have met a similar fate.

"Listen," Jan went on. "I know I told you not to, but I'm going by her place before coming to the restaurant tonight. And if I find her I'm going to beat her senseless, then drag her into the car with me."

"Sounds good. Because if she doesn't show…"

"If she doesn't show, we won't be celebrating."

Ashley's phone beeped, indicating she had another call. She told Jan goodbye and answered the incoming call.

"Ashley?"

It was David Wharton.

"David! Why on earth did you take so long to call me back?"

"I've been busy. Did you ask Sharon Dupre about that property?"

"Yes, and she's supposed to be pulling the file for me today."

"Good. I'll see you tonight, then."

"No, you won't. I'm having dinner with friends. We're celebrating my new job."

"I've got to see you. I've got to talk to you."

"I'll be out late."

"Then invite me to dinner. I'll be happy to celebrate your good fortune."

"We may not wind up celebrating. I have another friend who's missing."

"One of the girls from the hospital? Karen? Or Jan?"

She was surprised he knew both of them by name. But then, he had spent hours there, watching, not to mention that he was a reporter, trained to notice details.

"I don't want to talk about it right now."

"Fine. But I have a lot to tell you. Please, give me a chance. Let me come with you tonight so I can talk to you."

She sighed and told him where they were going. She would take a minute and talk to him. If she didn't like what he said, she would have Arne and Gwyn and the others around her. A table full of "almost" cops. And Len, who could even arrest him if he seemed dangerous.

Her lunch hour was over by the time she hung up. She went to spend time with Mandy, who showed her how to photograph a body from different angles and left her taking photos of a mutilated dummy. She spent an hour working on the project and was finishing up what she hoped would be a roll of good shots when Mandy stuck her head in the door. "Phone for you—I think you should take it." The older woman was smiling.

Ashley hurried to the phone, hoping against hope that it would be Karen. It wasn't, but it was good news. Nathan Fresia was on the phone. He was elated. Stuart wasn't conscious yet, but the scanner monitoring his brain had picked up activity that had given the doctors hope that he might awaken in a matter of days. She told Nathan how delighted she was, then felt a sudden sense of unease. "Nathan...was this knowledge made public?"

"I don't think so. But the hospital staff knows, and whatever cops were on duty."

"Since even the cops think someone meant him harm, it might be best to keep quiet about this. Let people think there's no chance of a quick recovery."

"You're right, you're right. I'll see that nothing else is said. I won't leave him for a minute."

"I'll be by tomorrow," Ashley promised and rang off.

Five o'clock rolled around. Still no call from Karen,

and then, when Ashley tried to get hold of Jan, she couldn't reach her, either.

Len Green, out of uniform, handsomely dressed in khaki trousers and a brown knit shirt, appeared in the small space that had been allotted as her office. "Ready?"

"I have my car here, Len."

"I know. I'm going to follow you home, then we'll take my car and meet the others at the restaurant."

"But I can drive myself."

"Everyone knows you don't drink and drive. And we intend to get you blitzed tonight."

"I don't want to get blitzed. In fact, I won't be doing anything if Karen doesn't show."

"You still haven't heard from her? I'm sure it's nothing. She was excited about tonight. I'm sure she'll show."

"I'm glad you feel so confident."

He shrugged. "Come on, I'll follow you home."

"All right. But you'll have to have coffee at the bar or something and wait for me. I want to shower and change."

"I'll wait forever," he told her.

Friday evening, and Bordon remained unconscious.

Jake refused to break his vigil at the man's side. He'd had a number of talks with the surgeon, who had given him an extensive list of the man's injuries. The liver, pancreas, stomach and intestines had all been damaged. Bordon had lost an incredible amount of blood, and then there had been internal bleeding. They had done all they could, but the man had little more than a ten percent chance of surviving the next forty-eight hours. He could regain consciousness any time, or he might never regain it.

Jake had to go on the chance that he might.

The other inmates were questioned extensively during the day. Every one of them denied wanting to harm Bordon. Despite strip searches and a thorough search of the cafeteria, the weapon that had inflicted such heavy damage had not been found.

During the long hours of the day, Jake had taken a few minutes here and there to walk out in the hall and get in contact with the force in Miami-Dade. The night shift had given way to day, and Marty had come on duty.

"So Bordon was practically skewered, and he's still hanging in," Marty had said. Jake could imagine his partner shaking his head over the irony that a criminal might survive, while innocent people died every day.

"He's hanging in—barely."

"Well, I've got things covered here," Marty told him, and began to tell him all he had learned. Skip Conrad had found prints belonging to Jake, Marty, Nick, Ashley and a number of other people whose prints were on file, all of whom had had reason to be on the boat. Skip had also commented on the lack of prints in many places, which might well have meant that someone had been painstaking in their efforts to make sure no incriminating fingerprints were found.

Marty had seemed puzzled about his request regarding John Mast and the plane crash, but he promised to get the information and did so quickly, calling Jake back within the half hour. There was excitement in his voice when he called. The reports issued out of Haiti, where the plane had gone down, had stated that there were no survivors. And that was the assumption. But only eighty of the plane's eighty-eight passengers and crew members had been retrieved from the ocean. John Mast's body had not been one of those identified. Because of the circumstances of the crash, he and his fellow unidentified passengers had been presumed dead.

"He's out there, somewhere, Marty, I know it," Jake said.

"Maybe, Jake. Maybe. You going to stay up there until Bordon dies?"

"I have to wait it out, Marty."

"I understand. But listen, I'll keep going with the property investigations. If you need me, call."

"Right."

He'd let his partner go, realized that he'd forgotten to tell him to keep Franklin and the others up to date on the information, so he made a call to the FBI man, who promised to get right on a search for John Mast, and to Blake, who would see that a report was written out and circulated. When he finished speaking with Blake, he started back toward Bordon's bedside. Then he hesitated and put a call through to Ashley's cell phone. She didn't pick up. He called the bar. Katie answered. Nick and Sharon were out, as was Ashley. "She came home, showered and left again. Big celebration tonight for her promotion," Katie told him.

"Yes, of course."

"I'll tell her you called."

"No, that's all right. I'll catch her later."

He hung up and returned to Bordon's side. He glanced at the priest, who had come into the room and was saying prayers.

The priest had told Jake that Bordon had, indeed, been to church regularly.

"Father, has he told you—"

"No. He wasn't much for confession. Not that I could tell you even if he *had* said something, but no, he didn't tell me about any crimes."

"Thanks."

"Pray for him, Detective. That's what I'm doing. He did find a love for God, you know, in the last few months."

Jake nodded. He prayed, but he knew his prayers were different from those of the priest. He prayed only for Peter Bordon to live long enough to give justice a few answers.

At seven, Ashley could stand it no longer. She left Arne, Gwyn and the others at the table and went outside. Neither Jan nor Karen had arrived yet.

She felt someone standing behind her. Len. Unease swept over her as niggling suspicion found root.

"You know where she is! Len, you left with Karen from the hospital parking, you brought her home. You were in her house, and then you followed me when I went out there. Because you were afraid that I'd find something." She was startled to find that she was having a hard time controlling her temper. She continued more evenly. "You touched everything in that house when you were in it with me, and that way, when her disappearance was investigated, there would be a reason your fingerprints were on everything. Where the hell is she, Len? *What did you do to my friend?*"

"What?" Len said, stiff and tense.

Other customers were arriving. People stopped to

stare at her, and at Len. His cheeks were pink with embarrassment.

"Len, think about it. You look suspicious. Where
is Karen, what did you do with her, where is her bo—
where is she?"

Something in his eyes changed then.

And she thought that it was guilt. Fury and guilt.
There was nothing he could do to *her*, because they
were in a very public place.

"If you hurt her, you are one sick slime!" she accused him.

Then she felt the tap on her shoulder. She spun
around and to her amazement, saw that Karen, as red-
faced as Len, was staring at her.

"Ashley, I'm right here."

Almost nine o'clock. Bordon remained unconscious.
Jake rubbed the back of his neck. A different prison
guard came in. Dr. Matthews had just been there, reading the chart, checking the IV. Bordon was still breathing; his heart was still beating.

Warden Thompson came through. "Detective, maybe
you should get a hotel room for the night. Get yourself
some real sleep for a few hours. If there's any change
at all, someone can call you."

"If there's any change at all and someone has to call
me, it may be too late."

Thompson nodded. "I understand." He hesitated.
"There will be a guard with you all night. If you need
anything…"

"Thank you."

So he sat. Exhausted, he tried to adjust his length to
the hospital chair. There was no way to get comfortable

in it. He'd sat awake many nights. This one just seemed longer than most. And more painful. Last night...

He'd been on the road. But the night before that he'd slept in his own bed. With Ashley at his side. In absolute comfort, red hair teasing his nose, his chest.

She was like a sudden flame in his life. She meant far too much to him, and he worried too much about her. Not that it mattered. She didn't want to see him.

He flicked out her drawing again. The accident, the highway, the body.

The figure in black.

He reminded himself that it was a sketch, a quick sketch at that. But then, that was her talent. A few lines on a piece of paper, and everything seemed to be conveyed. The positions of the cars and the body. The broken, pitiful form on the asphalt.

And the figure in black. Just lines, pencil lines. But what he saw was eerily reminiscent of what he had seen all those years ago, visiting the property that had belonged to the People for Principle.

He stood, stretched, nodded to the prison guard and went out to the hallway. Late again, but Carnegie wouldn't mind. He put through a call to the old cop.

Carnegie answered.

"Still at it?" Jake queried.

"Me? I hear you've been sitting in a hospital all day. It's been all over the news, of course. Papa Pierre, one-time leader of the People for Principle, embezzler, tax evader...connected to the brutal slaying of three women, perhaps the prison mastermind behind the death of a fourth. Bordon still alive?"

"Just barely."

"You may be wasting your time."

"Yeah, I may be."

"Well, I've got some good news from here."

"Yeah?"

"Doctors say there are indications the Fresia boy might be coming out of it."

"That's great. Does Ashley Montague know?"

"Nathan Fresia called her, and a few people found out before we got it straight that we didn't want anyone out there knowing his condition was improved. Of course, if one person knows...well, we've got men watching, day in and day out. And I've got an APB out on that so-called David Wharton fellow."

"Carnegie, I've got something for you, too. It doesn't quite add up yet, but I've got a sketch of the accident. And there's someone standing on the side of the road, someone in a black hooded robe."

"Jake," Carnegie said slowly. "You do that sketch yourself? That was how those crazy People for Principle dressed."

"Right, and I think that one of their members, presumed dead, is walking the streets of Miami. A man named John Mast. He supposedly died in a plane crash, but his body was never found. He might just be your David Wharton."

"How does it all add up, though? The victims associated with the cult were women, and their throats were slashed. My boy was struck by a car."

"I don't know how it adds up, but I'm starting to think it just might. Anyway, Bordon may still manage to say something. I'll wait it out. When I get back, I'll start moving heaven and earth to find Mast if he is alive and out there. I don't know why... I can't help thinking they might be one and the same."

"Gut instinct?" Carnegie said.

"Yep. Gut instinct."

They rang off. Jake walked back into the hospital room. He sat, watching Bordon die. Once, he would have thought that watching the man die slowly would give him some sense of justice. He couldn't have known then that he would be praying for the man to live.

Despite the fact that Ashley felt like an idiot, her party was a success. Every one of her classmates turned out for it. She was lauded with silly toasts. Everyone agreed with Arne's comment that the rest of them would have been fired for coloring in class, but Ashley had been turned into a heroine. Despite the ribbing, she had a great time.

She had wanted to sit at the opposite end of the table from Len, but he had parked himself beside Karen, who was next to her on one side. Jan, across the table from her, had heard the commotion and been profusely apologetic that she hadn't called once she'd gotten Karen to explain their friend was all right, but they would be a little late because of traffic.

The whole story had come out at the table.

"You knew I would show up tonight!" Karen said, looking meaningfully at Len, who, in turn, stared at Ashley, shaking his head.

"I knew where she was. I had promised not to tell," he said.

"So where were you?" Ashley demanded.

"Lord, try to keep a secret," Karen murmured. "Well, heck, I should just announce it to the entire restaurant."

"Karen, do you know that I scraped little specks of

something out of your bathtub and had them analyzed, and they were *blood*?"

"Jesus!" Len exclaimed. "I guess I didn't know until this moment how close I came to spending the night in jail."

"Oh, you wouldn't have gone to jail—you just would have had to tell the truth," Karen said.

"What *is* the truth?" Ashley demanded.

"Liposuction."

"What?" Ashley said incredulously.

"Well, you know, I've always thought my butt was way too fat. And I knew that if I told you and Jan, you'd give me a speech about plastic surgery being stupid and dangerous and say that my thighs weren't really fat."

"But it's an outpatient procedure," Ashley said. "Why didn't you go home last night?"

"I did go home. Late. And I didn't answer any calls because I was popping pain pills, not being the kind to enjoy suffering. And don't let anyone fool you. I have on this ridiculous…girdle thing, and the only reason you can't tell is because I'm wearing a skirt."

Ashley was still staring at her incredulously. "You told Len that you were having liposuction, but you didn't tell Jan or me?"

"I didn't mean to tell him." Karen glanced at Len and smiled warmly. "We just got to talking, and it came out."

"You go, girl!" Gwyn applauded from the other side of the table.

"Well, now you all know," Karen said lightly. "I should have just taken out an ad in the *Herald*. But seriously, it's wonderful that you guys care about me enough to worry."

"She'd better suck up to us both," Jan said, and everyone at the table laughed, and then the conversation moved on.

Ashley opted for three margaritas in a row—she wasn't driving. It had turned out to be a great night. Stuart was starting to recover. Karen was fine. All was well, except....

She had never felt more alone. Maybe because she had never felt quite as *together* as when she'd been with Jake.

He'd said he would be back tonight, but his plans had changed. Her classmates had brought the news. Peter Bordon had been knifed in a prison fight. He was dying and Jake was staying by his side.

She sipped her margarita and watched Karen and Len. They were laughing. Their eyes were alive when they looked at one another. Karen's surgery had probably curtailed her sex life for a while, but Ashley suspected Karen hadn't wasted any time the night Len had driven her home. No wonder he had seemed to know her house so intimately.

Maybe Len had harbored a real crush on her for a while, but now his arm was angled over Karen's chair. His smile for her appeared both warm and sincere. She was happy for them both. Just lonely for herself.

At last time wound away and the party began to break up. Ashley had been so relieved to see Karen that she had forgotten David Wharton's insistence that she tell him where she was going to be, but now she realized he'd never shown up. Too bad. The party was over and Jan was going to take her home.

Karen was going with Len. Being Karen, she took a minute to whisper to Ashley and Jan when they rose to go. "Can you believe I went through with this surgery *now*? He was amazing in bed! I have to admit, I've never been so vocal in my life, but he's built like Atlas. I was screaming from the minute I saw him."

"Spare us the details," Jan said firmly.

"No problem, because we're leaving. Len?"

"Good night all," Len said, waving as he and Karen started toward the door, hand in hand.

"Doesn't that just beat all?" Jan said. She yawned. "We need to get going, too."

"Right. Thank you, everyone," Ashley said, as Jan grabbed her arm.

But when they stepped outside the restaurant, David Wharton was there. Ashley nearly crashed into him.

"Hi. Boy, I'm really late, aren't I? The party is over, I see."

Ashley introduced him to whoever was still around and of course to Jan, who seemed more than appreciative.

"Hey—did your other friend show up?" he asked Ashley.

"Yes, she did, she was fine."

"That's a relief," he said. "What happened to her?"

"A long story," Ashley said.

"Liposuction," Jan told him, then turned away for a moment as Gwyn asked her something.

David grinned. "Can I give you a ride home, Ashley? We can talk."

She hesitated. He lowered his head, his voice low. "C'mon. I can hardly be planning to do you in when at least half a dozen would-be cops know you're leaving with me."

"All right. Jan, you're off the hook," she called out. "David is going to drive me."

"Okay. Good night, then." As Jan hugged her, she said, "Ash, my Lord, first Len and now him? How do you do it?"

"It's not what you think."

"Hey, I'm not Karen. How do you know what I'm thinking?" Jan winked at her, told David it was a pleasure to meet him and waved to the others. Ashley started across the lot with David Wharton. They reached his car, and she climbed in the passenger seat. After he had put the car in gear and reached the road, she stared at him, frowning.

"What's going on?" she asked.

"A great deal. Did you know that Stuart is showing signs of improvement?"

"Yes. How do *you* know?"

"I have my ways," he told her. "And Peter Bordon was seriously injured in a prison brawl."

"Yes, I heard. What does that have to do with Stuart?"

He stared at the road and swore softly at a car that cut him off. "Let's wait until we get to your place. Did you find out about the property?"

"Not yet. Sharon hadn't been back yet when I went home to shower, but the files should be in my room by now. She was going to leave it for me."

"When we see it, I'll explain what's going on."

"David, this mystery stuff is getting annoying."

"We're almost there."

He parked at Nick's. It was Friday night, and the place was jumping. He hesitated in the car.

"What is the matter with you?" she demanded.

"I don't want to be seen."

She sighed. "We can go in through the house entrance, though Sharon and my uncle may be around."

"Let's chance it."

"Why don't you want to be seen?" she asked, her eyes narrowing suspiciously.

"Because Nick's is always full of cops, and you know I'm persona non grata with them."

They went through the house. As Sharon had promised, the file was on Ashley's bed. David picked it up, not noticing that there was a second one underneath. He sat on Ashley's bed, eagerly looking through the papers. "Caleb Harrison was the buyer," he said, perplexed.

Ashley studied the information in the other file. A chill swept over her, along with a surge of fury. She stared at him, and he must have felt the anger emanating from her, because he looked up, too. As he did, something hard settled over his features.

"Ashley—"

"You son of a bitch! You own the property next door!"

She was furious, but something about the way he looked alarmed her. She turned to head out of her room.

She didn't reach the door. He was behind her instantly, grabbing her around the waist with one hand, strangling the scream that would have torn from her lips with the other.

Chapter 21

Midnight. Jake dozed and woke, dozed and woke. His muscles stiffened and cramped each time he sat in one position too long.

Still Bordon clung to life.

Jake stared at the clock for a while, then watched Bordon's face. Little tubes ran into his nose, keeping oxygen flowing through his lungs. An IV dripped life-sustaining fluid into his bloodstream. Neither was going to save his life. The gray pallor of his features was proof of that.

Twelve-thirty. He went to walk in the corridor to loosen up his muscles. He was nervous every time he did so, afraid that Bordon would awaken for the few seconds he was gone. But having spent endless hours by the bed, time in which to think, wonder and rationalize, he was becoming increasingly certain that events that seemingly had no connection just might be an interlocking key, the solution to both mysteries.

Despite the hour, he called Skip. No surprise, Skip had been sleeping, and he had to think for several minutes—and Jake had to repeat himself several times—before he seemed to understand Jake's questions. "Yeah...the computer was an area that seemed to be wiped clean of prints. Oh, yeah, and your phone and the answering machine."

Jake thanked him, apologizing for the hour. Skip told him no problem, a statement that obviously wasn't entirely sincere.

Jake started to head back to his chair, then hesitated and called Nick's place.

He was glad when Nick answered the phone himself.

"Nick's."

"Nick, it's Jake Dilessio."

"Yes?" Nick said carefully. His niece might be twenty-five, but Nick couldn't help feeling like a protective father. "You want to talk to Ashley? You can call her on her cell. But I guess you know that."

Jake hesitated. He wasn't sure that Ashley would answer her cell phone if she saw he was calling. But he wasn't certain he wanted to talk to her right then, anyway. On the one hand, he was still feeling frustrated and incredibly angry. He was also wondering if he was slightly insane to feel such a proprietary sense of protection and concern, as if she were in his care. As if he had the right to know her every movement.

"I don't need to speak with her, Nick. I just wanted to...make sure she was home. That she was all right."

"She's a big girl, Jake. She stays out as late as she wants. But I guess you know that."

"Nick—"

"She's home, Jake. I heard her going through the house about twenty minutes ago."

Jake hesitated. "Thanks," he said. He wasn't certain what to say to Nick. He didn't want to worry an old friend needlessly. "Listen, Nick, this is the situation. I'm up here in the center of the state."

"I heard. The Bordon incident has been on the news all day. Reports have his condition as critical."

"He's dying," Jake said flatly. "I'm sitting here hoping against hope that he'll say something before he does."

"I see. What about that corpse you have on your hands? Think he ordered the execution from prison?"

"I did—once. Now… I don't know. What I'm sure of is that the food fight was caused to cover the killing of Peter Bordon. And the thing is, I found a sketch Ashley did of the accident that landed Stuart Fresia in the hospital. There's a figure on the side of the highway, someone wearing a black cape and cowl. That was the uniform worn by members of Bordon's cult. I've also discovered that a former cult member who'd been presumed dead may have survived the plane crash that supposedly killed him. I know. I'm probably stretching things, but there was a reporter hanging around the hospital after Stuart was admitted, and according to Carnegie, the investigator on the case, he isn't checking out as who he says he is. I keep wondering if he could be the guy from the cult. Anyway, I'm concerned for Ashley."

"She's in for the night, I'm certain. I'll talk to her in the morning, though. It's all right to tell her what you've told me, right?"

"Yes."

"I'll keep my eye on her."

Nick was quiet for a minute. Jake waited, thinking he meant to say more. Or maybe he was waiting for Jake to say something. Finally he filled the silence.

"I'll be back in Miami as soon as I can. If anything comes up…let me give you Carnegie's direct number. You know how to reach Marty, and if you can't reach him…let me give you a few other names."

"I'll grab a pen. Damn…where the hell is a pen? Sharon? Shit. There she goes. Sandy, you got a pen there? No…hey, Curtis! Okay, here we go. I got a pen."

Nick took down the names and numbers Jake gave him. They rang off.

Jake headed back into the hospital room. The prison guard was still standing at the end of the bed. Jake nodded to him and slouched wearily in the chair. A moment later, the doctor came in. He studied his patient, opening his eyes, checking his pulse.

"How's he doing?"

"I think you can see," the doctor said with a shrug. "One way or another… I don't think he has more than ten hours left."

Ashley's next move hadn't been learned at the academy. It had been taught to her at a women's defense class she had attended with Jan, who thought she should learn what she could since she spent so much time on the road.

It was a good maneuver, a back kick with centered force. And she caught him just where she meant to.

David Wharton released her immediately, howling in sudden pain, falling to the floor in the fetal position.

"What on earth did you do that for?"

Ashley stared down at him. His reaction stunned her. "You attacked me."

"I didn't attack you. I was trying to stop you from leaving. I need you to listen to me."

"Talk, then."

"I can't talk. I'm dying."

"You're not dying. You're just hurting a little."

"A little? I'm in agony."

"All right, so you're in agony. It will fade."

"The hell it will. I'll never have children."

"I'm sure you'll still have children—if you live long enough. If you have something to say to me, you'd better say it fast. I'm going to call the police."

"You *are* the police."

"I can't haul you off to jail. When I call 9-1-1, they'll send someone who can."

"Ashley, please!"

"Talk."

"I'm trying. Do you have any idea what this feels like? You've never been kicked in the balls." He eyed her with pained reproach. "And I'm starting to think you have them, too."

"Talk."

"Yes, Ashley, I own the property next to the commune. I bought it with Stuart."

"What?"

"He was on to something. He didn't want to use his name. There were reasons why it was better to use mine. But hell, I didn't have the money. Stuart did."

"Why did Stuart want that property?"

"He was investigating the commune."

"That's not what you said before."

"Not exactly."

"If you have something on those people, why not tell the police."

He managed to edge himself up against the foot of the bed, gritting his teeth and wincing. "Because if the police go in, they won't find anything."

"Perhaps because nothing is going on."

David Wharton closed his eyes and shook his head. "It only happens on certain nights."

"What only happens?"

"I don't know. But I think Stuart does, and that's why he was drugged to the gills and pushed out on the highway."

Ashley had been leaning against the door, arms crossed over her chest. There was enough sincerity in his words that she found herself believing him.

She shook her head. "David, this is ridiculous. You've got to go to the police. They don't have to run in like gangbusters—"

"I can't go to the police, Ashley."

"Why?"

He stared at her for a long time, then let out a soft sigh.

"Because there's at least one cop out there who's dirty."

It was closing in on one-thirty, when the crowd generally started thinning out. Nick usually gave last call at two on a Friday night, and the place cleared out by two-thirty, three at the latest.

Tonight, one-thirty was still a happening time.

He knew for a fact that Ashley had come home. He'd heard her going through the house. Soon after the phone call from Nick, Sharon had gone in, too, saying she was exhausted. She'd been exhausted an awful lot lately.

He should have felt secure. There was crime in the area, sure, but the marina itself tended to be safe. Boaters looked after boaters. Most of his clientele had been coming in for years. The place was practically a historical monument.

Jake's phone call, though, had unnerved him. He pulled his keys from his pocket and opened the safe behind the bar that held a .45. It was right where it belonged. The gun was always under lock and key, because he would rather be robbed a thousand times over than have one of his employees shot in an attempt to defend the place.

Curtis was with Sandy at the bar. Nick had let Katie go early that night; she'd been serving as manager often enough lately that she deserved an early night.

"Hey, guys, keep an eye on the place for a minute, huh?" Nick was certain they were three sheets to the wind already, but they could manage the bar for a few minutes.

He slipped into the house. He checked his own room first. Sharon was in bed, apparently asleep. He walked through the house to Ashley's door. He knocked tentatively.

"Ashley?"

The door swung open. Ashley stood before him, smiling. "Hey, Nick, what is it?"

He felt a little foolish. "Just making sure you're all right."

"I'm fine. Just a little...tired." She yawned, and he noticed that her eyes were slightly unfocused.

"Had a few drinks, huh?"

"Three." She showed him with her fingers. She smiled. "I'm going to get some sleep."

"Talk to me in the morning, okay?"

"Sure."

He kissed her on the forehead. She caught his shoulders and kissed him on the cheek. "Good night, Uncle Nick," she told him.

"Good night. Sleep tight. Don't let the bedbugs bite."

He hadn't said that in years. She grinned. "I won't."

She closed the door. He heard it lock.

Strange… Ashley had never locked her door before.

Ashley waited for several moments, listening at the door, until she was sure Nick had gone on. Then she turned back to David Wharton. He was still on the floor; however, color seemed to be returning to his cheeks.

"You're full of it," she told him icily. "And I *am* going to see you arrested."

"Ashley, think of Stuart."

"I *am* thinking of him."

"There was an attempt on his life. He's in danger. Real danger."

"What on earth makes you think there's a dirty cop involved in this whole thing?"

He hesitated. "I heard someone talking once. But no one would believe me."

"*I* don't believe you."

"Why? Look, Ashley, I know how dedicated you are. I know your father was probably a great cop. I know that ninety-nine percent of the guys on the force are honest. But hell, cops are people, too. There are temptations.

And there are clever crooks. And where better to hide than behind a uniform?"

"You still haven't given me one solid thing to go on."

He hesitated for a second, then plunged in. "All right, let me try to explain. Along with big business, Stuart started looking into weird religion cults, trying to find out how many people really sacrificed chickens and why there were so many bizarre offshoots of established practices."

"Caleb Harrison said they weren't a religious cult."

"Trust me, he's practicing a brand of religion. A few other guys work that property, but it's mainly women."

"David, if he owns the property and they want to live there and work it, I'm not sure there are any laws against it."

"Probably not—not laws that are enforced, at any rate. There are some oddities still on the books, you know."

"You better keep talking, because I'm still lost."

"Stuart got into the commune. Someone had recommended it to him as a modern-day form of ancient living. He became convinced that Caleb Harrison hadn't bought the place with his own money, and that Harrison himself didn't really know what was going on. We bought the land next to them to watch what was going on."

"And what *was* going on?"

"Boats…at night. But you never knew which nights. They seemed to be random."

"It's not illegal to have a boat in a canal," she snapped.

"It is if the boats are being used for illegal activities."

"What illegal activities?"

He shook his head. "Can't be marijuana—the goods are too small. Probably heroin. What I'm sure of is that it's a bigger operation, but really well handled. Small planes slipping under the radar, coming in from South America and making drops in the Everglades. Then someone picks up the goods, and they're brought in little by little."

"You need to tell this to the police."

"You're not listening to me! If the police go in, Caleb Harrison will show them his prize tomatoes. Maybe they'll meet a few people living and working there. They won't find anything else, because Harrison himself is probably in the dark. Hey, he's got the lifestyle he wants. Why would he question a benefactor who asked him to do nothing but live on the property and grow produce?"

"The cops—"

"You can't call in the cops, I told you that! There's definitely a cop in on it."

"How can you be so sure?"

"I told you—I heard talking."

"All right, just what do you suggest?"

"I want to catch them in the act."

"Catch them in the act—how? You don't know when anything goes down, assuming you're right and someone *is* smuggling drugs. Why not put the police on the alert, have them stopped before they ever reach the property?"

"No! Not even if you're sure you're talking to an honest cop. If you stop the drugs coming through the Everglades, you've done nothing but stop some small-timers who don't know a damn thing. You're not going to get the mastermind behind what's going on—the person with enough power and influence to seize Stuart, shoot him up with heroin and throw him out on the highway."

"David, we've got to bring someone in on it. You must know that. You came to me."

"I came to you because we have to figure out a way to get Stuart out of that hospital before he's killed."

"He's being guarded. His parents are there all the time."

"He's being guarded by *cops*."

"There's got to be someone we can trust."

"Ashley, even if you go to the higher-ups the word could filter down. Don't you understand? We have to find out what is going on, before Stuart winds up dead." He fell silent suddenly, then rose, walking toward the door to the outside.

"Someone is out there," he said softly.

"David, this is a bar on a busy Friday night. There are probably lots of people out there."

He shook his head. "No," he mouthed. "There was someone…listening to us."

"All right, let's go and have a look. There are always a few cops in the bar."

"No cops," he insisted.

"All right, I'll get my uncle Nick."

She turned toward her door. He caught her shoulder. "Ashley, wait. I've got to get out of here. You get your uncle, and you look around the place, and then you lock up like Fort Knox before you go to sleep."

"David, just wait. I'll make sure no one is slinking around. My uncle was in the army. He was the first person to take me to the shooting range. He'll get his gun, we'll walk around, make sure everything is safe, all right?"

"Ashley, I'm begging you to believe me. We have to figure out what to do or Stuart will wind up dead. Please…trust no one."

"I shouldn't trust sworn officers of the law, but I should trust you?"

"I'm trying to keep Stuart alive. Look, I promise, I'll get more information. I swear, I'll do whatever it takes. Give me another day. And if I can't come up with something substantial, you can go to someone you really trust. And then, God help us all."

"All right, sit tight. I'm going to get Nick. We'll look around."

She left David Wharton in her room, wondering if she was insane to trust him. She couldn't help but feel he was telling the truth, at least as he believed it to be.

But a bad cop…?

Cops were people. It could happen.

She walked through the house and into the bar. There were a few people finishing their last drinks.

"Nick?"

"Ashley, you're still awake."

"Yeah…just barely. Can we take a walk around the place?"

"Why?"

"I don't know. I heard noises."

"It's Friday night."

"Humor me, please?"

"Sure."

Nick opened the safe and took out his gun. He held it close to his thigh so as not to draw attention to the weapon as he escorted her out to the terrace and around the circumference of the property.

"What did you hear, exactly?" he asked, when they discovered nothing and no one.

She shrugged. "Oh, rustling, I guess. Nothing, really. I'm sorry to have bothered you."

"You haven't bothered me. You've never bothered me. But I think we need to talk. Really talk."

She nodded. Her head was pounding. She didn't know what was true and what wasn't anymore. She should be calling the cops right now. But what if David Wharton was telling the truth, the whole truth and nothing but the truth? She could be endangering Stuart's life....

They had reached her outer door. Nick turned the knob. To Ashley's surprise the door opened. Then she knew. David Wharton had bolted. He probably didn't trust her any more than she trusted him.

"Ash, you're worried that someone is outside, and you left the door open?"

"I didn't mean to," she said sheepishly.

He stepped inside, gun drawn, motioning her back. He quickly discovered that her bedroom bathroom and closet were empty. He even looked under the bed.

"Find anything?"

"Dust bunnies," he told her.

She grimaced. "I need to vacuum."

"I need to check out the rest of the house."

"I'll come with you."

"I've got the gun, and I still have three or four cops out there. I'll be fine. But you lock yourself in. Both doors."

"I won't sleep unless I go through the house with you."

He sighed and shrugged. "All right."

They went through the house slowly, checking every closet, every nook—Nick even looked under his own bed, which woke Sharon.

"Anything wrong?" she asked sleepily.

"No, baby. Go back to sleep," Nick told her.

She gave him a half smile and closed her eyes again.

"Well, no one here," Nick said. "Ashley..."

"Thanks!" she said softly, then gave him a hug and returned to her room. She desperately needed some sleep. She couldn't even think straight anymore. Every bit of her training and knowledge screamed that she needed to talk to someone.

And yet...

Instinct. Instinct was holding her back.

She locked herself in her room, but before going to bed, she stared at her phone. She sighed, bit her lip and decided on one call.

Nathan Fresia answered, sounding exhausted.

"Nathan, hi. It's Ashley."

"Ashley...do you know what time it is?"

"Yes, I'm sorry. You're with Stuart, right?"

"Yup. Lucy is doing great, though. She'll be here in...in just a few hours."

"Nathan, this is strange, but humor me, please. Make sure that one of you is with Stuart every second. Unless his doctor is there or...just stay with him every second. Even when—even when the cops are around."

"What is it, Ashley?"

"There's no one who loves Stuart as much as you two do. So...?"

"We won't leave him, Ashley."

"Not for a minute. Okay? I'll be in tomorrow, all right?"

"All right. Maybe he'll wake up tomorrow and you'll be here. That would be wonderful."

"Yes, yes it would." She hesitated. "You're certain Stuart is fine?"

"I'm staring at him right now. His color is good." Despite his exhaustion, Nathan sounded excited. "Ashley, I'm praying...."

"So am I," she said softly. "Good night, then. I'll see you tomorrow."

Stuart was fine. His parents wouldn't leave him. Not even a cop could slip in and harm him, not with the hospital personnel around and Stuart's folks keeping vigil. It was still hard to believe a cop could be involved in his situation.

Why? Cops were people, too.

She was going to head straight to the hospital the next morning. And while she was there, she would make her decision about what to do with the information David Wharton had given her.

Her heart quickened. Jake would be back....

Maybe. Peter Bordon might linger for days.

Maybe she should go to the hospital right now. She would close her eyes for just a second, then get up and go in.

Mary Simmons was on breakfast duty. She enjoyed baking bread. While she kneaded the dough, she thought about the world and the peace she longed to find.

Her life was good here. Quiet. And she prayed as she worked.

She was startled when Ross, a young member of

the Krishnas, came in to find her. "You have a visitor, Mary. He says it's urgent."

"The cop?" she asked.

Ross shook his head. "No. He's—"

He broke off. The visitor had followed him in. She stared at him and gasped.

"Mary?" Ross said uncertainly.

"It's—it's all right."

"Can we speak privately?" the man asked.

"Yes, of course. Ross...?"

Ross nodded warily but left them.

"John!" Mary said incredulously.

He strode over to her, going down on one knee, taking both her hands. "Mary, dear Mary, I'm so sorry to come here...to disturb you. You've found what you wanted, haven't you?"

"I think so," she said, gently moving her fingers through his hair. "I thought you were dead."

"I was very close," he admitted. "And then...letting the world think I was dead seemed like a good idea."

"But, John..."

"Mary, I need your help."

"I can't help you. I can't help anyone."

"You *can* help me. You're the only one who can."

"John, I have a life here."

"Mary, you need peace, and you'll never have it unless you help me. I'm close...so close to those scumbags who nearly destroyed all our lives. You've got to help me."

"John... I can't!"

"Mary, for the love of God! Don't you want...revenge? Justice against those who used us—all of us?"

"John... I don't want to go to jail. Do you want me to do something...illegal?"

He looked into her eyes. "Yes. Illegal, but necessary."

She sighed, closing her eyes.

Then she removed the apron she had tied around her waist.

"I guess you have a car?"

"Better than a car," he assured her, his engaging grin coming into place.

"I found God."

Jake jerked his head up. He wondered if he had imagined the words. Peter Bordon hadn't moved. His eyes remained closed.

Then he saw the man's lips move.

"I found God. I found God."

Jake leaned closer. The words were little more than a whisper. His eyes opened, but he was staring straight ahead, as if seeing nothing. "I found God," he suddenly cried out. "Dear God, have you found me? Forgive me!"

Jake looked up at Dr. Matthews who shrugged. "The man is dying," he mouthed, then added in a whisper, "He's delirious. It probably won't do you any good, but try asking your questions."

"Peter, it's Jake Dilessio. You needed to talk to me."

Bordon's lips twitched. "Jake." He tried to turn to look at Jake but couldn't quite manage the feat. "Pain... pills...can't think. God...they say God forgives."

"Peter, I need you to help me."

"Didn't kill... I didn't kill...but I...knew."

"Peter, who did the killing? Let us stop him. Peter, they say that God forgives. Help us. In the name of God."

"Something in me...pills, not pills, couldn't swallow

pills…but the pain…oh, God, it will be good not to feel the pain. God… I found God…has God found me?"

"Peter, help me," Jake repeated urgently.

The man swallowed with great effort. Then he almost managed to turn to Jake, and Jake was amazed to see that tears had pooled in his eyes. "Your partner… Jake. Didn't know… Nancy…she came…she was with me… no, no, didn't kill…didn't kill, but I knew…"

"Peter, I can see your sorrow, see your remorse. Help me. I need names. I understand. Nancy came out to see you. You didn't know her, because she hadn't been at the property before, but someone there knew who she was and what she was doing. Who was it, Peter? Please."

Bordon mouthed something.

"What? Please, Peter, for the love of God."

The dying man's eyes were closed again. Jake longed to grab him and shake him by the shoulders, but he was afraid that any movement would kill the man when he still might speak.

"Peter, help us," he said urgently. "A name, Peter. I need a name."

Again the man's mouth moved. "So beautiful."

"What was beautiful? Who was beautiful, Peter?"

"Partner… She was beautiful. I told her I was sorry."

"I know you're sorry, Peter. Help me catch her killer…yours."

"Cops!" the dying man shouted suddenly.

"Peter, give me a name! Other people could die," Jake said, his voice grating with desperation.

"Jake…your partner…sorry…sorry…didn't want… God forgive me…"

"He's just ranting," Dr. Matthews said quietly.

"He said he'd have me killed…proved it…dead man…dead man…"

Bordon's lips kept moving. No sound was coming. Then, "Jake…" Barely a breath.

Jake's ear was nearly against the man's mouth as Bordon's lips kept moving. Then went still.

A moment later, Dr. Matthews came over and examined the man. He closed Bordon's eyes.

"He's…"

"Gone," Matthews announced. "I'm sorry, Detective Dilessio. You'll get nothing more from him. He's beyond human judgment and pain. He's dead."

Chapter 22

Just after opening, Katie called out to Nick that Sharon was on the phone.

He excused himself to the customers he'd been serving and picked up the receiver.

"Nick," Sharon said softly.

"Hi, baby, what's going on?"

"I…need you to come and meet me."

"Sharon, we've just opened. It's Saturday afternoon."

"Please."

"What's the matter? Is something wrong? Can you tell me?"

"Not—not on the phone."

She'd been acting so strangely lately. More strangely than ever now, it seemed. He looked around the place. Already jumping, and they'd barely opened the doors.

Katie was there, though, and a full staff. Ashley was still sleeping, but if Katie got desperate, she could wake her.

"Nick, I—I need you. I'm afraid. I'm afraid to even talk to you once I see you in person. But I have to. I have to get this out…now. Today. Whatever comes after."

"All right, all right…of course, if you need me, I'll be right there. I need an address."

She gave it to him.

"What kind of a place am I looking for?"

"You'll know when you get here," she told him.

"You're crazy, absolutely crazy," Mary told John Mast. "The hospital's too busy. There must be hundreds of visitors."

"We need those hundreds of visitors."

He adjusted the surgical mask he had just stolen from the supply room. He studied Mary, who was stuffing a strand of her hair under her cap. Good. No one could see anything but her eyes. Pretty, pale blue eyes. Nondescript, along with the scrubs she was wearing.

No one would recognize him either, because only his eyes were visible. He had donned contacts. He was pretty good with makeup. Shaggy, graying white brows, easily attached. He'd checked his reflection, and he'd done a good job. He'd be judged as a man of at least fifty by any witnesses.

"You're crazy," she repeated.

"I'm not crazy. Just desperate," he said. "Well…it's almost showtime."

Jake was on the road home by two.

Exhausted, he forced himself to stop for coffee at the hundred-mile mark. What little he had gleaned from

Bordon whirled through his mind. His list of "facts" waltzed before his eyes, along with a number of week-end vacationers and huge semis.

At the turnpike rest stop, he grabbed a sandwich and more coffee, then headed back to his car, eager to reach home. He had a strange feeling that he couldn't get there fast enough. Like an itch, an intuition that gnawed at him physically.

As he walked across the lot to his car, there was a dull pain in his heart, as well. Bordon hadn't given him any names, but he had admitted his own complicity, though he'd denied the physical act of murder himself. Not a surprise. But where Jake had once believed Bordon had been issuing the directives, he now knew that hadn't been true at all.

Bordon had been murdered. It might take the prison officials some time, but they would find out just who had started the brawl that had killed him. Jake couldn't wait for that news, though, so…

Fact: Peter Bordon had been with Nancy Lassiter. He must have been the man with whom she'd had con-sensual sex the night she had died. She'd been on to something and willing to bend the rules to get to the truth. She'd been a good cop. His heart ached to think of the moral dilemmas she must have faced as the night progressed.

And all the while, she'd had no idea she was going to die.

As he sat down, he noticed the pad on the passenger seat. He set his coffee in the cup holder and picked up the notebook. He flipped the pages. His own notes. The picture of the scene of the accident that had convinced him the cases were related. He frowned, realizing that two pages were stuck together.

He forced them apart, and his heart skipped a beat.

Ashley had done another sketch. And it was of John Mast, also known as David Wharton. The man who'd been hanging around the hospital. Sending the cops on wild-goose chases.

He broke out in a cold sweat, fumbling in his pocket for his cell phone. He tried Ashley's cell first. Her voice mail picked up. "Whatever you do, Ashley, stay away from David Wharton. Do you understand? Stay away from him. I'm on my way home." He hesitated. "Whatever you're feeling about me right now, Ashley, it doesn't matter. I believe that man was involved with the murders of four women and possibly the attack on your friend." He hung up, then tried the bar. He prayed that Nick would pick up. He didn't.

Katie came on. Nick was gone; she didn't know where.

"Ashley?"

"Ashley slept until noon, can you imagine? Then it was a zoo here, and, let me think,,,"

"Is she still there, Katie? It's urgent that I talk to her."

"No, no, that's what I was just about to tell you. She left for the hospital about an hour ago."

"Great. Thank you."

He tried the hospital, and went through a series of recordings and instructions to push different numbers, none of which got him anywhere. He swore, hung up and pulled the car out onto the highway.

He called Carnegie and told him he was certain that the man who had been calling himself David Wharton was really John Mast, former cult member, presumed dead, but alive and well. "Ashley has been talking to him pretty recently. I need you to get to the hospital yourself and tell her to be careful. It's imperative that we find him—now."

He'd covered another thirty miles when Carnegie called back. "Jake, I'm at the hospital. Something is going to break soon. The doctors are convinced Stuart Fresia is coming out of the coma. All sorts of brain activity and stuff I don't understand. Anyway, they've taken him for some kind of a scan or something. They think he could be talking by tonight."

"What about Ashley Montague?"

"She was here just a few minutes ago. She went to be with her friend's parents during the scan."

"Did you tell her what I told you?"

"Yes. She assured me that she'd hang around until you get here."

Jake exhaled. "Keep her there. No matter what, keep her there."

As he drove, he played everything in his mind, again and again. Every word that Bordon had said. Every fact, every supposition. Then he saw that his message light was blinking, and he frowned. Someone must have called while he was talking to Carnegie. He didn't recognize the number on his caller ID, so he quickly hit the message key. "Jake." She sounded very stiff. Well, they hadn't exactly parted on good terms. "I got your message from Carnegie. Sorry—I've managed to lose my cell phone. I've had some strange conversations with David Wharton. I know you say he's John Mast, and I guess it could have been bull, but…he sounded sincere. All right, go ahead, tell me I'm an inexperienced idiot, but he's convinced that there's a cop involved somewhere. Or cops. I'm here. At the hospital. I—I have to admit, I don't know who to trust anymore. If…for any reason you don't see me, I left you something. In a 'tight' spot. I—I'll see you when you get here."

He almost veered off the road.

He heard Bordon shouting again. "Cops!"

No. It couldn't be.

His stomach churned and tightened. That was just Mast, blowing smoke. And yet…

He looked at the speedometer. Bordon had been with Nancy. He knew about her killing; he might even have witnessed it. But he hadn't carried it out. *So beautiful… your partner…*

Screw the speed limit. Broward cops liked to ticket Dade cops. Not today. He turned on the siren and floored the gas pedal.

John Mast knew the hospital layout better than the back of his own hand. He had known how to approach the cop at the door, the Fresias, even Ashley Montague, where she sat in the room with Stuart and his parents, waiting, hopeful. He had Stuart's chart, and he'd given the right papers to the floor nurses. He had copied Dr. Ontkean's signature to a T, and he was calm, cheerful and able to carry out his mission with no trouble whatsoever. He was friendly to the on-duty cop who had challenged him at the door, assuring him that he was certainly welcome to come along and guard the patient during any medical procedure, and convinced the Fresias to go to the cafeteria for coffee.

It was once they started walking down the hall that Ashley began to look suspicious. "This isn't the way the sign said. I thought they did the CAT scans closer to the emergency room."

"Is she right?" the cop following them demanded.

John glanced at Mary. This was her department. He prayed she wouldn't falter. He needed to leave the hospital with Stuart, and that meant keeping everyone calm until he could deal with them.

Now that she was involved, Mary had things under control. "We're being especially careful with this patient," she said to Ashley, sounding as certain and assured as could be.

"Through here," he said, and looked at the cop as he waved Ashley into the room ahead of them. "If you want to give me a hand, pushing the bed around the corner there..."

He nodded at Mary. She drew a hypodermic needle from her pocket and stuck the cop in one quick fluid motion.

He was slumping over before Ashley even noticed. Just then she turned back, frowning. "I'm no doctor, but this isn't—"

She broke off when she saw the cop lying on the hospital floor. But by then Mary was at her side, a second needle drawn from her pocket. Almost instantly, Ashley slumped down beside the cop.

"Good job, Mary. We're halfway there. We've got to get her up on the gurney with him, then pull the sheet up over their faces."

"Why do they have to be covered?" Mary asked.

"The best way out of here is through the morgue," he told her.

Mary lowered her head. "Let's move, then."

At first she was in a fog. Reliving the events before the world had gone black. From the very beginning. Waking late, so late. She couldn't believe it. She never slept that late. She'd showered quickly, hurried out to have a word with Nick, only to find that her uncle was gone and Katie was swamped. She'd helped Katie until the lunch crowd had thinned out.

Still no Nick. She was irritated. She couldn't call him, because he loathed cell phones and refused to carry one. She'd tried Sharon's number but only got her voice mail.

Then to the hospital. Seeing Stuart's parents. Carnegie coming by, to warn her about David Wharton. She'd tried to get Jake, but had only been able to leave him a message. There had been a policeman on duty—whom she had then looked at suspiciously. Still, Stuart's parents…happy, hopeful. Vigilant. They'd all been allowed in the room at once, and they had chatted quietly.

And then…

The technicians who had come to do the scan. Charming, answering questions, though their voices were muffled behind their masks, reading the chart and happy to have the cop accompany them.

And that, she realized, was what had done her in. She should have recognized David Wharton—especially after Carnegie's warning. She had done so, but too late. She'd been an idiot. She should have recognized his eyes, even with the contacts and the fake eyebrows.

She was awake, she realized suddenly. Conscious. She didn't dare open her eyes at first. She lifted her lids incredibly slowly.

"Ashley?"

She heard her name, as if from a distance. And the voice….

There was a face hovering over hers. She opened

her eyes fully. Neither her mouth nor her brain wanted
to work at first.

"Stuart?" she said incredulously.

"Yes, it's me."

He wasn't more than five miles from the hospital
when Carnegie called him. He listened in astonishment
as he heard that Stuart Fresia had been kidnapped. He
barked out questions like a drill sergeant then and knew
he owed Carnegie an apology. But that would have to
come later. Right then he listened to everything Carnegie knew. Everything had appeared to be in order.
The technicians had come with a chart and a signed
authorization, they had cleared everything through the
nurses' station. They had even invited the cop to accompany them.

The cop had been discovered in an old procedure
room. He still hadn't shaken off the anesthesia that had
been shot into him. So far, they hadn't found Ashley or
Stuart. The hospital was, of course, crawling with police,
who were conducting a nook-and-cranny search, but so
far, they'd come up empty.

"If she's here…if they're here…we'll find them,"
Carnegie assured him.

"They aren't there," Jake said flatly. "Keep looking.
Keep me informed."

"Jake, the kidnappers were an older man and a
woman of about thirty-five or forty. Mrs. Fresia described them for me. The nurses agree with the description. So it wasn't John Mast."

Jake doubted that, but he held his peace on the matter. There was still too much he had to sort out in his
own mind.

"Are you still heading over here?" Carnegie asked.

"No."

"Then—"

"I'm going to find them."

"Jake, *you* keep *me* informed, you hear?"

She jerked back, suspicious as hell, and banged her head. She was lying next to Stuart. He was white as a ghost and looked like a refugee from a POW camp. But he offered her a wry smile and asked, "You all right?"

Staring at him, she shook her head. She tried to rise. Dizzy, she fell back. She realized that David Wharton— or John Mast—was standing at the foot of the gurney, along with a woman she'd never seen before. The woman had been the female tech, of course. She was slim, with huge, soulful eyes and brown hair.

"What the hell is going on?" she demanded sharply.

"She makes a good cop, huh?" Stuart said weakly. "We could be hardened criminals, but she's still going to try to tonguelash us into quivering jelly."

"Ashley, I'm sorry," John Mast said. Both the white eyebrows and contacts were gone.

"Hi, I'm Mary," the young woman said.

"You do realize you're guilty of kidnapping and God knows what else?" she said. "And you—you son of a bitch!" she said, staring at the man. "And you're John Mast. I doubt there even *is* a David Wharton."

"Ashley, I don't have much strength, but I'll try to explain," Stuart began.

"Save what strength you have," John Mast advised him quickly. "She's still too groggy to beat me to pieces. I have a few minutes to explain."

"You lied to me," she told him.

"Yes, but for a good reason," he protested quickly. "I had to. I had to get to know you. Yes, I'm John Mast. And yes, I went to prison, along with Bordon, for bad bookkeeping. But I wasn't part of what was really going on. Back then, there were things I kept my mouth shut about because Peter Bordon warned me we'd be killed if we didn't just go to jail, do our time and keep silent about whatever we knew until we were in our graves. You may not believe this, but I really don't know who killed those women. All I know is that at least one of them is a cop. I was in the house the night Nancy Lassiter was there, I saw her briefly, with Peter. Peter…liked women. I thought she was just someone he had charmed off the street. I pretty much ignored what was going on, stayed in my own room. Then, late that night, I heard the door… heard someone coming in, berating Peter. Peter was an idiot. Peter had picked up a cop. And he was damned well going to help make sure that she wouldn't leave. Not only that, she could finger the guy yelling at Peter, because they worked together. That's how I know there's at least one cop involved."

She shook her head. "You're telling me that a cop murdered Nancy Lassiter?"

"I'm afraid so," John said. "But there was another man there that night, too. I didn't see him or the cop, though. I—I never opened my door. I have to admit I was terrified. But I heard a third voice. And I figured that had to be the man Peter always called the cult's 'godfather.' I knew that something went on at times, but I never knew ahead of time when that would be. I was always locked in on those nights. And the girls and the others…they were locked into their quarters, as well. And the godfather had something to do with it, whatever it was. Anyway, the police had already been hounding us, because of the murdered girls. But Peter and I, we weren't the ones killing the girls." He hesitated and took a deep breath.

"Peter knew they were being killed, though. And he knew why. But he kept silent. He knew that the murders were being made to look as if they were for some kind of religious transgression, but they weren't. That was just a cover-up. They must have seen something they weren't supposed to, so they had to die." He was silent for a moment. "Everyone thought I died in a plane crash when I got out of prison, and I figured it was safer to let them. I washed up on shore with another man's identification. He was a few years older than me, but…it was easy enough to find forgers to get me some decent documents to go with what I already had."

The anesthesia was beginning to wear off. Ashley inched up, rubbing the back of her head. "Sorry—we kind of dropped you getting you into the ambulance," Mary explained.

"Great," she muttered, then looked at Stuart to see how he was doing. What was his involvement in all this, anyway? He was lying down, his eyes closed. He looked unconscious. "Stuart," she said anxiously.

His eyes flew open. "Sorry, I'm just trying to rest. I've—I've been conscious for almost twenty-four hours, actually. I just didn't dare let anyone know. Not even my parents," he said sadly.

"They might have given him away," John Mast explained.

"Did you know?" she asked sharply.

"I only knew I had to get him out of the hospital before someone succeeded in killing him."

"Okay. And, Mary, who are you?"

"I was a member of the cult," she said, and added, "The women who were killed were my friends."

Ashley digested that. "I'm sorry," she said after a moment, then she shook her head. "Where are we? And why did you knock me out and kidnap me?"

"We need you. And also because you insisted on coming to the procedure with me," Stuart said. "So we had to do something with you. Plus you're a cop."

"I'm not a cop," she said wearily. "I just work for them."

"Whatever. You have connections."

"All right—where are we?"

"At the house, of course," John said.

"What house?"

"Next to the commune."

"You do realize that eventually you'll be tracked down here?"

"Eventually," John agreed. "But hopefully not until we've got proof."

"Proof of what? And how are you getting it?"

"There's something going down tonight."

"How do you know that?"

"Our neighbors are having a sing-along. They'll all be up at the front of the property while something goes down in back. Ashley, don't you see? They're being used in the same way. The same 'godfather' has financed Caleb, and all he has to do is not pay attention to what goes on behind his property now and then. And if we can get proof of what's going on, then we can tie that to the murders."

"Okay, fine. But let's back step a minute. Da—John, how did you meet Stuart?"

He shrugged sheepishly. "I really did write an article about two-headed aliens."

"We met at the paper," Stuart explained.

Ashley rubbed her neck again and sat up. "Okay, listen, I believe you. But we need real help here. We know there are two utterly ruthless men out there who will kill without batting an eye. We have to call in the police."

"Ashley, how many times do I have to tell you?" John asked. "At least one cop is involved. And we don't know who the dirty cop is."

"One bad cop doesn't mean the whole force is evil. There's got to be someone we can trust."

"Who?"

"Dilessio," she said quietly. "Jake Dilessio. You know he's legitimate."

"Oh, yeah, he's legitimate. He was down my throat like a cougar. Especially after his partner died. He's the reason I went to jail."

"Why didn't you tell him his partner had been at the house with Bordon?"

"I was afraid," John Mast said simply. "I was just twenty-one. And Bordon assured me that I'd be killed."

"So why are you trying to solve things now?" Ashley asked.

"I died once already, in that plane crash," he said. "When I washed up on the beach, I knew I had to find out who had destroyed so many lives."

"Then let's call Dilessio."

"It's pointless. I tried. I left him an anonymous message with enough hints that he should have gotten the point, but nothing happened."

"The answering machine," Ashley murmured, remembering that Jake's mysterious intruder had apparently checked out his messages.

"What?"

"He never got your messages. Look, I know Jake isn't a dirty cop. And we've got to get help from somewhere."

"Yeah, great—we call him, he calls headquarters, and the murderer will know exactly where we are. He'll come all right—and he'll bring backup, and we'll all wind up shot," John said bitterly. "Besides, he lives at the marina."

"So do I," Ashley reminded him, puzzled.

John shook his head. "Don't you see yet? It's obvious. Something's going on at Nick's place, Ashley. I wasn't lying last night. Someone was sneaking around."

She hesitated. Jake had been sure that someone had been on board his boat. Nothing had been taken, but the intruder had been accessing his computer files, listening to his messages, learning from them, erasing them. She herself had been pushed overboard. And someone had been in her room....

Sharon.

Sharon, who had promised to talk to her that afternoon. But she hadn't been back by the time Ashley left for the hospital, and then... Then everything had gone crazy.

"We've got to call Jake," she repeated. "I'm certain that we can explain the situation."

"Before he tells half the city?"

She didn't have a chance to answer. John suddenly stiffened. "Shh," he cautioned.

They could all hear it then. A slight rustle along the outside wall.

"Might be the cops already," she whispered to him.

"We have to protect Stuart," he whispered back. "Mary, you stay with him. Ashley... I'm going out there. I have a gun. Stolen, I'm afraid. But I know how to use it."

Ashley started to follow him out of the room, then hesitated. "Mary, push that dresser in front of the door after I leave. In fact, throw anything you can in front of the door, and block that window with the highboy, do you understand?"

"Of course," Mary said, her eyes widening as she realized the danger she was in, looking after a man with the strength of a starved kitten.

Ashley nodded, hoping Mary was stronger than she looked. As she stepped out the door, she heard the scrape of furniture across the floor. Mary could handle herself.

She hurried after John Mast then, realizing she didn't even know the layout of the house. It was small, probably old, more like a one-story hunting shack than a true home. There was the bedroom they had been in, another beside it, a living room/dining combination, and a kitchen. There was a door out the front, and another that opened off the kitchen.

She was dismayed to see that night had fallen. If someone was outside, they were at the disadvantage. "The lights," she murmured. "We need to turn off the lights."

He nodded and moved back, hitting a switch. The lights were extinguished.

They stood in darkness for what seemed like a very long time. Listening. It was almost pitch-black at first. Then Ashley discovered that she could dimly make out John Mast's silhouette. He was holding what looked like a .45. She held her breath, then made a dash across the room to the kitchen, sliding along the wall that separated the kitchen from the dining area.

Again she listened....

Then, with a tremendous crash, the door flew open. Flashes of powder sparked in the darkness as John Mast's weapon went off.

And fire was returned from the door.

Jake jerked his car to a halt as close to his boat as he could get. He jumped out, loped down the docks, and burst into the *Gwendolyn*. His first strides took him straight to the shower; he discovered that he'd been left two real estate folders. He noted the addresses and was ready to head straight out at a gallop, but forced himself to pause. He pulled up the old files on his computer. He scanned the reports and the newspaper articles.

He hit the button on the answering machine that supplied a readout of his calls over the last week. He knew his visitor had been erasing his messages.

It didn't matter; he had what he needed. He had the answer—on at least a major piece of the puzzle. But he still had to be extremely careful.

He left the houseboat and put through a call to the one person he knew he could trust beyond a doubt. The one person who could supply him with what he needed most.

As he headed toward his car, he was startled to see Nick Montague come running out of the bar, racing to stop him. He paused, frowning, hoping Nick wasn't in the mood to engage him in battle for some reason.

Nick wasn't.

"I'm coming with you," he said, heading for the passenger door.

"Nick, this isn't—"

"I'm a Vietnam vet, I've got my service revolver, and I'm good with it," Nick said simply. "Look, I don't know everything that's going on, but I know they've got my niece. And I know where they've gone."

"So do I," Jake said.

Nick glared at him. "Sharon gave me the addresses Ashley had asked her about. Where did you get them?"

"Ashley left them for me," he said. He looked at Nick. "We're not going straight there."

"She's in danger!"

"A head-on assault will put her in greater danger," Jake said. Nick stared at him, and, after a moment, slowly nodded.

"You haven't called in what you know, have you?" Nick asked.

"Not to Miami-Dade."

"So who's dirty?" Nick asked after a moment.

"I think I know, but I'm not certain. And I think we have more than just a rogue cop to deal with. I think someone else, someone we see around here all the time, is involved."

Nick digested that, as well.

"Want to tell me the battle plan?"

There was a scream; Ashley heard a thud as someone fell. John rushed forward. "Wait!" she warned.

Too late. She heard shots, then a grunt escaped John Mast. She saw his body fall limply, as if he were a rag doll. She winced. She had cried out and given away her location. There was only one escape. The kitchen door.

She ran out of the house, trying to gain her bearings in the darkness. There were trees everywhere. Rows between the trees, the fence to her right...to the rear, the swamp and the water.

She couldn't head to the front. She would run right into an ambush. She tore along the rows of trees. She wasn't certain, but she thought that whoever had shot John Mast was alone. She *was* certain that he would come after her. At least that would leave Mary and Stuart safe. For a while. As long as she could lead the killer on a merry chase through the groves and into the Everglades.

She could hear the footsteps thrashing after her in pursuit. She kept moving. She reached the end of the groves, and the grass almost immediately grew higher. She gritted her teeth, praying it wasn't sawgrass or she would be cut to ribbons before she could move another few feet.

Not sawgrass, not yet. She was still on solid ground, trees ranging ahead of her. She kept moving. A massive spiderweb suddenly tangled around her. She nearly screamed. She held back, berating herself. Terrific. Would-be cop done in by a spiderweb. Clawing at the shreds that were still clinging to her, she kept going.

Suddenly she could hear voices. They were coming from ahead of her. Past a copse of trees, the terrain suddenly changed. The earth sloped down to the canal.

There were men there, men talking quietly, unloading plastic cartons from two small canoes pulled up on the muddy embankment.

They were clad in black, entirely in black. They blended with the night.

She slowed her gait but was still running. The men were ahead of her, a man with a gun was behind her.

Suddenly she heard one of the men carrying the cartons give a little shriek. She strained to see what was happening.

It was then that she hit the trip wire.

It had been strung low between the trees that marked the property line. She hadn't seen it, hadn't had a clue of its existence, until she went sailing through the air and landed hard in the muck.

She kept herself from crying out, but her foot was still tangled in the wire. Silently, she struggled up and started to free herself.

She was suddenly aware of a shadow looming over her. The man who pursued her was also clad in black. She looked up slowly, aware that she couldn't be more vulnerable.

"Hello, Ashley," the man said softly.

Chapter 23

Life was ebbing away. John felt it seeping from him. He wasn't dead. Not yet. But if he didn't get help soon, he would be.

He'd forced himself not to scream with the pain of the bullet that had torn through his flesh. He prayed that no vital organs had been hit. He prayed for the strength to find the gun that had slipped from his fingers as the bullet hit.

Reaching…inching, his blood leaving a slimy trail behind him as if he were a worm. He needed the gun. The man would be back.

After he found Ashley.

He paused, gasping in pain, his agony as much for what he thought he had done to her as it was for the pain that raged through him like a brush fire. She would die, and it would be his fault. And if he didn't get the gun…

Then Stuart and Mary might die, as well, and all their efforts would have been in vain. Their killer knew how to fix a crime scene. It would look as if Ashley had fought them, killed them…but not before they had killed her in return. And the murder of Cassie Sewell would be credited to him.

The gun…just an inch away now.

"Hello, Marty," Ashley replied. She wondered whether to try to fake it out or not and decided to give it a shot. "Thank God you're here. Is Jake with you?"

"Well done, Ms. Montague. If you hadn't been so gung-ho on being a cop, you could have tried out for the silver screen."

She nodded. Well, she'd had to try. "If you're going to shoot me, this looks like as good a time as any."

"It would be. Except that you're going to get me into that room where Stuart Fresia is lying. I could try to shoot through the door, of course. But they've got the place barricaded, don't they?"

"Yup." She was amazed that she sounded so calm. Her heart was thundering with terror, with remorse. This was it. Any minute now, he would fire. His aim would be true. She knew what a bullet looked like once it had exited the human body. Now she would know what it felt like entering.

"Come on, Ashley. Up."

He caught her by the arm. She gritted her teeth. He was powerful, far more powerful than his laid-back act had made her expect. His fingers bit into the flesh of her upper arm. Since her foot was still caught, it felt as if he had dislocated her shoulder.

"The wire, Marty," she said. "Sorry, but I can't go anywhere with you while I'm still caught."

He bent down to undo the wire and gave her the only chance she was going to get.

He still had the gun. She had nothing but desperation.

She brought her knee up, slamming it against his groin with all her strength. The blow had the desired effect. He wheezed out a cry of pain, falling forward.

And she moved. Like lightning. She somehow tore her foot free, and she ran.

The first bullet must have missed her head by inches. She heard the whine as it passed her by and went thudding into a tree. In agony or not, he was up. More shots came flying into the trees. He was on the move. And she had no idea where she was running, except into the darkness.

She surged forward and discovered that the trees were beginning to thin, the ground turning soft and boggy under her feet. With every step, her feet sank deeper. She was grateful for her jeans and sneakers—she had entered an area with sporadic patches of sawgrass. And here, as the water rose around her, she could come across all kinds of creatures that were no longer common in the city, driven away by concrete and civilization.

Water moccasins dwelt in these waters. Alligators. And the darkness...

She stumbled upward. Ground, solid ground beneath her feet. A little hammock stretching stalwartly into the canal.

Another bullet sped by her, only the sound telling her that he was still close, too close, behind.

Then, out of the darkness, something reached for her. Terror leapt into her throat. She opened her mouth to scream.

"Shush!" A hand closed over her mouth; strong arms embraced her. Filthy, soaked, covered in mud, she blinked and stared at a man who was as filthy as she was.

The hand loosened on her mouth.

"Jake?" She mouthed the word incredulously.

"Get behind me. Behind those trees."

She pulled back, shaking her head. "Jake, it's it's Marty," she whispered.

"I know."

Then, to her amazement, he stepped forward. "Marty!"

There was silence for a moment. Ashley swallowed hard. Jake had given away his position. Marty could shoot him easily.

"Jake?"

In the almost pitch darkness, she made out Marty's form as he moved forward. He'd shed the black he'd been wearing. He was in his typical work suit.

It was oddly lacking in mud stains. "Jake, man, I'm sorry. It's Nick's niece. She must have gotten into drugs or something. She helped pull off the kidnapping at the hospital. She's in on this whole thing."

"I'm going to give you one warning, Marty," Jake said softly. "I wanted to just haul off and shoot you, but...well, truthfully, I haven't figured out yet who your partner is. You're not the one who's been on the *Gwendolyn*, and I want to know who was. When I realized you'd killed Nancy, I wanted to shoot you in both knee-caps, then rip your heart out. But..."

"But what?" Marty said. "But I have a gun, maybe? Maybe you're the big hotshot detective, Jake, but I do just fine on the target range, and now I've got the drop on you. Everyone admires Jake, respects him. He's the guy with the instincts, the one who can sift through the garbage, and find the golden clue. I can't tell you what it's been like, watching you day after day, *working with you*, watching you eat your heart out over Nancy Lassiter. But you didn't figure it out, Jake."

"Well, Marty, actually, I did. A little late, I grant you, but—here I am. Will it make you feel better to hear it? I do feel like an idiot. Bordon did give me something the first time out, without really saying anything. Smoke and mirrors. The cult meant nothing. And then, when he was dying, he kept saying 'your partner.' At first I thought he meant Nancy, of course. But then I began to realize he might have meant someone else. So I went home, pulled up a few records. The thing that cinched it was the newspaper report on the day Nancy was found and her car was pulled from the canal. You were the first cop on the scene. You were a vice cop back then, so I had to ask myself what you were doing there. Are you the one who actually killed the women, Marty, or your partner?"

Marty grinned and shrugged. "You still don't know who that is, do you, Jake?"

"I have a hunch."

"You don't *know*."

"Did you kill the women, Marty?"

"Yeah, Jake, I killed them. Nosy women. Their own fault. They shouldn't have been snooping around."

"The last victim…she showed up at the commune next door and saw something she shouldn't have, right?"

"Jake, you're just brilliant," Marty said sarcastically. "And Nancy? You killed her, too, didn't you?"

"You should have seen her face when she saw me in that house, Jake. She was stunned. Smart girl. She caught on quick. Too bad for her. I killed her. And when I finish with you, I'm going after your little redhead. Now, she's a problem. Those drawings of hers… I had to get her out of the way whether you came into the picture or not. That picture of Cassie Sewell was…hell, it was scary. And who the hell would have thought she'd be a friend of that idiot reporter I drugged up and threw on the road? Go figure," he said casually.

"I hate to say it, Marty," Jake said, his voice extremely quiet. "I hope they give you the death penalty."

"They haven't got me yet, Lone Ranger."

"You're under arrest, Marty. And you will go to trial."

"You've got a gun, Jake. I've got a gun. Let's count to three. But what if you shoot me? What happens when I'm dead? You'll still be searching, Jake. Because there's still someone else out there."

"I'm not going to kill you, Marty."

"Right. *I'm* going to kill *you*." He laughed bitterly. "Look at you, Jake. Out here alone again. Blake gets pissed at you all the time, you know. Hell, I think he feels sorry for me, working with you. 'That Jake,' he'll say. 'He was such a loner. We had a whole task force, but Jake thought he could solve it all himself.' Well, guess what, Jake? Dumb move this time."

"Marty, put the gun down."

"Jake, you're going down. I think I can take you, and if I can't, well, see you in hell."

"Drop your weapon."

"What, no warning shot?"

"Drop your weapon. You're under arrest. You have the right—" Jake began.

Marty pulled his .38. He was fast. Jake was faster. The shots were deafening. For long seconds Ashley grasped the tree in a death grip. Long seconds that seemed an eternity of smoke and left both men still standing.

Then Marty fell, face first, into the muck.

The world seemed frozen. Ashley wanted to run to Jake but she heard movement in the brush behind her and started to swing around instead. A man was standing there, with ink-dark long hair, his face smeared with muck, just as Jake's had been. Hazel eyes, the only brightness about his face, peered steadily at her. Panic seared through her. An arm fell on her shoulder. She tensed, ready to fight.

"It's all right, Ms. Montague," he said, his voice as soft as a whisper on the breeze. "Leave him be. Just for a minute. There's someone to see you."

She looked past him. For a moment she thought she had stepped into a horror movie. *Night of the Swamp Men.* Other figures were moving toward her. They seemed completely confident and at home, moving silently through the water and along the embankment. Amazingly, she recognized one of them.

"Uncle Nick?"

"You bet, Ash."

She ran, or rather, stumbled to him and found herself caught up in his arms. He held her closely. Neither spoke. The others—five, she counted—hovered in back, silent. And then she heard a noise and turned.

Jake was walking toward the body of his fallen partner. He knelt down, placing his fingers against the man's throat. He stayed down for several seconds; then he rose. "He's dead," he said wearily, walking back toward them.

Ashley wanted to scream. She wanted him to realize it was better that Marty was dead than he was.

"*He's* dead," she managed to say quietly instead. "But there are drug smugglers. I saw them. I—"

"It's all right, Ashley," Jake said. His voice still sounded as dead as Marty was. "Marty was wrong about one thing. I knew I couldn't be the Lone Ranger. That's Jesse Crane behind you. And some of his men, Miccosukee police."

The hazel-eyed man gravely nodded an acknowledgment. Something about his solemn demeanor reassured Ashley, and suddenly her mind started working again.

"We need an ambulance. David—John Mast has been shot. He may be dead. I don't know. And Stuart Fresia and a woman named Mary are barricaded in the house."

"I'll radio in, get an ambulance out immediately," Jesse Crane said.

Jake had already started moving, running hard despite the foliage. Ashley took off in his wake, Nick and a number of the others behind her.

When she reached the rear of the house, the kitchen door was standing open. Jake had already gone tearing in. She raced after him, reaching the entry just behind him.

"John, no!" Ashley cried quickly. "It's me! And Jake Dilessio. And more cops. Good cops."

Bloody fingers eased off the gun as John Mast struggled to stay upright. Jake hunkered down at his side. John looked up, groaning.

"Dilessio. It's you. Oh, Jesus. Ashley will tell you. I kidnapped her and Stuart, but I swear to you, I was trying to protect him."

"Shut up, kid," Jake said. "Save your strength." John winced as Jake tore at his shirt, looking for the wound, trying to stanch the flow of blood.

"What are you going to do to me this time?" John said.

"Nothing, except get you an ambulance. And maybe take you out for one hell of a night on the town—assuming you survive, of course."

John stared at Jake, then slowly smiled. "I'll survive, Detective. I'll survive—just to take you up on that invitation."

"I thought you might say that."

John frowned suddenly. "Are you sure I'm not dead already? I hear music. A hymn, I think."

Ashley listened, then smiled.

"It's the sing-along next door," she said, shaking her head.

The people of the commune were keeping their covenant, singing away at the appointed time.

They would see no evil, hear no evil, speak no evil. Maybe they had sensed it was the only way to stay alive.

The singing would stop soon. The place would be swarming with police.

4:00 a.m.

The place had been swarming with cops for hours. The sirens had screamed; lights had blazed; rescue vehicles had come and gone. Both John and Stuart had been rushed to the hospital. Mary Simmons, shaken, had still calmly answered every question with steadfast honesty. She'd admitted to her part in the kidnapping, apologizing profusely. It didn't matter if she went to jail or not, she said. She'd done what she had to. Her beliefs compelled her to act to save Stuart's life, because she knew the killers wouldn't stop trying to get him.

Despite her part in the affair—and the fact that, at a later date, the D.A.'s office might press charges—Mary Simmons was at last allowed to return home.

Jake seemed to have more explaining to do than Mary. Ashley heard some of it, though not all. He was taken to task for not informing his own captain of his intended actions, and he explained over and over again that the only way he could be certain he wasn't bringing in one of the very men who meant to kill Stuart Fresia was by reaching outside the department.

He didn't seem to mind explaining, and he kept his temper. Perhaps because everyone realized that a brutal murderer had at last been brought to justice in the swamps, and a major drug ring busted, he was only verbally reprimanded.

There were a few moments when he sat at the back of a police wagon with Ashley and said, "What I really dread now is the paperwork."

She set a hand on his knee, telling him, "I'm so sorry."

He was silent for a moment, then shrugged. "I really didn't want to kill him. Not just because we're still not sure who his partner, the one with all the money, is, but because… I always thought that if I found the person who killed Nancy, I'd want to rip his throat out. But Nancy believed in the law. And I found out tonight that I do, too. I didn't want to kill him. I wanted him to stand trial for what he did. I'm sick at the thought that a man the public trusted, a man I worked with day in and day out, could be so brutal, so devious. Now there will be an inquest, this will all be in the papers, and good cops will suffer because one cop was bad." He met her eyes, his expression haunted.

"Cops have gone bad before, and I know they'll go bad again. But it's not the norm. And I hate that people will think it is. And when I think about it, I'm sick all over again, because if anyone should have been able to see Marty for what he was, to recognize him…it was me."

She had a feeling there was nothing she could say that would make him feel any better regarding Marty. She curled her fingers around his. "You saved my life. Your timing was incredible."

His fingers closed around hers. A half smile curved his lips. "I hate to admit it, but you were doing pretty well on your own."

"I couldn't have outrun him forever. He had a gun, I didn't."

He was quiet for a long time. "You know, eventually you really should finish at the academy."

She smiled, but she had no chance to respond, because Captain Blake was back; he needed Jake again.

It was another hour before they were able to leave. Marty's body had been removed to the morgue, and the drug smugglers had been taken to headquarters where they would be questioned for hours.

She was glad to see that, despite the fact that there was still a piece of the puzzle missing, Jake was determined to leave things to the other members of the department, and especially to the men in the task force.

He drove his own car. Nick was in the back; Ashley sat up front with Jake. When they reached home at last, Nick got out of the car first, and when Ashley and Jake crawled out more slowly, Nick said to no one in particular, "Okay, even I know this is one weird request." He turned and looked at Jake. "Just sleep in my house tonight, will you? I'd like to know you're both close." He stepped ahead of them then, twisting his key in the lock and entering the house.

Ashley felt a cool breeze stir her hair. It would still be a while until sunrise. She wished she weren't so exhausted, that she could make it to watch morning come.

"So...what do you say? Mind sleeping in the house?" she asked. "It's not that I'm the nervous type, but hey... there's nothing like backup."

"Everyone needs backup," he said softly. "Besides, the opportunity to see your room is a definite temptation. Hey, do I get the first shower?"

"Um," she said thoughtfully. "I'm not that magnanimous. How about *sharing* the first shower?"

"It'll do."

As it happened, they were both sporting a number of bruises and sawgrass cuts. They pointed them out to one another, then did things to make them feel better. When they emerged, the laughter stopped suddenly, and they stared at one another for several long moments.

"So...this is your bed, huh?"

"This is it."

"Ashley."

"Hmm?"

He wound his arms around her, buried his face against her neck, held her tightly. And began to move.

She had thought she was exhausted, but it was

amazing just how awake, aware and vehemently energetic she could become.

Later, they remained together, side by side, yet curled together as one. She felt his fingers against her hair, gently smoothing it back.

"I have to admit, I'm probably always going to be a bit of a chauvinist asshole where you're concerned."

"That's all right. I'll just keep putting you in your place."

"Just so long as you know."

She sat up suddenly, looking toward the windows.

"The sun is about to rise."

"It rises every morning."

"This morning, I'd like to see it."

Jake's clothing was caked with muck; he had to resort to one of her bathrobes, but he did so with only a slight grimace.

They sat on the dock together. She leaned against his shoulder. "It's so beautiful. I've never seen that shade between gold and red before."

"I have."

"Oh?"

"It's the color of your hair."

She looked up and met his eyes then smiled.

"This is scary as hell, but…"

"Spit it out, Detective."

"I'm falling in love with you, Ashley."

She rested her head against his shoulder again. "Well, Detective, you should have figured this one out. I've already fallen in love with you. I think it all started the minute I spilled that coffee on you."

"Ashley, have we seen enough of the sunrise?"

She smiled. "You bet. You look good in a business

suit, in your cutoffs…but man, when you're wearing my pink robe…"

He let out a laugh, stood and pulled her to her feet.

The sun had risen fully by the time they fell asleep.

Late Sunday afternoon, they awoke. Ashley, opening her eyes, saw that he was already awake and staring up at the ceiling.

"What's wrong?" she murmured.

He laced his fingers behind his head. "I keep thinking about who Marty's partner was. I keep trying to do the Sherlock Holmes thing. You know—eliminate the impossible, and what's left, no matter how implausible, has to be the answer. I can't seem to eliminate anyone."

"From…?"

"Being on the *Gwendolyn*. Being the money— and power—behind the murders and the drugs."

Ashley hesitated. "Sharon has been acting very strangely."

"Sharon?" he said skeptically.

"You don't think it could be her? She's got money—don't know how much, but her wardrobe is probably worth more than what a cop makes in a year. She was the one who sold those properties, and she was the first one to recognize Cassie Sewell from my drawing. Are you doubting she could be guilty because she's a woman?"

"No, I've known too many brutal and cunning acts perpetrated by women for that. And you could be right," he said. Suddenly, he rose, heading for the shower. He spun to face her. "Don't you dare join me. We've got to get started."

"Started doing what?"

"Eliminating the impossible."

* * *

Ashley was grateful that Katie was working, because she was able to get both Nick and Sharon to join Jake and her in the living room. Sharon was all maternal, asking if she was all right, telling her how she'd hardly been able to sleep after hearing what had happened.

Ashley thanked her for her concern, then plunged right in. "What's been going on with you?"

Sharon stared at her, going pink, then turned to Nick.

"Sharon, why were you really in my room?" Ashley demanded with exasperation. "What were you planning to talk to me about? And what was your appointment yesterday morning?"

"Oh, Ashley, I—I went to the doctor's office yesterday morning. I couldn't believe it at first, and I was so afraid of how Nick and you would feel, but... I'm pregnant."

Ashley blinked. "Pregnant?"

"Nick and I are going to have a baby." She paused to meet Nick's eyes, basking in his smile. "I know I shouldn't have been in your room, but I thought if I could get to know you better, get a sense of the private you, I could get closer to you, and then maybe you wouldn't mind so much that..."

She was definitely still overtired, Ashley realized. And so relieved. She burst into laughter. She laughed so hard that tears stung her eyes.

"Oh, no, Nick! She *is* upset. Ashley, I know Nick's been like a father to you since you were a little girl, and you've been like an only child..."

"I'm not upset," Ashley managed to say at last. "I'm re-lie—" Jake stared at her sternly. She caught herself and started over. No need to let Sharon know she had been a suspect, however briefly. "I'm elated. I'm thrilled for you both. I can't wait to have a little cousin." She rose quickly, hurried over to Sharon and hugged her tightly. "I couldn't be happier."

Nick, looking slightly embarrassed, rose to accept her hug. "It's scary," he said huskily. "I'll be bald and on arthritis medicine by the time the kid graduates from high school. But... I'm thrilled. And I'm thrilled that you're thrilled."

"We're all thrilled," Jake said, rising, as well. "Sharon, Nick, congratulations. Is there any decent champagne in that bar of yours, Nick? My treat." He slid an arm around Ashley, who was still shaking with relieved laughter.

Sharon begged them both not to say anything yet. She was nervous about carrying the baby and didn't want to make any announcement until she had passed the first trimester of her pregnancy. One way or the other, though, she and Nick had decided to get married. They were planning the wedding, which would be very small, on a Sunday morning, right there on the docks, in three weeks.

Jake and Ashley promised to keep their secret, then agreed to stand up for them at the wedding.

"What now?" Ashley whispered to Jake.

"Let's go fishing."

"Is that a Sherlock Holmes thing, too?"

"No, it's when you throw a baited hook in the water, and try to catch fish." He grinned. "I need to clear some cobwebs. Fishing always helps."

That night, when they'd come in with a nice supply of snapper and a few kingfish, Jake returned to his place, showered and put a call through to Ethan Franklin.

"I need your help. You're a computer whiz. I need you to find out everything you can about a couple of guys."

"You got it. And on this one, I'll even work nights and Sundays."

"Thanks, Franklin," Jake said, and gave him a list of four names.

On Monday morning, when Ashley walked into work she was smothered with hugs and congratulations both on being alive and on her part in the huge bust. She demurred, reminding them that she hadn't exactly solved anything; she'd been kidnapped from the hospital, sedated, along with Stuart Fresia. Captain Murray walked by and barked at everyone to get back to work—they were the police department, they were supposed to be solving crimes. But as everyone scattered, he set an arm on her shoulder and said three all-important words. "Good work, Montague."

Later that afternoon, while she was in the darkroom, there was a tap at the door. The entire forensics department was standing there, along with several members of her one-time trainee class. They'd gotten her a cake. And she was awarded a little banner Gwyn had made on her computer, declaring her an honorary member of their graduating class.

Monday night was great. Stuart was up and walking, so the two of them, along with Jake, Karen, Jan, Len and even Mary—who had dressed up for the occasion—were able to visit with John, but only for a few minutes. His nurses were strict. "Leave it to me to get the battle-ax," John moaned. "But once I get out of here, if I'm not under arrest, well, I'll be free. Really free, like I haven't been in years."

"And what then?" Jake demanded.

"I'm going to write one hell of a story," he said.

Stuart cleared his throat.

"Okay, so we're going to share a byline," John said, and they were all able to laugh.

They went to dinner as a group when they left the hospital. And then, for Ashley, there remained the wonder of being a twosome and returning to the *Gwendolyn* with Jake.

It was the next night, about seven, when they were arguing over the proper method of cooking the snapper they had caught, that Jake suddenly went silent.

Ashley frowned.

"Someone's out there," he mouthed.

He walked silently to the door and threw it open.

Brian Lassiter stood there, his hand raised as if he had been about to knock.

"Hey. Have you got ESP, Jake?"

Jake shook his head. "Heard you coming."

"Oh." He glanced in and saw Ashley. She had seen him a few times at Nick's and knew he had been Nancy Lassiter's husband, but she didn't know him at all.

"Hi, Brian. I'm Nick's niece. Ashley."

"I knew you looked familiar. Hi, how are you?" He looked at Jake again. "Can I come in?"

Jake opened the door wider.

"Want a beer?" Jake asked.

"Soda— I'm driving."

Ashley went to the refrigerator for a Coke, then brought it to Brian. He nodded to her with a small smile and looked at Jake. "I came to say thanks."

Jake shook his head. "No need to thank me for doing my job, Brian."

"Yeah, there is," Brian said. "I loved her, and it hurts just a little bit less to know the guy who did it won't be doing it again. And I know I owe you an apology." He paused, then went on resolutely. "You may doubt me, and that's all right, but I'm quitting drinking…and I'm going to get married again. I hope you'll come."

"Congratulations, Brian," Jake said.

"Ditto," Ashley agreed. "Hey, want some snapper?"

Brian looked a little uneasily at Jake. "I… Hey, why not?"

So he stayed. And though Jake was courteous, he was quieter than usual.

When Brian left, Ashley asked Jake what was wrong.

"He's rich," he said simply.

"He's an attorney," she reminded him.

"Yeah."

"Do you still hate him for hurting Nancy?" she asked softly.

"No," he said after a moment. "We all hurt her." He turned away, retreating to his desk, then into the bedroom. Ashley decided to take care of the dishes. Later, she tiptoed into the bedroom. She was startled by the strength of his arms when he grabbed her.

Later that night, his phone rang. He rose and padded out to the living room, and she heard him speaking for several minutes. When he returned, she asked him what was going on.

"It was Franklin, my FBI guy. He's gathering some information for me."

"Oh?"

He lay down beside her, pulled her close again and shrugged ruefully. "You'll be happy to hear that Brian Lassiter's finances are as clean as a whistle. He's a shark, out to get what he can, but he's a legitimate shark."

She smiled in the darkness. She was happy, because she was certain the knowledge made Jake happy.

She knew he was still deeply disturbed, though. Thus far, the questioning of the men taken into custody during the drug bust had revealed little. They were all from South America, as were the drugs, and they denied knowing who had paid to get them into the U.S. or who was dealing the drugs in the States.

In other words, they still didn't know who'd been working with Marty.

"The answer is right there, in front of me. How can it be happening so close without my seeing the truth?" he asked her softly.

"You can't let it drive you crazy."

"I can't stop it," he admitted.

She let him be.

The following morning, she woke early, kissed Jake and told him she had to run back to her room to get ready for work. He mumbled something, and she left him, pausing to switch on his coffeepot before she left. Just then his phone started ringing, and she heard him pick up. She was curious who it was, but she had no time to waste.

She let herself out and sprinted across the lawn to her room, then quickly showered and dressed in the browns that were her forensics wear.

Her hours were later now, but it seemed that she was always running a few minutes late anyway.

Maybe they should set the alarm a few minutes earlier. *They...*

She liked that concept. It was very nice being *they.*

She hurried into the house, wondering if Nick had risen yet.

No. He and Sharon were sleeping later, too. She smiled, thinking it would be fun to tease Sharon about it being natural for old pregnant people to sleep late.

In the kitchen, she switched on the coffeepot, wondering why they didn't just buy a pot that turned itself on automatically. She drummed her fingers until the coffee began to drip, then moved the pot and slid a cup in its place, shaking her head at the mess she made but determined to have a quick cup of coffee anyway.

It was light. For a moment, all she saw was a figure in the doorway, eerily reminiscent of the black-robed figure she had seen standing on the other side of the highway at the scene of Stuart's accident. The figure moved, and she gave her head a shake. It was just Sandy, and he was actually wearing a pair of trousers, a polo shirt and a jacket.

"Hey, Sandy," she said, "I'm running out. Nick and Sharon are sleeping. Help yourself to coffee, and make sure you lock the door on your way out. I'm running late, as usual."

"It's love," he told her.

She shrugged. That's what happened when you lived at a marina. Everyone knew your business.

"Hey, did Jake ever get anything back from that fingerprint fellow the other day?" Sandy asked.

"No, just prints of people he'd known had been there. You really do know everything that goes on here, don't you? Were you down at his boat when Skip got there? Did Nick have you let him in?"

"Naw. I just saw the guy from my boat. Well, too bad for Jake. It must be driving him crazy, knowing he's still missing a piece of his puzzle."

He's still missing a piece of his puzzle.

That wasn't common knowledge. Of course, around here, people talked. Sometimes, too much.

"It is. See you, Sandy," she said, and headed out the door. As she started to close it, she looked toward the water. From where she stood, she could see Sandy's boat. Jake's was much farther down, across from her wing of the house.

Sandy couldn't possibly see the cabin door of Jake's boat from his own. Of course, he might have seen Skip leaving with his oversized briefcase. And he might be lying, he might have been down by the end of the docks, just being nosy.

Suddenly she remembered standing just where she was now, talking about cops.

I listen to the cops in Nick's place, he had said. He knew them all. Jake Dilessio hadn't come around all that much until he had moved his boat, and yet Sandy had been able to tell her all about him.

Air seemed to escape from her lungs in a whoosh. Sandy? Impossible. He was a fixture. He was…ancient.

I listen to the cops in Nick's place.

Right. He talked to them all the time. He was always with one of them. No one would ever notice if he spent time talking with Marty Moore. No one would ever realize he was listening because he needed to know what was going on with the Miami-Dade force.

As the thoughts crossed her mind, she became uncomfortably aware that he was behind her. She stiffened, then started to turn, but stopped when she felt a gun against her ribs.

"Does that beat all or what?" he said quietly. "All this time, and I slip up on something really ridiculous. But that doesn't matter. I didn't come for coffee this morning. I came to get you. You barely gave yourself away, Ashley. If I hadn't come specifically to take you for a nice long ride, I'd have had to wonder if you actually figured it all out or not. You see, I'm all set to fly away, Ashley. Far, far, away. I've taken things here as far as it's safe for me to go. Made some good money, that's for sure. But…it's gotten way too hot. It started to unravel when that friend of yours didn't die on the highway like he was supposed to. Then there was Bordon. I should have had him killed years ago. Counted on Marty, though." He laughed. "He was a damned good partner. Got shot and went down without giving me away. Someone else is going to figure it out eventually, though, maybe soon. Dilessio, probably. Too bad I couldn't have killed him. Ashley, no work for you this morning. You're coming with me. Be real good and quiet, and I might let you live."

"When I don't show up for work, people will start looking for me. In fact, when they see that my car is still here—"

"It won't be here. You're doing the driving. We're going, Ms. Montague. Now."

She didn't protest; she had just seen an entirely different side of a man she had thought she knew well. His voice was different, the way he talked was different, even his stance was different. It was as if the years had dropped away.

"Where am I driving you?"

"An airstrip."

She took a deep breath, twisting slightly, trying to get a glimpse of the gun.

"Glock," he said. "City of Miami has been known to issue them, but maybe you've never handled one, since

Miami-Dade doesn't much like them. No safety. Pretty powerful weapon. It gives a clean kill."

"Want me to call in late to work?" she asked, trying to overcome her sense of shock and fight down a rising wave of desperate fear. She had thought Marty was cold-blooded, but the change in Sandy was more than chilling. Marty had done the killing. Peter Bordon had conspired with him. But this was the man who had given the execution orders.

"You've got a cell phone. We'll call from the road. We should really go, before Jake or your uncle shows up. I need one hostage, not two. I won't blink to shoot either of them, and I think you know that."

She had no chance of living if she went with him, and she knew that, too. But the thought of him seeing Jake or Nick—or Sharon!—and shooting them like dogs was far too vivid in her mind.

"Hey!" came a sudden cry. She was startled to see Jake, wearing only bathing trunks, come walking around the far edge of the terrace.

The gun jabbed more deeply into her ribs. "You've got two seconds to get rid of him," Sandy said. "Cry out and you're both dead. Trust me, a Glock is a damned good weapon. I can kill two people in a matter of seconds."

"Sandy, hey," Jake said, smiling pleasantly. "The coffeepot on the *Gwendolyn* is broken. What the heck did you do to it, Ashley?"

"What did I do to it?" she repeated.

"Did you make coffee?" he asked. "Sandy, look at you. Spiffy. Hey, did you come by for coffee, too?"

"Coffee's made," Ashley said quickly.

"Great. I'll just go pour myself a cup. Have a good day at work."

Sandy had maneuvered her just outside the doorway, hiding the gun with his body. Jake was smiling as he started past them. "Sandy, why don't you have a cup with me?" he asked.

"Can't, I'm in a hurry."

"Oh?"

"As a matter of fact, Ashley was going to drop me at the bank on her way to work."

"Is that a fact?" Jake started into the house. Ashley felt the gun at her ribs edge away as Sandy shifted his hold so as not to be seen.

Jake paused in the doorway. Ashley gritted her teeth, desperate not to give herself away.

"Ashley," he said suddenly, his eyes steady on hers. "I needed to ask you about something. I was talking to John Mast, and he was telling me about another talent you have. In fact, you mentioned it to me one day— suggesting that you could give me a demonstration."

She frowned, then realized what he was saying.

She smiled. "I showed John."

"Show Sandy."

"Jake, I haven't got time," Sandy said impatiently.

"Now!" Jake said.

Ashley slammed her leg back, her heel catching Sandy hard between the legs. As he gasped for air, Jake made his move. Fast. So fast that she screamed, not a warning, but a startled cry of surprise. One minute Sandy was standing at her side and Jake was in front of her. The next second, Jake had thrown his full weight against Sandy, and the two of them were down in the sand and the gravel.

Sandy was trying to aim the gun. A shot went off, flying wild. Jake slammed Sandy's wrist hard against the ground. Another shot went wild.

"Damn it, drop the weapon!" Jake warned.

"Fuck you!" Sandy spat back, struggling against the power of Jake's hold, determined to fire until he could fire no more.

"Drop it! Ashley, get inside before—"

A bullet thudded into the door frame, far too close to her head. She didn't go in; she flew around the two men, kicking the sand and gravel into Sandy's face.

"Drop the weapon," Jake repeated. He slammed Sandy's wrist against the gravel once again. The Glock went skidding away at last.

"Get up," Jake ordered roughly. He rose himself, catching Sandy's jacket lapels and dragging him up.

"I'm up, I'm up…." And he was up—halfway. His face was red; he held out a protesting hand and started coughing violently. He gasped in a breath and started coughing again, his entire body shuddering.

"Shit," Jake swore. "Ashley, call 9-1-1. This bastard is not going to die on my watch."

Ashley reached into her bag, searching for her phone.

Just as her fingers closed around it, Sandy's coughing abruptly stopped. At the same time, he made a lunge to escape Jake's hold, diving into the dirt for the Glock.

Jake swore. Sandy reached out for the gun. Grabbed it. He turned. By then, Jake was pointing the little snub-nosed .38 he'd stuck into the back of his waistband.

"Sandy, don't—" Jake began angrily, his finger on the trigger.

A gun exploded.

Sandy dropped back into the dirt.

Jake hadn't fired.

Ashley and Jake both jerked around, staring at the

door. Nick was there, his service revolver in his hand, still smoking.

"Sorry, Jake. I had to do it. He might have gotten a shot off first—because he knows you're an ethical cop. I'm not a cop. That bastard would have killed my niece. And he's been using me, my bar, for years. Besides, I think he's still alive. Sharon just dialed 9-1-1," he said. "Hey, the coffee is done."

Nick took the Glock from Sandy's nerveless fingers and went into the house. Ashley stared at Jake incredulously. "How did you know? How did you figure it out at just the right moment?"

"That phone call was Franklin. I had him checking into Sandy, and he found the proof I needed. He likes single malt whiskey, by the way. Remind me to send him the best bottle I can find."

He ducked down, checking the pulse in Sandy Reilly's neck. "Nick's right, he's still breathing."

They heard the sound of sirens.

"You should go have some coffee with Nick. In a few minutes, we're going to be talking for hours again. And the paperwork... Man, there's going to be a lot of it."

She shook her head, offering him a rueful smile. "I'll wait for you, Jake. Because...do you know what this means? Last piece of the puzzle. It's over—really over."

Epilogue

The ceremony was just as wonderful as she'd hoped, Ashley thought.

Her own name had never sounded more wonderful to her ears.

And when she walked down the aisle...the feeling was just incredible.

Everyone who counted was here to share her happiness. Nick, Sharon and her adorable new cousin, Justin Montague. Karen, still with Len. Jan, with John Mast. The two had met, disliked one another so intensely that they'd had to see one another again to finish an argument and had been together since. Stuart was there, along with his parents. Jake's dad, whom she had gotten to know well and liked immensely. There were also a slew of police officers in attendance, including Gwyn, Arne and the rest of her original class.

And, of course, Jake was there.

He was the first to congratulate her on the fact that after a year of working as a forensic artist, she had been able to take the time to go back and finish up at the academy. Her job wasn't going to change, though; both civilians and sworn officers worked in forensics.

The picture-taking seemed to last forever. There were shots with her friends, with her family, and with Jake. And one of her alone. The picture Nick especially wanted, to go beside that of Ashley's dad.

Then there was a huge celebration at Nick's. For all twenty-eight new officers and their families. Nick had insisted.

And finally…

Finally there was the moment when she and Jake returned to his boat. She was amazed at the way he'd set it up. There were balloons and flowers. And a big bottle of champagne.

"Oh, Jake! It's wonderful," she told him, turning into his arms.

"You missed the box by the champagne," he pointed out.

And she had. A tiny box. She picked it up curiously. He took it from her fingers, opened it, pulled out the ring and said, "Not quite as exciting as a badge…but I hope you'll accept it. Nick suggested platinum instead of gold, said it would go better with the badge. That is, of course, if you're willing to accept it."

She stared at the diamond, then into his eyes.

"It goes beautifully with the badge," she assured him, and threw herself into his arms. Then she drew away for a moment. "Actually, it's been something I was afraid I was going to have to ask you."

"Why? I knew you wanted to get through the academy first."

"Well…you know my new cousin, Justin?"

"Yes."

He stared at her blankly for a moment. Then he smiled slowly. "Wow!"

He repeated the word, then pulled her into his arms.

"So eloquent," she murmured.

"Wow? That isn't enough?"

"A few more words would be great."

"How about—I love you? And I'm grateful that you've agreed to spend your life with me. I'm incredibly proud of you. And I'm elated that we're going to be parents. Anything you want to add to that, Officer Montague?"

She leaned back in his arms.

"Wow."

* * * * *

HOTSHOT P.I.

B.J. Daniels

To the man I share my life,
my love and my dreams with.

Prologue

Clancy didn't know what had awakened her. She blinked, confused by the moonlight streaming across the third-story balcony, even more confused to find herself standing at the narrow log railing, staring down at Flathead Lake.

Waves lapped at the dock in the small bay below the island lodge. Clancy's heart rate accelerated along with her growing apprehension as she realized what was so terribly wrong.

The view. She shouldn't have been able to see the bay from this angle on her bedroom balcony. Behind her, the door to her family's lake lodge stood open. Past it, furniture huddled under sheets like ghosts. A corner of one sheet flapped softly in the night breeze. Clancy stared at the room, frantically trying to orient herself in a place haunted with childhood memories. The garret on the third floor—a room that hadn't been used in years for anything more than storage.

The early June breeze stirred the sheets and ran like a chill across her skin. She looked down, surprised to find she wore nothing but her nightgown. Her feet were bare—except for the sand. It was happening all over again! Fear raced ahead of her thoughts. Where had she been? What had she done *this* time? With growing panic, Clancy became aware of something heavy clutched in the fingers of her left hand.

A bronze sculpture of a cowboy, one of the first she'd ever made. It had been on the mantel downstairs. She shuddered as she realized how she and it must have gotten up here.

She hadn't sleepwalked in years. But the terror of waking up not knowing where she was or where she'd been wasn't something she'd forgotten from her childhood. She remembered with horror the last time she'd walked in her sleep. The night of the fire.

Clancy turned, wanting only to get back to her bedroom on the other side of the lodge, and realized she wasn't alone. Her heart slammed against her ribs. She fought back a scream as the moonlight spilled across the garret. Someone was on the couch. Sprawled, legs out at an odd angle. She stepped into the room, flipping the light switch. And stopped.

The bronze slipped from her fingers, hitting the hardwood floor with a thud, as she recognized the boots. Bright red cowboy boots. With wet sand on them. Just like her feet. Her heart thumped like a drum, filling the silence of the room.

Dex Westfall lay on the couch. His dark hair, normally coiffed to perfection, was now matted to the side of his head. Blood, once the color of his boots, stained the sheet covering the couch. His eyes stared, vacant, empty.

Clancy stumbled back, suddenly aware of the stickiness on her fingers. She stared at her left hand, her terror accelerating. How had she gotten blood on her? Her gaze leaped to the cowboy sculpture lying on the floor. Her heart rate rocketed, her pulse now a deafening roar in her ears. She didn't need anyone to tell her that the dark stain on the bronze was Dex's blood or that her former boyfriend was dead.

It was happening again. Only this time, her worst nightmare had come true. She'd killed someone in her sleep.

Chapter 1

Ignoring the overdressed stranger on the dock, Jake Hawkins loaded the cooler full of groceries into his twenty-five-foot fishing boat, then reached for his tackle box and new rod and reel resting at the woman's high-heeled feet. He noted with no small amount of satisfaction that she'd finally gotten the message. Beneath the huge hat, she pursed her thin, lipstick-red lips and stripped off the large designer sunglasses to give him the full effect of her icy baby blues. The look she gave him shot off more sparks than all the diamonds weighing down her body.

He smiled to himself. From the moment he'd found her waiting for him on the dock beside his boat, there hadn't been anything about Mrs. Randolph L. Conners that he liked—from her wealthy smugness to her condescending certainty that he was about to go to work for her. And he especially didn't appreciate being bothered on his day off. It was Monday and he was going fishing for a few days. And nothing was going to keep that from happening.

"Like I said, I don't baby-sit heiresses," he repeated as he turned away from the Galveston skyline to take a whiff of the gulf breeze. "Especially heiresses who have just murdered their boyfriends." The gulf shimmered in the morning sun, beckoning him. He couldn't wait to hear his twin 150-horsepower engines rumbling as he crossed the water, the wind in his face.

"I don't think you understand, Mr. Hawkins," Mrs. Conners said, enunciating each word carefully. "I'm not hiring you to baby-sit. I'm hiring you to see that my niece is exonerated."

Jake pushed back his Houston Astros cap and laughed. She wasn't hiring him at all. He didn't have the time or the inclination. Not even the money could entice him right now. Not when he had a well-deserved fishing trip planned. "You need a good lawyer, not a private investigator. But I can give you a few names—"

"I already have the best lawyers money can buy," she said, sounding pained that she had to explain everything to him. "I need someone with your...talents."

He prided himself on what he called his hunches, and right now one was riding up his spine like a centipede wearing spiked heels. While his hunches were seldom wrong, he hoped this one was; he had a bad feeling that somehow he was going to end up working for this woman.

"My talents?" he repeated, also hoping he was wrong about where she was headed. He shook his head as if he didn't get it.

Exasperation gave her a pinched look that reminded him of one of those mean little hairless dogs. "I want you to prove my niece's innocence, Mr. Hawkins. Whatever you have to do. Whatever it costs. My niece will not be convicted of murder."

Jake jumped from the boat to the dock with a thud. "If you think you can hire me to tamper with evidence..." He found himself looming over her, his blood pressure up and running.

She tilted her head back ever so slightly until he could see her eyes shaded beneath the hat. If she felt even a little bit intimidated, it didn't show; her gaze glittered with brittle-hard certainty. "You misunderstood my intentions."

"Like hell I misunderstood," Jake said, locking his gaze on the woman. "If your niece is guilty, then she deserves to do time. And from what you've told me—"

"You are wrong, Mr. Hawkins," she said, her voice as hard and gritty as gravel. "My niece is a Talbott. A Talbott does not go to prison."

Talbott? He felt a jolt of recognition shoot through him. He squinted at her, telling himself Talbott was a fairly common name. Not that it mattered, he reminded himself; he wasn't going to take this case. But still he couldn't shake off the rotten feeling tap-dancing at the back of his head.

"Do you understand what I'm saying, Mr. Hawkins?"

He understood perfectly. The niece was an embarrassment and too good for prison. He couldn't believe the gall of this woman. And now she wanted someone to go in and clean up the mess. At any price. Well, she'd picked the wrong man. "Like I said, I can't help you. It's my day off and I'm going fishing."

Jake flung his duffel bag into the boat, hoping Mrs. Randolph L. Conners would take the hint. But he wasn't averse to throwing her into the gulf if he had to.

She squared her shoulders, straightening her expensive suit. "I'm sure after you've given it some thought you'll change your mind, Mr. Hawkins."

He pointed to the shore. "Don't count on it."

She smiled. "We'll see."

Fighting to control his temper, Jake watched her walk away. He hated having someone raise his blood pressure, especially this early in the morning and on his day off.

As he went to untie the boat, he noticed the envelope on the bow, underneath the cellular phone the woman had surreptitiously left to hold it down in the light sea breeze. The envelope was creamy white; the address engraved. He slipped it from under the phone, not surprised to find his name hand-printed on the clean white surface or the paper smelling of her expensive perfume.

He figured the envelope would be full of old family money, but it felt a little too light. Maybe she'd written him a check. Jake ripped open the envelope, planning to do the same with the check.

But it didn't contain a voucher of any kind. Nor were there any crisp large bills inside. Instead, there was a single sheet of paper, folded neatly. On the sheet were printed the words: Deer Lodge. September 30. 9:00 a.m.

At the bottom was her neatly signed signature: Kiki Talbott Conners.

Kiki Talbott. He should have known. With a curse, Jake crumpled the paper and threw it into the water, feeling his plans crumple with it. The phone began to ring. He looked out across the gulf, suddenly reminded of a photograph that used to sit on the mantel of his family's Flathead Lake lodge in Montana. Memories flooded him. Bittersweet memories that he'd spent ten years trying to forget. He picked up the phone.

"I've left you a ticket and triple your normal first week's salary at the airport," Kiki informed him in her no-nonsense tone. "Your flight leaves in less than two hours. You'll have to hurry."

"And where exactly is it you think I'm going?" Jake asked, anger making his words as hard as stones.

"Montana. You can buy anything you need when you get there," she continued. "Of course, I will reimburse you for all expenses."

"Montana?" Jake swore and pushed back his baseball cap, dread making his body ache as if he had a bad case of flu. "I think you'd better tell me just which niece of yours we're talking about." He held his breath, waiting for the other shoe to drop.

Sea gulls squawked overhead; the gulf breeze tickled the sandy blond hair curling at his neck.

"Clancy Jones. Her mother was a Talbott. Her father was—"

Jake let out an oath. "I know who her parents were, for hell's sake. And I know who *she* is! You don't seriously believe that I'm going to help *her*?"

Kiki's tone was coldly calm. "Mr. Hawkins, you're very good at what you do. One of the best. That's why I've hired you. That's why you're going to do whatever you have to do to get my niece exonerated—in spite of your...former connections with her."

Jake walked over to his duffel bag and, cradling the phone against his shoulder, dug through his clothing. "Lady, the only reason you're *hiring* me is because you have something to hold over my head, and you damn well know it."

Jake thought he heard a hint of emotion in her voice when she finally spoke. "Please understand, I will do whatever I have to do to protect my niece. Including helping you on September 30. Or hurting you. And believe me, I'm in a very good position to do either."

Jake carefully lifted the .38 nestled in its worn shoulder holster from the duffel bag. He wondered if Kiki had any idea what kind of man she'd just hired. Or how big a mistake she'd just made.

"How do I know you'll hold up your end of the bargain?" he asked, glad she wasn't still on the dock, afraid of what he might have done.

She let out a long, impatient sigh. "I'm a Talbott, Mr. Hawkins. Please don't confuse us with the Joneses. Our word is our bond."

"Right."

"One more thing, Mr. Hawkins," she said, dropping her voice. "Because of your less-than-amiable association with my niece, I might offer you a tip as to how to best handle her—"

"Look, Kiki," Jake said as he snugged the .38 to his ribs. "I have a little tip for you. You can force me to take this job, although it's not the smartest thing you ever did. And you can force me to take your money and waste my time trying to find evidence that your niece isn't guilty of murder. But you can't tell me how to do my job."

"Now, Mr. Hawkins—"

"The truth is, Kiki, you can only buy so much with your kind of blackmail. And you've already bought more than you can handle."

Chapter 2

Awakened from a troubled sleep, Jake rolled over, forgetting where he was, and banged his head on the balcony railing. That rude awakening and the once-familiar view reminded him exactly where he was. As soon as he'd landed, he'd rented a boat to get to Hawk Island and his family's lodge. And he was there because of Clancy Jones.

Having no intentions of staying long, he'd just rolled his sleeping bag out on the balcony, wishing he was on the deck of his boat. The truth was he couldn't stand the thought of sleeping inside the lodge. It felt too musty and confining, brought back too many memories.

He'd gone to sleep cursing Clancy, while glaring through the railing at the only other dwelling on this side of the rugged island—an almost identical log lodge nestled in the pines across the small bay.

A single light had shone in one of the rooms on the second floor of Clancy's lodge until the wee hours. He'd seen an occasional shadow and wondered if she was alone. Angry that he couldn't sleep, either, he'd speculated on what she might be doing still up. Working in her studio? Or trying to sleep and not think, like him?

At one point, he'd considered going over to see her, getting it over with. But it was late, and he told himself waiting until morning was the best plan. He'd finally dozed off, only to be dragged from sleep by a loud noise, which did little to improve his disposition.

As he stared across the moonlit bay, trying to figure out what had awakened him, a movement jarred his attention into focus. Something was thrashing around in the water off the end of Clancy's dock. He saw what appeared to be a head surface, heard the choked cry before it disappeared again. Clancy?

Shedding his bedroll, Jake leaped from the end of the balcony, dropped onto the beach and took off at a run. He saw the head materialize again, dark against the silvery surface of the water, heard the cry for help and pushed his legs harder. All the time his mind raced ahead of him; the swimmer couldn't be Clancy. She swam like a trout and was much too smart to be swimming—drowning—at this hour of the night.

He sprinted down the weathered dock to the end as the person emerged once again—yards beyond his reach. Having no time to consider the consequences, he dove in. The sudden shock of the cold water brought him wide awake; he surfaced, gasping for breath. Just ahead of him he could see the swimmer start to disappear under the dark water again. He swam hard and reached out to grab the only thing he could. Hair. It was long enough he could bury his hand in it.

But to his surprise, the swimmer pulled him under with a force that almost made him lose his grip. Immediately he realized his mistake. The silly fool was struggling, fighting him, and he remembered why he'd never considered the lifeguarding profession. Too dangerous. At least in the private eye business you knew who you were dealing with: murderers, crooks, cheaters and liars. Not some novice in over her head in deep water, panicked to senseless desperation and determined to take you down with her.

Jake got a tighter hold on the hair and a grip on one flaying arm, and with all his strength kicked toward the moonlit surface. At first nothing happened, then they both rose in a rush, the swimmer choking and coughing as they surfaced. Jake used a no-nonsense half nelson to drag the person to the dock and, none too gently, hoisted the obviously feminine body onto the worn boards. He felt a moment of relief. This woman, whoever she was, wasn't Clancy. Not with *that* body. Her wet clothing molded to her curves—dangerously enticing, fully developed curves.

She leaned over the edge of the dock, fighting for breath, her dripping shoulder-length hair in her face. Slowly, she raised her gaze, sending a shock wave through him.

Clancy? Even under the wet mop of blond hair, even in the shimmering silver of the moonlight, there was no doubt about that face. Her hair was longer. Not quite as blond. But that face. That cute little nose. That slightly puckered, almost pouty mouth. That wide-eyed, curious deep brown gaze. If anything, she was more beautiful than he remembered. And certainly more…filled out. And in all the right places. That adorable seventeen-year-old tomboy he'd known was now one hell of a good-looking woman.

But he wasn't sure what shocked him the most. Seeing the change in her after all these years. Or realizing she was the swimmer he'd had to rescue. What had happened to the Clancy he used to know, the one who was much too smart to swim alone in the middle of the night?

"What the hell were you doing swimming at this hour?" he demanded, anger following his relief that Clancy was all right. He needed her alive, he told himself. His relief had nothing to do with any old feelings from their past, he assured himself, ignoring the flashes of memories of the two of them as kids. They'd been so close—best pals. More than that. Kindred spirits. The truth was, he'd thought he was in love with her.

"Swimming?" she said, choking. "You think I was swimming?" She coughed, then leaned back, her gaze settling on him with suspicion. "Someone tried to drown me."

"Wait a minute," he said, holding up his hands. "I was the one who fished you out of the drink." He felt something cold sprint up his spine as he looked into her eyes.

"Someone grabbed me and—" Clancy glanced around in obvious confusion, her eyes wild with fear. "You dragged me out?"

"Yeah." Jake studied her for a moment, wondering how long it would take her to acknowledge that she knew him. "About this *someone* who tried to drown you…you might notice there seems to be just the two of us on this whole side of the island." He glanced toward the still water, then at the empty shoreline, then at her again.

"Thank you for helping me," she whispered, still looking disoriented. And more than a little scared.

He'd known seeing her again was going to trigger a lot of old emotions, emotions he couldn't afford. He quickly reminded himself that Clancy hadn't only perjured herself on the witness stand and helped send his father to prison ten years ago, now she was facing a murder rap of her own. Forget that cute kid he used to build sand castles with on the beach and catch trout with off the end of this dock. Someone had bludgeoned Dex Westfall to death, and from what Kiki had told him, the police thought that someone was Dex's girlfriend, Clancy Jones.

"So what were you doing out here on the dock at this time of the night?" he asked, unable to keep the reproach out of his voice. He was wet and tired and didn't appreciate being awakened in the middle of the night. Especially by this woman.

"I heard someone…calling me." She sounded dubious.

Welcome to the club. "Someone calling you?" He glanced at the still water beyond the dock. The pines etched a dark, ragged line against the night sky. Then he looked over at her again. "Someone called you, so you walked down to see what they wanted in the middle of the night?" Perfectly logical.

He saw her look toward her lodge, her eyes widening. He followed her gaze, surprised to see that not a single lamp glowed in any of the windows. She hadn't turned on a light before coming down to the dock?

"I suppose you didn't recognize the voice calling you or see the person who pulled you into the water?" he asked, not even trying to hide his disbelief. He could read most people as easily as he could the cover of a tabloid from across the floor of a good-sized minimart. Clancy Jones was lying through her teeth, but for the life of him, he couldn't imagine why. He reminded himself that lying seemed to come easy for her.

"Whether you believe it or not, someone tried to drown me," she said, her voice breaking. She didn't sound any more convinced than he was, but she *was* scared. He could see it in her movements as she got to her feet, nervously tugging her wet clothing away from her body.

For the first time, he realized she wasn't dressed for a night swim. She wore a T-shirt and a pair of leggings. Both were wet and molded to her body. An amazing body, Jake grudgingly admitted. Her feet were bare, and she still wore her watch and a single gold bracelet. Both looked expensive. He ignored the voice of reason that questioned why she would have gone swimming wearing an expensive watch, why Jake had had to pull so hard to bring her to the surface. The questions wedged themselves in the back of his brain, a reluctant sliver of doubt.

"Right," Jake said. "And where is that someone now?"

When he raised his gaze to her face, he saw that she was staring at him again. Squinting, actually, as if the moonlight was too bright.

"Who are you, anyway, and what are you doing here?" she demanded.

He tried not to let it hurt his feelings. Why should

she recognize him or even remember him? She'd only spent the first seventeen years of her life living right next door to him, spending most every waking moment with him from the time she could walk. And it wasn't as if he wanted to believe he'd made an impression on her just because she had on him. True, there'd been that kiss, the first for both of them, on this very dock, and she'd said she loved him, but hey—

"Jake Hawkins," he said, surprised at the hurt and anger he heard in his tone. And the bitterness. "Not that there's any reason you should remember *me*. But perhaps you haven't forgotten my father. Surely you recall that your testimony sent him to prison ten years ago."

"Jake." It came out a whisper. She seemed to wobble a little as she squinted harder at him. "It's been so long...you sound so different...and—"

He rolled his eyes. "Forget it." For a moment, he just glared at her, mad, irritable and just plain out of sorts. He shifted his gaze to the lake. Lights flickered on the mainland. The air smelled of fish and pines. He should have been at sea, drifting with the night clouds, catching stripers and sailfish. He should have been at peace, breathing salt air, not standing on a dock in the wee hours of the morning with a woman who'd forced him to remember things he'd only wanted to forget. A woman, who unlike him, seemed to have put at least some of that past behind her.

"Why now?" she asked quietly. "After all this time?"

Fueled on a mixture of hurt and anger, he answered, "Your aunt Kiki sent me to save your butt."

"What?" The surprise on Clancy's face was worth the flight to Montana. It was almost worth missing his fishing trip. "You met my Aunt Kiki?"

"The Wicked Witch of the East herself." He'd never completely believed the stories Clancy had told after one of her required trips back East each spring to visit her rich aunt. He did now. "She's everything you said she was. And then some."

"I don't understand," Clancy said, frowning. "Why would Aunt Kiki send *you*?"

"Probably because I'm a private investigator and your aunt thinks her money and I can dig up evidence that will keep you out of prison." Even as he said it, he realized it didn't make that much sense to him, either. He had a hunch, one he was holding off like a bad cold. He told himself not to look a gift horse in the mouth. Kiki had provided him with the perfect opportunity. Why question it?

Clancy met his gaze; tears glistened in her eyes. "I see."

He realized she did see at least part of it: one of the only reasons he was here was because Aunt Kiki had procured his services. He thought it would give him more satisfaction than it did to hurt her. What had she expected? That he'd come back and forget what she'd done, forgive her? Not likely.

"It's unfortunate that you've wasted your time," she said, her words so faint, he almost missed them.

Wasted his time? What was she saying, that she killed Dex Westfall, that she was guilty?

She straightened, her glance shifting from her bare feet to his face. "The last thing I need right now is... *you* helping me."

He stared at her. "It's not like you have a lot of choice in the matter. I doubt there's a line of private investigators knocking down your door to take *this* case."

She let out a small laugh; her hand fluttered for a moment in the air between them. "Jake, we both know you're not here to save me. Admit it, you'd love nothing better than to see me behind bars."

He started to admit it, but she didn't give him the chance.

"What was my aunt thinking?" With a dismissive shake of her head, she turned and headed down the dock toward shore. "Consider yourself fired."

"Wait a minute!" he called after her. "You can't get rid of me just like that."

She didn't even turn around.

Jake stood on the dock, shaking his head in disbelief as he watched her stride toward her lodge. Fired? He'd never been fired in his life. Especially by some woman who didn't have the good sense not to go swimming in the middle of the night. A woman who had the audacity to make up a story about an attacker calling her down to the dock to drown her— Jake glared at Clancy's ramrod back as she retreated up the beach. Once a liar, always a liar, he thought.

"Fine," he called after her. "Fire me. Say hello to my father when you get to prison."

Her lodge door slammed, leaving him standing alone in the moonlight. He cursed and started toward his own lodge. Matching her angry strides, he stomped down the beach but quickly slowed to a limp. The bottoms of his feet hurt like the devil from racing across sand, rocks and rough wood to save a woman who didn't even recognize him. He cursed himself for not only his unappreciated heroics, but also for that moment of weakness he'd had when he first saw Clancy again. For just that instant, he'd actually cared. How could he have forgotten, if for even a moment, the part she'd played in helping send his father to prison? He assured himself he wouldn't forget again.

Clancy fell back against the door she'd just slammed and tried to stop shaking. She'd promised herself she wasn't going to fall apart; she'd already cried too many tears and it had accomplished nothing. But just when she thought things couldn't get any worse—Jake appeared.

She hugged herself to hold down the shudders that welled up inside her. Confusion clouded her thoughts. Someone *had* called her down to the dock and tried to drown her. Or had they? She closed her eyes, searching through the darkness of her memory, fighting desperately to remember. Could it have been just a bad dream? But it had seemed so *real*. The hand coming out of the water, grabbing her ankle, pulling her into the water. Once she hit the water, she'd been wide awake. But had there really been someone else in the water trying to drag her under? Or had it been Jake fighting to bring her to the surface? It had happened so fast. And yet she remembered the voice. It had been familiar. Jake's voice?

Her eyes flew open at the thought. No, it hadn't been Jake's. His voice had a hint of a southern drawl.

Jake. A rush of emotions assailed her. Memories, as sweet as the warm scent of summer. Regrets that made her heart ache. She'd never expected to ever see him again. Never expected to have these old feelings come back with such force. Then to find him on her dock tonight. And now of all times.

She moved to the table to retrieve her glasses, anxious to be able to see clearly again, wishing she'd had them on earlier. Or at least had her contacts in. All she'd gotten was a blurred impression of Jake. Medium height and muscular. She smiled, remembering the boy she'd grown up with, the boy she'd fallen so desperately in love with.

She thought about the betrayed, angry look he'd given her that day at the courthouse ten years ago. Tonight, she'd heard that same anger and bitterness in his voice. He still blamed her for his father going to prison. And now he'd come to Montana to help her? She couldn't possibly let herself believe that.

But Jake had saved her life tonight, hadn't he? Clancy shivered, remembering the dark water and the hands pulling her under. Or had they been Jake's hands trying to pull her toward the surface? If there had been an attacker, where had he gone so quickly?

She shivered, hugging herself tighter. Right now she needed a hot bath and dry clothing. She didn't want to think about the fact that she'd walked in her sleep again; she particularly didn't want to think what could have happened if Jake hadn't been there.

She hurried upstairs, anxious to get out of her wet, cold clothing. But as she disrobed and stepped into the hot shower, exhaustion pulled at her, making her thoughts as clouded as the steam that rose around her.

She yearned to be warm and dry. To wrap herself in one of her mother's old quilts. To curl up in front of the fireplace. To forget everything. And sleep. She closed her eyes and leaned back against the shower wall.

Jake quickly showered and changed into warm, dry clothing, hoping it would soothe his anger and frustration. It had done neither by the time he dialed the private number Kiki had left for him at the Kalispell, Montana, airport along with another cellular phone. She'd evidently anticipated that he'd chuck the first one into the gulf, which he had. It bothered him that Kiki thought she knew him so well.

Kiki Talbott Conners answered on the fifth ring. With more than a little satisfaction, he realized he'd awakened her from a sound sleep.

"What time is it?" she groaned.

Way past *his* bedtime, he knew that. His eyes felt as if they had sand in them. "A quarter after three."

"In the morning?"

"That could explain why it's still dark out." He could just imagine her in a huge satin bed at the Bigfork condo she'd rented, surrounded by plump pillows and pampered poodles. "Your niece and I just got reacquainted."

"At *three* in the morning?" Kiki demanded, grogginess turning quickly to surliness.

He walked to the window. "It's a long story." It looked as though all the lights in Clancy's lodge were on. What was she doing still up, he wondered. And why all the lights? What was she afraid of? Surely she wasn't buying into her own lies about a mysterious killer who came out of the water like a shark from *Jaws.* "Let me cut to the chase. Your niece doesn't want me on this case."

"That surprises you?" Kiki asked, adding an audible "humph."

"Perhaps she thinks you harbor a grudge against her."

Kiki's words snapped his attention back like a short rubber band. "Of course I have a grudge against her. And for a damned good reason." He raked his fingers through his hair, remembering what Clancy had said on the dock, *What could my aunt have been thinking?* Exactly what Jake wanted to know. "Which brings me to the reason I called. Knowing that, why in the hell did you want me up here?"

A faint tinkling sound broke the silence. She was pouring herself a drink. He felt as if he was going to need one, too. Kiki had enough money to buy the best private investigator in the galaxy. And if she wanted evidence tampered with, she could have bought that, too. For a price. But not from Jake Hawkins. So why hire a man who had every reason *not* to help her niece?

"The reason I hired you is the same reason you're not going to quit," she said simply.

He wanted to tell her just how wrong she was but that damned hunch of his was doing the lambada across the back of his neck to a little ditty called "Here Comes Heartache."

He heard her take a sip of her drink, taking her time. "Come on, Jake," she said impatiently. "You know the reason."

"Blackmail." He had a bad feeling that Kiki knew all the blackmail in the world couldn't make him do something he didn't want to do. He had his own personal reason for being here, and his hunch machine told him Kiki knew that, had known it all along. So what the hell had she hired him for?

Kiki sighed deeply. "Jake, we both know why you're in Montana, and it has nothing to do with blackmail."

He couldn't believe he was playing this game with her. "Why don't you spell it out for me, Kiki." He held his breath, afraid she was about to validate the strongest hunch he'd ever had.

"You're in Montana because you think Clancy's the key to proving your father's innocence."

Bingo. Jake squeezed the phone and closed his eyes. Clancy *was* the key. Had always been the key. She'd lied on the witness stand to protect her own father and let Jake's go to prison. And now Jake had Clancy where he wanted her. He'd taken this case for one reason only: to get the truth. And as certain as the coming sunrise, he'd do whatever he had to do to get it out of her.

He stared across the bay at Clancy's. "My motives for being here don't worry you?" he asked Kiki incredulously.

"No," she answered in that tone he'd come to despise. "I've seen how deep your loyalty runs. Unlike your mother. She could never forgive your father for disgracing her. She moved the two of you to Texas. She never visited him in prison. She forgot Warren Hawkins as if he'd never existed." Kiki sounded so damned sure of herself. "You, on the other hand, can't let go of the past. You believe in your father's innocence and would do *anything* to prove it. The same way you can't let Clancy go to prison for a murder she didn't commit."

"I wouldn't be so sure of that," he said, moving away from the window. Kiki thought he was a crusader for injustice? He wanted to laugh. Didn't she realize it was Clancy who'd done him the injustice? The woman was a liar; she'd proven that tonight. How could Kiki be so convinced Clancy hadn't killed this Dex Westfall guy? Blind loyalty? He'd once felt that for Clancy, and look what she'd done to him and his family. No, he suspected with Kiki it was simply a matter of saving the Talbott name.

"I'm quite sure of you," Kiki said, her tone downright haughty.

He wanted to tell her what a fool she was. After all these years, she'd just offered him the perfect opportunity to get what he wanted. The truth. And revenge at the same time. "What makes you think you know me so well?"

Kiki let out a long sigh. "I heard about how wonderful you were for years, Jake Hawkins. Did you forget that for a long time, my niece foolishly thought she was in love with you?"

Kiki hung up before he could respond. Not that he had a response for that one, anyway.

Clancy's eyes popped open at the sound of the phone ringing and realized she'd dozed off standing in the shower! Panic came in hot pursuit of the realization. What if she'd fallen into one of her deep sleeps and sleepwalked again—this time totally naked?

Whatever it took, she had to stay awake. She cranked the shower handle and let out a shriek as the cold water made her skin ache. But just as she was being revived, the phone began to ring. She quickly turned off the water and reached for a towel.

Dripping, she hurried to the phone and picked up the receiver. "Hello." She could hear breathing at the other end of the line. "Hello?" There was no answer. Just what sounded like soft, labored breathing. "What do you want?" she demanded. No answer. Clancy slammed down the phone. A prank call. Someone who'd read about her in the paper. She'd get her number changed. Maybe even get an unlisted number.

She sat on the edge of the bed, suddenly too tired

to move. The soft warmth beneath her beckoned her to crawl in, to cover her head and escape for a few hours in sleep. She stood and headed back to the shower, not about to make the same mistake she'd made earlier. After spending two nights in jail, she'd been running scared and not thinking clearly. She'd been so desperate she'd called her aunt Kiki who'd pulled strings and got her out right after the late afternoon bail hearing Monday. Clancy's plan had been to go to Bozeman and Dex's apartment as soon as she got out on bail. She'd come straight to the lodge to pick up a change of clothing. Unfortunately, after she'd hurriedly packed and started to leave, she'd spotted the flicker of a flashlight at the Hawkins's lodge and spotted the blue outboard tied at the dock. She'd assumed the county attorney had put a deputy on her.

She knew she was only out on bail because of Aunt Kiki and her money. She figured maybe the county attorney had gone along with the bail to please Kiki but had put a deputy on her to cover his political posterior.

So Clancy had foolishly sat by the window to wait him out—not knowing it was just Jake Hawkins, not some deputy, watching her. And she'd fallen asleep and sleepwalked.

She stepped back into the shower and let the icy cold water beat her body wide awake. She didn't dare let that happen again. Nor could she afford to wait until morning to leave. Although she didn't relish the idea of crossing the lake in the dead of night, Jake had left her no option. She'd wait until she could be relatively sure he was asleep, then she'd take her boat to the mainland marina where she kept her car. From there she'd drive to Bozeman, go to Dex's apartment and— She wasn't sure what she'd find there, but hopefully something that would prove she was innocent.

Sometimes she could almost forget about the upcoming trial. Almost pretend none of this was really happening. Then she'd get a flash of Dex Westfall sprawled on the couch in the garret. Murdered. And her standing over him with the murder weapon in her hand. One of her own sculptures.

Her heart told her she hadn't killed him. But reason argued: how do you know you didn't? You were asleep. And look at all the evidence against you.

Exhaustion tugged at her, beckoning her to the one place where she didn't have to think. Sweet slumber. But with sweet slumber came somnambulism, and she feared her nocturnal wanderings. Look what had happened tonight. What *had* happened tonight? She wasn't even sure. Her hands shook as she pulled on a pair of jeans and a T-shirt.

She clung to only one hope. That somehow she could prove her innocence. And the only place she knew to start was with Dex. She had to find out everything there was to know about him, including why he'd ended up dead in her garret.

She told herself going to Bozeman, to another county, wasn't really violating her bail. And anyway, she'd be back before anyone even knew she was missing. If she was lucky. But she'd take extra clothing, just in case. In case she found out something that would prove she had killed him and she decided to make a run for it?

Clancy was coming down the stairs, her hair wrapped in the towel turban-style, when she heard the pounding at her back door.

"Clancy, I know you're still up," Jake called. "You might as well open the door."

She pulled the towel off her head, shook out her hair and used the tip of the damp towel to clean her glasses. Maybe he was coming to tell her he was leaving, going back to wherever her aunt had found him. Hadn't she wished for the opportunity to really see him before he left?

If only her other wishes were granted that easily, she thought as she opened the door to find him standing on her step. He'd changed out of his wet jeans; he wore chinos and a white T-shirt that accented his broad shoulders and his tanned, muscular arms. A Houston Astros cap was snugged down on his sandy blond head; his hair curled at the nape of his neck still wet from a shower. His clean, spicy smell engulfed her.

"It's late," she said, but he didn't seem to be paying any attention. He was staring at her as if he'd never seen her before. The same way she was staring at him.

Her earlier impression of Jake hadn't done him justice. He'd been cute at nineteen; now he was strikingly good-looking. Strong features. A full, sensual mouth. Expressive gray eyes. A man with character. He had the kind of face she'd love to sculpt. A mixture of toughness and tenderness.

"You wear glasses," he said simply, sounding pleased.

She didn't tell him she'd worn glasses since she was fifteen—just not around him when she was a girl. "I can't see much without them."

He smiled then. "That's nice." He leaned one broad shoulder against the jamb.

She wasn't sure what she wanted him to say. Goodbye? Or maybe that he was sorry he'd hurt her. Or even that he understood she'd only done what she had to at the trial. "It's late," she repeated.

"Yeah," he said, the smile dissolving as if he'd suddenly remembered why he'd come over. "It's about your case."

She stared at him, telling herself she shouldn't be surprised. "I thought I fired you."

His frown deepened. "Your aunt hired me, and she's the only one who can fire me. And trust me, as much trouble as she's gone to to get me here, there isn't much chance of that happening."

Clancy could only assume her aunt Kiki had lost her mind.

"So now that we have that settled..." He glanced past her into the lodge.

"Yes, I guess that settles everything." She yawned openly, not that the Jake Hawkins she used to know could take a hint.

"Except for one thing," Jake said, his voice deadly soft. "I had a fishing trip planned that your aunt interrupted to get me up here." He held up his hand to silence her before she could tell him what he could do with his fishing trip.

"Let me give it to you straight. I'm here for only one reason—to get the goods on you," he said, his gaze hard as his body looked.

She swallowed, the cold hatred in his voice making her heart ache, her eyes burn with tears. Only stubborn determination kept her from crying. She wasn't about to let him see how much he'd hurt her ten years ago, how much he could still hurt her.

"I'm going to find evidence I can use against you," he said. "And then you're going to tell me the truth about what you really saw the night of the resort fire, the night Lola Strickland was murdered."

Clancy started to tell him she *had* told the truth, but she knew it would be a waste of breath. He hadn't believed her at the trial, why would he believe her now?

She looked into his eyes, wondering what had happened to the boy she'd loved, the boy who had loved her. She saw nothing in all that gray but bitterness. But instead of hating him, her heart broke as she thought of all the years he'd suffered. Because of his father. Because of her. Jake should have trusted her. He should have known she wouldn't lie, she wouldn't hurt him or his father, and she wouldn't have thrown away their love without a fight, the way Jake had.

"In the meantime," Jake said, "you and I are going to be inseparable until you're acquitted—or sent to prison."

She bit back a curse. "You're making prison look better all the time."

His gaze met hers. "I think I know why you lied about my father, but no matter the reason, you're going to admit it to me. And very soon." He touched the brim of his baseball cap. "See you in the morning."

She slammed the door and dropped into a chair at the table, feeling incredibly tired and despondent. Aunt Kiki had brought Jake back knowing how he felt about Clancy, knowing how she'd once felt about him. That old familiar ache seized her heart in a death grip. How Clancy *still* felt about him.

Tears welled up in her eyes and spilled down over her cheeks, bitter on her tongue. She wiped at them. She still loved him. Through all the hurt, she'd never stopped loving him. Could never stop loving him. But like him, she felt betrayed. And angry with him for not trusting her. She knew she'd have to draw on that anger to keep Jake from knowing how she felt about him— and using it against her.

Emotional exhaustion and lack of solid sleep stole at her strength. She leaned her head on her arms and closed her eyes, telling herself she'd rest for a while, just until she could be sure Jake was asleep. Crossing the lake at night seemed less dangerous now. Much less dangerous than facing Jake Hawkins. If there was more incriminating evidence out there against her, Jake would find it.

She wished with all her heart that she could turn back the clock, back before the night of the fire and Lola's murder, back when Jake loved her. She closed her eyes. And saw Jake come sauntering up the sandy beach, sixteen and suntanned, that grin she loved on his handsome face. And she ran out to meet him, as carefree as the breeze that rippled the surface of the lake.

Clancy opened her eyes, shocked to find the sun streaming in through her bedroom window. Even more shocked to find herself curled in the middle of her bed, the quilt rough with sand from her bare feet. She lay perfectly still, her mind frantically trying to recall when she'd come to bed. No memory.

That's when she noticed her left hand clenched into a fist, as if she held something that might try to escape. With dread, she slowly uncurled her fingers. There in her palm lay a single tiny blue bead.

Her heart pounded. There was nothing unusual or unique about the bead. Except Clancy knew where it had come from. With a tremor of terror she remembered

Friday night when Dex had called and demanded she meet him at the Hawk Island Café on the other side of the island.

He'd been holding a necklace of colored beads when she'd walked up to him. The outdoor café was empty that late at night and that early in the season. Dex sat at a table in a flickering pool of light from the Japanese lanterns strung overhead. She had looked at the necklace with growing dread, thinking it was another present, wishing she hadn't agreed to meet him.

He must have seen the expression on her face, because he gave a bitter laugh as she took a seat across from him.

"Don't worry, it's not for you," he'd said, holding up the string of beads for her to see. With a jolt she realized she'd seen it somewhere before. The tiny beads were pale blue. A handmade ceramic heart hung from the center of the necklace. It was painted navy with a smaller pink heart in the middle.

"Where did you get that?" Clancy asked, trying to remember where she'd seen it before.

"It's part of my mother's legacy," Dex said.

His mother? "What are you doing here?" Clancy demanded, wishing she'd never come, wondering how he'd even known where to find her. She'd never told him about the family's lake lodge. When she'd broken it off with him in Bozeman, she'd thought she'd never see him again. She felt a chill as she watched him hold the necklace up to the light and smile.

"What do you want, Dex?" Clancy asked with dread.

His eyes narrowed as he glared at her. "You're part of that legacy, Clancy."

She felt her fear level rise. How could she not have

seen this side of him from the very start? "I thought we'd agreed not to see each other again."

"*We* agreed?" He reached across the table and grabbed her arm, squeezing it until she cried out in pain.

"Leave me alone, Dex. I'm warning you—"

He squeezed harder. "If you think you've seen the last of me you're—" He looked past her, seeing something that made his eyes widen. He released her arm almost involuntarily. She turned to look but saw nothing in the darkness beyond the café.

He lowered his voice. "I'm not leaving this island, Clancy. Not until I get what I deserve." He'd hurried off, leaving her sitting, head reeling, wondering what he'd seen in the darkness that seemed to frighten him. And what Dex thought he deserved.

Just hours later, he'd turned up dead in her garret.

Now she stared at the tiny bead in her palm, knowing this had to be one of the beads from the necklace. Apprehension rippled through her as she stared at her sandy feet. Something had triggered her night wanderings again. And she couldn't seem to stop them. Now she'd returned from sleepwalking with a single bead from a broken strand. When had it been broken? And where had she found this one blue bead? Even more frightening, how had she known where to look?

She slid her legs over the side of the bed and staggered into the bathroom. As she dropped the bead into the toilet and flushed, she watched it disappear with growing terror. She couldn't keep kidding herself. Like the broken string of tiny blue beads, her life was coming unraveled.

Chapter 3

Clancy glanced warily across the bay at Jake Hawkins's lodge. The shades were drawn; she could catch no sign of movement behind them. The blue outboard was still moored at his dock, a boat she assumed he'd rented to get to the island. She looked at her watch, surprised to find it was earlier than she'd thought. Then she turned her gaze again to Jake's lodge across the small bay. The coast looked clear. She picked up the overnight bag and her purse and opened the back door, expecting Jake to suddenly appear and block her escape.

As she stepped out onto the small back porch, she glanced apprehensively behind the lodge. While she found no one hiding in the lilac bushes that brushed the back side of the building, she did see something that stopped her cold. Slowly she put down her purse and overnight bag and moved toward the first lilac bush.

Some of the branches along the lodge side of the bush
had been broken. They hadn't been yesterday afternoon
when she'd returned from jail. She was sure of it. She'd
stopped on the porch to dig out her key and picked up
the sweet scent of the lilacs, now in full bloom. And
she wondered where she'd be this time next year when
they bloomed. In prison?

Clancy brushed back the branches, not surprised
to find the grass beneath the kitchen window crushed
where someone had stood, looking in. Through the glass
Clancy could see her coffee cup at the table, the chair
pushed back from where she'd sat last night. Someone
had stood on this very spot, watching her!

She crashed her way out of the lilacs as if the person
was at her heels. Scooping up her purse and overnight
bag, she rushed down the beach toward her dock. Who
had been at the window? The same person who'd called
her down to the dock and tried to drown her? It hadn't
been a dream, her mind screamed. No more than the
crushed grass beneath the window.

With relief she passed the old boathouse, and Jake
didn't jump out of the shadows to stop her. All that
stretched ahead now was the dock and her boat waiting beside it. The sun danced on the slick surface of the
lake, golden. The tall pines shimmered, a silky green at
the edge of the water. She took a calming breath. The
air smelled of so many familiar, rich scents. Safe scents
she'd grown up with. But she was no longer safe. From
Jake. From the phantom in the lake. From the real live
person who'd stood looking in her window. As long as
she kept sleepwalking, she wasn't even safe from herself.

She reached the dock without incident and started
down it, walking as quickly and quietly as possible. A

sudden flash of memory tormented her. A hand coming out of the water. Grabbing her ankle. Pulling her. She walked faster, fear dogging her steps.

Just a few feet ahead she could see her boat, a yellow-and-white inboard-outboard; a coat of dew on the top and windshield glistened in the morning sunlight. Once she reached it and started the engine, Jake wouldn't be able to stop her. The thought buoyed her spirits.

She shot a parting glance toward his lodge. Jake must still be asleep. He'd been so adamant about shadowing her every step last night, this seemed almost too easy. She smiled to herself, imagining his surprise when he woke and found her gone, as she untied the bow and started to swing her overnight bag into the hull.

"Good morning!"

Clancy jumped, nearly tumbling backward off the dock. She swallowed a startled cry, pretending she wasn't trying to get away and his catching her wasn't a problem. Jake grinned up at her from the bottom of her boat, where he lay sprawled on a sleeping bag, his arms behind his head.

"Going somewhere?" he asked, raising an eyebrow at the overnight bag still clutched in her hand.

She cursed under her breath.

"If you're set on a life of crime, Ms. Jones, you're going to have to be more devious," he said, getting to his feet. "And jumping bail." He wagged his head at her. "Bad idea."

Clancy groaned. This man was the most irritating— She took a breath, trying to still her anger as well as the silly sudden flutter of her heart as he vaulted effortlessly from the boat to join her on the dock.

"Level with me, Clancy," he said, his voice as soft and deep as his gray eyes.

The sound sent a tiny vibration through her, igniting memories of the chemistry between the two of them as teenagers. She wondered if it was still there and hastily brushed that errant thought away.

Having to deal with this man on top of everything else was too much, she told herself. She didn't have the time or energy for this. Nor did she need the constant reminder of what she'd lost ten years ago—or how much more she had to lose now.

"Where are you going so early in the morning?" he asked as he stalked toward her, backing her against the edge of the dock, trapping her.

Clancy had to tilt her chin back to meet his gaze. He'd cornered her in more ways than one. And she acknowledged that it wasn't going to be easy to get rid of him. But getting rid of him was exactly what she had to do if she held any hope of clearing herself.

"If you must know," she said, coming up with the first plausible explanation that popped into her head, "I'm going to see my lawyer."

Jake pushed back his baseball cap. "Good, I need to see your lawyer, too."

She shot him a look. "You're going like *that*?"

He glanced down at his rumpled chinos and T-shirt, then looked up at her as he rubbed his blond, stubbled jaw. "It kind of makes me look dangerous, don't you think? Like a man who has nothing to lose?" He gave her a slow, almost calculated smile. "And anyway, what choice do I have? If I were to shower, I'd barely have the water turned on before you'd be hightailing it to wherever you're in such a hurry to get to."

That was exactly what she had in mind. She wished he didn't know her so well.

He stepped back to allow her room to get into the boat. "But I'm a reasonable man. I'll even let you drive your boat."

"You're so thoughtful," she said, but didn't move. Outwardly, she gritted her teeth and fumed. Inwardly, she plotted. She would dump Jake. And soon. She had to. She just didn't know how yet.

When Clancy didn't make a move to get into the boat, Jake swung back in and offered her a hand. He'd hoped his disposition would improve with daylight. It hadn't. If anything, the late-night adventure, his phone conversation with Kiki and trying to sleep in the bottom of a cold boat with his clothes on had left him even more irascible. Add to that, the gall of Clancy thinking she could get away from him this morning.

He'd been on this case less than twenty-four hours, and he felt as if he'd been beaten up by somebody twice his size. He didn't like the feeling he was being manipulated by not one, but two females. Kiki had hired him for reasons he could no more fathom than he could walk on water. And Clancy. At one time he thought he'd known her better than he knew himself. But that was years ago and a lot of water under the bridge. For all he knew, she was a killer. Let her rot in prison for all he cared.

You've become a cold-hearted bastard, haven't you, Hawkins. Reluctantly, he admitted it was true. Something had died inside him that day at the trial. He'd lost Clancy, and he'd lost his father. Only, Clancy had voluntarily chosen to leave; his father hadn't.

He watched her flick a glance at his outstretched hand but make no move toward it or the boat. Instead, she brushed her hair back with her fingers and looked toward shore as if she were thinking of making a break for it. Silently, he dared her to try. So help him, he'd take her over his knee and—

"Clancy," Jake said softly. "There're a few things you should know. One, I hate being lied to. Two, these dirty little secrets of yours? I'm going to know them all before I catch a plane back to Texas, and you can bet the farm on that." He extended his hand again. "And three, if you try to run again, I'll track you down no matter where you go, and you won't like it when I find you."

He flashed her a smile. But to his surprise, she took his hand, stepped into the boat and came right up to him. If he'd thought he could intimidate her, he'd been wrong. Her gaze met his, challenging him, daring him to take her on.

"Jake, there're a few things *you* should know," she said as softly as he had. "One, I don't have the time or energy to lie to you. Two, I have no intention of helping you send me to prison. And three—" her smile deepened "—I'm going to ditch you just as soon as I possibly can." She moved past him to slide behind the wheel. An instant later she started the boat.

Jake smiled to himself as he took a seat next to her. He'd forgotten how much he'd liked Clancy Jones's spunk as a kid. He was glad to see it was one of the things that hadn't changed about her. Unfortunately, it didn't alter the fact that she'd lied about his father or that she was lying to him right now about not jumping bail. If she wanted to play hard ball, he'd play, too. But he doubted she was going to like his rules.

* * *

They picked up the expensive bright red Mustang convertible he'd rented with Kiki's money at the mainland marina. The marina was one of several his father and Clancy's had owned as partners. Jake saw Clancy raise an eyebrow as she climbed into the car's leather seat and realized he'd dropped another notch or two in her estimation.

"Doesn't it bother you to take my aunt's money on the pretense of helping me?" Clancy asked.

"No," Jake replied, angry to discover that what she thought of him mattered.

"I thought you hate being lied to," she said. "Or do you overlook it when you're lying to yourself?"

He floored the gas pedal, sending gravel flying as he headed into town. Beside him, Clancy smiled. Jake cursed. What an impossible woman! He'd expected her to still be that cute little tomboy he'd grown up with, someone he thought he could handle—not some beautiful woman who knew how to push all his buttons. He swore to himself. What had made him think this job was going to be easy?

She smiled, seemingly amused. "You're certainly wide awake this morning. I don't remember you being such a morning person."

He didn't want to be reminded of their past or of the foolish, love-struck nineteen-year-old he'd been. Not that he was about to let that past distract or dissuade him from what he'd come to Montana to do. He'd come to settle an old score, and he had no intention of taking any trips down memory lane along the way.

"I'm *forced* to be wide awake at all hours around you," he said as he pulled out into the traffic and headed for the office complex. "Want to tell me why you were about to jump bail? Or do you want me to guess?"

"Guess," she said, looking out the side window.

"Look, why don't you just level with me. I'm going to find out, anyway."

She glanced over at him, and to his surprise, her eyes glistened with tears. "What if you're wrong, Hawkins? What if I didn't lie about your father?"

He felt a sharp stab at his heart, followed instantly by an unexpected desire to take her in his arms and comfort her. What was it about this woman that made him feel protective? Had always made him feel that way?

He shoved away the desire, the same way he'd shoved her away ten years ago. "You lied and we both know why."

She shook her head and looked away.

"You could tell me the truth now and save us both a lot of grief," he said, letting the old rancor replace any warmer feelings he might have had for her.

"And save you the satisfaction of blackmailing it out of me?" She shook her head. "Not a chance, Hawkins. Let's find out just how good a private eye you really are."

Jake drove toward Kalispell, furious that she could still get to him. He blamed it on that silly childhood crush he'd had on her. He'd opened up, letting her get closer than any other person in his life. Now he bitterly regretted having done that. It made him vulnerable. And it gave her the upper hand.

Okay, so she wasn't going to make it easy. She was going to make it pure hell. But what she didn't seem to realize was that he'd already been to hell and back because of her. And it was payback time.

* * *

Clancy breathed a sigh of relief when Jake finally pulled up in front of Lake Center, a large old hotel that had been made into an office complex. All she wanted to do was to get out of the close confines of the car and put some distance between the two of them. With a little luck, a lot of distance.

But as she started to open her door, he grabbed her arm. She pretended she didn't feel the jolt from his fingertips that seared her bare skin.

"I wish I didn't know you so well, Clancy," he said, sounding as though he meant it. "Whatever's on that conniving mind of yours, forget it. We're going to see your lawyer and find out what evidence they have against you."

She gave him what she hoped was one of her most innocent looks. "All right. But I'm starved. Why don't I go get us some breakfast at that café up the block and bring it back. What can I get you?"

He laughed as he opened his door and got out. She stepped out of the convertible, only to find him waiting for her. She watched him lock the car, her overnight bag in the rear seat. Then he linked his arm with hers and steered her toward the building's front entrance.

She didn't resist the gentle strength of his persuasive hold on her. It wouldn't have done her any good if she had. But while she also wouldn't admit it under Sodium Pentothal, she liked the feel of his skin against hers; she liked his touch, as dangerous as it was to her future, to her heart. And she glimpsed something in his expression that made her wonder if he wasn't as immune to her touch as he wanted her to believe.

"Geez, Jones," he said as they headed for the elevator. "Breakfast? A bit too predictable and not very imaginative. But a nice try, nonetheless."

Too predictable, huh? Not imaginative enough for him? Well, she'd see what she could do about that.

Jake studied Clancy as they stepped into the elevator and she pushed the third-floor button. She'd been like a kid in church, squirming in her seat on the way into town, glancing at her watch every few moments, tapping her toe to a nonexistent tune. She reminded him of a woman about to jump off a ledge. Actually, more like a woman about to jump bail, he corrected himself.

As the elevator climbed slowly to the third floor, Jake wondered what Clancy would have done this morning if he hadn't been there to stop her? With the depth of her bank account, she could probably disappear without too much trouble. At least for a while. But why run? Unless she was guilty of Westfall's murder and knew she was headed for prison.

But wouldn't a woman who planned to disappear forever take more than a small suitcase—or nothing at all—and buy what she needed when she got there?

The elevator doors thumped open, and it suddenly occurred to him that there might be a man—a man other than Westfall—in Clancy's life. That could explain the small suitcase. Jake realized he knew nothing about the nature of Clancy's relationship with the deceased. Kiki had said Clancy had dated Dex. But that didn't mean Dex was the only man, now, did it? Clancy could have dozens of men on the string.

"You don't mind if I step into the ladies' room a moment to freshen up, do you?" Clancy asked, breaking into his thoughts.

He grinned at her, hoping it hid his true feelings. "I'd hate to see you any fresher than you already are, but hey, it's all right with me since I'm coming along. Not that I don't trust you."

She scowled. "You can't seriously plan to spend every waking moment with me?"

"Every waking—and sleeping—moment." He took her elbow as they headed down the hall.

"That might be a bigger job than you think," she said cryptically. "And I suppose you want me to believe you're doing this for my own good, right?"

He held open the door to the ladies' room for her. "How can you doubt it?"

She shot him a drop-dead look.

"The truth, Jones, will set you free," he said, and smiled.

"Or send me to prison for life." She took only a quick glance into the rest room before she added, "I think you're right. I'm fresh enough."

As he let the door close, Clancy took his arm and smiled up at him as if he'd actually done something that pleased her. One side of her mouth crooked up a little, her brown eyes glinted with mischief, and just the hint of a dimple dented her left cheek at the corner of her lips. Jake had forgotten her smile could pack such a wallop. It hit him in the chest, taking away his breath and knocking him off guard.

He stumbled. Her smile deepened; humor glinted in her gaze. If he'd had any doubt before, he didn't now. She knew damned well the effect she was having on him, and she loved it. This was war. And for a moment, he wished there was another way, other than all-out war, to settle things between them.

He stared at her, wishing he could find the answers he needed in that face of hers. If only he could look into those brown eyes and know everything he wanted to about her. Like why she'd lied about his father. If she'd killed her boyfriend. Where she'd been going this morning in such a hurry. Why she'd betrayed him.

Instead, all he got were more questions from that adorable face of hers. And more suspicions.

She brushed against him as she stepped past, the silkiness of her skin sparking responses in him he didn't want to be feeling. Her scent filled him, branding his senses. He watched the provocative sway of her hips as she walked away from him. He assured himself he could handle this woman, that it would be a pleasure giving her some of her own medicine.

But that little voice of reason that kept him honest suggested the best thing he could do would be to get this case over with, pry the truth out of Clancy and head back to Texas lickety-split.

He swore softly to himself as he opened the door to the office with the sign that read Attorney Tadd Farnsworth, and watched Clancy waltz through, her bottom filling out her jeans in a way that should have been against the law. Clancy played him like a cheap guitar, but made him feel like he was a fine Gibson. Jake promised himself he'd have her dancing to his tune—and soon.

Chapter 4

"Jake? Jake Hawkins?" the handsome, prematurely gray-haired man said, coming around his large desk. "I didn't know you were back in town." Tadd Farnsworth's smile was as quick as his handshake and just as slick.

"I didn't know I had to check in at the border," Jake said, taking the attorney's outstretched hand.

"And Clancy," Tadd said.

Jake thought Tadd held her hand a little too long, his look a little too sympathetic and seductive.

Jake told himself he would have liked Tadd Farnsworth if the man hadn't been the prosecuting attorney who sent his father to prison. But he knew that wasn't true. At one time Tadd had been a regular at the island resort, always sporting a fast new boat, always a hit at the parties Jake's mother threw at the lake lodge. Jake remembered only too well how taken his mother had been with Tadd. That was plenty reason to make Jake dislike the man.

Seeing the way Clancy smiled at Tadd, Jake could see that even ten years older, Tadd still had a way with women. He decided he liked him even less.

"I was sorry about your mother, Jake," Tadd said as he returned to his chair behind his desk. "I heard she passed away a few months ago. My condolences."

"Oh, Jake," Clancy said. "I didn't know. I'm so sorry."

Jake nodded and took a chair beside Clancy. He didn't want to talk about his mother. Especially with Tadd. Nor did he want to talk about his father. He pulled his business card from his wallet and tossed it on the desk. "I'm here on the Dex Westfall case."

Tadd picked up the card. His eyes widened. "I'd heard Kiki had brought in some hotshot private eye." He laughed. "I'll be damned. So you're a P.I." He shook his head. "Interesting, her choice of investigators, wouldn't you say?"

No kidding. "I'd like to see what evidence you've got so far."

Tadd nodded. "Sure you wouldn't like some coffee? Or maybe a stiff drink?" His smile slipped a little as he looked from Jake to Clancy and back. "You're not going to like this case."

"There isn't much about it I've liked so far," Jake said. Clancy mumbled something under her breath and looked at her watch.

"Don't worry. This won't take long," Jake assured her.

"Do I look worried?" she asked with wide-eyed innocence.

The attorney excused himself and returned a few minutes later with a large manila envelope. He placed it on the desk in front of Jake and returned to his seat without saying a word.

Jake opened the flap, pulled out a stack of papers and flipped through them. He let out an oath without even realizing it.

"Told you you weren't going to like it," Tadd said.

The case against Clancy was overwhelming.

"I think I will take that coffee," Jake said to Tadd.

Jake sat stunned as Tadd buzzed his secretary. It had been one thing telling himself the woman who betrayed him was a killer. It was quite another to realize it might actually be true.

"Why didn't the sheriff just hang her on the spot?" Jake asked Tadd after he took a sip of the coffee the attorney handed him, happily discovering it to be heavily laced with bourbon.

"Would have a hundred years ago. If she'd been a man." Tadd chuckled. "Instead, she's a woman. And a Talbott to boot." He shot Clancy a smile to say he was just kidding, but with one look from her, it died on his lips.

Jake wondered if she realized that she'd be cooling her heels in a cell right now if it wasn't for Aunt Kiki's money and the illustrious Talbott name. Not to mention what Kiki must be paying Tadd. Jake wouldn't be surprised if Kiki wasn't also making a large donation to the Tadd Farnsworth for County Attorney campaign for added incentive.

Jake thumbed through the rest of the evidence, including a list of Dex Westfall's belongings from the murder scene: a bloody western snap-front shirt, a pair

of jeans and red cowboy boots. No socks. No underwear. Jake raised an eyebrow. Had Dex gotten dressed
in a hurry for some reason? Or was that his usual attire?
Jake made a mental note to ask Clancy.

There was also a list of items found at the cabin Dex
had rented at the Hawk Island Resort, including Dex's
wallet, watch, keys and some loose change.

"He didn't have his wallet or keys on him the night
of his murder?" Jake asked Tadd, suspecting even more
that for some reason Dex Westfall had dressed in a
hurry.

"I guess he didn't need them," Tadd said. "No place
to spend money and he sure couldn't drive anywhere.
He probably took one of the island trails to Ms. Jones's."

"You don't know how he got there?" Jake asked,
surprised.

"Does it matter?" Tadd said. "He got there. We know
that."

Everything mattered, Jake thought. What Dex hadn't
done was drive. There were no cars or roads on Hawk
Island. That left two other options: he could go by boat
around the island to Clancy's. Or he could take one of
the many mountain trails. Because the sheriff hadn't
found a boat at the scene didn't mean Dex hadn't had
someone drop him off. And that meant maybe he'd
planned to have that same someone pick him up again.

Dex was last seen with Clancy after the resort café
closed on Friday night. That meant there wouldn't have
been any place on the island for Dex to spend money.
But Jake still thought it odd Dex hadn't taken his wallet. Most guys would grab their wallet, keys and watch
out of habit. Some things you just felt naked without.
Like underwear.

The wallet, according to the report, contained less than thirty dollars. He glanced through the photocopy of the items—a Montana driver's license, a few credit cards. Jake frowned. No photographs. Not even one of Clancy, the guy's girlfriend. No family photos. No receipts or junk like most people carried in their wallets. No mementos.

Dex Westfall's belongings reminded Jake of a new subdivision. No feeling of history. Everything of Dex's had been marked on the sheriff's list as in new condition. Jake found himself wondering just who the hell this guy was and what Clancy had seen in him as he glanced at Westfall's driver's license photo again. The guy was almost too good-looking. Jake had never figured Clancy for that type, but then, he reminded himself, he didn't know Clancy anymore. He looked over at her. For instance, what was she thinking about right now? He realized how little he knew about her. It worried him. A lot.

Taking out his notebook, Jake jotted down Dex's social security number and address from his driver's license, and took down the credit card numbers. He put everything back in the envelope and looked up at Tadd.

"What do you know about this guy?" Jake asked.

Tadd shrugged. "No more than what's here, and we won't know until his next of kin are notified." Jake noted Clancy's sudden rapt attention and wondered why this subject would interest her when nothing else about her case had.

"There's one other thing," Tadd said. Jake felt the bad news coming even before Tadd opened his mouth. "You should know the sheriff has two witnesses who overheard Westfall and Clancy arguing at the marina café the evening Dex Westfall was murdered. Both said they heard Clancy threaten Dex."

Jake groaned inwardly.

"One is a waitress at the marina café," Tadd continued. "The other is Frank Ames. You remember him?"

Yeah, Jake remembered the tall, pimply-faced kid six years his senior. Frank had always had a major chip on his shoulder, one that Jake had more than once wanted to knock off. Jake's father had given Frank a job at the resort, wanting to help him. But Frank's hostile unfriendliness had forced Warren Hawkins to let him go, making Frank Ames all the more bitter.

"Frank owns the resort now," Tadd said. "Maybe you'd heard."

"No, I hadn't." Jake hadn't heard anything about Hawk Island since the day he promised his mother he'd never say his father's name in her presence again. It had been the day they left Flathead Lake, right after Warren Hawkins had been convicted of embezzlement, arson and one count of deliberate homicide. They'd left town on the whipping tail of a scandal that had rocked the tiny community. Kiki had been right; his mother had insisted they leave without stopping at the Montana State prison in Deer Lodge to see his father even one last time.

Jake had kept his promise to her; he'd never mentioned his father's name. But several times a year he'd visited Warren Hawkins in prison. Jake had wanted to reopen his father's case and do some investigating on his own, but Warren had asked him not to. Jake had left it alone, not wanting to hurt his mother any more than she had been.

But now she was gone. And he was back in Montana thanks to Aunt Kiki. Back on Flathead Lake. And that hunch of his was knocking at the back of his brain, demanding to be let in. Demanding that he follow it, no matter where it might lead. Clancy was his ticket as surely as Tadd Farnsworth was a born politician. It was just going to be harder to get the truth out of Clancy than he'd first thought.

"Can I get a copy of this and the autopsy report?" Jake asked, tapping the envelope with his finger.

Tadd nodded.

"Give me a call when it's ready." He gave Tadd the number from the cellular phone Kiki had given him.

"Here's my home number," Tadd said as he took out a business card and wrote on the back. He handed it to Jake. "In case you come up with something." He sounded more than a little doubtful that would happen.

Tadd pushed his intercom button and instructed his secretary to make Jake a copy of the Dex Westfall case, including the latest on Clancy's sleepwalking defense.

"What?" Jake snapped, telling himself he must have heard wrong. He glanced over at Clancy; she met his gaze for an instant, then looked away, her body suddenly tense. Jake cursed under his breath. What else had Clancy and her aunt failed to tell him?

"I guess you didn't know," Tadd said, smiling sympathetically at Jake. "Clancy was sleepwalking the night Dex Westfall was killed. That's why she doesn't remember what happened."

Jake stumbled to his feet, feeling the weight of the world settle around his shoulders. He took Clancy's elbow and steered her out into the hall.

"Sleepwalking?" he demanded the moment the door closed behind them. He couldn't believe what a chump he was. Even when she'd lied on the stand, he'd figured she only did it to protect her own father. If Tadd was opting for a Twinkie defense like sleepwalking, it meant only one thing: Clancy'd killed Dex Westfall and she damn well knew it.

"Sleepwalking?" Jake demanded again, trying to keep his voice down.

"I guess I shouldn't expect you to believe me," Clancy said, jerking her elbow free of his grip. She started down the hall, but he grabbed her shoulder and whirled her around to face him.

He let his gaze rake roughly over her, telling himself not to be fooled by that face of hers with its cute little button of a nose or the crocodile tears in those big brown eyes. He pulled her into the first alcove and blocked her retreat with his body. "Another murder and you just happened to be sleepwalking *again*?"

Clancy found her gaze locked spellbound with his. There was something commanding about him. He demanded her attention, and ever since she was a girl, she'd been unable to deny him. She looked into his eyes; they darkened like thunderheads banked out over the lake. Everything about him, from his eyes to the hard line of his body, warned her of the storm he was about to bring into her life. Jake Hawkins was a dangerous man, one she'd be a fool to trifle with.

"I walk in my sleep. I have ever since I was a child."

He stared at her, suspicion deep in his expression. "Sure you have."

She wanted to slap his smug face. "I assume you've never walked in your sleep."

"No." He made that one word say it all.

She reminded herself that people who'd never sleep-walked didn't understand, couldn't understand. But she wanted Jake to, needed Jake to.

"It's frightening, because when you wake up you don't know how you got there. You don't recall getting up. Suddenly you are just somewhere else, and you don't remember anything. Not even where you've been." She met his gaze. "Or what you've done."

"How come I never heard about you sleepwalking when we were kids?"

She glanced away. "I was…ashamed. Wandering around at night in my pajamas, not knowing what I was doing. It was something I didn't want anyone to know about."

Jake nodded, eyeing her intently. "And you're trying to tell me that the night Dex Westfall was murdered you were walking around in your pj's, sound asleep, and you don't remember killing him? Not that you didn't kill him, but that you don't remember because you were sacked out?"

"I'm trying to tell you the truth," she said angrily, and wondered why she was even bothering. "Sleepwalking isn't something I have control over. It just… happens. Like last night."

"Last night?" He dragged his fingers through his hair. "You mean last night on the dock when you were sure someone pulled you into the lake and tried to drown you? Now you're telling me that you were asleep?"

She didn't like his tone. "I was walking in my sleep." She took a breath and looked away. He'd never given her the chance to explain ten years ago; he'd just assumed she'd lied on the stand and he'd cut her off without a word. Without a goodbye. "Just like I was the night of the fire."

"How convenient that you were asleep at the murder you committed," Jake said, bitterness oozing from his every word. He slammed a palm to the wall on each side of her. "And how inconvenient for my father that you just happened to wake up in time to see him kill Lola Strickland."

"Yes." She ducked under his arm and ran down the hall, blinded by tears and regrets. Behind her, she heard him. The sound was a low, pained howl, the cry of a wounded animal. It tore at her heart. She wanted to take him in her arms, to comfort him. But nothing she could do or say would do that. She'd told the jury the truth. She didn't know what else had happened that night at Hawk Island Resort because she'd been asleep—walking, but sound asleep. Sleepwalking had always been her private shame. A frightening weakness that was best kept a secret. Until the night Lola Strickland was murdered. Now that horrible memory had come back to haunt her—just the way her sleepwalking had come back.

Jake slammed a fist into the wall, too stunned to chase after her. Sleepwalking? She'd been sleepwalking the night of Lola's murder *and* the night Dex Westfall was killed in her garret? And last night on the dock? His brain tried to assimilate this information but couldn't.

That's why her story had sounded like a lie. Could she really not remember anything? Was that why there'd been so many holes in her story? Because she'd been asleep? His mind refused to accept it. Just as it had ten years ago. She was lying. Again. Sleepwalking! Again.

He charged after her, only to run headlong into a group of students on some kind of career day. The teacher tried to gather her flock, but they scattered like errant chicks. Jake forced his way through to reach the elevator door just as it closed. He watched the numbers overhead to make sure Clancy was headed down before he took off at a run for the stairs. She didn't really think she could get away from him, did she?

He burst out of the stairwell and into the main lobby as the elevator doors were closing again. He raced over to them, slapping the doors open and startling the only occupants, an elderly couple.

"Sorry," he said. "I was looking for a blond woman. About five six. Cute." Incredibly sexy. And innocent-looking. He started to make a curvaceous outline with his hands, but stopped himself. "Nice figure. Wearing a navy shirt, jeans and sandals?"

They both gave him a knowing smile. The elderly woman pointed across the hall to a door marked Women. "She seemed a little upset," the woman said, clearly blaming him.

"Thanks." As the elevator doors closed again, Jake made a beeline for the bathroom, cursing himself for letting Clancy out of his sight for even an instant.

He stormed through the doorway, propelled by a flammable fuel of high-grade anger. "If you think I'm going to believe this latest story of yours—" he said, taking up the conversation right where they'd left off.

His voice echoed off the tiled walls. A half-dozen women looked up, startled. Clancy wasn't at either of the two sinks powdering her nose. That left only the row of four stalls.

"Sir, you're in the wrong rest room," one woman politely informed him as if he didn't know.

He politely informed her that he didn't care, then he leaned down to look for Clancy's sandaled feet in the occupied stalls. No Clancy. The last stall appeared empty; someone had put a handmade Out of Order sign on it.

Most of the women had the good sense to flee from the room, though they did it in high indignation, telling him in no uncertain terms what they thought of his behavior.

You want to see bad behavior, he thought to himself, *wait until I get my hands on Clancy.* A couple of women stayed to give him grief. He ignored them, waiting for the stalls to empty out. As he glanced around the room, he assessed the situation. There was only one door. Clancy hadn't had time to come back out.

Jake waited for the last woman to exit. As she stomped past, he noticed that the summer breeze coming through the open window at the end of the room smelled sweet with the scent of freshly mown grass. Jake could hear the sound of a lawnmower buzzing just outside at ground level. In front of the window, someone had upended a trash can.

Jake cursed himself and his stupidity as he pushed open each stall door on his way to the window. All the stalls were now empty, just as he knew they would be. And on the corner of the metal window frame was a small scrap of navy blue material that perfectly matched the shirt Clancy had been wearing.

Damn her hide, she'd given him the slip.

Chapter 5

Clancy caught the first flight out of Kalispell. She thought she'd feel safe once the plane was in the air. Instead, she couldn't shake the feeling that someone was after her. And not just Jake Hawkins.

She glanced around at the other passengers but saw no one she knew. No one even appeared remotely interested in her. As the plane banked to the east, she looked out the window and told herself she had to calm down and think clearly. Her life depended on it. And yet she'd never felt more afraid, more alone.

Except for one other time in her life. The night of the resort fire. The night Lola Strickland was murdered. Clancy closed her eyes and tried to fight back the painful memories. But the memories came, edged with one penetrating truth: she'd walked in her sleep that night, just as she had the night Dex Westfall died.

It had been late that night ten years ago when she'd come down the stairs, awakened by the sound of her parents arguing. Her parents never argued. Until that moment, she'd led an idyllic life on the island. The only dark spot in her whole childhood had been her required yearly visits back East to see Aunt Kiki and get a little culture so she didn't grow up a wild heathen. Clancy had hated the visits, the stiff, prissy dresses, the long, boring lessons in social graces, her aunt's endless lectures on the value of money and the Talbott name.

But it was her aunt's low opinion of Clancy's father that made her call Kiki the Wicked Witch of the East. Kiki had always thought her sister had married beneath the family name when she'd married Clarence Jones. Clancy idolized her father.

Clancy had stopped on the stairs when she heard her father's voice saying that he couldn't go to the police, wouldn't go to the police. Warren was his best friend.

But her mother had argued that Warren was stealing from the businesses and had been for some time. Clancy felt a sick, sinking feeling, knowing that their lives had suddenly changed and would never be the same again.

When her father left by boat to meet Warren at the resort, Clancy followed by land, afraid for her father for reasons she couldn't explain then or now.

But when she reached the resort office, she could hear her father and Warren inside and decided to wait in one of the boats tied at the dock. She'd fallen asleep.

Later, she'd woken only to find that she'd walked in her sleep. To this day, she had no idea where she'd been or what she might have seen. All she remembered was waking to find herself standing outside the office.

Her father's boat was gone. Inside the office she could hear voices raised in anger. From the shadows, she watched in horror as Warren Hawkins struggled with Lola Strickland. Lola stumbled backward into an adjoining room. Both figures disappeared for a few moments, then Warren emerged at a run. Behind him the office burst into flame, and within seconds the fire consumed the building.

Just thinking about that night brought back the incredible regret. Lola's death and Warren Hawkins's arrest ended the life she and Jake had known on Hawk Island. Jake and his mother left Flathead; Jake left hating Clancy. Clancy's parents had moved to Alaska to start over. They'd lost everything. Kiki purchased the lodge at Clancy's pleading. Clancy had foolishly hoped her family would some day be reunited there. Two years later her parents were killed in a small plane crash outside of Fairbanks.

Clancy didn't come back to the boarded-up lodge for years and then only occasionally. At first the bad memories were just too painful. Then the good memories started to surface again.

She opened her eyes and looked out the plane window. She'd had such hopes when she'd returned. Had she made a mistake coming back? Was there a curse on the island and her? Some debt not yet paid?

She felt a chill as she thought of Jake. He'd believed his father's version of what happened that night. Warren Hawkins testified during the trial that he knew nothing about the missing money. After Clarence Jones left, he'd gotten out the books to go over them. Warren was in charge of that part of the businesses in the partnership with Clarence, but he'd turned a lot of the responsibility over to Lola, he'd said.

Warren said he'd heard someone in the adjoining office. When he'd gone to check, he saw two suitcases outside the door and found Lola cleaning out the safe.

He'd tried to stop her. Lola had poured gasoline around the office, obviously planning to cover her tracks. In their struggle, she must have lit the gas. The room burst into flames. That's when Warren swears he saw someone move in the shadows; someone else was in the office by the back door. When he ran out, Lola was still alive. He thought she was right behind him.

Warren said the other person in the office that night must have taken the money from the safe, because it wasn't found in the debris from the fire and Lola certainly didn't get away with it. That person must have also murdered Lola. In the autopsy it was found that Lola had died from a head wound—not from the fire. That made Warren look all the more guilty.

In the end, the jury didn't believe there was another person in the office that night. Nor did they believe Lola set the fire. It looked too much like Warren had embezzled money from the businesses and tried to cover his misdeeds with the fire. Lola, who was leaving the island, just happened along at the wrong time. All of the joint businesses' books were destroyed in the fire. Warren couldn't prove his innocence. Nor could the police prove his guilt.

Clancy's testimony had clinched it. Warren was convicted of embezzlement, arson and deliberate homicide. He got sixty years at the state prison at Deer Lodge.

And because of Clancy's testimony, Jake had walked out of her life without a word. The hurt from that still made her heart ache. And now— Now he'd come back. For revenge.

Just what she needed, Clancy thought as the plane descended into Gallatin Field outside of Bozeman. An old boyfriend with a grudge on top of all her other troubles.

At the airport, Clancy rented a car and drove the

eight miles into Bozeman to Dex's condo. She felt as if time were running out. Jake wouldn't be far behind her, she knew that. And he'd be furious. Boy, was that putting it mildly.

But she hoped that by the time he tracked her to the airport, discovered she'd flown to Bozeman and rented a car, it would be too late for him to stop her. By then she'd have searched Dex's place and hopefully found something that would help her case. Though she couldn't imagine what.

There was also the possibility that Jake would go straight to the county attorney. By the time she reached Bozeman, the police could be looking for her, as well.

Either way, she needed to get this over with as quickly as possible.

Dex owned a condo on the southside of town, set back against a hill overlooking Sourdough Creek. Clancy parked and sat in the car for a moment, watching the quiet street. No other vehicles cruised by. She told herself she was just being paranoid. No one was after her. Except Jake. And maybe the entire Bozeman police. And possibly the person who'd tried to drown her last night.

She picked up her purse from the seat and got out, closing the car door behind her. As she walked toward the front door of the condo, she searched the street. A florist's van passed by; the driver never even looked her way. She could only hope the spare key was where it had been the last time Dex locked himself out. Carefully, she slid the large flowerpot slightly to one side. Nothing but dust. She pushed it a little farther and was relieved to see the key.

Quickly she scooped it up, slipped it into the lock and turned. The door swung open.

Clancy stepped into the high-dollar condo, wondering whether the police had already been here, whether they'd already searched the place and found something that would further incriminate her. The cluttered condo didn't surprise her as much as the man who came out of the kitchen.

"Excuse me," he said, sounding annoyed and a little frightened by her intrusion. He was short, with rumpled dark hair and sunless pale skin, and he was wearing nothing but shorts. "How did you get in here?"

Her first thought was that the condo had been sold. Her second was that Dex had a roommate she hadn't known about. A roommate who was looking more than a little anxious.

"I'm a friend of Dex Westfall's," she said quickly, not sure that was exactly accurate, but it beat the alternative. That she was the woman the police had arrested for Dex's murder.

"Dex Westfall," the man said, shaking his head. Had he heard Dex was dead? She felt her heart rate accelerate. Worse yet, had he heard about her arrest? "I suppose he gave you a key."

She shook her head, wondering how she was going to explain what she was doing here. "I used the one under the flowerpot."

He swatted the air with the pancake turner in his hand. "Did Dex tell everyone where to find the key to my condo?"

"*Your* condo?" Clancy thought she must have heard him wrong.

"Dex Westfall was only house-sitting for me for a few months," he said, his tone increasing in both volume and irritation. "I come home to find he's run up my phone bill and failed to pay the utility bills, and now

the police want to talk to me about God knows wh—"
Behind the man, smoke curled out of the kitchen. He
spun around and charged out of the room.

Pans clanged into the sink. A kitchen fan came on. A
few moments later, he stalked back into the living room.

"Look," he said, his face flushed. "The guy's a dead-
beat. Just give me the key and tell Dex I don't want to see
him or any more of his girlfriends around here, all right?"

He didn't know Dex was dead. "The police called
you?"

"I got a message on my machine," the man said. "I
haven't had time to call them back." He seemed to resent her questions, but also seemed resigned to answer
them. No doubt he felt sorry for a woman stupid enough
to fall for Dex Westfall. "I just got back yesterday from
Australia. I haven't even had time to unpack yet." He
held out his hand for the key.

Clancy noticed the stack of newspapers by the door.
Magazines and junk mail were piled high on a telephone
table by the door. "Did Dex leave any personal items
here?" she asked as she handed over the key. "He has
something that belongs to me."

The man rolled his eyes. "Dex isn't completely stupid. He packed up and got out just before I returned
home. Did you check his apartment?"

She stared at him. "His apartment?"

"You don't get it, do you," he said, his face growing red-
der. "Dex Westfall is a lying sleazeball. You aren't the first
woman to show up looking for him. Or the last, I'm sure."

No, she *hadn't* got it. She realized how little she knew
about the man she'd dated. The man she was now accused of murdering. "Where is his apartment?" Her
voice came out a trembly whisper.

He reached over to snatch a scrap of paper and a pen from the phone table and scribbled something on it. "If you loaned him money, forget it. I'm sure it's long gone. Just like I would imagine he is. This is the address he gave me."

Clancy took the piece of paper. It had a northside apartment address on it.

"If you should catch up to him, tell Dex— Never mind, it wouldn't do any good," the man said disgustedly.

She figured he'd find out just how right he was as soon as he returned his calls.

He moved past her to open the front door. "Good luck," he said as she stepped outside, then he closed and locked the door behind her.

Clancy stumbled to the rental car and sat for a moment, too shaken to drive. She remembered the first time Dex had brought her to see his new condo. *His* new condo. He'd told her what a great deal he got on it. He'd insinuated that he'd purchased it with their future in mind and even talked about how easy it would be to build on a studio for her.

He'd been lying through his teeth. To impress her? Or con her? But out of what?

She started the car, anxious to get to Dex's apartment. Maybe the police didn't know about it yet. Maybe he'd left something that would help her.

Dex Westfall's apartment turned out to be a basement rental in an old run-down part of town. Clancy circled the block and, not taking any chances, parked behind the house. A short, worn path led from the alley to the basement entrance. Clancy stepped down the crumbling steps and peered through a dirty window into what looked like the furnace room.

"Can I help you?" The voice was elderly and shrill, with an irritated edge to it.

Clancy spun around to find a wrinkled woman; her pink curlers clung haphazardly to her washed-out gray hair. Her eyes were narrowed and mean.

"I'm looking for Dex," Clancy said, adding what she hoped was a friendly smile.

"Humph! Isn't everybody." The woman jammed her small fists down on her hips and glared at Clancy. "And just what do you want with him?"

"I'm his…sister," she said quickly. "I'm worried about him."

"His sister?" The woman eyed her. "Not much resemblance that I can see."

"Different fathers," Clancy said, caught up in her whopper.

The woman puckered her lipstick-cracked lips. "He owes me rent."

Clancy opened her purse. "How much?"

It took all of Clancy's charm, most of her cash and more flagrant falsehoods to get into the apartment. To her surprised delight, it didn't sound as though the police had been there yet. But then, they had their killer; they weren't looking for clues in Bozeman. Or maybe they'd only gotten as far as the condo, because that was the only address they had for Dex.

"Last thing he said to me was that he'd be back with enough money to buy this house and me with it," the woman said with a huff. "I've seen his kind before. Fancy dresser. Full of himself. Full of bull, that's what he was." She looked up at Clancy as she unlocked the apartment door. "Too bad you can't pick your relatives, huh? Don't take anything." With that, she left, her worn slippers shuffling up the cracked concrete steps.

Clancy closed the door and turned to look at Dex Westfall's apartment. Under the golden glare of a single bulb overhead, the cramped studio apartment looked seedy at best. An old couch hunkered against a dark paneled wall next to an overstuffed worn chair and a small kitchen table and two metal folding chairs. A blanket was neatly folded at one end of the couch. Dex's bed?

An old, hump-shouldered refrigerator kicked on in the kitchen area of the room, clanging a little before it settled into a tired, noisy thrum. Clancy reminded herself that she didn't have much time. Jake would be after her. And by now the man at the condo could have called the police back.

But still she didn't move. She stared at the apartment, trying to connect it with the man she'd known. Or thought she'd known.

On the makeshift counter next to the fridge was a sink and a hot plate. Not far from it stood a tall, homemade pine closet, a bent wire hanger caught in its door. Past it, through a narrow doorway, she could make out a toilet, shower stall and a bathroom window, trash and dead weeds blown in on the outside.

This was the kind of cheap apartment college kids rented while they attended Montana State University. They hung posters on the paneled walls, had loud parties and spent most of their time playing hackysack over at the park or studying at the library. There was no way that Dex Westfall had ever lived here. There had to be a mistake. Even if Dex was short of money—

She reached to free the coat hanger from the closet door. The last thing she expected to find was any of

Dex's clothing inside— She'd been right. All of his clothes were gone. But what she saw sent a shock of horror through her.

The wall at the back of the empty closet was covered with papers and pictures, all thumbtacked to the wood. One photograph in particular caught her attention. She shoved back the half-dozen bent metal hangers dangling from the galvanized pipe rod. It was a photo of a young woman.

Clancy moved closer, panic making her movements stiff, unsure. The photograph was of her. Next to it was a ten-year-old newspaper article about Lola Strickland's murder and Warren Hawkins's trial. Clancy's testimony had been highlighted.

Her heart slammed against her ribs as she saw that the entire back of the closet was covered with articles about the trial and that summer. She felt her legs quake beneath her and all her blood seemed to rush to her head. She reeled and caught herself, grabbing the closet for support. A photograph fluttered to the floor. Mechanically, she reached to pick it up.

It was a shot of her in a dark green suit coming out of the gallery where she used to work in downtown Bozeman. She stared at the photo. It was a candid shot, taken from the other side of Main Street. She squinted as something in the picture caught her eye. A silver spot on the jacket's lapel. The pin her Grandmother Jones had left her when she died. Clancy drew the snapshot closer. She remembered that day! It was the last time she'd worn the pin. She'd gone to lunch and when she returned to work, the pin was gone. Lost. She'd run an ad in the paper, but the pin never turned up.

Her heart began to pound harder. It was the same

day she'd met Dex. After lunch that afternoon. She'd been so upset about losing her Grandmother Jones's pin. And this man had walked into the gallery, looking for a sculpture. He didn't know the artist's name, just the artist's work. And he had to have the sculpture.

Clancy had been startled by Dex's good looks, his charm, his passion for an artwork he'd only glimpsed in a gallery window. And even more startled and pleased when the artist's work he was dying to purchase turned out to be her own.

Clancy gripped the photograph tighter. Dex had purchased one of her most unusual—and most expensive—sculptures. Then he'd asked her out for dinner that night, telling her he wanted to know more about the artist who did such magnificent work. And unlike her usual cautious self, she'd accepted.

Tears rushed to her eyes, fed by fear rather than regret. Fear and a fresh sense of panic. Dex had taken this picture of her *before* he'd come into the gallery, *before* he'd pretended he hadn't known the name of the artist he was searching for, *before* he'd ever met her.

Her pulse thundered, drowning out the thrum of the refrigerator, drowning out everything but one single thought: Dex Westfall had known her! From that very first day. He'd known who she was. From the newspaper articles about the trial. He'd known. And he'd come after her.

Clancy clung to the edge of the closet. Why her? She let the photograph drop. It drifted to the bottom of the closet, where it lay staring up at her. A play program lay beside it. A play Clancy had attended. Just days before Lola's death.

A thud overhead pulled Clancy back. Pretty soon the landlady would be down here, wondering what was keeping Clancy so long. But Clancy continued to stare at the pictures and newspaper articles, shocked by Dex's deception.

Carefully she moved away from the makeshift closet. The hangers rattled softly behind her. She glanced toward the small, dusty ground-level window over the sink, that feeling that she was being watched even stronger than at the airport. She shivered, urging herself to finish her search and get out of there.

The rusted bathroom cabinet was empty. So was the chest of drawers she found tucked back in the corner. It seemed obvious that when Dex had left, he'd had no intention of coming back. He'd pretty much taken everything. Except for his wall of mementos. A shudder of apprehension rocked her as she stood before the closet again. Why had he thought he wouldn't need them anymore?

That's when she spotted the letter. The letter she'd written him, warning him not to contact her again. He'd tacked it on the closet wall, still in its envelope. She reached for it at the same time she heard the creak of the door opening behind her. Clancy grabbed the envelope, folding it in her hand as she turned, and smiled to greet the nosy landlady.

But the dark silhouette that filled the doorway was much larger than the landlady and much more threatening.

"Jumping bail *and* destroying evidence?" Jake asked, that touch of a southern drawl doing little to take the edge off the anger in his voice. He stepped to her side in two effortless strides and, grasping her wrist, plucked the letter from her hand. "You're just damned and determined to go to prison, aren't you, Clancy Jones?"

Chapter 6

Jake hadn't thought past finding Clancy. Hadn't thought of anything but catching her. And now that he had, he stood scowling at her, uncertain as to what to do with her. Several thoughts crossed his mind, surprising him in both content and fervor. "I ought to—"

Clancy stepped back as he advanced on her, stumbling against the open door of what looked like a home-made closet.

Jake stopped dead when he saw the bulletin board Dex had constructed on the back wall and recognized the subject. "What the—?" He swore under his breath, that hunch of his doing the Charleston in a bright red sequined outfit.

He shot a questioning look at Clancy and noticed how pale she'd turned and realized it wasn't even his doing. "Would you like to tell me what's going on?"

She didn't get a chance to answer. Car doors slammed out front. A moment later, someone pounded on the front door of the house overhead. The screen door creaked open and a woman's high-pitched, irritated voice demanded, "Don't tell me Westfall is in trouble with the law, too."

"Cops." Jake swore and glanced around for a way out. He grabbed Clancy's arm and shoved her toward the bathroom. "I know how fond you are of climbing out windows." He popped open the bathroom window, pushing aside the garbage and weeds, and hoisted Clancy up and out. A few moments later, he was through the window himself and leading Clancy down the path behind the house.

"Is that your car?" Jake asked, hardly waiting for her affirmative response before he asked for the keys, opened the passenger door and shoved her inside. He climbed into the driver's seat, quickly started the car and pulled away.

"Where's your—"

"Parked up the block," he said. "Don't worry, I'll call the rental agency to pick it up." His second rental car on this case was the least of his worries.

A few safe blocks later, he threw on the brakes, startling her, startling himself, at the depth of his anger with her.

"Do you realize the position you've just put me in?" he demanded, unable to keep from yelling. "It's not bad enough that you jump bail and I cover for you. Now I'm withholding evidence from the police on top of it."

"I didn't ask you to cover for me," she said. "You might recall, I fired you."

He narrowed his gaze at her. "Thank you for reminding me of that. I'd almost forgotten." The fact that she hadn't asked him to protect her, that he'd done it all on his own, only made it worse. Far worse. And to add insult to injury, she didn't even appreciate his heroic gesture. He reminded himself she hadn't appreciated it last night, either. One of them was a damned slow learner.

"I just compromised myself and my career, put my P.I. license on the line for you," Jake told her, laying it on a little strong.

She didn't look impressed. "Let's not forget why you're really here." She glared at him. "To get the goods on me, isn't that what you said?"

"I don't remember you being like this," he snapped, forgetting he didn't want to be reminded of their past. He didn't want anything to weaken his resolve, and thinking about the two of them back then definitely made him weak sometimes. "You've grown into an amazingly irritating woman."

"Thank you," Clancy shot back.

Irritating. Conniving. Underhanded. Devious. Sneaky. All traits of a criminal mind, he noted. A murderer's mind. Why else had she jumped bail to get this damned letter? Wasn't that what really had him upset? That the reason for that mountain of evidence against Clancy was because she'd killed Dex Westfall.

He jerked the letter from his pocket where he'd shoved it before the impromptu climb out the window. "Is this what you didn't want the police to find?"

She started to say something, but he cut her off with a slash of his hand through the air between them. He pulled the letter from the envelope and quickly read it. There was no doubt it would be damaging in court. Clancy had dumped Dex in the letter, warning him not to contact her, to leave her alone. It sounded angry. And Jake couldn't help but wonder what the guy had done to prompt this letter. Was Dex the reason she'd quit her job at the gallery and moved back to Hawk Island? Jake suspected he was.

But the letter wasn't damaging enough to jump bail, to chance getting caught by the police, to climb out two windows in one day and race halfway across the state with the cops— and him—close at her heels.

No, Jake thought, glancing over at Clancy, nor did she look much like a criminal. She looked ashen. Shaken. Scared. He remembered the collection on Dex's back closet wall. "I take it you didn't know he had all that stuff on you?"

She bit her lip and shook her head.

Jake considered how he would have reacted to finding a closet wall covered with his life, complete with candid photographs. He thought about the guy tacking all that stuff up;

Dex Westfall had to have been one weird bastard.

"He was obviously obsessed with you." Jake could understand that. "What is it you think he wanted?"

She shook her head. "He planned our first meeting." Her voice broke. "From the very beginning, he planned it all. But why?" She started trembling as if the summer day had suddenly turned ice cold. He felt a chill himself. But fear was a much safer emotion than what he felt as he watched Clancy try desperately not to cry.

That was the thing about the Clancy he'd loved, he recalled. All tomboy tough on the outside but tender and soft on the inside. Before he could consider how stupid it was, he pulled her into his arms. She resisted at first, her body stiff, almost brittle. He pulled her to him, gently rubbing his hand up and down her back. Slowly he felt her soften in his embrace, felt her let the tears out, her face buried in his shoulder. Her back warmed under his hand. He could feel her heart pounding next to his. He concentrated on the rhythmic rubbing of her back, forcing his thoughts to focus on Dex Westfall, a man he was beginning to hate, instead of the soft, wonderfully feminine feel of the woman in his arms.

The crying stopped; so did the trembling. She pulled away. He sat for a moment, less surprised by the sharp jab of desire he felt after having her in his arms than his longing to kiss away her tears, to protect and shelter her.

He growled at himself in disgust. Lust he understood. Clancy was one hot-looking woman. But anything beyond that would mess up his head—and his whole reason for being here. Just as she'd pointed out. He wasn't going to let anything change that.

He started the car, wondering about Dex's relationship with Clancy. In his business, he'd heard a lot of hard-luck stories from women who'd been screwed over by men. This was one story he wasn't anxious to hear. He had a feeling he was going to want to have killed the guy himself. "Let's get some coffee."

"How did you find me?" Clancy asked, cradling the coffee mug in her hands. He'd picked a truck stop just outside of Bozeman. Clancy looked small and vulnerable in the pea green upholstered booth, but some of her color had come back and she seemed a little less shaky.

"I added up a few things," he said, eyeing her over his coffee. At first, he'd been too furious to figure out anything. The fact that she'd run made her look guilty as hell. Not that everything else hadn't already made her look that way. The fact that she'd outsmarted him didn't help matters in the least.

But then he'd calmed down enough to replay it all in his head. From when he'd first seen her, hurrying toward the boat, anxious to get somewhere. The small amount of clothing she'd packed. He'd gone through the suitcase she'd left in the back of his rental car, hoping to find an address or phone number inside. No such luck. Instead, there was only what looked like enough clothes for an overnight stay. She hadn't planned to go far or for very long. An extra pair of jeans, a sweatshirt, one change of underwear, and a toothbrush and toothpaste.

Nor had she planned to go anywhere fancy. He happily threw out the boyfriend theory. No sexy nightgown. He added the fact that she'd seemed terribly anxious all morning, worried. She'd needed to get somewhere and in a hurry.

In the end, he'd felt a little better. Because unless he missed his guess, he knew where'd he'd find her.

"I placed a couple of calls, found out you'd taken a plane to Bozeman," Jake said simply. "It was just a matter of getting Dex's home address."

She looked up, surprised. "How did you—"

He smiled. "You'd be surprised what a motivated P.I. can find out. And I was *very* motivated after your devious departure."

"So, was it imaginative enough for you?"

He saw the beginning of a smile on her lovely face. "You want me to admit that you outsmarted me, don't you." He wagged his head at her. "All right, Jones, you got me. You happy now?"

Clancy smiled, her face transformed, sunshine after a storm. "You *are* good at your job, Jake."

He returned her smile, recognizing a reluctant compliment when he heard one. "It's what I get paid for." He hadn't meant to say that.

Her smiled faded. "Yes, I haven't forgotten that," she said, looking into her cup. "Or what really motivates you."

They finished their coffee, then he drove them to the airport where the small plane he'd chartered was waiting. He stopped for a moment to speak to the pilot, then ushered Clancy onto the plane. "I couldn't help but overhear. I didn't know you had your pilot's license," Clancy said as they boarded the plane.

"There are a lot of things you don't know about me, Clancy."

She was starting to realize just how true that was, she thought, hugging herself as if the afternoon had gone cold. Jake's arms around her had left an imprint, one she didn't want to forget. How could he have such compassion for her when at the same time he held such hatred for her? He'd just possibly postponed her going back to jail, and at the same time, risked his license and a brush with the law. She wondered if he even understood himself.

Still, she had been glad to see him when he showed up at Dex's. She'd needed someone desperately, and there was Jake. Just like old times. She'd almost run into his arms. Almost forgotten the bad blood between them.

"Thank you for helping me," she said, meaning it. "Again."

He mumbled something under his breath, then motioned to the empty plane. "Sit anywhere you like."

She headed for a window seat near the wing. Jake disappeared into the cockpit to speak to the pilot. A few moments later the plane began to taxi out to the runway. She was fumbling with the seat belt when Jake took a seat beside her. "I guess all of this sleuthing has made me a little nervous," she said, all thumbs. He took the seat belt strap from her and with practiced smoothness locked it into place.

"Try not to worry," he said, buckling up his own.

She clenched her hands together, her nerves a steady vibration running through her body like the whine of the plane engine as it readied for takeoff. The engine revved and the plane roared down the runway.

She looked out the window at the endless blue sky instead of at Jake's bottomless gray eyes. Only a few clouds huddled over the Tobacco Root Mountains. The rich green valley floor raced to the foothills and the pines. Below her, rivers ran to meet at Three Forks, the Jefferson, Gallatin and Madison converging to form the Missouri.

"Tell me about Dex Westfall."

She snapped back around in surprise, having momentarily forgotten the trouble she was in, both with the law and Jake Hawkins. "To help you put me in prison?"

Through the window across the aisle, the sun glistened, blinding white off the plane's wing as the pilot banked toward Flathead Lake and home.

"Come on, Clancy, you know I don't want to see you go to prison." He almost sounded like he meant it.

"Right. You'd much rather see me hang."

Jake pulled off his cap and raked his fingers through his hair. "Look, I'm still going to get the truth out of you, but in order to do that, I need to find something that proves your innocence. I don't see any way I can do that without your help." He slapped the cap back on his sandy blond head. "The way I see it, that puts us on the same team."

"Not hardly." She locked her gaze with his, wishing for the look she'd seen earlier, wishing for the old Jake, the one she'd once trusted with her life, the one who'd trusted her. "I'm fighting for my life, Jake. You're fighting for redemption. You want me to tell you that you were right, that I'm a liar, and that I betrayed you and your father." His jaw tensed, his gray eyes darkened. "You want me to tell you that you didn't make a mistake ten years ago. Well, I'm sorry, Jake. You're wasting your time if that's all you came to Montana for. I didn't lie. And you'll have to judge just how large a mistake you made."

Jake stared at her for a long moment, then, unsnapping his seat belt, he stalked off to the front of the plane without a word.

Clancy sat stunned, surprised by what she'd said to him, surprised even more by her raw anger. She felt the same way she had the last day of the trial when Jake had pushed himself to his feet, his gaze finding hers just before he walked out of the courtroom—and her life.

That day she'd expected him to come back. She'd been wrong. Today, she told herself she was smarter: she didn't expect him to come back for the rest of the flight. He'd said he wanted the truth, but look how he reacted to it. She cursed him for the coward he was and had worked herself up into a pretty good mad by the time he returned. She probably would have shared a few more choice words with him, but those words died on her lips when she saw what he'd brought her.

"I had the pilot pick us up a little something," he said, handing her a soda, a bologna sandwich and barbecue potato chips. Her childhood favorites; he'd remembered. "I figured you haven't had any more to eat today than I have."

All she could think to say was "Thanks." She hadn't realized just how hungry she was until that moment. She took a bite, aware of his gaze on her as he sat down with an identical lunch, just as they had a zillion times as kids.

They ate in silence, Clancy intent on her sandwich right down to the last bite. "I feel like a prisoner on death row eating my last meal."

"Clancy."

The way Jake said her name made her catch her breath. That single, simple word broke down the barriers she'd built around her heart. She could forget the past. She could forgive. If only he loved her again.

"Yes, Jake?" she asked softly, wiping the last of the bread crumbs from her lips. When he didn't answer, she glanced over at him, half hoping, half afraid.

She found his gaze soft, his eyes a rich light silver. She wasn't sure, but his expression seemed as hopeful as she knew hers must be. Did he want to believe in her? Was there a chance he could forget vengeance and remember what they'd shared before the trial and really help her?

In the length of a heartbeat, whatever she'd witnessed in his expression died. It blew out like a fledgling fire in a strong wind. "Jake." It came out a plea.

He shook his head, the moment lost, then looked past her to the plane window. "I forgot how incredible the sunsets can be in this part of the country."

Clancy turned to the scene outside, disappointed that he'd decided not to say whatever had been on his mind just then. The sunset was indeed spectacular. She couldn't remember the last time she'd seen anything so beautiful. Slivers of sunlight pierced the clouds like daggers of gold. The growing darkness dipped the peaks in deep purple while the dying sun painted the sky with a pallet of pinks.

The sight stirred something in her, giving her a feeling of strength and renewed hope. The sandwich helped, too. So did the truce, however uneasy, between them.

"I don't know what I can tell you about Dex Westfall," Clancy said after a moment. She didn't kid herself that Jake was on her side. But she needed his help. It was that simple.

"Dex planned our first meeting," she said, feeling a shudder at the memory of the bulletin board on the back of the closet. She told Jake about the day in late February when Dex came into the gallery pretending to look for the artist of a sculpture in the window.

Jake raised a brow when she told him she'd accepted a dinner date that very evening with a man who was a total stranger. She couldn't tell Jake that she'd been starved for a man in her life after Jake left her, but had never found one who even made her heart pitter, let alone patter.

"Dex was charming. He said and did all the right things." He'd swept her off her feet. At first.

But he never made her ache inside for him. Never made her deliriously happy at just the sight of him. Never made her want more. Like Jake had. Nor had his kisses ever made her feel the way nineteen-year-old Jake Hawkins's had. Nor had the kisses of any other man she'd dated.

"We dated for a few months," she said. "I never knew that much about him. He didn't like to talk about his past. All he told me was that he was raised in eastern Montana, on a farm. His parents were very poor, and once he got away from there, he'd never gone back."

"Why do you think he wanted to meet you?"

Dex had led her to believe he was as lonesome as she was. "He said he'd been looking for me all his life. At least that part was true." She grimaced at how gullible she'd been. "He told me he loved me."

"No kiddin'?"

She narrowed her gaze at Jake. "That surprises you?"

"On the contrary, in case you haven't looked in a mirror lately, you're not a bad-looking woman."

His compliment, although not eloquent by any means, warmed her nonetheless.

"What about you? Were you in love with him?" He balled up his sandwich wrapper and didn't look at her.

Did it bother Jake that she might have loved another man? Well, he needn't worry; there'd only been one love in her life, was still only one.

"I was flattered by the attention," she admitted honestly. "At first." At what point had the attention become too much?

"What made you finally write him off?" Jake asked.

She bit her lip. She'd literally written him off, and Jake had the incriminating letter in his pocket to prove it, not that the sheriff needed more evidence to convict her. "I just didn't want to see him anymore."

"So you were running from Dex when you went back to the island to live?" Jake asked.

She knew it had been more than that. Dex had frightened her in a way she couldn't even explain. But she'd also wanted to go home. She'd wanted to go back to a time when she'd felt safe. And loved. And that time had been on Hawk Island. "It felt like it was time to go home," she said.

Jake said nothing.

She'd had an uneasy feeling about Dex that she hadn't been able to throw. Now she realized she'd been right not to trust him. She felt almost a sense of relief to have her misgivings about Dex confirmed. Unfortunately, all that insight came too late. Dex was dead. And she'd be going to trial soon for his murder.

"Do you think he thought you had money?" Jake asked.

She'd considered that. "What money? I'm a struggling artist."

"Hardly," Jake said. "I've seen your work in galleries in Texas."

"I do all right, but not well enough for a man to want me for my money. And my parents lost everything after…what happened."

Jake winced. "And they blamed my father, I'm sure."

"No," she said with conviction. "They were horribly saddened by what happened to Warren." She looked over at him. "You lost your father to prison, but you can still see him. I lost both of my parents."

Jake looked away.

"The only thing I own is the lodge at the lake, thanks to Aunt Kiki," she said, then had a thought. "Unless he figured he could get his hands on Aunt Kiki's money."

Jake shook his head, seemingly happier that the conversation had returned to the case. "Kiki would have been a long shot. You're not her only heir."

She nodded, biting at her lip. "I still don't know what he wanted or why he came to Hawk Island." She looked out the window. The dying sun rimmed the mountains with gold. A deep purple filled the valleys and spilled over into the foothills. "That's why I went to Bozeman, to try and find out. Not to get that letter."

"Tell me about the night Dex showed up at the island."

She hugged herself against the memories of that night and related to Jake how Dex had called, insistent that he had to see her. She'd agreed to meet him at the café just to get it over with. Jake frowned when she told him how strangely Dex had been acting, talking about his mother, playing with that string of beads. Her legacy. "He said I was part of that legacy."

Jake's frown deepened.

She brushed her hair back from her face and took a calming breath. "I thought maybe he'd been drinking. He wasn't making any sense. Then he glanced past me into the darkness and saw something that...scared him."

"Something or *someone*?" Jake asked.

"I don't know, I turned, but whatever it was—if there was anything at all—was gone. Suddenly he became very agitated and said he had to go. He wasn't leaving the island until he got what he deserved."

"And maybe he got it," Jake said, his gaze intent on her face.

"I didn't kill him." She glanced away. At least she didn't believe in her heart that she'd killed him. "Why would I kill him in my sleep? What possible reason could I have had?"

Jake could think of a half-dozen reasons a woman might kill a man. And he figured a woman could think of at least six more without even being asleep. A woman who thought she could get away with murder because of her sleepwalking history could have any reason she wanted for killing Dex Westfall.

Well, Clancy might be able to dupe Tadd Farnsworth, who couldn't see beyond her shapely body and her aunt's money. But Jake Hawkins wasn't that easily fooled. He'd known Clancy. Maybe not as well as Dex had— Not wanting to continue with that line of thinking, he pulled a magazine out of the back of the seat in front of him and pretended interest in it he didn't feel.

After a few moments he looked over and realized the futility of his charade. Clancy was sound asleep. He stared at her beautiful face, peaceful in sleep, and wondered. Did she really sleepwalk? Did she kill Dex? Was it in her sleep?

He reached across the aisle for the manila envelope he'd tossed there earlier. He'd placed a call to the librarian while he was waiting to charter a plane. The envelope had arrived by courier shortly before his takeoff from the Kalispell airport. It contained photocopies of stories about sleepwalker murder cases. He'd been shocked by what he read on his plane ride to Bozeman.

Jake read case after case of what was known as homicidal somnambulism. One story, from medieval times, was about a woodcutter who thought he saw an intruder at the foot of his bed and, picking up an ax, killed his wife, who was asleep beside him.

The whole concept was too alien for Jake. Sleep-related violence. Out of the millions of Americans who had sleep disorders, only a small percentage became violent, picking up axes, guns or sculptures to kill while sound asleep.

He glanced over at Clancy, who was still sleeping peacefully, and tried to picture her. Her eyes would be open, her face bland. She'd be unresponsive to everything and everyone around her. In a hypnotic trance, functionally blind, the articles had said. She would pick up the sculpture, go up the stairs to the garret. Dex Westfall would be waiting for her up there. Who knew what for. And she would bludgeon him to death.

Her brain would be awake enough to allow her to do all of this while the rest of her mind would remain unconscious to everything that was happening. She would wake to find herself standing over Dex's body and be horrified at what she'd done.

Jake shook his head. How could Clancy have stayed asleep through such a violent act and then have total amnesia from the time of falling asleep until waking? It was much easier to imagine her killing her boyfriend in cold blood.

They were approaching the Kalispell airport when Clancy stirred and looked up at him wide-eyed. "I fell asleep?" She sounded horrified by the idea. "I didn't—"

"Sleepwalk?" he asked, tucking the manila envelope away. She really didn't think he bought this, did she? "No, you didn't leave your seat."

He had his own theory on Dex Westfall's murder. One he didn't like to admit, even to himself. "Dex was seeing other women, wasn't he?"

She seemed startled, and he told himself he should have felt like a louse, catching her off guard, half asleep. He didn't.

"Yes," she said quietly.

"A jury might read that as possible motive. The woman scorned. You know?"

Clancy shook her head. "It wasn't like that."

Right. "When did you find out about the other

women?" he asked, already knowing the answer and realizing how damaging it was going to be in court.

"Right before I left Bozeman, I found a note from some woman. I don't doubt there were others. The man he house-sat for mentioned Dex's other girlfriends. But I just used that as an excuse to break off the relationship. I'd been trying to break up with him for several weeks."

Jake scoured a hand over his face. He needed a long, hot shower, a shave and a few hours of uninterrupted sleep in a real bed. "A note?"

"It was from some woman Dex had met in a bar."

"Some woman he'd—" He didn't have to finish; she anticipated this one.

"Some woman he'd been…intimate with," she admitted.

Jake groaned to himself. "Where is the note now?"

She shook her head.

The note would turn up, providing the prosecution with possible motive. Couple that with the letter in his pocket. "You wrote him a letter and broke it off right after that," Jake said, not even needing confirmation.

"Yes. Dex just wouldn't take no for an answer, so I thought if I wrote it down— Now I know he was after something else."

"Tell me about Friday night, the night you found Dex in the garret."

She shifted in her seat and looked out the window again. "I left him at the café and went home a little after ten," she said mechanically. Obviously she'd already re-counted this story numerous times to the cops.

"Did you go by boat?" he asked.

"Yes." She seemed to be waiting for another question, but when none came, she continued. "I couldn't sleep. I went to my studio and worked for a while."

"Were you more angry or afraid?" Jake asked.

"What?" She sounded surprised by his question and not the least happy that he'd interrupted her again. She obviously wanted this over with as quickly as possible. "Why would you ask that?"

"I remember the year you started sculpting," he said, wishing he couldn't remember. "You used to work when you were upset."

"Both angry and afraid. I remember locking the doors. I never lock the doors at the lake."

"Then, you thought he might come over?"

"I guess I was worried that he might," she admitted.

"How do you think he got in? Did he have a key?" He felt her gaze burn his skin. "Did he come by boat or walk?"

"I didn't give him a key, if that's what you're asking." Her voice broke. "I don't know how he got there, what he was doing there, or how he got in. I don't know anything. I went to bed around midnight, exhausted. The next thing I remember is waking up to find Dex dead." She shuddered and hugged herself against the memory.

Classic homicidal somnambulism. No memory. Confusion. Horror at having done it. Right. "The murder weapon was in your hand. How do you think it got there?"

She didn't answer. Jake glanced over at her. He knew that look. He remembered it only too well as a kid. He'd stepped over the line.

"You don't believe me," she said. "You don't believe anything I tell you."

He could hear the anger in her voice. And the hurt. He just didn't expect the hurt to affect him the way it did. Damn her. He couldn't afford these feelings.

"You think I killed him?" Her face was flushed, but he had no idea whether it was from anger or something else. Like guilt.

"*You* aren't even sure you didn't kill him," he pointed out carefully. Then he went a step further, telling himself he had no choice. "It could have been a crime of passion."

"Passion?" she cried.

Jake wanted to back off. But he had to get to Clancy somehow, he had to get at the truth. "Don't tell me it didn't hurt you. The guy screwed around on you. You thought he was the man of your dreams. You were in love with him. He turned out to be a jerk. A jerk who wouldn't leave you alone."

Her eyes flashed. "You're wrong." She glanced away. "I wasn't in love with him. I just wanted him to leave me alone." She raised her gaze to Jake's. He could feel the heat of it. "How can you possibly hope to find something that proves my innocence when you believe I'm a murderer?"

Good question. And one Jake had worried about himself. He studied her for a moment. "I don't know what to believe," he said honestly. "All I know for sure is that Dex Westfall is dead and the cops think—maybe with good reason—that you did it." He flicked the torn sleeve of her navy blouse. "And all you've done is dupe me. For all I know I'll turn my back again and you'll be gone, maybe for good this time."

"You're wrong, Hawkins. And I'm going to prove it, with or without your help."

Jake looked over at her, admiring her determination if nothing else. He didn't even want to think about what Clancy had told him. Or the things she'd told him that she hadn't meant to. Dex Westfall had hurt her. He'd had other women. He'd played her for a fool from day one. And he wouldn't leave her alone. He'd even followed her to the island. And what had Clancy done about it?

Did he really believe she could kill someone? Not the girl he'd known. But what did he know about this woman? Nothing, he told himself. And he'd been in the P.I. business long enough to know that anyone could kill—given the right circumstances. And the fact that he knew Clancy had already lied at least once, didn't help her defense.

As the plane made its descent into Kalispell, Jake placed his hand over Clancy's. He came up with several good reasons for doing it. None of them had anything to do with any feelings he might have once had for her.

The night air smelled of Montana summer. It was warm with a gentle breeze that stirred Clancy's blond hair as they walked to the Mustang.

"Tell me something, Hawkins," Clancy said as he opened the passenger-side door for her. "Has there ever been a case you couldn't solve?"

"No. And this one won't be my first."

He watched her climb into the car and started to close the door, but stopped as something caught his eye. "What did you do to your ankle?"

Chapter 7

Clancy stared down at the scrape on her right ankle. Fear shot through her. "I don't know."

Jake touched his fingers to the discolored skin, tenderly, caressingly. She flinched.

"Does it hurt?" he asked, jerking back his fingers, obviously surprised by her response.

She shook her head, unable to speak. Hurt had nothing to do with her reaction to his touch. The pain of his fingers on her skin was a dull ache—far from her ankle.

"How did you get that?" he asked, frowning as he inspected the injury.

She flinched again, this time from a flash of memory. A hand coming out of the water. Grabbing her ankle. Pulling her—

"Last night," she whispered, staring out into the darkness. "On the dock when I was walking in my sleep—" She closed her eyes, trying to remember the moment when she'd awakened. It always felt like coming out of a fog with nothing ever very clear. Silver. A flicker of something silver coming out of the water. Then the hand and a sharp pain as the fingers reached out of the water and clamped around her ankle. Her eyes flew open. "He was wearing something silver on his wrist. It must have been a watch and it scraped my ankle."

Jake stared at her. "*Who* was wearing a watch?"

"The man who tried to drown me last night," she said, relieved she wasn't losing her mind. "When he grabbed my leg and pulled me into the water, his watchband must have skinned my ankle." She shivered, her relief short-lived. If it hadn't been a dream, if she wasn't crazy, then the scrape and the memory added up to something far worse. "Oh, Jake, I was right. Someone really *did* try to kill me."

Jake stared at Clancy, unsure how to respond. He realized she believed what she was saying, but the evidence was against it. If there had been someone else there last night, where had he gone? Wasn't it more likely that she'd scraped her ankle when she fell from the dock into the water? And the memory of the hand and the watch? Part of a dream. She'd said she was walking in her sleep. If a person could believe that. Jake operated on solid evidence, not even putting much stock in his hunches, no matter how right they ended up being, until he had tangible proof to go with them.

"You think I'm making this all up?" Clancy snapped. "Then, how do you explain the scrape?"

He knew sharing his explanation with her right now would do him more harm than good. "I can't." He barely got out of the way before she slammed him with the car door. He walked around to the driver's side and climbed in, wishing he could think of something to say that would cool her ire. Instead, he feared that anything he said right now would be wrong. So he kept silent, a male trait that he knew often only made her madder. But he'd risk it, he decided. It seemed the safest thing to do.

They drove with the windows down out past the lights of the city, past Christmas tree farms and tiny resorts until they were running along the shoreline of Flathead Lake.

Through the pines, Jake caught glimpses of the lake. It never failed to move him. The largest natural freshwater lake west of the Mississippi. The most beautiful. Incredibly clear by day. But by night, there was something haunting about it. Especially when the lights of the tiny communities nestled around it shimmered at its shoreline as they did now.

Jake felt a dangerous pull deep within him. A pull for this place. And the people in it. One in particular.

Out of the corner of his eye, he could see that Clancy still had a good mad going. She wouldn't even look in his direction. That was probably just as well, he thought, dragging himself back from places he couldn't afford to go.

The moment he pulled into the marina parking lot, Clancy had her door open and was halfway out of the car. "You wouldn't believe me even if you caught someone with a knife to my throat," she said, slamming the door behind her.

She was gone before he could get in a word. "Women." Jake grabbed her overnight bag out of the back and followed her down to the docks where they'd tied her boat that morning. It seemed like days ago now.

Music and the smell of fried foods filled the night air. A band at Charley's Saloon a few doors down cranked out country, while french fries sizzled in hot grease at the Burger Boat across the street. It was June, and the small resort community bustled with tourists and locals. Kids cruised the drag, honking, squealing tires, revving engines, yelling at friends. Summer on the lake. Jake felt a stab of envy, remembering when he and Clancy were kids.

Clancy was already in the boat, behind the wheel, waiting. Waiting, he realized, because he'd taken the key that morning. He grimaced. If he didn't have the key in his pocket, she'd have left him in a heartbeat.

He stopped on the dock for a moment, trying to figure out what he was going to say to her. In the distance he could make out the lights at Hawk Island Resort. They flickered on the water, beckoning him, drawing him back to the island just as Clancy had. He untied the boat and hopped in.

"It isn't that I think you're making anything up," he said, sliding into the seat next to hers. Voices carried across the water, followed by laughter. "I believe you *believe* that's what happened."

"So you think I'm…what? Crazy?" She reached impatiently for the key, obviously annoyed that he'd taken it to begin with.

"I've never walked in my sleep, but I've had some doozy dreams where I couldn't tell reality from dreamland," he said, dropping the boat key into her hand. "They scared the hell out of me, they were so real."

Her fingers closed around the key. "But this *is* real,

Jake. Someone is…after me." Her gaze shifted to the darkness beyond the shoreline. "This morning I found a place in the lilac bushes next to my kitchen window where someone had stood looking in. Someone's stalking me, just like Dex was. And I have no idea why." She flicked a look back at him. "You *do* think I'm crazy."

"No." That was the last thing he thought. "I think you're scared. And for a good reason." Someone *was* after her. Jake Hawkins. But he'd check under the lilacs. He was sure it had just been some kind of animal. "You're facing a murder rap. Anyone in your situation would be running a little scared."

Tears of frustration stung her eyes as she glared over at him, the skepticism in his tone still ringing in her ears. "You think that's all this is? I'm just running a little scared? There's a mountain of evidence that says I killed Dex Westfall. I can't sleep at night because my dreams force me to wander to places I don't want to go. Now someone is trying to kill me." She fumbled the key into the boat's ignition, her fingers trembling with anger, frustration, fear. "And you say you can understand why I'm running a *little* scared? Great, Jake. At least on top of all that you're not here to help send me to prison."

She turned the key, the motor rumbled to life, and she gave the boat full throttle, roaring out of the marina, ignoring the no-wake buoys.

They raced across the smooth, dark surface of the lake. The night air felt cool and sweet, the speed of the boat pleasurable. Jake sat silent, his face dark with a scowl that she knew meant she'd hit a nerve. It gave her some satisfaction. But she knew she'd be a fool to rely on Jake Hawkins for anything but more heartache.

She felt her anger slipping away as the early-summer night soothed her senses, the lake calming her as it always had. But nothing could chase away the fear at the edge of the darkness. Someone out there wanted her dead.

Clancy pointed the boat toward Hawk Island. The wind from the speed whipped her hair. She let it blow away her thoughts, let the steady throb of the motor lull her, promising her she had nothing to fear on such a beautiful summer night, on an island that was her home.

But as they rounded the end of the island, Clancy saw a light flickering in her lodge and knew differently. "Look!" she cried.

"What?" Jake asked, suddenly alert.

"A light in the garret. Didn't you see it?"

It was obvious he hadn't, but still, as she pulled back on the throttle, he reached over and shut off the running lights.

"Are you sure it wasn't just a reflection?" he asked.

She ground her teeth together. "It was a flashlight. Someone's in the garret."

"Don't go to the dock," Jake said. "Pull into the beach."

She did as he said, silenced by fear as she steered the boat to the nearest stretch of shoreline and cut the motor. She had seen a light. She wasn't starting to imagine things as Jake kept insinuating.

As they reached land, Jake jumped out and pulled the boat up on shore. Clouds hid the moon, pitching the narrow stretch of beach into darkness. Jake tied the boat to one of the pines that grew almost to the water's edge. "I'm not leaving you here alone," Jake whispered as he gave her a hand out of the boat. "Stay behind me, and if anything happens, get to cover."

Clancy followed Jake along the beach, hugging the rocky cliffs and the pines, her anger at him dissipating quickly. What would she have done if she'd come home alone? She'd sworn she wasn't going to rely on Jake, but right now she'd make an exception.

Water lapped at the shore as they crossed behind Jake's lodge. The light in the garret room had flickered like a firefly caught in a jar. What was someone doing in that room, the room where Dex had died? She felt a chill, although the summer night was exceptionally warm.

They were almost to her lodge when an owl let out a hoot. Clancy jumped, grabbing Jake's arm. He patiently unhooked her clawlike grip and motioned for her to stay low behind him.

They crept the last few yards in silence. Darkness draped the back of the lodge. Clancy held her breath as they climbed the steps and crossed the old wooden porch. The boards groaned under their weight.

"Is that your bike?" Jake whispered, motioning to the black mountain bike by the back door.

She nodded.

Jake tried the door. Locked. Clancy shook her head; she hadn't locked it. She could remember locking it only once in her life. And that night it hadn't kept Dex out, had it?

As she stood on tiptoe to reach above the door for the key, Jake groaned next to her. "Great place for a key. No one would ever look *there*."

Feeling Jake's reproachful gaze on her, she quietly slipped it into his waiting fingers and pressed against his back as he inserted the key in the lock. If he thought for a moment she was going to let him out of her sight, he was sadly mistaken. As she clung to him, she felt something hard. A gun.

The door creaked open. Jake drew the gun. Her heart dropped to her knees as she realized the danger she was putting him in.

"No," she whispered. He stopped and she collided with his back.

"What?"

"I don't want you getting killed because of me."

"How thoughtful of you. Now, shut up."

He turned and started across the kitchen floor, with her right behind him. Something thudded, and Clancy let out a squeal before she realized the sound had just been Jake crashing into her microwave cart.

"Quiet!"

"Jake," she pleaded, suddenly more afraid for him than herself.

"Stay right behind me," he commanded as he headed up the stairs. "And be quiet."

Clancy held her breath, afraid to breathe, as they started up the stairs. She followed, her heart in her throat, her hand gripping a handful of Jake's shirt. They were almost to the top when she looked back. She let go of Jake. The front door stood partway open. Starlight slipped through the crack and splattered onto the living-room floor. Clancy reached for Jake but he was several steps ahead of her. A shadow moved into the light.

"Jake." It came out little more than a whisper.

The shadow turned into a dark figure in a hooded sweatshirt. It looked up at her. A startled, pained cry escaped her lips. She caught only a glimpse of the face beneath the hood. But it was enough. Clancy screamed.

The figure disappeared out the open door and into the darkness as quickly as it had appeared.

Clancy dropped to the stair, her gaze locked on the wedge of light still spilling in from the night.

"Clancy!" Jake cried, charging down the stairs to her. "What is it?"

She heard him groping for the light switch but couldn't answer him. Instead, she stared after the intruder, too stunned to speak.

The living room was suddenly flooded with light.

"Are you all right?" Jake demanded, pulling her to her feet on the stairs. She fell into his arms. He held her tightly. "What happened?"

She stared over Jake's shoulder, her gaze fixed on the open doorway and the darkness beyond it. "I saw him."

"Who, Clancy?" Jake asked, pulling back to search her face.

She looked up. "Didn't you see him?" she asked, knowing he couldn't have. Pleading with him to say he had.

"Who did you see, Clancy?"

Her mouth opened but no words came out. She closed her eyes, willing away the image of the man in the dark hooded sweatshirt. "It was Dex Westfall. He's alive!"

Chapter 8

Jake grabbed Clancy's shoulders and pulled her around to face him. "You saw Dex Westfall?" he demanded. He watched doubt flicker across her face. Worry settled in his stomach like a chunk of granite.

She tried to avoid his gaze. "I only got a glimpse so I can't be completely sure—"

"Clancy?" Jake asked, pleading.

She swallowed. Tears brimmed in her eyes. "It was Dex. I swear. It was Dex."

His grip tightened. "The *late* Dex Westfall?" He felt her flinch and let go of her, realizing he was hurting her. He led her down the stairs. The front door stood open.

"I know it sounds...crazy." She seemed to hesitate. "How could I have seen him when he's dead? I didn't get a really good look at him. He was wearing a dark gray hood that hid part of his face, but—" Her gaze flipped up to his, her eyes full of pleading. "It was him, Jake."

That rock of worry in his belly turned into a fifty-pound boulder. He went out on the deck and looked down the beach. Empty. He came back in and had barely closed the door when the breeze blew it open again, making them both jump. This time Jake closed the door and locked it.

"I know what you're thinking," she said, her voice barely a whisper.

Jake doubted she had any idea what he was thinking. He wasn't even sure himself.

"But I know what I saw," she said, the look in her eyes scaring the devil out of him. "It was Dex Westfall."

The cynical private eye side of him argued that Dex Westfall was dead; Clancy couldn't have seen him. She'd probably imagined it, or dreamed it, or she'd gone off the deep end.

But the man who'd fallen for her years ago made a good case that Clancy Jones had been one of the most rational, sensible and credible people he'd ever known. She might be a murderer, but he had his doubts that she was crazy.

"I'm telling you, Dex is alive," she cried. "Don't you see what this means? I didn't kill him."

Jake didn't want to burst her bubble, but it was time for a reality check. "If Dex isn't dead, then whose body did the sheriff find upstairs?"

Clancy blinked. Her face fell. She turned away from him to stare out the window. "I don't know. And no matter whose body it is, the sheriff thinks I killed him, right?"

That about sized it up. Jake knew how desperately

Clancy wanted to believe she hadn't killed anyone. But the bottom line was someone had died in the garret upstairs and Clancy had had the murder weapon in her hand.

"If Dex is dead…" Her eyes turned dark with pain, her features drawn with fatigue. "Then his ghost has come back from the grave for me."

Jake glanced toward the darkness outside, his mind flashing on an image that freeze-dried his blood. The face of the woman his father had gone to prison for murdering. What if Lola Strickland's pretty face suddenly appeared outside his window one night? He shuddered at the thought. And reminded himself that no one came back from the grave. Not Lola. Not Dex.

He turned to lean with his back against the window, the last of the adrenaline ebbing. His body felt tired, his mind exhausted, as he settled his gaze on Clancy. Had someone been in the lodge tonight or had Clancy just imagined it? Like the person who'd tried to drown her last night?

"You first saw the light in the garret?" Jake asked after a moment. All he wanted to do was sit down, close his eyes, catch a few winks. He was too tired to think, too tired to try to figure out anything tonight. With effort, however, he pushed himself off the wall. "I'm going upstairs to take a look around. Why don't you—"

"I'm coming with you."

He looked at her, surprised she would willingly go back to the scene of the crime. "Look, I'm not wild about going up there. If I were in your shoes—"

"I'm coming with you," she repeated.

He nodded, recognizing that old familiar glint of persistence shining like a searchlight in her eyes and the stubborn way she stood when she wasn't about to budge an inch.

"There's nothing up there but old furniture," Clancy said as he led the way up the stairs to the third floor.

Old furniture. And bad memories.

The tiny room was indeed filled with furniture, Jake saw as he turned on the light and stepped through the open doorway. The single overhead light did little to illuminate the room. Shadows pooled everywhere. With the furniture covered in white sheets, the room had a ghostlike quality. Or maybe it was just the fact that Clancy believed Dex Westfall had come back from the dead that made it seem that way. It was enough to spook even nonbelievers, Jake thought.

The only bare piece of furniture was a couch in the corner under the eaves. The sheriff's department had obviously stripped it, taking the blood-stained sheet and cushion as evidence, but left behind the couch.

"I'm not sure this is a good idea," Jake said, turning to shield Clancy from the view.

"I have to do this," she said, her tone brooking no argument. "Besides, I'm the only one who knows if something is out of place up here."

He nodded and stepped out of her way. As he watched her walk into the room he thought to himself: here is a woman to be reckoned with.

With all the courage she had, Clancy looked toward the couch where she'd found the body. Her fingers flew to her lips to stifle the cry that rose from deep within her. Memories of that night flashed before her, flickering images of horror. She staggered. Jake reached for her.

She motioned him away. "I'm fine," she said, knowing that if he touched her now it would be her undoing. She hugged herself to still the trembling, her gaze scanning the room, trying to remember every detail.

Before the night of the murder, she couldn't remember the last time she was in this room. How could she know if something was missing? On top of that, Kiki had hired a cleaning crew after the sheriff's department finished taking prints and collecting evidence.

Clancy stared at the garret. Bits and pieces of memory floated back from Friday night.

Dex— Her gaze leaped back to the couch. It had been Dex, hadn't it? Something had made her think it was, but what? The bright red cowboy boots. The moment she saw them she'd known it was Dex because of those stupid boots he loved. But had she really looked that closely at his face? All that blood— She shook her head, frustrated at her inability to remember any more.

As she walked around the room, she quickly realized it was impossible to tell if an intruder had been here. But how desperately she would have liked to prove he had.

She pushed open the balcony doors and stepped out, immediately assaulted by a memory. She gripped the railing. "Oh."

"What?" Jake asked, joining her.

She shuddered as she stared out at the lake. "Friday night," she said as it came back to her. "I remember waking up on this balcony." She glanced down; her head spun just looking at the dizzying drop to the rocky beach below her. "What was I doing out here?"

Jake followed her gaze from the rocky beach below to the lake, sprawled to the horizon, a dark, silent pool, its slick, silken surface a reflection of the star-splattered sky overhead. He had no idea what Clancy had been doing out here. No idea what she had been doing in the tiny room beyond them just moments before Dex Westfall died. God, how he wished he did.

"I remember standing here not knowing where I was at first," she said. "The view was all wrong."

"What do you mean 'all wrong'?"

"I thought I was on my bedroom balcony." But it was next to her studio and at the east end of the lodge. She couldn't see this bay from it.

Turning slowly, she moved back through the open doorway as if she were still sleepwalking. "At first all I saw was the furniture. The white sheets were blowing in the breeze from the open doors and I realized I was in the garret."

Jake followed her, watching her face as she relived the night of the murder. She stopped, her gaze going to the couch. "Then I saw him in the corner." She looked down at her left hand. "I guess that's when I realized I had the sculpture in my hand. I dropped it on the floor. My feet—"

"What was wrong with your feet?" Jake asked.

"I must have been to the beach, because the tops of my bare feet still had sand on them." All of the shore around Flathead Lake consisted of small flat rocks—no sand. But Hawk Island had sandy beaches.

"What the hell were you doing on the beach at two-thirty in the morning?" he demanded, then shook his head. "I forgot. Sleepwalking."

If she heard the doubt in his tone, she didn't respond to it. "Dex's boots had sand on them, too."

"Maybe he followed you up here." An unpleasant thought skittered past. "Or maybe you'd been on the beach together."

She stared at the stained arm of the couch as if there were things there she could see that he couldn't. From the horrified expression on her face, he was damned glad he couldn't see them.

"Where had I been that night?" Clancy asked, shifting her gaze to Jake. "I hadn't sleepwalked in years."

Not since the night of the resort fire, Jake thought bitterly. The night Clancy saw his father kill Lola Strickland. Or at least that's what Clancy would have him believe.

"Why would I suddenly start sleepwalking again after so many years?"

Jake wished he knew. He wished he could believe she sleepwalked at all. "What's the last thing you remember before you fell asleep?"

"I had been working late in my studio. I have, or I guess, that's *had* now, a show planned in August at a gallery in Bigfork. I was finishing up one of the pieces for the exhibit. As I headed up to bed, I couldn't help thinking about Dex, worrying about why he'd shown up here." She let out a long sigh. "That's the last I remember."

"Did Dex wear underwear?" Jake asked.

"What?"

"He wasn't wearing underwear the night he was murdered. Is that usual?"

"I would have no idea," Clancy said, turning away. "I didn't— I'm sure he wore underwear, but the subject never came up."

Jake smiled to himself, more pleased to hear that she had no idea than he should have been. "Unless I miss my guess, someone interrupted Dex that night, either from his beauty sleep or some other unclothed activity. He pulled on his jeans in a hurry and headed for your place."

"Who? Why?" Clancy asked.

"That's what we have to find out."

Framed in the balcony doorway, her hair shone golden, her face a pale porcelain. It surprised him just how beautiful she looked standing there. How small and fragile. And so terribly defenseless. Protecting her seemed as natural as breathing and had ever since they were kids. He felt a pull so strong, the force threatened to draw him to her against his will.

"I think we'd better get some rest," Jake said, stepping past her to close the balcony doors. He could smell her scent as he passed. It made him weak. He took a deep breath of the night air and closed the doors. When he turned, he found Clancy standing at the top of the landing, staring down the stairs.

"I'll stay here in the lodge with you tonight," he said, surprising himself even more than her. "If that's all right with you," he added. "I need a good night's sleep, and that boat of yours isn't all that comfortable."

"You think I'm going to run off, Hawkins?" she asked, too tired to let his lack of trust do more than give her heart a twinge. The memory of Jake lying in the bottom of her boat, however, did offset the twinge some.

"I thought you could use some company," he said softly.

She studied his handsome features, trying to read motive in those bottomless gray eyes. The thought of staying alone tonight frightened her more than she wanted to admit. But was he suggesting staying here to watch over her? Or to keep her from jumping bail again? Did it even matter?

"I thought you didn't believe in ghosts," she said, reading nothing but concern in his eyes.

"I don't," he said. "Nor do I believe in taking chances until we know just what we're up against."

We're up against? Just hours ago, she'd warned herself not to rely on Jake Hawkins. But right now his words sounded better than a hot shower. After everything they'd been through today, couldn't she let herself rely on him for just one night? This whole day had made her realize what an incredibly strong, caring man Jake Hawkins was, just like the boy he'd been that she'd always loved so much. Only, she wasn't a girl anymore and he wasn't a boy. "You can take the spare bedroom. The sheets are in the hall closet. You know where that is."

He nodded. "Same place as my lodge."

He followed her down the stairs to the kitchen and, opening the refrigerator, pulled out two cold beers. He twisted the cap off one and handed it to her.

She took a sip, surprised at how good it tasted. "You don't believe Dex is alive and that he might be the one trying to kill me?"

His gaze, as warm and gentle as the summer night outside, brushed over her face. The kindness in his eyes made her want to cry. Slowly he twisted off the cap on his own beer. "The cops would know if it wasn't Dex's body," he said reasonably.

"Yeah, I guess so." She took a long draw on the beer. It tasted good. She leaned against the wall and closed her eyes. The beer made her drowsy.

"Why don't you go take a long, hot shower," Jake suggested. "I'll make sure everything's locked up for the night. Leave your door open."

"Thanks." She opened her eyes. His unruly sandy blond hair hung down on his forehead; the blond stubble at his jaw gave him a rugged, almost dangerous look that she found disarming. And appealing. Suddenly there seemed a million things she wanted to say to him, but she couldn't seem to sort them out. Nor did she trust her emotions. Not tonight. Maybe she'd tell him how much she appreciated him being here. Tomorrow. When she wasn't feeling so vulnerable. Or so tired. "Good night." She set her bottle on the table and turned to head for the stairs.

As she passed the telephone she noticed that the message light on the answering machine was flashing.

Clancy stepped over to it, hit rewind, then play. "Clancy?" Tadd Farnsworth's voice filled the room. "I didn't want to leave this on your machine, but I haven't been able to reach you and I wanted to be the one to tell you. The sheriff's having trouble getting a positive ID on the body you found in your garret. All he knows for sure is that the guy's name wasn't Dex Westfall. Dex Westfall never existed. At least not until five months ago."

Chapter 9

The color drained from Clancy's face. Jake watched her strength and sanity empty with it. He knew only too well what it was like having his world crumble under him, no longer sure what to believe, who to believe. Wasn't this what he'd wanted for Clancy? In that dark, malevolent part of his heart, hadn't he longed for her to suffer the way he had? And now she knew what it was like to have her life destroyed overnight. So why did he feel like dirt?

He watched Clancy try to dial Tadd's number. On her second attempt, Jake took the phone from her trembling hand and hung it up.

"I don't understand," she said, her voice breaking.

Jake understood. It was just as he'd suspected. The brand new clothes. The leased car. The new-subdivision feel. No roots. No Dex Westfall.

He also knew that if the sheriff didn't get a positive ID in the first twenty-four hours, it could take a while to put a name to their John Doe—if they ever did. Clancy might never know who died in her garret. Nor why the man had stalked her.

"I have to call Tadd," she said.

Jake shook his head. "You have to take a hot shower. I'll call Tadd. I'll come up when I'm through."

Clancy nodded, looking shell-shocked and terribly vulnerable. She stumbled toward him.

He felt a rush of tenderness for her. He pulled her into his arms, aware of her soft fullness, her wonderful warmth, her need so like his own. She raised her gaze to his, her eyes as dark as her lashes. The look in those eyes—

Without thinking, he dropped his mouth to hers, hungry to taste her, hungry to feel her body molded to his. He knew her kiss would taste of sunshine and summer. Her arms would offer comfort and sanctuary. That's what he needed tonight. That's all he needed.

But when his lips met hers, there was nothing safe or comforting about it. The kiss fired his blood, sending desire streaking through his veins at the speed of a grass fire. He became a part of the blaze, losing himself in the heat and the hurry. Losing himself in her. The realization burned to the bottom of his black heart.

With a silent curse, he pushed her away. "Go take your shower. I'll be up in a moment, to tell you what Tadd says."

She stood just looking at him. He felt like the bastard he was. But he'd better get used to it. He would see a lot more hurt in those brown eyes before he was through with her. When she turned and ran up the stairs, he had to kick down the urge to go after her. He slammed his fist against the wall and cursed Clancy for the love he'd seen in her eyes. It changed nothing between them.

He waited until he heard the water running upstairs before he dialed Tadd's home number. It was answered on the second ring.

"Where's Clancy?" Tadd demanded.

"Here, at her lodge," Jake said. "What's this about Westfall?"

"Fake ID, nothing matches up, not his name, social security number or prints," Tadd said.

No prints on file? Then he'd never been in the armed services or in trouble with the law, Jake figured.

"The sheriff's sent out flyers to all law enforcement agencies across Montana and the Northwest. Maybe someone will recognize him."

"Clancy told me he grew up in eastern Montana, poor farming family. There might be some truth to it," Jake said. He'd found that people who lied often mixed in a little truth with their lies, just enough to hang themselves. He wondered if that was the case with Clancy. Would her lie about his father get her hung?

"I'll see that fliers get sent to the smaller towns back there," Tadd said.

"Anything new?" Jake needed to find out if Tadd had heard about Clancy's little trip to Bozeman.

"It looks like we might be dealing with some kind of nutcase." Tadd let out a long sigh. "The police in Bozeman found a closet wall full of background material on Clancy, including all that old stuff about your father's trial and Lola Strickland's murder. The landlady said Dex's sister had been there, paid his rent. Funny, but the sister's description sounded almost familiar." Bingo. "I thought Kiki hired you to keep Clancy in line."

"No," Jake said, his jaw tightening. "Kiki hired me to try to prove that Clancy didn't kill Dex Westfall—or whoever the hell he was."

Tadd didn't say anything for a moment. "How's Clancy holding up?"

"How do you think?" Jake snapped miserably. He hesitated, some old loyalty making him want to protect her. "Clancy thought someone was in the garret tonight."

"Someone broke into the lodge?" Tadd asked.

"Not exactly." Did he really believe there'd been anyone there earlier, especially someone who looked like Dex? "No sign of a break-in." In fact, the lodge had been locked, something Clancy said she hadn't done. Jake figured she'd just forgotten she'd locked it. Except for the front door, which had probably blown open.

"Was anything taken?" Tadd asked, sounding confused.

"We haven't searched the whole house, but it doesn't look like he was your run-of-the-mill burglar. There're valuables sitting all over and they weren't touched." Jake assured himself he owed Clancy nothing but grief for what she'd done to him. Clancy's lawyer needed to know about everything, even if Jake didn't like the guy. "She swears the man she saw in the house was Dex Westfall."

"Right," Tadd said. He laughed, then must have realized Jake wasn't joking. "You aren't serious?"

"Dead serious."

"Come on, we might not know who he is, but we do know he's not up and walking around."

"At least some guy isn't up and walking around." Jake pulled off his baseball cap and raked a hand through his hair. He felt one of his bad feelings doing a little polka at the back of his neck. "Could you send me copies of that stuff tacked up on the guy's closet wall and one of those fliers?"

Obviously following Jake's line of thinking, Tadd let out an oath. "The guy she knew as Dex Westfall is dead. Clancy IDed him the night of the murder. He was her damned boyfriend. Don't try to tell me that maybe her boyfriend's alive and we have someone else on the slab in the morgue."

"Then it can't hurt for her to take another look."

Tadd groaned. "I'll get you a flier," he said, not sounding the least bit pleased. "Just try to keep her in the county in the meantime." He hung up.

Jake stood at the living-room window, staring out at the lake. He liked the quiet and the darkness. And the lake had always given him a sense of peace. Tonight it made him restless. Was the guy Clancy had known as Dex Westfall still out there? Or was it just Clancy's guilt making her see him everywhere she turned?

Long after he heard the shower stop running, Jake couldn't bring himself to go upstairs. His body felt leaden with fatigue. But the truth was, he didn't trust himself around Clancy tonight. It would be too easy to take her in his arms. Too easy to let her get to him. He felt a need for warmth tonight, and he'd seen the same need in Clancy's eyes. Along with love. It was the love that kept him from going upstairs.

He sat, put his head on the kitchen table and shut his mind to that kind of thinking. He thought of the past, letting the bitterness swell inside him.

* * *

The hot shower did little to soothe Clancy. Her body ached with a need like none she'd ever known. She'd seen that same need in Jake's eyes. So why had he pushed her away? Because he wasn't about to make love to a woman he thought a liar? And a murderer?

And yet she came out of the bathroom half expecting to find Jake sitting on the edge of her bed, waiting for her. Half hoping. She reminded herself how much it had hurt when he'd walked away from her all those years ago. When would she ever learn?

She went to her dresser and, slipping off the silk robe, drew a long cotton nightgown over her head. She couldn't trust her heart to Jake Hawkins ever again, but nor could she seem to stop it or her body from aching for him. She lay on the bed, staring up at the ceiling, wishing there was some way she could prove to him she wasn't the woman he believed her to be. If only there were some way to show him that she would never have betrayed their love. Never.

She closed her eyes, too exhausted to worry about the goblins that waited for her on the edge of sleep.

Jake jerked around at the sound of soft footfalls behind him. For a heart-stopping instant, all he saw was a ghost—a figure shrouded in white coming from the kitchen. "Clancy?" He hadn't heard her come downstairs, hadn't heard her come into the kitchen, and he realized he'd fallen asleep at the table.

She looked up but didn't seem surprised to find him sitting alone in the dark. As she stepped into the shaft of light that spilled down the stairs, he caught his breath. She looked so beautiful, her face shiny and squeaky clean from her shower, her blond hair still damp and dark, lying in tendrils against her cheek. The long white nightgown cupped her full breasts and floated around her slim ankles. His gaze fell on her inviting curves for a moment, then flicked down to her feet and the floor behind her. She was leaving sandy tracks on the hardwood floor.

"What were you doing outside?" Jake asked, his pulse suddenly thundering in his ears.

Her gaze shifted to him and he looked into her eyes. An icy wind wrapped around his neck like the hands of an assassin. "Clancy?" She didn't answer. She stared past him, through him. Then slowly she turned and headed up the stairs.

He hadn't believed her story about walking in her sleep. He still wasn't sure he did. He hurried after her, not knowing what he planned to do.

He found Clancy curled in the middle of her bed, her eyes closed, her breathing soft and rhythmic. As he stepped closer, he could see the sand still on her bare feet. She'd been outside on the beach. Doing what? He cursed himself. He'd have to keep a closer eye on her.

As he started to pull one corner of the comforter over her, he noticed her right hand balled tightly into a fist. It was the sand between her fingers that drew his attention.

Carefully, he touched her hand, expecting her to wake. She moaned softly in her sleep and her fingers opened like a flower to the sun. In her palm lay a single blue bead.

The sun came up, filling the room with golden sunshine and warmth. Jake woke, sprawled in a chair at the foot of Clancy's bed. He sat up slowly, his body stiff and sore. What he wouldn't give for a good night's sleep in a real bed. He'd opted for the chair, pulling it over in front of the doorway, because he didn't want to leave her alone again, even for a moment. He'd hoped the morning light would bring him some peace. Instead, he woke with the same haunting questions he'd gone to sleep with.

He studied Clancy's face. She looked so tranquil, he envied her restful sleep. His dreams had been filled with dark shadows lurking at the edge of his subconscious. He'd awakened at the slightest sound, a creak of a floorboard, the cry of an owl outside the window.

He couldn't shake the memory of Clancy sleepwalking. He'd never seen anyone do that before. It was weird. And spooky. He could understand why it frightened her so. He couldn't imagine waking up and finding sand on his feet and realizing he'd been somewhere and had no memory of leaving his bed. And yet a part of him was still skeptical, even though he'd seen it with his own eyes. Hadn't he?

He tiptoed out of the room and down the hall, anxious to get a hot shower, a shave and a change of clothes before Clancy woke.

He was dressed in jeans, toweling his hair dry, when she stuck her head into his bedroom doorway.

"Good morning," she said, and smiled tentatively. She wore jeans and a blue shirt the color of a summer sky. Her hair was pulled back with a ribbon, and there was a freshness about her, as if the sunshine coming through her window had renewed her spirit.

"How did you sleep?" he asked, tossing aside the towel to pull on a fresh shirt.

"Great. For a change." Her smile faltered. "Did you call Tadd? The last thing I remember, you were going to come up and tell me what he had to say. I must have fallen asleep."

"You were sacked out by the time I came up," he said truthfully. "I didn't have the heart to wake you."

He ran a hand through his hair, studying her. She didn't seem to remember her little jaunt on the beach last night. Or maybe she was waiting for him to say something. Not a chance.

Last night he'd pocketed the bead, brushed the sand from her bed and covered her with the comforter. At the time, he'd wanted to protect her. But this morning, his suspicious mind wasn't ready to accept her sleepwalking. Not yet. If she'd staged it for his benefit, she'd made a fatal error. He suspected she no more sleepwalked than he did. And if he could prove it, he'd have her right where he wanted her. That kind of thinking made him feel more in control than remembering the way her lips had felt on his.

"Why don't I fill you in over breakfast." He smiled at her, noticing with regret that she'd resurrected the wall between them, her defenses safely back in place.

He told himself he should have taken advantage of the situation last night. What had made him think he might be vulnerable to her, a woman who'd betrayed him and still refused to admit that she'd perjured herself? He could have made love to her last night and maybe gotten to her and the truth. He promised himself he wouldn't pass up the opportunity if it presented itself again. *When* it presented itself again.

"What exactly did you say you were making us for breakfast?" he asked as he followed her down the stairs. He told himself sleeping with her would be a means to an end. Nothing more. And that the only reason he found himself looking forward to it, was because it would mean getting this case over with and returning to Texas.

Clancy busied herself in the kitchen while Jake made a small fire in the woodstove to take the chill off the room. The sun hadn't reached that side of the lodge yet, and even though it was summer, it was still cool in the morning. As she listened to him whistling to himself as he stacked kindling in the stove, her heart cried out for the old Jake. Was there any of him left in this hard-nosed cynical private investigator?

"Buttermilk pancakes, my favorite," Jake said, taking a sniff over her shoulder. "Not with huckleberry syrup?"

She smiled at the pleading in his voice. "Of course."

He rolled his eyes toward heaven. "I may never leave here."

Clancy knew that wasn't true. She'd felt an urgency in him to get what he wanted from her and get out quickly. She wondered what would happen when he didn't succeed?

They ate in silence, Clancy watching in amusement as Jake scraped up the last of the syrup and pancake from his plate before pushing it away with a satisfied sigh. He'd always loved her pancakes.

"Fantastic," he said, giving her a smile that warmed her more than the sun now beginning to shine in through the kitchen window. The smile faded as his gaze met hers.

She knew what was coming. "Can I get you more pancakes?" she asked as she stood. She didn't want to think about Dex Westfall or the upcoming trial or who she thought she'd seen on the deck last night. In the light of day, she wanted to believe she'd been mistaken about the face looking anything like the man she'd known. She feared she was losing her mind; she didn't want Jake to tell her those fears were well founded. "It won't take but a moment to fry up a couple more."

"Clancy." He took her hand and pulled her back to the table. "We have to talk about it."

Resigned, she sat.

He filled her in quickly about the phony name and social security number. "Whoever he was, he was carrying a fake ID that said he was Dex Westfall."

"But no Dex Westfall ever existed." She wasn't surprised after finding out that he'd lied about the condo, lied about everything as far as she knew. "Then, who was the man—"

"The sheriff should know in a few days, and maybe then we'll know what he wanted with you. I asked Tadd to send us the flier they're distributing. That way—"

"I'll know if the dead man is at least who I thought was Dex Westfall," she finished for him.

"Exactly. Meanwhile, we have work to do."

Work sounded good. She needed to do something. And the thought of doing it with Jake definitely had appeal. Especially since, as he'd said, she was running a little scared.

"I need to interview the two witnesses who overheard your conversation with Dex that night at the café," Jake said. "I was hoping you could tell me what you remember."

She leaned over her coffee cup and stared down into the black liquid.

"Tell me everything, no matter how trivial it seems," Jake instructed.

She nodded, remembering the summer night air, still remembering the sickening fried smells coming from the café. "Someone had been in the café working, cleaning the grill, I think. The air smelled of old grease. But the café was closed. There weren't any customers around. Dex was sitting at one of the tables on the deck. It was fairly dark."

"You're doing great," Jake encouraged her.

She drew a breath, letting it all come back. She told Jake again about the necklace, the legacy from Dex's mother, and how he had said Clancy was part of that legacy.

"What kind of necklace was this?" Jake asked.

Clancy looked up to find him watching her closely. "It was a string of beads like the hippies used to make and wear." She blinked. "Jake, how could there have been two witnesses who overheard the conversation? There wasn't anyone around."

"What about the person cleaning the grill?"

"Whoever was in the café couldn't have overheard us. We were sitting too far away."

"Did Dex give you any indication as to why he wanted to meet you?" Jake asked.

"No. I got the impression he had something he wanted to talk about, but whatever he'd seen in the darkness changed his mind." Clancy took a sip of the now-cool coffee. It tasted as bitter as the memory of Dex.

"What color was this string of beads?" Jake asked.

She looked up, surprised by his question. "Pale blue, with a tiny dark blue ceramic heart hanging from the center. Why?"

He shrugged. "Just wondering." He got up to take the dishes to the sink.

"The strange thing about the necklace was that I thought I'd seen it before," Clancy said, joining him. She shrugged and looked over to see Jake watching her.

"I'm sure it doesn't matter. I just remembered something else. The clasp was broken."

"You think the beads are important in some way?" he asked.

"Maybe. The other night—" she picked up the dishrag, avoiding Jake's gaze "—I walked in my sleep again. When I woke up, I had one of the beads in my hand. I don't know where I found it. I just have a feeling that finding the rest of the beads might be a clue as to where Dex went that night."

Jake took the dishrag from her. He still didn't believe she walked in her sleep, she realized. She felt a hefty jolt of irritation. Why had she bothered to tell him?

"I'd like you to come with me to the resort," Jake said after a moment. "You'll have to wait in the boat while I talk to the witnesses."

Clancy told herself she shouldn't be hurt and angry at his lack of trust in her. "Let me see if I understand this: you'd like me to tag along so you can keep an eye on me, but stay out of the way so I don't hurt my case," she said, summing it up quite nicely, if she said so herself.

"I just don't want you staying alone. Or I could call your aunt Kiki to come over from her condo in Bigfork—"

"Don't even joke, Hawkins," she said. "Of course I want to tag along with you."

She didn't tell him that she had no intention of sitting by casually while he did all the investigating. Her life was at stake, and she had a couple of things she wanted to check out on her own.

He shoved back his Astros cap and grinned, probably thinking he'd won. That it was his favorite hat was no secret to her. It looked as if it was the first thing he put on in the morning and the last to be discarded at night,

and had been for years. The bill was stained and faded
from the elements. The once-white *H* had bled into the
once-bright red star. Even the cloth-covered button on
top was missing.

When she came back from brushing her teeth, she
found him outside by the lilac bushes, hunkered down
at the edge of the window. "Did you find anything?"
she asked.

He shook his head as he straightened. She tried to
hide her disappointment as she turned and headed toward the dock.

"How did you get into the private investigating business?" Clancy asked when they reached the boat.

"You want to drive?" Jake asked, holding up the key.

She gritted her teeth, reminded that every time they
stopped anywhere he'd taken the key for safekeeping.
"Why don't you drive," she said as sweetly as she could
muster. "*You* have the key."

He either ignored her sarcasm or missed it. But something told her he hadn't missed it.

"When I first moved to Galveston I met this old
private eye who fished off the same pier I did," Jake
said as he pulled the boat away from the dock. "We became good friends. He taught me everything he knew
about people and secrets." Jake pointed the boat out of
the bay. "'Everyone has a secret,' he used to say. 'All
that separates murderers from ordinary people is that
they have secrets they'd kill to keep.'" They rounded
the end of the island, the sky as clear blue as the water
was green. "He used to say I was a natural private eye.
Cynical and determined. If someone has a secret, I'll
find out what it is. Or die trying."

She felt his gaze on her and wished she hadn't asked.

Chapter 10

To Jake's surprise, Hawk Island Resort looked much as it had when he and Clancy were kids. The store and café had been rebuilt on the same spot overlooking the marina. A row of six original cabins that hadn't burned still stood in the pines off to the right. Jake felt a rush of nostalgia, followed by nausea. There were too many memories here. Just as at his family's lodge.

Although it was early in the season, a few boats had already been moored in the bay when Jake eased into a slip at the docks. The air smelled of motor oil, gas and fish. "You want to wait here or at the café?" Jake asked.

"I'll stay here and catch some rays."

Clancy leaned back into the seat and closed her eyes. He studied her for a moment, wondering if it was safe to leave her alone. "I want to be able to see you at all times, Clancy. So I know you're all right." Then, feeling like the louse he was, he pulled and pocketed the boat key. Her eyes flickered open; he didn't like the look she gave him.

"I won't be long," he said, unable to think of anything to say in his defense. She mumbled something he figured he didn't want to hear, anyway, and headed up the pier.

At the outdoor sinks, a man cleaned fish from the full stringer of lake trout he'd caught. Jake was surprised when he saw who it was.

"Nice catch," Jake said, extending his hand to the man. "How have you been, Johnny?"

Johnny Branson looked up from his work. A smile crinkled his leathery face as he wiped his hand on his pants and took Jake's hand in his. "Jake Hawkins. I'd heard you were back."

Johnny was a large man with a full head of graying hair. He'd always reminded Jake of a Newfoundland puppy. Friendly. Loyal. And a little gangly. The former sheriff looked as though he'd lost some weight since Jake had last seen him. Johnny had been best friends with Jake's and Clancy's fathers since grade school. It had been Johnny who'd had to make the arrest and take Warren to jail. The strain of the trial had shown on Johnny, but the years since hadn't seemed to have been kind to him, either.

"I heard you retired right after the trial," Jake said.

Johnny nodded as he went back to cleaning his fish. "I'm a fishing guide now," he said, holding up a twenty-pound trout. "It suits me."

"Looks like business must be good," Jake said, not sure how to broach the subject on his mind. "I was hoping to talk to you while I'm back on the island. About my father's case."

Johnny didn't look up. "After ten years, can't be that much to say anymore, can there?"

He figured Johnny didn't want to drag up any of that old misery any more than he did. Johnny had taken his friend's conviction particularly hard.

"I was hoping you might be able to answer some questions I still have."

"That what brings you back?" Johnny asked, squinting past Jake to where Clancy waited in the boat. Idly, he rubbed the blade of his fish-gutting knife across one thumb pad.

"That and this mess with Clancy," Jake answered honestly. "I need to know if you thought my father was guilty."

"The jury thought Warren was, that's what mattered," Johnny said, cutting a clean slit up the fish's belly.

"I need to know what you thought. What you still think," Jake said. "Was justice served?"

"Life dispenses its own form of justice," he said as he ripped the guts from the large lake trout.

Jake shook his head. "I became a private investigator to ensure that justice gets done once in a while on earth. I'm too impatient to wait and let God set the record straight at the pearly gates." He met the man's gaze. "Just tell me if you think my father was an embezzler, murderer and arsonist."

Johnny chewed at his cheek for a moment as he looked out at the lake. "Sometimes people do things out of desperation, out of a feeling of helplessness and unhappiness." He wanted to shake the big man and demand he answer his question, not dance around it. "Are you saying that's what happened to my father?" Jake asked, shocked by what sounded like an indictment against his father.

Johnny tossed the cleaned fish into the pile with the others. "I'm saying, leave it alone, son. No good comes from digging up the past."

The same thing Warren Hawkins had said to him. Jake walked away, heartsick and shaken. Not by Johnny's words as much as by the bitterness he'd heard in the man's voice. Was he really ready to find out the truth about his father? About Clancy? No matter how it came down?

As he walked up the steps to the resort store, he glanced to the right, to the west end of the island. The Branson home sat at the edge of the cliffs. A wide deck ran across the front with an elevator platform next to a long flight of wooden stairs that dropped to a dock at the water. Jake could make out a figure sitting near the edge of the deck. Johnny's wife Helen, her wheelchair glistening in the morning sunlight.

Clancy waited until Jake was out of sight before she made her move. She headed for the row of cabins against the hillside, having spotted a cleaning cart parked in front of number three.

Johnny Branson waved to her as he left in his boat. She was shocked by the change in him. He looked so much older and slighter than he'd been. She wondered if Warren Hawkins's trial hadn't made him age more rapidly. She was thinking about the trial and the effect it had had on them all as she took the trail to cabin three.

"Hello?" Clancy called, sticking her head into the cabin's open doorway. Like the other five cabins, number three was small, with twin beds against the knotty-pine wall and a marred night table and lamp between them. A girl of about fifteen looked up from her bed-making, the tail of a sheet in her hand.

"This cabin isn't ready yet," she said quickly. "Check-in isn't until noon."

Clancy smiled and stepped inside. "I don't need a cabin. Actually, I need to find out if one of your guests left anything behind."

The girl let go of the sheet and straightened, but she didn't look all that happy for the interruption. "If they did, it would be in lost'n found. I can show you."

"It would have been cabin six," Clancy said. "On Friday."

The girl stopped in her tracks and looked up, her eyes narrowing. "That was the guy who got murdered."

"So what was he like?" Clancy asked casually.

The girl rolled her eyes. "A major hunk. But kind of a real pain."

"Yeah?"

"He was always bossing me around, asking me to run here and there for him."

It was obvious she hadn't really minded. "What did he want you to do?"

"Get him things and take messages— Why are you asking about him, anyway?"

"It isn't every day there's a murder on the island."

"He didn't die here, you know," she said.

"That's what I heard. But he stayed here a day and a night, right?"

"Two nights," the girl said.

Two nights? Dex hadn't called her until the second day?

"So he had you running errands for him," she said, knowing she had to tread softly. "I hope he tipped you well."

The girl shook her head. "That part stunk, too."

"Really? If he had you taking messages to people…"

The girl looked wary. "You with one of those weird newspapers?"

This time it was Clancy's turn to shake her head. "No, the truth is, I dated the guy for a while," she said truthfully.

"No kidding?" The girl looked at her with misguided respect.

"That's why I wondered if he left anything behind, a message or letter, maybe…for me."

The girl gave her a sympathetic look. "Sorry, when the police finally let me clean the cabin, I didn't find anything." She went back to her bed-making.

"What about the messages he had you take for him?" Clancy asked.

"It was just one. I took it to the marina and left it under a bait can beside the repair shop."

Interesting place to leave a message. "What night was this?"

"The first night. Thursday."

"Didn't you wonder who it was for?"

"It didn't have any writing on the envelope."

Clancy took a long shot. "Was the envelope sealed?"

The girl looked up and grinned. "Yeah. I couldn't make out anything, even holding it up to a light. I didn't dare open it."

Clancy laughed. "Thanks for your help." She had more questions, but the girl was heading for her cart and another cabin and Clancy didn't want to press her luck. "Do you mind if I take a look around cabin six, just in case?"

* * *

Jake found Frank Ames in the pumphouse behind the café, bent over, banging on a pipe, swearing.

"Frank?" Jake called over the racket.

He looked up, the wrench in his hand falling silent. Not much had changed about the tall, pimply-faced kid Jake had known. He was still thin, his narrow face pockmarked, his expression one of open hostility. "What do you want?"

"Just to ask you a few questions." He held out his business card. When Frank didn't bother to reach for it, Jake stuffed the card into Frank's shirt pocket.

Frank glared at him from dark, deep-set eyes that were just a little too close together. "Do I look like I have time to answer questions?" he demanded.

Jake had always wanted to knock that chip off Frank's shoulder. Only now, Jake's father wasn't here to keep him from doing it.

Frank must have realized that. "Hell," he said, pushing himself to his feet. "Make it snappy."

"You told the sheriff you overheard Clancy Jones talking to a man in the café Friday night," Jake said, disappointed Frank had given in so easily. He really wanted to thump that mean, nasty look off Frank's face.

"You know that or you wouldn't be here."

Jake smiled. He might get the opportunity to thump Frank yet. "What did you hear?"

"I already told the sheriff—"

"Tell me, Frank," Jake said between gritted teeth.

Frank slowly wiped the grease from his hands onto his worn jeans. "They were arguing about something."

"What?"

Frank shot him a contemptuous look. "How should I know?"

"You were listening to their conversation."

"I just happened to overhear Clancy threaten him, that's all."

"What exactly did she say?"

"I don't *exactly* remember." He shook his head at Jake's stupidity. "I got better things to do than memorize my customers' conversations."

Jake took a step toward Frank. "Try to remember."

"She said it was over between them. He said it was over when he said it was over. She said he was hurting her and he'd better leave her alone or else."

"Not bad for a conversation you can't remember," Jake said. "Where exactly were you when you overheard this conversation? I thought the café was closed."

He gave him a nasty sneer. "I was walking by."

Jake nodded. "This waitress who overheard this same conversation—"

"Liz Knowles. She's up at the café."

"Was she walking with you?"

"I think it's time for you to leave, Hawkins." Frank turned to go back to his plumbing problems.

"One more question. How was it you were able to buy this resort?"

Frank picked up a pipe wrench from behind the pump and hefted it into both hands. "I'm through answering questions. You don't own this place anymore. Your old man's behind bars, your girlfriend's a murderer, and you're nothing but some punk P.I. who doesn't know squat. So don't you come around here hassling me no more—or you'll regret it."

Jake smiled and pushed back his baseball cap. "One of these days I'm going to kick your ass, Frank. And that's a promise."

* * *

Clancy knew there probably wasn't anything to find in cabin six, but she still had to look, and she hoped the cabin girl's curiosity would get the best of her.

Just as the girl had said, the cabin wasn't locked. Nor did it look much different from number three. Except the beds were made. Clancy glanced around in all the corners, under the beds and behind the door. Nothing, just as she'd thought. Then she took a closer look, inspecting the cracks between the worn pine plank floor and the crevices between the floor and baseboard. No tiny blue beads.

Disappointed, she stood for a moment in the middle of the room, thinking about Dex. Where were the rest of the beads from the necklace? It was obvious the necklace hadn't been broken here. Some of the tiny beads would have gotten caught between the floorboards. Common sense told her she'd find the beads closer to home. They were near enough to the lodge that she'd walked to them in her sleep. But where? And what did the broken beads signify? Probably nothing. Her sleepwalking was often illogical, she reminded herself.

It made as little sense as Dex coming to Hawk Island. If it was to see her, then why hadn't he called her the first day? Why had he waited? And whom had he left a message for on the dock? As far as Clancy knew, Dex didn't know anyone up here but her.

"Find anything?" the girl asked from the doorway.

Clancy smiled to herself, glad she hadn't been wrong about the girl's curiosity. "Is it possible the message he wrote was for some woman he'd met here?" she asked, knowing that was more than a possibility.

The girl looked away.

Clancy knew she'd hit paydirt. "Dex always had a way with women."

The girl looked up, a smirk on her young face. "There was this one waitress."

Of course there was. "Which waitress?"

"Liz. Liz Knowles."

What a sleaze Dex had been! All the time he'd been dating her he'd been seeing other women. Then he'd come to Hawk Island supposedly to get her back and he was making time with one of the waitresses at the resort. Maybe she *had* killed him. "So the message from Dex was probably for her?"

The girl shook her head. "I passed Liz on my way down to the docks. She was already headed for his cabin."

"Maybe Liz just missed the message or picked it up later."

The girl brushed a speck of lint from her sweatshirt and, looking at the ground, shook her head. "Later I went to check. The message was gone. Liz hadn't left his cabin."

"Do you know if anyone else came to Dex's cabin that night?" Clancy asked on impulse.

"No." The girl looked disgusted, and Clancy realized her impulse had been right. The poor thing had hung around outside the cabin waiting for Liz to leave. All Clancy could think was how lucky the girl had been that Dex hadn't taken advantage of her schoolgirl crush.

But if the message hadn't been meant for Liz Knowles, then whom? Clancy felt a sudden chill as she remembered that night at the café when Dex had looked past her into the darkness and seen someone. Or something that had frightened him. She wondered what Dex had had to fear. And from whom. The person who killed him? "What about the night he was killed?"

"I had to work at the café. But I know Liz planned to go to his cabin that night."

Clancy remembered what Jake had said about Dex not having any underwear on when he was found dead. Liz Knowles might be the explanation for that. But if Jake's theory was right, who had interrupted the two?

"The only time he left the island was that first afternoon Thursday," the girl was saying.

Clancy's head snapped up. "He left the island?"

She nodded, looking unhappy. "He was all dressed up."

The girl obviously figured he'd had a date. She was probably right. "Do you know where he went?"

She shook her head.

Clancy had a thought. "He came back and *then* wrote the message you took to the dock that first night?"

She nodded, looking miserable. "He was in a really good mood."

The first thing Jake noticed when he left the pump-house and Frank was that Clancy was no longer in the boat. In fact, she was nowhere to be seen. He swore under his breath. This should not have come as a surprise. No, this was absolutely predictable. Anyone who knew Clancy would know better than to think she'd just sit idly by in the boat as he'd asked her. She'd never done anything he ever told her. Needless to say, that part of her hadn't changed a bit.

He spotted her finally by the cabins, talking to a cabin girl. Questioning a cabin girl, he corrected himself. Damn her hide. Well, at least he could see her, and she was all right. For the moment. He'd take this up with her when he finished interviewing Elizabeth Knowles.

The Hawk Island Resort café was actually little more than a grill that served burgers, hot dogs, fries and soft drinks. All the seating was outdoors at wooden tables under a canopy of pines and Japanese lanterns. Cheap plastic checked tablecloths flapped in the summer breeze. A woman in her early twenties in shorts and a tank top was busy putting out condiments.

"Lunch isn't served for another half hour," she said when she saw Jake. She had the harried, tight expression of a young woman who was already tired of her summer job and it was only early June.

"I'm looking for a waitress named Knowles."

She looked up.

He saw fear flicker in her eyes.

"I'm Elizabeth Knowles."

He asked her the same questions he had asked Frank. But got different answers.

"What makes you think they were arguing about money?" he asked, his interest piqued not only by the difference in how she and Frank related the conversation, but by this woman's obvious sympathy toward Dex.

Elizabeth shrugged. "He said she owed him money. But it sounded like she'd dumped him, too, and he was upset about that."

Funny, but money had never come up in the conversation, according to Clancy. And Frank. Jake glanced around the café. "Where were they sitting?"

She pointed to a far table at the back edge of the deck flanked by two large pines.

"And where were you when you heard this conversation?"

Her gaze flickered away. "I was working. I had to close the café that night."

She must have been the waitress Clancy saw cleaning the grill.

"You couldn't have heard their conversation from inside the café," Jake said quietly.

She flushed to the dark roots of her blond head. "I wasn't. I was…in the trees. I had to run an errand."

Right beside the deck. "Did you see anyone else while you were there?"

She shook her head. "I was only there a few minutes."

"Just long enough to overhear their entire conversation," Jake said.

"I gotta get back to work," she said, turning to walk away.

"What was so interesting about that conversation that you hid in the pines to listen?"

Her steps faltered, but she didn't stop or turn around. Nor did she deny it. "I was just curious," she said flatly. "There's no law against that."

No, if there was a law against curiosity, Jake would be doing time right now, he thought as he watched Clancy hurry down the dock to her boat. What had she learned from the cabin girl that had put a spring into her step? More important, how could he convince Clancy she wasn't going to be doing any more investigating on her own?

Clancy stretched out in the back of the boat, pretending to be asleep. It was hard to do since she couldn't help but steal a peek at Jake from under her large straw fishing hat. Jake strode down the dock, his cap pulled low over his eyes, his jaw set in concrete. She didn't have to see his eyes to know he was furious. Or to know who he was furious with. Obviously he knew that she'd left the boat.

"I thought you agreed to stay here where I could see you," he said the moment he reached her.

She leisurely pushed back her hat and looked up at him. "I *did* stay in the boat. For a while." She grinned, too pleased at what she'd discovered to hold it in any longer. "Don't you want to know what I found out?"

"Dammit, Clancy, I won't have you messing up my investigation with your amateur sleuthing." He glowered at her.

"I found out some pretty good stuff," she said. "For an amateur, of course. Dex was romantically involved with one of the waitresses."

"Liz Knowles."

She stared at him. "How did you know that?"

"She's one of the witnesses who overheard your conversation with Dex."

Clancy sat up. "Really?" How interesting. "Wait a minute, why didn't I see her that night?"

"She was hiding in the pines right beside the deck."

Excitement coursed through her. "Then, she wasn't the person Dex saw in the darkness. It *was* someone else, just as I suspected." She hurriedly told Jake about the note the cabin girl had left under a bait can and how Dex had been on the island an extra day and night before he contacted her. Also how he'd left the island Thursday to meet someone, maybe a date, and returned in a good mood. "That's when he left the note."

She waited for Jake's reaction, expecting him to be as excited about this as she was. He bent to untie the boat, and, if anything, he seemed more angry.

"Don't you realize what this means?" she demanded. "Dex knew someone else on the island, someone he left a note for. He also left the island to meet someone. It's a lead."

Jake looked up, leveling his gray-eyed gaze at her. "Clancy, I realize telling you what to do is a waste of my breath," he said. "But it would help if you'd let me do the job I've been hired to do. And if you'd just stay put like you're told. This is my case, and whether you believe it or not, I know what I'm doing."

"No wonder I keep firing you," she said in exasperation. "This may be your case, Jake, but it's my life. Even if I trusted you to do the job my aunt hired you to do, which you have already admitted isn't why you're here, I couldn't stay put. Someone tried to kill me. The sheriff isn't even looking into other leads because he believes he already has his killer, and you don't believe I'm innocent any more than he does. If I stay put, I might end up dead. At the very least, in prison for life."

Jake jerked off his cap and raked his fingers through his hair. "Dammit, Clancy, sometimes I'd like to —" He slapped his cap back on his head and leveled his gaze at her. "You were always like this. Too independent, stubborn and fearless for your own good. Remember that time you went swimming off Angel Point in the storm?"

She'd almost drowned. Probably would have if it hadn't been for Jake. She'd only done it because he'd told her not to. What he was saying was true. Often in the past, she'd let her stubborn pride get her into trouble. "You're wrong, Jake. I'm not fearless. I'm scared to death."

In one swift motion, he pushed off the boat and stepped in. "You should be scared. There's already been one murder. If you didn't kill Dex, or whoever he was, then the killer is still out there. It's too danger-ous for a—"

"Woman?" She raised a brow at him.

"Amateur," he said with that soft southern drawl.

She pushed back her sunglasses to glare up at him.

"We'll discuss this back at the lodge." He tossed her the boat key. "You can drive."

She caught the key easily enough but bristled at his tone. It sounded as if he thought he was going to have the last word on this. He was even going to let her drive her own boat. And then take the key again when they got to the lodge. She tossed the key back to him. "Some things aren't debatable," she said, pulling down her sun-glasses as she stretched out on the seat in the sun again.

She heard him mumbling as he started the boat and pulled away from the resort. She had the feeling that Jake Hawkins was used to women he could mold like soft clay. Well, not this woman. And he had a fight on his hands if he thought he could.

It was more than her stubborn pride, Clancy told herself. She was tired of feeling like a criminal. And while she appreciated Jake's help, she had no intention of letting him investigate her case alone. She had to prove her innocence. And she couldn't depend on any-one to do it for her. Not even Jake Hawkins. Especially not Jake Hawkins.

Jake slowed as they rounded the island. Clancy pre-tended to sleep until she felt the boat bump the dock. She sat up, studying Jake out of the corner of her eye to see if his mood had changed.

He still looked irritated with her, but as he passed on his way to tie up the boat, he handed her the boat key. That simple sign of trust touched her more deeply than she wanted to admit.

"Jake?" She started to tell him that she was glad he was here. That she liked being around him, even when he was ill-tempered. That his being here made her feel like she had a chance to prove her innocence. He gave her strength. And hope. Even if he was here for all the wrong reasons— "Thanks."

He grunted in response and offered her a hand out of the boat. "I still don't want you interfering in my investigation."

She smiled. "But you're smart enough to know that I will whether you like it or not."

"You are the most disagreeable woman I've ever—" Before she knew what was happening, he grabbed her and hauled her out of the boat—and into his arms, into his kiss. It was a kiss that brooked no arguments. He took her lips, the same way he took her body to his. Her lips responded to his demands, parting of their own volition to allow him access to her. Against her counsel, her body answered his, molding its softness to his hardness.

"Excuse me?"

Clancy's eyes popped open as she recognized the voice and realized it was directly behind her. Abruptly Jake broke off the kiss and swung Clancy around, shielding her before he realized just who had joined them in the small bay.

"Sorry to interrupt," her attorney said from his boat, which now bumped the edge of the dock. Funny, but Tadd didn't sound sorry. Nor could Clancy remember hearing his motor when he pulled into the bay. She had a feeling he'd cut his engine and drifted in when he'd seen the two of them kissing.

But then she'd heard nothing but the throb of her heart against Jake's chest, felt nothing but his lips on hers. Now she felt her face flush, wondering how long Tadd had been watching them.

"I'd ask you how the investigation was going but I can pretty well see the course it's taking," Tadd commented.

Jake swore and released Clancy. She stumbled and fought to regain her composure.

"Did you bring the flier?" Jake said a little hoarsely.

Clancy tried to still her pounding heart, not even kidding herself that it was Tadd's sudden appearance that had caused it to pound, not Jake's unexpected kiss.

"Why don't we go up to the lodge," Tadd said, his look growing serious. "I've got some news you might want to sit down for."

Chapter 11

Clancy led them into the living room. Tadd took a seat on the western-style couch her family had bought when she was a child. It had horses embossed in the thick leather and wide wooden arms. She stood, too nervous to sit, remembering the night of the resort fire when she'd come down the stairs to find her parents sitting on that same couch, arguing about Warren Hawkins and the missing money.

Clancy had that same sick feeling now as she looked at Tadd. He sat on the edge of the couch, at odds with the warm, inviting character of the room with its large rock fireplace that Jake now leaned against, the rich golden pine floors, the bright-colored rugs.

Tadd pulled a sheet of paper from his shirt pocket. "The sheriff needs to know if this is the man you knew as Dex Westfall," Tadd said, unfolding the flier.

Clancy found herself unable to move. Instead, Jake crossed the room, took the paper from Tadd's hand and brought it over to her.

She could feel his gaze on her as well as Tadd's. She took the flier in her hands, a zillion thoughts whipping through her mind. The last thing she wanted to do was look at the photograph she knew she'd find reprinted on the sheet of paper. What if it wasn't the man she'd dated? What if it was?

She braced herself, her gaze flicking to Jake, his look sympathetic, supportive. She looked at the face in the photo. Her heart leaped into her throat.

"Is that the man you knew as Dex Westfall?" Tadd asked again.

She nodded, looking away from the dead man's face to stare into the darkness of the empty firebox.

Jake took the flier from her. "Are you all right?"

She nodded, avoiding his gaze. She wasn't all right and wondered if she'd ever be all right again. The man she'd known as Dex Westfall was dead. So who had been snooping around her lodge last night? Who had she seen who looked like Dex? Who'd run out of the lodge? Who had pulled her into the lake and tried to drown her?

"Have you got an ID on the body yet?" Jake asked Tadd as he handed back the flier.

Out of the corner of her eye, Clancy watched Tadd carefully fold the sheet of paper and put it into his shirt pocket. He's stalling, she thought, and faced him, realizing he'd brought news. Bad news.

"The sheriff got a positive ID from the family this morning," Tadd said. "What Dex told you, Clancy, about being raised in eastern Montana on a farm turned out to be true."

The air in the living room crackled. "Who was he?" she asked, her voice no more than a whisper.

Tadd's gaze shifted to Jake. "His real name was Dexter Strickland."

"Strickland?" Jake asked.

"Strickland?" Clancy repeated, the name not registering.

It was Tadd who answered. "Dex Strickland was Lola's son."

Lola. A chill stole across her skin. "Lola Strickland, the resort secretary?" The woman Jake's father had gone to prison for murdering.

Clancy looked over at Jake. He stood, his muscles tensed, all his attention on Tadd.

"Dex was her son?" Jake asked, sounding not all that surprised.

"I never knew she had a son." Was Clancy the only one shocked here? "I didn't even know she'd ever been married."

"No one did," Tadd said. "Dex lived with his father on a farm near Richey. The father had custody. I guess Lola just up and disappeared one day, leaving her husband to raise his infant son alone. Allan Strickland never heard from her again."

"What about during the trial?" Clancy asked. "It was in all the papers. Surely he would have heard about his wife's death."

"From what I can gather, Allan Strickland's farm is pretty isolated," Tadd said. "But you're right. He knew about her death. He says he was trying to shield his son."

Clancy's legs wobbled beneath her. "If Dex was Lola's son…"

"The murders have to be connected," Jake said.

"We don't know that," Tadd said. "But it could explain why Dex had the newspaper clippings of the trial in his closet and why he might have wanted to meet Clancy."

"Why Clancy?" Jake asked.

Clancy saw the pain etched in his face and wished with all her heart that she wasn't responsible for him being here, for him having to relive all this. They were talking about the woman his father had been convicted of murdering.

Clancy wanted to reach out to Jake but knew she was the last person he'd take sympathy from. Especially right now.

"Why wouldn't Dex come after *me*?" Jake demanded. "If he wanted retribution, it was my father who…he believed killed his mother."

"Who knows what Dex had in mind?" Tadd said. "Maybe he was just looking for some connection to his mother."

"Or to his mother's murder," Jake interjected.

That seemed more a possibility now that Clancy thought about it. "He did say something that night about his mother's legacy and how it linked the two of us."

"But what was that legacy?" Jake asked.

"Well, it seems to be death," Tadd said quietly, making the hair stiffen on Clancy's neck.

Dex had stalked her. With a shudder, she realized Dex was still stalking her. "Did Dex have any brothers?"

Jake's gaze swung around to meet hers.

"I already thought of that," Tadd said. "I asked Allan Strickland if there were any more like Dex at home."

"And?" Jake asked impatiently.

"Dex didn't have any siblings."

Clancy felt the air rush out of her. The floor wavered and threatened to come up to meet her.

"You should sit down," Jake said, suddenly appearing at her side.

She gave him the best smile she could manage. "I'm okay. I'm more worried about you."

He seemed surprised that she would be worried about him right now. He returned her smile. "Thanks, but I'm tough."

She knew that. And tender. Her heart ached to take some of the pain from those gray eyes. She wished she *had* lied on the stand about his father. At least now she could rectify things. "I think I'll get a drink of water."

"I'll get it for you," Jake said, already heading for the kitchen.

She stopped him. "Please, I need a little fresh air. A few moments alone."

He studied her for a long moment, then nodded.

Was he worried about her? Or just worried she'd jump bail? She felt a stab of annoyance. Just when she let down her defenses, he'd remind her again exactly what his stake in her case was. Revenge. Nothing more. She was on her own, now more than ever.

She left the two of them in the living room and went straight to the porch, where she gulped the summer afternoon air and tried to quit shaking. Dex was Lola Strickland's son. She couldn't even comprehend all the ramifications of that. What had Tadd said? Maybe he was just looking for a connection to his mother. Or to his mother's murder, Jake had added. Is that why he went to so much trouble to get close to her?

A connection. Like the string of beads. Dex said the beads were a legacy from his mother. But Lola was dead, and all of her belongings had burned in the fire. So where had he gotten the necklace? From someone who was still on the island who'd known Lola? Or someone on the mainland?

That silly necklace, why was it so familiar? The memory came in a flash. The string of tiny blue beads. Light glinting off the small dark blue ceramic heart. Clancy knew she'd seen them before. Now she knew where.

The memory brought her little pleasure. She'd seen them the night Jake Hawkins had promised her *his* heart. That's why the tiny navy heart had stuck in her memory. She reminded herself that not only had Jake broken that promise—he was now on the island to, as he put it, get the goods on her.

Grabbing her mountain bike from where she'd left it against the porch railing, Clancy took off up one of the trails without thinking of anything but reaching her destination and getting back before Jake missed her. If she was right, she might have some answers to keep her out of prison when she returned.

The lodge seemed empty after Clancy left. Almost eerie. Jake found himself pacing, too keyed up to sit.

"I'm worried about Clancy," Tadd said, leaning forward as he watched Jake wear out the rug in front of him.

"You should be," Jake said, stopping his pacing for a moment. He fought the urge to check on Clancy again.

Not long after she'd gone outside, he'd looked out to find her standing on the back porch. He wanted to give her the space she'd asked for, but not too much. She couldn't get into too much trouble for a few minutes on her own back porch in broad daylight, right?

"She thinks someone is trying to kill her," Jake said, resuming his pacing. He told Tadd about the near drowning incident and filled in more detail about last night's supposed intruder. "She thinks someone who looks like Dex Westfall is still stalking her."

Tadd gave him one of those calculated lawyer looks. "Is that what you think?"

Jake didn't know what to believe. "There's a scrape on her ankle, and if you'd seen Clancy's face last night— She saw something," Jake said in Clancy's defense. "Someone. Someone she thinks looks enough like Dex to make her believe he's still alive."

"You don't believe Strickland's come back from the dead?" Tadd inquired.

"Of course not." Jake pulled off his cap and rumpled his hair with his hand.

"At some point, Clancy's going to have to see a sleep specialist and have some extensive tests run on her," Tadd said. "If we can prove she has a sleeping disorder. That Dex's death was the result of noninsane automatism, an act committed by a sane person but without—"

"Intent, awareness or malice," Jake interrupted. "I know, I've read about it." He shook his head at Tadd. "If Clancy killed Dex, it wasn't in her sleep. Dex Strickland stalked her, lied about who he was, cheated on her. All the more reason for Clancy to want him dead. Add to that the mountain of evidence against her—"

"I *have* to sell the jury on the sleepwalking defense or she's going to prison," Tadd interrupted.

Jake groaned, realizing how true that probably was. "Unless I can find some evidence that proves she didn't kill him." And if he couldn't? Then he'd have no bargaining chip. Funny how that didn't matter as much as it had just a few days ago. "She thinks Dex has come back from the grave for her."

"Ever read any Edgar Allan Poe?" Tadd asked.

"There's no heart thumping under the floorboards here. Unless it's Lola Strickland's."

Tadd gave him a long look. "You think Dex came back to either avenge his mother's death or solve her murder?"

"You have to admit, both are possibilities," Jake said. "But if he believed my father was guilty, why wouldn't he come after me instead of Clancy? Unless he believes Clancy's father, Clarence Jones, is somehow involved."

"That's what you think, isn't it?" Tadd said as he got to his feet. "Maybe you should solve one murder at a time, preferably the one you're being paid to solve."

"The murders are connected."

"Maybe. Maybe not. My only concern is for my client. What's yours?"

"Clancy," Jake said, realizing that was true. "But these murders are connected."

His entire theory rode on the premise that the two murders were connected, and Dex turning out to be Lola's son only supported that. The hunch discoing at the back of his brain was that whoever killed Dex had killed Dex's mother. Clarence Jones could have embezzled the money, either used Lola to do it or killed her because she found the discrepancy, and started the fire to cover his own misdeeds. Warren Hawkins had come along after the fact, just as he said, and tried to save Lola and the books to prove his innocence.

But Clarence and Lola were dead. And Warren was in prison. So where did that leave Jake? All the prime suspects were now out of the picture. Too many things were blowing holes in his hunch.

Not only that, ten years ago he had found it easier to believe that Clancy had perjured herself than he did now—perhaps being around her had altered his perspective.

"I don't see how the murders could be connected," Tadd said.

"Clancy's the connection," Jake insisted. "Maybe she saw something that night that someone doesn't want her to remember."

Tadd lifted a brow. "They waited ten years to shut her up?"

Jake admitted it didn't make a lot of sense. But what did about this case?

Tadd let out a long sigh. "I'm worried about Clancy's mental state. I'm concerned she might be on the verge of a major breakdown. The sooner we get to trial, the better."

"I beg your pardon?"

They both swung around at the sound of a sharp, female voice from the doorway.

"Kiki!" Jake said. Her name came out like an oath.

"I can assure you my niece is not on the verge of a major breakdown, as you so delicately put it," she said firmly. She stormed into the room, giving them both withering glares. "Nor is she a murderer."

Jake wondered how long she'd been standing in the doorway listening. He didn't have to wonder long.

"If my niece says someone is trying to kill her, I expect you to believe her," Kiki said, biting off each word.

Tadd was on his feet, trying to explain himself, but Kiki cut him off.

"How can you fools *not* believe her?" Kiki snapped, some of her highly bred composure slipping. "Clancy's no murderer. She didn't care enough about the man to kill him. Asleep. Or awake." She narrowed her eyes at Jake. "Why aren't you out looking for the real killer instead of sitting around speculating on Clancy's mental health?" She shook her head in disgust. "Where is my niece, anyway? I came by to see how she was doing."

Jake stared at Kiki. "Didn't you pass her on your way in? She was out on the porch just a—" He was already racing toward the back of the lodge. He pushed through the door and out onto the porch. "Clancy?" She was nowhere in sight. A breeze rippled the water. The tops of the tall pines swayed overhead. Her boat was still at the dock. The beach was empty. He glanced around, thinking she might have just gone for a walk.

Then he noticed her mountain bike was gone. He swore, knowing he'd never be able to catch her on foot. Nor did he have any idea which trail she might have taken. The island was a labyrinth of trails.

"It's a small island," he heard Tadd trying to reassure Kiki. "How could she get into trouble on such a small island in broad daylight?"

"Find her. Hurry." The emotion in Kiki's command clutched at Jake's heart. He felt the tentative strum of a hunch at the base of his spine. He knew the name of this tune. Trouble. And Clancy, as usual, was right at the center of it.

Chapter 12

Clancy rode up the narrow mountain trail through the cool pines. The sun sliced down, making patterns of gold on the dry pine needles covering the path. The trail climbed the steep terrain through a series of switchbacks to the top of the ridge. The exertion felt good; she pushed herself harder, stopping at the top to catch her breath.

The lake stretched for miles, a mosaic of blues and greens. The Mission Mountains rose up from the valley floor to the east. Pines, dense and dark as the ones around her, edged the other side of the lake as far as the eye could see. To the north, boats churned the water in a bay near the resort. Laughter and the roar of engines drifted up the mountainside, making Clancy ache for happier summer days.

She headed down the main trail that ran along the

ridgeline. Occasionally she'd catch a view of the lake from the dense pines. The island was a web of narrow trails; most she'd ridden at one time or another during her childhood. Ridden with Jake, she thought. Back when their lives had held nothing but promise.

As she rode, she tried to understand everything she'd learned over the last few hours and where she fit into it. Some things started to make an odd kind of sense to her. Why Dex had stalked her. Why he'd followed her to the island. This is where his mother had died, and Clancy Jones had been the only witness.

That is what tied her to Dex Strickland. The same thing that distanced her from Jake.

Jake and Tadd split up and, lacking a bicycle, Jake began his search for Clancy on foot. Tadd opted to go by boat. Her bike tires had left no tracks on the needle-covered path, so Jake had no way of knowing which way she'd gone or where she was headed. He took the trail directly behind the house.

He stormed up the trail, that hunch of his dancing to that same old little ditty. Clancy was the key. Had always been the key. Now that he knew Dex was Lola's son, there was no doubt in his mind that their deaths were connected. Nor did he have any choice but to dig into the old murder and his father's case.

What bothered him like a bad headache just getting started was his father. Why had Warren Hawkins asked him not to get involved? Well, Jake was involved now. And he was going to learn the truth. About his father. About Clancy.

But first he had to find her. She couldn't have gone far, he told himself. Jake couldn't believe she'd taken off again. He knew the shock had thrown her—just as it had him. But if she really believed someone was trying to kill her, how could she have taken such a chance?

Because she was too impetuous, independent and stubborn for her own good. But Jake knew he was partly to blame. He'd made it clear to her that she couldn't trust him. She was alone and scared. Now he had to find her before she got into more trouble.

Clancy cruised down the mountain on a narrow trail that came out directly behind Johnny and Helen Branson's place at the edge of the cliffs.

Helen spotted her as she came out of the pines and waved from the kitchen window for her to come on in.

Helen was petite with short blond hair that showed no gray, blue eyes and fair skin. Unlike Johnny, Helen didn't look as though she'd aged at all the last ten years. In fact, Clancy noticed with surprise, Helen looked as if she might be closer to thirty than she was fifty.

"I hope I didn't catch you right at dinner," Clancy apologized as she was met with the smell of pot roast.

"Don't be silly," Helen said from her wheelchair in front of the stove. Johnny had built the house to accommodate Helen's disability; everything was wheelchair level. "Stay for dinner. Johnny should be here any moment. We'd love to have you."

Clancy's stomach growled, and she remembered she hadn't eaten anything since breakfast, but she declined the offer. She had to get back before Jake called out the National Guard.

"Maybe some other time," she told Helen. "I just stopped by to ask you something."

"I heard about all that nasty business. I've been so concerned for you."

"That's why I wanted to talk to you. You remember Lola Strickland, the secretary at the resort?"

Helen frowned. "Why, yes."

"That man, the one who was killed upstairs at my lodge. His real name was Dex Strickland. He was Lola's son."

Helen's eyes widened. "My word. The woman had children?"

"One," Clancy said. "A son."

"But how can that be?" Helen asked. "I never saw her with a child, and she certainly never talked of children."

Clancy felt a surge of hope. "Then you did know her fairly well?"

Helen chuckled. "It's a small island, dear. Everyone knew her. But it sounds like you know more about Lola than I do. I didn't even know she had a son."

"Oh, I thought you might have befriended her," Clancy said.

"What would make you think that?" Helen asked as she turned to take a peek into the oven at her roast.

The smell was enough to make Clancy drool. "I remembered that you were both involved in the Flathead Community Theater Company in Bigfork that summer."

Helen laughed. "I just did some of the makeup and helped with costumes."

"Didn't Lola star in one of the plays right before her death?" Clancy asked.

Helen frowned as she reached into the refrigerator and pulled out a bowl of salad. "It's been so long, but now that you mention it, I think she did. Why do you ask?"

"I remember the play," Clancy said, suddenly hesitant. Earlier her theory had made sense. Right now it seemed silly. "I wondered if you knew what happened to the necklace she was wearing opening night?"

"A necklace?" Helen asked in surprise. She wheeled over to the dining-room table by the window with the salad. Clancy noticed the table settings for the first time. Fresh flowers, cloth napkins, candles and fancy china?

"Is it your anniversary?" Clancy asked, even more ashamed for interrupting Helen's cooking.

"Oh, dear, no." Helen smiled. "I just wanted to spoil my husband tonight. He's been a little under the weather lately."

Clancy felt tears pool in her eyes. They threatened to overflow and spill down her cheeks.

"I'm so fortunate to have a man like Johnny," Helen said, straightening the napkins she'd folded by each plate. "We've been married for almost thirty years. We were childhood sweethearts, you know." She turned and seemed surprised to find Clancy near tears. "Are you all right, dear?"

Clancy hadn't thought much about true love, marriage or love-ever-after. Not since Jake had left the island ten years ago. Dex certainly hadn't made her realize what she'd been missing. But standing here, smelling pot roast, seeing this romantic dinner scene, having earlier kissed her own childhood sweetheart—

"What's wrong?" Helen asked again.

Clancy made a swipe at her tears. She was exhausted. Overstressed. Overemotional. But then, why wouldn't she be? She was a suspected murderer who wasn't even sure she was innocent, and a dead man was after her. That would make anyone a little teary at unexpected moments. "I'm fine." She wondered how many more

times she could say those two words before she started
to scream.

"You're not fine," Helen said, taking her hand. "Tell
me what's wrong."

Clancy found herself pouring out her heart. From
Dex's death, to the hand coming out of the water and
scraping her ankle with the silver watchband, to Jake.

Helen smiled kindly when she finished. "It sounds
like Jake being back might be putting even more stress
on you. You have feelings for him, haven't you?"

Clancy tried to deny it and couldn't. She brushed
away her tears, feeling relieved to be able to talk to
someone who believed her. "Thanks for listening to
me."

"Anytime, dear. I'll always have a strong shoulder
for you to cry on. Now, what can I do to help you?"

"Was there anyone else involved in the theater company that summer who might still be around?" Clancy
asked.

Helen seemed to think for a moment. "Frank Ames.
I believe he helped with some of the scenery." She
straightened one of the place settings. "Why are you
looking for a necklace of Lola's, dear?"

Clancy knew it sounded ridiculous. What could a
string of tiny blue beads have to do with finding Dex's
murderer? "I just thought she might have given it to a
friend. Or left it with someone for safekeeping."

"You thought I was that friend." Helen smiled
kindly. "I was probably as close as anyone to Lola, but
I wouldn't say we became friends. I'm sorry, dear."

Johnny came in then. "Clancy, what a nice surprise.
Something sure smells good. I hope you're staying for
dinner."

"Pot roast," Helen said, sounding pleased. "Wash up. I tried to get Clancy to join us, but she can't. I want her and Jake to come to dinner soon."

"Real soon," Johnny called as he headed down the hall.

"What did this necklace look like?" Helen asked.

"Tiny blue beads. Like hippies used to wear. There was a small handmade dark blue ceramic heart at its center."

Helen seemed surprised. "I thought maybe it was diamonds. You made it sound so important."

Clancy knew she must seem irrational, worrying about a string of beads at a time like this. "Dex had it the day he was killed. I just wondered where he might have gotten it." And where it was now.

"I wish I could have helped," Helen said.

Clancy thanked her and made a hasty goodbye, promising she'd come back soon. Once on her bike, she headed for home.

The air felt cool against Clancy's flushed cheeks. It had been hot in the kitchen, she assured herself. She wasn't flushed and embarrassed about her silly behavior. Crying over nothing. As she rode through the shadowy trees, she made excuses for her tears back in Helen's kitchen. They had nothing to do with Jake Hawkins. Nothing at all, she told herself.

Jake reached the top of the ridge and stood for a moment, scanning what little of the island he could see through the dense pines, disappointed Clancy was nowhere to be seen. Down the mountain at the resort, an American flag snapped above the treetops in the wind; whitecaps dotted the water beyond the bay. Jake wondered if Clancy had gone back to the resort. Or if she was just out riding and thinking. Or maybe making a run for it?

He'd tried not to think on his hike up the mountain. It made his head hurt, trying to put together pieces of a puzzle he'd spent ten years trying to solve. Worse yet was worrying about Clancy. And that latest stupid kiss.

Not that he regretted either kiss. Unprofessional, yes. Totally out of line, unquestionably uncalled for. And yet he couldn't get either one out of his head, let alone out of his blood. He'd planned to do more than kiss her when the opportunity arose. But the kiss on the dock had been as unexpected for him as it was for her. The real problem, however, was the effect it had on him.

Now he was out wandering in the woods looking for the most frustrating woman in the world. Stubborn. Hell-bent determined. Too brave for her own good. Grudgingly, he admitted he admired her.

Under normal circumstances. But now he worried that Clancy might not have just gone for a bike ride. He worried she might have taken off. Tricked him again.

There was one way to find out. If she'd run, she'd need a boat to get her off the island. As he hurried down the trail, he realized he'd spent most of his time on this case chasing that woman.

At the resort office, the clerk assured him that no one matching Clancy's description had rented a boat.

Jake used the phone to call the lodge, hoping Clancy had returned by now. He hadn't seen Tadd since they'd split up to search for her. Aunt Kiki quickly informed him that neither Clancy nor Tadd had returned.

He hung up, more worried. Unless he missed his guess, Clancy was still on the island. The question was where?

As he started to leave the phone booth, he remembered the Bransons and dialed their number.

"Clancy was here, Jake, but she left just a little while ago," Helen told him. He could hear the clatter of dishes in the background and apologized for interrupting her dinner. She assured him they were just finishing. "I invited Clancy to join us, but she said she had to get home."

He hung up, wondering why she'd gone to the Bransons', and started back up the trail. So she was headed home. That was a good sign. He told himself he'd known she hadn't taken off again, at least not far. But he still felt a sense of relief that lifted his spirits. All right, maybe he'd started to trust her a little and he was glad she hadn't broken that trust by skipping the island to parts unknown.

Come on, Hawkins. When are you going to be honest with yourself? You desperately want to believe in Clancy's innocence. You're such a chump, you even want to believe she didn't perjure herself at your father's trial, that maybe there's another explanation.

Jake cursed his own foolishness. As he topped the mountain and started down the other side, he spotted Liz Knowles. Two things struck him as odd. One was the way she was dressed. The other was her hurried pace. He went after her on the side trail she'd taken, wishing he had enough time to tail her secretly and find out where she was headed in such a hurry.

"Hello," Jake said, catching up to her.

She jumped, startled. Scared, too, he noticed. Like a turkey on Thanksgiving morning. He couldn't help but wonder if he was the cause of her fear. Or someone else. After all, if the cabin girl was right, Liz had spent some quality time with Dex right before his death.

"You haven't seen Clancy, have you?"

"Clancy?" She wore a freshly ironed shirt with matching shorts and sandals. Her hair was pulled up, her lips painted pink, her cheeks flushed with blusher, and she smelled of perfume. He figured she had a date and must be meeting him on the trail somewhere since there was nothing but rocks and trees the way she was headed. She seemed a little overdressed for a roll in the pine needles.

"Clancy Jones, the woman you said you overheard threaten Dex Westfall on the day he died," Jake said through gritted teeth.

"Why would you ask if I'd seen her?" The drone of a dirt bike broke the stillness. Liz glanced up the mountain, her look agitated. He was keeping her from something. "I don't even know the woman. Of course I haven't seen her." When she looked again at Jake, she seemed all the more anxious to be on her way.

He decided to let her go. She started down the trail, turned once to see if he was following her, then took a side trail that headed off to the west. He had a feeling that wasn't the way she'd intended to go, that she'd changed her plans because of him.

Jake headed down a trail that would eventually lead him back to Clancy's lodge. As he walked, Clancy crowded his thoughts. Flashes of her making pancakes. Lounging in the boat with that silly fishing hat hiding her eyes. Standing in his arms. Looking up at him, her eyes filled with— He stumbled and swore. Love.

Clancy heard the buzz of a dirt bike coming up the mountain. The engine whined, the bike bucking as it climbed the steep terrain. The sound grew louder. She felt a chill and realized how dark the sky had gotten. Shadows hunkered in the pines. A wind blew up from the lake, swaying the tops of the trees. She pedaled faster through the growing darkness of the approaching storm, anxious to get back to the lodge. And Jake. Her sense of security ebbed with the light.

She was almost at a trail that dropped down to her lodge when she heard the dirt bike behind her, saw its headlight flicker in the trees in front of her as the bike gained on her. The bike was coming up behind her fast. Too fast. Didn't he see her? She took a side trail, stopping partway down the narrow path, waiting for the motorbike to go by.

She didn't realize she'd been holding her breath until she heard the biker stop. Clancy looked up to see a figure wearing a shielded dark helmet standing astride an old motorbike. She couldn't see his face behind the helmet, but she could feel him staring at her. Her heart thundered at the thought of whose face was hidden behind the shield.

She jumped on her bike and took off down the tree-lined trail, wanting only to get home. Above her on the mountainside she heard the bike motor rev. In horror, she realized he was chasing her. Panic tore through her. She pedaled as if the devil himself were at her heels. But when she stole a glance back, the trail behind her was empty, and she could hear the whine of the dirt bike dying off into the distance.

Clancy's heart thumped wildly in her chest. Paranoia. Maybe Jake was right. She *was* imagining things. Her legs felt weak and shaky from her scare. What had made her think that biker was chasing her? Was it the same thing that had made her think someone had tried

to drown her? The same thing that made her think she
saw a light in the lodge last night? Made her think she
saw Dex?

The sky darkened to charcoal overhead. In the distance, she heard the rumble of thunder. The wind picked
up, whipping the tops of the pines. Ahead, the trail
forked, the trees opened a little. The path to the left
circled up the mountainside to the east end of the island, the one on the right dropped rapidly in a series of
switchbacks to the beach and her lodge. Clancy relaxed.
She'd be home soon. An image of a furious Jake filled
her mind. Even he would be a welcome sight.

A bolt of lightning splintered the sky above the treetops, making her jump. Thunder boomed, drowning out
the sound of the dirt bike.

The biker appeared in a flash of movement. Leaping
from the pines. All she saw was a blur. All she felt was
the bike hit hers. A scream caught in her throat. The
ground came up to meet her. She hit it hard, knocking
the air from her lungs. Then she fell, tumbling down
the steep mountainside.

Chapter 13

As Jake wound his way through the dense pines, he heard the unmistakable whine of the dirt bike again. It cut through the softer evening sounds, irritating his already fried nerves. He cursed himself with each step. He was handling things poorly. He should have stashed Clancy with her aunt Kiki. Or had her bail revoked. At least if she was in jail, he wouldn't have to worry about her. And right now, he was worried.

One of his faithful hunches pounded at the back of his brain to a little ditty that had started the moment Kiki Talbott Conners had set one high-heeled foot on the dock beside his boat in Galveston. It reverberated like the thunder overhead and promised a darkness far beyond the storm bearing down on the island.

Thunder rumbled and the sky darkened like night. Clancy's skin was cut, scraped and gouged as she fell, plunging down through brush and branches, dirt and rocks. She fought to find purchase, grabbing at anything, everything, to keep from tumbling all the way down the steep mountain to the beach below. Finally, when she thought she'd never stop, she plunged over a large, old fallen log, decayed from the years, dropped into a hole rimmed by a thicket of fresh new pines and slammed to a halt.

That's when she felt the pain. It shot through her, making it hard to tell if she was seriously hurt or not. She tried to get to her feet, but her body screamed with pain for her to lie still a little longer.

Overhead, thunder clapped with a startling closeness. She glanced around to see that she'd fallen into a hole below the rotted log. Squirming away from the prickly pines, she leaned back against the warm earth, stared up at the blackened sky above her, and assessed her injuries. None fatal, few that required more than a bandage. She'd been very lucky. Again.

She replayed the accident over in her head. Then slowly she sat up, her heartbeat accelerating to breakneck speed. It had been no accident. The biker had waited in the pines and deliberately hit her. But why? And where was he now?

She glanced up the mountainside but couldn't see past the fallen log blocking her view. Suddenly the day seemed too quiet. In that deafening silence before the storm, she heard a sound above her that congealed her blood. The soft scuffle of footfalls, half stumbling, half sliding, coming down the mountain.

A flash of lightning electrified the sky and illuminated the darkness. The light died in an instant, leaving thunder to rattle across the treetops. Dirt showered down on her, cascading over the log, as someone drew closer. The biker. Her mouth went dry, her pulse pounded so loudly she feared he could hear it.

She didn't move, just waited, knowing that any moment he would peer over the log and see her lying there.

A voice in her mind, which sounded a lot like Jake's, yelled for her to move under the log. And yet she waited, with a sickening sureness that he'd find her before she could move. Then the lightning splintered the sky; thunder boomed. Clancy scrambled under the log, wedging herself into the small, narrow space between rotting log and earth. She held her breath and waited.

A boulder cartwheeled over the top of the rotted log with a resounding thump, then crashed through the new pines below her and on down the mountainside to the rocky beach below. It was followed by the thud of boots on top of the hollow-sounding log. She could almost feel him standing up there, looking down the mountainside, looking for her. To finish the job?

Rain splattered on the ground next to her, large, hard drops that pummeled the earth. Clancy closed her eyes, praying he wouldn't come any farther down the mountainside. If he did, he'd surely see her and—

She squeezed her eyes tighter, concentrating on Jake's handsome face, the sound of that soft southern drawl, the feel of his arms wrapped around her. She prayed for Jake, clinging to the log and hope as she waited.

The first drops of rain pelted down, angry and wet, as Jake would soon be. He told himself that when he found Clancy, he'd wring her neck. He'd bodily carry her to her aunt's for safekeeping. He'd take her over his knee and—

The dirt bike. It took Jake a moment to realize why the sound had pulled him from his frenzied thoughts. Its engine. Revved to the max. He looked up to see the headlight coming out of the blackness of the storm. The light flickered wildly as the bike roared down the pine-lined trail. Jake had only a moment to realize its rider didn't see him, couldn't see him in the rain and the darkness. He leaped from the path as the bike sped past.

Jake watched it go, not surprised to see Liz Knowles on the back of the bike, her russet hair blowing in the wind.

He cursed the biker and his close call. Then he turned and headed down the trail, following the path he knew would take him directly to Clancy's lodge. He hadn't gone far when something glinted in the trail ahead.

Dread clamped down on his heart as he thought he recognized the object at the edge of the trail. His breath caught as he drew closer. A bicycle, broken and twisted. His legs forced him forward, his mind arguing it wasn't Clancy's. Couldn't be hers. Clancy's ruined bike lay mangled at the edge of the steep drop-off in the rain.

"Clancy!" Jake screamed her name, a cry of fear and anguish, hope and despair. He stumbled past the bike to stare down the mountainside. The wind howled in the pines; rain bit into his skin, hard as stones. He bent down, saw the tracks where she'd slid down the mountainside and practically threw himself down the slope after her.

Clancy thought she heard the high-pitched whine of the bike fade. But she stayed wedged beneath the log, afraid to move. Had he really left? How could she be sure?

In the end, it was thoughts of Jake that made her slowly edge out of her hiding place. The wind whipped the pines, making them groan. The rain splattered down, wet and cold, promising a torrent shortly. She looked up, half expecting to see the biker standing on the log above her, his body in silhouette, his face as black as the shield he'd hidden behind earlier.

But no one waited on the log.

Had he really gone? And more important, who was he? Why did he want to harm her?

Clancy pulled herself to her feet. Her body throbbed with so many pains she couldn't isolate one from another. Her right hip ached with a dull throb where she vaguely remembered hitting it on something as she tumbled down the mountainside. The rain stung her skin, but she hardly noticed. She thought she heard her name on the wind. She thought she heard Jake's voice because she'd wished it so.

Jake's heart threatened to burst from his chest as he slipped and fell his way down the mountainside. He didn't even realize he'd screamed her name until he heard her call out to him and look up. He saw her just below him.

Her face was covered with a mixture of dirt and blood, her clothes were torn and stained, her hair a nest of weeds and decomposed wood. He thought she'd never looked more beautiful.

"Clancy?" His voice came out a whisper and was quickly carried away by the wind. "Clancy."

He stumbled down to her, grabbed her and pulled her into his arms. "Oh, baby. Are you all right?"

He felt her nod against his chest as she tightened her hold on him. Relief washed over him, making him weak. The rain began to fall in sheets, drenching him and everything it touched.

"He tried to kill me again," she said, her words muffled against his chest. "The man on the dirt bike. This time you believe me, don't you?"

He pulled back to look into her face. Words stuck in his throat. "Yes," he whispered. "I believe you." He swept her up into his arms and took her to the closest shelter—his lodge.

Clancy couldn't stop shivering as Jake kicked open the door and carried her up the stairs, straight to his room and the shower. She leaned against him as he got the water going, refusing to give up the warmth of his body or breach the bond between them even for a moment.

He turned and, without breaking contact, pulled her into the shower with him. The warm water felt wonderful, but not as wonderful as Jake as he drew her to him. He cupped her face in his hands. His mouth dropped to hers, taking her as his own, possessing her in that single kiss in the same way he'd possessed her heart for more than a decade.

His lips lingered on hers, savoring her, seducing her with his lips, his tongue, his breath. He drew back. She looked up at him, breathless from the kiss, from the look in his eyes. "Jake," she whispered, a plea.

Slowly, his gaze on hers, he unbuttoned her shirt, opening her bare skin to the warm water and the fire of his touch. She leaned into the spray and him, letting the water wash away the dirt and blood, letting Jake wash away the years of hurt.

He caught his breath as her shirt dropped from her

shoulders to the shower floor. His gaze alone hardened her nipples, making them ache with longing. He reached to unhook her bra, freeing her breasts to his gaze, to his touch, to his mouth and the rough, wet feel of his tongue.

Warmth sprinted from her hardened nipple through her body, making her weak. She ached for the feel of his skin on hers as she hurriedly unbuttoned his shirt, pushing aside the wet cloth to brush her palms across the solid wet heat of his flesh.

With a groan, he stripped off her jeans and panties and dragged her to him. Her pulse matched the thunder outside as he backed her up against the shower wall, trapping her there, her body now at his mercy. She surrendered as he devoured her swollen breasts, sucking her nipples red and hard. Then his mouth trailed down her belly to her open thighs, where he consumed her with the same kind of desperate need. She buried her fingers in his hair, arching against his mouth, as a hot current raced through her. There was no need for words; for once, they completely understood each other. There were no walls. No fences. Nothing to keep their hearts from running free.

"Jake," she whispered as she unbuttoned his jeans. A plea. A promise.

Jake stepped out of his wet jeans and lifted her, hip to hip. He breathed her name, husky with desire. "Clancy." Not a question. An affirmation. He thrust her against the shower wall, his gaze locking with hers. She gasped as he filled her so completely, and with each drive, he took her spiraling up, the water pounding them as the rain beat down on the skylight overhead. As the thunder rumbled and lightning lit the sky, he took her higher

and higher, further and further, until they both soared
like hawks over the island.

Jake said nothing as he pulled her into his arms. She
buried her face in his shoulder, hugging him tightly,
grazing his skin with a kiss. He placed a hand on the
back of her blond head and gazed down at her. So small.
So strong. So beautiful. He should have been surprised
by his feelings for her. But instead he was more surprised by her feelings for him. After everything he'd
done to her, she still loved him.

She leaned back to look up into his eyes. Then she
picked up the bar of soap and gently glided it over his
skin, lathering his shoulders, his chest, his belly.

He watched her eyes, still dark with pleasure, and he
knew he had to have her again. One time would never
still the need inside him. He doubted a hundred thousand would.

He took the soap from her and slowly slid it over her,
from the pounding pulse at the hollow of her neck, over
her luscious, full, rounded breasts, down to the hollow
of her stomach, to the silken V of her thighs.

She groaned softly, her eyes darkening as her hands
trailed over his skin.

He pulled her to him, their bodies slick and slippery.
He buried himself in her again, losing himself in her
body, in her eyes, in her.

Clancy came out of the bathroom, her wet hair curled
at her neck, her skin pink and bare except for the towel
wrapped around her. Jake tossed another log on the fire
and closed the screen.

"Do you want to go home and get something on
your scrapes and scratches?" he asked as he closed the

distance between them. "You must hurt all over from your fall."

She shook her head. Thunder boomed overhead, rattling the windows. Rain streaked the glass and pounded the deck. "I've never felt this wonderful."

He laughed as he swept her up and carried her to his bed. Before he joined her, he picked up the cell phone and dialed Clancy's number. Kiki answered on the first ring.

"Clancy's fine," Jake said. "She'll be back in the morning. Go home." He hung up and pulled Clancy into his arms. They lay together watching the storm rage outside, the fire crackle and glow inside until they fell asleep, spooned together in the middle of the bed.

The next morning, Clancy woke to find Jake propped up on one elbow, looking down at her. He smiled as he brushed hair back from her forehead and planted a kiss between her eyes, then dropped to place one on her lips.

She lay on her back, watching his face. When she'd first opened her eyes she'd caught him frowning down at her. She'd gone to sleep happier than she could ever remember being. Now she felt as if an elephant had just sat on her chest. "What is it?"

He seemed surprised by her question, then his smile faded. "You really don't miss anything, do you?" He trailed a finger across her shoulder.

She could almost hear the wheels turning in his head as she sat up, pulling the sheet over her bare breasts and leaned against the headboard, bracing herself. Outside, the storm had let up. The lake lay slate gray and flat. Water dripped from the eaves. In the distance, Clancy could see a slit of blue sky on the horizon.

Jake pulled himself up and leaned back against the wall next to the bed so he could face her. "Clancy, I've never been closer to anyone than I am to you."

She feared what was coming. She promised herself she wouldn't cry. "Why don't you just say it. This was a mistake."

She started to get up but he grabbed her arm and kept her on the bed.

"No, dammit, I'm trying to tell you that making love to you has made me realize that now more than ever, I want— I *need* to know—"

She knew the words before he said them.

"The truth. I have to know, Clancy. For my sanity's sake. For...our sake."

She stared at him. For a few hours she'd forgotten why he'd come back to Montana. Didn't he say he'd get the truth out of her at any cost? "Is that why you made love to me?" she asked. She shoved him away and got out of bed, anger soothing the dagger of hurt that was stuck in her heart. "Is that what this was all about? You thought if you got me naked and in a weakened enamored state, maybe I'd break down and confess everything?" She remembered her clothes were still on the shower floor, soaking wet.

"No! Dammit. You're not listening to me."

"Oh, I hear you just fine, Jake." She jerked a pair of jeans from Jake's closet. From the few items of clothing he'd brought, he obviously hadn't planned to stay long. Just get the truth out of her—whatever it took, even seducing her. Then he'd be gone back to Galveston. Oh, what a fool she'd been. Did she really think making love meant anything to him? Just a means to an end.

The jeans were way too big, but that didn't stop her.

She tugged them on, grimacing at her aches and pains. Just hours ago, she'd felt nothing but pleasure in Jake's arms. But this morning, her sore body reminded her painfully that some things hadn't changed. Making love with Jake had solved nothing.

"Dammit, you're wrong," Jake said, flying out of the bed to tower over her. "You think last night was just part of my plan?"

She looked up at him. "Don't tell me it didn't cross your mind."

His gaze slithered off. "I'll admit it did cross my mind but—"

"That's what I thought." She shoved her way past him to the closet and jerked one of his shirts from the hanger.

"Listen to me, woman. I used to imagine making love with you." He took her bare shoulders and drew her around to face him. "Nothing in my imagination would ever come close to actually being with you."

"Now, if I'd just quit lying to you, everything would be perfect, right?" She shucked his hands from her shoulders and tried to get the shirt on without him seeing how hard she was shaking. She didn't want him to see how much he'd hurt her. She didn't even want to admit it to herself.

"Where do you think you're going?" Jake demanded, stomping around to face her in all his nakedness.

She pushed past him. "Leave me alone, Hawkins."

"I can't stand this between us. Can't you understand that, Clancy?"

She angrily thrust one arm into a sleeve, then the other, making him have to step back to keep from getting slugged. "Nothing I can say or do will ever convince you."

"You can't just stomp off. Not now." She stepped back when he reached for her. He raked a hand through his hair and let out a frustrated curse. "Are you forgetting that someone tried to kill you?"

She fumbled with the buttons, not caring which holes they went in. "No, Jake, something like that doesn't exactly slip your mind, especially when I'd been telling you someone was after me all along and you didn't believe me." She stuffed her feet into her wet sandals and headed for the door.

"Just a minute, you aren't leaving like this. Let me get dressed. You took off by yourself yesterday and look where it got you."

She turned to see him hopping on one foot as he tried to pull on a pair of jeans. He looked so flustered, so much like the boy she'd fallen in love with. She cursed the emotions that drew her to him, the heart that threatened to break at just the sight of him. "Damn you, Hawkins. There are worse things than having a crazed killer after you. Like having a crazed ex-boyfriend who pretends to want to help you. Especially one you've been in love with your entire life." She turned and left, slamming the door on the way out.

"Where have you been?" Aunt Kiki demanded the moment Clancy slammed into the lodge. "Are you all righ—" She glanced from Clancy's flushed, scraped and scratched face to Jake's shirt, improperly buttoned with one tail hanging lower than the other. Clancy had to hold up the much too-large jeans with one hand.

"I'm fine," Clancy snapped, sweeping past her, feeling like a teenager caught necking. "Someone on a dirt bike tried to kill me. Other than that—" She turned and walked to her aunt, whose eyes widened in obvious disapproval at this inappropriate display of emotion. "And *someone* brought Jake Hawkins back into my life. If the guy on the bike doesn't get me, Jake will convince the state to hang me instead of just send me to prison. Other than that, I'm just fine. Didn't Jake tell you to go home?"

Kiki looked highly offended, but then she often did. "I don't take orders from Mr. Hawkins. And believe me, *this*—" she waved a hand at Clancy's postcoital condition "—isn't what I had in mind when I hired him."

It gave Clancy some satisfaction to see how displeased her aunt was over Clancy's liaison with Jake Hawkins. "Sometime you'll have to tell me just what it was you *did* have in mind when you hired him. In the meantime, I will just continue to assume that you've lost your mind."

Clancy turned and, with all the dignity she could muster, limped toward the stairs, her body hurting with each step.

"By the way," Kiki said behind her, "your lawyer called. It seems he fell while looking for you and broke his leg. He's at the hospital but said he plans to be home later. You might want to call him. That's if you are still interested in not going to prison."

"Actually, prison is looking better all the time," Clancy said without turning around.

She heard her aunt sniff in disapproval, then leave quietly. Always the Talbott, she thought, thankful that she had enough Jones in her to rant and rave and show some good, honest emotion.

Clancy started up the stairs, changed her mind and went back to lock all the doors. The last person she wanted to see again was Jake Hawkins. She'd much prefer Dex Westfall's ghost.

As Clancy climbed the stairs, she concentrated on the pain from her fall instead of the warmth inside her where Jake had been. Her skin still simmered from where his skin had touched hers. She used anger as a salve. What had she thought? That once they made love, Jake would realize she couldn't have possibly lied? That she was a woman who would never betray her man? That he'd been wrong? Oh, sure. A man as stubborn, intractable and incorrigible as Jake Hawkins? Fat chance.

Jake took a few frustrating minutes to try to find a shirt, then gave up and went after Clancy, realizing that all he'd done in the three days since he'd hit Montana was chase this woman and he was getting damned tired of it.

He threw open his front door to find Kiki poised under the dripping eave ready to knock. It didn't take a genius to see that she was madder than an old wet hen. She glanced at his bare chest with distaste. She was lucky he hadn't come to the door stark naked. He almost wished he had just for the shock value, although he doubted much could shake up Kiki.

"What?" he demanded. Before she could speak, he added, "Whatever it is, I don't have time for it."

"Perhaps we misunderstood each other, Mr. Hawkins," she said, her look darker than the storm that had passed through. "I hired you to help my niece, not seduce her."

He bit back a nasty retort and tried not to bite off her head. "It's none of your business who Clancy…sleeps with or doesn't." In his case, it would be "doesn't" in the future, he was sure, but he wasn't about to tell her that.

Kiki narrowed her gaze at him. "Please don't be offended, but you're not right for my niece. She deserves better than some…private investigator. Her mother married poorly. I won't let that happen to Clancy. I hope that's clear enough for you."

"Marrying your niece isn't even an option," Jake snapped.

Kiki's look would have frozen boiling water. "How nice to hear. Do you know who killed Dex Westfall yet, Mr. Hawkins?"

"No, as a matter of fact, I don't. If I could keep your niece from disappearing every time I turn around, I might be able to find out."

"See if you can do that." With a haughty flip of her head, she turned and headed for her boat.

Furious, he slammed out of his lodge and stalked the distance to Clancy's. *Some private investigator.* The nerve of that woman. He'd marry anyone he damned well pleased. As he stormed up Clancy's steps, he wasn't sure who he was the most angry with. Kiki. Clancy. Or himself.

He'd blown it, plain and simple. The case. But mostly Clancy. And, he realized with a start, he didn't give a damn about anything else. But she was right; what the hell was he doing making love to her when he still thought she was a liar and possibly a murderer?

Because I'm in love with her! He felt like he'd been struck by lightning. *You're in love with a liar and a possible murderer?* He stood for a moment, trying to get his bearings. He'd prove she was neither, dammit. He'd prove it to himself and then… And then what would he do? Throw himself at her mercy? Good luck.

But first he had to get back into her good graces somehow. It wasn't going to be easy. But for once, he thought he knew what to do.

* * *

Clancy was curled up on the couch in her robe, a heating pad on her back, a bag of crushed ice on one ankle, her scrapes, scratches and cuts disinfected and bandaged, when Jake burst in.

"I thought I locked that door," she demanded.

"Like everyone else in the world, I know where you keep your key."

She gave him a sour look. "Did you come to make love to me again to see if I'd crack this time?"

He cocked a brow at her. "I want to make love to you again, yes. But not for the reason you think."

Her look, as she got up to escape to another room, said his chances of that weren't good.

"But I'm not going to make love to you," he said.

She stopped and raised a brow at him. "No kidding."

"You were right. There's enough going on in your life right now without me complicating things by making mad, passionate love to you. We have a killer to find." He moved toward her, wanting desperately to take her in his arms and do exactly what he was about to promise he wouldn't. "We have to concentrate. For now. So, I promise I won't even kiss you." He reached out to run his thumb along her lips. "Or make love to you. Not until you ask me to."

"Well, there's no chance of that." Clancy took a ragged breath. Just when she thought things couldn't get any worse, he'd promised not to even kiss her until she asked him to. Right. How could she be around him and not beg him to kiss her, beg him to make love to her? Prison was starting to look like a picnic.

"So, we'd better get back to business. We have to

go to the resort and talk to Liz," Jake said. "She knows who was driving that bike."

Clancy told herself at least now he believed someone really was trying to kill her. She supposed that was something. Although, she did wonder about this sudden turnaround of Jake's. What was he up to with this promise of his? Something.

Out of the corner of her eye, she looked into his wonderfully handsome face and felt her dark mood lighten like the blue sky through the window. Even as a kid she could never stay mad at him.

"All right," she said, hoisting herself up from the couch. The parts of her body that weren't bruised, scraped, scratched or gouged, ached. All of her still ached for one man. She gave Jake a resigned look. "Let me get some clothes on."

He gave her a wide berth as she passed. Fool that she was, she already missed his touch.

It looked like off-season at Hawk Island Resort. The storm that had hammered the island most of the night still had everyone curled up inside their cabins. Only a handful of hard-core fishermen bailed their boats at the docks for a morning fishing trip. Everything dripped, wet and cold. June in Montana.

"I'd tell you to stay here—" Jake started, then smiled "—but what would be the point? You might as well tag along. One look at that scraped-up face of yours and Liz is bound to talk."

"Thanks a lot," Clancy said, climbing out of the boat and sweeping past him.

But when they reached the café, the only person

banging around at the back of the small kitchen was Frank Ames.

"What do you want?" Frank said, glancing up from the dirty grill.

"We're looking for Liz Knowles," Jake said.

Frank cursed and continued scraping the grill with a large metal spatula. "Isn't everybody."

"What does that mean?" Jake demanded, amazed at how quickly he could lose his patience with Frank.

Frank gave him a smirk. "She didn't show up for work this morning."

A bad feeling settled in the pit of Jake's stomach. "When was the last time anyone saw her?"

"I wouldn't know," Frank said, throwing down the spatula in disgust. "What's the big deal with you, anyway? I'm the one who has no waitress."

Jake leaned over the counter toward Frank, hoping he wouldn't have to cross it to get what he wanted out of him. "Did you check her cabin?"

Frank had the good sense to look a little nervous. "Of course. She hadn't slept in her bed. One of the cabin girls said she had plans last night with one of the dock boys. He says she never showed up for their date. She probably left the island with some guy she met. Happens every summer." He turned back to his dirty grill.

"Who has a dirt bike on the island?" Jake asked.

Frank stopped scraping and turned around slowly. "Why?"

Well, that answered that question. "Who besides you?"

Frank looked suspicious. And worried. He laid down the spatula again. At this rate, he'd never get that grill cleaned. "No one. Why?"

"Someone on a dirt bike tried to kill Clancy," Jake said.

"What?" His gaze shot to Clancy, surprise registering in his expression when he saw her injuries. "Just a damned minute here," he said to Jake. "You're not pinning me with that. I haven't ridden that bike since last summer."

"Where is your bike?" Jake asked. "I want to see it."

Frank ripped off his apron and threw it down on the counter. With a mean look, he led them to the back of his place and a dilapidated shed. Frank swung the door open and stood for a moment staring into the semidarkness inside.

Frank's shoulders sagged. He swore but didn't turn around.

Jake stepped past him to look inside the shed. Junk had been piled waist-deep in a U-shaped heap that left only a small, narrow space at the center. Just small and narrow enough for a dirt bike. But there was no bike.

"Someone stole my bike," Frank said. "Not that I'd expect you to believe me."

Jake didn't. "How could someone take it? Where was the key for it?"

Frank avoided his gaze. "I always left the key in it and the helmet on the seat."

"That's handy," Jake said.

"It was handy," Frank snapped.

Jake couldn't believe this. "And I suppose everyone knew the key was in it?"

Frank kicked at the shed door in answer. "No one's ever stolen it before, so why would they now?"

"Is there any reason anyone would want to incriminate you in a murder?" Clancy asked from behind him.

Frank's head flew up. "You mean someone took my bike to make it look like I tried to kill you?"

"Bingo." Jake watched Frank's eyes widen in surprise, then narrow in meanness.

"No. No one." The lie seemed to catch in Frank's throat. "That's the craziest thing I've ever heard."

"If Liz turns up, have her call me," Jake ordered.

Frank nodded distractedly.

Jake would have given a penny for his thoughts.

On the boat trip back to the lodge, the sun burst through the clouds, making the morning golden if not exactly warm. A few thin clouds scudded across the blue. A light breeze rippled the top of the water, bringing with it the smell of wet pines.

Jake's obvious disappointment in not finding Liz or the bike hung like a dark cloud over him. Clancy knew he was worried about Liz. Had Liz seen the biker run Clancy off the trail? Is that why she'd disappeared? Then, what had she been doing on the back of the bike just after that? She must have known Clancy's assailant. Did that mean Liz was part of whatever was going on? She *had* spent time with Dex.

Clancy felt a shiver as she and Jake walked up the beach toward the lodge. As hard as she tried not to, she kept seeing Dex's face beneath that bike helmet.

As Clancy opened the door, she could hear the phone ringing. She raced to it. "Hello?"

Silence.

Her heart began to pound. Another one of those crank calls. She motioned for Jake to pick up the extension in the living room. "Hello? Is anyone there?"

For a moment all she could hear was the labored

breathing. Then came the distinct sound of a match being struck as the person on the other end of the line lit a cigarette and took a long drag. "Please say something," Clancy urged.

"Clancy Jones?" The hoarse voice was a woman's. At least Clancy thought it was. "I need to talk to Clancy Jones."

"This is Clancy."

"I need your help." The woman sounded scared. And maybe a little drunk. Clancy wondered if that wasn't why she'd finally decided to speak rather than hang up like she had the other times.

"My help?" Clancy asked in surprise.

"My name is Glenda Grimes," the woman said. Clancy could hear her tapping nervously on something as she spoke. "You don't know me. I'm Lola Strickland's sister. Half sister."

Clancy looked across the room at Jake. His eyes widened in surprise. He nodded for her to keep talking.

"What can I do for you?" Clancy asked.

"Could you come up to Somers? I've got to talk to you. It's about Dex. I know who killed him."

Chapter 14

Jake turned off Highway 93 and drove the Mustang through downtown Somers, a community with little more than a bar, post office, café and hardware store. He drove up one of the dirt streets to the top of a rise and parked in front of a small dilapidated cottage overlooking the highway.

"Are you feeling all right?" Jake asked. "You've been awfully quiet."

"Just thinking." Clancy brushed her hair back from her face and gave him what she hoped was a reassuring smile. After what Jake had told her, she was worried about Liz Knowles. She agreed with Jake; there was a killer out there and she felt if they didn't stop him, he'd kill again. As she opened her car door, she hoped Glenda Grimes really did know something that could help them.

A woman in her sixties answered the door with a cigarette and a beer. She held little resemblance to her half sister, Lola. A bright-colored scarf tied around her head hid most of her frizzy dyed red hair; a faded chenille robe the color of dirt hid most of her body, except for a pair of bony bare feet poking out the bottom of the robe, the toenails painted bright red. The same color as the lipstick smear on her beer can.

"Yes?" the woman asked, suspicion as much a part of her face as the wrinkles.

"Glenda Grimes?" Jake asked.

Eyes narrowed, she looked from Clancy to Jake and back. Clancy could smell her perfume. A mixture of cigarette smoke, beer and perm solution. At one time, she might have been pretty, Clancy thought. But not as pretty as Lola.

"What do you want?" She had the voice of a woman who'd spent a good deal of her life on a bar stool. She took a drag off the cigarette and blew the smoke out the corner of her mouth as she eyed them.

"I'm Clancy Jones." It didn't seem to register at first, and Clancy felt her initial rush of hope dissolve. Either the woman was a crackpot or Glenda Grimes hadn't called her at all.

Glenda looked around warily before she settled her gaze on Jake. "Who's he?"

"He's a private investigator," Clancy said, then added, "and a good friend of mine."

Glenda studied Jake for a moment, then glanced past him as if she thought someone might be watching them. Hurriedly she pushed open the screen and ushered them inside, closing and locking the door.

And Clancy thought *she* was paranoid.

Clancy stepped into a small, cramped living room. The place was filled with…stuff. Every flat surface had something on it from chipped figurines and old perfume bottles to ashtrays with the names of Montana bars.

"All I have is beer," Glenda said, shuffling into the cluttered kitchen to swing open the door of an old fridge with so many magnets on it Clancy couldn't tell the color.

Both Clancy and Jake declined, and Glenda finished the beer in her hand and pulled out a fresh one. It was obvious she'd already had a few as she came into the living room.

"Sit down." She motioned to a broken-down couch in a dark corner and dropped into a faded chair across from them. Clancy watched her put her beer next to an overflowing ashtray beside her chair. Her fingers trembled.

"There's something I don't understand," Clancy said. "If you have information about Dex's murder, why did you call me instead of going to the police?"

The woman took a drag off her cigarette, then fumbled it back into the ashtray. She popped the top on the beer and took a long drink as if she thought it would steady her nerves. Clancy wondered what Glenda Grimes had to be nervous about.

"You're the one they arrested for Dex's murder, right?" Glenda asked.

Clancy nodded, wondering where this was going.

"I figured you'd care more than the police about who really killed Dex."

That made an odd kind of sense to Clancy. "On the phone you said you knew who killed him."

Glenda reached for another cigarette, fingers shaking violently. "I did."

"You?" Clancy asked incredulously.

"I wasn't the one who bashed his head in, mind you, but I killed him just as sure as you're sitting here." Glenda reached for her beer and a tissue.

Clancy shot a look at Jake. Glenda Grimes was a crackpot, just as they'd feared. A morose woman who cried in her beer and blamed herself for her nephew's death. Another dead end.

"Why should you feel responsible?" Jake asked.

"I was the one who got him all stirred up about the past." She started to cry. "Got him digging into things that should have been left buried."

"What kind of things?" Jake asked.

Glenda just shook her head and cried. "I've never been to Vegas. I'm an old woman. I want to go before I die. That isn't too much to ask, is it?"

What did that have to do with Dex's death?

"So you really don't know who killed your nephew," Jake said, getting to his feet. "Why did you call Clancy and waste her time?"

Glenda wiped her tears and narrowed her eyes at him. "I don't know who actually killed him. But I know why," she said, anger making her cheeks pink.

"Why?" Jake demanded. When she didn't answer, he swore softly under his breath. "Two people have already died. If you really do know something—"

"Somebody doesn't want all that old stuff about Lola coming out again. You've got to find the murderer before he finds me." Glenda finished her beer as if it were an antidote.

"Why would someone want to kill you?" Jake asked. "What is it you know?"

"It isn't what I know," she cried. "It's what he might think I know. Don't you see, I talked to Dex and he figured it out. If the killer finds out I talked to Dex, he might think I know more than I do and come after me."

"Wait a minute," Clancy interrupted. "How do you know Dex figured it out?"

Glenda studied the end of her cigarette. "He came by here the night before he died. He told me he knew who killed his mother."

Jake shot Clancy a look she recognized instantly. Total disbelief. "He didn't tell you who that person was?"

"He didn't want to get me involved," Glenda said. "Just believe me, Dex was positive he'd figured it out."

"Based on what?" Jake demanded.

Glenda shook her head. "He'd collected everything he could find on his mother's murder."

The newspaper clippings, Clancy thought.

"He'd even hatched some lamebrain scheme that involved getting to know Clancy, thinking, I guess, that she might know something. I told him the rest, about the trial, his mother..." Glenda said with a look of disgust.

Clancy thought of the beautiful, dark-haired woman who had worked at the resort office. "I don't remember very much about Lola. Can you tell us what you told Dex?"

Glenda let out a long sigh, making Clancy think it was going to be a long story. "Lola looked like her daddy. All that dark hair, those dark secretive eyes, a face that stopped traffic."

"You didn't have the same father?" Clancy asked.

"No, my daddy died when I was young. Mama remarried and had Lola." Glenda wagged her head. "Lola was spoiled, wild and foolhardy from the get-go. She ran off at sixteen and got herself into trouble. Then she goes and runs off again after Dex is born." Glenda leaned back, as if that pretty much covered Lola's entire life history.

"Did you see much of her when she lived on the island?" Jake asked.

"She'd stop by just to lord it over me. Tell me about the parties she'd been to, important people she'd met."

"Do you know where she was going the night of the fire?" Clancy asked.

Glenda raised a brow. "She *thought* she was taking off with her lover."

"Her lover?" Jake and Clancy asked in unison.

Glenda seemed surprised by their surprise. "Lola always had a lover, but this time she thought she'd met her Prince Charming." She rolled her eyes. "But he turned out to be just another loser."

"You knew who this man was?" Jake asked

"Lola never told me, just that I'd find out soon enough and I should expect fireworks," Glenda said. "Lola loved drama in her life."

"You think he was married," Jake said.

Was Jake thinking of his father, Clancy wondered. "Could be why Lola kept him a secret." Glenda made a production of lighting another cigarette. "Who knows? But I can tell you this, he was no Prince Charming."

"What makes you say that?" Clancy asked.

"Where were his suitcases if he planned to run off with her?" Glenda asked. "All her talk about how sweet he was, loving, caring, considerate. I knew he sounded too good to be true."

"You think he's the one who killed her?" Jake asked.

"He could have been," Glenda said as she got up and headed for the fridge. "Probably over the money."

Clancy and Jake exchanged a glance. "What money?" Clancy asked first.

"The money Lola stole." Glenda gave them a look as if to say they weren't as bright as she'd hoped.

"Are you talking about the money that was missing from Clancy's and my father's businesses?" Jake asked. The money Warren Hawkins had gone to prison for embezzling. "Lola stole it?"

"If there is one thing Lola loved even more than men, it was money." Glenda dug around in the fridge. "I wonder if she ever really planned to run off with this guy."

"What do you mean?" Clancy asked.

"She could have led the guy on, planning to double-cross him all along," she said as she slammed the fridge door and popped another top. "Maybe he found out and killed her."

"If you thought Lola embezzled the money, why didn't you come forward during the trial?" Jake demanded.

Clancy could have cut the tension in the room with a dull knife.

Glenda came back into the room, sat and dug another cigarette out of a half-empty pack. "Why? I don't know she did it. Why get involved in something I didn't know squat about?"

"You were her sister," Jake shot back.

"Half sister. Maybe I didn't want anyone knowing I was related to her. It wasn't like she told anyone about me. Anyway, she'd made someone mad enough to kill her. I didn't want to get involved."

"But you did get involved," Clancy pointed out.

"When you told Dex. Why did you decide to tell what you knew now?"

Glenda looked toward the front door as if she expected someone to come bursting in at any moment. "I want to go to Vegas before I die."

It took Clancy a moment. "You told Dex because you thought he would uncover the missing money."

Jake swore.

Tears filled Glenda's eyes. "How did I know it was going to get Dex killed?" she demanded. "I just thought he might be able to solve the mystery of what happened to that money."

"What made you think the money was even still around?" Jake asked, sounding surprised. "It had been embezzled over a period of time. What makes you think the embezzler didn't spend it as fast as he stole it?"

She shrugged. "I figure if Lola stole the money, she would have been real careful. She'd know better than to spend it. So she'd hide it somewhere. She was probably going to pick it up that night but she got killed. Her lover might or might not have known where she'd hidden the money. Either way, he probably didn't have time to rehide it before he was arrested for her murder."

That was quite the theory, Clancy thought. *If* Lola took the money.

"But now Warren Hawkins is coming up for parole," Jake said, an edge to his voice. "You wanted to get to the money before he could. Just in case he was that man."

Glenda took a swig of her beer.

"Wait a minute," Clancy said, frowning at the woman. "You're saying now that you don't believe it was Warren Hawkins?"

"Someone murdered Dex because he was getting too close to the truth," Glenda said with certainty.

Jake shook his head. "You had to have told Dex more than this for him to figure out who killed Lola."

"I told you everything I told him," Glenda said stubbornly. "When he came by, he wasn't here long. We talked, he looked through a box of junk Lola left here, but he didn't take anything except for some silly necklace, and he left."

Clancy's head jerked up. "Necklace?"

"What box of junk?" Jake demanded with a pained look.

"What did this necklace look like?" Clancy questioned.

"Just a string of beads," Glenda said.

Clancy felt her heart rate accelerate. "Pale blue with a navy ceramic heart in the center?"

Glenda nodded, eyeing her suspiciously. "How did you know that?"

"Dex showed me the necklace. He said his mother left it to him."

The woman snorted. "Lola didn't leave him nothing. She couldn't have cared less about the boy. It was just some stuff she dumped here and a few personal things the police turned over to me after the fire."

So Glenda had come forward after the trial to collect her sister's valuables. Only they hadn't turned out to be valuable.

"You should have seen the way that boy rifled through that box," Glenda was saying. "Like he thought she'd left him buried treasure or something." Glenda wagged her head. "It was pathetic to see—"

"You still have the box?" Jake interrupted.

"It doesn't have a thing in it that's worth anything," she said. "That's probably why Lola left it with me."

"I'd like to see the box," Jake insisted.

With effort, Glenda pushed herself out of the chair and went into one of the rooms off the living room. She returned a few minutes later with a shoe box and handed it to Jake. He set it on the coffee table and carefully removed the contents. Clancy slid closer.

Glenda was right. It contained little of monetary value. Several pressed dried roses. Ticket stubs from the local theater. A faded fishing lure. A plastic bubble with fake snow falling over a fat, red-cheeked Santa. A cheap dime-store mood ring. A pair of tarnished silver half-moon earrings. An envelope of photographs from the resort, mostly scenic, Clancy noticed as she flipped through them. A stack of play programs, ones Lola had had roles in. A handful of greeting cards. It reminded Clancy of the kind of things a young girl keeps from her first love affair.

It seemed odd that Dex would take nothing but the bead necklace. Had he just taken it because it belonged to his mother? Then, why didn't he take some of the other things? "Was the necklace in the box when Lola gave it to you?"

Glenda shook her head. "She must have been wearing it. The cops gave it to me with that ring and those earrings." She pointed to the mood ring and the half-moon earrings Jake had pulled out of the box. "That's the lot of her belongings," Glenda said with disgust. "And all that talk about her ritzy friends."

Jake handed Clancy the photographs he'd found. She leafed through them, stopping in surprise at a photo of Lola with a man she recognized. The man stood next to

Lola on the dock in front of the resort, his arm around her shoulders, a smile on his face as he looked down at her. There was what Clancy would describe as a longing in his eyes. The man was Tadd Farnsworth.

"Could this have been Lola's Prince Charming?" Clancy asked.

Glenda squinted at the photograph, then shook her head. "Why the fuss over keeping it a secret if she was going to pose right in front of the resort with him?"

Clancy had to agree. She suspected Lola's great love had been a forbidden one. She just wondered why.

Jake glanced through the greeting cards, then handed them to Clancy. They were all in the same hand, all the kind of cards a man in love might buy a woman, all with the same inscription: "With love, your Teddy Bear."

Glenda nodded with a smirk. "Teddy Bear. Can you believe that?"

It didn't sound to Clancy like anything a grown man would call himself, but what did she know about men? She put the cards back into the box.

"Do you think Teddy Bear was this man she planned to run off with?" Jake asked.

Glenda shrugged. "If a guy who calls himself Teddy Bear doesn't have something to hide, who does?"

"This stuff meant something to her," Clancy said, glancing at the odd items from the box. "That's why she brought it here." But why? Was she worried that something might happen to her? Was there a clue in this box as to who killed her and had Dex recognized it? Then, why had he taken only the necklace, which hadn't even been in the box?

Out of the corner of her eye, Clancy saw Jake slip one of the cards into his pocket when Glenda wasn't looking. Clancy hoped he hadn't taken it because he'd recognized the handwriting as his father's, and that Teddy Bear was Warren Hawkins. If Glenda's theory was right, Lola's lover was still on the loose—and a killer. And if that were true, then Warren Hawkins had gone to prison for a murder he hadn't committed.

"Do you mind if we take this photograph?" Jake asked, holding up the one of Lola and Tadd.

"Take the whole box," Glenda said. "I want it out of here."

Chapter 15

Clancy was too quiet as they left Somers. Jake drove along the lakeshore, his own thoughts tangled. The storm had left the day cooler than usual, but Jake cracked his window, anyway, to let in some of the fresh air. He found himself going over what Glenda had told them, trying to fit the odd-shaped chunks of truths and lies together. It made his head ache.

"Glenda Grimes knows more than she's telling us," Jake said with a silent curse. He looked over at Clancy when she didn't respond. "Want to tell me what's bothering you?"

They'd gone a few miles along the Flathead Lake shoreline, everything lush and green after the storm. He suspected Clancy had seen him pocket the card. She didn't miss much. Or was he losing his touch?

"You've never believed your father was guilty," she said quietly. "So who did you think was?"

Jake knew this discussion had been coming for years. Actually, he was surprised they hadn't gotten into it sooner. He pulled the Mustang over at the first wide spot and turned off the engine. Sunlight flickered on the water. A canopy of clouds still hung over the mountains. It had seemed clear to him. "Your father," he answered.

"That's what I thought." She didn't sound angry, just sad.

"It was the only thing that made sense," Jake admitted. "I knew you wouldn't perjure yourself except to protect your father."

"That's what you think I did, knowing what it would do to you?" she asked. "Jake, I adored my father. But I didn't love him as much as I loved you. I would never have lied for him. He wouldn't have let me."

Jake felt a pain at heart level stronger than any he'd ever known. "At the time, all I saw was that either you'd lied to save your father or that my father was not just a thief, but a murderer and an arsonist."

"And now?" Clancy asked.

He shook his head. "Now everything seems different than it did then." Because of the large amount of money that was missing, it seemed that one of the two partners, Warren Hawkins or Clarence Jones, had to be guilty. "Maybe Lola did embezzle the money. All I know is that now I can see that there might be another explanation, even though Lola's dead and the money's never turned up."

"Maybe she spent it or gave it to someone. Maybe it's still hidden somewhere like Glenda thinks it is."

He looked over at her. "You don't want my father to be guilty any more than I do, do you."

She smiled. "I never did, Jake."

"The problem is, if Lola had been skimming that much money from the businesses, my father would have caught it." Warren Hawkins had been in charge of the financial end of the businesses.

"Your father may have been...distracted," Clancy said.

He glanced over at her. Had everyone known about the problems his parents had been having or just Clancy? He'd always believed his parents would have worked things out if his father hadn't gone to prison. Now he wasn't so sure of that. He knew they'd been having financial problems partly because of the way his mother had liked to live, throwing large, extravagant parties. She loved to entertain, and there was nothing wrong with that. They could afford it. Couldn't they?

"I thought we'd stop by Tadd's and ask him about that photograph," he said as he started the Mustang.

"You think he's Teddy Bear?" Her tone made it clear she didn't.

"His name is Theodore."

They found Tadd at home, his leg up and a ballgame on the television.

"How's the leg?" Jake asked, taking the chair Tadd offered. He noticed Clancy didn't sit. She'd gone to the mantel, where she seemed to be inspecting a series of framed photographs.

"Hurts like hell," Tadd said, grimacing. "Doctor says I'm lucky I didn't break my neck." His gaze followed Clancy. "How are you, Clancy?"

She turned. "Sore, but otherwise just glad to be alive."

He nodded, and continued to watch her inspect the photos. "The sheriff called. They found the dirt bike."

"Where?" Clancy asked.

"Paradise Cove." Tadd seemed to hesitate. "They also found Liz Knowles's body."

"Oh, no," Clancy said, slumping down into a chair by the fireplace. "She wasn't…"

"She'd drowned," Tadd said. "She was wearing the bike helmet."

Jake slammed a fist down on the arm of the chair. "No way. Someone else was driving that bike when I saw her. Whoever it was killed her as sure as I'm sitting here. Don't tell me the sheriff thinks it was an accident?"

"He's waiting for the results of the autopsy," Tadd said. "But it looks like Liz might have ridden the bike off the cliffs and drowned."

Jake swore. "What about the bike?"

"Belonged to Frank Ames, all right. He's sticking to his original story that someone stole it."

"With Liz gone, we don't know who was driving that bike and we can't prove Frank's lying," Jake said.

Tadd nodded. "I think Frank Ames is up to his neck in this. I asked for a copy of the police report." He reached beside his chair, picked up a manila envelope and handed it to Jake. "These are the photocopies of the evidence you asked for along with Dex Westfall's autopsy report and copies of the clippings from Dex's closet wall."

Jake took the envelope but he didn't open it. He studied Tadd, a dozen suspicions buzzing around in his head like angry wasps. "Where were you when Liz went off that cliff, Tadd?" Jake asked, trying to keep the accusation out of his tone.

Tadd's eyes widened. "What?"

Jake saw Clancy tense. "You used to own a dirt bike. I remember when you raced in local competitions. You were pretty good."

Tadd let out a laugh. "You can't be serious. I haven't ridden in years. I'd kill myself."

"Or break your leg," Jake added.

"Wait a minute," Tadd said, holding up his hands. "Why would I want to kill Liz Knowles and my own client?"

"Because of Lola," Jake said quietly.

"Lola?" Tadd asked, looking uncomfortable.

"We had an interesting talk with Lola Strickland's sister this morning in Somers," Jake said.

Tadd looked surprised. "Lola had a sister?"

"Half sister. Glenda Grimes. She told us she thinks the person who killed Lola also killed Dex."

"You're not accusing me?" Tadd laughed. I told you what happened. I got out of the boat to look around and fell. Fortunately I wasn't far from the boat and could get to the hospital. I had the doctor call as soon as I could."

"Lola's sister told us something else interesting," Jake said. "The night Lola died she thought she was running off with some man she'd fallen in love with."

"No kidding," Tadd said.

"Were you that man?" Jake asked.

"You aren't serious. I was engaged to marry a senator's daughter. Why would I run off with Lola?"

"Because you were in love with her," Clancy said as

she reached into her pocket and pulled out the photograph Glenda had given them. She handed it to Tadd.

He took it with obvious reluctance and stared down at it for a long moment. "Where did you get this?"

"From a box of special mementos that Lola left at Glenda Grimes's house. This was in the box along with numerous cards from her Teddy Bear."

He looked up and seemed surprised at their expressions. "You think I'm Teddy Bear?" Tadd asked, sounding amazed.

"Isn't your real name Theodore?" Jake asked.

Tadd groaned. "I've never been called Teddy in my life. I certainly wouldn't call myself Teddy Bear."

"We think the man who wrote the cards is the same one Lola planned to run off with," Clancy told him.

Tadd laughed. "You've got the wrong man."

"But you did have an affair with her," Jake said.

Tadd let out a groan. He met Jake's gaze. "Okay, I had an affair with her. But it was just that, a brief affair. When she threatened to go to my fiancée, I bailed out."

"But you never married the senator's daughter," Clancy pointed out.

Tadd nodded. "When I broke it off with Lola, she went to the senator. Not only did Suzanne drop me like a hot rock, it set my political career back a good ten years."

"What did you do about it?" Jake asked.

Tadd laughed. "It was too late to do anything. I'd lost Suzanne and the senator. By then, Lola had already moved on to her next victim. Lola didn't go long without a man," he said bitterly. "I got over it." He looked up and must have seen their skepticism. "Come on, you don't really believe I was Teddy Bear. I'm a lawyer. I'd never put anything in writing."

Jake didn't want to, but he believed him. He'd also compared the handwriting on the back of the business card Tadd had given him with the note on the Teddy Bear card. The handwriting wasn't even close.

"Any guesses who this Teddy Bear might have been?" Jake asked.

Tadd shook his head. "I'll tell you who used to have it bad for Lola. Frank Ames. He was always hanging around her like a lost puppy." He turned his gaze on Clancy. "Well, are you going to fire me?"

"You have more reason than any other attorney to keep me out of prison. The upcoming election and Aunt Kiki's money. That's good enough motivation for me."

"I've been doing some research on sleep disorders," Tadd said. "Did you know that severe stress or some type of trauma often triggers sleepwalking?"

"You mean like being arrested for murder?" Clancy asked sarcastically.

"I was thinking more like Dex Westfall showing up on the island," Tadd said.

"Or showing up at the lodge after he's dead?" Jake asked.

Clancy waited until they reached the car and Jake started to pull away from the curb before she asked, "I've walked in my sleep again, haven't I?"

"Yes."

"Oh, my God." She buried her face in her hands for a moment. "What did I do? Where did I go?" When he didn't answer, she looked at him. "Why didn't you tell me?"

He shrugged.

"You thought I was faking it." She turned to look out the passenger-side window, a volatile mix of emotions making her want to strike out at him.

"I'm not sure where you went—somewhere on the beach," Jake said. "You had sand on your feet. And—"

She looked over at him, her pulse rate accelerating. "And what?"

"You had something in your fist. A tiny blue bead."

Clancy let out a groan. "You weren't going to tell me?"

"I haven't really had a chance."

"You could have said something when I told you about the necklace and my other sleepwalking episode when I came back with a bead."

Jake said nothing. But then, what could he have said in his defense?

"Don't you realize your lack of trust in me is hampering this investigation? Can't you, the professional P.I., see that?"

"I should have told you."

No kidding. "Just like you should have told me about the card you took from the box."

He reached into his pocket. "Here." He handed her the greeting card. "I was going to tell you."

"Sure you were." She opened the card, wondering if that were true. The card was like the others in Lola's junk box. Only this one had a sailboat on the cover with a man and a woman watching a sunset. They presumably were in love. Inside it read: Each day with you is a dream come true. It was signed: Your Teddy Bear.

"Do you recognize the handwriting?" Clancy asked.

"It's not my father's, if that's what you're asking." His

voice had an edge to it. He knew that was exactly what she was asking. "You want to talk about trust here?"

He was right. But it was that lack of trust between them that was breaking her heart.

Jake took the card from her and turned it over and returned it to her. Written on the back in an entirely different hand were the words: I have to talk to you. Meet me at the usual place. Frank.

Clancy looked up at Jake. "Frank and Lola?"

"Lola seems to have been a busy woman. Makes you wonder, doesn't it? I'd like to pay Frank a visit. What do you think?"

"Why not?"

Clancy could feel the weight of the few days' events on her sore and aching body as they parked the car at the marina and went by boat to the island resort. She wanted this case over with as quickly as possible so Jake could go home to Texas. Being around him wore down her heart. She told herself it would be easier not to see him. Not to be near him. Not to hear his voice. Not to know he was just down the hall.

Frank wasn't in his cabin. He didn't come to the door when Jake knocked and the door was locked.

"He's not home" came a male voice from the darkness.

Clancy recognized the youth as the dock boy she'd seen working the day before. "Do you know where he is?" she asked.

The boy shrugged. "He left earlier by foot." He pointed to the mountain.

Frank didn't seem like the hiking kind.

"You didn't happen to be around the night Dex West-fall was murdered?" Jake asked.

The boy looked up, surprise in his expression.

"I was wondering if Dex might have taken a boat out that night."

He shook his head. "The only time Mr. Westfall left the island was that first day. He rented a boat."

Jake looked disappointed. He thanked the boy and they started back down the trail.

"Mr. Westfall did have a visitor who came by boat the night he died, though," the boy added from behind them. "A woman."

Clancy stopped and turned slowly. "Can you describe this woman?"

The boy smiled. "Oh, yes." He proceeded to describe her in detail.

Clancy shot a shocked look at Jake.

Jake swore. "Kiki." He turned to the boy. "About what time was this?"

He shook his head. "It was late, well after dark. She went up to Mr. Westfall's cabin. I didn't see her leave."

"Did you tell the sheriff this?" Clancy asked.

The boy shook his head. "No one ever asked me. I figured it wasn't important."

Jake thanked him again. They walked back to their boat. "Kiki?" Jake exclaimed the moment they were out of earshot. "Had your aunt ever met Dex?"

"Not that I was aware of." She bit her lower lip, feel-ing sick. "You don't think she—"

"Is somehow involved in his death?" Jake asked. "No, but I've thought from the very beginning that Kiki knew a lot more about this than she told either of us."

* * *

Jake docked the boat in front of Kiki's rented condo in Bigfork. The condo hung over the water, a huge monument to commercial development. Clancy didn't wait for him to tie up the boat. She jumped out, charged up to her aunt's door and pressed the doorbell.

Kiki opened the door in a caftan with a champagne-colored poodle under her arm and what smelled like a banana daiquiri in her hand. "What a nice surprise," she said.

"You might not feel that way when you find out why we're here," Clancy said.

Kiki raised a finely sculpted brow as Clancy stepped past her. "Can I offer you something to drink, dear?"

"I'd love something to drink," Jake said from behind her, although Clancy noted Kiki hadn't offered him one.

Jake closed the door, then he and Kiki followed Clancy into the living room.

Clancy spun around to face her aunt. "What were you doing on the island the night of Dex's murder?"

"I'll fix that drink myself," Jake said to Kiki, and headed for the wet bar.

Kiki set the poodle down. It was the only color in the room. Everything else was white. Even the marble fireplace was white.

"Visiting Dex Westfall," Kiki said, and took a sip of her drink.

"Where's the ice?" Jake called from the bar.

"In the bucket," Kiki called back, her voice sounding a little strained.

"I didn't even know you knew Dex!" Clancy cried.

"I made his acquaintance shortly after the two of you met," Kiki said, walking over to sit in one of the large white chairs in front of the fireplace. "I offered to pay him not to see you anymore. Are you sure you wouldn't like something to drink?"

Clancy gasped. "You tried to buy him off?" Her aunt had always interfered in her life, offering unwanted advice, but this was way beyond that.

"What was I to do?" Kiki asked, nonplussed. "He wasn't the right man for you."

"Did he take the money?" Jake asked from the bar.

"No," Kiki said in disgust. "He said he deserved much more and he intended to get it."

"Aunt Kiki, I can't believe you'd do such a thing," Clancy said. "What else did you do?"

"If you're asking if I killed him, of course not," Kiki said. "But I can't say I'm sorry he's dead. He was a deplorable man."

"If he refused your money the first time, why did you go to the island to see him?" Jake asked as he joined them. He handed Clancy a glass of brandy she hadn't asked for and went to sit across from Kiki.

"To offer him more money," Kiki stated flatly. "I knew he had a price, I just had to find it."

Clancy rolled her eyes. Life was so simple for her aunt as long as she could solve her problems with money. While she almost appreciated Kiki's efforts, she resented her aunt's continued attempts to control her life. Had always resented it.

"Dex didn't take it?" Clancy knew no large quantity of money had been found in Dex's cabin or on his body. Although, she was surprised that Dex hadn't taken her aunt up on the offer.

"The opportunity didn't present itself," Kiki said

with a sigh. "I caught him with some woman and did the next best thing."

"Let me guess," Jake said. "Blackmail."

Clancy glanced over at him, keyed to the way he'd said "blackmail." Was that how Kiki had gotten Jake to Montana? She felt sick.

"While blackmail is always a possibility," Kiki said, smiling at him, "it really wasn't necessary. He was planning to leave the island that night, anyway."

"But he didn't," Jake pointed out.

Kiki shot him a dour look. "Something must have kept him from it. Someone. He told me his business on the island was finished. He seemed quite pleased about leaving."

"Who was the woman?" Jake asked.

Kiki shrugged. "I never saw her, but I smelled her perfume. It was expensive."

"Did he look like you'd interrupted something?" Jake asked.

"He was clothed, if that's what you're asking," Kiki replied primly. "But yes, now that I think about it, I did see him kick something under the bed. A pair of white Jockey shorts, I believe."

Kiki didn't miss a thing, Clancy thought, and took a sip of the brandy. It burned all the way down. She took another.

"I was astounded to hear the next morning that he'd been murdered," Kiki continued. "Even more appalled to learn the sheriff thought Clancy had killed him."

Clancy drained her glass and stared dumbfounded at her aunt. "What do you do when you can't buy what you want or blackmail someone to get your way?"

Kiki studied her niece for a moment. "The problem's

never come up." She glanced pointedly at Jake. "But I could see how it might."

He finished his drink and got up to take Clancy's empty glass from her fingers. "You ready to go?" he asked her.

"Yes." She marched to the door, opened it and stopped to look back at her aunt. "One of these days you're going to go too far. Maybe you already have."

Jake tipped his baseball cap at Kiki on the way out. He didn't say anything until he and Clancy reached the boat. "She's something, isn't she?" he said, and laughed.

"It's not funny, Jake."

"Oh, come on. It's her way of trying to protect you. As strange and twisted as it is. And you have to admit, her instincts about Dex were right."

Clancy spun on him. "How can you defend her?" She narrowed her gaze at him. "How did she get you up here, anyway? Money? Or blackmail?"

"Money?" He sounded insulted.

She studied him for a moment, remembering that she'd heard his father was coming up for parole soon. "If not money, then it had to be blackmail. Initially."

He tried to look insulted, but she knew her instincts had been right. "What makes you think I didn't come up here because I wanted to?" Jake demanded.

Clancy glared at him. "I remember how mad you were that first night when you had to save me from drowning. Then, when you realized you could get revenge—"

"Hey." He grabbed her and spun her into his chest. "You're wrong. Maybe at first. But surely you realize it isn't like that anymore."

"Isn't it?" she asked, looking into those gray eyes. The lights from the marina came on, making them gleam a slick silver. She felt the strength of his grip on her arm as he pulled her to him. For a moment, she thought he'd kiss her. Hoped he would forget his promise. Hoped he'd take her in his arms and tell her he believed her.

With an oath, he let go of her and climbed into the boat without another word.

Clancy said little on the boat ride back to the island.

"I need to do some work," she said the moment they walked into the lodge. Jake watched her disappear up the stairs to her studio, kicking himself.

He couldn't stand the wall between them. But at the same time, he seemed incapable of tearing it down. He cursed himself and went to his room just down the hall from Clancy's studio. He dumped the envelope of evidence in the middle of his bed. He had to find out who killed Dex and keep Clancy from going to prison. Maybe, if he got lucky, he'd also find Lola's killer. For his father. For his own sanity. But he wondered if by then it would be too late for him and Clancy.

He picked up the cellular phone and called Tadd.

"I need to know if Frank Ames inherited a bunch of money. Or maybe won the lottery. I need to know how he bought Hawk Island Resort. Now."

"Tonight?" Tadd croaked.

"Tomorrow would be fine," Jake said.

"I'll put my secretary on it at daybreak."

After Jake hung up, he felt restless. The lodge seemed uncommonly quiet, the summer night almost too still. He didn't want Clancy to think he was checking up on her. But he couldn't help himself. He couldn't get her off his mind any more than he could forget the feel of her in his arms. Or her steadfast conviction that she hadn't perjured herself, hadn't lied about his father.

Quietly, he sneaked down the hall. Clancy's studio was a second-floor addition that overlooked the bay. It had been a surprise birthday present from her father for her fifteenth birthday. Johnny Branson, who'd been a carpenter back then, had built it. That was before he ran for sheriff.

Jake heard music filtering through the open doorway. He stopped. Classical? He and Clancy had grown up on country music. The long-haired stuff coming off her stereo only reminded him of how much had changed between them. He was wondering if she ever listened to country anymore when the song ended and another came on. A Don Williams tune. One he used to know all the words to. He smiled to himself. Maybe things hadn't changed that much.

The actual studio was a large room with a bank of windows on three sides to catch the light. As Jake peeked in, he remembered the times he'd come here, moving quietly, hoping not to disturb her. He remembered how seriously she'd taken her sculpture. That's one reason he'd loved to watch her work.

Now he stood at the edge of the doorway, just looking at her. Watching the way her fingers molded the mound of clay on the table in front of her. She pinched, prodded, slicked and smoothed. Her fingers strong, her movements precise. He studied her face, not surprised by the intensity of her expression. Clancy had been fourteen the summer she confessed to Jake she wanted to be an artist. She'd felt it was a frivolous desire. How many artists actually made a living with their work?

But Jake and her parents had encouraged her. And surprisingly, so had her aunt Kiki. Kiki saw to it that Clancy got her first sculpting lessons. Jake could still remember Clancy's first work. It was crude but showed potential, her art teachers had said. Hell, one of her first pieces was a part of the breakwater at his beach house in Galveston, he thought with a curse.

Clancy frowned now as she stepped back to inspect her latest creation. She wore her glasses instead of her contacts. He liked them on her. They made her look even more sexy, if that was possible. The frown deepened as if she wasn't quite satisfied with it. That would be the perfectionist in her. She stepped forward again and began to reshape and resculpt, working quickly, meticulously, totally immersed in the clay and the vision inside her head, totally oblivious to everything else. Including him.

So intent on studying her, Jake hadn't even noticed the sculpture she'd been so engrossed in until she suddenly pushed it back to inspect it again. The back of it faced him. A bust of a man's head.

She gave the sculpture a turn. It slowly revolved around on the lazy susan. Jake caught his breath as he saw the face she'd molded into the clay. The likeness was so striking it shocked him.

It was *his* face in the clay. Younger. His nose straighter than he remembered it. His face far more handsome than he'd ever been. But he could see the resemblance to the boy who'd grown up on this lake with Clancy.

It unnerved him, reminding him too much of the past and the way things had been between them.

He stepped back into the hallway, pressing against the wall. Emotions surged through him, waves that threatened to wash away everything he'd believed, everything he'd held on to for ten years, everything he'd let go of ten years ago. What if he'd been wrong?

He thought about the sculpture, the man she'd somehow captured in the clay. He felt moved and, at the same time, torn.

He sneaked back to his room. Clancy's phone rang. He heard her pick it up. He listened to her tell Helen about Lola's half sister. From the conversation, it seemed Helen didn't know about Glenda Grimes, either.

He turned his attention back to the evidence on the Westfall case. The answer was here, somewhere, and damned if he wasn't going to find it.

Jake sifted through the pile of papers again, his head aching from lack of sleep and the craziness of this case. At some point, he could always feel the pieces start to fall into place. There'd be that rush as he started to see glimpses of a pattern. But not in this one.

He pushed back the papers and stretched, surprised, when he glanced at his watch, at how much time had gone by. Surely by now Clancy had gone to bed. But he hadn't heard her.

He walked down the hallway. Her door stood open. He peeked in. The covers were thrown back on her bed. Her shoes were by it on the floor. But her room was empty.

This time, he made noise as he went down to her studio. But when he rounded the corner, she wasn't sitting at her worktable. The sculpture of him wasn't on the table anymore, but a large mound of battered-looking clay sat in its place. His face was long gone. And so was Clancy.

Panic rocketed through him. "Clancy?" He raced down the stairs, calling her name as he went. "Clancy?"

The kitchen door stood open. He charged outside, wondering how much of a head start she had on him.

That's when he saw her. She looked ghostlike walking down the beach, her long white nightgown billowing around her bare ankles. He went after her, telling himself she was fine. But he couldn't throw off the bad feeling.

He'd almost reached her when she suddenly stopped and, in slow motion, bent to pick up a small piece of driftwood in her path. An icy chill shot up his spine as she started walking again, the driftwood dangling from the fingers of her left hand, forgotten.

He felt a stab of shock as he caught up with her and looked into her blank face, the face of a sleepwalker.

"Clancy?" She moved along on some agenda, programmed like a robot. The only problem was that the program was often flawed, senseless. Or was it? Was Clancy headed somewhere she really wanted to go? But she was headed for the end of the island and the cliffs.

"It's time to go to bed." He touched her arm. Hadn't he read that you shouldn't wake a person who's walking in her sleep?

But she didn't wake. Nor did she fight him. He turned her toward the lodge, then trailed along beside her. Almost home, something must have clicked, some kind of wake-up call. She blinked. "Where—"

"I'm here," Jake said quickly.

She turned in surprise to see him there. Tears flooded her eyes. "I did it again," she whispered. "Where did I go?"

"Just down to the beach. I saw you and brought you back."

She looked down, startled to find the piece of driftwood in her hand, and dropped it quickly as if it were a poisonous snake. She began to shake.

Jake swept her into his arms and carried her inside

the lodge and up to her bed. He sat beside her, holding her hand until she fell asleep again.

He took the chair, positioned it in front of the door, and made himself as comfortable as possible. It was going to be a long night.

Chapter 16

Thursday morning, Jake woke to the ringing of a phone. He hurried down the hall to his room and picked up the cell phone. "Yeah?" He could hear a television in the background.

"No inheritance. No lottery," Tadd said, sounding as sleepy as Jake felt. "No bank loans. Frank Ames couldn't have bought a candy bar with his earning power before he purchased the resort."

"Then, how did he?" Jake asked, starting to wake up.

"Good question," Tadd said. "As long as he put the money down as income on his tax returns, he's legal and there's no way we can track it. Hold on." Jake heard Tadd turn up the volume on the TV. "Lola's sister lives in Somers right? Glenda Grimes?"

"Why?" Jake asked, afraid he wasn't going to like the answer.

"Her house is on fire and her neighbors think she's inside."

Jake hung up and raced down the stairs to turn on the television in the living room. Glenda Grimes's home was nothing but a ball of flames.

"What is it?" Clancy asked from the stairs. She still had on her nightgown, her expression worried and afraid. Not as worried and afraid as Jake was for her at this moment.

"Glenda Grimes," Jake said, turning off the TV. "She didn't make it to Vegas."

Clancy stood in the hot shower, letting the water pound her skin. Desperately she tried not to think about Glenda. Had Jake been right? Had Glenda known more than she'd told them? Well, her secret had died with her.

Clancy shifted her thoughts to something more pleasant. Jake. Knowing he was just outside the door gave her a sense of security and well-being. She'd seen her own fears mirrored in his face. Was she next?

When she reached for the soap, Clancy had a quick flash of her shower with Jake. Her skin tingled, and that ache low in her belly almost brought her to her knees. Having him right outside the door made her more aware of her naked body. Having once had it, she now ached for Jake's touch. She remembered his fingertips on her skin. His mouth. His tongue. The weight of his body on hers. She groaned.

"Clancy?" Jake asked on the other side of the door, his voice full of concern. "Are you all right?"

"Fine!" she called back quickly, and turned up the cold water. Well, he wasn't going to make love to her until she asked, and she couldn't ask until he believed that she wasn't a liar and a murderer. The way things were going she would never know the feel of him again.

When she came out of the shower wrapped in her modest robe, she heard Jake on the phone. He hung up when he saw her. "What is it?" she asked.

"I just talked to the sheriff's department."

"Arson?"

Jake nodded. "And deliberate homicide. Glenda was inside. She'd been bludgeoned to death before the fire was started."

Just like Lola. Clancy clutched the front of her robe, the look in Jake's eyes making her more afraid.

"We've got to find this guy, Clancy. And soon."

Clancy couldn't agree more. "How would you suggest we do that?"

He hesitated. "Helen was close to Lola. Didn't you say they were involved in summer theater together?"

Clancy nodded. "You think Lola might have confided in Helen about this mystery lover of hers?"

"Maybe." He rubbed a hand over his stubbled jaw. His hair hung over his forehead. He looked as though he hadn't gotten a lot of sleep last night.

Clancy felt a twinge of guilt for that, but had to admit Jake Hawkins had never looked more handsome to her.

"Even if Lola never told her, Helen still might recognize something in Lola's keepsakes that at least would give us a lead," he said, and stopped. "What are you smiling about?"

Clancy quickly looked away. "I was just thinking that I could make us some breakfast while you—"

"Do I look that bad?" Jake asked.

She shook her head. "You look—" Sexy. Seductive. Wonderful. "Fine."

He grinned. "I won't take but a minute. Promise me you'll be here when I get back."

Clancy had to laugh. "I promise." There was no place she wanted to be more than with Jake, she thought with a curse.

Jake was as good as his word. He was back by the time she had the eggs and toast ready. He'd showered, shaved and changed into a shirt and chinos. He looked good enough to eat.

"Not bad," she said, sliding a plate of food in front of him. As she sat across from him and picked up her fork, she realized her sudden hunger had nothing at all to do with food.

"We're going on the assumption that Teddy Bear killed Lola, right?" Clancy asked as they took her boat to the Bransons'. "And he's still killing to keep his secret?"

The lake's surface mirrored the clear, sunny sky overhead. The air smelled fresh and clean. In the distance, she could hear a boat's motor running.

"Because he's never come forward, I think that's a pretty good assumption," Jake said. "Or he knows who did. I'm not sure how Frank Ames fits into all of this. I talked to Tadd this morning. No one knows where Frank got the money to buy the resort."

"You think it's the missing money?" Clancy asked.

"Maybe," Jake said. "If it is, then Frank had to have someone on the inside embezzling it for him."

"Lola." Clancy looked up at the cliffs as they rounded the end of the island. The Bransons' place sat on the highest bluff, with the elevator Johnny had put in for Helen running from the dock up to the house. There were also wooden stairs that switchbacked up the face of the cliff.

"Clancy, could you see Frank Ames as Teddy Bear?" Jake asked.

Clancy laughed. "Not hardly. But maybe Lola did. Frank would have been a lot younger. From what Tadd said, Frank had a huge crush on her."

"Yeah, it sounds like she enjoyed attention," Jake agreed.

"Maybe she encouraged that attention," Clancy said.

"That's what I was thinking," Jake said as he pulled alongside the Bransons' dock. "Especially if Frank could be useful to her."

"Like helping her hide the embezzled money?"

Jake looked over at Clancy. "Yeah. Then maybe he got greedy. More than likely he found out she was seeing other men. I mean, Frank's note to Lola is on the back of one of the cards. Frank could have decided to get rid of Lola and keep the money for himself."

Clancy tried to imagine Frank's face behind the motorbike helmet, in the water off the end of the dock as he dragged her under, beneath the sweatshirt hood as he ran out of her lodge. But all she could see was Dex Strickland's.

Jake closed the door on the cagelike elevator and pushed the button. It lurched with a noisy groan and began to climb. He'd been disappointed to note that Johnny's boat wasn't tied at the dock. Jake had hoped Johnny would be here.

The elevator grumbled to a jerky stop. Jake opened the door and Clancy stepped out.

"I've always wondered why Johnny would build up

here, especially with Helen's handicap," Clancy said quietly.

"You have to admit, it's an amazing view," Jake said, joining her at the railing. "And it's isolated. I get the impression that since the accident they pretty much keep to themselves."

Jake stood on the top deck. He couldn't help but admire the Bransons' house. Johnny had always been a master carpenter, but he'd outdone himself on this place.

It was built on three levels, all connected by ramps in such a way that they didn't call attention to Helen's handicap. Along the side of the house were three decks set at the same levels as the house, also with ramps. It gave the place a spacious feel. Each deck had a view, but the top deck, where he and Clancy stood now, was the most panoramic.

They found Helen in the pool on the second deck, swimming laps.

"Sorry, I didn't hear you come up," she said from the side of the pool. "I force myself to get exercise every day, and today was so beautiful—"

"Don't let us keep you from it," Clancy said.

"No, actually, I was just finishing," she said, hoisting herself up onto a step.

"Here, let me help you," Clancy said.

"No." Helen smiled to soften her words. "I have to do it myself. I refuse to be an invalid."

"You look great," Clancy said as Helen lifted herself into the wheelchair, making it look effortless.

"So what are you up to this morning?" Helen asked, pulling a white robe around her shoulders.

"We brought something we'd like you to look at," Jake said, indicating the small shoe box under his arm.

"Come on in," Helen said. "I think Johnny put some coffee on before he left."

They followed her into the living room, which opened up into the kitchen to the left and what looked like bedrooms off to the right. It had that same open, airy feeling inside as it had out. A two-way radio near a large window squawked as they went past.

"Where's Johnny?" Jake asked. "Fishing?"

"No, he had a doctor's appointment," Helen said on her way to the kitchen. "He hasn't been feeling well lately."

Jake saw that Clancy had stopped in front of a glass cabinet filled with trophies. He joined her, noticing a photograph of a smiling Helen beside a balance beam.

"Gymnastics. It was my first love," Helen said from the kitchen. "Then I got into theater and met Johnny and found my true love."

Clancy followed Helen into the kitchen. "You and Johnny both were actors?"

Helen laughed and shook her head. "Johnny on stage? No, he built sets. That's how we met. I'd seen him around at school, but he was so shy. So I joined the drama club, hoping he might notice me. I liked acting, but found helping with the costumes and makeup put me closer to Johnny. The rest is history, as they say."

Helen poured them both a cup of coffee. "Sit down," she said, motioning to the table set against the big bay windows.

"I've been so worried about you," Helen said to Clancy. "Have they got any closer to finding out who killed Dex Strickland?"

Clancy shook her head. "That's why we're hoping you might recognize something in the box. It contains Lola's things."

Helen looked surprised. "Lola's? I thought all of her belongings burned in the fire."

"Not everything burned," Jake said. "Some things were saved from the fire, the rest were in this box of… keepsakes that Lola left with her sister before her death."

"This half sister you told me about who lives in Somers?" Helen poured herself a cup of coffee before joining them at the table. "A son and a half sister we knew nothing about. I sometimes wonder if I knew Lola at all."

"Her sister died in a fire early this morning," Clancy said.

"I saw something on the news, but I had no idea that it was Lola's sister," Helen said. "Oh, how awful. What was her name, Linda Grimes?"

"Glenda," Clancy corrected her. "She told us yesterday that Dex had figured out who killed his mother. We think that person murdered Dex because of that."

"And probably Glenda," Jake added.

Helen looked shocked. "You mean, you don't think the fire was an accident?"

"No," Jake said.

"Well, I'll try to help in any way I can," Helen said.

Jake pushed the box over to her and watched as Helen riffled through the items.

She frowned. "Why would Lola's sister have hung on to this for all these years? It doesn't seem to contain anything…important." She picked up one of the cards. "Teddy Bear?"

"Do you have any idea who that might have been?" Clancy asked. "Glenda seemed to think that he was the man Lola planned to run off with the night she was killed."

"I knew she was leaving the island, but she planned to run off with some man?" Helen asked, sounding surprised. "That is certainly news to me. Lola seemed to date a lot of men, but none for very long."

"Glenda thought Lola had embezzled the money from the resort. This man might have been someone who helped her."

"Lola?" Helen shook her head, her look full of sympathy as she shifted her gaze to Jake. "I know how badly you want to clear your father's name, but that just doesn't sound like the Lola I knew. Did this Glenda person have proof of any of this?"

Jake stared into his coffee cup, his mood as dark as Helen's coffee. "No. That's why I was hoping you might recognize something in the box. If we could figure out who the man was—"

"I'm sorry, Jake," Helen said. "Lola never mentioned him to me, and you'd think she would have."

"For some reason she kept him a secret," Clancy said.

"You're sure she didn't…dream him up?" Helen asked. "I mean, Lola loved acting, playing different roles. It suited her. She didn't seem happy with real life. Never satisfied with what she had, whether it was a man or a job. That's why she told me she was leaving the island. She said she needed a change." Helen took a sip of coffee. "No, if her 'Teddy Bear' existed, he wouldn't have stayed with her long. It's a shame. She was a very beautiful woman, but so…needy and dependent. That puts a lot of men off."

The sun hung high in Montana's big sky as Clancy and Jake headed back to the lodge. Clancy couldn't help thinking about Helen's last remark and how lucky Helen was to have a man like Johnny. Clancy doubted Johnny could have loved her more. Just seeing that kind of love made Clancy ache inside for what she and Jake had had.

Jake said little on the boat ride back, and Clancy knew he'd hoped Helen would provide one of the missing clues. Finding the elusive Teddy Bear was proving much more difficult than Clancy had hoped. She wondered if maybe Helen was right; maybe Lola had made the man up. Hadn't even Glenda said he sounded too good to be true?

Jake brought the boat into the dock and Clancy jumped out to tie it up. She could feel Jake's frustration. It matched her own. They were no closer to finding out who had killed Dex Westfall, and her trial was coming up quickly. Without some sort of new evidence—

As Clancy bent down to secure the stern of the boat, she noticed something shiny in the water beyond the dock.

"Jake?" she said.

He joined her and squatted to look into the clear green water. "I'll take a look." He stripped off his shirt, then slipped out of his Top-Siders and reached for the zipper on his chinos.

"I'm going in with you," Clancy said, pulling her shirt over her head.

Jake stopped undressing. "You sure that's a good idea?" he asked, raising a brow. "You wouldn't purposely try to get me to break my promise?"

She mugged a face at him, slipped out of her skirt and sandals, down to her bra and panties, and dove into the water. It felt cold after the hot sun and the heat of Jake's gaze. Was that exactly what she was doing? Trying to get him to break his promise?

Jake did a shallow dive and came up next to her. They dog-paddled for a few moments just looking at each other, neither touching. His bare shoulders glistened, slick with water. They were so close she could feel his legs churning the water in front of her. It brushed her thighs, sparking a need to feel his skin against hers again. Desire flashed in his eyes as bright as the summer sun overhead. In that instant, the water no longer felt cold. Her skin ached, hot and sensitive to his gaze.

He groaned and dove into the water. She followed. Jake reached the bottom first, scooping the object into his hand. He looked over at Clancy and gave her a thumbs-up.

They burst to the surface almost in unison. Clancy watched as Jake inspected the object in his hand, then passed it to her. She stared at the silver watch for a moment, then up at Jake.

"Just as you described it," he said. "A flash of silver."

Proof that someone had tried to drown her that night. She smiled in relief and swam to the dock, hoisting herself up. Sitting on the edge of the dock, she turned the watch over in her hand. She heard Jake dive under the water and saw that he'd disappeared from sight. She looked down at the watch; something on the back caught her eye. Lettering. An inscription. She read the words in shock. Then realized Jake hadn't surfaced yet.

Getting to her feet, she stared into the clear water but couldn't see him. Where had he gone? She clutched the watch and waited for him to reappear, suddenly worried. How long could he stay under?

Just when she was about to dive in to search for him, he reappeared beside the dock.

"You scared me," she admonished.

He grinned up at her, his eyelashes jeweled with water droplets. "Sorry. I think I know where your attacker disappeared to that night." He pointed to the dock beneath her. "There're large air pockets under here between the flotations where he could have waited until we were gone."

Jake lifted himself onto the dock beside her, making her uncomfortably aware of how little they had on and just how wet and body-conforming their clothing was. She could feel Jake's gaze caress her, traveling across bare, wet skin to what was no longer hidden beneath her underwear. The air stilled around them. Time stopped.

"Dammit, Clancy, you can't do this to me."

"Do what?" she asked innocently.

He threw himself back into the water. She reached down and grabbed his hair, gently pulling him to the surface. She handed him the watch. "It's inscribed."

It seemed to take him a moment to drag his gaze from her to the watch. He flipped it over. "To Frank, love Lola," he read. His gaze flew up to Clancy's. "You have to be kidding."

Jake called Tadd with the news about the watch.

"Even with the watch and the motorbike, I'm not sure the sheriff has enough to hold Frank," Tadd said. "It would help if we had something more tangible."

Jake agreed. "Clancy and I will go over the evidence. Maybe there's something we've missed."

After he hung up, Jake dumped everything he'd collected on the Dex Strickland murder case in the middle of the kitchen table. But his attention was on Clancy. He felt a pull toward her stronger than the gravity on Jupiter.

"Where do we begin?" She leaned toward him.

He could smell her scent. It brought a rush of memory—the feel of her skin, the sound of her voice as she pressed her body to his, the look in her eyes as they made love. Damned if he couldn't still see her on the dock, wet and in that skimpy underwear. Why had he made such a foolish promise?

"Here's Dex's autopsy report," he said, trying to concentrate on the report. "This is interesting. Dex was struck from the right. That would indicate he was hit by a right-handed person."

"I'm left-handed, and the sculpture was in my left hand when I woke up. But that really doesn't prove anything, does it?"

"It helps," Jake said, flipping through the report. "If we have to go to trial, everything that puts doubt into the jurors' minds will help."

Clancy picked up a stack of photocopies of all the newspaper clippings, photos and other materials Dex had tacked to his closet wall. He saw her shudder as she sorted through them, quickly passing over an old play program from the summer Lola died. Jake recognized it. It was the play he'd taken her to the night he told her how much he loved her and that he wanted to marry her.

"You don't have to do this if you don't want to," he said. But she didn't seem to be listening.

"Look at this," she said, stepping over so he could see. It was a newspaper article. The headline read Local Woman Injured in Wreck Near Angel Point. Jake saw that it was an article about Helen Branson. The subhead read Sheriff's Wife Critical After High-Speed Rollover.

Jake read over Clancy's shoulder. Johnny Branson was driving at a high rate of speed when he lost control and rolled down an embankment. Helen was thrown from the car. She was listed in critical condition at the local hospital. Johnny was uninjured.

"It's dated the night of the resort fire," Clancy said in surprise.

The night Lola was murdered. Jake scanned the story again for the time of the accident. "It would have been just hours after the fire and Lola's murder."

Clancy looked up at him. "Dex had this tacked on his closet wall, too?"

"Johnny was the sheriff, and it was the same night as Dex's mother's death."

Clancy moved away from the table to look out into the night. "Johnny was driving the car," she said. "I didn't know that. How awful for him to know that he was responsible for Helen being in a wheelchair for the rest of her life. Why was he going so fast on that road, I wonder?"

"And what were they doing on Angel Point that time of the morning?" Jake said.

Clancy shook her head. "He was probably upset after what had happened at the resort, having to arrest one of his best friends. I guess I never realized how many lives were affected by what happened that night."

"Neither did I." Jake got up to take his empty cup to the sink. He'd been so filled with anger for so many years. He hadn't even thought about the other people who'd lost something that night. He leaned over the sink for a moment. Like Clancy. She'd lost her family first to Alaska, then to a plane crash. Her pain had been amplified by him walking out on her. And he'd spent the last ten years in his own kind of sleepwalking. Pretending he could forget about her.

He glanced over at her, remembering the way she'd looked last night on the beach. Her eyes open. Her expression glazed. Picking up that piece of driftwood in her path and not even realizing what it was.

He felt goose bumps on his arms as a chilling thought whipped past. Had she picked up that driftwood the same way she'd picked up the murder weapon the night Dex was killed? He remembered what he'd read about the total amnesia sleepwalkers experienced from the time of falling asleep until waking. The confusion on waking.

"Clancy," he said, excited by how right this felt. "Last night on the beach when you were sleepwalking, you picked up a piece of driftwood in your path. What if that's exactly what you did the night Dex died? If that's how you ended up with the murder weapon in your hand?"

Clancy stared at him.

"Don't you see? You must have heard someone upstairs. Still asleep, you walked up there. The murder weapon was in the middle of the floor. You picked it up and went to the balcony." Jake shuddered. "The killer must still have been in the room. Clancy, that's it. You must have seen him. That's why he's after you now."

"But I can never remember anything about my sleepwalking episodes."

"The killer wouldn't know that," he pointed out. "He may be afraid that you'll remember." The thought came out of left field, fast and hard. "Oh, my God. Clancy, if I'm right and the same person killed Lola and Dex, you might have seen him *both* times." Jake slapped a hand to his forehead. "You could have seen him the night of Lola's murder when you were sleepwalking. God, Clancy, that could be what woke you up."

"And he waited ten years to come after me?" Clancy asked in disbelief.

"No, he felt safe. Then Dex turns up, asking questions, maybe even actually knowing who the killer is. Dex could have tried to extort money from him. Or maybe just threatened to go to the cops. Remember what Kiki said about Dex being in a good mood and saying his business on the island was completed and he was leaving?" Jake stood, pacing the floor, excited by the way the pieces seemed to fit. "He thought he was getting money. And somehow the killer got him to go to your garret, then killed him and set you up."

Jake pulled off his cap and raked his fingers through his hair. "And you played right into the killer's hands, picking up the murder weapon."

"Oh, Jake, is it possible?" Clancy cried. She got up to get them more coffee, excitement in her movements.

More than possible, he thought as he watched her, his heart so full of love for her that it felt as if it would explode. And she loved him. He believed that with all his heart. Then, how could he not believe everything else she'd told him?

"I know you didn't kill Dex Strickland," Jake said, feeling a rush of emotion as he knew something else in the only place it mattered. In his heart. "And I know you didn't perjure yourself at my father's trial."

She didn't turn. Her hand clamped down on the handle of the coffeepot as if she needed support.

"I believe you, Clancy," he said.

"But?" she asked, her back still to him.

"But I believe my father, too. There's an explanation for what you saw that night, because I know in my heart that you didn't lie."

She turned slowly, her eyes welling with tears as she looked at him.

In two strides, he came around the table and pulled her into his arms. "Oh, Clancy," he breathed against her hair. "I love you," he said, thumbing the tears from her cheeks. "God, I would give anything to have never hurt you." He drew her closer. "I'm so sorry I didn't believe you. Can you ever forgive me?"

She drew back to look up into his face. "I love you, Jake. I've always loved you."

"I know." He held her to him tightly, promising himself he'd never let her go again.

"Kiss me, Jake. Please. Then make love to me."

He laughed softly. "I thought you'd never ask."

They made love in front of the fireplace. Slowly. Gently. Touching each other as if for the first time. Lovers at long last.

Later Jake cooked steaks on the barbecue and they sat on the front deck watching the sunset. Jake felt a contentment he hadn't known in years. Not since he'd left Flathead and Clancy.

He sat holding her hand, watching the last of daylight disappear behind the mountains, when he heard a sound behind them.

"Did you hear that?" Clancy asked, turning to look back into the lodge. Jake's gaze leaped to the window behind them as Clancy let out a startled cry. A figure moved through the shadows of the unlit living room, headed for the back door.

"Stay here," Jake commanded without thinking. Had

he had time to think, he would have asked her, pleaded with her, begged. Because commanding Clancy had always proved a mistake. But there wasn't time to beg. Jake wasn't about to let the intruder get away. Not again.

He circled around the side of the lodge just as the figure broke into a run down the beach. Jake tore after him, stretching his legs and lungs with everything he had in him, closing the distance.

The figure headed for a rental boat pulled up on the beach on the other side of Jake's lodge. Jake knew he had to reach him first.

The moon had just started up the backside of the Mission Mountains. Dusk lay deep in the pines. Jake concentrated on only two things: the dark figure running up the beach and the shoe box tucked under the man's arm. The man raced for his life. It was a race Jake wasn't about to let him win.

Just before the thief reached the boat, Jake made a flying tackle. He caught the man by the lower legs and brought him down hard. Not hard enough, Jake thought, scrambling to his feet.

The man tried to get up. Jake put a boot toe into the man's ribs and flipped him over onto his back, noticing that he wore a dark hooded sweatshirt, the hood up, hiding his face. Next to him was a crushed shoe box. Some of Lola's keepsakes had tumbled out when he'd fallen.

Grabbing the scruff of the man's coat collar, Jake jerked him to his feet and, pulling down the hood of the sweatshirt, finally got a good look at his face. The man held no resemblance to Dex Strickland.

"Frank Ames." Jake swore and tightened his grip on the man's throat. "I ought to kill you right now with my bare hands."

Chapter 17

Fear shone in Frank's eyes. "You wouldn't do that." He didn't look in the least bit convinced.

"Wanna bet?" Jake demanded. "You're the one who's been trying to kill Clancy."

Frank shook his head violently. "That's not true."

Jake shoved Frank down into the sand again. "Don't lie to me, Ames. I swear—"

"I'm telling you the truth," Frank cried, gasping for breath. "It wasn't me. Why would I want to kill Clancy?"

"That's what I want to know. We found your watch near the dock where you tried to drown her," Jake said, getting angrier by the minute.

"What watch?" Frank asked, almost sounding surprised.

"The one Lola gave you."

"Lola never gave me a watch."

Jake towered over him. "It was engraved. 'To Frank, love Lola.' Ring any bells?"

"I don't know what you're talking about."

"Are you also going to deny you were in the lodge tonight?" Jake demanded.

Frank swallowed and took a shaky breath. "Helen told me you had some of Lola's things in an old shoe box."

Jake wondered why Helen had told him that.

"I wanted to get my letters back."

"Your letters?" Jake asked. Frank couldn't be Teddy Bear. "Personal letters."

"Love letters?" Jake demanded. "You sent Lola love letters? How did you sign them?"

Frank looked confused. It wasn't a new look for him. "I signed my name."

Not Teddy Bear. "I want them back. They're mine."

Frank thought Lola had saved his letters? What would make him think that? Unless— "You're not trying to tell me that Lola responded to your sick fantasies."

That mean look Jake had seen many times before showed up on Frank's ugly face. He flushed with anger. "It wasn't like that. She cared about me. She talked to me when other people wouldn't. We were friends."

"Were you friends with Liz Knowles, too?" Jake demanded.

Frank frowned. "She was my waitress, that's all."

"How did she end up on your motorbike, then, Frank?"

"Maybe Liz was the one who stole it and chased your girlfriend. Did you ever think of that?"

"No." Jake figured Frank would finger anyone to

save his own neck. "What possible motive would Liz have had?"

Frank shook his head. "I'm supposed to know that?"

"Look, Frank, I saw Liz on the back of your motorbike not long before her body was found in Paradise Cove," Jake told him. "Someone was driving that bike. I think it was you."

"Well, you're wrong."

Jake tried another tack. "I found a note you wrote Lola to meet you at the 'usual place.' Where was that?"

"It was just this little stand of pines," Frank mumbled. "She liked it there. Not that it's any of your business."

Jake had had about all he could stand. He moved toward Frank, determined to get the truth out of him. "Not that it's any of my business, but where did you get the money for the resort?"

Fear crossed Frank's face as he groped in the sand behind him. "I don't have to tell you nothing," he said, coming up with a hefty chunk of driftwood. He scrambled to his feet, brandishing the weapon, then turned and made a run for it.

Jake would have gone after him but Clancy grabbed his arm.

"The sheriff's on his way," she said. "Let him handle it."

Chapter 18

Jake hung up the phone and pulled Clancy into his arms. "Tadd just called to say the sheriff picked up Frank Ames at the airport this morning. He was trying to make a run for it."

Clancy buried her face in his shoulder. "Then it *was* Frank?"

"He hasn't confessed, but the deputies found a mask at his cabin, and last night he was wearing a dark hooded sweatshirt."

"Mask?" Clancy asked.

"It's the kind of thing they use in the movies," he told her. "It's eerie how much it looks like Dex Strickland," Tadd said.

She stared up at him. "Frank went to the trouble of having a mask made that looked like Dex Strickland just to scare me?"

Jake tightened his grip on her. "I don't think he did it to scare you. More than likely it was to trigger your sleepwalking. Tadd agrees with me that Frank had to have been in the garret that night and saw you sleep-walking. He couldn't chance that you'd remember seeing him, not again. Nor did he need another murder on his hands. So, by triggering your sleepwalking, he could make your death look like an accident."

"They're sure it was Frank?"

Jake had been a little surprised himself. Frank didn't seem smart—or patient enough—to use Clancy's sleep-walking to his benefit. "With the mask, the hooded sweatshirt and his watch that we found off the dock, Tadd thinks the county can make a pretty good case against him for attempted murder," Jake said. "Tadd's convinced they'll be able to tie him to Lola's murder and the others." He brushed a kiss into her hair. "Do you realize what this means? You're finally safe."

She hugged him tightly. "I was thinking more about what it will mean for your father, Jake."

"Yeah." Jake pulled back to look at her. "I'd like to tell him about this in person."

She nodded. "I really need to get back to work. I might still be able to make my art show in August."

Jake knew Clancy wanted to give him time alone with his father and he loved her for that. But it was hard to leave her, even with Frank locked up in jail. He thumbed her hair back from her forehead and planted a kiss between her eyes. "I'll be back before you know it." Jake didn't tell her he had one stop to make on his way to the prison.

After Jake left, Clancy poured herself a cup of coffee and went out on the deck. The sun felt warm as she leaned against the railing to stare out across the lake.

The water shimmered, gold. No breeze stirred the surface. Only an occasional boat made waves that lapped softly at the shoreline. Why did she feel so antsy? The killer was behind bars. Jake loved her.

She went back into the kitchen to pour herself another cup of coffee and wandered the lodge, trying to put a finger on what was bothering her. According to Jake's theory, Lola had embezzled the money with Frank's help, Frank had found out about Teddy Bear, taken the money, killed her and burned down the resort.

But how did Clancy explain what she'd seen that night, ten years ago, when she woke up on the docks? She saw Warren Hawkins and Lola fighting and Warren push her. Jake had tried to blame it on the confusion she normally felt when she suddenly awakened in a strange place. That she hadn't really understood what she'd seen. Or had she?

She took a sip of the hot coffee and stared at the lilac bushes framing the window. Something didn't feel right. The other time Frank had come to the house, he wore a mask to make him resemble Dex Strickland. Why hadn't he last night?

Don't buy trouble, she told herself. All the evidence pointed at Frank Ames. Just as all the evidence in Dex's death had pointed to her, she reminded herself.

Not even the coffee could take away the sudden chill in the room. Clancy put down her cup. What was it that tugged at the back of her brain? The necklace. Why hadn't the rest of those tiny blue beads turned up? *Did it really matter?* she asked herself. Yes.

Frank Ames looked like a man who belonged behind bars, Jake thought as he watched the deputy bring the prisoner into the room.

"What the hell do you want?" Frank demanded when he was ushered into the small interrogation room. "You aren't going to leave me alone with this guy?" Frank asked the jailer who brought him in.

"You can always call a cop if you need one," Jake told Frank as the jailer went to stand just outside the door. "Okay, Frank, we're alone. Whatever you tell me will just be my word against yours. But I need to hear the whole story. Start with Lola and why you killed her."

Frank eyed Jake warily. "I've already told you. I loved Lola. I wouldn't have touched a hair on her head."

Jake took a seat at the far end of the table.

Frank seemed to relax a little. But he sat as far away from Jake as he could get.

"Come on, Frank," Jake cajoled. "Lola hurt you. She fell for someone else—and planned to leave the island and you to run off with him. I'll bet you wanted to kill him, too."

"There wasn't any man," Frank said adamantly. "She flirted with guys sometimes. But it didn't mean anything. I was the only one who really cared about her and she knew that." It was all Jake could do to keep from going for Frank's throat. "We're not going to get anywhere if you keep lying to me, Frank."

"You're lying to yourself," Frank said nastily. "You want to wrap up this case, get your old man out of prison, clear your girlfriend. You want it to be me so badly that you're blind to what's right in front of your face." Frank shook his head at Jake in disgust. "What kind of killer would use his own motorbike, leave his engraved watch at the scene of the crime, hide the mask he used in his top dresser drawer? How stupid do you think I am?"

Jake decided he'd better not answer that one. Nor would he listen to that little voice at the back of his head arguing that Frank was making sense. No one was that dumb, not even Frank Ames. Maybe especially Frank Ames.

No, Jake thought, Frank was smart. He'd played it this way on purpose. Making it look too obvious. "Who would want to frame you, Frank?"

He stared down the table at Jake. "I can think of only one person. Your father."

"My father?" What kind of bull was this?

"But since he's still in prison, someone on the outside would have to be setting me up for him," Frank said. "Maybe that explains why you've been dogging me. You're working with your old man."

Jake slammed a fist on the table, making it rattle and Frank jump. "That's a crock, Frank, and you know it. Why would my father want to frame you?"

"Where have you been, Hawkins?" Frank said, coming back like a mean, cornered snake. "You're supposed to be this amazing private eye."

He leaned toward the man, reminding himself that Tadd had gone out on a limb for him, pulling a lot of strings so he could be alone with Frank.

"Why don't you spell it out for me?" Jake said, also reminding himself he'd promised not to lay a hand on Frank, let alone give in to the urge to kick Frank's scrawny behind.

"Where do you think I got the money to buy the resort?" Frank asked in that cocky, "about to get his butt kicked" tone. "Why don't you ask your father?

"What?" Frank shook his head, sympathetically. "I got the money from your father."

"My father didn't have any money after the fire. Especially to loan you. He fired your sorry butt."

"A loan?" Frank's laugh almost changed Jake's mind about thumping him, cops or no cops, promise or no promise.

"He didn't fire me," Frank said. "I quit after I found out what was going on. Your old man paid me to keep my mouth shut."

Jake felt like he'd been kicked in the gut. He gripped the edges of the table and bit off each word. "What did you have to keep your mouth shut about?"

Frank got up and shuffled around the table to put the most distance between them, all the time eyeing the door. "I caught him skimming the money from the businesses. He paid me to keep quiet. I invested every dime of it and waited. I told you your old man was an embezzler."

"You're lying," Jake growled.

"I've got the proof. I stole the doctored books." A smile curved Frank's thin lips. "You were right, Hawkins, Lola did play me for a fool. I thought she was in love with me and I made the mistake of telling her about your father and how he'd been skimming money from the businesses. Then I found out that she was leaving the island with some man and had told Clancy's old man about your father, his partner and friend, so Clarence Jones wouldn't think she'd been taking the money." Frank let out a bitter laugh. "So I went to the resort that night and I took the books before your father could destroy them."

Jake leaned into the table, sick at heart. His internal arguments that Frank was lying fell on deaf ears.

"So you see, Warren didn't destroy the doctored

books in the fire because he couldn't find them. That's probably what he was fighting with Lola about when Clancy saw him. He must have thought she'd taken them. That's probably why he killed her. In the end, they both got what they deserved. And I got the resort. So who's the fool now, Hawkins?"

Clancy hadn't been into the storage room in years. She waded through musty old weathered orange life jackets, past rods and reels and water skis, to the dusty boxes at the back. The one she wanted, of course, was on the top shelf.

She pulled out another box to stand on and reached up for her mother's old hatbox, remembering Lola's box of mementos. Clancy's was much the same. A box that most people would think was nothing more than junk. Little things that would remind her of summers spent on the island. With Jake.

As she stepped down she noticed that the large box she'd used for a stool held her father's yearbooks. Clancy pulled his senior yearbook from the box and carried it and the hatbox upstairs to the kitchen where there was more light.

Not ready to delve into the box and all those memories just yet, she opened her father's yearbook.

When she found her father's senior picture, her eyes filled with tears. He looked so young, she thought as she ran her fingers over his face. Oh, how she missed him. He hadn't been handsome by most standards, but he had been to her. He'd been voted class clown, she noted with a smile.

She found another photograph of her father with his two best friends, Warren Hawkins and Johnny Branson.

She looked up their senior photographs. Johnny appeared uncomfortable in an outdated brown suit and garish tie. She studied his face, remembering what her father had told her about Johnny. He'd had to go to work at a young age to help support his family and was always ready to help anyone in need. He'd been voted nicest guy in the class.

She turned a page and found Warren Hawkins. His smiling photograph was in stark contrast to Johnny's. Captain of the football team. Star quarterback. Senior class president. Voted by his classmates as most likely to succeed.

As she thumbed through the yearbook, she looked for Helen. What had her maiden name been? Clancy thought she was a couple of years younger than Johnny. She found Helen in the sophomore section. Helen Collins. Her hair, a pale blond, was long and straight. A pretty girl. No wonder Johnny had fallen for her. Talk about contrast. Johnny had come from one of the poorer families around Kalispell; Helen from one of the richest.

Clancy started to close the book when she noticed a group photograph. The drama club. Johnny Branson would have stood out in the back row for his size alone, but no one could miss the smile on his face.

Helen Collins stood in front of Johnny in a simple shift, her hair hanging past her shoulders. She smiled into the camera. It tugged at Clancy's heart just looking at the two of them. Childhood sweethearts. They had married right out of high school.

Clancy pushed aside the yearbook and opened her treasured hatbox. Like Lola's box of keepsakes, it was filled with memories from summers of love. An odd-shaped smooth rock that Jake had picked up off the beach and handed to her. The lure she'd caught her largest fish on; Jake had netted it for her. The photo he'd taken of her holding it. Ticket stubs from movies, concerts and plays.

Clancy spotted a play program, the same one she'd seen in Dex's stuff on the back wall of his closet, she realized. Clancy remembered that play. For two reasons. It had been a special date. Jake had surprised her with dinner on the mainland and then a play at the community theater in Bigfork. It was over dinner that he'd told her he loved her and wanted to marry her.

But the play was also where she'd remembered seeing Lola wearing the bead necklace. As she'd sat next to Jake, with him holding her hand, everything about the play had been magnified. Not that she could remember the name of the play or even what it was about. But she remembered the necklace. Probably because of the tiny handmade ceramic heart. It had caught the light at the end when the cast and crew took their bows. It had stuck in her memory because she and Jake had promised their hearts to each other that night.

She opened the play program. The photographer had taken a large wide-angle shot of the cast and crew. Clancy found Lola in the front row. Her heart sank. Lola's neck was bare. Why had Clancy been so sure that's where she'd seen the necklace before?

Clancy's gaze fell on another woman in the photo. Around her neck was the tiny string of beads, the stage lights catching on the ceramic heart. Helen Branson had been wearing the necklace the night of the play. Not Lola.

Jake drove into the state prison yard under the heat of a summer sun. His head ached. He kept telling himself he couldn't believe anything Frank said. Frank would do anything to cover his own behind. The problem was, he believed him. Hadn't Jake always prided himself on being able to tell when someone was lying? Well, he'd been wrong about Clancy. Could he be wrong about Frank, as well?

"Jake," Warren said, sounding surprised and nervous as he was ushered into the visiting room. He started toward his son but stopped as if suddenly scared. "What's wrong? Nothing's happened to Clancy—"

Jake shook his head. "The sheriff just arrested the man he believes killed Lola and Dex Strickland."

Warren slumped into the nearest chair. "Thank God they finally found the killer. Who is he?"

"Frank Ames."

Warren looked surprised. "Frank Ames?"

Maybe it was his father's look. Maybe it was realizing earlier that Clancy would never lie to him. Or maybe it was that bad feeling, thumping at the back of his brain. But he knew. "You lied to me."

Warren sat perfectly still, his gaze locked with his son's.

"It was you all along. You stole the money. And you let a slimeball like Frank Ames blackmail you."

Warren's eyes swam behind tears. "I tried to warn you. I asked you to stay out of this."

Jake felt his stomach turn to stone. "Frank thinks you're orchestrating all the evidence against him from here. He actually thought I might be a part of it."

"That's ridiculous," Warren said.

"Why, Dad? Why did you do it?"

He suddenly looked years older. "I was losing your mother, Jake. I knew she was unhappy and I thought more money would keep her. I planned to pay it all back.

But then Frank found out and I found myself getting in deeper and deeper. I didn't know how to stop."

Jake swore.

"It just got so crazy after Lola was murdered. I wanted to tell the truth, but I was afraid it would make me look more guilty. Then it was too late."

"Mother knew." Her attitude toward his father suddenly made sense.

"I told her. She couldn't forgive me. It didn't matter that I did it for her. What about you, son? Can you forgive me?"

The pain was too raw right now. Jake just kept thinking about Clancy. "Clancy saw you arguing with Lola that night, just like she swore she had."

Warren nodded. "But I didn't kill Lola. I swear to you. When the fire started, I got out. I thought she was behind me. I realize now, whoever was in that adjoining room started the fire and killed Lola."

Jake stared at his father, unable to believe anything he said. A mystery person in the adjoining room. For years he'd wanted to believe that. But he hadn't believed Clancy, who'd told the truth. Now he wanted desperately to blame his father, to blame someone other than himself, something other than himself for all those years of lack of trust in the woman he loved.

"The killer is after Clancy," Jake said. He moved to the door, needing desperately to get back to Clancy. What had started as a notion, jitterbugging at the back of his mind, was now a death march. The killer was still out there.

Jake stopped at the door, all his fears pounding him like hail the size of walnuts. He thought of Clancy alone at the lodge. If Frank hadn't killed Lola— If Warren hadn't— "Who was Lola in love with?"

Warren slumped into a chair. "He wouldn't hurt Clancy."

"Are you willing to gamble Clancy's life on that? Because if you are—" Jake opened the door to leave.

"Wait."

Jake looked back at his father. He could feel time slipping away. He had to get to Clancy.

"He loved Lola," Warren said more to himself than Jake. And Jake realized his father had sat in his cell for ten years having this same argument with himself. "He couldn't have killed her."

"Who?" Jake demanded, losing his patience with this tangled web of misplaced loyalties.

"Johnny Branson."

"Johnny?" Jake cried.

"He fell head over heels for Lola. He'd never loved anyone like he loved her, but in the end he made the right decision. He was going to tell Lola that night that he couldn't leave Helen."

"Johnny was meeting Lola at the resort office?"

"He'd already been there when I found Lola," Warren said. "She was very upset, so I figured Johnny had told her. But I swear to you, she was alive when I left that room."

"How do you know Johnny wasn't still there?" Jake asked.

Warren blinked. "Johnny loved her. He's the kind of guy who wouldn't hurt a fly."

The phone rang, making Clancy jump. She glanced at the clock on the wall, surprised how long she'd been working. The rest of the morning had passed in a blur of creative expression.

Clancy stretched, content with the work she'd accomplished. It hadn't taken her long to get back into it.

She'd always worked best when something was bothering her. While her fingers shaped the clay, her subconscious worked on any problem on her mind. Like the string of beads. Clancy could see where Helen might not remember a cheap bead necklace after ten years. But how had Helen's necklace ended up in Lola's keepsake box? Not that it probably mattered, she told herself as she wiped her hands and went to answer the phone. The killer had been caught. With any luck, Frank would confess and this nightmare would be behind her.

"Clancy?" Tadd asked. "Is Jake there?"

"No, he's gone to Deer Lodge to see his father. Why? Is there a problem?"

"No, I just wanted to talk to him. When do you expect him back?"

Clancy glanced at the clock on the wall. "Any time, actually. What's going on, Tadd?"

"It's Frank Ames. The sheriff had to release him for lack of evidence."

She sat down hard on the stool at her worktable. "Lack of evidence? What about the watch, the hooded sweatshirt, the mask?"

"Frank had an alibi for the night you said someone tried to drown you, Clancy. He also had an alibi during the time Lola was murdered. Everything against him is circumstantial. The sheriff couldn't hold him. Also, that watch you found off the end of the dock. It might have been ten years old, but the engraving on it wasn't, the lab says."

Someone had planted the watch off the end of the dock? Who had even known about the scrape on her ankle? Jake. Tadd. Helen. Helen had probably told Johnny. Clancy glanced through the window at the lake shimmering under the summer sun. "When was Frank released?"

"Not long after Jake's visit this morning. I just heard about it and wanted to let you know."

Jake had gone to the jail to see Frank? "I thought you were so sure Frank was the one."

Silence. "There's been some new evidence. An eyewitness got the license plate number from a car that was seen near Glenda Grimes's just before the fire. We're waiting to get a name from the Department of Motor Vehicles. Their computer's down. I'll call you as soon as it comes in. Do you want me to send someone out there to stay with you until Jake gets back?"

Another call beeped on Clancy's line.

"No, I'm fine," Clancy said. "My aunt's coming over. That's probably her calling now."

Absently she pulled the play program out from under her sculpting tools and opened it again to the photograph, thinking about the necklace.

She clicked to the other call. "Hello?" As she answered, she pulled the photograph closer, noticing that Helen wasn't looking at the camera but off to her right. She looked upset and seemed to be glaring at—

"Clancy?" It wasn't Kiki's voice. "It's Helen, dear."

"I was just thinking about you," Clancy said, wondering if it had been ESP or just a coincidence. She looked more closely at the photograph. Helen was definitely looking at someone else. Clancy followed her gaze over to… Lola? Or— Clancy blinked. Or was Helen glaring at the man standing next to Lola? A big teddy bear of a man, Clancy thought with a jolt. That man was Johnny Branson.

"I hate to bother you." Helen sounded upset.

"Is something wrong?" Clancy asked, her heart

pounding as she stared at the photograph. Johnny Branson. Teddy Bear?

"I was digging around and I found something I think you should see. Can you come over?"

What had she found? Something to do with Lola's death? Or had Helen found a receipt for the engraving of a silver watch?

"Helen, does this have something to do with Johnny?" she asked, voicing her worst fear.

"Yes." Helen sounded close to tears.

Clancy looked down at the play program photo. "I'll be right over."

"Please hurry." Helen hung up.

Jake left the prison and headed for the airport, his chest aching with worry. As he drove, he dialed Clancy's number on the cell phone. No answer. Then he tried Helen Branson. The phone rang and rang. Jake hung up and dialed Tadd Farnsworth's office.

"Can you get the sheriff to send a deputy to Clancy's right away?" Jake asked.

"Clancy's?" Tadd said. "I just tried to call you to tell you about Johnny."

"What about Johnny?" Jake asked, dread settling in his chest.

"There's an eyewitness who saw a car parked near Glenda Grimes's house right before the fire. When the Motor Vehicle Department ran the plates—"

"The car's registered to Johnny Branson," Jake said.

"How did you know that?"

"Johnny is Teddy Bear."

"No kidding?" Tadd sounded genuinely surprised.

And Warren had been so sure that Johnny couldn't hurt a fly. Right. "You said you tried to call me earlier."

"I talked to Clancy and warned her that Frank's been released. He had alibis for the nights in question. The sheriff couldn't hold him any longer."

Jake swore. As hard as he tried, he couldn't convince himself that Frank Ames wasn't a danger to Clancy. "Did you tell her about Johnny?"

"I hadn't received the information yet from DMV the first time I talked to her. I tried a few minutes ago, but there was no answer."

"Tadd, I'm worried about her. Something's wrong. She said she was going to spend the day in her studio."

"When I talked to her she told me her aunt was coming over," Tadd said reasonably. "In fact, she got a call from Kiki while I was on the line. Maybe the two of them are outside and can't hear the phone."

Jake wanted to believe it was that simple.

"If you're worried about Johnny Branson, the sheriff sent a deputy out to bring him in for questioning. The deputy should be there by now."

Jake tried to relax but knew he wouldn't be able to until he had Clancy safe in his arms. "I'm in Deer Lodge. I'm flying out on the first plane I can charter." Or steal. "Call me when Johnny's in custody."

Chapter 19

"Helen?" Clancy called after her knock at the kitchen door went unanswered. A warm wind blew off the lake, whispering through the tops of the pines at the edge of the deck. Large white cumulus clouds scudded across a backdrop of clear blue. Clancy knocked again and tried the door. Locked. She headed up the ramp to the second level, wondering if Helen was in the pool, swimming laps. That seemed odd, considering how urgent the woman had sounded on the phone.

"Helen?" Clancy called again. The pool glistened a pretty turquoise blue, but Helen was nowhere around. A knot of worry settled in Clancy's stomach. She'd told herself all the way over that she was just jumping to conclusions. Just because it had looked like Helen was glaring at Johnny and Lola in an old photo. Just because Johnny had changed so much since Lola's death. Just because he was indeed a big teddy bear of a man. That didn't mean that he was Lola's lover. Helen could have found out something else about Johnny—

Clancy had started toward the ramp to the top deck, but stumbled to a stop as something in the crack between the boards caught her eye. She knelt. More than a dozen tiny blue beads were wedged between the wood of the deck. Using her thumbnail, she dug one out. Her hand shook as she held it up to the light. This was a bead from the necklace. Helen's necklace. The one Dex had had the night he died.

She held the single bead in her palm, all the ramifications of finding it here battering her brain. This is where the string of beads had been broken. Dex Strickland had been here.

To see Johnny? To talk to him about Lola's murder because he was the former sheriff? Or because Dex thought that Johnny Branson had been in love with his mother and had killed her?

Clancy straightened, suddenly even more worried about Helen. What had she found out about Johnny? That he really was Teddy Bear? That he was the one who'd killed Lola? That he'd killed three more people to keep his secret?

Her steps quickened. Where *was* Johnny now? Had he returned from fishing? Clancy had ridden her mountain bike instead of coming by boat to avoid the climb up the cliffs by either the elevator or stairs. She hurried up the ramp, anxious to get to the top deck so she could see if Johnny's boat was tied at the dock.

Helen sat at the far edge of the deck, her back to Clancy, her wheelchair facing the lake. She wore her white terry-cloth robe, the hood up. The wind whipped at one corner of the robe tucked around her legs.

Something about the way the woman sat made Clancy hesitate. Her shoulders were slumped forward, her head bent as if she were crying. If Clancy was right about Johnny and Lola— She tried to imagine what Helen must be feeling. Betrayed. Johnny had been her life. She must be devastated. How could a woman accept that the man she'd been married to all these years was a murderer?

"I came as quickly as I could," Clancy said as she approached Helen from behind. The woman had probably been sitting here, waiting, expecting her to arrive by boat. "Are you all right?"

When Helen didn't respond, Clancy laid a hand on her shoulder.

"Helen? It's Clancy."

Helen suddenly slumped forward in the wheelchair. Clancy rushed around to help her. "Helen," she cried as she knelt in front of her and gently pushed her back into the chair.

"Oh, my God!" Clancy threw herself backward, slamming into the deck railing. Her feet slipped out from under her and she sat hard on the deck floor at the foot of the wheelchair as a high-pitched scream shrieked from her lips.

Jake dialed Clancy's number again as he turned into the mainland marina. It was answered on the first ring.

"Kiki?" he asked. "Where's Clancy?"

"I was going to ask you the same thing," she said. "I just got here— Just a moment. Clancy left you a note. It says, 'Sorry. Helen called upset. I'm going over there. I think I know who Teddy Bear is and that Helen's figured it out, too.'"

Jake swore and hung up as he swung into a parking

space beside the deputy's car. But it was the boat tied at the dock that stopped him dead.

He climbed out of the Mustang and walked down to the dock. Johnny Branson looked up from his boat and smiled.

"You must be that special fare I'm supposed to pick up," Johnny said.

Jake shook his head.

Johnny looked around and frowned. The marina parking lot was empty except for Jake's and the deputy's cars. Johnny seemed to study the cop car for a moment, then turned his attention to Jake. "That's funny," he said, still frowning. "I was supposed to meet a client here more than half an hour ago."

"Have you seen Clancy?" Jake demanded.

The older man looked surprised. "No, why? What's wrong?"

"I just got back from Deer Lodge."

Johnny's gaze dropped to his feet. "How is Warren?"

"How do you think he is?"

When Johnny raised his head, worry etched the man's thin face. Worry and a deep sadness that Jake knew only too well at this moment.

"He's the one who embezzled the money, but you knew that, didn't you?" Jake said, trying hard to hold down his anger. What had happened between two best friends that one would let the other go to prison for a murder he didn't commit?

Johnny slumped back against the side of the boat.

"You were Lola's lover. You were Teddy Bear." Jake had spent the last few hours trying to put it all together, but it still didn't fit. He told himself he was just too close to it. "You went to the resort that night to meet Lola. The two of you were taking off."

Johnny shook his head. "I went to tell her I couldn't go with her. I couldn't hurt Helen."

Jake stared at the former sheriff. At one time he'd been a big bear of a man. Now he looked frail and broken, a man worn down by secrets and sorrows. With a shock, Jake realized that Johnny Branson looked like a man who was dying. Jake knew that look; he'd just recently watched his mother die. "Cancer?"

Johnny raised his head slowly and nodded.

"How long?" Jake asked.

"I won't see fall."

Jake looked out over the lake, then back at Johnny. Jake's father was right; Johnny didn't seem like much of a killer. Nor could Jake understand why a man with only three months to live would keep trying to cover up a ten-year-old murder.

"The cops have an eyewitness who saw your car at Lola's sister's house just before Glenda Grimes was murdered and her house set on fire," Jake said. "A deputy is at your house now with a warrant for your arrest."

Johnny's gaze flicked up. He glanced toward the island, worry in his eyes. Jake followed his gaze, a thought hitting him between the eyes like a brick. A dying man *wouldn't* keep killing to protect himself. Jake felt his heart lunge in his chest. He swore and looked again at Johnny's gentle face.

"You didn't kill Lola," Jake said, the first thing he'd been truly sure of. "My God. Who told you to pick up a fishing client here?"

"I probably just got it wrong."

"Who, dammit?" Jake demanded.

"Helen said Frank Ames set it up—"

"Call her." Jake vaulted into the boat and handed

Johnny the two-way radio. "Dammit, call Helen now. Clancy's on her way there. Helen phoned her and asked her to come over."

Johnny stumbled to the radio. Just as Jake had feared, Helen didn't answer.

Jake shoved Johnny aside to start up the dual engines on the large, powerful fishing boat. It would be faster than his rental boat. He only prayed they could reach the island in time.

"You don't understand," Johnny said as they sped across the water. "Helen loves me. She's always loved me. She was so pretty and popular. I was poor and a… nobody. She made me somebody, don't you see? She gave me everything. And look what I did to her."

Jake's fears multiplied with each beat of his heart. He could see. That's what frightened him so. "You fell in love with someone else. That's not the same as murder."

Johnny's eyes clouded over. "Helen didn't know I'd changed my mind about leaving her. She didn't know."

The island grew closer, but Jake's fear grew with it.

"I was going to tell the truth," Johnny said. "Then after the accident— We were arguing. I was driving too fast. It was all my fault."

Jake could see only too clearly why Johnny had covered for Helen all these years. "She's killed three more people, Johnny. How long were you going to sit back and let her keep killing?"

He frowned. "She couldn't have killed them. How could she? A woman in a wheelchair?"

Jake had asked himself that same question. He picked up Johnny's binoculars. The home Johnny had built Helen high on the cliffs shone in the afternoon sunlight as Jake glassed it with the binoculars. The deputy's boat was at the dock. So was a bright red jet boat. "Whose jet boat is that?" Jake asked.

Johnny took the binoculars. "Frank Ames's."

Jake's heart dropped. "Maybe Helen had help." Someone like Frank Ames. Had Helen been Frank's alibi? That would explain how he'd gotten out of jail and why he was at Helen's now. To collect whatever amount she'd agreed to pay him. With a fresh rush of fear, Jake reminded himself that Helen had called Clancy to come to the house.

"Try the radio again," Jake commanded, praying that Johnny would be able to stop Helen. But who would be able to stop Frank Ames? Jake assured himself that a deputy was there—everything was fine. Except the hunch stomping at the back of his neck said everything was not fine. Not fine at all.

In horror, Clancy stared at the face beneath the hooded robe in the wheelchair. Not Helen's face. But a man's. A man Clancy didn't recognize. Couldn't have recognized. The face purple, tongue protruding, eyes bulging. Around his neck was a white cord. The same white cord Clancy had seen Helen tie around her slim waist the day before. The cord was now taut around the strangled man's throat.

Unable to pull her gaze from his face, Clancy stumbled to her feet. The wind caught the edge of the robe and whipped it open. Clancy's heart thudded against her rib cage as she backed her way along the railing toward the house. The man wore a uniform from the local sheriff's department. Clancy's heart rate rocketed upward. His holster was empty.

"Helen!" she screamed, frantic to put distance between her and the death in the wheelchair, her brain tangled and confused. Where was Johnny? She looked over the side of the railing, down the cliff to the dock floating in the dark green of the lake below her. Two boats. Neither was Johnny's fishing boat. Two boats? Her thoughts came like bullets. A Sheriff's Department boat. But who did the other one belong to?

Clancy inched her way along the railing toward the house without consciously realizing what she was doing. Who had killed the deputy and put him in Helen's wheelchair? Where was Helen? "Helen!"

Clancy's shoulder slammed into the glass door to the living room. *Run!* The deputy was dead. Helen wasn't answering; she'd answer if she were still alive. The killer was still here. His boat was still at the dock. *Just get out of here. Get help. Don't go in the house.* She glanced toward her bike, leaning against the deck railing, but her feet seemed incapable of moving another step. She slumped against the glass door. Panic made thinking almost impossible. Where was Helen? Who else was up here?

The door began to open. Clancy felt her breath catch in her throat as she found the strength to push away from the glass. She turned, in slow motion, hoping to see Helen in her wheelchair, praying to see Helen. The sun ricocheted off the glass. Behind it nothing but darkness. The door slid open slowly. Clancy felt a scream rise in her throat.

Frank Ames stood in the doorway, smiling, his shirt soaked with blood. Clancy screamed.

Frank stumbled toward her, his face contorted in not a smile but a grimace. He tried to speak but the words came out slurred. All Clancy caught was one word, "Helen," before Frank lurched forward and fell at her feet.

Clancy would have turned and run, but she heard a faint cry for help from within the house. Helen. She slipped past Frank's lifeless body into the living room. Empty. "Helen?"

"In here," Helen called from the front part of the house.

Heart hammering, Clancy rushed into the master bedroom.

Helen lay on the floor near the bed.

"Where's Frank?" she cried as she pulled herself up to a sitting position to lean back against the foot of the unmade bed. A bloody baseball bat lay on the floor beside her.

"I think he's dead," Clancy said, rushing to her. "Are you all right?"

"He tried to strangle me," Helen said, her hands going to her throat. She jerked off the scarf that had been wrapped around her neck and cast it away from her in disgust as she reached for a smaller wheelchair near the bed.

Clancy didn't mention the deputy, strangled outside in her other wheelchair. "Here, let me help you."

"Don't worry about me," Helen snapped, shooing her away. "Call Johnny. I need Johnny."

Clancy rushed back into the living room but went to the phone instead of the radio. She punched out 911 before she realized the line was dead. As she hung up, she noticed the drawer in the desk, partially closed on a stack of papers. Unconsciously, she opened the drawer to push the papers in. Her gaze fell on the word *Sleepwalking*.

She pulled the drawer open a little farther. There were dozens of photocopies of articles about sleepwalking. One sentence, underlined in red, leaped out at her. "Sleepwalking episodes are often triggered by severe stress or trauma."

Clancy's heart thundered in her ears as something else in the drawer caught her eye. A tiny ceramic heart. The heart from the necklace.

Clancy staggered and grabbed the desk to keep from falling. Helen's necklace. It had been the clue all along. Dex had had the necklace. And the old play program. He *knew* it was Helen's. That's why he'd come here.

The two-way radio squawked. Clancy jumped.

"Helen?" Johnny's voice came over the radio. "Helen?" Desperation laced his voice. She could hear the boat's motors in the background and the sound of his boat's hull slapping the water as it crossed the lake.

"Clancy?"

A chill streaked across her skin at the sound of Jake's voice. She lunged for the radio. "Jake? Where are you?"

"We're almost there. Clancy, thank God, you're all right. Where's Helen?"

"In the bedroom. But there's a deputy here— He's dead, Jake. And Frank—" The elevator. It groaned and clanked as it climbed the cliffs. Clancy could feel the hysteria rising like lava in her throat. "Someone's coming up the elevator."

"Clancy, listen to me—" The radio crackled.

The elevator clanged to a stop. Clancy turned slowly, afraid of who she'd see in the contraption. The sun caught on the dull metal, then passed through the bars. The elevator stood empty.

"Clancy, do you hear me?" Jake yelled over the radio. "Get out of there! Helen killed Lola. Get out of there! Now!"

Clancy turned to look toward the bedroom as she set down the radio receiver. "Helen?" She moved cautiously toward the open bedroom doorway. "Helen?" A deathly quiet fell over the house. Her pulse thrummed in her ears. She fought for each breath. At the edge of the doorway, she peered around the corner into the bedroom.

Helen was gone. So was the wheelchair and the baseball bat.

Chapter 20

Clancy stumbled to the door and stepped gingerly over Frank. The top deck was empty except for the deputy. He sat slumped over in the wheelchair, the wind snapping the tail end of the robe. Helen was nowhere in sight, but Clancy knew she couldn't have gone far.

Cautiously, she walked to the back edge of the deck to look down past the pool and the lower deck. Her bike still leaned against the railing. If she could reach it—

She could hear Jake's words in her head saying he was on his way. He would be at the dock soon. Take the elevator down to the dock and wait for him. She turned and looked back at it still sitting empty at the edge of the deck. Then she hurried over to it and pulled open the door. She stared at the empty elevator for a moment. Why had Helen brought it up? Just to slow down Johnny and Jake? Or for another reason?

Don't get in the elevator! Clancy stumbled back, no longer sure she could trust her instincts. *Take the bike. Get to the resort and call for help.* She turned and fled, racing down the ramp past the pool. She thought she heard a noise behind her but she didn't turn. She reached the railing and grabbed her bike.

"No, Clancy," a voice behind her said calmly. "That's not the plan."

Clancy turned slowly, expecting to see Helen at the edge of the deck in her wheelchair. The last thing she expected was to see her standing with the deputy's gun pointed at Clancy's heart.

The wind had picked up as they neared the island. Waves hammered the bow and spilled into the boat, drenching them both. Jake didn't slow down. A million thoughts raced around in his brain. All the things he wanted to do with Clancy when they got out of this mess. Ahead he could see the dock. They were almost there. *Hang on, Clancy*, he cried. *I'm coming!*

"You can walk!" Clancy cried, unable to take her eyes off a Helen she'd never seen before. "You were never paralyzed!"

"I was for a while." Helen moved closer, leveling the gun at Clancy's chest. "But after a few weeks I started to get some feeling back in my legs. The doctors said I might, but Johnny worried that I never would."

"He doesn't know?"

Helen cocked an eyebrow at her that implied Clancy was smarter than to ask a silly question like that. Of course he didn't know. Helen motioned with the gun for Clancy to start moving up the ramp toward the house.

"Let's go out on the deck where we can see when Jake and Johnny get here."

"You stayed in a wheelchair all these years to keep Johnny?" Clancy asked in amazement as she stood staring at Helen.

"With Johnny fishing most of the time, it wasn't hard to keep up the charade. I learned from the master," Helen said. "I watched how Lola entrapped Johnny with her helplessness. Did he want a woman who was strong and resourceful? No, he wanted one who was inept, dependent, hopeless. Someone he'd have to spend his life's energy taking care of." Helen's gaze turned hard. "All I did was pattern myself after Lola. She was what he wanted. So I became her. Totally dependent on him for my very existence."

"You killed Lola!"

"I had no choice," Helen said, seeming surprised by Clancy's reaction. "I didn't know Johnny had gone to the resort that night to break it off with her. But it's probably just as well. I wanted her out of our lives forever and at any price. Unfortunately, for Lola the price was death." She motioned for Clancy to get moving.

Clancy started up the ramp. "And Dex? Was that his price, too?"

"He was just like his mother," Helen said. "He wanted something that didn't belong to him. In his case, it was my money. He thought I'd pay for his silence."

Helen shook her head as if the whole thing saddened her. "He called to say he had something of mine. I didn't believe him at first. He said he had proof. I told him to leave it under a bait can on the dock. Dex just figured Johnny would pick it up for me. He couldn't know that I'd come myself."

The message the cabin girl had taken to the dock. It had been for Helen.

"It was a drawing of the necklace and a demand for money," Helen said.

"How did Dex get the necklace?" Clancy asked, wondering how Helen's necklace had ended up in Lola's belongings after the fire.

"I had it on the night I went to the resort to deal with Lola. She tore it from my neck in the struggle."

That's when the clasp was broken, Clancy thought as she tried to walk more slowly, stalling for time, for Jake.

"I just assumed it had burned in the fire," Helen continued, sounding distant, as if the past no longer mattered. "The police must have found it and, thinking it was Lola's, given it to the family. It was the only proof that I'd been at the resort the night Lola was murdered."

Clancy felt a chill race across her skin and turned to look at Helen. "That night at the café. Dex saw something in the pines. It was you. Out of your wheelchair. Walking. No wonder he'd looked so frightened."

Helen smiled. "I enjoyed playing with him. Later I surprised him and his girlfriend at his cabin. I was in my wheelchair and convinced Dex he'd only imagined seeing me standing in the pines."

That would explain why Dex was killed sans underwear.

"You agreed to pay him off?" Clancy asked, remembering what Kiki had told her about Dex's mood.

Helen nodded distractedly.

"Then, how did the beads get broken at your house?" Clancy asked.

Helen looked up in surprise as if the question had pulled her from other thoughts.

"I found the beads from the necklace caught in your deck," Clancy said.

Helen smiled. "How very observant of you. Dex made me so angry, coming to the house when I told him not to. It was a good thing I'd given Johnny something to help him sleep. I grabbed the beads and..." She looked across the pool, her eyes suddenly full of tears. "The necklace broke. Johnny made it for me while we were in high school. He gave it to me the night he asked me to marry him."

Clancy thought she heard the roar of a boat on the wind. Helen must have heard it, too. She motioned with the gun for Clancy to head up the last ramp to the top deck.

Clancy felt sick inside. Jake would be here soon. But soon enough? "How did you get Dex into my garret?"

"Dex thought Lola had embezzled the money from the resort and hidden it somewhere. I just told him it was in your garret and where you kept a key, over the front door."

Jake had been right; everyone in the world knew about the key.

"And Dex believed you that *I* had the money at the lodge?"

They reached the top deck, and Clancy felt time running out as quickly as beach sand poured from between her fingers.

"Dex was like his mother. Greedy, but not particularly bright," Helen said, not unkindly. "I followed him to your lodge. I didn't know you would come sleepwalking in and pick up the sculpture I'd used to kill him. I remember your mother saying what a sound sleeper you always were. She thought that was one reason you sleepwalked."

Helen had always known about her sleepwalking. "Weren't you worried that I'd remember seeing you?" Clancy asked.

"Of course not, dear, I'd seen you sleepwalk before, the night I killed Lola. I passed you on the dock and you looked right at me."

Clancy turned to stare at her, realizing Helen had spared her that night on the dock only because Clancy had been walking in her sleep. "Then, why did you frame me with Dex's murder if you felt you had nothing to fear from me?"

"I was just buying time, dear." She frowned. "But then you came over asking about the necklace and I knew, as badly as I didn't want to, I'd have to stop you."

Clancy's eyes widened in horror as she realized this soft-spoken, caring woman she'd known most of her life had become a cold-blooded killer. "You tried to kill me." Even now, Clancy found it hard to believe.

Helen wagged her head. "It grieved me terribly, dear. You were the last person I ever wanted to hurt."

Clancy felt repulsed as she noticed the silver bracelet on Helen's slim wrist. "It wasn't a watch that scraped my ankle but your bracelet. After I told you I thought it was a watch, you planted the watch off the end of my dock to make it look like Frank Ames did it." Clancy stared at her in abhorrence. "You couldn't have been the person who ran me off the trail on the motorbike," Clancy said, thinking Helen had to have had an accomplice. Frank?

"I'm quite capable of riding a motorbike, dear," Helen said, sounding offended. "I used to be an athlete, remember?"

Yes, and Clancy had forgotten what excellent shape Helen had kept herself in all these years. She remembered seeing Helen hoist herself into the wheelchair. The woman had incredible strength for her age. And Clancy realized Helen Branson was capable of anything. Including another murder.

"Frank figured out that you were the one framing him," Clancy said.

Helen seemed not to be listening. "That young waitress saw me take Frank's bike and thought to cash in on my misfortune." Helen tsked to herself. "So unfortunate. But it doesn't matter now, does it, dear? Time has run out."

Clancy had reached the edge of the top deck. The wind whistled across the mountain, whipping her hair into her eyes. She backed the last few feet to the railing as Helen indicated her to do, intensely aware of the gun pointed at her heart, but thinking more of the cliff behind her.

"Helen, you can't expect to get away with this," Clancy cried.

"Oh, I don't dear. I'm just cleaning up a few loose ends. Tidying up." Helen stepped around Clancy to look down the cliff, but the gun never wavered. "Don't do anything foolish, will you, dear." She smiled as she glanced up. "I always thought you and Jake Hawkins would make a fine couple."

Clancy could hear a boat motor growing louder over the howl of the wind. She felt tears sting her eyes.

"They're almost here. It's almost over." Helen looked up at Clancy. "Johnny's dying of cancer. He thinks I don't know." She smiled sadly, her eyes bright with tears. "I'd hoped for just a little more time with him."

Clancy glanced past Helen in shock. Frank Ames was no longer sprawled in the living-room doorway. He stood behind Helen, blood running down into his left eye as he reached out a hand.

Jake was out of the boat the moment they reached the dock. He didn't bother with the elevator but took the stairs, two at a time. Below him Johnny stumbled from the boat. Jake heard him try the elevator. It groaned but didn't move. Helen had locked it on top to slow them down. Behind him, he heard Johnny running up the stairs. Jake ran faster.

Helen smiled as she saw the startled expression on Clancy's face. "You really don't think that old ploy is going to work, do you, dear? I'm suppose to see that look on your face and then turn around so you can jump me and take the gun away. Really, Clancy, I thought you were more intelligent than that."

Frank laid a hand on Helen's shoulder. Surprise, then fright, registered in her eyes. She started to wheel around. Clancy lunged for the gun and, grabbing Helen's wrist, fought to wrestle the pistol away. Helen swung her body to catch Frank in the face with her elbow; he fell backward, hitting the deck hard. The gun went off, the shot echoing across the deck.

Jake had neared the top of the stairs when he heard the shot. His heart in his throat, he drew his .38 from the holster at his ribs and bounded up the steps, fear racing him up the last few.

Clancy still wrestled with Helen for the pistol, but her concentration broke when she spotted Jake. Helen wrenched the gun from Clancy's grasp and was raising the barrel to point it at Clancy when his foot came down on the last step.

"Drop it!" he yelled over the wind, ready to fire if Helen hesitated for an instant.

The gun dropped from Helen's hand and hit the deck with a thud.

Jake rushed over to scoop it up. Then pulled Clancy to him. "Are you all right?" His heart slammed against his ribs, making each breath a labor.

She nodded.

Helen smiled as she saw Johnny lumber up the last of the stairs. She ran to him. He took her in his arms and held her, seeming only mildly surprised that she could walk. Jake looked into the big man's face and saw the pain. And the silent plea. "Let me take her in."

Jake nodded.

"It's all over, Helen," he said to his wife, hugging her to him.

She nodded and turned to look back at Jake and Clancy. "Yes," she said. "It's all over."

"Shall we take the elevator down?" Johnny asked Helen.

She looked up at him, her face full of love. "Yes. That's exactly what I thought we'd do."

They walked arm in arm to the elevator.

"Jake," Clancy cried softly. "No, you can't let them—"

Jake pulled her closer. "Let them go, Clancy," he whispered. Johnny helped Helen into the elevator and stepped in after her, closing the door behind them. He turned to look at Jake, tears in his eyes. Then he pushed the button. The elevator dropped like a rock.

Epilogue

The wind whipped Clancy's hair as she watched the Galveston skyline grow smaller behind the boat. She brushed her hair back and breathed in the smell of the gulf, letting it fill her lungs as she looked at her husband.

Jake stood on the bridge of the thirty-six-foot trawler steering them toward the endless horizon, his Astros baseball cap cocked back, his tanned hands strong and sure on the wheel.

Her husband, she thought, and smiled as she joined him.

"What are you smiling about, Mrs. Hawkins?" Jake asked as he pulled her closer.

She liked the sound of that, loved the feel of him. "You," she answered. For so long, Clancy thought she'd never smile again.

The days after Helen and Johnny's deaths had been as

dark as the days after the resort fire and the loss of her parents. But unlike then, Jake helped her through those early summer days, piecing together what had started ten years before and finally ended on the Bransons' deck.

Some of the answers died with Helen and Johnny. Others were locked in Clancy's subconscious. Had she really walked along the cliffs all the way to Helen's in her sleep to return with a single blue bead, not once, but twice? Had part of her known all along it was Helen? Is that why she'd continued to walk down the beach each night?

Whatever the reason, the sleepwalking had stopped as abruptly as it had started. She knew that as long as she could curl up with Jake each night, she would have no reason to walk anywhere in her sleep again.

Frank had lived and become a hero, taking credit for saving Clancy's life, although Clancy knew now that Helen had never intended to harm her or Jake at the end. But Frank seemed happier than he had in years. Maybe he'd finally gotten rid of that chip on his shoulder. Or maybe he'd just finally laid Lola's ghost to rest.

With Tadd's help, Warren Hawkins's case was reopened. He got out of prison in time for their wedding and stood next to his son as Jake promised to love, honor and cherish.

Their lives had been different as they'd left Hawk Island. Like Johnny, she and Jake had once seen the world in blacks and whites, rights and wrongs. Now they could see the grays.

It had been Jake's idea to marry as soon as possible. "Life is too short," he'd said. "We've already lost enough time. Let's not lose any more."

"Aunt Kiki isn't going to like it," Clancy had pointed out.

"Oh, you might be surprised. I think I finally figured out why she hired me to investigate your case."

Kiki had cried at the wedding, then presented them with the thirty-six-foot trawler. "Go see the world, and when you get back, I'll have the nursery ready at the lodge." Clancy had assured her that wouldn't be necessary. Not yet, anyway.

Clancy snuggled against her husband and looked back to see the Galveston skyline disappear behind them. When she turned back, Jake was gazing down at her as if just looking at her brought him joy.

"Did I ever tell you about these hunches that I sometimes get?" Jake asked.

She shook her head and grinned up at him. "I don't believe you ever have."

He rubbed at the back of his neck. "How do you feel about twins?"

"Twins?" Clancy cried.

"Twin boys. Born nine months from now."

She laughed. "You really don't put any stock in these hunches of yours, do you?"

"Nah," he said as he put the boat on automatic pilot and led her down to their cabin. "None at all."

* * * * *

We hope you enjoyed reading

Picture Me Dead

by *New York Times* bestselling author

HEATHER GRAHAM

and

Hotshot P.I.

by *New York Times* bestselling author

B.J. DANIELS

Both were originally MIRA® and
Harlequin® Intrigue stories!

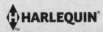 **HARLEQUIN**®

INTRIGUE

Edge-of-your-seat intrigue, fearless romance

From passionate, suspenseful and dramatic
love stories to inspirational or historical,
Harlequin offers different lines to satisfy
every romance reader.

New books available every month.

 HARLEQUIN®

www.Harlequin.com

She couldn't see the bastard behind her but knew he was
waiting. Waiting to watch her die as her strength gave out
and she couldn't support herself anymore.

She tried to yell—even if someone came rushing into the
room, it wasn't going to do much more damage than her
swaying here until her strength gave out—but the sound was
cut off by the rope over her vocal cords. If she wanted to
yell, she was going to have to use one hand to pull the rope
away from the front of her throat. That meant supporting all
her weight with one arm.

Her muscles were already straining from the constant
state of pulling up. Supporting her weight with one arm
wasn't going to work.

But she'd be damned if she was just going to die in front
of this bastard.

She swung her legs up, trying to catch the upper part of the rope, but failed again. Even if she could get her legs hooked up there, she wasn't going to be able to get herself released.

She heard a low chuckle to her side. Bastard. He was enjoying this.

And then the alarm started blaring.

Masked Man muttered a curse and took off up the stairs. Lillian felt her arms begin to shake as the exhaustion from holding her own weight began to take its toll. If it wasn't for the rigorous SWAT training, she'd already be dead.

But even training wouldn't be enough. Physics would win. Her arms began to tremble more and she was forced to let go of the rope to give them a break.

Immediately the rope cut off all oxygen.

When everything began to go black, she reached up and grabbed the rope again. It wasn't long before the tremors took over.

She didn't want to go out like this. Wished she hadn't squandered this second chance she'd had with Jace in her life.

But even thinking of Jace, with his gorgeous blue eyes and cocky grin that still did things to her heart after all these years, couldn't give her any more strength.

She reached back up with her arms and found them collapsing before she even took her weight. Then the noose tightened and jerked around her neck, pulling her body forward, all air gone.

Blackness.

Will Jace and the team get there in time to rescue her? Find out when USA TODAY *bestselling author Janie Crouch's* ARMED RESPONSE *goes on sale August 2018.*
Look for it wherever Harlequin® Intrigue books are sold!

www.Harlequin.com

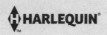

HARLEQUIN®

INTRIGUE

EDGE-OF-YOUR-SEAT INTRIGUE, FEARLESS ROMANCE.

Save **$1.00**

on the purchase of ANY Harlequin® Intrigue book.

Available wherever books are sold, including most bookstores, supermarkets, drugstores and discount stores.

Save **$1.00**

on the purchase of any Harlequin® Intrigue book.

Coupon valid until October 31, 2018.
Redeemable at participating outlets in the U.S. and Canada only.
Not redeemable at Barnes & Noble stores. Limit one coupon per customer.

52615883

5 65373 00076 2 (8100)0 12378

® and ™ are trademarks owned and used by the trademark owner and/or its licensee.

© 2018 Harlequin Enterprises Limited